THE HUCKSTERS OF HOLINESS

THE HUCKSTERS OF HOLINESS

RON GORTON

BART
NEW YORK

Published in association with Bryans & Bryans.

ISBN: 1-55785-108-5

First Bart Books edition: June 1989

Bart Books
155 E. 34th Street
New York, New York 10016

Manufactured in the United States of America

PROLOGUE

CHRISTMAS DAY, 1977. The breaking dawn saw a drizzle of rain falling onto rolling hills. Two monks, in brown, hooded robes, slowly moved through the mist in quiet meditation. Suddenly distracted by the cawing of crows, they altered their course and walked cautiously toward a thicket of woods. Through a cluster of trees and with the mist rising in a ghostly vapor, they came upon the macabre. The two monks stood—frozen in horror.

Sixteen-year-old Ron Rebuck, Jr., and his mother stepped out of the police car. They were quickly escorted by a cadre of police to a waiting Jeep that would take them into the woods, to the site of the crucifixion.

Shortly thereafter, the Rebucks got out of the Jeep and followed the local sheriff a short distance on foot to the scene of the tragedy.

As they crested the hill, June Rebuck refused to look up, but kept her eyes fixed on the ground as she walked. The sheriff, realizing the futility of trying to persuade her to leave and spare herself the gruesome sight, physically pushed reporters out of the way as he guided her along the trail of sorrow.

At the foot of the cross, her eyes still on the ground, her arms around her son, June suddenly felt the jolting vibration of his body. Ron Rebuck, Jr., had seen his father and was weeping bitterly.

"Take me to him . . . Take me to your father," his mother pleaded.

The deputies standing nearby caught the sheriff's signal

5

for them to withdraw. It was a courtesy that would enable Ron Rebuck's wife and son to be alone in their grief.

As the boy's sobbing intensified, June Rebuck finally looked up. Her body quaked. She turned ashen pale, as though the blood in her veins had stopped flowing. Feeling her falling, her son tightened his grip around her waist, but she tore loose from his hold and fell to her knees, her head close to the face of the man who'd been her partner in life . . . the face of the man she'd loved and lived for. She gently wiped away the blood from his nose and that which had caked around his mouth, then began to kiss the cold face, over and over.

Ron Rebuck looked from his mother to the pathetic figure of his father—his arms and legs extended, his hands and feet nailed to the rough wood with railroad spikes. The rain, like a million tears, dripped onto the nude body.

As his gaze moved higher, the pupils in young Ron Rebuck's eyes began to gleam—a burning gleam reminiscent of his father's. As he stood there, his body frozen, he could not tear his eyes off the sheet that hung loosely above the cross, its crude letters painted in red that spelled out the words, "THE ANTICHRIST."

PART I

IN THE NAME OF GOD?

CHAPTER 1

HAUNTING, WHIRLING, black clouds rimmed with silver blotted out the light of the moon. Below, the heaving surface of a fierce ocean pounded a beach of fine white sand. A southerly gale packing fifty knots of force lashed the tropical growth along a usually serene coastline. The only intruder on a scene of primal grandeur was an observation tower clinging to the rim of a time-tortured cliff, its huge beacon eye probing the darkness.

Two men clad in wet suits fought the riptide, evading the prowling light, then emerged on shore as if tossed from the ocean's maw, melting into the changing patterns of shadow and shape. High above, the driving wind tore at the tower. The rusted metal casing of the powerful searchlight rattled at its hinges. From the tower, an olive-skinned man wearing a military soft cap looked out and saw nothing.

Two miles out in the midnight hell, the silhouette of a low-riding vessel slipped into the deep. Toward the battered shoreline, five frogmen rode the treacherous waves in their I.B.S. raft. Thrust from the unrelenting sea, they beached the craft with practiced ease, then moved in the night shadows to the foot of a hill whose summit became the base of the cliff. Working with swift efficiency, they buried the raft, then moved decisively past whipping saw grass and under wind-laced trees toward the cliff and its pencil of light.

The rendezvous had been set by precise coordinates at a cluster of trees 150 feet below the ridge, and now the five frogmen with faces camouflaged in black, green, and gray paint waited like a grouping of statues. Unaffected by the slashing wind, their eyes were fixed with an almost predatory concentration on the looming structure.

A flashing red light from within the tower reflected in their eyes. The two advance scouts, who'd left the raft a quarter-mile offshore, had secured the observation tower, and the men of the second wave huddled around their leader, who promptly removed a plastic pouch from the belt on his wet suit. Another shone an infrared light on a detailed topographic map of this slice of rugged Central American coastline. A finger pointed to a double *XX* below the boldfaced words circled in red: "Operation Black Eagle."

Inland, beyond the cliffs, beyond the rolling hills of a verdant upland, a cross soaring fifty feet high defied a wind bent on sacrilege. A short distance from the cross, a paved road came to a circle where the fluorescent glow of white stripes marked a helicopter's arrival and departure point to and from the Valley of the Holy Spirit. The road went on, undulating through a wonderland of lush growth under barrage from a relentless wind. It continued to a wooden bridge that arched gracefully over a waterfall. Here, a sharp fork in the road cut into dense jungle. In the distance, through the trees, a light flickered from the sprawling ranch house the Right Reverend Cody Walker called home.

The main road ended abruptly at a wall of earth pierced by a tunnel. A series of cherub-faced angels mounted on both sides of the passageway bore sconces whose shimmering flames accented the soft hues of a trail carpeted with orchids. The seduction of the senses was completed by the subtle intrusion of religious music piped softly through unseen speakers. At the tunnel's end, two immense statues of mythic winged creatures guarded a door of celestial size. Two angels, with their arms spread wide and beckoning, bade welcome to the newly arrived citizens of the Valley of the Holy Spirit.

What appeared beyond the door was a stark contrast which numbed the senses. The Valley of the Holy Spirit, outwardly the picture of spiritual tranquility—what Cody

10

Walker's stateside henchmen promoted in their slick, four-color brochures as "The place where angels come to rest and play"—was a cruel facade. Row after row of dilapidated metal shanties housed the elderly, the infirm, the brainwashed, and the desperate. At each corner of the dreary compound, what appeared to be harmless water towers were, in fact, security posts manned by guards armed for war. "Cody's Commandos," vigilant beneath flat-topped roofs, stood behind intense spotlights which constantly roamed the grounds of the squalid living quarters of the "parishioners" below.

In the name of God, Cody Walker and his disciples sought out the lonely, the elderly, and the despondent from the ragged edges of organized religion. Vulnerable in their disenchantment with a fundamentalism which had failed them, their bodies and souls Walker recruited into his legally chartered Church of Living Angels. *In the name of God,* he fleeced them of their holdings and benefits and set them to cultivating the religion's lucrative cash crop: a local hybrid of the cannabis plant potent enough to satisfy the sensate tastes of jet setters from Malibu to Monte Carlo. *In the name of God,* Cody Walker promised them heaven on earth and delivered hell.

A bedraggled stick of a woman broke away from the clutches of her feeble husband and fell at the feet of the nearest guard, babbling for compassion. She cried out the names of her children, as if they could somehow forestall a sadistic enactment of nightly penance. With total disdain, the guard rained blow after blow upon the hysterical woman groveling at his feet. His companion turned on the woman's protesting husband, a toothless gargoyle, who crumpled to the wooden floor with the fixed stare of death in his eyes. From hut to hut, the whippings were as passionless as the tropical storm buffeting the Valley of the Holy Spirit.

Reverend Cody Walker sat in a reclining chair in a richly furnished sunken living room. Wrapped in a robe of burgundy velvet, he peered through gold-rimmed glasses

11

at the young girl washing his feet in a cloisonné basin. His slender hand gently stroked the adolescent's long black hair until she reluctantly raised her Latin eyes and saw the glow of contentment radiating from Walker's ugly face.

A balding, middle-aged man seated on an overstuffed sofa put the document he'd been reading in an expensive attaché case. But his attention was focused on the human gift, the compliant compliment of a ranking official in the government's pro-U.S. dictatorship. He watched her wipe Walker's feet with a soft, gold-trimmed towel. "Cody, are you quite finished?" he asked, drumming his fingers impatiently on the arm of the sofa.

Walker toyed with the sculptured curves of a Waterford crystal wine glass. He waited for his late-evening ritual to be completed before responding to the restless man. "Counselor, you just continue to dot the *I*'s and cross the *T*'s and don't concern yourself with the Valley of the Holy Spirit."

The heavyset man waited for the young girl to glide from the room before speaking his mind. "Contrary to your belief, Cody, everything here is not Shangri-La. There are problems. And you are not immune to them."

Walker sipped the 1956 Chateau Margeaux Cabernet Sauvignon with the relish of a man enjoying the sybaritic peace only affluence can bring.

"Cody," the lawyer pressed, "it is hardly a secret that you and your church are on Washington's hit list. The Feds are harassing your people in the States. And some of them are buckling under, telling some nasty stories." He rose from the sofa and walked toward the cult's self-proclaimed messiah. "Cody, for Christ's sake, you've got millions stashed in Swiss accounts. Tell your key people you've got to go on a pilgrimage, the Holy Land, anywhere. Just get the hell away from here before they nail you."

"Nail me? Hit list? Who do you think you're speaking to, a mobster?"

"Cody, I don't have to tell you who or what you are."

"From here on, Counselor, you shall address me in the same dignified manner you would a Billy Hale."

"Billy Hale was never into goddamn concentration camps!"

Walker leaned back in his chair, deep in thought.

"Look, Cody, I am deeply interested in your welfare."

"And you very well should be, Counselor. Yes, indeed. For whatever ails *me* will most certainly ail *you*."

The attorney moved a hand across his pudgy face. He looked long and thoughtfully at Walker, then returned to the sofa where he took out a single document from the attaché case, inspecting it briefly. "Cody, I have come down from New York with what I consider to be vital information, information that could result in your collapse. Dammit, Cody, what does it take to get through to you?"

"A possible suggestion is for you to stop speaking as if everything here is in a state of chaos."

"Cody, what you are doing is criminal. There's not a jury alive who wouldn't convict you of nearly every inhumane act known to mankind."

"Spare me, Counselor. Your sudden attack of conscience grows tiresome."

"You sit there, having your feet washed, drinking expensive wine, totally divorced from the atrocities you're inflicting upon people you keep enslaved—and you have the gall to talk of conscience?"

"Such a bleeding heart," said Walker, finishing the wine.

"Cody, I want you to get on that phone and call whomever you're paying off in this banana republic to make immediate arrangements for the release of those people."

Walker laughed sardonically and calmly placed the empty wine glass on an end table. "Am I to believe that after three years you have only now removed the blindfold from your eyes? No, Counselor, you have taken your thirty pieces of silver too many times."

"It won't work, Cody; I am only your attorney. *Correction*, your church's attorney."

"If you are really naive enough to rely on that fact to save you, you are greatly mistaken. You are involved, Counselor, right up to your parasitic ass."

"Not so, Cody. I have not as yet crossed over the legal line."

"Stop fooling yourself. You're well beyond the point of no return."

The attorney held out the document for identification and spoke in a calm, professional manner. "This letter will confirm my resignation as attorney for the Church of Living Angels. I shall follow up with a more detailed letter once I have returned to—"

Suddenly, the muffled rumble of an explosion shook the study floor. The windows rattled. Cody Walker's fingers clutched the chair's leather armrests. The bewildered attorney turned pale.

Beyond the compound, past a double barbed-wire fence, the two-story building housing the security force had erupted in flames that raged out of control. The wounded cried out for assistance. Survivors of the initial blast crawled over dismembered human bodies in a vain attempt to escape the gale-fanned flames. A man ablaze ran stiffly into the woods, howling like the wind.

Within the compound, at ten-second intervals, the watch towers disintegrated in fiery eruptions. For brief moments, the spotlights revealed their violent bursts. Amidst the flying wreckage, bodies rose into the stormy night in a grotesque light show—before the generator was gutted by a blast of fire from an automatic weapon. The dazed, delivered congregation swarmed out of the huts.

A scattering of guards with weapons drawn searched frantically through the glow of firelight for the invisible intruders. Forming a ragged squad, they moved in the direction of the tunnel. Hysterical members of the congregation who strayed into their paths were beaten with pistols or lashed by whips. Once separated from the vanquished citizenry, the guards ran for the sanctuary of the tunnel. From within, savage bursts of enfilading firepower cut them down. The rows of angels surveyed the carnage with sweet, frozen smiles of Renaissance innocence.

Cody Walker darted from room to room as if lost in a maze. He stormed past the attorney into the hallway and entered the kitchen, where he glared at his servants huddling close to one another like cowering dogs. Their bulging eyes froze upon his hand—the shaky hand gripping a Walther P38 pistol. He fled from their presence down the hall. Suddenly, sensing the presence of someone behind him, he quickly spun about. The attorney's face twitched as he looked into the pistol's black hole.

Walker slowly lowered the weapon and headed toward his den. "Cody," the attorney said, following him, "it's over." Like a burst of buckshot, the words cut into Walker's back. He stopped and turned with fear pouring from his eyes.

"Cody, you're trapped. There's no place to hide."

"Another word and you shall meet the devil."

"The devil? I already have, Cody. I already have."

"Don't push me, you fool!"

"Shoot me? No, Cody, that's not your style. You don't shoot people. You bleed 'em to death. Besides, you must realize I'm your only hope."

Walker burst into his den with the squat-legged attorney fast at his heels, and quickly locked the door behind them. With the pistol firmly lodged in his hand, he rested his free hand on an ivory-inlaid desk.

"You have to act, Cody, and act fast."

Walker stared blankly at his lawyer.

"I'm talking about money, Cody, and a lot of it."

"People are here to murder me, and *you* speak of money?"

"Money buys everything, even the saving of *your* life."

The attorney seated himself at the desk, rapidly ripping open drawers until he found what he was after: a piece of church stationery. Sliding a pen from his jacket pocket, he proceeded to write rapidly while he spoke. "My guess is the CIA is behind this. Whomever, they couldn't have picked a better night. They've knocked out your communications. You can bet they found the whereabouts of your heliport. The only chance of saving your ass is for me to make a deal on your behalf."

"A deal with *whom*?" Walker asked desperately.

"It doesn't matter, Cody. I want the numbers to the Swiss accounts, the bank deposits in the States, and the valuables in that safe behind the holy picture. You must sign everything over to me. I'll get one of the servants to witness. It's—"

"Parasite!"

The startled attorney looked up to see the twisted lips, the frenzied eyes of a man erupting with uncontrollable rage.

"Parasite! Parasite!" Walker bellowed repeatedly.

The condemning word shrilled in the lawyer's ears. For a fleeting moment, a bewildered grin came to his beefy face when the thunder with which he flirted exploded in his chest, toppling him backward onto the deep pile carpet. The raving Walker stood over the lifeless man, shouting out damning verses from the Bible. When words finally failed him, he pumped two more rounds into the bloody carcass of the dead lawyer.

A rustling sound from the hallway brought him out of his delirium. He cocked and aimed the pistol at the door.

His ears tuned to perceive the slightest sound, Walker heard only the raising of the wind and brief torrents of rain. He found himself staring at the painting which dominated the room: a painting of Jesus in the popular conception of the Man of Sorrows. The release of adrenalin which flushed his cheeks was not a sudden hot flash of the spirit; rather, he was looking through the painting, visualizing the wall safe it concealed, picturing the thick stacks of large-denomination bills piled in neat rows. The money he kept on hand to bribe various government officials kindled a brief flame of hope. He sprang toward the painting when suddenly the lights went out.

He stood rigid, mesmerized by the unexpected. His eyes leaped about the blackened room. The Swiss clock on the wall was silent. The sweat trickling from Walker's forehead fogged his glasses. Yet his will to survive was augmented by the pistol in his hand as he waited in the darkness.

A massive figure bolted through the window. Hysteria

16

flooded Walker's mind like a wild river. He flattened himself against the wall in a crouch, squeezing off a round. The missile bored into a wooden shelf, sending books flying. In a desperate move, he blindly fired the fifth of six bullets as he rushed toward the broken and jagged glass. A blinding beam of light caught him in the eyes, bringing him to a paralyzed halt. From out of the darkness, a powerful hand gripped his slender wrist, forcing the pistol downward. The intruder's other arm coiled around his chest followed by the swift action of an immense leg which clamped across his knees. Unable to see the painted face of the towering man who held him with bullish strength, Cody Walker tried in vain to look away from the blazing light in his face. "In the name of God, don't kill me," he pleaded.

From across the room, behind the light, a voice repeated, "In the name of God?"

"Yes . . . yes. In the name of God," Walker whimpered.

The light drew closer and still closer until its streak of uneven brilliance encompassed the painting of Christ on the wall above. Again came the voice, "In the name of God?"

"Yes . . . yes, whoever you are! Yes, yes, sweet Jesus, yes!"

Held by what seemed a superhuman strength, blinded by the light in his face, and intensely aware of the weapon still clutched in his useless hand, Cody Walker realized the futility of further reply. He was barely conscious of his hand being guided upward to where the gun's barrel pressed coldly against his pounding temple. His numb index finger was forced onto the trigger and overlapped by the larger finger of his captor when the voice behind the light thundered for the final time, "In the name of God?"

The room plunged back into blackness. The eyes of Christ glittered strangely in the dark, and over the din of the sounding wind rose the final word, "AMEN!"

CHAPTER 2

THE SUN'S RAYS glinted off the gold cross mounted on the hood of the custom silver and black Lincoln. Billy Hale frowned from behind a morning paper with the blaring headline: CULT LEADER SLAIN! He had read the article several times and wondered why he felt such concern over the bizarre demise of a man he had known little and respected less.

The electric window responded to his touch, and he savored the clear Virginia air gentled by a late Indian summer. The once-handsome face known throughout the world had suffered the ravages of time. His face now crisscrossed with wrinkles and lines and the famed lantern jaw sagged visibly. All but the clear, blue, hawklike eyes had been mortified by life's great imposition. He would wryly compare his snow-white hair to Moses', whose mane, according to the movie epic *The Ten Commandments*, turned white when he descended from the Mount. Billy Hale had been to the mountain. He knew all there was to know about his life's calling, and now, in his seventy-third year, he was more of a revered elder statesman than a force in the exploding world of evangelism.

The limousine pulled off the Shenandoah Mountain road and into the Hale estate. It penetrated acres of pines framing a sparkling brook before coasting into a circular drive fronting a splendid Tudor home of pale gray brick accented with black shutters. Hale's long-time chauffeur and sometime valet, a slender, middle-aged man named Emile, opened the back door of the Lincoln and handed his boss a marble-headed cane, then watched the old evangelist challenge the steps leading to a double door of sturdy oak.

For the next two days, Billy became a virtual recluse in a rustic, lodge-sized room where a multitude of busts, all representing figures from the Bible, stood about like ghostly sentries. Only recently had he reluctantly given in to installing any form of communication in a place where he'd once found sanctuary from a hectic schedule paralleled by few.

Having retired from the religious arena as the undefeated champion, he'd now become the grand spectator. And for the past two years, other than infrequent speaking engagements, important religious commemorations, and occasional guest television appearances, his time was spent in deep reflection and the composing of books.

Billy Hale sat back in the soft leather chair, a token of esteem from former President Richard Waters, whose picture hung above a massive stone fireplace. The portrait sat amid a gallery of world-class names, all of whom were beholden to Billy, according to their handwritten testimonials. He ran a hand through white hair that curled slightly over his shirt collar, then rubbed the white stubble on his unshaven face as he closed his bloodshot eyes to think through another difficult decision.

A gentle rapping on the door returned him to a conscious state, and he opened his eyes to see his wife, Doris, peer into the room before entering with a tray bearing his lunch. She placed a liverwurst sandwich and glass of milk on the table next to him, then perched gracefully on the armrest. Neither spoke as they sat in silence, holding hands.

Billy could not remember a time when their love had soured. For forty-five years she had been his staunchest admirer, the partner in life he depended on. Like all married couples, they'd had their ups and downs. The loss of their only child, a boy with Down's syndrome who'd died of pneumonia at age thirteen, was a cross they bore together.

Billy slumped deeper into the chair, looking away from the face which still retained traces of youthful beauty. She would be seventy in March, three years his junior, but looked much younger. She waited for him to speak, and the words came in a soul-searching tone. "Doris, I believe the time is fast approaching when fundamental religious beliefs can no longer enjoy their ancient heritage."

"There will never be a substitute for the Holy Bible," she replied fervently.

"It's the eighties, Doris, a decade of great change. World religion can no longer ignore progress. How long will life's traumas, and death itself, keep people close to God? The better educated people become, the more the Bible loses its potency."

"Billy, eat your sandwich—please."

He ignored her plea and moved from the chair with his head bowed in thought—limping to another. "People are challenging scripture, Doris. No matter what any evangelist, priest, minister, or rabbi tells you, religion's greatest ally has always been death. The love of God is truly the fear of God."

He turned from her questioning eyes. Again he nervously left the chair. The distaste of his thoughts became evident on his face. "Electronic religion," he said. "Jimmy Christian's 'God Loves Everyone, Everywhere Club,' Harley Lombard's 'Ministry Of Might,' and on and on and on. Not to mention the faith healers and their like. To think I once fretted over calling my TV ministry 'Campaigns for Christ.' "

Without his cane, he hobbled toward a large oak desk. "If only there was a true champion upon the religious scene . . . there's no one, Doris. They're all carbon copies of one another: Jimmy Christian, Wallace Langly, Veep Siler, and yes, Harley Lombard. All with their five-hundred-dollar suits, three-hundred-dollar shoes—TV *stars*. And what do they really say? Send me your money, and I'll pray for you. . . . Give, give, give. It's like watching a sea of hands and mouths."

He stopped in front of the bow window and gazed at a stand of tall spruce and Virginia pine. "I swear, if Harley Lombard or Jimmy Christian told their TV audiences they needed ten million dollars for the building of a pole to reach heaven, they'd get it."

Using the desk for balance, he eased gingerly into a chair with a gold cross embossed on its rich leather. He opened the desk drawer and brought out a thick stack of letters. "From pastors throughout America. They want me to help bring about some temperance to religious broadcasting before Jimmy, Harley, and the rest of them turn Christianity into an assembly line."

He dropped the letters on the desk, brushed them away, and folded his hands. "Apparently, they're losing many of their flock to the seemingly endless run of evangelical TV shows. They're worried, Doris. Without adequate attendance, financial support from their congregations, their churches will go under. How ironic; they're asking me to intercede. *Me*, who started it all."

"Billy," she protested.

"It's a fact. I was the first to bring televised evangelism into the American home. Whatever fame I've received has come through the electronic media."

He rose to his feet. This time she brought him the cane, and they returned to the comfort of matching chairs. His eyes drifted towards the TV. "Would you believe it has come to a point where local churches are advertising their televised Sunday morning services? Doris, if I could have known *then* what my television campaigns would eventually lead to—"

"*Billy*, stop persecuting yourself."

"I was blinded by my own greed, by a thirst for power—as Harley and Jimmy are now."

"Your television ministry brought great hope to millions of people."

"For how long, Doris? A day? A week? A month? Was it worth the millions they contributed? Who really benefited?"

She could not reply. This was a side of Billy Hale's nature even she didn't know.

"*Reverend* Jimmy Christian, *Reverend* Harley Lombard, *Reverend* Doc Thran Tho and, oh yes, *Reverend* Bill Hale. Reverend . . . It's clearly becoming more and more a misnomer." Billy paused as if studying her. "A last hurrah, is that what you're thinking, Doris?"

"I'm thinking you needn't prove a thing."

He looked away from the determination chiselled on her face. "Perhaps you're right, Doris. Besides, who really cares to listen to the fears of an old man?"

His inner struggle was far from over and she waited patiently for his next words. They were oddly toneless when they came. "I stepped away from the religious spotlight because I felt I had said and done all that I possibly could. I had no regrets. My life as an evangelist was certainly fulfilling. Believe me, Doris, I looked forward to retirement. But little did I realize how time could play such hell on one's mind, how inactivity could be such a curse."

"Billy, let things run their course. You've earned your retirement."

"My coming out of retirement will largely depend on Harley Lombard and Jimmy Christian. I intend to pay them *each* a visit."

"Billy, I won't hear of it. The doctor—"

"There's more, Doris . . . First there was the bizarre death of Jason Everson two months ago, and now this Cody Walker thing—I swear it's just the beginning of things to come. I can feel it . . . feel it in these old bones."

"What things?"

"There are no faces, no battlegrounds. Nothing but dark clouds—but I can damn well hear the drums."

"Billy," she said, shaking her head. "You said the exact words before that terrible Ron Rebuck ordeal. I wish you wouldn't—"

"Doris," he said, cutting her off, "what do you call a man driven to champion a cause against something *he* started?"

CHAPTER 3

THE YOUNG LIEUTENANT nursed his rising impatience in a room without windows. For the past two hours he'd cooled his heels in room 1424-B within the vast maze of the Pentagon. More cubicle than room, it was furnished with a small metal desk, two folding chairs, and a black phone. A lone painting of an early-American naval battle hung on a drab wall. Room 1424-B was obviously a seldom-used confessional in the vast cathedral of the Joint Chiefs of Staff.

The door flew open and the young lieutenant snapped to attention. A senior naval officer carrying a leather attaché case swaggered into the room and seated himself at the desk. "As you were, Lieutenant," he said, dropping the briefcase on the desk. "I'm Commander Hamlin. Hope I haven't kept you anchored too long."

The commander twirled the twin combination locks on the brown leather case, flicked the latches open, removed a document, inspected it, then handed it to the young man. "That, Lieutenant, is a copy of your official orders for the period commencing September twenty-third through October eighteenth of this year. I'm sure you will notice it's signed by your superior officer, Commander O'Donnell."

The lieutenant's eyes froze on the words "Operation Deep," but they had no immediate meaning. He skipped down to the signature of his commanding officer. The officious scrawl was genuine—or an expert forgery.

The commander ignored the lieutenant's heightened curiosity and replaced the document with another. "You now have in your possession an affidavit signed by the captain of the submarine you and your SEAL team were aboard. The captain has testified that at no time during your orientation exercise did you or any other member of the SEAL team leave the ship.''

The blueprints for a cover-up burned through the fog in the lieutenant's mind.

''Just place that on the desk,'' said the commander, sorting a fresh set of papers into order. Grouping them together, he held them before the young man's suspicious eyes. ''These, Lieutenant, are signed statements from each member of your SEAL team who was aboard the submarine.'' He handed them to him. ''You will note they corroborate the affidavits you've previously examined.''

The lieutenant searched the names for one in particular. It was there: the ragged signature of Ike Vesper, his chief petty officer and most trusted friend. He searched for a clue that would prove it was signed by a man under duress, but he saw none.

The commander retrieved the papers and neatly arranged them on the desk, then removed a single document from the briefcase and flashed his best cocktail-party smile. ''Yes, Lieutenant, this one is for you.''

The lieutenant coldly regarded the smug expression on the commander's face and purposely let the outstretched hand holding the document dangle before accepting it.

''Sign where your name appears, and you will be on the night flight to California.'' The commander rushed his words, annoyed by the junior officer's impertinence.

The document set forth the same disclaimers as the others, and the young officer found himself wrestling with indecision. It was not unusual for a SEAL to receive orders for a covert mission at a locale far removed from the briefing rooms at SEAL Base I or its extension in the Philippines. But for a junior officer to be summoned to the Pentagon, the fountainhead of all SEAL orders, and there ordered by an obnoxious commander to deny involvement in a mission that should have made national heroes of every man in his unit, was an order he would not obey. He looked up at the commander, whose cocksure expression turned to an instant burn as the lieutenant ripped the disclaimer into confetti.

Bristling with silent rage, the commander stuffed the surviving depositions into the briefcase and reached for the phone. He punched three numbers, snorted, and waited. "Yes, this is Commander Hamlin. The admiral is expecting my call." His steely eyes fell on the lieutenant. "Admiral Church will be expecting you. Fifth floor. Fleet operations wing."

The lieutenant had stepped into the long corridor when the commander's voice brought him to a halt. "Unless you get smart in a hurry, I wouldn't make plans for Christmas in California. You might be in Washington for a spell, *Mister*."

An efficient WAVE tiptoed into the plush office of Rear Admiral Lester Church. She waited until he acknowledged her presence before speaking. "The SEAL lieutenant is here, Admiral."

The silver-thatched, ruddy-complexioned man leaned back in a leather swivel chair. He toyed with a U.S. Naval Academy ring and looked at her absently.

"Shall I have him wait?" she finally asked.

"No . . . no, send him in. And, Madge, hold *all* my calls."

The lieutenant entered, scanning the large and orderly room. Sensing his presence, the admiral feigned deep concentration on the report he was reading. "Be seated," he commanded.

The young man removed his hat, revealing a shock of dark brown hair. He waited until the WAVE secretary closed the door behind her, then stepped smartly to within a foot of the desk and stood at rigid attention.

The admiral looked up at the brash young officer who chose to stand. He examined the handsome, rugged face and paused at the piercing hazel eyes, which reminded him of a predator's. The admiral's attention shifted to the insignia sewn on the upper left sleeve of the officer's dress blues. It was the proudly worn patch of the Navy's elite and mysterious special force: an eagle with extended wings, a musket and trident gripped in its talons.

"All right then, son, we'll both stand," said the admiral, who picked up the folder from the desk and walked slowly to the opposite side of the room. He stopped in front of a bookshelf stacked with thick volumes of naval and maritime law. "More than likely you are wondering why I sent for you. Let's just say I'm concerned over the welfare of a damn good man. I have been going over your record, Lieutenant, and I must say I'm quite impressed. It's one you should be proud of."

Admiral Church moved away from the bookcase and stood in front of the farthest window. "It's a sorry thing when one's own country cannot publicly acknowledge its true heroes. Apparently, our sense of heroism has fallen to the level of honoring hostages. Unfortunately, we're living in sensitive times, Lieutenant. There's not a politician in this town who isn't fearful of a witch-hunting press. Those damn liberals! Who'd believe this country would fall prey to the insolent demands of minority groups and sellout artists. Are you following me, Lieutenant?"

The lieutenant offered no reply, and the admiral inched closer to the window. Any impression of sympathy vanished as he struck the folder with the back of his hand. "You are obviously not getting the message, son. People are trying to help you, but you're too bullheaded to realize it." He put the folder in his other hand, then waved it before the lieutenant's unblinking eyes. "Are you willing to play craps with this? Seven years of distinguished service? Because if it comes to the point of all hands overboard, *you* will drown."

The admiral looked through the window at a late-November sky threatening snow. Expecting the young officer to say something, he became aggravated by his silence. His words now came with a rehearsed cadence. "The United States Government did not participate in, nor did it have any previous knowledge of, an attack on that so-called 'religious community' in Central America. 'Operation Black Eagle' exists only in *your* mind."

The admiral spun from the window. He searched the lieutenant's expression for a flicker of understanding, a hint of acquiescence. But the young man's face remained impassive. "The official report from the country's own government states that the October raid on the mission, known as the Valley of the Holy Spirit, was the exclusive work of left-wing terrorists. According to the report, the cult leader, a man known as Reverend Cody Walker, murdered his attorney, then turned the gun on himself—despite an earlier, inaccurate report to the contrary. Apparently Walker took his life to avoid torture at the hands of the terrorists. Is that clear enough for you, Lieutenant?"

He paused, anticipating what the lieutenant might believe he had overlooked. "If you're thinking about the frogmen those liberated wretches saw and heard, they were English-speaking mercenaries. Men without a country. Hired by the radical elements inflaming Central America. *Now* is the picture complete, Lieutenant?"

Their minds locked in mental combat until a trace of guilt softened the hard lines around the admiral's mouth and eyes. "Sign those damn papers and be done with it! Don't push it, son. All the tracks are covered. Believe me."

There was no evidence that the words had produced their intended effect. Again the admiral looked out the window and sighed. "Apparently your silence indicates indecision. I suggest you return to your hotel and do some *serious* thinking. That's all, son. You're dismissed."

The admiral waited for the young man to leave, then slowly returned to his desk and wearily sank back into the swivel chair. Placing the folder before him, his sturdy fingers tapped on the cover, which read: LIEUTENANT RONALD A. REBUCK, JR. For a moment he sat there, dogged in thought. He reached for the phone and decisively punched the button to a line that did not go through the Pentagon switchboard, a direct line seldom used. His fingers dialed numbers known only to a select few. A voice crackled on the other end of the line. Admiral Church's message was brief and somber, "He's all yours, Sam."

CHAPTER 4

BILLY HALE'S limousine veered off the Virginia interstate and onto a dirt road, leaving a trail of dust and stones. The ornamental cross on its hood flashed like white fire. The Lincoln slowed at the entrance to the sprawling construction site that would soon be known as Christ Town.

Billy looked at the pretentious gate dominated by two wrought iron portals, each pivoting on a blue and gold hemisphere of the earth. Arched above the gate, the name G.L.E.E. CLUB (God Loves Everyone, Everywhere) connected the spheres in a semicircle of fluorescent letters.

Billy thought about his unannounced visit to Jimmy Christian. The fact that he'd traveled over a hundred miles to impose his unsolicited wisdom on the young evangelist came from an undefined compulsion and nothing more. He realized that his coming out of retirement would not truly depend upon his visits to the warring evangelists, Jimmy Christian and Harley Lombard. He did not need the powers of a deity to know the result before the deed. Was he simply bored? He asked himself time and time again. God, he hoped not.

The swarm of construction workers paid little heed to the shiny vehicle as it crawled along the winding road, the high gloss of its finish collecting a film of dust. Bulldozers and cranes clanked and groaned. Billy closed the window, shutting out the choking dust and deafening sound of the heavy machinery. He noted the various half-finished buildings and those nearing completion. Among the most imposing was a futuristic, white concrete structure fronted by

28

a sign reading: "Future Site of the G.L.E.E. Club Communications Center." He sighed, realizing all too well the building's great importance. Along with the computers, the *telephones* were the bread and butter of any successful religious organization. If the Catholics ever replaced bingo with 800 numbers, Hale thought, they would dominate the religious world.

The limousine finally entered the driveway of a 150-year-old Virginia Colonial whose heritage depended on which realtor's story you believed. A guard, dressed in a powder-blue and gold uniform, emerged from the white-columned entrance to challenge the unexpected visitor. Recognizing the famous face, he stepped briskly to open the door for Billy, but was waved off by Emile, the chauffeur.

Billy mouthed a silent greeting and unleashed the familiar grin which had turned on millions for so many years, then carefully stepped from the car, easing his weight upon the cane's marble head. He had taken two steps forward when a sharp flash of pain shot from his damaged kneecap to his hip. Through gritted teeth came a wounded smile.

From above, at a window, a woman's scrutinizing eyes watched through oversized glasses. Beth Staples moved gracefully from the window, tall and sensuous. The woolen skirt and sweater only half disguised the curves of a statuesque body. She placed a smooth, white hand on the golden clip that held her reddish brown hair in a bun. Behind the large glasses, emerald eyes were set above a slightly upturned nose.

Beth avoided the bovine gaze of Frank Buckmaster—Jimmy Christian's TV sidekick and personal whipping boy—and made an inconspicuous approach to the massive desk where their boss, Jimmy Christian, sat looking like a dwarf king perched on his throne. Four men in business suits were seated in captain's chairs wincing at the fire and brimstone he was raining on someone over the phone. "Pervus, what kind of horseshit preacher are you anyway? . . . Don't con me, Pervus. Your quota stinks! The worst in the south . . . What? . . . I don't give a damn about your lousy Christmas pageant. You deliver or I'm cutting your take to five percent."

Beth waited patiently until Jimmy Christian slammed down the phone and finished cursing under his breath. She approached the desk, bent low, and whispered in his ear.

"Billy Hale? *Here*?"

She nodded.

"Why? What's he doing here?"

"Shall I send Bucky?" she asked.

"No. He'll only get into one of his Biblical bullfests. The *great* Billy Hale will just have to wait." He sharply turned his attention on a moon-faced, middle-aged man. "Yes or no?" he demanded.

"Impossible. Take a miracle," said the president of W.O.G. (World of God), a subsidiary company to the parent G.L.E.E. Club.

"What the hell do you think I do around here?"

"Jimmy, before I could acquire prime time, there'd have to be a bona fide guarantee Jesus Christ was the guest star."

"You make it sound like I'm trying to hitch a bale of cotton to a pissant." Christian turned to a slender, white-haired man. "Do I have the money?"

"Only if you put a hiatus to construction. And even then you could be short," the chief accountant revealed.

"Hiatus, my ass!"

"You don't need a telethon, Jimmy," said the youngest of the group, a husky public-relations type with an acne-scarred face. "Juice the daily Glee Club tapings with the 'I'm broke' bit. Blame it on the government. The FCC. The devil. Hell, it works every time."

"Jimmy, why not regional? Maybe ten, even twelve states," the ministry's attorney suggested.

Jimmy raised a hand signifying he had heard enough, then looked at each of the sullen faces before him. "You people have been associated with me long enough to know when I get an idea, it's as if I've been goosed by God himself. . . . We go for it. Night of the Disciples. Four hours. Prime time. A live mini-telethon from our new studio complex." Before the skeptic media buyer could raise an eyebrow, Jimmy leered into the man's pumpkin face. The words seared like flames. "*God* needs this night. *Jesus* needs this night. *I* need this night. Do you goddamn well understand?"

A diminutive woman bounded into the room, forcing the departing quartet to step back and give her passage. "Shit!" said Jimmy, pounding his palm onto the desk. "What now?"

Cora Lee Christian, the former Cora Lee Turner, was once part of the Turner Sisters, a third-rate country-western group, fourth act on hillbilly western tours, who recorded for a regional label in Atlanta. She now ran the music end of Jimmy Christian's operation, a tax-exempt subsidiary that not only booked gospel acts and celebrities who'd found Jesus, but produced and sold records on an international scale.

They were a perfect couple. Not only did they have the same crab-apple cheeks and bantam figures, but the same high-pitched voices. Strangely, both had identical pouty lips until they opened up to sing hymns or to exhort donations. Actually, she looked more like Jimmy Christian's clone than his wife. Perhaps the most distinctive physical difference between them, other than gender, was the hair. He had the latest Italian cut, perfectly even without the plastered-down look: she had something which appeared more like a helmet than a hairdo.

"Daddy, *we've* got trouble!" she whined.

"Cora Lee, I'm busy. Billy Hale's downstairs."

"*Daddy* . . . we've got *big* trouble."

He closed his eyes and slumped back in his chair. "What kind of trouble, Cora Lee?"

"Mary Lou Busby's pregnant."

"Who in the world is Mary Lou Busby?"

"My lead singer in the choir."

"Is *that* what you rushed in here to tell me?"

"Mary Lou Busby, a sweet Christian child, was taken advantage of by that fast-talking ni-gro with his shiny suits."

"Jeremiah Jones?"

"I warned you, Daddy. Told you not to have a ni-gro on your board of governors."

He looked past her at Beth Staples, eager for her help. "Damn it, Cora Lee. There are twelve trained spiritual ministers in the building and you *had* to bring this to me. Especially with Billy Hale waiting—"

"*Daddy* . . . Mary Lou is engaged to one of *your* ministers."

"Gee-zus Christ!" Jimmy brought a closed fist down on the desk. "Cora Lee, how do you know Jeremiah Jones got her pregnant?"

"She told me. And Mary Lou doesn't lie."

Jimmy's eyes blared with anger. "That stupid black sonovabitch! All I need is a scandal. It's got to be taken out of Virginia. Beth, get on this right away. Call what's-his-face—that smut publisher in New York."

"Jack Winters?"

"Promise him something. *Anything*. He'd sell his mother to publish one of our born-again books."

"Are you talking about an abortion, Daddy?"

"Cora Lee, we're not the Catholic church. We're not losing soldiers."

"Kick him out of the Glee Club," she demanded.

"Are you crazy? Jeremiah Jones is good for better'n three million a year from the black communities."

"What about Mary Lou?"

"Get a backup singer."

"Daddy, I can't. She holds the group together."

"A voice that comes from the Lord," Frank Buckmaster said as Jimmy burned him with his eyes.

"Cora Lee, I can't keep Billy Hale waiting *any* longer."

"Does that mean you're going to do nothing about that . . . that *coon?*"

"Cora Lee, for Christ's sake, not now!"

Beth Staples placed a delicate hand on the tiny woman's elbow. "Cora Lee, why don't we discuss this privately?"

"But what about—"

"Everything will be fine. Just fine," Beth consoled.

Cora Lee's truculence gradually subsided. Beth enjoyed that kind of calming influence over her and commanded her respect. She had become a sturdy bridge between the frequently bickering Jimmy and Cora Lee Christian. Many a night, Beth would be awakened and summoned to Lord's Lake, the Christian residence, to bring about a semblance of peace to the feuding couple.

Jimmy let out a loud sigh and brought his little hands to his face, careful not to mess his hair. Cora Lee was always a war. A simple conversation would inevitably turn into a shouting match. And his effort to convince her she would be a great singing missionary somewhere in the Amazon was a hope gone dry. "Getting like a damned zoo around here," he said to himself when, through the openings between his fingers, he noticed that Frank Buckmaster was staring at him with the devoted attention of a Saint Bernard. "Why are you standing around like a statue of shit? Get Billy!"

The reception lobby looked more like the inside of an advertising agency than a ministry. Yet, despite his personal feelings, Billy Hale harbored a grudging admiration for Jimmy Christian. Certainly the young evangelist had made it happen in a relatively short time. Of course, his apprenticeship didn't find him stumping through an endless procession of cities and towns, living in second-rate hotels and boarding houses and performing night after night in damp circus tents, musty halls, and mosquito-infested ballparks. Jimmy Christian did it all from an air-conditioned TV studio. The five hundred stations airing daily in his G.L.E.E. Club network were far more than Billy Hale's best. At his peak, Billy had reached fewer than three hundred outlets. And those carried only his quarterly TV campaigns.

Billy was courteous. He smiled and waved and exchanged pleasantries. But he was beginning to feel like some old master on exhibit for the G.L.E.E. Club personnel, all eager to see at close range the man who epitomized the word "evangelist." Billy picked up a book with Jimmy Christian's face pictured below the shiny cover's title, *My Friend God*. "Is he?" Billy said softly to himself.

He knew the uncomfortable wait was nearing an end when the portly man dressed in a pink shirt with a dazzling blue bow tie waddled down the stairway, grinning broadly. " 'Light is sewn for the righteous and gladness for the upright in heart,' " quoted a breathless Frank Buckmaster.

"Psalms 97:11," Billy Hale responded, rising and extending his hand.

Buckmaster ignored Billy's hand and embraced the man he revered.

"Long time, Bucky."

"In sweet Jesus' name."

Billy remembered when Bucky, as he was known to the religious crowd, was once heralded as the golden voice of southeast Ohio during the magic days of radio. Billy had converted him during one of his campaigns, and Bucky had subsequently spent years with the Billy Hale ministry. Billy was forced to let him go when a fondness for alcohol clouded his sense of responsibility. Now, as Billy looked at the triple chin, the paunch of a Santa Claus, he wondered if Bucky had licked the battle over the bottle in his employ as a fat Robin to the evangelizing Batman, Jimmy Christian.

"Jimmy's sorry you had to wait, but the Lord's work must be done."

"I'm sure," Billy said dryly, hobbling after him.

Stepping into an awaiting elevator, Billy was surprised to see Buckmaster standing outside its entrance. "Surely you're coming with me?"

A sudden flush came over an already florid face. Bucky could have lied and made up an excuse about having to lose weight. But he didn't. Instead, he confessed, "I'm not permitted to use the elevators."

"Bucky," said Billy, reaching for his hand. "It's all right. I will take full responsibility."

Jimmy Christian sprang from the chair. "Billy, Billy,

Billy," he sang, clasping Hale's hand with both of his own.

"Praise the Lord!" Buckmaster bellowed. "The two greatest Christians in modern history."

"God knows I'm surprised to see you," said Jimmy. "Figured you would have waited until the completion of our new G.L.E.E. Club home, or at least 'til the studio unveiling."

"Something's bothering me. Thought it best to get it off my mind and *into* yours."

Jimmy's nod of dismissal at Buckmaster did not escape Billy. "No reason for Bucky to leave. We go back a long, long time."

"So I've been told *many* times," said Jimmy as he waited for Billy to be seated in a cushioned chair, then took a seat across from him and the glowing Frank Buckmaster. "Must be terribly important for you to make a trip to see me."

"You're moving too fast, Jimmy. Much, much too fast." Billy wouldn't leave him dangling. "You found a formula and it's working. But slow it down. Incorporate some temperance."

"Temperance?"

"Yes, temperance. Along with humility, it is a requisite of our profession."

Jimmy leaned forward to meet the challenge in Billy's hawklike eyes. "You didn't come all the way from your Shenandoah home just to tell me what you're telling me. What's truly on your mind?"

"I've said it. I feel you're moving too fast and saying too much. Leaving yourself wide open. Becoming a target. Son, you can only get so big before they come down on you."

"They? Who are they?" Jimmy smiled.

"*They*, as in those who engineered the deaths of Everson and Walker," Billy replied.

"As far as Everson goes, he apparently died of suffocation in that fire. And as for Cody Walker—why, the man was a fraud, a charlatan!"

"An enemy of the Lord!" Buckmaster roared.

"Who once was closely associated with the Jimmy Christian television ministry," Billy reminded them both.

Jimmy leaned forward. He would not be intimidated by someone who had come uninvited—a man he considered to be an artifact from the past. He shot out of the chair and moved with short steps about the office. "It's been over four years since I publicly disassociated myself with Walker. Anyway, from what I've read lately, he committed suicide."

"I'm inclined to believe the *initial* report," said Billy.

"Whether he did or didn't, his death was justice. For crying out loud, Billy, what does Cody Walker have to do with me anymore! His so-called ministry degenerated into a sick cult. I continue to spread the word of God, of our Lord, Jesus Christ, into the homes and hearts of millions every day."

"Amen," Buckmaster punctuated.

"The sick, the invalids, I bring Christ to *them*. They depend on *me*. I am their daily communion."

"Let's not get too carried away. The sick and the invalids are also financial contributors."

"And what about your donors, Billy? Did you exclude the sickly?"

"No . . . no, I'm afraid I didn't."

Jimmy returned to his chair, brought a hand to his tightly groomed brown hair, and laughed. For whatever reason, Billy was taunting him. He was sure. Tired of acting the role of an amiable host, he would deliver some gibes of his own. "Billy, I get the feeling maybe you don't understand where it is. I mean, the way of the world. Since your *retirement*, things have changed. Evangelism, like everything else, has to keep up with the times."

Billy could recite the lines, yet he let him ramble.

"What I'm building here is of the greatest magnitude. *Christ Town*. My God, man, this will be the Evangelical World Center!"

"Praise God," Buckmaster intoned.

Billy smiled. "Most enterprising. Quite a courageous undertaking. Christ Town . . . *the* Evangelical World Center. Yes, indeed. I'd sure like to believe you, Jimmy. I truly would. But I've been following your activities. You're smooth, cunning, a slick salesman. I'm sure you could show the boys in the Vatican how to improve their holdings . . . and you're greedy, son. Greedy."

The younger evangelist's lips tightened. "I just trust in the Lord, *Reverend* Hale."

" 'The righteous shall be glad in the Lord, and shall trust in Him,' " Buckmaster echoed.

"Psalms 64:10, isn't it?" said Billy. "He that loveth silver shall not be satisfied . . . Ecclesiastes."

They sat in silence until Jimmy turned away. "What more is there to say? I can only thank you for the . . . advice."

"No charge," said Billy, groping for his cane.

"By the way, have you given thought about the honorary chairmanship of my church, Billy? Perhaps I neglected to mention, but *fifty thousand dollars* a year for expenses goes along with it."

"Most generous," said Billy, struggling to rise. "My memory's a little faulty these days; who are the people that sit on your board?"

"Tommy Sunday's nephew for one. Tommy was a dear friend of yours, wasn't he, Billy?"

"A dear, dear friend."

"A martyr for Jesus," said Buckmaster.

"He was that," Billy agreed. "Tell me: this nephew, didn't he take over Tommy's ministry?"

"His radio crusade is aired through our subsidiary network."

"Been reading about his oil ventures."

"He's done well, Billy."

"Mixing religion with oil?"

"Takes a tremendous amount of capital to ensure doing the Lord's work *these* days."

"Rising costs, of course."

Jimmy ignored the snide inference. "Phil Hartman sits on the board."

"The former national security advisor convicted of fraud and perjury?"

"Born again, Billy."

"Before or after he wrote his best-selling book?"

"*Buddy Reeves,*" said Jimmy.

"The manufacturer of CB radios?"

"Johnny Clay."

"The country singer, drug addict, and wife-beater who—terribly sorry, I forgot. *Another* born-again Christian."

"Then, of course, we have Reverend Jeremiah Jones."

"Jeremiah Jones," Billy repeated, "the one-time champion of black rights who's a frequent visitor at the White House." Leaning on the cane, Billy moved away from the chair. "I must hand it to you, son. Every soul you mentioned has made headlines."

"The Lord chose who Jimmy would have on the board. He prays and receives their names," Buckmaster singsonged.

"There's one more," Jimmy said in a voice richly laced with sarcasm. "Abe Margolis."

Billy Hale stopped in his tracks. "The *Rabbi?*"

"The *evangelist,*" Jimmy corrected.

A scowl wrinkled Billy's face. "Abe Margolis is a fraud."

"The Lord's fraud," chimed Buckmaster.

"How did you buy him, Jimmy?"

"He saw the light. Quite possibly the same light the apostle Paul had seen. I'm sure you wouldn't consider ever contradicting *that* light. Especially when you preached of it so many, many times."

"Son, the only light Margolis sees is the light of gold. What's his take—twenty percent of every Jew he converts to Christianity? Bah!" Billy limped past Frank Buckmaster and turned painfully at the door. "Jimmy, I think I could hold you up for a quarter of a million dollars. If for nothing more, to lend some respectability to your church's board." He shifted the cane to his other hand. "Take the advice of an old veteran. Go forth with something besides God. Like caution."

*　　　*　　　*

38

It was a furious Jimmy Christian who watched the limousine pull out of the driveway. He paid little attention to Buckmaster waving goodbye with both hands, nor did he hear Beth Staples enter the room.

"Everything has been arranged," she informed. "The girl leaves tomorrow for New York."

When he didn't reply, she came to his side and followed his glare—taking in the limousine winding its way through the maze of construction. "I gather Dr. Hale's visit was not entirely upbeat."

He moved away from the window, stopping at his desk. He looked aimlessly about the room, then targeted in on the scale model of Christ Town which took up a full corner of the spacious office. He was drawn to it.

"He comes out of the blue. Unexpected. *Uninvited.* Then has the gall to chastise me, lecture me, like I'm some school kid."

"About what?" she asked.

"Billy Hale, a w ed-up Billy Hale, tells *me* I'm rushing things, and arns me that I could end up like Everson and Walke Me!" He turned to look at her. "Who else is doing what I'm doing? What other person on earth is building *Christ Town?*"

She couldn't tell him what she really thought. How Billy Hale, despite his retirement, was still the grand name in evangelism. How Jimmy Christian, in his best day, could never duplicate the electricity and magnetism Billy Hale projected. How most of the religious critics and experts felt that Jimmy Christian and his chief rival, Harley Lombard, came out of the evangelist litter of mediocrity. None of them was endowed with the grace and style of Billy Hale. "Jimmy, you must remember that Billy has built his fame over a great number of years," she said reassuringly.

"He's never reached the heights *I* will. Once the world sees Christ Town, they'll think Billy Hale lived in the Stone Age. *Harley Lombard's* behind that old man's visit. Harley's panicked. He's afraid of drowning in my wake. You can bet he asked Billy to come snooping around." He turned to where she could see hurt building in his eyes. "Twice I've asked that old man to be on my board. *Twice*, Beth! . . . I don't need him. Never did. He wipes Harley Lombard's nose, not *mine*. When, when did he ever help me? When did *anyone* help me?"

She let his last remark slip by. It was the price she paid to be the administrative aide of an egomaniac. But she would never forget that there was a time when he was shunned by his peers, who wrote him off as a brash young man who should leave evangelism to the experts. Nor would she forget when he changed his name from Jimmy Clarendon to Jimmy Christian, or how he begged her to help him enact his dream of blanketing the world with his religious television network. She would not forget how she left her job in sales at a Cleveland television station to become the efficient and quiet force behind the G.L.E.E. Club's success. Help him? Without her, he would never have come this far. What mattered to her was that *she* knew he knew.

" 'You're getting too big, *son*. Incorporate some temperance,' " Jimmy mimicked. "Two men die and Billy Hale thinks some religious upheaval's upon us. Doesn't he know everyone wants to be a Christian these days? Even the president speaks of being a good Christian. You don't hear him saying, 'Be a good Jew.' Billy Hale had his day in the sun. It's my turn, Beth, and *no one* is going to keep me from it."

She expected him to pout, since he was predictable after unleashing his wrath. To her surprise, however, she saw that other look she had recently learned to identify. For the past six months, he'd been coming on to her. So far she had been able to deflect his advances, to fight off his desire with the elusiveness of a cat. And now, once again, he approached her with a horny pleading in his eyes.

"Beth, I need you. God knows, I need you. You're the only person in the world I can communicate with." He moved closer, and she stood erect, prepared. Unlike any time before, he boldly placed his hands on her waist. He hoped to look manly, she knew, but the odd smile that parted his lips, the cherubic, clean-shaven cheeks and the dark brown eyes devoid of sparkle made her think of a little boy trying to put the make on an experienced woman. "Beth, you know I don't drink or smoke. I'm not on dope. Beth, I'm so goddamn frustrated."

"I'm not your outlet, Jimmy."

"Beth, when? For God's sake, when?"

"Jimmy, take your hands off me!"

His hands had slipped from her waist to fondle an ass that drove him wild in his dreams, but she pushed them away. He gazed longingly at her breasts, but the stern denial in her eyes stood him off. Defeated by her glacial lack of response, he slowly turned, his face crimson with rejection.

Beth Staples smiled inwardly. She would let the Mary Lou Busbys of the ministry spread their legs for the glory of God. She had come this far without the anointment of Jimmy Christian's pecker. Besides, he didn't have what it would take. He wasn't alone. And until someone did, she was *nobody's* woman.

41

CHAPTER 5

LIEUTENANT RON REBUCK, JR., sat alone in a corner of the crowded, dimly lighted hotel bar. Dressed in a yellow turtleneck and brown leather jacket, he blended into the crowd of Christmas Eve revelers in downtown Washington, D.C. Without the uniform, he looked far removed from the U.S. Navy, and his sun-washed good looks hadn't gone unnoticed by the sexy redhead seated at the bar flashing a silky leg through a black slit dress. But Christmas Eve with a hooker was not the Christmas present the young lieutenant had in mind.

He surveyed the busy scene of tinsel and holly, the animated crowd of drinkers. He let his eyes wander over the melange of boisterous government workers, trolling singles, closet homosexuals, and blatant screamers, the usual collection of not-so-gay divorcées. It was the same old game, Rebuck thought, the one played nightly in gin mills and body shops from Portland, Maine, to Portland, Oregon, and all the vast span of America in between. But beneath the cheerful facades, the hollow laughter, wooden dialogue and tired smiles, the intruder loneliness was knocking at their hearts. He was sure of it. He could hear the knocking.

It was nine o'clock, and Rebuck identified the cocktail-hour holdovers from their business-day attire and advanced states of intoxication. The most recent arrivals were dressed more casually for the evening's long haul. He wondered why these people weren't home with their families. *Home*, he thought. For the past seven years, his mailbox had read,

"SEAL Base I, U.S. Navy, Coronado, California." It was all the home he'd desired.

The SEALs were his life. Belonging to the select Sea-Air-Land special force created by John F. Kennedy during the early 1960s—when men with keen intelligence and the physical stamina of a horse became the SEAL prototype—was a source of considerable pride for Rebuck. After all, though operating under the Navy umbrella, the SEALs were known as an elite entity which ranked with the world's finest.

Rebuck rarely drank to excess, but he had decided to make an exception to suit the calendar and the extraordinary circumstances surrounding his presence in Washington, D.C. The fact that he was under virtual house arrest was overridden by the significance of a day which marked the eleventh anniversary of his father's bizarre and brutal murder. Catching the attention of a waitress dressed in a green tank suit and pantyhose and complete with a red-and-white Santa's hat, he signalled for a refill.

"What *was* that?" she asked, approaching.

"Sebastiani. Bring the bottle."

"Can't. How about two glasses?"

He nodded, grumbling over the word "can't." It didn't exist in the SEAL dictionary; neither did the word "deceit." Yet for the past twenty-eight days he had been assigned to the Pentagon, where he sat in a cubbyhole of an office with nothing to do but think. At night he was restricted to the confines of his hotel, where he would think some more. And about what? Becoming part of a cover-up? He bit down on his lip as, once again, his mind flashed back to that night of wind, stealth, and the deadly execution of a hit on an obscure but dangerous religious cult. He remembered his swelling sense of pride—not only in himself and his fellow SEALs, but in his country—when their mission had been successfully completed. With his own eyes he'd seen the wretched men, women, and children they'd liberated from a cult of horrors. For the life of him, Rebuck could not understand why the truth of this particular mission should be denied by his own government.

His thoughts ran next to Ike Vesper. Only he and Ike, his chief petty officer, knew the truth of what had happened to the Reverend Cody Walker, whose death had vaulted him into national infamy. And if Ike's signature *was* attached to those affidavits, he must have been drugged—all six foot five, two hundred fifty pounds of black is beautiful.

He'd been unable to reach Ike at his Coronado apartment, and calling him at SEAL Base I had proved equally fruitless. Either Ike was not getting his messages, or he was unable—or unwilling—to return his calls. But it didn't seem right. For the past two years, they had been almost inseparable; Ike had become the older brother Ron had never had. After the fourth Mrs. Vesper took a permanent leave of absence, Rebuck did all but move into the apartment.

Rebuck watched the waitress fend off the advances of a drunk on her way back to his table. Mumbling curses under her breath, she set the two glasses of wine before him. But Rebuck had no room now for anyone's troubles but his own and looked past her toward the bar. The redhead was now the object of an aggressive man's advances. He had locked onto their activity, observing what he thought to be two people quibbling over the price for a fast lay, when the severity of his own problems suddenly came back to him.

Rebuck let his thoughts drift into a maze of wishful thinking. Maybe this was all some kind of test to measure his qualifications for a dangerous, sensitive mission. He was staring into the wine when a hush fell over the three noisy drunks at the next table. Rebuck looked up and saw that the redhead had left the bar and was walking toward him.

"Two glasses? Where's your date?" the redhead asked, revealing flawless white teeth.

"I'm here by myself."

"Can I join you?"

He half motioned for her to be seated, placed a glass of wine before her, then lit a thin, pungent cigarillo—all the while studying her. He had seen hookers the world over, from teenaged vamps in Latin America to European grand-mothers. Yet there was something about this one . . . she didn't fit the traditional mold. Perhaps it was the kid gloves she wore, or her hair, set in what might be de-scribed as "virginal pageboy." Whatever it was, he won-dered why with her face and figure she had to grind for C-notes in some bar when she could run with millionaires.

She seemed to read his mind and said, "Don't believe it. I fuck for fun."

"Just great. Getting plenty of it?"

The glitter in her eyes didn't match the smile. She sipped the wine. "You have good taste. The question is, do you taste good?"

"Miss . . ."

"Trudy, Trudy Ballin."

"Trudy, all I want is to get through this lousy night. Maybe another time, another adventure."

She ignored his dismissal. "I know so much about you," she said, a harder edge to her voice. "It's like we've already met."

"Sure," Rebuck said, assuming a conspiratorial tone of his own. "Paris, two years ago . . . George Cinq Hotel. Where I woke up in the morning with my wallet missing and your note, 'Off to Monaco.' "

She laughed too loudly; an attention-commanding laugh, he thought. He sat back and looked suspiciously at the wide, forced smile when she spoke firmly through clenched teeth. "You're hot." Her eyes darted about the room. "Don't look around. The men next to us are not the Three Wise Men—they're Feds. The woman behind you is a notorious double agent. The—"

"*Hey*! Trudy, or whatever your name is—can it!"

She laughed at her poor attempt to play a woman of intrigue and reached for his right hand, softly stroking the palm as she studied it. "You have friends. People who care. I see a man. A very important man. He's most eager to meet with you."

"And *you* can take me to him?"

"Shall we go?"

Rebuck folded his arms. He wasn't going anywhere to meet anybody. Everyone involved officially in his career knew exactly where to find him.

She read the boredom in his eyes and shot him an icy look. Her voice was threatening as she returned her attention to his palm. "I see another man. He *doesn't* like you."

"I think I've seen this movie before," said Rebuck, retrieving his hand.

She didn't seem in the least bothered by his rejection but, to his surprise, began to slowly work on the wine glass as if it was some object of hard-core passion. Snaking her tongue suggestively along its smooth rim, she then blew gently on the wine's surface as if to remove its chill. At the next table, the three men she called federal agents abruptly ended their boisterous conversation and watched the performance with leering admiration.

Through the haze of alcohol, Ron Rebuck's instincts retained their cutting edge. He was drawn by the movement of a man making tracks toward their table. Rebuck quickly sized him up: middle-aged, neatly dressed, average height, medium build, and if he was carrying a weapon, it had to be a blade, because there was no noticeable bulge under his buttoned jacket.

"Take a cocaine break, sonny," the man growled. "Red and me got some unfinished business."

Rebuck looked past the intruder, beyond the redhead's smug grin to where the head bartender alerted the lounge's hired "tuff."

The man bent over and thrust his face in Rebuck's. "Do I have to kick your ass out of that chair, Junior?"

Rebuck gently slid his chair back as the man's fist whistled past his face, grazing an ear. Rebuck's reaction was swift as he grabbed the man's tie, spun him around, then drove his face down onto the table's hard surface, splintering the bone in his attacker's nose.

The huge bouncer was fast upon the scene. Perhaps irked by having to work on Christmas Eve and needing to take his frustrations out on someone, he vetoed normal persuasive conversation and charged what he thought to be just another wimp filled with whiskey courage. But his bull's rush at Rebuck was met by a sharp kick to the knee, followed by a swift reversed spin kick which landed jarringly against the bridge of his nose. Another kick to the pit of his stomach doubled him over, and a knee to his face put him on his back. To his bloody misfortune, he had come upon someone whose frustration was far greater than his own.

Rebuck tossed a wadded twenty-dollar bill on the table and, without another glance at the smiling redhead or the two battered men, walked out of the bar and into the hotel lobby.

He stopped at the desk and asked the clerk for his messages, but there was nothing in his box. Ike Vesper still had not returned his call, and his frustration seemed endless. He didn't have to report back to his Pentagon cubbyhole until Tuesday at 0700 hours—three days away —so he decided to isolate himself in his room, somehow get through the night, and first thing in the morning leave Washington, D.C., before he was driven to kill somebody.

His orders limited him to a hundred-mile radius, and he wondered how far it was to Little Creek, Virginia, and SEAL Base II. He was sure to find some of his friends there, men he'd trained and served with. He decided to give it more thought after he'd found out the exact mileage. In either case, he wouldn't stay cooped up in this damn hotel for the next three days. He swore as he passed the elevator and headed for the stairway. In his present state of mind, he'd prefer to walk the six flights up to his floor rather than chance being trapped in a lousy lift.

Reaching his floor, Rebuck looked down the hall to see whether anyone was lingering outside his room. During his enforced sabbatical, he'd battled a rising tide of paranoia; he felt that every move he made was being watched by someone. After this latest episode, brawling over a redhead right out of a James Bond movie, he knew he'd better get himself a weapon. Proficiency in the martial arts was one thing, but fighting off bullets with hands and feet was another. The hell with civilian law, he thought. Without a gun to defend oneself, the odds for survival dropped too much for his liking.

He made it to his room without incident and flicked on the light. A pair of long silky legs filled his eyes. He slowly worked his way to the redhead's face.

"What kept you?" she purred.

He looked beyond where she was sitting. "Who've you got hiding in the bathroom, King Kong?"

"It's just you and me, Lieutenant Ron Rebuck, Jr. One on one."

After all that had been happening, he was only mildly surprised that she knew his name and rank. "How did you get in here?" he asked, looking around his room.

She uncrossed her legs, revealing more thigh and playing on a seductive smile. "Tell me, who taught you how to kick like that, a kangaroo?"

"Red, you're going to have to take your act somewhere else. I can't handle any more nightmares."

She came out of the chair. For the first time, he realized how tall she really was: five-nine, maybe ten. "You call *this* a nightmare?" she said, whirling in place.

For a moment he was mesmerized by the long, shapely legs Hanes couldn't improve upon—those amazing breasts beneath the tight black dress, so inviting, waiting to be unveiled, kissed and fondled—and the superb ass that could create thunder in any man's mind. Perhaps the fact that he was bordering on some kind of quiet nervous breakdown was what provided the sudden antidote to his rising desire. He wearily took off the leather jacket and hung it in the closet next to his dress blues, then turned to see her gazing unabashedly at his crotch.

"God, I bet you're hung," she said in a taunting, pornographic voice. She seemed to put a little extra into her sway as she walked to the double bed and sat on its edge. "All right, Lieutenant, before I drive you to the point of tearing my clothes off and fucking my brains out, perhaps I *had* better get on with the whys and wherefores." She watched as Ron Rebuck plopped into a chair. His smirk had no effect on her. "Like I said, my name really is Trudy. And *yes*, the man who hassled you was a set-up. Poor Bernie," she giggled, "hope he doesn't have a concussion to go with that broken nose."

Rebuck's sour expression persisted. Yet she smiled and continued. "I apologize for the B-movie tactics, but I *had* to get you out of that bar before the vino did cuckoo things to your head. Before you got involved in conversation with those men at the next table."

"The three Feds?" he said, sarcastically.

"Precisely. You must realize that the biggest ears are in Washington."

"Just who the hell are you—Mata Hari?"

"Close. And you, Lieutenant, happen to be a walking time bomb."

"You got that right."

"We figured if you were going to explode, tonight was the night. We just couldn't take that chance."

"*We?*"

"Shortly. You will find out shortly." She noticed he was looking at the handbag which matched her alluring ensemble. "No, Lieutenant, no tape recorder. It isn't necessary. This room is bugged and your phone is tapped."

Rebuck now saw her in a new perspective. At last, he hoped, he'd get some answers. She had told him enough to make him believe she knew much more. And he would get it out of her—by force, if necessary. He sat back in the chair, controlling his impatience. "What's it all about, Red?"

She returned his question and piercing gaze with a slow, suggestive smile, then rose from the bed and slithered out of her dress, exposing a flawless back and hips. She dropped back onto the bed and removed her boots and delicately rolled the nylons down her legs. Clad now only in a shiny black bra and panties, she stretched out on the bed, her sensational legs arched in an erotic display of pure temptation.

Ron Rebuck watched intently as she rose to her knees,

unhooked her bra and, with a lurid wickedness, rolled onto her stomach. He would not allow himself to be driven over the sexual edge and into an emotional freefall, yet he couldn't tear his eyes from the firm, pointed tits, and the rise of an ass some men would die for. He suffocated the urge to succumb to the world's oldest trap. For not even she, this wonder woman, could speedily repair the short circuits in his battered mind.

It was his move and she appeared overly confident when, suddenly, a loud rapping noise filled the room. Again it came: three firm knocks on the wall from the next room. Before he could possibly react, she had sprung from the bed and was at the door to the adjoining room.

For the second time in one night she had caught him unprepared. And *twice* was death reborn in his line of work. He rose from the chair, wondering what this peculiar woman with more sides to her than a magician's box was up to, as she unlocked and pushed open the door to the next room. She turned in the doorway, facing Rebuck with a diabolical expression on her face. "Sam's waiting," she said.

He quickly realized the only protection he had was her, and with lightning speed, he grabbed her. She was no match for his quickness as he spun her by the chin, then pushed her into the darkened room, a forearm around her delicate neck.

Rebuck heard what he thought to be the sound of a creaking chair. It was followed by a commanding voice. "The clock started at 2200 hours. You've got less than nine minutes, Lieutenant."

For fifteen seconds there was dead silence. Then another movement in the darkness found him tightening his grip on the woman's throat until she gasped for breath. Rebuck could just make out a ghostlike figure when a slender ray of light emanating from the lamp in his room fell on a pair of military shoes. His eyes remained fixed on the feet inching toward him, closer and closer, until a shadowy silhouette materialized before him. Rebuck smelled the leather-scented cologne when a flicking sound exploded in his ears like a cannon, followed by the flame from a cigarette lighter which shone in his eyes like a bonfire. And then he saw that face—the unmistakable face of a man special forces the world over called "The Vampire."

Rebuck's arm dropped immediately from the redhead's neck, his protective shield surrendered to a legend as he looked into the cold steel eyes of the feared SEAL captain—Claude Gemmer.

Suddenly, the door shut behind them. They were alone. To be so close—within arm's length—to a man who, rumor had it, possessed the eyes of an owl and the cunning of a mythical vampire, had Rebuck wondering how many throats Claude Gemmer had slit under the cover of darkness.

They sat across a small table lit by an overhead light which hung from a copper link chain. Ron Rebuck looked upon the leathery face with scar tissue about the nose and under the narrow eyes and fought off his feeling of intimidation. Throughout his tour of duty, he had only once met the highest ranking and most valorous of all SEALs. It was during graduation from BUD, Basic Underwater Demolition, when the captain, then a commander, presented him with the prestigious Iron Mike award. He was thrilled to have received this honor from a man his SEAL instructors considered their ultimate hero. But he'd had trouble believing all the stories dealing with the captain's heroics until Ike Vesper confirmed his exploits in vivid, gory detail.

Vesper had served under Gemmer in Vietnam, and he often told one story which explained why the Viet Cong had put a bounty on the head of every SEAL—and promised a fortune to the man who killed or captured Gemmer. According to Ike, Gemmer's nightly ritual was to slip from the camp perimeter, alone, and melt into the jungle to stalk snipers and infiltrators. He always returned before dawn . . . but not before he'd spilled enemy blood.

The captain's lips parted, and Rebuck thirsted for words that might finally resolve his dilemma. "The pussies at the Pentagon, at Defense, didn't know diddly shit about Operation Black Eagle. Your orders, Lieutenant, were as false as a padded bra."

"Operation Black Eagle was an unauthorized mission?"

The captain nodded.

"How? How did it all come down?"

"In what sense, Lieutenant?"

"My orders . . . my C.O., Commander O'Donnell, the sub's captain, Admiral Church, my SEAL team . . . were they *all* in on it from the start?"

The captain's face was an unrevealing mask. "You will resign your commission to join our team," he said, quickly raising his hand to stifle the objection forming on Rebuck's lips.

"The papers have been drawn up and your resignation approved. Shortly after the new year, you will be a civilian."

Rebuck sat in silent rage. His words came fast and sarcastically. "Is that *your* order or the Navy's?"

"Doesn't matter. You *will* resign."

"Is that a threat, Captain?"

"Threat? No, Mister, that's a fact!"

The wiry captain sprang from the chair and walked with a noticeable limp past a window to a darkened corner of the room. His voice came from the shadows. "You're not dropping anchor on plans that took years to develop. You've been chosen, Mister—by me, *personally*."

"Chosen for what, Captain?" Rebuck demanded.

"To head up a special task force here on the East Coast. To become part of an organization that cares about this country's future."

The captain moved out from the shadows and limped back to the chair. His face was hard as nails. "Never again will the United States be held hostage by pissant countries or religious crackpots. Your mission—yes, Lieutenant, Operation Black Eagle—made damn sure there wouldn't be another Jonestown."

"Captain, the SEALs are my career, my *life*. You can't just shoot down—"

"*Lieutenant*! . . . You only have one option."

Rebuck looked long and hard at the cruelty written on every line of Gemmer's face, at the thin tight lips, the scar tissue resulting from too many skin grafts. "Captain, that option sounded more like a death warrant."

"*Didn't* it."

"Are you people afraid I might spill what I know to the newspapers? Is that why I've been kept prisoner in this hotel?"

"You're not the kind. Besides, you'd never get the chance."

"And I suppose that if I don't resign, I get dropped over the Kremlin wall or shot out of the sky—is that how you blackmailed my men? Ike Vesper, he really bellied under?"

"Ike Vesper served under me before you ever heard of the SEALs. I taught him, like he taught you."

Ron Rebuck's eyes narrowed with suspicion.

"Who do you think appointed Vesper to be your nurse-maid for the past two years? That's right, Lieutenant. And while you're thinking about that, chew on this. Your name didn't come out of some hat. There's many a good man in the SEALs, Black Beret, and Second Marine Recon who fill my requirements. But you have that something extra." Gemmer paused, and Rebuck was locked to the evil smile which suited the captain's marred face. "You see, Lieutenant, I know all about your father, and those who killed him. You could say I'm tuned into the personal hell you've been living with, that piece of *pure* hate in your heart."

Gemmer paused for effect before playing his trump card. "And should you have any thought of disobeying me, Lieutenant, I want you to remember this: your mother, June Rebuck, is completely safe. . . ."

CHAPTER 6

CHRISTMAS CAME AND WENT. It was the start of a new year, another dent into the eighties, another presidential election year. For many, it was another beginning to 365 days of "Is this all there is?" It was another year for five thousand more people to become hermits. Billy Hale would not be among them. The new year found him on the interstate again, this time in Ohio.

The voice cut through Billy Hale's dream. "We're here, Chief," Emile, his chauffeur was saying.

Billy awakened from his nap in time to see the sign: WELCOME TO CHARITY—POPULATION 160,000. Moments later an immense billboard read, HOME OF THE RIGHT REVEREND HARLEY LOMBARD AND HIS WORLD CATHEDRAL. It featured a large and flattering picture of Harley Lombard superimposed on a photograph of the majestic cathedral. "Have mercy," Billy muttered, contemplating his dinner meeting with his close friend and protegé.

Harley Lombard stood nude before a full-length mirror in one of two master bedrooms within his majestic ministry-owned home. His coal-black eyes scrutinized the reflection of his protruding belly and the roll of fat girdling his waist. He swore to reduce his consumption of alcohol and eliminate desserts. He would not become a candidate for a coronary; not now, not at his peak, when he considered himself the undisputed king of world evangelism.

A close inspection of his face brought an approving smile. Evangelically speaking, his face could not have been more appropriate. His features were distinguished but not regal. His only facial blemish was a peculiar red blotch on the tip of his nose. Although he was fifty-two, Lombard had the unlined appearance of a man in his early forties, a face both the suspicious young and reactionary old could trust. The smile broadened; his face had hardly changed since the days when it all had started, when he was Billy Hale's protegé.

Harley Lombard padded along the plush earth-tone carpet and entered a high-ceilinged, oval-shaped room lighted by a crystal chandelier. He pushed his palm against a leather-sheathed toggle switch recessed in the cedar-paneled wall. There was a soft hum, and the solid-appearing wall became seven panels that retracted like the petals of a tulip, exposing seven partitioned roomlets housing his wardrobe. He touched the switch a second time and a full-length mirror whirred silently into place, ready to reflect his sartorial decision.

He emerged from the dressing suite in a blue, crushed-velvet smoking jacket with the gold initials *H.L.* monogrammed over the right breast. A white cashmere turtleneck covered his bull-like neck, and tailor-made houndstooth pants draped over the tongues of Gucci shoes. He completed the fastidious ritual by slipping a large, rococo ring on his finger, and his face swelled with pride.

"I only make forty thousand a year," he would counter critics of his lifestyle as if the wolves were at the door. The expensive clothes and jewelry, the real estate holdings, the two Mercedes and the Porsche Turbo Carrera, the gourmet food he ate and the imported wines he drank were all purchased through the tax-exempt Harley Lombard Ministries.

Lombard delighted in speaking of the hard times he had endured before the building of the World Cathedral. He would drone for hours about the days when his suits were store-bought, when his feet were shod by Thom McAn, when he preached from the stage of a leaky, rented auditorium. Lombard would listen to the busy hum of his World Cathedral offices and recall the days when his entire staff had been comprised of Andy Gaines, two part-time shills, and his wife, Wilma Mae, who doubled as a secretary and beat up on the piano while belting out religious songs. Never once did he mention how Billy Hale saved him from a life of pastoral drudgery and guided him along the road to evangelical stardom.

Wilma Mae Lombard, the former Wilma Mae Babbitt, beloved daughter of the late Reverend and Mrs. Jesse Babbitt, was an indispensable personality in the Harley Lombard Ministry. In addition to her musical input, her mother-and-apple-pie image made her as effective a solicitor as her vibrant husband. She stood in a bedroom no less opulent than Harley's, furnished in Elizabethan decor with contrasting contemporary touches. Tall, noticeably erect, she actually resembled a living mannequin. When she walked, she gave the impression that if she were to come to an abrupt halt her body would topple into sections. Sorting through wig after wig in a closet much like her husband's, she chose an Eva Gabor piece, then, as if by the numbers, she sat in a powder-pink chair before a parlor mirror framed with star-shaped lights.

"Harley," she called in a husky voice as she applied polish to long, false fingernails. She called his name again and twice more before sensing his presence at the door. Her chestnut-brown eyes projected displeasure. Her voice made it more definite. "Your *thing* called. Says it's important."

Harley moved into the room and stood behind her. "What is it between you and Andy Gaines? You're always bad-mouthing him. The man has been with me for almost twenty years. What do you know that I don't?"

"I know he's never been married."

"What's that supposed to mean? Jesus was never married; most of the popes never married; *I* almost didn't marry."

She dropped the nail polish on the table. "You're the one who gets revelations." Her eyes were drawn to Harley's ostentatious ring. "You're *not* going to wear *that?*"

"That?" said Harley. "You call a petrified splinter from the cross Christ died upon *that?*"

"Harley, you're a fool. Billy Hale will *never* kiss it."

"Forget the ring, Wilma Mae. You called Andy Gaines a *thing*. I want to know why."

"I don't want to talk about it any further. I'm angry enough. Billy Hale calls and I have to change my whole day."

"Change what, your bridge date with a pack of female hyenas?"

She turned stiffly from the mirror like a woman whose neck was in a brace, her cheeks flushed with anger. "You're not the man my father was, Harley Lombard."

Billy Hale had been a frequent dinner guest in the Lombard home. On this night, the evangelist realized he had been an inattentive visitor who had taken no more than casual notice of the dining room's uncommon elegance. The candelabras were matching seven-branch antiques, their light flickering softly off rosewood paneling accented with amber-hued carriage lamps. Original oils of English hunting scenes tastefully enhanced the room's British men's-club informality, as did high-backed chairs upholstered in deep red leather and the high gloss of the parquet floor.

Lombard's English-born butler poured steaming coffee into Hale's demitasse and bowed at the old evangelist's nod of appreciation.

"Tell me, Wilma Mae, how is my godson?" Billy asked.

"Matthew has been serving the Lord in Africa for two years. He reminds me so much of my father in his missionary work."

"Your father was a pastor in Toledo, not a missionary," Harley snapped.

"One needn't be in Africa or India to be a missionary." She looked directly at Billy. "My father did the work of the poor in Toledo. I'm sorry you never had the opportunity to meet him, Billy. He was a wonderful, wonderful man."

"I'm sure," said Billy, smiling at his coffee.

"He didn't have any great World Cathedral. Just a

simple church . . . By the way, Billy, have you noticed Harley's ring?"

"No, I haven't."

"Show Billy your ring, Harley," Wilma Mae insisted.

More indignant than embarrassed, Harley extended his hand to Billy, revealing a massive gold ring topped with something which resembled a miniature trophy case surrounded by diamonds.

"According to Harley, a genuine piece of the cross Jesus died upon is fixed between the diamonds," Wilma Mae said cattily.

"That's wonderful," said Billy, attempting to mask his disinterest. "Harley, when are you going to show me your chapel? I've been coming here for years but I've still yet to see it."

Wilma Mae smiled like a Cheshire cat. "Yes, Harley, *do* show Billy your chapel."

"A chapel's a chapel. You see one, you've seen 'em all," Harley replied quickly.

"Not *your* chapel," Wilma Mae gloated.

Billy looked at his watch. "Emile will be coming for me within the hour and there is something I would like to discuss with you, Harley."

"You're not staying overnight, Billy?" Wilma Mae asked with surprise.

"Perhaps Harley neglected to mention it, but I made previous arrangements to spend the night in Cleveland. I'm delivering the eulogy for an old friend in the morning." Billy folded his napkin. "Now, what do you say we visit your chapel, Harley?"

"Billy, really, it's much more comfortable in the living room."

"But it's *so* comfortable in your chapel," Wilma Mae persisted, looking away from her husband's steaming face. "Billy, when Harley had the chapel built, he did it in parts, so—"

"*Wilma Mae*, Billy doesn't want to hear about it!"

She spoke on over his grumbled objections. "When something goes wrong in the *chapel*, would you believe

58

Harley blindfolds the poor worker, leads him by the hand to whatever needs fixing, then puts a screen around him so he can't see anything but what is to be repaired?"

Billy Hale rose from his chair. "Harley, Lucifer himself couldn't stop me from seeing your chapel."

It was a gaping Billy Hale who stood at the open oak door decorated with two angels carved into the wood by a masterful hand. He shook his head as if to clear what he believed to be a mirage; for in the center of a two-thousand-square-foot room, reposing under a twenty-foot dome, lay a gigantic, sunken, marble-tiled Jacuzzi. Hot water rainbowing from the pouting mouths of cherubim fed the five-thousand-gallon pool. "Harley, Harley," he moaned.

The Venetian tile walls of the chapel were indented by seven alcoves, each with an arched entrance flanked by statuary. Anticipating Hale's angry reaction, Lombard had vanished into the first alcove. Knowing he would sooner or later have to face an inevitable confrontation with his long-time mentor, and unwilling to be lectured and chastised, Harley loaded up with fortitude and came out on the offensive—speaking rapidly. "When I opened the door, it activated a super computer. Come and look, Billy. Had it designed by an electronics genius from West Germany."

"I'll take your word for it," Hale groused.

"Show you how it works," said Harley, giving the scowling Billy a wide berth.

"Must you?"

"Let there be life," Harley said in a somber tone. His vocal command activated the computer within the first alcove. "Adam," he called, and Jacuzzi jets sent warm water swirling. "Gabriel," he trumpeted, and symphonic music wafted from hidden stereophonic speakers. "Peter," he commanded, and the domed ceiling filled with a firmament of glittering stars.

Billy limped to the edge of the pool and looked into the swirling water at the contoured marble lounge with its surface-level headrest, as twinkling stars swarmed above and tranquil music filled his ears. He waved a forceful hand. "What magic word turns this off?"

"The one to conclude a prayer," Harley said.

"Amen," said Billy. "Amen, amen, a thousand times amen!"

The stars faded, the music furred into silence. Billy waited for the gurgling waves in the pool to subside before he spoke. "All of this—for what purpose? Tell me baptismals, I'll strike you with this cane."

"No matter how it appears, this is *my* chapel."

"You mean private *spa*."

"I mean chapel, Billy. Like the pope has *his* and I have mine."

"The pope's chapel *is* a chapel. A place where he privately worships. An altar, a place for meditation."

"Medieval, Billy. *Strictly* medieval. A little on the pagan side, don't you think?"

"You're impossible," said Billy, who turned away from the brooding face to study the bizarre setting. The alcoves piqued his curiosity. "I know I will be sorry for asking, but what in God's name do you have in *those* rooms?"

Harley excitedly ushered Billy into the first alcove, where the old evangelist viewed the computer with its flashing digital lights. But was he not the pioneer? Was he not a major figure in its rise from toy to tool and the first evangelist to use computers? It all came hauntingly to mind and he hastened from the room.

The second alcove featured high-intensity heat lamps and a battery of air jets emanating from an oval wall and used exclusively to dry oneself. Billy felt this was a luxury mankind could do without and left in a huff.

The next alcove led to a room that was much larger than the previous two and, to Billy's amazement, was religiously oriented. The walls were effectively lighted and alive with costly religious paintings. Harley knew Billy was at last taken in. "Impressive, Billy? Religiously inspiring?"

"Financially inspiring, as well," Hale grunted.

Harley moved briskly past the fourth alcove and stood at

the entrance of the fifth, waiting for his hobbling guest. "The environmental sauna and grooming parlor," Harley proclaimed, grinning widely.

"Really?" said Billy, pausing at the entrance to the alcove Harley had passed by a trifle too swiftly. "What, pray, is in here?"

"Only a bathroom."

"*Only* a bathroom?"

"Just a john, Billy."

"Just a john, you say. Like your chapel is just a chapel?" He beckoned Harley to approach. Their eyes collided. "Harley, show me your 'just a john.' "

The room was electronically activated by their body heat and shimmered with an aqua afterglow. A strain of classical music first crackled through speakers inserted into the wall, then came in smoothly, without flaw. Harley's feet sank into an ultrathick, blue-green rug made of cut velvet pile. He walked toward what appeared to be a throne, an actual throne worthy of some Biblical monarch—an impressive structure of rare, aged cocobolo wood inlaid with gold.

Billy Hale couldn't decide whether to laugh, cry, or shout out some cutting verse from the Bible as he surveyed *the holy crapper*.

"No toilet paper," said Harley in all seriousness.

"For God's sake," Billy said over the building resonance of the "Hallelujah Chorus." "This . . . this is preposterous. Have you lost all sense of value, man? What in God's name has possessed you?" He moved next to Harley and looked down at the soft, flesh-textured seat. Was it eccentricity or was it egotism? At this point, Billy no longer cared.

"Billy, see, you press this when you're finished. Like this." He pushed a button recessed in the chair's right armrest. A mist rose from the throne's bowl as the water began to swirl, and Billy smelled a lilac fragrance. Harley pressed another button on the left armrest, and Billy watched while a mild spray of gentle soap preceded a miniature geyser of warm water. "The loins are cleansed," Harley gushed like a man who had just invented electricity. Moments later, a strong force of warm air completed the process.

"I have but one question," Billy said. "How do you explain *this* to the IRS?"

"I told you, it's all part of my chapel," Lombard said, a wounded tone in his voice. "Billy, I'm going to tell you something known only to me and God."

"Don't associate God with your selfish acts!" Hale said sharply.

"When I was growing up in Kentucky, we were poor and didn't have bathrooms. The whole family had to use an outhouse."

"Harley, I, too, used an outhouse when *I* was growing up."

Harley would not be deterred. "When I was seven, seven years old, sitting in that outhouse in the freezing cold, well, an angel came to me."

"With wings, of course."

"The angel told me—straight-out told me—I would receive many revelations in my life. They were to appear in the place where I bathe. And Billy, I've had revelations, visions right in this very room."

"Harley, look at me. Who do you see?"

"Billy Hale, of course."

"Try to remember that."

"Now, now wait. Wait a minute. What about all the revelations *you* had? The ones you wrote about in your books and told the world about over television?"

"Harley, there are revelations and there are *revelations*. Let's not confuse greed with spirituality." He spun from Harley's view, gritting his teeth at a sudden stab of pain in his leg. "I need to sit for a spell," he aimed his cane in the throne's direction, "and I'll be damned if it's there."

They reached the entrance to the largest den, and Billy happened to look beyond the Jacuzzi pool at the lone alcove across the way. He pointed to it. "What do you have in there?"

"Huh? Oh, in there . . . ah . . . just a storage area, Billy," he answered, a nervous tremor in his voice.

"Storage? With iron grating covering the entrance? No, no, Harley. *Don't* tell me."

Billy moved through the entrance and looked with distrust into what was obviously a sitting room. Its overall design, including the heavy tapestries, was borrowed from ancient Rome. Jarred by the sight of the biggest chair he had ever seen, Billy first thought it to be a prop from a movie, but its purpose became obvious when he saw three floor-level, contoured sofas—all facing the massive structure.

"Over here," said Harley. "Sit here." He pointed to the mammoth seat with an array of black and white computer keys implanted in both armrests.

"I shall *not* sit in *that*. Nor will I lie on *those*," said Billy, who looked about the room and noticed a folding chair set off in a corner.

"Billy, please. I'll sit there, you—"

Hale fetched the chair, placed it before his embarrassed host, and sat down. The web of pain gradually vanished from the corners of his eyes and he sighed softly. But his face grew stern as he saw Harley perched in the gargantuan chair. "No more buttons. No more of this nonsense. I mean it! And stop flashing that ring in my face. I *won't* kiss it."

If Harley Lombard admired anyone, it was Billy Hale. He was perhaps the only human on earth who could cut through Harley's thick hide and penetrate his bulldog stubbornness.

"Harley, I want you to take a hiatus. Call it a sabbatical."

"Sabbatical?"

"I want you to leave your television ministry and the cathedral. Get out from under the religious spotlight for a while. At least for a year. Possibly two."

"For what reason?"

"Call it a warning."

"Warning about what?"

"I believe you are a potential target."

"Target? Me?"

"You, and others."

"You shoot at targets. Who in hell wants to shoot at

me?'' He drew a large cigar from an inside pocket of his smoking jacket and lit it with a crucifix-shaped lighter made of gold. ''Cuban, Billy. The Vatican gang has nothing on me.''

Nothing but two hundred billion dollars, Billy was tempted to say, but he would not encourage Harley to use the Vatican as the rationale for his blatant extravagance.

Harley puffed hard on the cigar and a cloud of smoke screened his face. ''You say I'm a target.'' He fanned the smoke. ''What have I done to become someone's target?''

''I have nothing more than a hunch. Call it a gut feeling.''

''A feeling. *Just* a feeling?''

''That's right, Harley. What's more, I believe the never-ending religious TV shows flooding the airwaves are heading for a crash. And your quarreling with Jimmy Christian over who will dominate religious broadcasting isn't helping matters.''

''*Now* you're speaking about a target. That little cockroach is begging for a war.''

''Then what?''

''Then *what?* He's stealing my eyeballs and you ask, then what?''

''Harley, take a vacation.''

''You're not thinking right, Billy. I take a vacation and that bandit will have my entire network.''

''Let him.''

''Do you really expect me to turn the other cheek?''

''Why not? Christ did.''

'' 'Christ did,' '' Harley mimicked. ''Come on, Billy, you know as well as I, if Christ was alive today, he'd be doing the same as me, preaching over TV.''

''In a multi-million-dollar cathedral?''

''Was that aimed at me?''

''Do you think so?''

''Billy, your thinking's off by billions. The *Vatican*, the *Mormon* church—how can you compare my ministry with that kind of clout?''

''Harley, do you—''

''*When* the pope and his college of con men turn their

treasury over to the poor, *when* the Mormon chiefs give Utah back to the United States, *then* I'll do my preaching in the streets.''

"Enough!" said Billy. "Despite your eccentric behavior and ridiculous Vatican-inspired craving for luxury, I am deeply fond of you. Whereas I didn't expect Jimmy Christian to listen to my advice, I came here hoping to express my fears to someone I thought I had a very close rapport with."

Harley looked at Billy with growing suspicion. "Billy, what is it? I mean, really? This hunch, intuitive warning, what truly brought it on?"

Their roles were now reversed. Billy was on the defensive and he had to look away from Harley's earnest face. "I guess I would be less than honest not to admit that Cody Walker's death, coming so soon after Jason Everson's, has added a great deal to my fears."

"As I understand it, Everson died in a freak fire, and Walker killed himself."

"There's more to these deaths than we have been led to believe."

"From what I read, the Walker thing had a happy ending. Besides, Cody Walker was a cult leader. He gave up his television ministry years ago. And Everson was hardly in my class."

"Harley, think back eleven years ago. What happened then could very well repeat itself. The world has become much more sensitive."

From the penitent way Harley rose from the chair, Billy knew he had finally gotten through. The sorrowful expression on Harley's face was further assurance. His voice was punctuated with remorse. "How many times I got on my knees to thank the merciful Lord for sparing me."

Both men vividly remembered the hell they had shared. It had been billed as the "Night of Light" at the Hollywood Bowl, where, under a moonlit sky, Billy Hale, surrounded by a virtual *Who's Who* in evangelism, told a jam-packed audience of Bible-believing fundamentalists that his antagonist, Ron Rebuck, Sr.—a man who claimed to be the Archangel Michael's messenger and who had called the Holy Bible a portrait of sadism and facts for fiends—was the Antichrist.

How well they both remembered the thunderous and inspirational singing of "Onward, Christian Soldiers" by the zealous throng of humanity, when death came in the form of a mortar shell lofted from a nearby hill. Their "Night of Light" became a night of horror when the deadly missile struck the wing of the stage; when the evangelist Norville Riggins, who vigorously led the tumultuous voices in song, was no more; when the feisty evangelist Tommy Sunday was decapitated and his head sailed into an audience of terrorized people; when the fallen Billy Hale crawled painfully from the battered stage with a leg shattered by shrapnel; and when Harley Lombard came out of the temporal Hell with nothing more than a nosebleed.

"Billy, Rebuck's a memory. A dead item. Besides, what did he really leave the world? A goofy book about angels that never turned religion around. . . . A mission somewhere that's become a poor man's Hare Krishna." He returned to his throne, confident he had detected the cause for Billy's fears. "I don't mean to be disrespectful, but—"

"Why is it ever since I've retired I keep hearing people tell me that? I'm not a saint or some old revered holy man. Forget sanctimony and say what you have to say."

"Well, maybe . . . maybe you're living too much in the past. Just because one evangelist dies—rather strangely, I'll admit—and a cult leader kills himself—"

"He was murdered. But go on."

"What I'm trying to say is that you're haunted. Being inactive, your mind is inventing the fear of things which don't exist. *Evangelism*, thanks to you, has advanced to where it is today. Think of it, Billy: just one of my sermons, just *one*, reaches more people than all of the sermons Christ ever gave."

"I have been aware of your intention to rival the pope, but *Christ*, Harley?"

"C'mon, Billy, you know I didn't mean it that way."

"I will not deny that I'm haunted." Hale tapped lightly on his throbbing knee. "But, as usual, you think of the aftermath and never the genesis of things."

"Genesis?"

"What I'm saying is that you, I, and others in our profession were directly responsible for what happened eleven years ago. Through our greed—yes, I said greed— and through our flaunting of Christianity over the airwaves we presented ourselves as targets. Being as overexposed, and as controversial as both you and Jimmy Christian presently are, plants thoughts in the minds of fanatics. And fanatical people do fanatical things."

Harley's confidence withered. He gazed upon the wise old man who had never once steered him wrong. "Billy, did you come here to scare me?"

"Most definitely."

"And you seriously believe I'm a target?"

"You, *and* others."

"Uh-huh, okay, let's just say you're right. Of course, I don't believe you are, but anyway, let's say your fears *are* warranted."

"Go on, Harley," Billy said.

"Have you got a solution?"

"For you?"

"For *me.*"

"Take a long vacation."

"Will you *forget* the vacation."

Billy studied the face of a man seeking direction. "The other remedy takes a great deal of courage. You know, Harley, the kind our Lord Jesus Christ possessed."

"What, Billy, what?"

"Accompany me to Washington."

"Why Washington?"

"Join me in lobbying against the excesses of religious broadcasting."

"You . . . you want me to lobby against *what?*"

67

CHAPTER 7

IKE VESPER DRIFTED about SEAL Base I in a daze. He had just returned from a month of unexpected duty in the Philippines and could not bring himself to believe the news that Ron Rebuck had resigned his commission. Vesper knew how much the SEALs meant to him. It didn't make sense. Rebuck loved the SEALs with a devotion which bordered on the pathological. Something was wrong. And he took his suspicions to the base commander.

"Lieutenant Ron Rebuck, Jr., resigned his commission effective January fourth." Commander O'Donnell was exact in reply. When Vesper pressed for more information, the base commander shuffled some papers and said, "That will be all, Chief."

Ike Vesper paced the rooms of his Coronado apartment with feelings of intense foreboding and desolation. Ron Rebuck was family. They had defied the twin taboos of rank and race and had forged a solid bond of friendship. On duty, they followed the caste distinction between officer and enlisted man. But in their free hours, Rebuck was "little brother."

His huge black hand reached for the phone as an idea occurred to him. But he released the receiver from a strangled grip when a glimmer of uncertainty filled his eyes. He remembered Rebuck had not seen his widowed mother in many years. Through their nightly rap sessions, Rebuck had said enough for Ike to understand why it was an only child would remain so distant from the woman who had brought him into the world.

Apparently, the sight of her crucified husband had been too much for June Rebuck. After her breakdown, she'd been confined to a sanitarium for many years, while Ron moved in with his grandmother before going off to U.C.L.A. Vesper understood from Rebuck that visits to his mother threatened her delicate emotional balance. The first few times he'd gone to see her she'd suffered lesser but still damaging breakdowns, and a doctor had explained to him that his strong resemblance to his father, and the memories of that last night which he inevitably stirred in her, were not only impeding her recovery but endangering her life. So Ron had stayed away, writing her occasionally . . . hoping that some day he'd see his mother again. Ike knew she'd been living in Connecticut for the last few years, with a nurse in attendance virtually around the clock. No, Ron wouldn't have gone there—and Ike had no wish to risk upsetting Mrs. Rebuck by calling.

He went to the fridge and allowed his frustrations to become intertwined with the consumption of food as he finished off enough snacks for a crowd, washed them down with two bottles of Coors beer, flipped the television knob, then stretched his six-five frame out on a beat-up couch and listened to the rumbling sounds his stomach proceeded to make.

As he stared at the forgettable movie on TV, Operation Black Eagle swooped through his drifting thoughts and came to roost in his mind. He replayed the meticulous planning: the swift, violent hit during a raging storm, then the perjurious documents he and other members of Ron Rebuck's SEAL team had been forced to sign "in the interest of national security." The breakup of a team that had functioned with superb efficiency, his unexpected orders for temporary duty in the Philippines, and Ron Rebuck's mysterious summons to the Pentagon presented him with a thorny conclusion. Whatever was coming down, Ron Rebuck had not played the man's game. Finally, at about 2:00 A.M., the mundane dialogue of the movie put him to sleep.

Morning came, and after a cup of black coffee laced

with a liberal belt of Sauza Gold Tequila, Ike reported to SEAL base determined to learn Ron Rebuck's whereabouts. He asked for some of the leave time he had accumulated, but a Lieutenant J.G. shot down his request. He was to see the old man—and on the double.

"You shall depart for Baja at twelve hundred hours," said an unsympathetic Commander O'Donnell. "You will dress in civilian attire. Sport clothes. You will be issued a station wagon with California plates. It will be conspicuously loaded with fishing gear. You will drive to Ensenada using the tollway. Once in Ensenada, you will register at the Palacio Motel. You will be met in the lobby by a Mexican national who will make himself known with the code words 'Teddy Roosevelt.' He will then drive you to a private residence where you will receive further orders from a man whose authority you will recognize and obey without question. That will be all, Chief Vesper."

A vital element of Ike's longevity in the navy was that he knew better than to question orders. With three years to go for his twenty, he wouldn't make waves. The search for his best friend would have to wait.

Traffic was light on Interstate 805 as Vesper drove across the border at the San Ysidro port of entry. He followed the looping road skirting the clutter of downtown Tijuana which fed onto Baja Frontera's pride: the four-lane, divided tollway hugging seventy-five kilometers of rugged coastline. He distinctly remembered it was here, in this tourist mecca, where he and Ron Rebuck had celebrated Rebuck's graduation from Basic Underwater Demolition. It was here in this Yankee spending spot with its breeding ground for countless legends that their bond of friendship was knotted.

Cruising along the ocean-washed escarpments past isolated condo complexes, Vesper recalled the first time he had set eyes on the handsome young ensign, Ron Rebuck. Then a BUD instructor, he delighted in making life miserable for trainees, particularly candidates who were officers. Rebuck, a young man with defiance in his eyes and a confident swagger, was no exception. Ike had pushed him the hardest, worked him the most, and never resisted an opportunity to intimidate him. Yet the tougher and more demanding he had become, the more Ron Rebuck seemed to thrive. It soon became a mutually perpetuated challenge—the savvy instructor and seasoned veteran who had done it for real in Vietnam against an inexperienced ensign fresh out of UCLA, who strangely made the pro feel as if the apprentice could do it better.

Three years went by before he saw Rebuck again, when both were assigned to a crack SEAL Ranger team. And for the past two years he had served under Lt. Ron Rebuck, observing with quiet pride Rebuck's skill of command, his cool leadership in the hairy situations which often developed during clandestine missions. A sign telling him Ensenada was two miles ahead brought him to the business at hand.

There was nothing palatial about the Palacio, which sat in ramshackle shape at the ocean end of Ensenada's action strip: a colorful gauntlet of storefront restaurants, souvenir shops, strolling mariachi bands, taverns, and the seemingly never-ending run of liquor stores. He double-parked the Ford wagon directly in front of the Mexican motel and stepped out into the bright sunshine, unaffected by the pungent odor wafting from a local fish-processing plant.

In a lobby populated with natives, Ike Vesper stood out like an oil sheik at a bar mitzvah. The Palacio did not receive many six-foot-five black guests. Ike registered and paid in advance for a room he would never see, then ambled over to a bulletin board festooned with flyers advertising night clubs, guided tours, and fishing boats for charter. Deciding it was as good a spot in the lobby as any for the Mexican to make contact, he noticed a coffee-hued man fold the paper he was reading and make his approach with the slyness of a thief.

The Mexican's suit was shabby, there were food stains on the white shirt which was opened at the collar, and his moustache was noticeably uneven. The mousy manner in which he presented himself matched his build, and the way he singsonged, "Teddy Roosevelt, señor," brought a slight grin to Ike's face.

The Mexican indicated he was to drive, and Ike gave him no argument. They'd soon left the helter-skelter of downtown midafternoon traffic for a residential area in the hills above the city which offered a spectacular panorama of the blue-green Pacific. The Mexican drove in silence and that was fine with Ike. Until he knew the players and the game, he would waste no energy on guidebook Spanish-English small talk.

"Teddy Roosevelt" turned onto a private road and they jounced to a dusty halt at a wrought-iron fence some hundred yards down a lane surrounded by the water-starved ground cover of the Baja hills. The Mexican slipped him a humble smile and gave a long blast on the horn followed by two short ones. The gate rattled open and they drove slowly on to a sprawling stucco ranch where the lush landscaping betrayed the presence of a subterranean sprinkling system.

As Ike looked at the entrance door trimmed with burnished copper, that feeling, the particular kind which antedated combat, chilled his bones and stole his breath. The Mexican broke the silence with excited Spanish gibberish and pointed anxiously to the door. Ike would not be rushed, and allowed his suspicions and the growing wish that he'd armed himself to become gradually tempered by a will to obey orders. He had not taken a step from the car when the Mexican pulled away and sped off with *his* station wagon. "Mysterious little bastard," Ike cursed. But it wasn't for him to speculate, he quickly reminded himself. He was on assignment. It would all come down in the house before him.

A woman with high cheekbones, attired in the traditional floral print dress of the peasant class, opened the door and motioned him into the foyer with a slight bow. As she led him down a long hall, the smell of cleaning detergents swamped his nostrils. He continued to follow her down the narrow hallway, allowing himself only a brief glance at the rooms they passed, when she finally stopped, meekly pointing to a screen door leading outdoors.

Ike Vesper's gaze did not venture farther than a voluptuous redhead clad only in a one-piece black bathing suit—this despite the rather chilly early-January weather. He hardly noticed her male companion, seated some ten feet beyond her sipping languidly at a bottle of Mexican beer.

"Welcome to Mexico, Chief," she said, rising from a chaise longue.

Her licentious approach was met by Ike's lustful stare, which hungrily took in the full and rounded breasts overlapping the suit's bodice and the tight waist to long golden legs. She was the kind of woman who could make a man forget his name, and the expensive oval sunglasses hiding her eyes added to the aura of mystery.

"Something to drink?" she asked with a wickedly provocative smile.

He declined with a mild shake of his head.

She reached for his hand and led him in the direction of her companion, and he couldn't release his eyes from the gyrating behind that even the most extravagantly endowed sisters he knew would envy. "This is Hans. Hans, meet Chief; Ike Vesper," she said, as if she had known Ike for years.

The man merely raised his bottle in a diffident salute. Ike read him with a single sweep of his eyes. Thirtyish, blond hair mowed into a crew cut, wiry and well muscled, lifeless eyes, an arrogant expression fixed on his face: Ike felt certain the man belonged to one special force or another. He had seen enough of such men to recognize the common traits.

"Make yourself comfortable, Chief," the redhead said. "Sure you won't have a drink?"

Once again he silently declined, and watched her move around the kidney-shaped pool guarded by a low brick wall. He was instantly reminded of what his grandma told him to stay clear of when growing up in Mississippi. This one was the true prototype—the kind which got a black boy hung.

She ordered drinks over a white cordless phone, then returned to her chaise, where she sat facing him with her legs slightly elevated and much too far apart. Vesper could not help but notice the swell of her pubic bone and a silken wisp of auburn hair. "Do you like stories, Chief?" she asked. "Short stories?"

He regarded her impassively, remaining silent. He would let her do the talking. Hopefully, he would pick up a hint as to when the *man* would arrive with his orders. Commander O'Donnell hadn't said anything about some big-titted redhead.

She saw him glance at Hans, who appeared oblivious to it all. "Hans isn't the talkative type," she said. "We met in Acapulco. Hans is a man without a country. Don't you find that interesting, Chief?"

A mercenary, Vesper thought. He knew a few SEALs who had left the service to fight for pay. It was always a seller's market when it came to dirty little wars in some African or Central American shithole.

A slim-waisted male servant in a white embroidered shirt appeared bearing a tray holding another margarita and bottle of beer. He served the drinks without a word and departed without any gratuitous response.

Vesper now watched her tongue lick along the rim of salt which crusted the glass. "At first I thought Hans would be a challenge," she purred. "And it's true he was no pushover, Chief, but like the rest, he bought my act . . . isn't that right, Hans?"

Hans permitted himself the luxury of a grin.

"Hans thinks I'm some rich widow who killed her sugar daddy by fucking him to death."

There was no reaction on Hans's face. The smile had been replaced by the familiar smirk.

"He thinks my name is Theresa. Theresa Blanchard." She looked at Hans. "Enjoying the story, Hans?"

Hans laughed mirthlessly at what Ike could only assume was an inside joke. What in Mississippi mud was this lady talkin' on about, he wondered.

"Actually, my name is Trudy—I'm what you might call a trapper. Hans, *please* pay attention."

"Beautiful," he replied in a heavy Germanic accent.

"Is my story boring you, Chief?" she asked.

Ike continued to contemplate her in silence, wishing she would take off the dark glasses so he could see her eyes. Green, he bet, *reptile* green.

"Maybe you'll get hooked on the punch ending," she said as if confident he would. She took a long sip of her drink, drawing it out for all its effect, and waited until only the hum of the pool's filtration system and the shrilling of distant gulls were heard before speaking. "Poor Hans," she said, a new, chilling inflection in her voice. "He'll never get laid again . . . you see, he doesn't know it, Chief, but he's living the last day of his life."

Shit, Vesper thought. This is all a honky performance for my benefit. She's piling up the bullshit and her stone cowboy is spreading it out. Where the *fuck* is the man in charge?

Ike did not realize their little party had expanded until Hans rose suddenly from his chair and began to inch toward the brick wall. Two men, sidearms drawn, converged on Hans, who vaulted the four-foot wall with the agility of a gymnast, vanishing into the dry undergrowth. Ike remained keyed on the two men, who made no attempt to pursue Hans but calmly returned to the house.

It was she and he alone, and neither spoke. She looked at her watch, a Piaget, then came off the chaise. He watched her pick up the phone and speak in a voice he couldn't hear. Nor did he want to. She no longer gave him lustful thoughts. She was a cunt.

"Chief," she said, returning to the chaise, "Consuela will show you to your quarters. I'm sure you'd like to freshen up before dinner." She withdrew a mirror and lipstick from a straw purse. "Later in the evening, you will receive your orders . . . from Sam."

Sam, Vesper thought, who the fuck is *Sam*? But he had not broken his silence since arriving at this strange rendezvous and he wouldn't now.

Consuela, the woman who had led him through the house, appeared at the screen door. He decided to keep her waiting until the redhead looked at him. But she kept toying with the mirror. Finally, he gave in and got up. As he reached the screen door, to his surprise the redhead called after him.

"Oh, *Chief*! Please give my love to that handsome Ron Rebuck."

The room seemed to be closing in on Ike. But it wasn't the close dimensions which played hell on his mind. *Sam*. Who was Sam? And the redhead's casual mentioning of Ron Rebuck: what did she know that he didn't? She made it sound as if he would be seeing Rebuck. It had to be an intimidation course he was going through. A test of mind games to see if he could qualify for some very important assignment. It had to be, he kept telling himself over and over.

Ike dined alone. The single place setting on a captain's table in a bland dining room was a straight clue, the first since he'd arrived. A stocky woman with a polar-bear personality served him fried shrimp, lobster tails, and a cut of rare filet mignon. Three bottles of cerveza washed it down. He abstained from pie and coffee and sat back in the chair, wondering what was next, when "Teddy Roosevelt" appeared.

"You come with me!" "Teddy" insisted in his broken English, waving his arm like a traffic cop.

Following his impish guide, Ike entered a dimly lit room in a remote wing of the sprawling house. He heard his footsteps on the terrazzo tile floor echo off walls that were devoid of pictures. The room was completely unfurnished with the exception of an enormous rectangular conference table. He was thinking it was odd for only two chairs to be set at one end of so large a table when "Teddy" harshly pointed for him to take the chair nearest the wall, then did his vanishing act on cue.

For most of his adult life and all of his seventeen years of military service, Ike Vesper had been a man of action, trained to defeat an enemy in almost any situation requiring physical toughness. But from the first moment he had set foot in this house, a blanket of helplessness had cloaked him. He could not make sense of any of the puzzling events which had occurred since his arrival in Ensenada. The Palacio Motel, "Teddy Roosevelt," the woman who called herself Trudy, Hans, the two gun-toting torpedoes, the strange dialogue—it had all run together into a shapeless mass. All he could do, Vesper knew, was to hang tough and wait for his orders. Once he discovered why he was here and what was expected of him, all this bullshit could be filed away until some night when he and Ron Rebuck were swapping stories by a roaring fire.

A door swung open. A man lurched out, followed by the two men Ike had seen at the pool. It was Hans, and he was still in the yellow bathing trunks, now stained with blood. His hands were tightly bound behind his back and the two men shoved him toward the table.

Ike's bewilderment swelled as he watched them stuff Hans into the chair opposite him. Acting with the cruel efficiency of Spanish Inquisition priests readying a heretic for the rack, the two men tied Hans's knees together with heavy nylon line and shackled his ankles with the kind of irons once used on chain gangs. The cuts on Hans's face, the puffed lower lip of a mouth apparently parched from lack of water, and the eyes glazed with pain were all too realistic. Yet Ike could not totally unload the feeling it was just a well-staged act. Seconds later, that feeling was sunk by the entrance of a man with a pronounced limp.

Dressed in combat fatigues, stripped of all his insignia, Captain Claude Gemmer negated Ike's rising with a sharp gesture of his hand. Gemmer stood at the far end of the table, and Ike could manage only a weak look at this man he greatly feared, a man he believed to be the total destroyer, a man he believed could intimidate God himself—a man who looked at Hans through eyes revealing the colors of hell.

The deadly silence thickened. Seconds turned to minutes, and still the captain leered. But why, Ike wondered.

What had Hans done? Why was he bound and manacled? Why weren't his wounds being attended to? Most of all, why did he, Ike Vesper, have to witness whatever it was that was going on here?

"Did you really think I wouldn't find your yellow ass?" said the captain in a tone of voice that delivered chills.

Ike swallowed hard. His eyes pounced on Hans. The gravity of the captain's words would at least bring about a reply. Surely one that would blow away the storm of confusion raining on his mind. But the redhead was right when she said Hans wasn't the talkative type. He facially mocked the captain's threatening serve with an unspoken obscenity in return. Once again an intense silence captured the room, and Ike felt an impulsive need to rid himself of the beers he'd gulped down with dinner.

It was almost as if he was in a movie theater, Ike thought, watching the slow-motion finale of a horror movie starring the captain as the ultimate monster. He had trained under Claude Gemmer, served in combat under him in Vietnam, yet the man was still a complete enigma. No one knew him intimately, Ike knew, and no one desired to. And no one more epitomized the name "Vampire," given him by enemy and ally alike.

His attention stayed with Hans, for at best he could only sneak an occasional look at the captain. He had to admire the blond man's courage and wondered why the captain had called him yellow. Such bravery sparked a feeling of boldness within him, but the urge to speak out was stifled by the sudden actions of the two men, who bodily lifted Hans from the chair and held him rigid.

The captain approached the helpless man, slowly, menacingly. A look of hatred burned in his eyes, and as the blood rushed to his livid and narrow face, it looked to Ike as if the mass of scars was fresh from battle.

Without need of a spoken command, one of the men swiftly slipped an arm under Hans's neck, and Ike could see the splash of fear in the man's eyes. They lifted him by the manacled ankles and lowered him onto the table, pinning him into a helpless state. His eyes ballooned as he identified the surgical scalpel in Gemmer's upraised hand. Impossible, Ike thought. He wouldn't—certainly not with Vesper as a witness. But the impossible became reality as the captain suddenly plunged the scalpel into Hans's chest just below the screaming man's sternum, and slowly cut down past the navel.

Ike wanted to bolt from the room, flee from this grotesque scene. But his legs were as paralyzed as his mind. He could not even summon the strength to lift his hands and cover his eyes to blot out the sight of blood spurting copiously from the hemorrhaging wound. He could not muffle the gasping, sickening sounds gurgling from Hans's gaping mouth. Locked to the terror, Ike felt a soundless scream rise from his throat as what he now viewed seared into his frozen eyeballs. The captain had plunged his free hand into the bloody abdominal cavity and ripped out a handful of still-quivering intestines.

Vomit dribbled from a corner of Ike's mouth. What he now saw made his blood curdle, never to be forgotten. With his hand filled with bilious mesentery, the captain shook the yellow-green intestines dripping with fecal matter before dilating eyes that rolled back into the vacant stare of a welcome death.

Ike Vesper urinated uncontrollably.

CHAPTER 8

"WELCOME, WELCOME ALL to the God Loves Everyone, Everywhere Studio," Frank Buckmaster joyfully announced through rabbit teeth.

Inside a thirty-five-monitor control booth, the bearded director slapped his forehead. "He blew the opening. The walrus said studio instead of club."

"Heeeeerrrre'ssss Jimmy," Bucky sang out.

Jimmy Christian parted the curtain and sprinted to Bucky's side. With the musical fanfare by the twelve-piece G.L.E.E. Club orchestra building to a crescendo, he whispered, "I'm going to kill you." Jimmy then silenced the orchestra with a raised hand and shouted, "Praise God. Praise *Gee*-zus!"

The audience thundered a chorus of "Praise God" and "Praise Jesus" and Christian raised his arms like a man who would shortly ascend. "Turn the cameras. Let the people at home see the joy on the faces of Glee Club members who came to be part of this gloreee-us night."

"Praise God," said Bucky, as five new cameras panned an audience of senior citizens sprinkled with middle-aged worshippers. They had come from as far north as New York and Pennsylvania, as far west as Illinois and as far south as Florida. They were one thousand select members of Jimmy Christian's blue-chip monthly donors, who had each paid one thousand dollars for the privilege of attending the ceremonial unveiling of the multi-million-dollar studio complex.

The camera returned to Jimmy, who declared in a triumphant voice, "The Night of the Disciples! *You*, each and every one of you, are *Gee*-zus Christ's disciples! Do you know what it means to walk and talk with *Gee*-zus?'' He pointed forcefully into a camera before him. "*You*, you shall be his disciples this very night. *You* shall feel *Gee*-zus in your hearts.''

Billy Hale frowned. He was at home watching Jimmy Christian on TV, and he grumped aloud to himself. " 'Reap the Holy Reward,' 'Heavenly Harvest,' and now, 'The Night of the Disciples.' Another religious theme, another TV hustle. TV special, nothing. TV *payathon*.'' Billy knew the hustle well, and the part where Jimmy said "You will find Jesus in your *heart*" was a dead giveaway.

A blue phone buzzed softly and a flickering red light diverted Billy's attention. He picked up the receiver. "Yes, Doris . . . Harley Lombard? . . . All right, I'll speak with him.''

"Billy, are you watching?'' Harley asked in a voice to shatter one's ear.

"Trying to, that is, if I ever hear again.''

"I'm taping him, Billy.''

"For what purpose?''

"I've been tipped the little cockroach is gonna say some nasty things about me.''

"Harley, you are the farthest thing from Jimmy's mind.''

"What's that suppose to mean?''

"It's my bet the man's financially wounded. This Night of the Disciples is out of desperation.''

"You know this, Billy? Are you telling me Wonder Boy's going bust?''

"His Christ Town is in financial quicksand. Apparently he's running out of holy gimmicks and revelations.''

"Billy, from your lips to God's ears.''

"Harley, take that vacation,'' said Billy, hanging up and settling back to critically evaluate whatever Jimmy Christian had brewing.

Recording heavyweight Johnny Clay, a governor of Jimmy's ministry and its musical ambassador, electrified the audience with his foot-stomping country music. Backstage, a furious Jimmy Christian shadowed by a perceptive Beth Staples backed Frank Buckmaster against a stage prop. "You dumb shit!"

"What's wrong, Jimmy?"

"You numb-nuts! It's costing me millions for a live show and you said 'studio' instead of 'club.' "

"I'm sorry. God knows it was an honest mistake. There's no reason to shout at me. As Mark says in Chapter Eleven, Verse Twenty-five, 'Forgive if ye ought against any, that your Father in Heaven may forgive you.' "

The slap came hard across Bucky's face. "Once more," Jimmy threatened, wagging his finger in front of Bucky's tear-rimmed eyes, "fuck up *once* more. *Just* once!"

Jimmy stormed away, leaving Beth Staples to watch the shaken pitchman wipe tears from his crimson face. "He needn't have done that. Didn't have to humiliate me. But I will forgive him. As Jesus said, 'It is better to turn the cheek.' "

"Spoken like a true fool," Beth replied, walking away.

As he watched the show, Billy shook his head. He could predict Jimmy's next move. The expression on his face was the familiar look used by TV evangelists in times of self-confession, prior to the hard sell. It was that glowing pious look.

Jimmy didn't fail him. "Almost three years ago, I announced the plans to create an Evangelical World Center. A place where all who preach from the Holy Bible would gather in united force. Where young men and women would attend our seminary and receive the fruits of the Holy Spirit. Where Christ's disciples, *you* who are hearing my voice, would come to spend annual retreats. Where your faith would become impregnable."

Jimmy's voice cracked and Billy anticipated the tears. "The Christ Town theme park, where events from Jesus' life will be re-enacted, has been viciously attacked." Jimmy's voice now acquired a sobbing inflection. "There is only one with such destructive power. The Lord of Lies. The King of the Damned—*Satan*!"

"Who else?" said Billy, thinking of how many times he'd blamed the devil for his own failures.

"He came in *hard hats!*" Jimmy cried out. "He came as lawyers, bankers, in forms we couldn't detect."

Jimmy continued to blame the devil for everything that had gone wrong. His condemnations ranged from financial woes to mosquito bites. But Billy knew he was building a mood, craftily setting up his TV audience. Hale identified the smug look on Jimmy's face, the kind he, himself, had used so many times after his critics reported he was finished—when all the while he was palming four aces in his right hand and showing a pair of jacks in his left.

Jimmy ignored the man frantically waving a cue card at him. He was in spiritual motion and moved across the stage until he was standing under an immense wall map of the world. Dozens of miniature tricolored lights representing places on the globe the G.L.E.E. Club shows were seen flicked on and off. Seated at long tables directly beneath the map, five tiers of senior-aged men and women, some fifty in number, were anxious to man red, white, and blue phones.

"*We* shall, *you* shall, defeat the devil!" said Jimmy. "The Lord *Gee*-zus Christ needs our help. The Lord *Gee*-zus Christ who died on the cross for our sins, who asked only for our faith in return, now beseeches us—every man, woman, and child who hears my voice—to help Him build *His* town. *Christ Town.*"

He thrust out his arms and, in a voice strained with emotion, led his galvanized audience in song. The studio rocked with the inspirational anthem, "Bringing in the Sheaves."

The phone once more interrupted Billy's concentration on the telecast. "Who now, Doris? . . . Harley, again?" He didn't want to speak to him, yet picked up the phone. "Harley, if I need an interpreter, I shall call you."

"Just some thunder, Billy. Some electric hype before he drowns. What do you think?"

"I think the man might have something working."

"Billy, he's dead but doesn't know it."

"Then why do you sound so worried?"

"Worried? I'd bet the World Cathedral the cockroach falls flat on his ass. Christ Town? *Dump Town*. He's dead. *Finished*."

"Harley, I think the dead man's eyes just opened."

Preceded by a drum roll, the number "one million" lodged in the slots of a twelve-by-twelve-foot totalizer machine. Above the giant scoreboard, letters emblazoned in red spelled out *Christ Town*. Silver spangles flashed around the words, giving a Hollywood special-effects illusion. But as far as Jimmy's super-motivated audience was concerned, the letters had been chiseled by the invisible hand of God.

Jimmy wiped away his tears with a dark handkerchief embossed with small white crosses. He made a dramatic attempt to speak, but was too emotionally coiled. Seizing the opportunity of his rare loss for words, Cora Lee bounded to the evangelist's side. "One million dollars!" she shouted gleefully in her high-pitched voice. "One million, Bucky," she repeated, noticing Frank Buckmaster's wary approach.

Before she could bungle it, Jimmy made a speedy recovery. "A million-dollar *beginning*," he clarified. "A million given to *Gee*-zus from Glee Club members here with us tonight. *Praise* God!"

Jimmy ignored Cora Lee's obvious desire to sing her solo and darted forward. This was his kill and he had no intention of sharing the spotlight. "*Gee*-zus called my soul. The Son of God called my mortal name. It was Christ our Lord who instructed my body and soul to reveal His great expectations."

A smarting Cora Lee boldly advanced toward him and he moved even further forward, teetering on the edge of the stage. "Christ, the Savior of us all, now asks every Christian to give in His name. To give willingly for the building of *His* town." He pointed to the rows of operators. "Light up those phones with pledges to the Lord!"

A bedlam of "Hallelujahs" mixed with "Praise God,"

"Praise Jesus," and "Praise Jimmy," soared from a thousand throats and reverberated through the studio. Christian waited for the demonstration to end, then directed his words to the TV millions at home. "That new refrigerator, stove, car, suit, dress *must* wait. Can *any* deny Him?" A threatening expression enveloped his face. "Come that day of judgment, shall *He* deny *you?*"

Beth Staples smiled callously as she watched Jimmy's performance on the control booth monitors. She thought about the money, the millions he had raised, and wondered how much more people would continue to give. The majority of his donors were senior citizens living on fixed incomes. Just how much could he bleed from them?

She had seen him take gambles in the past, but none like this. She knew the G.L.E.E. Club treasury was tapped. It had taken virtually all of the ministry's financial resources to complete the studio complex. And if he didn't score big with this Night of the Disciples, how long would the unpaid contractors listen to his promises and his requests for them to trust in the Lord? Already some of the contractors had yanked their crews and would not return until either the Lord or Jimmy paid up.

But she knew Jimmy was on to something, and for the first time in their association he had purposely excluded her. Ever since he had attempted to manhandle her, she could feel the coolness he generated, and the question of trust weighed heavily upon her mind. Her thinking was suddenly disrupted by a male technician who entered the booth. Noticing the videotape cartridge under his arm, her curiosity soared as he headed directly to the bedraggled director.

"Merciful God in heaven," said Billy Hale, unwilling to believe his eyes. Seated on the kind of dais used by TV talk show hosts, Jimmy Christian's taped guest was the aging industrialist C.D. Pittman. The eccentric, a blatant atheist and ruthless businessman, clearly one of the nation's richest men, was an enemy of long standing. If an election for a mortal devil was held, C.D. Pittman would be Billy's candidate. He despised the man and had attacked his ethics and godless morals on every continent. His dislike for C.D. Pittman, a man who'd been widely quoted as saying the wealthy had a responsibility to keep down the lower class—even though most of the employees of his various corporations were of that class—had once grown to such an obsession that Billy had overstepped the boundaries of fair criticism in a published assault on the man. Only Billy's close friendship with then-President Richard Waters kept him from being slapped with the largest libel suit in history. To the present day, Billy wondered what it had taken for Waters to keep it out of the courts.

"C.D.," said Jimmy, "when did you become a born-again Christian?"

"When I realized God was not dead."

"Faker!" Billy shouted in his den. "When you realized there was money to be made."

"Praise God," said Jimmy. "Would you tell the millions who are watching us on television how you became directed to me and the Glee Club ministries?"

"I believe your undertaking of Christ Town is one of a vast spiritual magnitude. What do you people call it?"

"Divine ordinance?"

"Precisely. And although I have been known to be a skeptic, a nonbeliever, I could not dispute the powerful feeling which came over me."

"Praise God," said Jimmy, who allowed the billionaire to continue.

"I'm grateful for having been called. And to show my appreciation, I shall match every dollar you and your Glee Club receives during this Night of Disciples telethon."

"Praise *Gawd*," said Jimmy, falling to his knees, bawling like a baby.

A solemn Billy Hale pushed the phone's intercom button and dialed a number. "Doris, cut off all incoming calls . . . For how long? *Indefinitely!"*

CHAPTER 9

A GMC MOTOR HOME, shadowed closely by a black van, rolled along a country road flanked by acres upon acres of fertile fields carpeted with a thick mantle of white. It had snowed in this Lancaster section of south central Pennsylvania three times and January had yet to become history.

Mennonites, primarily those of the Amish sect, had settled this lush farmland in the late seventeenth century, and their spartan daily lives were strictly governed by church elders. They called their land the Valley of Divine Providence. But twelve years ago, controversy struck the valley when one of their own, Wilhelmina Krause, sold her five-hundred-acre farm to religious revolutionary Ron Rebuck, Sr. The God-fearing, agrarian society saw its tightly woven social and religious fabric threatened by the prospect of a secular mission rising on their hallowed land. To the present day, the superstitious and God-fearing Amish farmers referred to Michael's Mission as "Beelzebub's Garden."

The twenty-six feet of home on wheels, trailed by the black van, dipped off the freshly plowed main road and stopped before a faded sign. The letters, which once spelled "Michael's Mission," had been worn away, leaving only their ghostly outlines. The two vehicles moved slowly along the recently plowed mission road when they came to a bend. To the right, a stand of evergreens partially obscured a low outbuilding with the cement-block appearance of a cheaply constructed motel. Through the lush windbreak of pines, a rusty yellow school bus was barely visible. The motor home veered to the left, winding toward an old, three-story house where smoke, filtering through a chimney, wisped into a matching late-afternoon sky. Beyond the house, looming in the background, a large red barn was flanked by two silos.

From a covered porch, young men and women regarded the idling motor home with a mix of curiosity and suspicion. Ron Rebuck, Jr., looked through a tinted window, exploring their faces. He wondered what would induce young people like them to join the type of radical religious movement the media had labeled *cult*. Cutting off the engine, he slipped a navy peacoat over a blue turtleneck and stepped out of the motor home, setting foot on grounds he had once vowed never to tread upon.

A gaunt, freckle-faced young man stepped down from the porch and warily approached him. ''Is there someone you wish to see?'' he asked.

Rebuck shouldered past him without a word, and, for a brief moment, the young man considered a more forceful challenge—until he saw Ike Vesper's awesome frame emerging from the black van.

Ron Rebuck entered the house and looked about the large and meagerly furnished room with the freshly shellacked wooden floor. His eyes were lured to a large portrait which hung over a rough fieldstone fireplace. His body grew visibly tense as he neared the portrait. It wasn't the heat from the crackling logs which brought beads of sweat to his face, rather the fire in his blood as he stared deeply at the image of the mission's founder—his dead father.

Lost in the swarm of bitter memories, he seemed unaware of the bearded man who had moved quietly to his side. ''That is our founder,'' the man said reverently.

Rebuck kept staring at the portrait. He heard nothing but the heckling from his own soul.

The man stroked his heard thoughtfully. ''You wish to see me?''

Rebuck finally tore his eyes from the portrait and took in the face of a man in his early forties. He recognized the man's hangdog look. He had seen it before—when he was sixteen, at his father's funeral.

The mission director looked hard into Rebuck's eyes, then at the familiar portrait. Uncertainty slowly vanished from his face. "You are . . . my God in heaven . . ." He grasped Rebuck's strong forearms with both hands. Tears welled into the corners of his eyes. "Our founder's son," he joyfully announced to the confused spectators who had pushed into the room.

Ron Rebuck joined his father's successor in a room which reminded him vaguely of the one in the Pentagon where he had sat through another fateful meeting. Other than two uncomfortable wooden chairs which creaked like old bones, there was a desk that would puzzle the best of antique dealers, a manual typewriter from an era when the people who pounded it wore green eyeshades, a phone that was chipped in several places, and a solitary window so smudged and stained that natural light made a detour. The room was lean—much like the look in the mission director's eyes, Rebuck thought.

For almost five minutes, the director went on talking about himself, the mission, and how Ron Rebuck's father had spoken so often about him. He would have continued to expound over the works started by his father and later entrusted to him when Rebuck had heard enough of the man's random stream of reminiscing. "I didn't come here to talk about my father," he interrupted, tossing an envelope on the desk.

Startled by Rebuck's harsh manner, the mission director curiously inspected the envelope before removing its contents. The more he read, the more troubled he appeared. Once again, his bony fingers touched his scraggly beard. He looked up at Ron Rebuck with eyes more hungered than before. "This—this is all too surprising," he said. He waited for an explanation, but none was forthcoming and he continued. "If I was only aware of this, this codicil to your father's will . . ."

"You are now," Rebuck curtly responded.

"Yes, but who, besides you and possibly your mother, knew of this item deeding you the two hundred acres at the northeast tract? Certainly *I* was not privy to it. All we could find out about you was that you were in college somewhere in California." His long fingers clasped together; the document slipped from his sweaty hands. "As for your mother, ever since she permitted the interment of your father's body here in the mission's ground, it was made clear we were not to contact her. I understand that she was . . . not well, and have never violated that wish." He paused before continuing. "When I became your father's successor, the mission was in great disorder. It took months to sort out your father's affairs."

Rebuck studied the pathetic face resembling some missionary in the depths of never-never land. What he didn't want to hear now poured through the director's shivering lips. "For more than a decade, we have followed your father's path. His book is our inspiration. Our Bible. Come this fall, more of our men and women will join their fellow messengers in combatting the fear of a wrathful God."

"Don't preach to me, Mister!"

The director leaned back in the old wooden chair to recover from a blow he had not expected. But he would not be intimidated, not even by the founder's son. "We are not religious peddlers. We solicit nothing. We grow our own food and neither I nor my staff receive financial compensation. Whatever funds we've managed to obtain have come through our graduate messengers and a lady in Rome who desires to remain anonymous." He could see he was getting nowhere and once again relied on speaking in a soulful voice. "For the past ten years, the mission has survived. Barely survived. But unfortunately, its future here in Pennsylvania is coming to an end. I've been forced to sell the land."

"All but two hundred acres of it, perhaps," said Rebuck. "The fact is that *those* two hundred acres are mine, and I'm moving onto my property immediately."

The director decided it was neither the time nor the

place to contest an amendment he never knew existed. He rose. "We can discuss this codicil later. Right now, Michael's Mission must properly welcome the son of its founder. We—"

"*Damn* you!" Rebuck thundered. "My father's dead and done with." He moved toward the director in a slow and threatening manner. Placing his hands on the desk, he hunched forward. The fire in his eyes was genuine, and the mission director's haggard face grew paler. "The sooner you learn that I despise people like you, the better off things will be."

They assembled outside the office and onto the porch, fifty young men and women and a staff of five—to see the *son*. Ron Rebuck searched the faces of young men and women. In some way he could not put his finger on, they seemed different from the Moonies, Hare Krishnas, and the list of religious panhandlers that infested airports and busy city streets. There was nothing overtly false or plastic about them. Missing was the manic gleam in the eyes of the so-called "born-again" Christians.

A very pretty girl with auburn hair and sky-blue eyes captured Rebuck's attention. There was something about her, an aura which awoke a deep yearning; something recognized but indefinable. He wanted to speak to her, and was about to when he sensed the mission director's presence behind him. He quickly broke away, bounding down the porch steps.

"How'd it go?" Ike Vesper asked as Rebuck approached him.

Rebuck leaned against the van and pulled a tax map of the mission property from his pocket. Unfolding it, he studied it intently. He looked toward the northeast, toward the property his father had willed him. "We'll attach the snow plow to the van. Make our own damn road."

"Home, sweet motha-freezin' home," Vesper said, shivering at the bleak prospect.

The mission's populace watched in silent disappointment as the van plowed away undisturbed snow for the motor home to follow. The mission director did little to enlighten them. "He's the son of our founder. His father's blood runs through his veins. But this is a man filled with great hate."

CHAPTER 10

HARLEY LOMBARD LET the phone drop from his hand. It clunked onto a mahogany conference table. "Three days I'm up shit's creek and Billy kills the damn phones," the evangelist grumbled.

A slender man seated at the table calmly replaced the receiver on its holder, then resumed writing on a yellow legal pad.

Harley brought a hand to the back of his head and held it there, looking vacantly at the expanse of the World Cathedral library. "The little weasel pulled it off," he said, weaving through the large room highlighted by stained glass windows depicting religious events from the New Testament. "I haven't slept in two nights," he groaned. The natural redness on the tip of his nose brightened oddly. "What the hell are you writing?" he asked the man at the table.

Andy Gaines looked up. His soft eyes probed the gloomy face of his longtime boss. "When I think, I doodle."

"Jimmy Christian hits me over the head with a mountain, and you're doodling? Talk to me!"

"About what, Harley?"

"C.D. Pittman. Of all people, he gets C.D. Pittman . . . The cock-a-roach lands a *whale*."

"Why should it surprise you? Jimmy Christian is still a good investment. He's been in the public eye since he started building Christ Town over three years ago."

"Billy told me the son of a bitch was going lame." Lombard's feet were not in unison with his brain and he paced the library in a zigzag pattern. "How do I fight that kind of clout? What's to keep him from stealing *all* my shows? . . . Are you listening to me?''

''Harley, I'm listening.''

''Try Billy again.''

''Harley, face it. The man is out of reach.''

''Sure, when I need the old bugger, he's never there.''

Andy Gaines knew nothing was further from the truth. But he declined an opportunity to speak on Billy's behalf. It would only cause Harley to rant and rave, and Gaines was in no mood to be hassled more than usual.

''The hell with Billy! Why do I need him? Tell me why?''

''Harley, I think you can best answer that yourself.''

''Help me? My great benefactor?''

''Yes, I guess.''

''And who were Billy's benefactors?''

''I haven't the foggiest.''

''Do you think Billy just *became* a household name?''

''I wouldn't think anyone just becomes a household name, Harley.''

''Bankers, politicians, publishers. That's the kind of muscle Billy had behind him.'' He paused as if in deep thought and Gaines couldn't decide which troubled Lombard the most: Jimmy Christian's financial miracle or his inability to reach Billy Hale.

''Fifty-two,'' Harley said. ''I'm fifty-two years old. Second banana to Billy Big for so many years, and now that I'm number one, the *king* of Evangelism, an *insect* is going to knock me off my throne.''

''Maybe not, Harley.''

''I can't produce billion-dollar miracles!''

''Everyone knows whatever C.D. Pittman touches, he owns.''

''So?''

''Could be Jimmy Christian cut himself a deal with the devil.''

''Sold his soul? That kind of crap?''

''You certainly don't believe Pittman's born-again stuff? It's obvious he made a deal with Jimmy, and whatever the financial arrangements are, you can bet Pittman holds the trump cards.''

''Shit ass will still finish building Christ Town.''

''Most likely. But Pittman will hang him in return.''

''My nerves, my nerves,'' Lombard groaned.

The wheels were turning. Andy Gaines knew the look which preceded some of Harley Lombard's most outlandish, if not outrageous, ideas.

''Got to do him one better,'' Harley said half to himself. ''Something—something to grab the media by the balls. And *before* Easter.'' He moved closer to Andy Gaines. ''What happens when someone puts all his eggs into one basket?''

''Harley, I, ah—'' Gaines groped.

''You're not thinking! Don't I pay you to think?''

''Yes, I guess. And to do a hundred other things.''

''Smart ass. You're being Mister Smart Ass instead of thinking.''

''Harley, I'm sorry. I don't know what happens when someone puts all his eggs into one basket.''

''You know why?''

''No, Harley, I don't know why.''

''Because you are a follower. One of the mullet in this world. Look at you: what have you ever created? Not even a child. And why does Wilma Mae call you a thing?''

''A *what?*''

Harley quickly returned to what was bothering him the most. ''Maybe that little cockroach will get so involved with his religious Disney World, he'll become vulnerable. If what you said is gospel, his becoming a partner with a barracuda like C.D. Pittman just insures my bet.''

He paced the room again. He would think some, stop, shoot Andy Gaines a dirty look, then do it all over again. ''The timing couldn't be better,'' said Harley. ''Now's the time to come up with something.''

''Like what?''

''I'll think of it. I didn't get to be king of the hill by being an empty chair.''

''Revelation, Harley?''

" 'Bout damn time you got *something* right."

Andy Gaines took the insult in stride. During the course of one twelve-hour working day, he made it a point to count the number of insults Harley laid upon him. Today he'd quit counting after twenty-three.

Harley's eyes were shining. "This one has to be the biggest of them all. The kind that rolls with power. And when it comes, Jimmy Christian will be scabbing for pulpit money. And I don't need Billy to help me pull it off!"

He went to the door and opened it. The sound of musical voices infiltrated the room. The World Cathedral Chorus was practicing in the loft, and something more physical than a revelation came to mind. "Get me—you know what."

"A drink?"

"Nitwit, you know what I mean." He jerked his thumb in the direction where the music originated.

"You *find* it, *fetch* it, then *bring* it home," snarled Harley, slamming the door behind him.

Andy Gaines sat back in the chair, his pale, aquiline face locked in a pout. Today was his birthday, his fortieth. Yet he should have known Harley would forget. Only once in twenty years had he remembered and then Harley had promised a present. But he had to admit Harley had made good. He still had the loud yellow tie with the silk-screened image of Harley and the World Cathedral. No, he was aware that Harley was a complex man who rarely cared or thought of the needs and wishes of others, and he should have known to *expect* the expected.

He had spent half his lifetime working for Harley. For twenty years he had been his right and left arm, his pacifier, ego builder, and personal whipping boy. He lied, cheated, and defamed for Harley, but his more recent role of procurer was getting harder and harder for him to justify. Harley's instructions gnawed feverishly at his insides.

The young girl walked with reluctance down the hall, trailed by her troubled escort, Andy Gaines. She wore a denim skirt with black boots and her long blond hair was pulled back and tied in a bun. She wore no bra under a white blouse, and a pale blue sweater was draped loosely around her shoulders. She was five-foot-three and still growing. Although her body was that of a mature woman, the traces of acne on her face defined her age. She had only recently turned fourteen. More cute than pretty, she looked the part of the majorette who led her school band down the field on some autumn afternoon.

They reached the door to Harley's inner sanctum and if Andy ever despised his employer, it was now. He stepped in front of the trembling girl and knocked twice. There was a buzzing sound and the lock clicked open. He looked at the girl, whose frightened eyes seemed to seek his protection. For a moment he felt true grit. He wanted to take her by the hand, lead her safely from the cathedral, but the urge lost its sizzle. Stifled by his innate timidity, he cracked open the door.

He watched the small, pathetic figure inch past him into the room. He quickly shut the door, hoping to block the scene from his mind. But he knew he was the sheep who had led the lamb to slaughter, and that guilt would always be with him.

"Come in, little angel," Harley Lombard cooed.

She moved a step closer, then halted. "Reverend . . ." Unable to put the words together, she fell into silence.

"What's wrong?" Harley asked, sounding like a guardian father.

Tears began to form in her eyes, and the fatherly image he was trying to project was quickly replaced by the apprehension of a defendant awaiting a jury's verdict. "You *are* on the pill, aren't you?"

She let him hang for a moment, then nodded.

Greatly relieved, Harley's tone returned to a soothing inflection. "Tell me what's wrong. You know I will help you."

"Rev-Reverend Harley, isn't *this* wrong?"

"Wrong?" Harley sounded offended.

"I know you said I was an angel sent by God, but—but angels aren't people."

He slid off the couch and walked carefully to her side. He smiled thickly. "But you *are* an angel. Of course, not like the angels in heaven. But that's why God sent you to me. The strength you give me cannot be given by spiritual angels. Only people angels. Like yourself."

He led her gently to the couch. His hand slipped from her waist and came to rest on her rounded hips. "Without you, my fight against the devil would be lost."

She stood before him, confused. He sat on the edge of the sofa, clutching her slim waist once again. "You give me the strength, the power to do battle against the king of hell."

"But, Reverend, doesn't your wife give you strength?"

"My wife," he said with a tone of remorse, "she can no longer give me that power, the strength I need." He lowered his head, lying through his teeth. "My wife—has cancer."

"Will she die?"

"In time, in time," he said, rushing his reply.

"I'm sorry. Truly I am."

"Now do you understand why *you* are the one?"

"Yes, I think so."

"Then let us do what God wants us to do."

While she demurely folded her sweater over a chair, he dropped his pants, stripped off his shorts and lay back on the couch. When she turned toward him, he could see by her expression it wouldn't be that simple. This was not the day he felt like coaxing her.

"Reverend Harley, I—I don't want to . . . kiss . . ."

"Kiss?"

She pointed to his hardening penis.

"But that is part of the strength you give me."

"Reverend Harley, I *really* don't want to."

"Agreed," said Harley, who proceeded to stroke himself in anticipation while she unbuttoned her blouse and slipped it off.

Harley stared hungrily at her young tits—so round, so

pointed at the still undeveloped nipples—and the tempo of his stroking intensified. She was about to unfasten the buttons to her denim skirt, but had a change of mind. The lust within Harley grew incensed as he saw her edge toward him with the large, rounded bosom that jutted out from golden skin, an imploring look in her eyes.

"Can I leave my skirt on?" she asked with innocence.

He nodded, and she hitched up the skirt to reveal silk-smooth legs. The cheeks of her tight young ass spilled from white bikini panties.

"Forget the underwear," Harley rasped with burning impatience.

She lifted a firm leg and pulled the pubic area of her panties to the side, mounting him.

His hands clutched her young and unscathed ass, then rose to fondle her breasts while she rode him with slow undulations. All the while, she stayed from his face—unable or unwilling to look at him.

"My little angel," he uttered blissfully as she began to ride his glistening staff more rapidly. "What are you doing?" he asked breathlessly.

She didn't answer him.

He asked again with a rising urgency in his voice.

"I'm loving you."

"*No!*" Harley said. "Say the *word*. The *word!*"

"I'm . . . fucking you."

"Yes. And who are you fucking?"

"I'm fucking a reverend," she replied as though she had rehearsed the line.

"Faster," Harley moaned. "Faster . . . harder, *faster!*"

Her tempo increased until he could no longer feel her heaving breasts or grab onto her driving ass as the thrusting motion of her hips and her strong, scissoring legs pinned him in a willing helplessness.

"The pole, the pole. Up and down," he crooned frantically.

She lifted both booted legs until her dimpled knees were but an inch from his hairy chest.

"Harder!" he cried out, repeating the word again and again between sucking breaths.

The room seemed to vibrate with the wet slapping and pounding of her ass against his thighs. She took him deeply, as deeply as she possibly could. His entire body went rigid, then seemed to quiver. Every erotic nerve ending was on fire when he emitted a bull-like moan of ecstasy—and came.

She continued to hump him rapidly until he could stand no more. For the first time since mounting him, she looked directly into his perspiring, flushed face. "Reverend Harley, was the Mother Mary really fourteen when she had Jesus?"

CHAPTER 11

JESSICA TOWNE WAS THE least likely of the mission students to defy authority or willfully violate mission rules. A rather shy girl, she avoided center stage. But a visit to the man the mission director had taken to calling "the Stranger" had become a topic of heated conversation, and her activities were suddenly the object of scrutiny from fellow students. Her unwillingness to share her experience in the camp of Ron Rebuck, Jr., after she was intercepted and questioned by a fellow student on the trail, had heated the coals of gossip.

From the moment Ron Rebuck's eyes had met hers, she'd felt drawn to him, and an impulsive desire to know him had begun to burn within her from that moment. The very next day, she'd slipped off by herself and walked the mission's trails in the hope of finding this strange young man. She'd not been disappointed.

Jessica was arguably the loveliest of the mission girls. Slender, with a long tawny mane and radiant brown eyes, her beauty was natural, not in need of the enhancement of makeup or flashy clothes. She was born a country girl, and her open face, with its dusting of freckles and full, tempting mouth, would certainly turn the head of any red-blooded man long after the models in the "big city" had lost their applied sensuality. Simply put, Jessica had a glow.

Their one meeting had been brief but promising, despite the interruption in the form of Ike Vesper. Tonight, Jessica felt an even stronger, burning urge to see Ron Rebuck. Warmly dressed against the winter's chill, she slipped out of the dormitory and into the bitter February night. Trudging over snow dappled by a full moon which created stark shadows, she reached the trail behind the old mission house and moved toward what her fellow classmates considered forbidden grounds.

She wondered why the mission director had not said a word to her yet about her meeting with Ron Rebuck, since surely the gossip must have reached him. She knew that until he declared the trail to be off limits, or banned her from seeing the founder's son, she would continue to seek him out. Now, as she moved into the cover of the woods, she didn't see the bearded face looking out from an upstairs window of the mission house.

The attack dogs picked up her scent and their vicious snarls and attempts to leap the high fence brought an alert Ike Vesper from his trailer home. Once his flashlight illuminated her face, Ike shouted to the Dobermans, who whined submissively.

"He's not here, Little Girl," Vesper said.

She looked around the camp. There were no lights inside the motor home and the black van was gone.

Ike saw the deep frown of disappointment and asked, "Like some hot coffee?"

The other night Ike Vesper had acted as if she were a bad omen, and for him to take such a friendly attitude now struck Jessica as too dramatic a change of character. She shook her head and turned to leave, but he was upon her like a big cat. "Little Girl, I promise not to bite-cha."

Ike's smile, that of a protective brother, immediately put her at ease. She followed him, hesitating for a moment at the trailer's entrance. "It's cool, Little Girl," Ike said, reassuring her.

She sat at the kitchen table, watching him pour coffee into a mug, and wondered why Ron Rebuck lived in a motor home while Ike had the roomier trailer. She studied what she thought must be a communications system as she removed her scarf and gloves.

"That dude in charge, whattaya call him, Arch sumpthin'?" Ike said, placing the coffee before her.

"Arch-Messenger," she replied softly.

"You comin' here like this must be fuckin' up his mind."

She looked down at her cup.

"That word offend you, Little Girl?" He wedged his mammoth frame into a chair and sat across from her. "Tell me, Little Girl, what do you people do besides pray?"

"We don't pray," Jessica said.

"You *don't* pray?"

She nodded.

"Little Girl, you wouldn't be messin' with this nigger's head?"

She wasn't. He knew she was telling the truth, and now Ike Vesper was confused. He waited for her to speak again. "C'mon, open up," he said after a long silence. "Let it roll, save my black ass. I wanna be born again."

"We don't believe in that," she said, smiling.

He'd wanted to have some fun at her expense, to ridicule established religious beliefs, but she'd completely disarmed him. He took a sip of coffee, studying her over the rim of the cup. He liked this pretty, spunky girl, he decided . . . but he still wasn't about to let her off the hook—it wouldn't do her any good. "Little Girl," he started, "you're climbin' on a volcano, and when the motha blows, you might never come down. Are you gettin' my drift?"

"Are you talking about Ron . . . and me?"

"You're flashin' eyes at a statue."

"What are you trying to say?"

"There ain't nothin' you can do that'll light his fire."

As she sat in silence, Jessica's ardor was written on her face. Vesper recognized the look and smiled knowingly.

"Why are you smiling?" she asked.

"Autumn leaves, rainbows, waterfalls, me and my man walkin' hand in hand through a funky forest 'til death do us in? Little Girl, the story don't read that way. It ain't your fault, but ya don't sing his song. He's got a solo goin'. He can't handle duets."

She bit down on her lip, and he figured she was either too inexperienced or unwilling to cope with the bullet truth. Yet for some reason he felt obligated to tell her that Ron Rebuck was not her shining prince.

"He likes you, Little Girl. But he ain't for you."

"Did he tell you that?"

He wouldn't lie to her, but he regretted having played Uncle Ike and decided to put an end to the conversation and see her to the trail. It was no skin off his black ass if some dreamy-eyed honky bitch got burned. But then, it could mess things up if she hung around—and certainly the captain wouldn't be pleased.

"How old are you, Little Girl?" he asked.

"Eighteen—last October. Why?"

"Eighteen," said Ike, shaking his head.

"I know Ron must be ten years older than me."

"Ten years older?" Ike laughed. "Little Girl, as far as you're concerned, the man is goin' on a hundred 'n three." He could see the confusion building on her face and drew closer to her. "Little Girl, you're dealin' with a dude who's intense to the max. The cat got no future 'til what's stinkin' in his gut gets flushed. You be a smart girl and don't get involved. You stay away, before something bad happens."

Her silence and the wounded look on her face indicated he had come on too quickly and too harshly. He never did have much tact with women. "You gonna cry, Little Girl?"

"No."

"Tell me I'm full of shit?"

"Why? Should I?"

She listened, and he liked that. "Then you gonna take my advice?" he asked.

"What is the 'something bad' you're talking about?"

Ike held back what he wanted to say. "Believe me, Little Girl, you keep seein' the man, and you'll be an old woman before your time."

"Is Ron that bad?"

"C'mon, Little Girl, I'm walkin' you to the trail."

104

He quieted the dogs with a loud command and led her to the trail. He believed he had done the right thing, yet he felt sorry that he'd been so rough on her. He was about to say so when the sight of a frail, ghostly figure standing in the path ahead distracted him. It was the mission director.

"Thank you," Jessica whispered to Ike.

"For what, a lotta hurt?"

"For being honest."

To Ike's surprise, there was no confrontation between the girl and the mission director; no words were spoken when she passed him. Ike waited for the man to follow her, but he just stood there, staring at him. If he had something to say, why didn't he say it? Aggravated by the man's silence, irked at being challenged by a wimp, Ike strode toward the man. "You got something to say to me?"

There was a pathetic sadness on the man's face and a martyr's resignation in his eyes. Ike recalled a picture of Jesus Christ's face after his sentencing by Pontius Pilate, a holy picture his Bible-toting grandmother had burned into his memory. He stepped closer, towering over the smaller man. With one swat of his lion-sized paw, he knew he could knock that annoying holier-than-thou expression off the man's face.

Ike calmed himself. After all, he reflected, he had no reason to get involved with this so-called "man of God." Unlike Ron Rebuck, who would become incensed at the mere mention of religion or its merchants, Vesper had long ago forgotten his Baptist background. While he considered religion a means for rip-off artists to brainwash the young and spread fear through the minds of the elderly, it didn't affect him and, thus, he didn't let it bother him. To his thinking, the only thing almighty in religion was the almighty buck—but they sure weren't getting any of *his* money.

"Leave Jessica alone," the director ordered.

"Say *what?*"

"She is an innocent in the ways of the world."

"Back off, Spooky Man! You're jivin' with the wrong dude. Tell it to the man."

"If you are referring to Ron Rebuck, Jr., I'd like you to tell me how to talk to a man who hates as he does."

"Outta my zone, Spooky Man. Lay it on Rebuck. He's the cat you got to do business with."

"I have offered my hand in friendship. It is up to him."

Vesper sneered. "Friendship? Man, he don't want your kind of friendship. That just ain't where it's at. He's got no love for religious dudes. The way he sees it, it's chumps like you who murdered his old man."

"Surely he doesn't believe that!"

"Tell you what, Preacher Man, you go ahead and ask him."

"I will, given the opportunity."

Ike Vesper roared with laughter. The ragged vapor of his breath entered the cold night air and seemed to smite the man's face. "You do that, Spooky Man—you ask him about it," said Vesper, walking away. "You be sure to ask him about it," he repeated from a distance, leaving the mission director with the sound of mocking laughter in his ears.

CHAPTER 12

BILLY HALE LOOKED around the lobby of the brilliantly designed, futuristic triple-tiered building, searching for something religious in its motif. A large portrait of Jimmy Christian set amid heavenly clouds was the nearest to a spiritual theme that he could find. He waited in the background for a group of senior citizens congregated around the reception desk to disperse. He was in no mood for small talk or making new acquaintances and paid little attention to the tall, attractive woman stepping from an elevator until she moved decisively toward him.

"Dr. Hale, another surprise visit?"

He tried to place her.

"I'm Elizabeth Staples. Jimmy Christian's executive assistant. It will be some time before Jimmy's free. He's taping a show."

"That is the most refreshing thing I have heard today."

"Refreshing? I'm afraid I don't follow you, Dr. Hale."

"I was referring to the taping being called a show," he said, adding, "And call me Billy, please."

She grinned, and he wondered if she thought of him as an old hypocrite. His own TV "campaigns" had not been mere sermons.

"While you're waiting, would you like a tour of the building?" she asked.

"How about starting with the church?"

"Church?"

"Place of worship. With all this construction going on, there must be a church."

"I'm . . . afraid not," she confessed.

107

"An Evangelical World Center without a church?"

"Well, in a way you could say this building is a trinity."

"A *trinity?*"

"Computer-telephone center, studio, and offices," she said with that same likeable grin.

She had repelled his innuendoes with a sense of humor. Billy liked that and returned her smile. "I've seen computers and telephones before and never did take a shine to offices. So what say we see the show?"

"Would you think it advisable? I mean, *you*, Billy Hale, in Jimmy's studio? It could be most disrupting."

"Young lady, that is precisely why I have come."

Four hundred people sat in theater chairs beneath a web of overhead cables and lights in a TV studio on a technological par with those of the major networks. An attentive Jimmy Christian was seated behind a desk on a curved stage listening to a middle-aged, slightly cross-eyed man giving his testimony. Frank Buckmaster, who was seated on a sofa next to Jimmy's guest, nodded in agreement with everything the man said. All the while, five tiers of middle-aged and elderly women manned eighty busy phones. In the orchestra pit, the musicians seemed bored by it all.

"Yes, Jimmy, the vision was real," the man said woodenly.

"Praise God," said Bucky.

"I saw Jesus, just as I'm seeing you, Jimmy."

"And what did Jesus say to you?"

"He looked sad, Jimmy."

Bucky bit down on his lower lip.

"Did He say *anything* to you? Did *Christ* say anything to you?"

"Yes, He did, Jimmy."

"And what did Christ say to you?"

"He said many things, Jimmy."

"Surely, He spoke of *His* town. *Christ Town?*" Jimmy prompted.

"Yes, Jimmy. Yes, He did."

"Praise God," Jimmy said with relief in his voice. He

turned and looked directly into the camera. "The Lord, *Gee*-zus Christ, spoke of *His* town. *Christ Town!*"

"Praise God," Bucky said, leading the audience in applause.

Cora Lee Christian bounded perkily onto the stage before her cue and began to sing in a nerve-shattering voice. The studio filled with the words of a tune called "God Knows Every Little Thing You Do." Jimmy waited for her to get into the number, then left the stage and confronted a man standing in the wings out of camera range. "You call yourself a talent coordinator? Where did you get that idiot of a guest?"

"Visions *sell*, Jimmy."

"Visions sell when they're *rehearsed*. I didn't think the bastard would ever get to Christ Town." Jimmy scanned the audience. Club members who had come in tour buses and cars to attend a taping always suppressed his anger. He looked like a farmer surveying a good crop until his smile slowly turned to a frown. "Is that Billy Hale? By the door . . . standing next to Beth?"

"If it is, he looks like Moses."

"Oh, shit," Jimmy cursed, noticing Buckmaster stand up and peer toward the back of the studio. "Get the floor director. Fast!"

Buckmaster had drifted too close to Cora Lee. "Go away," she hissed between notes.

Bucky stared owlishly. "Cora Lee, *Billy Hale's* out there," he whispered.

"Get away from me," she said, prancing toward the footlights.

A young man wearing headphones relayed his instructions to the control booth and Jimmy reappeared on the stage. The music stopped and the attention of the audience was split between Cora Lee shouting at Buckmaster and the unexpected appearance of Billy Hale. Jimmy stepped between them and had to struggle to get the microphone from Cora Lee's hand. "Fire him, Daddy! Fire that blubber puss," she demanded, stomping her foot.

"Jimmy," Bucky protested, "Billy's *here* in the audience."

"Find a deep hole and jump in," Jimmy snapped.

Cora Lee seconded her husband's ire with a swift kick to Bucky's shin and he let out a loud yelp.

Beth Staples leaned close to Billy. "I see what you mean."

"I always keep my word," Billy replied in a less than serious tone.

Beth saw Jimmy nearing the front of the stage. Even from such a distance, she could recognize the familiar expression on his face: the kind which gave elementary school teachers conniptions. She knew Jimmy was up to something, and the video tape was rolling.

"We are honored," said Jimmy, "honored by the presence of a great man. A man who long ago was the pioneer of televised evangelism. A man whose worldwide television Campaigns for Christ made it possible for evangelism to reach out and touch people everywhere. Glee Club members here with us in this magnificent studio, and those of you watching worldwide, let us warmly welcome the one and only *Billy Hale*."

The applause sign wasn't necessary. The audience rose in a spontaneous ovation. Beth Staples was not fooled by Jimmy's gracious acknowledgment. She knew Jimmy had not forgotten Billy's last visit and how he thought the old man's needling him was strictly for Harley Lombard's benefit. She was sure Jimmy was setting a trap and that she would not have to wait long for it to spring, for Billy was now limping down the aisle.

Frank Buckmaster hovered at the top step, anxiously waiting to escort his hero onto the stage. His enthusiastic greeting was deflated by the combative look on Billy's face. "Bucky, I think you had better sit this one out," Billy half whispered.

Bucky did not understand, yet had the sense to back off as Billy mounted the steps, pausing to rest halfway. Followed by two rolling cameras, Jimmy Christian came swiftly to greet him. "Has the Lord sent you to inspire me?" he trumpeted.

Before Billy could reply, Jimmy pulled the mike back from his reach and spoke to his audience in a booming voice. "Billy Hale has come to inspire *me* in the completion of Christ Town. *Praise God!*"

Jimmy gestured for quiet with his free hand and the audience grew silent. Turning his attention to Billy, who stared at the hand holding the microphone, he asked, "Have you come as the Lord's messenger?" Once again, he danced away from Billy and addressed the audience with rising passion. "*Billy* has come as the Lord's messenger. *Praise God!*"

The audience responded with a throng of hallelujahs. Beth Staples thought Billy had made a foolish mistake. She was certain he had stepped into a lion's den. But Billy snatched the mike from Jimmy's hand. "The message I have for you is *not* from the Lord."

Jimmy Christian drew a finger across his throat. The red camera light winked out.

A determined Billy Hale stood by as Frank Buckmaster rapped persistently on Jimmy Christian's dressing-room door. "Jimmy, Billy wants to speak with you," he whined. "Jimmy?" He kept knocking on the door.

A late-arriving Beth Staples provided a remedy. She motioned for Bucky to stand aside, then simply opened the door.

Jimmy Christian was seated at a dressing table wiping the makeup from his face. He took only casual notice of the interruption until he saw Buckmaster. "You—out!" he roared. Despite his discomfort in Beth Staples's presence, he seemed to welcome Billy's. "Take a seat, Billy," he said. "All the traveling you've been doing must tire you out."

"I'll stand, thank you. By the way, Jimmy, nice try."

"Well, you'd be surprised how smooth it will turn out after the editing. What's on your mind, *this time?*"

"Your involvement with C.D. Pittman," Billy promptly replied.

Jimmy stood wiping his hands with a towel, then sat on a yellow couch at the far end of the posh dressing room. "From what I hear, he's an old enemy of yours. Isn't he, Billy?"

"He's that and more."

"Well, I wouldn't know about that. Your wars with C.D. were well before my time."

"Shall we dispense with the verbal sparring?"

"Sounds good, Billy. It will save us both a lot of *valuable* time."

"First, I believe your building of Christ Town is nothing less than a sham upon the public, a religious rip-off. I have never said so publicly for there is the remote possibility you could prove me wrong. But your association with C.D. Pittman has stuck in my craw."

"It seems a lot of things have been sticking in your craw, Billy."

"Pittman is a man who has practiced every evil known to mankind. He's a briber of politicians and a man known to hire mob killers to get his way. And I would think that you, who call yourself a man of the cloth, would know better than to get involved with him. For you to use his money to build a town in Christ's name is an outrage."

Christian waited for Billy to continue and was surprised when he didn't. "That's it? That's all?"

"*That* is enough."

"Well, I'm sorry, but I don't buy that bullshit. Are you forgetting those Mafia leaders, the ones who contribute so heavily to their church? Ever see *their* funerals, Billy? The whole Catholic enchilada. Besides, I really don't think my taking money from C.D. Pittman is any of your business."

"I think it is."

"Well, that's just the point." Jimmy rose from the couch and tossed the towel aside. "Your coming here, snooping around, is getting a little tiring." As he started to pace the room, Beth wondered how far he would let his show of anger run. "I mean, who asked you for advice? Just butt out, huh, Billy?"

"Don't sass me, young man," Hale said, feeling his face flush.

"Yeah? Well, who the hell are you coming here and telling me what I can and can't do? What is it, you've got nothing left to do but stick your nose in other people's business?"

"Now you just hold on there, young man. I came here in good faith—not to snoop, as you apparently believe. No matter how difficult it might be for you to understand, I have your best interest at heart. Pittman is no good. Whatever he touches, he corrupts. Get out from under him before it's too late."

"Well, I believe you're wrong. I mean, you *have* been wrong."

"Not in C.D. Pittman's case."

"Well, I think you are. He's your devil, Billy. Not mine."

"Do I take that as an indication you intend to continue your relationship with the man?"

"Bank on it."

"Then you leave me no alternative. Unless you divorce yourself from Pittman, I will have to stop you."

"*You?* You are going to come down on *me?*"

"As you say, 'Bank on it.' "

"You gotta be kidding." Christian looked at Beth. "Is he kidding?" His eyes flashed derisively. "You're washed up. Yesterday's news. Nobody takes you seriously anymore. You're an old man. People think you're senile."

"Jimmy, stop!" Beth said with alarm.

"Stay out of this, Beth. 'Bout time someone told him where he's at."

There was no stopping Christian now. She knew better than to try. He began to circle, and Beth wondered how long the seemingly undaunted Hale would endure the demeaning tirade. Jimmy was going for the jugular vein. She had seen it before. Yet Billy was big game, even for Jimmy Christian.

"Look," Jimmy continued, "there is no question you were once Mr. Great. I respect that. But you're not anymore. You're as passé as the collection basket. And just so you know how I really feel about you, I'm going to put it to you in a way you won't forget. Wipe Harley Lombard's ass. He shits enough to keep you busy."

The knuckles on the hand holding the cane matched the sudden ashen whiteness of Billy's face. He limped toward the bantam figure of Jimmy Christian. The young evangelist stood his ground, his sneering face only prodding an uncontrollable urge within Billy Hale. Beth Staples winced as the cane cracked against Jimmy's face and head, followed by another lusty blow that fell on the side of Christian's neck.

"Call the police!" Jimmy shrilled, trying to fend off the relentless cane with flailing arms.

Beth Staples would do no such thing.

114

CHAPTER 13

RON REBUCK DROVE the van slowly. He did not want to risk missing the road. According to the directions in the coded instructions, the cutoff was just ahead. He was searching intently for the turn when it loomed suddenly before him.

He braked the van to a stop and looked out at the moonlit landscape of the Maryland back country. A road patched with ice led to winter-stripped woods. Rebuck skillfully maneuvered the skidding van on the slick road and drove deeper, past meadows and hedgerows to an area thick with oak, pines, and hemlock. He noticed two spruce trees separated by a stone wall covered with frozen lichen and moss. A rusted gate which no longer swung on its hinges identified a tract of land rich in colonial history. Titled headstones marked the burial site of Revolutionary War patriots. Rebuck cut the engine and flicked off the headlights.

It was too silent, too eerie, as if this desolate, long-forgotten spot in the world was timeless. The prospect of meeting with a man who had eliminated so many names from the book of the living gave Rebuck a shiver of concern. He checked that the .357 Magnum was secure in a shoulder holster, concealed two throwing knives in the lining of his navy peacoat, and got out of the van.

The cold wind snapped at his face as he crossed the icy road and moved toward the wall most distant from the ancient gate. Using a towering spruce for cover, he slipped over the wall. Crouching low to the frozen ground, Rebuck surveyed the ghostly setting of the rendezvous. He tensed at the sudden sound of crunching snow. His heart pounded wildly. His hand went for the reassuring steel of the Magnum.

Captain Claude Gemmer appeared from behind a tombstone like an apparition. "Good evening, Lieutenant," he said.

Rebuck gazed at the coatless man wearing a dark turtleneck sweater, seemingly immune to the freezing temperature. He had no trouble rediscovering the sick grin on Gemmer's scar-laced face. Suddenly Rebuck felt an urge to blow him away, to rid himself of the man who'd ended his naval career and who now virtually controlled every phase of his life. He knew he would never have a better opportunity—but he also knew that he couldn't do it until his mother's safety was assured, and she had disappeared off the face of the Earth, as far as he'd been able to determine. No, he could only waste Gemmer in sheer self-defense.

"Take me on, Lieutenant?" Gemmer said.

Rebuck shrugged. "That's up to you."

"Come out from under that tree."

"First move away from the headstone, Captain."

"Not one step, Sonny."

Rebuck was sure the captain was armed, that hidden behind the tombstone a weapon was firmly clutched in his hand. But *he* had the drop on him, the first shot. So why did he feel the captain was giving him a sporting chance, as if he was the underdog? Was the man *that* confident? Was this one of the ways he intimidated his victims—by flaunting a suicidal courage? Impossible, Rebuck thought; Gemmer would never have lived this long.

Rebuck gauged the distance between them. He couldn't miss. But what if he did? He decided to wait him out, a SEAL tactic. Then Rebuck remembered, it was Captain Gemmer who had introduced the silent freeze he had studied in his classes on commando warfare. He had sworn never to let himself be intimidated by Gemmer again, never to let the captain screw up his head the way he had during their Washington hotel meeting. He would seize the initiative, careful not to do or say anything that could be construed as a weakness. "Why the cemetery, Captain? Why not a hotel room in Washington?"

"I have personal reasons," Gemmer replied.

"We've got nothing personal working."

"Ah, but we do."

"Bullshit, Captain."

"Lieutenant, if I wanted to end your life, I would have done so long before you set foot on these sacred grounds."

"Maybe not. Your flair for drama is world renowned. And I'm no longer a lieutenant. *Remember?*"

The captain stepped from behind the stone and Rebuck rose with caution. They moved forward almost simultaneously, both surrendering their cover, and silently measured each other under the light of a full moon.

"A .357 Magnum—it figures," the captain said, nodding at the weapon trained on his breastbone.

Rebuck focused on the mini machine gun the captain held at hip level. "I've heard you prefer more artistic ways of wasting people," he said, "like all those throats you've slit. Tell me, Captain, was any of it in hand-to-hand combat or was it always from behind?"

"Are you trying to intimidate me, Mister?"

"Does the switch in roles bother you?"

"Don't buck fate, Junior."

"Your threats are empty, Captain. You shot your load the last time we met."

The master assassin studied the youthful face, probing the intensity. The long steady fingers lightly caressed the trigger. Rebuck's eyes froze on the subtle movement. He would not retreat, nor would he say anything to defuse the confrontation. Nor did he realize that a thousand ghosts were chanting for the captain's demise. He was mentally and physically prepared to deliver that bolt of fire and survive, or receive Gemmer's savage burst and fall victim to eternal darkness.

The captain prolonged the taut drama for as long as he had intended, then let the machine gun drop into the snow. "Lay your weapon next to mine. We've got business, Mister."

A sensation of relief drained through Rebuck's body. He watched Gemmer limp off, moving among the headstones like some ghoul at home amidst the dead. Despite the captain's orders, Rebuck would not surrender his weapon and slid the Magnum back into its holster. He moved slowly and cautiously through the graveyard. Following at a distance, he saw the limping warrior step before one of the larger tombstones. Rebuck moved closer until he could see the name "GEMMER" chisled deeply into the stone, washed by moonlight.

"Do you believe there's something else, Lieutenant? Do you wonder how you will die?" Gemmer said tonelessly.

"A few minutes ago I was wondering about it."

"I have seen many die—seen them check out laughing, cursing, and yes, praying. Yet not once did I see anything but blood, guts, and waste leave the body."

"What does all this have to do with me, Captain?"

Gemmer placed a hand on the stone and slowly traced the letters of his name. "I too will join my father and his father someday, and the rest of the military Gemmers who are buried in these hallowed grounds."

The captain was deep in reflection, and Rebuck was surprised he would show a side of himself seldom, if ever, revealed to others. He wondered if this personal display was for the purpose of setting him up, catching him off guard—followed by the blast, a death sudden as a stroke of lightning.

"Of course, there's a chance I will live to be an old man and die of some cursed disease. But I believe differently, don't you?"

"I wouldn't know, Captain."

"I shall die a violent death. That much I know. And you, Lieutenant, how will you leave this godforsaken planet?"

"I don't think about it."

"Surely you must."

"I don't."

The captain ignored Rebuck's response and spoke in a softer voice, almost to himself. "The last great adventure

. . . the one experience all living creatures have in common. I have often wondered what type of person will do me in. Whoever, my executioner will have to be good. The best." His eyes left the stone and swung to young Rebuck's face. "Are you the *best*, Lieutenant?"

Rebuck would not permit himself to flinch and took the full brunt of the captain's stare. He felt as if his face was being pricked by needles. Yet this was only a man, he told himself. He would not back down and turn to jelly like Ike Vesper. But why did his legs feel so weak, why did he feel as if the strength was being sucked slowly from his body? And why did he imagine it was no longer the captain's face before him, but that of a deadly snake lulling him into a hypnotic state before the strike?

Rebuck watched the captain limp away. Suddenly, the air felt cold again. Before he could regroup his senses, he was startled by the sight and sound of the captain kicking at the frozen ground with his bad foot. The harder Gemmer kicked the more livid his face became.

"Do you know who God is?" the captain asked, frenzy in his voice. "God is a gun!" he thundered. "The *supreme* assassin!"

The captain was crazy, crazy from too many kills, Rebuck thought, as the enraged Gemmer limped toward him. The twisted lips, demonic snarl, and crazed eyes were too close. Still the captain inched closer, until the vapor of his breath commingled with his own.

"Do you think I'm insane?"

"I think you're completely off the wall, Captain."

"Affirmative. But unlike you, I'm able to control my insanity, turn it on or off whenever or wherever I choose."

"Why should your insanity interest me?"

"It's all relative. Your *problem*, Lieutenant? You know I'm well aware of it."

"Captain, if you've got business with me, get on with it. If not, I'm leaving."

"Be aware, I'm still watching over your loved ones, Lieutenant. The penalty remains the same."

119

"My ultimatum? I was wondering when you'd get around to it. You know, Captain, I think about it day and night."

Gemmer spoke in a surprisingly gentle tone. "Your problem—we must discuss it."

"The only problem I have is you."

"Don't play with me, Mister! You know what I'm talking about."

Rebuck clenched his teeth, and the veins in his neck bulged. The captain's roller-coaster moods, unrelenting psyche games, and sudden outbursts were getting to him.

"Tell me, Lieutenant, how did you feel when Ike Vesper wasted the Reverend Cody Walker? When he pleaded for his miserable life, did you cherish the moment?"

The words blasted Rebuck's ears, stirring the purgatorial coals of hate jailed within him.

"When you saw the splattering of the bastard's brains, did you imagine it was someone else?"

The captain approached him, exuding triumph. They stood toe to toe, squared off in silent, cerebral combat. Neither man flinched, and their minds framed parallel thoughts. The captain reveled in these moments of high-energy confrontation. His voice shattered the long silence. "I've had you waiting in the woods too long, Lieutenant. Your first assignment, Operation Dog Food, commences in a few more days. The particulars will be delivered to you through the usual channels. Be ready. That's it, Mister. Good night."

"That's not good enough, *Claude*. Unless I know what's coming down from the start, you know what you can do with your Operation Dog Food."

The captain turned away, hobbled a few steps, then pivoted back toward Rebuck. "For the first and *last* time, I will favor you," he said. "The target is someone who's been blackmailing our country for too long." Gemmer's steel-gray eyes flashed. The sardonic grin returned. "A force in religious broadcasting, Lieutenant," he added.

"The name?" Rebuck said.

"At the appropriate time," the captain replied, moving away.

120

"Besides Ike Vesper, how many men do I get for this operation?"

"You've been favored once, not again."

Rebuck caught up and kept pace with the limping SEAL legend. Neither man spoke while they walked through the snow. Then the captain turned and looked at him as if memorizing every line of his face. "You interest me, Lieutenant," he said. "Few people have. That is why I selected you to head up a very special team."

"For how long, Captain?"

They neared the Gemmer family's tombstones, and Ron Rebuck hungered for an answer, but the captain's mind had strayed elsewhere. "There is nothing more truthful than *pure* hate . . . nothing so honest when it strikes."

"For how long, *Captain?*"

"Pure hate is the thoroughbred of all feelings. I know. I have made a study of it." He searched Rebuck's face once more. "And your hate, unlike mine, is *truly* pure."

"*When*, Captain? How long before I'm free of your threats?"

"For as long as it takes."

"That tells me nothing."

"Obey and execute orders, and not only do you have my word that no harm will come to a certain party, but you will come out of this a rich man, as well. . . . And more, yes, you will gain something more precious than wealth . . . but why, why do I have the feeling you shall fail me?"

"Perhaps because you know I detest you. Because you know there is nothing I want so much as to be free of you."

The captain placed his hands on the stone, mumbling something to himself. The changing expression on his face mystified Ron Rebuck. The threatening glare had vanished, replaced by a searching, soulful look. But it lasted only a minute and then the sickly grin reappeared.

Before the captain could muster another equally unsettling performance, Rebuck moved out. He would not stay for a curtain call. He walked briskly toward the gate, his desire to put great distance between the captain and himself a compulsion. His pace quickened until he almost fell on the icy path. He was through the gate when a burst of chilling laughter preceded the captain's booming voice. "You're good, damn good, Lieutenant—but are you the *best?*"

CHAPTER 14

HARLEY LOMBARD'S REVELATION came in the sleek form of a woman named Sue Bergman. Her telephone call from Washington identifying herself as an attorney immediately kindled Harley's skepticism. And when she appeared at the H.L. Ministries Cathedral Tower in downtown Charity, that feeling was fanned into a blaze of suspicion.

"Don't you even take a leak while she's here," he ordered Andy Gaines. Lawyers made Lombard break out in a nervous rash. Before paying even routine legal fees, he would first inform his learned counselors of what Christ *supposedly* said in denouncing their ilk.

Just the day before, Andy Gaines had witnessed a classic shouting match between his employer and an attorney whose services were terminated after he had submitted a bill which Andy felt was reasonable. Unlike his predecessors, who'd endured Lombard's name-calling tirades until the check had cleared the bank, this lawyer not only failed to turn the other cheek, but matched Lombard word for insulting word.

"Hypocrite," Harley ranted.

"Parasite," the lawyer retorted.

"Fleecer," Lombard accused.

"Con man," the attorney responded.

"Buzzard."

"Vulture."

"Crook."

"Pickpocket."

Their immature broadsides reminded Gaines of two schoolboys arguing at recess, both afraid to fight. They had volleyed like that until Lombard resorted to his righteous routine. "That check you're holding represents hard-earned money donated by God-fearing, honest people. And when you cash it, may the money turn to blood in your filthy hands."

"And who the hell writes your checks—God?" the attorney said, slamming the door as he left. It was the only time Andy had ever seen Harley left speechless.

Sue Bergman carried herself with an alluring combination of sophistication and flair, a small but stunning woman in her middle thirties. The subtle sheen of her smoky, taupe-colored nylons complimented the tailored formality of her light fawn-gray suit. Her chic hairstyle gave her a windblown look and the casual way her bangs fell on her forehead emphasized expressive eyes. From the gold earrings to the rich patina of her classic Italian leather pumps, she radiated an aura of understated elegance.

It did not take her long to melt Lombard's glacial hostility toward the legal profession. He found himself in the presence of a woman who was attractive, charming, clever, keenly observant and, most impressive of all, a perfect lady. Sue Bergman was not the piranha Lombard had expected to meet. And, if the hovering presence of Andy Gaines bothered her, she hid her discomfort well. Harley liked that. He also liked her shapely legs and told her so with his eyes when she demurely crossed them.

"*Miss* Bergman?" Harley asked.

"It is now," she replied.

"No Ms.?"

"Reverend Lombard, a modern woman doesn't need another label."

Lombard was not completely at ease with today's emancipated woman. He tested her with another sexist question. "Miss Bergman, do you believe what the Holy Bible says about women?"

"Reverend Lombard, could you be hinting at the feud you had with that female rights activist?"

Jesus, Andy thought, she's done her homework on Harley. The confrontation with that particular woman had happened over a year ago.

"The Bible tells us women are subservient to men. Christ Himself cast women in a secondary role. If God had wished to create a woman first, He would have done so."

"Reverend Lombard, who am I to question the Holy Bible?"

"You'd be surprised how many do these days . . . I swear all these protest groups are backed by Commies. And why is it most of them are headed by Jews?" A frown furrowed his forehead. "Bergman, isn't that a Jewish name?"

She remained unflappable. "It's Swedish, as in Ingrid Bergman."

"Don't get me wrong," Lombard blustered. "I'm not some bigot." He looked at Andy. "Rabbi Glickman, isn't he one of my closest friends?"

Much to Harley's surprise, Andy didn't nod as he expected. His mind was set on putting this woman on the defensive before Harley said things he would later regret. "Miss Bergman, how might Reverend Lombard be of service to you?"

She ignored Gaines and spoke to the man she had come to see. "The association I represent feels you are the religious leader who can best help restore morality to the American way of life."

Harley smiled. "Flattering me, Miss Bergman?"

"If so, Reverend Lombard, you deserve it."

Harley's smile broadened. "Really, Miss Bergman, why me? Why not, uh . . ." He twirled a finger at Andy Gaines. "What's that preacher's name?"

"Jimmy Christian," said an obliging Andy.

"Reverend Lombard, the ARA was unanimous in their recommendation. They feel you are by far the most qualified."

Harley sat back in his chair, looking smug.

"Miss Bergman," Andy began, "could you tell us about this organization you represent?"

She studied Andy's face with her hazel eyes. "I'm terribly sorry, but I was sure my letter was self-explanatory."

She turned back to Lombard. "I know how valuable your time is, Reverend."

She was damned shrewd, Andy thought. Harley had read only the first paragraph of the letter and glanced at the impressive names on the letterhead. Assuming it was another political fund-raising letter in an election year, he had shoved it off on him. Harley had already received eight letters soliciting funds that very day and Gaines recalled his fit of pique. "Are these fucking people mad? I'm in the getting business, not the giving business," he grumbled. Lombard twisted the Biblical admonition that it is better to give than to receive whenever possible. His standard rationalization was, "You must receive before you can give." But the only time he gave was when his tax-exempt ministry was caught on some fine point of interpretation by the Internal Revenue Service.

Andy could feel the sting from Harley's shoe-button eyes, yet bravely continued. "Miss Bergman, I was referring to the origin and philosophy of the ARA: how it came about, the people involved."

"The American Recovery Association, Mr. Gaines, was founded five years ago. Our national headquarters is based in Dallas with branches in every state of the union."

Another John Birch Society. So that's her game, Andy surmised.

"The Board of Governors which appears on our letterhead leaves, I would assume, little to improve upon. As for the purpose of the ARA, surely, Mr. Gaines, you are aware of what has happened to this country."

"Not exactly," he said.

"I'm referring to the bankruptcy of leadership for the American people: government handouts to minority groups, massive welfare fraud, the new wave of uneducated immigrants, illegal aliens taking jobs from American citizens, the deterioration of our national defense." She turned her attention to the evangelist, who was watching her raptly. "How can we ignore the moral collapse caused by fuzzy, liberal minds who intend to make this nation into another Sodom and Gomorrah?"

A concerned Andy wondered if Harley realized that the Biblical names were mentioned solely for his benefit.

"Reverend Lombard, the president, along with those well-known left-wing senators and congressmen, must be voted out of office in the fall. Another four years of the present administration would be disastrous."

"Reverend Lombard is an evangelist, not a politician," Andy Gaines interrupted.

"Really, Mr. Gaines, *just* an evangelist? I am under the impression that since Billy Hale's retirement, Reverend Lombard has become *the* evangelist. Tell me, Mr. Gaines, would I be wrong to say the main thrust of the reverend's mission is to keep America a Christian, Bible-oriented society? Would I be in error if I said Reverend Lombard has great influence on millions of American voters?"

"He speaks to the people about God, about what the Bible teaches, not about their voting habits."

"Mr. Gaines, unless I stand corrected, weren't the Ten Commandments adopted by our founding fathers as the basis for the laws which govern our society? Are we not a nation under God?"

"Miss Bergman, I'm sorry, but I fail to see how all of this relates to Reverend Lombard."

"*I do*," said Harley as he moved forward in the swivel chair, his face glowing. "Andy, I'm sure you have some unfinished work to do."

Gaines looked imploringly at his superior. "If you don't mind, I'd like to—"

"Like now!" Harley snapped, pointing to the door.

When Andy Gaines slunk from the room, he could see the victorious gleam in Sue Bergman's eyes. Harley waited for the door to close, then turned to the woman and favored her with his most devious smile. "May I call you . . . Sue?"

CHAPTER 15

IT WAS ONE OF those spectacular days nature saves for spring. The temperature was in the upper sixties and a soft breeze carried the scent of flowers in bloom. This was not a day for heavy debates over God, world religion, and mysticism, rather a time for the students to take their amorous feelings out of the classroom and activate them in various love bunkers among the verdant meadows, secluded glades, and shining ponds within the sprawling mission grounds.

Ike Vesper had had his fill of girlie magazines. Ten weeks without a woman was nine weeks and six days too long. He had had several opportunities to lay some wordly lines on young and gullible mission girls, and he knew the chubby mission cook had not been taking her evening walks along the trail for exercise. But unlike Rebuck, he would not risk involvement with these mission females while they were out here on a potentially explosive assignment for the captain.

Ike Vesper had no control over Ron Rebuck's infatuation with Jessica Towne, though he'd tried to defuse what he perceived as a potentially dangerous situation. He had even tried to play on Rebuck's sense of chivalry, suggesting that Jessica was too young and too innocent for a man so involved with danger. But Rebuck knew his friend was coming at him from a deeper level of fear. "Little Brotha," Ike had said after one of Jessica's visits, "there ain't no antidote for the captain's bite."

"Not for cowards," Rebuck said, ending their conversation.

But with the word coming down that their first assignment was two days off, there was nothing to prevent Ike from hitting a crummy hotel for the night with a couple of fun girls he knew. Packing clothes suitable for the occasion, he came out from the trailer, tossed a tan suitcase into the black van, then moved with long strides to Rebuck's living quarters.

Rebuck was poring over maps and reports, and gave Ike's entrance little notice. Ike waited for Rebuck to look up before speaking. "Sink the homework, Little Brotha. Pack and track with me tonight. Get your mind off your troubles."

Rebuck looked up uninterestedly. "Have a good time," he said, returning to the papers Gemmer had sent that morning.

Rebuck's odd detachment lured Vesper closer to the table. He placed an enormous hand over the map Rebuck was reading. "What's happenin' to you, man? I know you're concerned 'bout your mom, and all, but there's nothing you can *do*. Man! You been actin' like some downtown nigger lookin' to burn a buildin'."

Ron Rebuck eased back into his chair. He gazed long and hard into Ike's face. "Question. What makes you think Captain Crazy's not just setting us up?"

"Those plans tell you that?"

"It's a fortress, Ike."

"Mighty Dude will spell it out when he's ready."

"We don't move unless the odds are in our favor and I know the target's name and case history."

Vesper frowned with annoyance. He punished a chair by letting his two hundred and fifty pounds fall into it.

"Ike, hasn't it occurred to you we're in the hands of a maniac?"

"The captain is what the captain *is*."

"Meaning?"

"The man does what the man says."

"You mean if he says he's going to kill someone, you can bank on it?"

"If the captain tells me he's gonna rise from the dead and suck out my blood, I'm a dead nigger."

"Amazing," Rebuck said sarcastically. He collected the reading material before him and stacked it neatly.

Ike's voice was earnest. "Little Brother, I know what you must be going through, but we got somethin' workin'. What we're onto beats a navy pension."

"Does it, Ike?"

"Whatcha talkin' 'bout, turkey? We're getting heavy line to do what the navy paid us shit to do."

"I don't give a shit about the money, Ike—and I don't think you do either."

"Well, you're dead wrong there," Ike said. "I figure in a couple years I'll have myself enough bread stashed to wing it to Tahiti. Find some shakin' sisters to take care of my black ass."

"*You* may love the money, but *I* don't like living under a madman's threats."

"But this madman's got you good. There's not a mothafuckin' thing you or I can do."

Rebuck pushed the papers aside. "Gemmer told me just enough. He's not the power you think. We're only one of the hit teams he watches over. Cut his string and the real clout behind him won't shed a tear. If I could only be sure she's safe . . . if I could just find out *where* she is."

"Man, you can't fight the devil. Ya know what happened to—"

"*Not* again, Ike. Not the 'poor Hans' story."

"Shit," Ike growled, moving for the door. "What's the fuckin' use?"

"Ike," Rebuck called after him, "one way or the other, sooner or later, we've *got* to kill the bastard." Vesper was out the door and never heard Ron Rebuck's impassive conclusion: "before he kills *us*."

The motor home was parked on a hill overlooking a picturesque lake, ten miles from Michael's Mission in the heart of Amish country. It was late afternoon and Jessica had spread a simple picnic lunch on a patchwork quilt.

Much to her surprise, Ron Rebuck seemed relaxed, almost happy. The truth was, he had fallen under the spell of her country-girl magic, and saw her as the lone bright spot in a nightmare existence. He had not told her as much, yet she could see he was irritated when she told him how the mission director had tried to keep them apart.

They had eaten in silence, then moved down the hill toward the lake, away from the parked motor home. Up to this point, he had not touched her, and when he now took her by the hand, she felt a tingle run through her body like never before. It was true—the movies she saw, the books she read, all telling how love swept people off their feet, and how pure love gave an inner peace shared only by the eternal. She bubbled with it now, hoping this splendid moment would never die.

He stopped and gazed at the cloudless sky. He seemed, Jessica thought, to be searching for something . . . or perhaps he was just staring idly into space, deeply submerged in his thoughts. She could only wonder. She would not ask and risk disrupting his mood.

They drifted farther along the bank of the lake when he finally cut into the solemnity. "Jessica, why are you at the mission?"

"To study."

"Why not at some college? A university?"

Jessica did not feel it was the time or place to tell him she was the oldest of ten children born into a West Virginia coal-mining family, about the poverty of her Appalachian upbringing. He released her hand and she could feel the tension building in his body. "How much is that mission creep ripping you off for?"

"It doesn't cost me a penny, Ron. Every year the new class is sponsored by classes that have graduated."

"Like a pyramid," Rebuck suggested, wondering what kind of scam was involved.

"Mr. Ragonese, the Arch-Messenger, is really a wonderful man."

"He's on your case and you call him wonderful?"

"He's only trying—"

"*Trying* to protect you? Save you from sin? He's a creep like the rest of them. They've all got their ears to your heart and their hands in your pocket, telling you ghost stories."

"Ron, the director isn't like that."

"The same. He's no different from the rest of them with their well-rehearsed piety. They all come from the same stinking mold."

"Ron . . . your father was a great prophet."

"Prophet? More of a Don Quixote. He never stood a chance."

"He left the world a great message."

"He left my mother a broken heart—left me a ton of hate. And what did it get him? At forty-three, he was labeled the 'Antichrist' and crucified in the name of God!" He picked up a rock and hurled it angrily into the lake. "Life's an imposition, a hand no one asked to have dealt. What kind of God would play with a stacked deck?"

The sun had slipped behind the greening hills, and they sat on a grassy knoll watching dusk breathe the stars to light. Jessica sat propped against his raised knees. She knew if Ron failed to drive her back to the mission soon, she would be missed and in deeper trouble then she was already. She would possibly be expelled; but in her state of mind, that of a love-struck eighteen-year-old, being with him was worth almost any consequence.

Her woman's instinct told her everything was perfect. It was the right time and the right place, Ron was the right man and she was ready with no thoughts to the contrary. His strong hands drew her close to him and she looked into the peculiar eyes with their distinct facets of brown, green, and yellow. He kissed her with tenderness and she craved more.

Rebuck led her through the deepening chill to the warmth of the motor home, and it was now Jessica who was reminiscing; the countless dreams, the boys in West Virginia who had tried, the girlfriends who had called her a prude, and the frustrations over saving herself for the right man were all skirmishes of the past. Now, as they lay beside one another on the convertible bed, with his lips pressed to hers, all of the reasons why she shouldn't lost their meaning. But as he rose from the bed and undressed, she hesitated. He stood nude, gazing down at her, expecting her to make a move. She had never undressed before a man. To expose her body to anyone other than the man she married was to violate a strict religious upbringing still deeply rooted in her mind.

Rebuck smiled, wondering if her innocence was truly genuine. He awarded Jessica the benefit of any doubt and flicked off the aircraft light above the bunk. He came to her side and she squirmed uneasily. His kisses were long, entrapping, and she became lost in a maze of sensuality. He had raised the material of her dress to her waist, and she trembled as his hands tugged at her panties. He moved slowly on top of her, so gently she could barely feel his weight. His kisses were no longer tender, but raw with whipping passion. She could feel the throbbing of his penis against her leg, then seeking entry, and she closed her eyes in anticipation. Then his heavy breathing slackened . . . he had become still—too still. She opened her eyes to see the peculiar expression on his face. All doubts of her innocence now vanished from his mind.

As he parted her legs and guided his hardened penis into the warm entrance to her vagina, she let out a gasping sound, reacting to the sharp pain, and locked her arms tightly around his neck. He entered slowly, carefully, and she could feel rather than hear his moan as she engulfed him. As he began to move within her, his strokes deepened and suddenly there was no longer any pain from his penetrating thrusts. She felt his hands grasp her buttocks and she began to moan in pleasure herself, moving to his rhythm until they were finally in perfect syncopation. She wanted to tell him, to shout out words she had never dared, to let him know how her newfound eroticism had reached a height she'd never realized existed. She hungered for his mouth and kissed him with savagery, her breasts aching exquisitely each time her nipples brushed against his chest. It was now she who burned with fervor, who unchained her inhibitions and was finally free in the wilderness of their splendor. Her legs encircled him, and she clung fiercely to him as the steady, driving motion he initiated was equalled by her own torrid movement. Her irregular moans of ecstasy accompanied a feeling of wild abandon, her breath coming in ragged gasps. She cried out as together they reached a sublime moment of climax in which all the stars in the heavens seemed to explode in her mind.

They showered separately: she first, embarrassed by the sight of her virginal bleeding, hoping he wouldn't notice. After he'd showered and rejoined her, she was intimidated by his silence, and wondered what was behind his inscrutable smile. Was she just another conquest, merely one girl of many who'd lost her virginity to this handsome, self-assured man? She hoped not. God, how she hoped not.

They lay down together on the bunk and Rebuck tugged at the large towel she'd covered herself with, laughing at how she tried to hide her nudity. She grinned back at him, sharing his amusement at her strong sense of modesty. Somehow, being here with him like this, she felt no shame, no sense of guilt or betrayal to her principles, only a cool inner breeze which blew against spreading sails of contentment. As she snuggled up to him, she realized he'd dozed off. Studying his face in repose, she discovered that Ike Vesper had been wrong when he'd told her Ron slept with one eye open, trusting no one. If it was true, then she was the exception.

She laid her head softly on his shoulder and had just closed her eyes when something from outside activated an awareness. Jessica turned to the window, parted the drapes, and saw lights winking in the distance. She became increasingly wary as the lights drew nearer, and then she was able to make out the shadows of men holding lanterns. She shook Rebuck awake. "Ron," she said, "someone's coming."

His eyes sprang open and he took in her concerned expression. Sliding off the bunk, he moved to the front of the motor home where he withdrew a .44 Magnum from beneath the dashboard. Gun in hand, he moved to the door, and the metalic click as he cocked it startled her.

"Ron," she said, peering out the window, "I think they're Amish or Mennonite. We're probably on their land."

"Religious bastards," Rebuck muttered, "they're like insects—*everywhere.*"

She pulled on her dress and picked up his discarded levis from the floor. The presence of the weapon in his hand frightened her. "I'm sure they're harmless," she said, but he didn't answer her. She could see him shaking as if racked by a sudden chill.

"Ron, Ron, please . . ." she pleaded.

He turned, and for a flitting second she saw the wildness, the madness in his eyes. As he bounded from the motor home, Jessica realized she was still holding his jeans.

Naked, Ron Rebuck moved without delay toward the five men wearing wide-brimmed black hats and dark clothes. Through the lanterns' light, the men appeared genuinely unconcerned by the long-barreled weapon in his hand and looked upon his nudity with unspeakable scorn. The Amish elder stepped forward to meet Rebuck's challenge. "You are trespassing on private property." As he looked past Rebuck to where Jessica stood bewildered in the doorway of the motor home, the bearded man's scowl deepened. "You must leave these grounds," he commanded.

His mind blazing with that particular kind of hate which Captain Gemmer had recently alluded to, Ron Rebuck came to within inches of the elder and held the barrel of the .44 Magnum under his bearded chin. Jessica ran frantically to his side as the elder's four companions stared speechlessly at the gun pressed against their spiritual leader's throat.

"Ron, no, *no!*" Jessica screamed, grabbing at his arm. It was like a steel vise, unmovable, and her fears heightened. The elder dropped to his knees, dislodging the pistol from under his chin. His action prompted the others to their knees as he began to lead them in soft, chanting prayer.

Rebuck's hatred soared to an even higher level of intensity. Driven by the burning memory of his father, whom the Amish and Mennonites had called the "devil," Rebuck swatted the wide hat from the elder's head and held the gun inches above the mass of scraggly white hair, his hand trembling noticeably in the eerie glow of the lanterns.

The night was filled with the sound of chanting voices as Jessica knelt by the elder and placed a gentle hand on the wrist of the man who controlled his fate. She saw the deadness in Rebuck's eyes, the face of a man possessed by some inner demon. Vaulting from the ground, she flung her arms around his neck, kissing him with a compulsion she did not understand. Rebuck slowly came out of his trance, turning to look at her as if seeing her for the first time. Exhausted, he turned and allowed her to lead him to the motor home.

As she wiped the sweat from his trembling body with a towel and watched as he pulled on his jeans, Jessica could only wonder at the depth of his hatred for these men of peace. She was too mentally fatigued to think about it right now. It had been a day like none other, and she needed to rest. But as she tiredly slumped into the dinette booth, Ron Rebuck quickly slid behind the wheel and started the engine. Flashing on the high beams, he floored the accelerator and drove the motor home directly at the fleeing Amish, who scrambled in all directions for the safety of their lives.

CHAPTER 16

JIMMY CHRISTIAN THREW the architectural rendering across the room. The construction foreman for C.D. Pittman Industries looked dismayed. Beth Staples retrieved the blueprint while Frank Buckmaster was relieved that for once somebody else had reaped the whirlwind of Jimmy's anger.

"You call this the right decor? It's the pits!" Christian thundered at the foreman. "Looks like some barbecue joint. It's supposed to be the Last Supper Restaurant, idiot!"

"Mr. Christian, I'm no idiot. I have my orders."

"It's *Reverend* Christian. And what do you mean, orders? *I* give the orders."

The foreman retrieved the drawing from Beth. The man merely shrugged and left the office under Jimmy's haughty stare.

"Incompetent fool," Jimmy cursed. "At the current rate of screw-ups, we'll never be ready for the opening."

"Not if you keep harassing the construction foremen," Beth retorted.

"What the hell's that supposed to mean?"

"I mean you refuse to bend one inch—as if you're worried about not getting all the credit for the building of Christ Town."

"I deserve all the credit," Christian boasted.

"Don't you think C.D. Pittman deserves a share? Jimmy, the man has fourteen construction companies working around the clock. He's even pulled crews from jobs in South America. He's working miracles to complete everything

137

on schedule. If you don't stop complaining and let the foremen do their work, Christ Town won't open this summer *or* the next.''

'' 'He healeth the broken in heart, and bindeth up their wounds,' '' Buckmaster quoted.

"Will you take a hike!" Jimmy shouted.

Bucky lifted himself heavily from the couch, then waddled from the room like an obedient Saint Bernard.

"God, how that man pisses me off," said Jimmy, dropping into the couch Buckmaster had vacated. A cloud of doubt passed over his face. "You know, Beth, I get the feeling you worry more about Pittman than you do me."

"Are you questioning my loyalty?"

"You seem to be taking a lot of interest in that old codger."

"Meaning?"

"You're never around when I need you—like this morning during the taping. Cora Lee was hogging the damn show again."

"For your information, Jimmy, I was keeping the peace between you and C.D."

"Another lunch with the old geezer?"

"Having lunch with C.D. was your idea, remember?"

"Yeah, but every day? If I didn't know better, I'd think you were having an affair."

"I didn't ask to be placed in the role of go-between."

"Spy. The role of spy," said Jimmy. "But what are we arguing about? I trust you more than anyone. You know that."

"Jimmy, C.D. has invited me—"

He cut her off. "The conception of Christ Town was my idea. Pittman smelled a potential gold mine. He wanted a piece of the action. I didn't go looking for him." He roared off the couch and began to pace. "People are beginning to think I have no investment in Christ Town. Remember *me?* I'm the one who broke ground for the Evangelical World Center three years ago. Twenty million dollars—twenty *big* ones, Beth—that's what I've got invested."

Twenty million dollars invested for the Lord, she thought to herself. "Jimmy, I know it's hard for you to admit, but before the project is completed, C.D. Pittman will have invested three times that amount just to bail you out. He also has a contract hanging over your head."

"Contracts have a way of being broken."

"With *C.D. Pittman?*"

"Look, sixty percent of Christ Town's first phase was completed before old Moneybags jumped aboard. The lakes were dredged, most of the land was cleared and excavated, some of the buildings were finished—including the Glee Club Communications Center."

"I don't see what any of that has to do with a contract obligating you to pay the interest on some very large notes C.D. is holding."

Before Jimmy could answer her, Frank Buckmaster burst into the office, excitedly waving a newspaper. "Jimmy, it's made the big print."

Christian ripped the newspaper from Bucky's hand. He couldn't miss the feature on the front page. The words suddenly became a blur and all he saw was Harley Lombard's spiteful face. He handed the newspaper to Beth. "Read it. Out loud—until I choke."

"Evangelist Harley Lombard, whose 'Ministry of Might' television show is viewed coast to coast by millions, plans to challenge politicians with fire and brimstone. Lombard yesterday announced the founding of Virtues, Incorporated, an organization which, Lombard said, will screen candidates seeking political office. Lombard said Virtues, Inc., will oppose politicians who fail to measure up to the organization's moral code. 'Candidates who are not worthy of the religious and moral trust of the American public will be denounced from Christian pulpits and voted out of office,' Lombard said during a press conference in Charity, Ohio. Reverend Lombard also said Virtues, Inc., was counting on strong support through media blitzing." She glanced at Christian for a reaction. "Shall I go on?"

"Lombard this, Lombard that," Jimmy mimicked. "Lombard *bullshit*. That old billy goat is behind this."

"I doubt it," Beth disagreed.

"C'mon, Harley's a ham-and-egger without Billy Hale to hold his hand. He's made some all-time bad moves whenever he didn't have Billy to whisper in his ear. And this Virtues, Inc., thing you can bet is not a Harley Lombard idea." He glowered at Buckmaster. "Why wasn't I aware of this? Why did I have to read it in the fucking *Washington Post?* Whatever happened to that great pipeline of yours?"

"*Pipeline,* Jimmy?" Bucky was totally confused.

Again Christian began to pace the room. "How does this hurt me? I mean why should I worry about Harley and his pissant do-gooders?"

"Scary," Beth muttered half to herself.

"What's scary?"

"Christianity and State."

"What's new about it?"

"The fact they obviously intend to flaunt it through the media."

"Good," said Jimmy, "it'll give the damn Jews and atheists something to worry about."

"Don't you think the Jews already have enough to worry about?" Beth was visibly annoyed.

"If you are not a Christian and not born again, the Bible tells us you will go to hell," Buckmaster grimly intoned.

Jimmy glared at him. "Where in the Bible does it say that?"

"In John 3:3, Jesus said, 'Verily, verily, I say unto thee, except that a man be born again, he cannot see the Kingdom of God,' " Bucky recited.

"No wonder religion spawns prejudice," Beth sighed, sitting wearily on the couch.

"Whatever," Jimmy said impatiently. "Billy's using Harley as his stooge. He's an old, old man who needs a last hurrah."

Beth disagreed. "I think Billy Hale will be just as surprised by Virtues, Inc., as we are."

"Beth, I'm telling you he's using Harley. Virtues, Inc., is his big comeback. But who cares? Who really gives a holy shit about Billy Hale?"

"I do," Bucky blurted.

The immediate shock of Frank Buckmaster defending his former employer reddened Jimmy's face. "*You* do? Isn't that marvelous? *You* care." He moved toward him. "Has your memory become as fat as your ass? He *dumped* you. *Fired* you."

" 'We know that all that happens to us is working for our good if we love God and are fitting into His plan,' " Bucky stubbornly held his ground.

"Beth, do you know what the hell he's talking about?"

"Romans, chapter eight, verse twenty-eight," Buckmaster proudly added.

Jimmy's eyes blazed. "Since you feel so strongly about defending your hero Billy Hale, maybe you should draw your next paycheck from him."

Bucky squared his shoulders and spoke with pride. "Billy Hale is a credit to God. I will always believe that." Jimmy would not have the satisfaction of shouting him out of the office this time. Bucky waddled from the room, slamming the door behind him.

Beth smiled. "Apparently there's more than jelly in Bucky's spine."

"Day by day, that dummy is getting more and more on my nerves."

"The man's totally devoted to you, Jimmy."

"He's a drunk. A fat, stupid drunk. And why should you stick up for him?"

"Maybe I understand him."

"*God* doesn't understand him."

Jimmy grew silent and Beth leaned back on the couch, wondering what type of mood he would switch to now. She knew them all. What she didn't know was that her dress was raised to mid-thigh.

"Beth, we've got to have a serious talk. One on one." He rushed to his desk and pressed the intercom button. "No calls. I mean, no one!"

Whenever Jimmy spoke in that tone, she knew trouble was brewing. With Bucky gone, she suddenly felt uneasy. Watching him lock the door to her private office, then make his way to the entrance of the spacious room, she became gripped with suspicion. "Jimmy, if you lock that door, I'm leaving."

He rested his hand on the brass doorknob. His fingers froze on the lock.

"I'm serious, Jimmy," she said in an even firmer tone.

"For Christ sakes, Beth, I'm not going to rape you. I just want to talk."

"Not behind locked doors."

She had trouble rising from the sunken cushion and he was fast upon her. "Beth, just talk," he urged, sitting close by her side.

Name, rank, and social security number, she reminded herself. Other than being twenty-six years old and born in Shreveport, Louisiana, she had told Jimmy little about herself. She had never invited him to her apartment, never dined alone with him, nor had he ever met any of her friends. Through the years, she had managed to avoid small talk with Jimmy, and she intended to keep it that way.

"Tell me, Beth, which is greater, a woman's fury or her curiosity?"

"I would say *Cora Lee's* fury."

"And yours?" He flashed his best little-boy smile, the one which charmed millions of television viewers and grated so on her nerves. He reached for her hand and held it chastely. "Beth, I'm going to divorce Cora Lee," he somberly informed her.

She snatched her hand from his. "You're not serious?"

"Most serious."

"For whatever reason?"

"Beth, isn't the reason obvious?"

The only thing obvious to her was his sly glances at her exposed legs and that he was sitting much too close. "Jimmy, I really don't think it's any of my business. I wish you wouldn't discuss it further."

"Beth, it's *because* of you."

She swallowed hard. "Me?"

142

"I know the reason why—why you won't let me make love to you."

"Jimmy, what *are* you talking about?"

"My being married prevents you. I admire that, Beth. I truly do."

"Jimmy."

"After Christ Town is running smoothly, when things have settled down, I'll divorce Cora Lee and marry you."

"Jimmy!"

"Beth, I live for the day."

"You're crazy. I'm not going to marry you."

"Why not? I'll be free."

"It has nothing to do with you being free."

"Then what? Am I ugly? Too short for you?"

"If you don't mind, I think I'd better leave."

Before she could stand up, Jimmy pivoted off the couch and was kneeling before her. She managed to stand, but his arms wildly locked about her legs.

"Jimmy, this—this is ridiculous! For God's sake, Cora Lee might come in."

"I hate her," he said, pressing his face against her covered thighs.

"Jimmy, let me go!"

"I can't," he moaned. "Jesus knows I can't!"

His arms slipped to her knees and she lost her balance, falling back onto the couch. With his chest braced against her legs, she saw his hand fumbling with his belt buckle. "Jimmy, so help me, I'll scream."

She tried to stand, but he used his leverage to push her back. The warning in her eyes could not intimidate him this time. "I want you, Beth. Want you *bad*. More than Moses wanted water," he panted, unzipping his fly.

Cora Lee Christian stepped briskly from the elevator leading to the executive reception lobby. The only occupant besides the receptionist was a brooding Frank Buckmaster, who sagged on a leather sofa like a sack of wet wash. He looked at Cora Lee sadly. She had not spoken to him since the "Night of the Disciples" fiasco, and whenever she would pass him by, he was to turn his face to a wall, a door, anywhere, as long as she did not see it. Unlike Lot's wife, he heeded her warning of turning him into a pillar of salt. But the face she looked into now was that of a man nursing a deep hurt, and her maternal instinct overrode her hostility. "What's wrong, Bucky?" she asked in a motherly fashion.

Bucky shook his head. He couldn't tell her because he wasn't sure why he felt depressed.

"Did Daddy yell at you again?" she asked.

"He didn't have to. Not this time."

"I forgive you, Bucky."

" 'Blessed are the merciful,' " he acknowledged, smiling wanly.

Cora Lee took Bucky by the hand. "Now let's go see Daddy. He'll forgive you, too."

They had rolled off the couch onto the carpet. Jimmy was on top of her, and his blue shirt was patched with damp spots of blood where she'd dug her sharp nails into his back. Still, Beth had the presence of mind not to scream. To do so would draw a crowd from the surrounding offices and Jimmy would only turn the bizarre scene around to his advantage.

He kissed her busily on the face and neck, but she prevented his lips from touching hers. She struck the sides and back of his head with both hands. But the more she hit him, the more his passion intensified. She felt his rigid appendage thrusting against her as she dragged herself along the carpet. She turned onto her side with a surge of strength. Frustration etched her face when he locked his short arms around her waist, keeping her pinned to the floor.

Her cotton dress was torn and the sight of her exposed legs brought a drool of saliva from Jimmy's mouth. The fingers of his right hand worked slowly down her mound until they located her clitoris and she arched her back as if jolted by an electric shock. Rage replaced her anger and

144

she clawed his cheek. Startled, Jimmy instinctively brought a hand to his bleeding face.

She managed to pull herself to her knees and looked back to see his eyes narrowed in a manic squint. Before she could stand, he lunged at her, knocking her to the floor. She tried to pull herself forward, but his weight against her back kept driving her downward until her chin rested heavily on the deep pile carpet. He straddled her legs and she lay motionless, frantically thinking of what she could possibly do or say to stop him.

The sight of her raised ass shredded what little was left of his reason. He tore at the tattered remains of her dress and tugged at her pantyhose until the nylons were halfway down her thighs. He stared hungrily at the tight-fitting pink panties and was so absorbed in his passion, so intoxicated by her soft, rounded ass, he was all but mentally paralyzed.

He had gone berserk and was trying to rape her. Any doubts to the contrary had now perished from her mind. She still felt she could successfully fight him off. Perplexed by his immobility, she looked back to see him staring at her ass with glazed eyes. She felt his hands relax and quickly lunged forward with a thrust of her arms. She tore away from him, but he reclaimed her waist. She managed to crawl forward a few feet, dragging him with her. But she was nearing the threshold of physical exhaustion. She crawled on, kicking her legs in a frantic attempt to break his grip, but soon weakened.

She now felt the damp warmth of his mouth kissing the back of her panties and it sent a wave of nausea through her body. Mustering one final burst of strength, she rolled onto her left side. But that gave him added leverage and he ripped off her panties, burying his face between her legs. She tried to wiggle free, but his arms coiled tightly around her waist. His tongue licked at her vagina with slobbering abandon as he moved a hand to her left breast. Seizing the opportunity, she lowered her face to the hand fondling her breast, and out of sheer desperation, bit deeply into his arm—and it was *he* who screamed.

The door swung open and Cora Lee burst into the room, trailed by a gaping Bucky. "What—what in a crow's nest is going on here?"

A disheveled Beth Staples felt only relief as Cora Lee surveyed with blazing eyes the proof of Jimmy's lecherousness. She felt no embarrassment, rather a sense of fair play knowing Cora Lee had the solid evidence before her, and that Jimmy had earned himself a hay load of trouble. Confronting an irate Cora Lee would be like taking on a tank with a pea shooter.

"I'm waiting," Cora Lee said icily, stomping her foot.

"Cora Lee, I'm sure your husband will have a fascinating explanation," said Beth as she picked up her tattered dress and retreated to her office.

Frank Buckmaster did not have to be told. He turned and tiptoed from the room.

Cora Lee placed her hands on her hips, looking the part of a plucky prosecutor. She glared at Jimmy, who sat on the floor with a subsiding bulge in his pants and a mouth twisted in both pain and guilt. He held his arm tightly, waiting for the tirade to begin.

"She said you'd explain. I'm wait-*ing*," Cora Lee shrilled.

Jimmy slowly got to his feet. He tucked in his bloodstained shirt, shaking his head as he stalled for time. Turning away from her, he buttoned his pants and zipped his fly.

"Too late," said Cora Lee. "You can't hide the evidence."

He made a move towards his desk, but she darted ahead of him and sat stonily facing him. "Let me hear you weasel your way out of this, Jimmy. But before you do, I want you to know that I may be a country bumpkin, but I am *not* the village idiot."

"Damn it, Cora Lee, you won't understand."

She pounded her pudgy little fist on the desk. "Guilty!" she shouted.

"I know it looks bad, but I had to find out."

Again, she pounded the desk. "Guilty! Guilty as hell!"

"It was the only way. I had to do what I had to do. If I didn't find out, it could have been devastating."

"Guilty!"

"We could have lost everything."

"Guilty!"

"Harley Lombard would've leaked it to the papers."

"Guilty!"

"C.D. Pittman—I hate to even think what *he* would have done."

"Guilty!" she thundered. "A thousand times guilty!"

"Goddamn it, Cora Lee. I had to find out for myself and I damn well did."

He circled the room furtively, checking that both doors were firmly shut. She was not taken in by his theatrics.

"Cora Lee, what I'm going to tell you cannot leave this room." He looked over his shoulder as if someone had materialized in the room. He then moved closer to the desk and lowered his voice to an almost conspiratorial whisper. "Cora Lee," he said, pausing for dramatic effect, "Beth Staples . . . is a lesbian!"

CHAPTER 17

THE PEA-GREEN, all-terrain van moved under an evening drizzle off the four-lane Jersey highway and traveled north toward Newton. Behind the wheel, Ike Vesper flicked on the wipers and looked at his front-seat passenger. Ron Rebuck could read his thoughts as he had done so many times when they were brother SEALs about to begin a mission.

Rebuck's attention shifted to the rear where five men sat bunched together, crowded by scuba gear, water-resistant weapons, and ammunition. A lone bazooka stood out among Stoner machine guns. Rebuck and three of the five men wore wet suits beneath coveralls, making up the frogman element of Rebuck's strike team. Ike and the remaining two wore cami-fatigues. Every member of Rebuck's team was highly proficient in demolition. They were paid assassins, chosen from around the globe by a discriminating Captain Claude Gemmer. Ron Rebuck took little consolation from the fact that both he and Ike Vesper were unwilling members of this infamous fraternity.

They were forty miles from their destination, and Rebuck consulted a condensed reconnaissance map. He felt Ike's glance and satisfied his curiosity with a reassuring nod. He then half closed his eyes to once again consider possible flaws in the invasion plans. He could find none. The information given him, if accurate—and he had no reason to doubt that it wasn't—was meticulously detailed. There would be no change of strategy. He knew the success of executing this operation depended chiefly on the element of surprise and on precise timing. And he and his team had extensively rehearsed penetrating what he had at first considered an impregnable bastion.

The north Jersey country estate with its three thousand acres of wooded hills and spring-fed lakes was but one of four palatial residences owned by Reverend Tho and his Church of Guardian Spirits. The spring and summer home of one of the world's most powerful and wealthy religious leaders was a three-story mansion of Japanese design contained within thirty-five acres and surrounded by three levels of security. A twelve-foot electrical fence, a thirty-foot-wide moat, and a twenty-foot concrete wall provided Reverend Tho with a veritable fortress.

Tho's castle was further secured by marksmen who manned three open towers with railed balconies and Asian tiled roofs that dominated the concrete wall at the north, south, and west angles of a diamond. A solitary bridge crossed the moat at its eastern apex. Floodlights embedded into the outer wall, together with the tower's spotlights, were activated nightly and could detect a jumping frog at a distance of one hundred yards.

At the compound's lone east entrance, the fence terminated at both sides of an intensely lighted wooden bridge which gave access across the moat to an ebony-pronged gate bisecting the high wall. Just beyond the gate, a guardhouse was situated in the middle of a brick road.

Blue-gray, diagonally laid tile walkways trailed around the grounds like the tail of a mythical dragon. The soft lights flickering from Gifu lanterns created an aura of tranquility and gave the red maples a more intense hue. The Japanese cherry, plum, and prolific pink and white dogwood created a floral beauty from a heritage older and more durable than man. Ancient ginkgos, transplants from the Far East, continued their vigil as they had for centuries. Meandering plants, illuminated by soft ground-level lights, helped to define the walkways and open areas which flirted with the clear spring's edge and abutted the arched footbridges. Rare peacocks strutted brazenly, screeching in unison when alarmed and treating onlookers to the retreating spread of their glorious fans. Large white Pekin ducks paddled leisurely on the surface of limpid ponds.

The main driveway, one of two roads fanning from the command-post gate, was flanked by the oaks, elms, and evergreens of the region.

The grounds closest to the mansion were a fairyland of waterfalls cascading from tiered bronze basins, gently flowing under lacquered bridges. Lanterns illuminated the imposing entrance where bonsai trees enhanced the decor of heavily carved twin doors from the ninth century. Oriental fretwork complemented the mansion's stucco and teak exterior while Japanese railings graced the polished walkways to the rear where a pool, encased like a jewel, continued beyond glass walls to the patio pavilion.

Thunder rolled across a leaden sky threatening a heavy downpour. Ike Vesper drove off the slippery country road, stopping before the entrance to a rutted dirt path. He then backed the van onto the path, cut the lights, and kept it idling alongside a large poster which forbade trespassing and warned of a high-voltage fence.

Ron Rebuck looked at his diver's watch: 20:55. It was nearing zero hour, and his anticipation was shared by Ike, who tapped his fingers on the steering wheel. Twice before he and his team had been turned back before reaching this point by a coded message aborting the operation. Each time Captain Gemmer's plant, the paid informant at the target's site, had failed to make vital contact.

Approaching headlights suddenly beamed on the road. Ike gripped the wheel. Rebuck's face tightened. Their ears became acutely tuned to the sound of a truck's motor.

The truck passed them a little too slowly to suit Ike. His gut feeling gave cause for alarm when the truck came to a stop farther down the road. "Shit," he cursed, hearing the shifting of gears.

The truck's whine in reverse was challenged in the van by the metallic sounds of automatic weapons fixed on ready. Ron Rebuck looked straight ahead as Ike reached into a compartment for binoculars with infrared lenses. He could see the logo of a shade tree on the door of the truck and underneath it the name MONROE TREE AND LANDSCAPE, INC. "Go away, Monroe," he whispered.

"Dammit, he must have seen our exhaust," said Rebuck.

"Go away, Monroe," Ike repeated over and over as the men raised their Stoners.

The driver was out of the truck and had started to walk across the street in the direction of the path. He was a young man with a full beard. Probably the father of a child with a wife who loved him, Rebuck thought.

"He's comin' too close," Ike said.

"We're not going to hit him," Rebuck decided. "We'll abort the operation first."

"He's moving back to the truck," Ike said with relief.

The truck's motor had faded in Ike's ears when he turned to Rebuck. "If that turkey kept comin' and we didn't waste him, how would you explain it to the captain?"

Just then the communication system buzzed softly. Ron Rebuck picked up the receiver. He responded to the message with a string of coded numbers and placed the receiver back in its cradle. His lips curved in a faint smile: Operation Dog Food was a go.

Reverend Tho dined among his six top-level aides in a room with fusima screens depicting majestic mountains, which slid into walls revealing a highly polished ebony nest of tables. Although he was Korean by birth, his tastes reflected the traditions of China as well as Japan. He was attired in a silk robe embroidered with colorful peacocks and seemed content to listen to the conversation of others. Yet he remained the dominant figure in the room. He was lord and master, and these ranking disciples led him to believe that they would not hesitate to commit the ultimate sacrifice on his behalf.

It was difficult for westerners to guess his exact age. The handsome round face with its smooth yellow-brown skin had been a common sight on the TV since 1981, when he'd brought his unique oriental style of evangelizing to American living rooms. But his person was not without flaw, for his head was noticeably too large for his small, plump body.

Since becoming an American citizen and successful televangelist, he had revealed little about his past. The Department of Immigration and Naturalization's file contained nothing unusual. The few books written about him focused more on his church than on its founder. A prestigious East-Coast newspaper had run a series of articles about Tho, emphasizing his crucial aid to American interests during the undeclared Vietnam War, but had failed to reveal his actual role. Apparently, the paper's investigative reporters had drawn a blank at the State Department, where Tho's dossier was deemed "classified."

Stories of missing children allegedly abducted by Tho's followers and held in missions against their wills, as well as incidents of a young woman returned to her parents in a box and of a young man so mentally lost that deprogramming was impossible, brought criminal allegations against Reverend Tho and his church from vengeful parents. But their prosecution proved fruitless. The church's top-notch legal staff had organized a brilliant defense that had vindicated Tho and his church of all wrongdoing.

Politicians, greatly influenced and supported by the major churches, had forced a congressional hearing on religious movements such as Tho's, which were considered "cults." Testimony given by former members of Tho's ministry and bereaved parents who had lost their children to various cult movements brought widespread criticism of Reverend Tho and his like. Representatives of the clergy from various traditional religious groups spoke of the shameful methods used by cults. They accused Tho, the most successful by far of the cult leaders and the only one who boasted a national television empire, of being an unworthy minister of the Almighty. But despite the steadfast opposition of organized religion and constant media harassment, Reverend Tho prospered. The most recent attempt to strip his church of its tax-exempt status had been thwarted by a political master stroke. Since organized religion was being regarded as more and more of a business, Tho's chief attorney offered a solution: the revocation of tax-exempt status for *all* religions. The political opponents of cults and nontraditional religious groups became strangely silent. Pastors and religious representatives greeted the proposal with loud indignation, but none cancelled their weekly collections. The congressional hearing limped to a close. The reluctance of even a conservative Supreme Court to tamper with the First Amendment had served Reverend Tho well. His weekly, coast-to-coast program doubled its income.

Reverend Tho cleared his throat and the room was silent. He spoke in English; what he called the language of money. "What about Congressman Telep?" he asked the aide seated to his immediate left.

"The congressman assures me he will oppose any further congressional investigating of our church. He understands his campaign for re-election will be *extremely* well financed."

Tho nodded without expression. "These congressmen must seek re-election every two years. We need to influence more senators and governors." He faced the man directly across from him. "Did Governor Salvino receive my gift?"

"He would not accept it, Excellency."

"Regrettable," said Tho. "Perhaps it is time we stop treating the governor with velvet gloves." He returned his attention to the first man. "Have we managed to infiltrate this Virtues, Inc., with our loyal communicants?" he asked.

"Excellency, they are better organized than most start-up movements. Their headquarters is extremely well protected."

Tho's composure crumbled. "People! Tell me of ways to *get to* these people," he commanded.

"Excellency, if I might, I'd like to suggest we let this Virtues, Inc., progress to a point where it becomes more vulnerable."

Reverend Tho snapped his fingers, wishing to hear no more. Within seconds, a parade of kimono-clad geishas glided gracefully into the room, bearing the next course.

Ron Rebuck and his frogman contingent infiltrated the western woods of the Tho estate. Flashes of lightning seemed to snipe at them as they moved through thick ground cover and approached a lake pitted by pounding rain. Ron Rebuck took visual aim at the harshly lighted outer wall of the compound before entering the water.

Saddled with Emerson rigs, Rebuck and his team stood in knee-deep water and clipped their lifelines onto the belts of their wet suits. The last man attached a neutral buoyant and hermetically sealed duffel bag to his waist. Ron Rebuck took a bearing across the lake, then adjusted his setting on the luminous compass head at the forward point of his tac board. Without hesitation, Rebuck submerged and led the closely trailing frogmen on a grueling journey of two hundred yards—six hundred feet of cold, black hell.

Ike Vesper waited until the van with the two-man support team drove away from the path fast puddling with water, then trekked into the rain-swept woods. Armed with a bazooka strapped across his shoulder, a Stoner machine gun in one hand and a large can of ammo in the other, he moved through the sheets of rain, avoiding the light's perimeter, and positioned himself upon the soaked ground where the vague outline of the west tower was directly in his line of vision. Here he would wait until the final phase of the operation, when he would clear the area for Rebuck's and his own getaway.

Without a light to guide him, Ron Rebuck moved blindly through the subterranean narrows. A light below the water's surface would stick out like a neon sign, making the assault team easy targets for the sniper in the tower. The luminous compass, depth gauge, and clock on the tac board were shrouded by rubber coverings and gave off no glare.

The depth gauge read ten feet. According to Rebuck's reconnaissance map, his bearing would take him to a rock ledge located in four feet of water. There the surging spring would produce an even stronger current. Somewhere below the ledge, a three-foot-wide passageway would give access under the lake's bank and the high-voltage fence, then into the moat.

Rebuck maneuvered through the water with such certainty, his fellow frogmen wondered if he had made this daring underwater run before. Despite the rain, Rebuck could see the spotlights' reflection above. But he knew the Emerson tanks produced no bubbles to reveal their presence. The depth gauge now teetered between four and five feet, and Rebuck felt the rising current. From this point, he would have to sense his way to the rock ledge.

The support team of two guerrillas had abandoned the van in a secluded spot away from the main road and penetrated the southernmost part of Tho's property. Loaded down with demolition devices, they were to wait for a signal confirming that the south tower had been secured before making their move.

Ron Rebuck had reached the rock ledge. He successfully located the passageway to the moat and fought the churning eddies at its entrance. Captain Gemmer's reconnaissance was without flaw. Yet Rebuck had no time to rest. He had completed only the first leg of his mission. The most dangerous part lay ahead.

The theater in Reverend Tho's home was a myriad of brilliant colors. The backs of the wide-cushioned chairs were upholstered with fuchia-colored leather, and the armrests were covered with black silk. Velvet drapes emblazoned with a fiery sunset marked the entrance. The theater walls were accented with parchment-covered lanterns suspended from a ceiling of exquisite brocade set within a gridwork of polished teak moldings. Carpeted steps led to the stage where a painted backdrop of geishas and traditional Kabuki figures was bracketed by drapes of regal purple.

While Tho quietly enjoyed the screen heroics of John Wayne, his disciples were considerably more demonstrative in their emotions. Engrossed in the action film, the theater's occupants were totally oblivious to what was transpiring outside.

The torrential downpour did not affect the compound's elaborate security mechanism; indeed, the storm enhanced the security force's preparedness. The six interior guards wearing hooded green ponchos dutifully slogged the grounds on foot patrol while their feathered counterparts, the easily spooked peacocks, clustered under toyland pagodas. The marksmen in the towers, wearing foul-weather gear, prayed the wind would not shift and blow the rain into their faces. Two rag-topped jeeps were stationed at the command post. Inside, the captain of the guard sipped hot tea and checked his closed-circuit television monitors which transmitted infrared images at night, while his subordinates jabbered through an oriental game played with dice.

Lightning flashed at longer intervals and the thunder was reduced to the sound of distant drums as the rain subsided to a soft, steady patter. The rim of Ron Rebuck's face mask cracked the moat's surface, then a second mask, a third and a fourth. Following Rebuck's lead, the invaders drifted toward the wall, trailed by slowly spreading ripples.

With their backs braced against the wall directly below the south tower, Rebuck and a second man removed their masks and scuba tanks, letting them sink to the moat's bottom. With the same quiet efficiency, the two remaining frogmen inflated a small black raft the size of a bicycle tire, while Rebuck reached into the buoyant duffel bag and retrieved a retractable aluminum pole with suction devices attached to each end. Rebuck then secured the pole to the smooth concrete of the wall, slipped into a backpack, fastened a holstered .357 Magnum and an encased silencer to the belt on his wet suit, took a final look at the two men in the water steadying the raft, nodded to his backup, and began to ascend the fifteen-foot section of aluminum, stepping on laterals at three-foot intervals.

His backup in the raft waited until he was halfway up before attaching a silencer to a nine-mm. Beretta. Slinging a Stoner machine gun over his shoulder, he followed Rebuck up the pole.

Above, in the tower, a guard sat on a stool beside a rifle rack. He was leafing idly through the pages of a men's magazine, stopping only at the graphic color spreads. A pinging sound brought a cold wave of reality to a lustful mind as he climbed off the stool and went to the observation portal of the tower. He peered down the fifty spiral stairs which coiled around a concrete pillar. He saw nothing, heard only the soft pelting of the rain, and had returned to the stool anxious to pick up where he had left off when he heard the sound again. This time, he reached for his rifle and moved cautiously to the railing overlooking the moat. He never heard the spitting sounds from two hollow-tipped bullets which tore into his chest.

Ron Rebuck went over the wall. His backup vaulted into the tower.

The ornate clock chimed the hour. It was 10:00 P.M. and the reverend's personal servants assembled in the lobby outside the theater. The last to enter was a four-hundred-pound Asian giant, a former sumo wrestler who presided over his fellow lackeys.

The film was still in progress when Tho walked briskly from the room. His evening movie was occasionally interrupted by a VIP dinner or an executive gathering, yet he had come to rely on it as necessary therapy. Accompanied by the sumo giant and a petite girl in geisha costume, he entered his private elevator, while his male servants traveled the well-guarded stairs leading to the master suite that occupied the entire third floor.

Ron Rebuck crouched in shallow water beneath a footbridge and wiped the moisture from the face of his watch. According to the detailed map he'd committed to memory, he had successfully infiltrated the inner gardens encircling the mansion. However, two guard-patrolled acres lay ahead, and he would have to make the perilous journey in ten minutes or risk losing contact with the plant. There was no turning back. To do so was certain to bring about a confrontation—a shootout he was sure to lose. Bolstered by the thought that the north tower had been secured, he was moving toward the creek's bank when he heard the voices of men approaching the bridge. Instinctively, he attached the silencer to the Magnum, crouched even deeper in the water, and held his breath.

He heard the bootsteps drumming across the bridge, then stopping halfway. Two guards taking a break spoke in singsong Korean, and Rebuck prepared himself for a confrontation. As the men smoked and chattered, he knew the loss of another minute could prove disastrous. He could not wait any longer. He would have to move on them, take them out and get to the mansion. As he rose slowly, the sound of a hacking cough stiffened his movement. A discarded cigarette passed his head and hissed in the water. Not until he heard the footsteps crossing the bridge did he loosen his grip on the Magnum and breathe normally.

Reverend Tho stood like a mannequin while his servants carefully undressed him. He came out of the dressing room in a terrycloth robe and reclined in a satin-covered chair. He closed his eyes, and the enormous sumo impassively massaged his head and shoulders while keeping a watchful eye on the servants performing their tasks in a bedroom dominated by an ostentatious bed befitting an Eastern monarch.

Tho waved a limp hand. The giant clapped loudly and there was a swift exit. Bowing servants retreated to the door followed by the giant, who bolted it behind them. The reverend was now ready for his final evening ritual.

The support team moved freely about the unguarded portions of the grounds, placing demolition charges along the electrified fence to provide a corridor of escape for the two frogmen who now occupied the north and south towers. The fifth member of the deadly underwater team wound his way through the slimy moat to the entrance bridge, where he attached timed explosives to various sections of the wooden structure.

Inside, the geisha gently removed Tho's robe, exposing his nakedness. He tested the water with his toes, grunted approvingly, and stepped into the Jacuzzi. She slipped from her kimono with a sensuous pirouette, and only when she had lowered herself into the tepid water did her spiritual master permit himself the luxury of a smile.

From behind a manicured hedge, Ron Rebuck stared at a second-story window sheltered by an upturned wing of the pagoda roof. Captain Gemmer's plant inside the mansion had yet to reveal himself, and Rebuck's concern mounted with each passing second. He began to envision the worse. Without the assistance of Gemmer's contact, he was stranded. And to remain behind this hedge any longer was a risk he couldn't chance. Just then he spotted the assault net unfurling from the open window and feathering to the ground.

Rebuck climbed the webbed nylon rope and slithered headfirst through the window. In a darkened room, vacated by its occupants who were attending the movie, he watched the outline of a frail man hurriedly retrieving the net. The man then led him into a lighted bathroom. Rebuck could tell by the Oriental's attire that he was one of Tho's trusted servants, and he wondered how the captain had got to him.

Rebuck watched the man unlock a door, then followed him through a narrow entrance to a room used specifically to house the pump and filtration system servicing the Jacuzzi on the floor above. The servant shone a flashlight on the bulbous protrusion of the tub's fiberglass shell, and a reassuring look came to Rebuck's face. Still without a word, the betrayer fetched a stepladder from a corner of the room, placed it below the ceiling's bulge, looped an extension light over a support beam, then turned to Rebuck. It was his show from here on.

Rebuck went through the backpack crammed with the tools of his deadly trade. His fingers sifted past a rolled burlap sack, a garrote, a flashlight and a half-dozen golfball-sized grenades before reaching the plasticene lump of a C-4 demolition charge. He carefully removed the hand-molded explosive and gingerly arranged it at the juncture of two vertical wood columns supporting the Jacuzzi's weight above. Setting the firing cap, he rushed from the room with the false servant at his heels.

Directly above, Reverend Tho luxuriated in the swirling warmth of the oval tub, running his fingers lovingly along the smooth glaze of the ornate porcelain tiles. The water was controlled thermostatically, and the diminutive geisha had sprinkled it with bath scents and mild imported liquid soap.

She guided him onto a raised corner seat, gently leaning him back so that his pelvic area was at water level. Her deft fingers began to softly stroke his miniature prick and massage his equally dwarfed balls. Tho watched her in the mirrored ceiling that reflected her performance. His pleasure intensified when her tongue began to flick the swollen head of his stiffening penis while her fingers tenderly pushed and pulled on the throbbing shaft. He began to moan softly, and his hairless belly rose above the water's surface as she enveloped the length of his reddening shaft in the contraction of her warm, moist mouth.

The explosion shattered the vertical columns into a blizzard of toothpicks. The protruding Jacuzzi base burst apart scattering jagged webs of fiberglass, followed by a deluge of water which tore the pump-house door off its hinges. Rebuck moved through the sodden devastation with Magnum drawn. He saw Tho moaning under a welter of plaster and shattered tiles. He was bleeding to death from gaping wounds, and his feet had been severed at the ankles. Close by, what was left of the geisha lay in a pool of crimson. She had been decapitated, and a small cylinder of severed flesh appeared to be caught between teeth clenched in death. Rebuck removed the debris that covered the semi-conscious Reverend Tho and knelt at his side. Laying the Magnum on the drenched floor, he slid a diver's knife from its scabbard and jerked the cult leader's head back by a wisp of hair. Tho's eyes sprang open. It mattered to Ron Rebuck that the glazed eyes looking at him were not those of a dead man. But blood gurgled from Tho's mouth and the pupils of his eyes dilated suddenly. Rebuck let the head fall back in death and rose with the blood pounding in his temples.

A puzzled look came to the traitorous servant's tawny face as he observed Ron Rebuck stuffing the reverend's body, including the severed feet, into the burlap sack. His consternation turned to panic, for such an action was contrary to the deal he had made. It had been firmly understood that he was to find the master's body *after* the assassin made his getaway. The captain had sworn not to blow his cover, and he had half of the money stashed in a safety-deposit box. He made a flimsy attempt to prevent Rebuck from taking the body, when a resounding battle cry acknowledged the presence of the sumo giant glaring down from the cavity above. Rebuck pushed the panicked servant aside, snatched the backpack at his feet, then hoisted Tho's remains over his shoulder, kicking the rubble out of his exit path.

Four hundred pounds of frenzied humanity leaped through the battered opening. The petrified traitor made a desperate lunge for the Magnum Rebuck had left behind, but was wrenched to a halt by the giant's powerful hand grasping his leg. Like a weightless doll, the traitor was lifted from the floor, then drawn like a magnet to a Herculean chest. Through terror-filled eyes, he saw the saliva dribbling from the sumo's frothing mouth. He gasped for breath, then felt the excruciating pain from the crunching of his ribs, followed by a flood of numbness as his spine broke like a twig.

Explosions shook the estate at ten-second intervals. Blue flashes arced along the ground where the high-tension fence had been crumpled by the blasts. Members of Reverend Tho's commando foot patrol who'd survived the initial withering bursts of machine-gun fire from the captured towers scrambled to strikeback positions under bridges and along the stream banks. Screeching peacocks were flushed from their shelters by the bedlam and cut down in the crossfire. Frenzied servants rushed from their quarters. Scantily clad off-duty sentries moved groggily inside their barracks to the weapons rack. Tho's chief disciples forgot their sacred allegiance and fled the mansion, racing one another down the driveway toward the command post and exit bridge. The captain of the guard triggered an alarm much like that which blared from fire stations. Armed with Uzi's, the captain and his men mounted the awaiting jeeps. Their fatal introduction to the war was swift, as the mined entrance bridge they were crossing blew apart in a blaze of pinwheeling timber, men, and machines.

Ron Rebuck stood next to the escape window, stooping under the weight of the burlap sack and its bloody contents. He looked out at the flares drifting downward, lighting the botanical battleground, then at his watch. In exactly thirty seconds the rescue chopper was to make its descent with searchlights sweeping the mansion. Two looped lines and a suspended hook were to hang from its landing skis. Rebuck steadied the sack and released the backpack from his free shoulder, placing it on the windowsill. The miniature grenades would further clear the area for his airborne getaway, and he had reached into the pack when a single blow from hands like concrete flattened the heavy door that led out of the room and four hundred pounds of raging trouble blocked his way.

Rebuck dropped the burlap sack and moved reflexively for an empty holster. For a flashing second, he saw the sneering face of Captain Gemmer instead of that of the bald giant. He stepped into a shadow away from the window and unsheathed his diver's knife. The sumo's tiny, cobra-like eyes followed his every move as he drifted deeper into the shadows.

Despite his tremendous bulk, the stalking sumo moved with the agility of a dancer. Cutting off Rebuck's escape route, he had him trapped in a corner and was primed to destroy this intruder who'd come in the night and robbed him of a comfortable life. He now advanced toward Rebuck in the wide stance of the sumo, ending each plodding footstep with a ceremonial stamp.

Rebuck gripped the knife at his side. He could hear the intense machine-gun fire from his men in the captured towers, then the building, welcome sound of the descending helicopter. Yet he was within arm's reach of the sumo and pressed against the wall. Strangely, the Asian was momentarily still. He was leering at Rebuck with those tiny eyes when the sudden roar of a turbo-jet engine, accompanied by the blinding probe of a searchlight, filled the room.

The startled giant tossed his massive head. He covered his eyes from the incredible light and Rebuck was off the wall in a blur of action. Plunging the knife under the sumo's breastbone, he tumbled to the floor and rolled toward the window, safely away from the hulk, whose bellowing could be heard even above the chopper's deafening sound.

Rebuck saw the dangling ropes dancing in the wind created by the huge rotor blades. The situation on the ground had not changed; his team was in firm control. Reverend Tho's foot patrol was still pinned down by intensive firepower from the frogmen in the towers. There was no immediate danger to the hovering chopper, yet any further delay would spoil a perfectly timed escape. He considered leaving his prize behind, but decided not to. He would follow Captain Gemmer's orders to the last detail.

He was stooping to hoist the burlap sack when, from the corner of his eye, he saw the crazed giant coming for him with his powerful arms striking at nothing but air. Rebuck scrambled to his feet and quickly reached into the backpack. His hand closed over a miniature grenade. Eluding the giant's swiping arms, Rebuck timed the sumo's rush and slammed his free hand against the knife handle jutting from a profusely bleeding chest. Rebuck felt a hot rush of air as the monolithic jaws sprang open, and he quickly ramed the live grenade down the giant's throat. He then yanked his hand free of the gagging brute's mouth and fled to the far side of the room where he dove to the floor behind a large sofa.

The explosion radiated downward. Chunks of flesh, bone, and brain matter flew everywhere. Eyeballs extruded from their orbits. Blood and fatty tissue splattered in all directions. It was as if the great head had been excavated from the neck up. Its total severance from the rest of the body left only jagged, bony remnants protruding from the shoulders. Rebuck stepped through the gore to the window, shouldered his bundle in a fireman's carry, and grabbed onto a length of the dangling rope, slipping into the awkward harness.

Ike Vesper knelt closer to the light's tentacles, steadying the bazooka. Zeroing in on the tower's marksmen through the cross hairs of his scope, he fired a strike. The medium-range missile blew the west tower into a mushroom of flame.

The machine-gun fire ceased and the survivors of Reverend Tho's ground force lurched out from their cover. The escaping Rebuck tossed mini-grenades into their midst, and the razor-sharp fragments from their blasts indiscriminately slashed flesh and vegetation alike. The chopper eluded the light flak of rifle fire from the late-arriving reinforcements and flew over the west wall, where Ike Vesper keyed the chopper's pilot to his presence with a blinking flashlight.

The hovering chopper dropped an escape line, then swept off with Ike, Rebuck, and their booty dangling like puppets from the bladed bird. It would take them to a deserted farm a few miles away. There, a blue panel truck would provide them with transportation for the final leg of the operation.

Neither the police nor the fire department had yet arrived at the scene of the burning battleground.

Ike Vesper kept well under the speed limit as the blue panel truck rolled into a small northeastern Pennsylvania coal town. They cruised through the sleeping village to its outskirts, where a neon sign at an all-night truck stop was partially clouded by rising fog. Pulling off the road and onto an entrance of broken pavement, the panel truck crept toward the rear of the cafe and stopped directly alongside a large and rusted garbage bin. Rebuck helped Ike drag the burlap bag containing Reverend Tho's mortal remains from the back of the truck and heaved it into the bin.

"This mothafuckin' mission is over," said Ike, wiping his hands.

"Park over there," Rebuck pointed, "in the shadows."

"Man, whucha sayin'? Our orders end here."

"And my curiosity begins," said Rebuck, climbing into the blue truck.

They sat in the shadows and neither said a word. Vesper kept looking nervously at the luminous dial of his watch. Six minutes had passed and Rebuck was still staring straight ahead like a man with an appointment he expected to be kept.

"Man," Vesper whined, "we gotta ditch this truck and pick up our van. We—" Approaching headlights cut him short.

Two men wearing blood-stained butcher smocks had stepped down from a meat truck. Snatching the body from the refuse, they hauled it to the rear of the truck, opened the twin doors, and flung it into the refrigerated storage compartment.

"Follow them," Rebuck said.

"*Follow them*," Vesper mimicked. "Sheeeeeeeit!"

They trailed the meat truck through swirling patches of ground fog. They had passed the dim outlines of old buildings clustered by what appeared to be holding pens when the truck vanished in another fold of mist and reappeared at the entrance to an industrial complex. A large sign dominated the facade of the main building. It read DAVIS MEAT PROCESSORS, INC. Smaller letters below added, THE BEST IN PET FOOD.

Reaching a knoll overlooking the hollow, Ike brought the panel truck to a stop. They could see the loading platform of the slaughterhouse and watched a light wind wrap gauze bandages of fog around a plant humming to life. Rebuck's curiosity was satisfied.

Vesper's face had broken into a broad grin. He tossed his enormous head against the seat and laughter rolled from him in booming waves. "Dog food!" Vesper gasped.

"Dog food on some grocery shelf! The motherfucker finally met his true callin'."

Ron Rebuck closed his eyes, mentally adding another chapter to the captain's flair for the bizarre, as the laughing Ike Vesper drove off into the mist.

CHAPTER 18

BILLY HALE HAD come to Washington seeking inside information. But for all he had learned so far, he might as well have stayed at home reading the newspapers and watching television. The man he had counted on to answer his probing questions had been cordially stonewalling him for twenty minutes.

Dan Kaiser looked more like an ex-tennis pro than an assistant director of the FBI. Remarkably handsome, he did not appear to be much more than forty, but his birth certificate spoiled the illusion by adding a decade. Tall and lean, he moved from behind his desk and took a seat across from Billy. He looked with admiration upon the man who had baptized his two children and been greatly responsible for the advancement of his career during the administration of President Richard Waters. Like Billy Hale, Kaiser was born and raised in Cullinan County, Virginia, and this visit by the county's most famous resident had taken him by surprise. It had been almost two years since he had last seen Billy Hale, when Hale had delivered a moving eulogy at Kaiser's father's funeral. He would never forget how Billy had skillfully involved the graveside mourners by drawing the presence of death from its isolated state with the sobering words, "we all shall follow. . . ."

"Billy, I'm sure you will agree," Kaiser said, "Reverend Tho was not the most popular of men. He had scores of enemies, both in this country and abroad."

"Well, at least you've told me *something*," Hale responded sharply.

"Did I?"

"When you said, 'he *had* enemies.' You either believe or know the man is dead."

"But I don't."

"Dan, you can do much better than that."

"I'd like to, Billy."

"Then why not begin by telling me what you and the bureau *really* know?"

"I've already told you that all the evidence suggests the attack on Reverend Tho's estate was accomplished by a highly trained team of terrorists."

"And what happened to Cody Walker—was that also the work of well-trained terrorists?"

"I thought we were discussing Reverend Tho. But as long as you brought up Cody Walker, I can tell you we have proof as to what happened down there. And until we gather sufficient proof in the Reverend Tho matter—"

"Proof." Billy cut him short, tapping his cane impatiently against the carpet. "If you had any more proof, it would jump up and bite you." He shook his head. "Bazookas, machine guns, grenades, explosives, a phantom helicopter and a siren to wake the devil in hell, and *still* the police didn't hear a thing."

Kaiser squirmed while avoiding Hale's hostile eyes. "There is the possibility that the local authorities were remiss in their duties."

"*Remiss?* I call it out-and-out collaboration."

"Now that's a little heavy, wouldn't you say?"

"Is it? I don't think so, Dan. Not when fifteen human beings lost their lives."

"It will all come out in our investigation."

"No, Dan. I don't think so."

The assistant director's poker face thawed into an expression of concern. "Surely you don't believe the Federal Bureau of Investigation would be involved in a cover-up?"

"Pray tell, what is considered a cover-up these days?"

"A cover-up is a cover-up. Today, yesterday, or tomorrow, the definition stands."

"Baloney, Dan. How many times have we heard that

'in the interest of national security' this or that had to be kept from the public?''

"Reverend Tho? National security? Billy, isn't that a little farfetched?''

"Reverend Tho was murdered. As were Cody Walker and Jason Everson. What's more, there is a definite connection between all three deaths.''

"Connection?''

"Their murders were sponsored.''

"Sponsored by whom?''

"By the government of the people, by the people, and for the people.''

"That's ridiculous!''

"Tell me why, Dan. Tell me *why* I'm wrong.''

The FBI man silently toyed with an ashtray on the coffee table. Hale hoped that he was finally making some progress. But when Kaiser spoke, the patronizing tone had returned to his voice. "Before you tell me the president is a Communist, let's put things in their proper perspective. Contrary to what the newspapers first published, Cody Walker's death was a suicide. He died from a self-inflicted wound and there were no other fingerprints on the gun but his own. We also know that he murdered the church's attorney before taking his own life.''

"And you honestly believe that?''

"Cody Walker was accorded the same rights as any American who dies on foreign soil. I can tell you this department conducted an intensive investigation and its findings were substantiated.''

"Cody Walker was killed to prevent another Jonestown. And you know it.''

Kaiser ignored Hale's statement and went on. "As for Reverend Tho, the list of people who want him dead could fill the District of Columbia telephone directory. We need a body, Billy, and until we find the man dead or alive, it remains a suspected kidnapping.''

"A body? How long has Jimmy Hoffa been missing? No, Dan, Tho's murder falls under blackmail. Just what did the S.O.B. do for American interests in Vietnam? Was

169

it so productive that he would be welcomed into this country and given a charter for his church with the IRS's stamp of approval?''

Kaiser scribbled idly on a note pad as he spoke. ''Billy, where on earth did you come up with such poppycock?''

''How much did it cost the American taxpayers for the charter of Reverend Tho's church? Ten million? Fifteen? *Fifty?*''

Kaiser slipped the paper into the pocket of his suit jacket and stood up. ''I wish I had more time,'' he said, glancing at his watch.

''I know, you have pressing business and this old man has taken up enough of your valuable time.''

Billy planted his weight on the cane and struggled from the chair. Dan Kaiser placed a hand on his elbow to steady him and noticed the disapproval on Billy's face.

''Next time you come to Washington, give me some lead time and we'll have you over for dinner. Cynthia would love to see you.''

''I'll do that,'' Hale said coolly. ''How are the children?''

Kaiser glowed with pride. ''Peter will be a senior at Georgia Tech and John just graduated from Virginia.''

''Time sure has a way of slipping by,'' said Billy, scanning the walls of the spacious office. Among the framed photographs, he searched for one in particular. ''I gather the passage of time also applies to former presidents.''

''Former presidents?''

''Richard Waters did a lot for you, Dan. I'm surprised you don't keep a picture of him on your wall.''

Billy Hale returned home late that evening, a thoroughly dejected man. His trip to Washington had been a total failure. Once more he had exerted precious energy on a dry run. He slumped into a bedroom chair, weary and defeated. His weary eyes watched his wife place a glass of warm milk on the night stand next to the bed.

''You look exhausted,'' she sympathized.

''I feel worse,'' Billy rasped.

She knelt at his feet and gently removed his shoes.

"You were right, right all along, Doris. I needn't prove a thing."

She rose and stood behind the chair. Nudging him forward, she helped him from his jacket.

"I've done nothing more than make a damned fool of myself. I've let myself become some prophet of doom. Harley Lombard must think I'm senile, I'm sure Dan Kaiser believes I should be committed—and I still can't believe what I did to Jimmy Christian."

"It might have done that young man a world of good," said Doris, folding his jacket over an arm and waiting for him to remove his trousers.

"It never should have happened—striking him with my cane like that. There was no excuse for my conduct. I took my hatred for Pittman out on Jimmy."

"Billy, you've tried. What more can you do?"

He handed her the pants. "I know precisely what I am going to do—nothing! That's right, Doris. Let Jimmy Christian build his Christ Town. Let the electronic ministries run their course. And Harley? Well, he'll just have to get himself another advisor. No more foolish trips. It will be a while before I leave these peaceful grounds again."

She began to empty his suit pockets, placing the contents on his bureau top: loose change, two small packets containing pills, his billfold, and a folded piece of note paper. "Billy, is this piece of paper anything important?"

"What piece of paper?"

She brought it to him. He unfolded it, and the hastily printed letters seemed to jump off the paper at him. He stared at the words, and as he let their implication sink into his weary mind, he felt a renewed surge of energy. And it was an inspired Billy Hale who read the note a second time. *"Can't talk—will be in touch—D.K."*

CHAPTER 19

VIRTUES, INC., WAS BEYOND the seedling stage and Harley Lombard was ecstatic over the rapid growth of what he had been assured was his brainchild. The organization had reached the point where Harley could pick and choose from a staggering list of clergy wishing to buy a ticket on his red, white, and blue return-to-morals train.

Sue Bergman, Harley's new advisor, had plied him with all the words necessary to fuel his mind with visions of power: real power, the kind no evangelist had ever attained. Harley envisioned himself becoming the Protestant pope, and his untethered ego soared to stratospheric heights. Sue Bergman proved to be a master of manipulation; although he was the puppet dangling from her strings, she made him feel as if he were the genius behind Virtues, Inc.

Andy Gaines was wise to Sue Bergman from the start. He saw through the soft but purposeful feline smile and the cool detachment of a poisonous snake. He never believed that she had just accidentally popped into Harley's life or that her original visit to Lombard's ministry was simply an incidental follow-up to a letter. Gaines was certain her appearance had been meticulously planned, and executed only after she had completed an exhaustive study of Harley and his Ministry of Might operation. Through Harley, she had found a virginal front for the American Recovery Association, the ultra-patriotic organization she represented. Andy Gaines had no doubt that Sue Bergman was a queen of deception and that Harley Lombard was being royally conned.

Sue Bergman's raids on the Cathedral Towers had been

swift and ruthless. Her slashing of personnel had included those with years of service. She had expediently replaced all but six of the ministry's fifty full-time employees with an influx of strangers. And then there was the matter of the eighteenth floor.

Andy was bitter about the purge of loyal ministry colleagues and blamed the pogrom on Harley. Even Sue Bergman could not have managed the wholesale firings without the evangelist's blessing. But Gaines felt he shared in the guilt by failing to relay his suspicions to Billy Hale. He was, after all, Lombard's trouble-shooter and flak-catcher, but he had let the situation go too far. Not even Billy Hale could exorcise this she-devil from Harley's grandiose vision of his destiny as kingmaker and universal pontiff.

Andy's new status as the ministry's resident nobody had begun after an argument over Billy Hale. Gaines had made the fatal error of telling his boss that excluding Billy from an undertaking like Virtues, Inc., and ignoring his telephone calls was a foolish mistake. He was certain that Harley would eventually need Billy's expertise and counseling. Once Andy had voiced his opinion, Lombard scalded him with a tirade which amounted to a repudiation of his mentor. Lombard called Billy an old man shadow-boxing with concepts of the evangelical past. As reward for his candor, Gaines lost access to Lombard's ears and Sue Bergman now had them both ensnared in her web. Andy knew that that was not all she had. The Friday-afternoon hookers and choir singers had been phased out, giving Gaines reason to believe that the woman had become Lombard's sexual pacifier. To accomplish that during her frequent visits to the Cathedral Towers, Gaines knew she had to be not only a tigress in bed, but a versatile seductress who could unblushingly satisfy Lombard's sexual kinks and fetishes.

Gaines was crushed but not really surprised when a Bergman flunky informed him that he had been relieved of his role as Lombard's chief administrative aide. Andy had correctly surmised that his head would be the last to roll from the block, and he knew that when the blade fell Lombard's ego would have been stroked to colossal proportions. Sue Bergman had managed to convince Harley that Andy had become a cancer within the ministry. Her cure was a coolly efficient replacement who had the thin-lipped countenance of a CIA agent.

Andy's only meeting with his successor had been brief and antiseptic. Lombard's new assistant was fortyish with a receding hairline, pin-striped three-piece suit, and plastic-framed bifocals. It was the unofficial uniform for Sue Bergman's ministry personnel. Andy thought his replacement was a pompous ass. When he asked why he had been handed the news of his reassignment by a messenger rather than by Lombard himself, the man only smiled vapidly. Andy never did get an answer.

Oddly, Sue Bergman did not evict Gaines from his office on the penthouse level of the Cathedral Towers. Andy wondered about that and hoped that she had not been able to persuade Lombard to completely terminate his service to the ministry. But he would never know, since Harley's luxurious office was off limits to all but Sue Bergman and the select few she authorized.

Later that afternoon, while brooding in his office, Gaines was surprised to see roly-poly evangelist Veep Siler ushered into Harley's suite. Siler was a Florida cracker who had amassed an impressive television following in the South. Although as a preacher he rated perhaps a six, in evangelical circles he was given a perfect ten when it came to wheeling and dealing.

Beneath his amply fleshed appearance of respectability, Siler maintained the lean efficiency of a greedy man. Billy Hale never trusted him and had warned Harley, "He's a meddler, always looking to capitalize on somebody else's deal." Siler was also a supporter of Jimmy Christian, and his presence in the enemy camp raised deep suspicions in Andy's mind.

"Veep," said Harley, "why is it I have the impression you're on some perpetual journey?"

174

"Just a country-boy evangelist doing the work of the Lord."

"Uh-huh. But why do I get the feeling you're looking to put the ultimate shaft to someone?"

"Be nice, Harley. I didn't come up from Florida to be insulted."

Harley grinned and stuck up a finger. "One more?"

"If it pleases you, Harley."

"Veep, you're looking more and more like some humongous pig."

The fat man smiled and leaned back in his chair. "And how are good ol' Billy Hale's tits these days? Still suckin' em, Harley?"

Lombard gritted his teeth. "Billy has nothing to do with Virtues, Inc. Only the *Lord* advises me."

"So true," Veep said sarcastically, "and the Big Guy is never wrong."

"Not in my case," said Harley. "Of course, I'm not convinced about yours."

"What does it take to convince you?"

"You tell me, Veep."

"Fair," said the obese evangelist, rising from the chair and walking about the spacious suite on spindly legs which miraculously supported his ample girth. His eyes darted from Harley to his walnut desk, and then to the walls and ceiling, before returning to his host. "Bugging me, Harley?"

"Do I need to?"

The fat man grinned crookedly. "Sure I'm not bugging you?"

"The moment you sat in that chair, I would have known."

Siler looked curiously at the chair he had been sitting in, then at Harley. "Into James Bond stuff these days, Harley?"

"Veep, I've got a *heavy* schedule."

Siler held a meaty hand aloft and went to another chair, inspecting it thoroughly. He moved it farther away from Harley, sat down and farted.

"Jesus, Veep. Did you have to let one loose?"

"If the Lord didn't intend for us to pass gas, we wouldn't."

175

"Shall we get down to business?" Harley said, annoyed.

"Of course. Your *heavy* schedule," said Veep, taking a white handkerchief from his suit jacket and wiping the sweat from his porky face. "I believe you've got a good thing going, Harley. This Virtues baby of yours has a fine, fine smell to it."

"Like waves of power?"

"Maybe a tidal wave."

"Veep, aren't you forgetting you're with Jimmy Christian's network?"

"The munchkin's up to his ass in Christ Town. The boy's become paranoid. Did you hear he lost his top girl?"

"No. What's more, I could give a damn."

"Between Cora Lee, Bucky, and Jaws, Junior's got to wind up a basket case."

"Jaws?"

"C.D. Pittman."

Harley remembered Andy calling Pittman a barracuda. He preferred Jaws. Barracudas tear at flesh, but sharks devour it whole. In the business world, Pittman was definitely a Great White.

Siler arched his thick eyebrows. "Where I come from, religion and politics go hand in hand."

"Still living in the Florida panhandle, Veep?"

"You know better than that, Harley. You also know I can deliver to Virtues, Inc., a born-again Christian state. If you didn't think so, this here meeting wouldn't have come about."

"I won't horse trade with you, Veep. My phones are backed up with calls from Florida. Everybody's trying to climb on the bandwagon. They've seen the light."

"You got cloud cover over south Florida. Unless you have someone in Virtues, Inc., who can—" Siler was interrupted by the chiming of a red phone on a glass table. He was visibly aggravated as he watched Harley move rapidly around his desk to answer it. "Thought we agreed on no phone calls," Siler said, clearly annoyed.

"Washington, Veep," Harley said, oozing self-importance.

The fat man had come to deal. He had hoped to sustain

a mood and didn't need this interruption. He muttered peevishly while Lombard spoke to his caller in soft, caressing tones. The conversation was brief, and Siler swallowed an impending insult when he saw the broad smile on Harley's face as he returned the phone to its cradle.

"Guess who's giving the invocation *and* benediction at the Republican Convention?"

The fat man returned his grin. "My, my, Billy Hale is truly dead. Long live King Harley."

"People better start believing it," Harley said. The news had excited him and set his ego aflame. "Virtues, Inc., will control fifteen, maybe twenty million votes. Maybe even more. *Jesus,* do you realize the kind of power I'll be holding!"

"Awesome," Siler said.

"Virtues, Inc., the third major national political party."

"The religious party," Veep added.

"We're going to boot that sorry sonovabitch out of the White House."

"He sold Christianity out."

"That jackass and *all* of those fucking liberals will be looking for work come fall."

"They'll have to get *legitimate* jobs."

Harley's face grew stern. "Are you being funny with me, Veep?"

"No need to get huffy."

Harley looked at his wristwatch, a Rolex with a twenty-four-carat gold band studded with tiny diamond crucifixes. "I've got an eight o'clock flight to Washington and quite a few things to do before I leave."

The fat man was now witnessing a side of Harley he had never seen before. Without Billy Hale around to protect Harley, Siler had been certain he could cut himself a lucrative deal. Stroke the man's swollen ego, slam the Jews, and he would have him cold . . . that had been his game plan, but the man had changed dramatically. His megalomania had advanced beyond mere ego and Siler knew he would have to proceed with more caution.

Harley picked up a large black notebook and thrust it at

Siler. His voice had a triumphant ring. "Florida, Veep. Facts and figures. Contains the names of the politicians Virtues, Inc., doesn't want elected and those it does."

"Ah, yes, Florida's hit list. Senator Lollar's sure to be number one. Who's after Lollar?"

Harley thumbed through the pages. "Senator Lollar and Congressman Michaelman. In *that* order."

"Lollar, possibly. But forget Michaelman. He's brought a ton of federal money into south Florida. Too much muscle, Harley. Besides, Michaelman represents a district, not the state."

"Don't give me that defeatist crap!" Harley slammed the book closed and tossed it onto his desk.

This was more like the old Harley he knew, Veep thought. Got to keep him provoked. "The cardinal sin any negotiator can commit, Harley, is to lose sight of reality."

"Veep, I don't need you to lecture me. Virtues, Inc., is against every immoral son of a bitch holding political office. Michaelman and his kind are what's wrong with America."

"Because he's a Jew?"

"Don't play on my words, Veep. Virtues, Inc., is against *anyone* who is pro-abortion, who tolerates pornography, homosexuality—"

"And anyone who opposes prayer in public schools," Siler recited. "Yes, Harley, I'm aware of the Virtues, Inc., commandments. And I don't have to read that book of wonders on your desk to understand why you need me."

"*Need* you?" Harley laughed. "I'm doing you a favor, fat man."

"Because we attended divinity school together, of course."

"That's one consideration," said Harley. "Another is the way Billy kept you out of deals in the past. You must have known it was Billy who didn't want your 'Kingdom and Glory' show with my network."

"The thought did occur to me."

"Look, Veep, I like you. Always did. You might have

screwed a lot of people, but you've always been on the square with me.''

''Was that what you might call a complimentary insult?''

''Harley Lombard doesn't forget favors. You once did me a big one and I owe you. But I want you to realize I could get a lot of heat for selecting you.''

''From whom, Harley?''

''That's not important.''

''From God, Harley?''

Harley sneered at him, casually walked over to his desk and sat down. Siler knew the silence could only work against him. ''All right, Harley, let's play hardball. The way I see it, you need me to organize your Florida people. Keep those preachers firing from their pulpits. You furnish me with the ammo and I'll give Senator Lollar so much flak he'll think he's flying a Messerschmitt over Israel.''

''We want him up to his ass in mud.''

''Quicksand, Harley.''

''And Michaelman?''

''I'll think of something.''

''Like maybe planting a story that the Jew is into Miami Beach hotel deals with Arabs?''

''Harley, if the price is right, I'll make it known he went down on Yasser Arafat.''

Harley folded his arms and looked directly at his old divinity school classmate. ''What's it going to be, Veep, a piece of the action or a flat fee?''

''What do those Florida collection figures project?''

Harley picked up the black book and studied a few pages. ''Between four and five million, conservatively.''

''You mean miraculously. My God, man, those pastors will have to hock their parishioners' homes to meet that kind of quota.'' He shook his head so hard his jowls rolled. ''I'm getting too old to chase miracles. The fee?''

''One hundred thousand tax free. And that's on the come.''

The fat man did some fast calculations. ''Fifty thousand guaranteed for best efforts, two hundred thousand on the

179

come, Virtues, Inc., picks up all out of pocket expenses, and exclude Michaelman.''

"No Michaelman?"

"Best efforts."

Harley nodded. "All right, Veep. You cut a tough deal. But what the hell, I'll take a chance."

"I'm overwhelmed by your faith in me, Harley."

"You're getting funny again."

"What about my 'Kingdom and Glory' show? My ministry has a lot invested."

"Stay with Jimmy Cockroach until I say different."

"Who's my contact with Virtues, Inc.? Andy?"

"*No*. He's got nothing to do with this."

"Did you dump Andy, too?"

"We got a deal or not?"

"Might I have forty-eight hours? I hate to break a longtime precedent."

"Forty-eight hours. Not a second more."

"How merciful," Siler said, ponderously rising from the chair. "Is Andy about?"

"Somewhere," Harley said disinterestedly, showing him to the door.

"Mind if I say hello?"

"If you want to take him, take him. He works cheap. Just remember, Veep, after forty-eight hours all bets are off."

"And a good day to you, Harley." Siler attempted a low bow. "I mean, Your *Excellency*."

Andy Gaines rested his head on folded arms. He did not hear his office door open, nor notice the pudgy face peering at him. But when the door closed, he looked up and saw the three-hundred-pound frame of Reverend Veep Siler.

"That bad, boy?"

"Oh, things could be worse, Veep. Maybe in Bangladesh."

The fat man scrutinized the room. "Take a walk with me, boy."

"Can't, Veep. Waiting for an assignment."

"What kind?" Siler asked.

180

"Wish I knew. Apparently I've been demoted to the status of chief pissant. Any idea what level comes below pissant?"

"Don't give me that sorry dribble. Get off that skinny ass of yours and walk me to the elevator."

Gaines felt strangely compelled to obey Siler's authoritative tone. Both Veep and Harley were domineering, but that was all they had in common. Veep was a far cleverer man who did not need advisors or counseling. He had a keen insight which usually kept him a step ahead of everyone else. Once Gaines had overheard Billy Hale telling Lombard, "The man acts, thinks, and looks like Sydney Greenstreet." Andy admired the corpulent duplicity of Greenstreet's roles, but felt the resemblance ended there. "Laid back" was a term which could never be applied to Veep's personality.

As they walked down the hall toward the reception area, Andy could not shake the feeling that he was being closely observed. A quick glance over his shoulder confirmed his suspicion. One of Sue Bergman's watchdogs had been stationed in an office doorway down the hall and was now following them.

The receptionist was speaking quietly into her phone and Gaines searched her face, wondering if she, too, was spying on them. *I'm getting paranoid,* Andy thought, when a smartly dressed man appeared out of nowhere and joined them at the elevator. He smiled courteously and pushed the "down" button. Gaines nodded, but Siler ignored the man's smile.

Suddenly, it struck Andy that Sue Bergman was not in the building. She was probably back in Washington, yet she had been informed of Veep Siler's visit—a visit that was not *authorized* by her. This was a Harley Lombard move, and Bergman had sent her spies into action.

An elevator arrived. The doors opened, and to Andy's amazement the hippo-sized evangelist stepped inside with the speed of a welterweight and blocked the bewildered man's entrance with a solid bump of his great belly.

"More than two in an elevator makes me nauseous. I'm sure you don't mind," Veep said without blinking an eye.

The door closed heavily on the man's stunned face and Andy smiled for the first time that day. But the smile vanished when Veep asked, "Virtues, Inc.'s, operations center—what floor?"

"Eighteenth."

There was no button for the eighteenth floor, and Siler gave Gaines a fishy look. "How do you get there?"

"The lobby and through Harley's office. But the guard downstairs won't let you on the elevator."

"Guard?" he asked, pushing the lobby button.

"*Armed* guard," Andy said.

"The eighteenth floor: reception center, remote cameras, scanners, electronically operated doors—CIA stuff?"

Andy nodded.

"Who does what on this eighteenth floor?"

"Veep, I can only guess."

"Haven't you been in there?"

"Tried. I was told I didn't have security clearance."

"Is Billy Hale in the picture? And don't lie to me, boy."

"No."

"In any capacity?"

"None."

"Has Billy been here? Seen what's going on?"

"Harley won't even take his calls."

"Then who in blazes is coaching the man? And don't tell me it's God."

"I'm sorry, Veep. I still work for the ministry."

The fat man laughed. "Loyalty? Stop thinking like a fool. Harley's put you on the slave block."

"I don't believe it."

"Only minutes ago he tried to pawn you off on me. Said you work cheap. Your next assignment will be cleaning out the World Cathedral's shithouse." The fat man studied Gaines intently. "How long have you been Harley's doormat?"

"If you mean, how long have I been working for Harley, twenty years."

"Twenty years," Veep sighed, shaking his head.

The elevator stopped in the lobby and Andy watched Siler push the "close" button. Veep's eyes searched Andy's face. "You're a faggot, aren't you, boy?"

"A *what?*" Gaines gasped, his face flushing.

"Gay. A homo."

Gaines was stuttering now. "How, how can—where do you get off—"

"*Don't* play-act with me, boy. I can tell a faggot when I see one. That shine under your lower lip gives you away."

Andy instinctively raised a hand to the area under his lip. The fat man grinned. Andy had fallen for an old "gotcha" ploy.

Siler released the "close" button, the doors slipped open, and Veep led Andy by the arm past an annoyed group of people impatiently waiting to board. From the corner of his eye, Andy spotted the man Veep had bellied off the elevator. He was speaking to a uniformed guard by the farthest elevator, the eighteenth-floor express. Gaines then noticed a man at the tobacco stand watching them over his newspaper. "Veep," he said, "you get the feeling we're in the Kremlin?"

"Don't get paranoid on me, boy. We're going to need each other."

They left the building with Veep still clutching Andy's arm. He led him to a silver Toronado parked in a tow-away zone, then drew so close to Andy that Gaines could smell his stale breath. "I'm at the Marriott. Suite 626. I'll be expecting you at seven thirty."

Andy pulled himself free of Siler's grasp. "Why in the world would I come to see you?"

"You need a friend. Someone to realign your thinking."

"If you don't mind, I prefer to work out my problems by myself."

"You can't, boy." He pointed toward the top of the building. "To them, you've become a potential danger."

His hand dropped to his side. His eyes gleamed earnestly. "To me, you're golden."

The Toronado pulled slowly up to the curb. A slim, blond man with a deep tan came from the driver's side to open the door for the waiting evangelist. "Rick, say hello to Andy. He'll be joining me for dinner."

Andy shook the extended hand and was disarmed by the driver's handsome, almost pretty face. The suggestive expression in the young man's blue-green eyes needed no further words. Andy clearly understood the message.

CHAPTER 20

A HIGH-STEPPING chestnut mare pulled the trim black buggy down the rural Pennsylvania road. A sleek white Corvette streaked by in a brief meeting of past and present. Strong hands gripped the reins while the carriage rocked in a sudden slipstream of wind. Without further violation to the tranquil surroundings, the buggy clickety-clacked off the road toward the entrance to the grounds the Plain People called evil.

Jessica Towne's mind wandered during the mission director's droning lecture on reincarnation. While he discussed the possibilities of an afterlife, Jessica pondered the life at hand. Her relationship with Ron Rebuck was in the open. The reaction of her fellow students had run the gamut from jealousy and hostility to her current unwritten status as a non-person. Though the mission director had yet to formally confront her and forbid the relationship, her peers had initiated disciplinary actions of their own. She roomed alone; no one spoke to her except by necessity. She was the subject of whispers and hostile stares.

She knew if she would stop seeing Ron Rebuck the silent treatment would lift. That if she were to come back to the flock and "baa" forgiveness, her life at the mission would return to normal. But only she lived with her feelings. Though she was somewhat shy by nature, and inex-perienced with men, she did not intend to live a life of celibacy. There was nothing in the doctrine of Michael's Mission that forbade intimate relations between men and women, and she was a young woman in love. If her fellow students couldn't accept that, so be it. She would not pander to their self-righteousness and jealousy.

Her mind turned to thoughts of Ron, and, as the director concluded the long lecture and invited class discussion, he saw the vacant expression in her eyes and called her name. There was no response, and he called on her again, this time in a louder tone. "Jessica," he said, "would you mind leading off the discussion?"

She remembered enough of the topic to offer a general statement. "I believe reincarnation would represent one more imposition upon man's soul," she said.

"Double jeopardy," said the director, slightly fazed by her negativism. Usually he could rely on her to choose the affirmative role.

The word "imposition" clung to Jessica's mind. She had heard Ron Rebuck use it—four days ago, on that unforgettable day when he had spoken of his father, of God and of hate. The day he had taken her virginity . . . and the day she'd seen his obsession manifest.

The director's attention was drawn to a classroom window. The class followed his gaze and looked out to see two men with wide-brimmed black hats stepping down from their horse-drawn carriage. Jessica gasped as she recognized the older, bearded man. Without question, it was the man Ron had assaulted in the woods. She slumped in her seat.

Rebuck called it "Operation Ultimatum." Since 9:00 P.M. the night before, they'd engaged in a search-and-destroy exercise with Ike as the hunter and Ron the hunted. Vesper had twenty hours to find Rebuck and "terminate" him. Using 170 acres of the 200-acre tract, Rebuck was required to make at least four territorial changes, none of which were to be less than fifty acres in lateral distance. The hunted had every reason to be an elusive quarry, for Vesper's weapons fired dye pellets that inflicted stinging wounds.

Ike played the exercise straight from the SEAL manual. Missing, of course, were the grenades and flamethrower

186

he'd use in a real war to flush his quarry. "Fucking Boy Scout shit," he repeated under his breath each time he thought back to 'Nam.

Deciding to lay back for a while, Ike unslung the shotgun from his shoulder, unfastened his cartridge belt and unclipped a holster containing a Luger-type pellet gun, and dropped them wearily by his side. He would wait it out, hoping to catch Rebuck on the move and blitz his carcass with buckshot. Rebuck's unwillingness to tell him what they were practicing for was pissing him off more and more as he thought about it, and at this point he'd had quite enough of the hide-and-seek bit.

Ike set the alarm on his wristwatch to go off in twenty minutes and closed his heavy eyelids. He was jarred back to alertness almost immediately by the sound of a woman's voice. Peering cautiously through the tangled undergrowth, he recognized the slender figure of Jessica Towne.

"Hey, Little Girl!" he shouted, rising to his feet.

Jessica knew the voice, but as Ike approached she blanched at the sight of his painted face, the battle fatigues, and the weapons.

"Stay cool, Little Girl."

He looked like he'd stepped out of an ad for the American military fighting man. "What's going on, Ike?" she asked.

"Practicin' for Halloween. Whattaya doin' out here, Little Girl?"

"I have to see Ron."

Ike looked at his watch. "The dude won't surface for two hours and . . . forty-three minutes."

"Ike, I *must* see him."

"Not 'less you're some kinda mole."

"Really, Ike, I've got to warn him."

"Warn him? Little Girl, whucha tellin' me?"

She looked away.

"Hey, what comes down on the man, comes down on me."

"Didn't Ron tell you?"

"Not ev'rythin'," he said, bluffing.

"Ike, he's here. The Amish elder. *Here* at the mission."

For the first time, Ike noticed she was trembling. Gently, he took her by the arm and led her toward the camp. "Little Girl," he said, "I think ya better tell Uncle Ike the whole story."

Ron Rebuck emerged from his subterranean hiding place at precisely 5:00 P.M. He carefully slid a grass-covered wooden lid over the six-by-six-foot hole in the ground and checked to make sure it blended with the natural surroundings. Brushing the dirt from his cami-fatigues, he proceeded southward to where he would rendezvous with Ike Vesper.

He reached the designated spot, a clearing distinguished by two trees intertwined, and waited. It was 5:05, the precise time for their appointed meeting. At 5:10, Vesper still had not shown. Disturbed by his friend's failure to complete the maneuver, Rebuck sprinted back to camp, slowing to a brisk walk as he reached it. Ignoring Ike, who peered at him from a hammock, he entered the sanctuary of his trailer.

As Ike lay in the hammock, strung between two trees by his trailer, he rehearsed questions that needed prompt answers. What Jessica had told him ran wildly through his mind. Rebuck was playing Russian roulette with the captain's gun, and all the chambers were loaded. He was testing the captain's patience, and that was like poking a spear at some Great White from a dinghy in mid-Pacific. Ike swung himself from the hammock, then walked heavily to Rebuck's trailer, geared for a verbal shootout.

Inside, Ike was greeted by the sound of running water. He would wait; what he had to say was too important to be shouted through a shower curtain. He idly glanced about the cramped but tidy quarters, and a yellow legal pad on the dinette table caught his eye. He moved across the living area and picked it up. Amidst Rebuck's doodlings was a single name, that of a famed evangelist. As Ike pondered its significance, he heard the water stop running.

Ron ignored Ike's hulking presence as he went to get a

towel from an overhead cabinet, calmly drying off his lean, muscular body. Collecting a navy-blue robe from a hook on the closet door, he put it on and strolled toward the convertible bed.

Ike tossed the pad aside. The muscles in his face were taut as he spat the words, "Ya did it, man. Ya put our names on a mothafuckin' mailbox!"

"Later," said Rebuck, crawling onto the bed.

"Ya blew our cover. Ya just bought us two—no, make that *three* tickets to Deadsville."

"I said later, Ike. When you tell me why you bugged out from the maneuver."

"You've put your own mother's life on the line, not to mention your ass and mine!"

"You quit in the middle of maneuvers, Ike," said Rebuck, stretching out on the bed.

"Don't shift tracks on me, Stone Man. The dude whose head ya were gonna blow away has been tellin' his story to the Mission Man."

"So what?"

"So *what?* I'll tell you so what—you blew our fucking cover!"

Rebuck sat on the edge of the bed. "What makes you so sure of that?"

"Ya got us fingered, fool!"

"Forget it."

"Shit," said Vesper, slamming his fist against the wall's teak veneer. "The po-leece are gonna put it together and come crawlin' up our mothafuckin' asses, and you say forget it!"

"It'll never happen," said Rebuck.

"Man, they're gonna light this place up like the Fourth of July. It's gonna look like the fuckin' Tet offensive all over again."

"Not a chance," Rebuck said. "I've been thinking about it, and it's obvious that Gemmer and whoever is pulling his strings are wired into the local police department." He took out a bottle of orange juice, poured a

189

glass, then sat down with it in the dinette booth. "Think— have we had a single problem with the local authorities?"

Ike couldn't dispute the fact that there had been no sign of police in the two weeks they'd been here, but he was in no mood to give in to Ron Rebuck's persuasive logic. "What happened in the past was *then*. What's happenin' now is *now*," he said.

Rebuck waited for him to slide into the booth before speaking. "Gemmer was right when he said his force was strong."

"Man, that should tell ya somethin'."

"It tells me the mastermind behind it all is someone who doesn't use pencils with erasers."

"That tells *me* a whole fuckin' lot."

"Remember when I said we didn't have a flag? I was wrong. We've got one, Ike. A red, white, and blue swastika."

Ike raised a questioning eyebrow.

"O'Donnell, Church," Rebuck continued, "they're all just drops in a pond. For sure, Gemmer's the enforcer. But I don't think he's any more than that. It's my guess that a hardline syndicate of conservative, wealthy people is behind this, footing the bill." He paused to search for a reaction on Ike's face. "Are you on board?" he asked.

"I jumped ship back at the flag."

"Swim back when you're ready to listen," said Rebuck, slipping out from the booth.

"Okay, I'm listenin'."

The sincerity in Ike's voice was not duplicated on his face. Nevertheless, Rebuck continued, "How long do you think the captain will need us?"

Ike shrugged, unable to respond.

"You don't know," said Rebuck.

"All I know is the money's good and the alternative ain't."

"For how long?"

"Aw, shit, man, say whucha mean."

"I'm onto the captain's plan, Ike. Remember my telling

you he said we were a *special* team? Well, I'm beginning to think he's making *us* his personal assassins.''

Vesper shook his head. "Little Brotha, as long as ya don't cross him, the man's as straight as cobra spit." He leaned heavily against the backrest, letting out a deep and pleading sigh. "Do what the man says and ev'rythin's cool."

"But it's not cool, Ike. We're expendable—and unless your head's a watermelon with pits for brains, you've got to know you'll never live to catch that dream you keep talking about."

"Shit," said Vesper, breaking out from the booth with a face scorched with anger. "Ya got a mothafuckin' bomb tickin' in your head, some kinda death wish, and you're tellin' this nigger *he's* crazy?"

"I'm telling you we've got to take the initiative against the inevitable. And if you're too intimidated to understand there's no *or* in Gemmer's 'do or die' ultimatum, then you're a fool."

Resting his big hands on the table, Vesper took a long time framing his words. He wanted them to be right. "Little Brotha, I never been ta college. I'm just a Mississippi farm boy who joined the navy for a better life. But I know when someone's a fool." He looked deeply into Rebuck's face. "It's not me who's playin' chicken with Captain Death. It's you—and you've got a hell of a lot more to lose than I do."

Rebuck paid no attention to Ike's roundabout advice and revealed some wisdom of his own. "Operation Ultimatum, Ike. It deals with survival. *Ours.*"

Vesper's jaw dropped. He did not need a telegram to understand. The words stuck in his throat. "Un-unauthorized? Man, ya tellin' me, unauthorized?"

"Operation Ultimatum is our lifeboat."

"Lookin' in holes, climbin' trees, poison ivy eatin' on my face—this was *unauthorized?*"

"It's our only chance of coming out of this deal alive."

"Two mothafuckin' weeks playin' hide and seek and it was all *your* idea?"

"Sit down, Ike. I'll—"

"Shit! You ain't tellin' me nothin' about some crazy scheme to blow my black ass away."

Rebuck shrugged. "You're not interested? Okay, then, you're not interested." As Ron rose to leave the booth, a human wall blocked his way.

"You can crash after listening to what *I* got to say."

"To the words of a puppet?" said Rebuck. He strained to get up, but Ike shoved him back. "Get out of my face, Ike," Rebuck said menacingly.

"You want to get it on?" Vesper replied, moving back a step. "Okay, if that's what it takes, but you're gonna listen to me, one way or the other."

Rebuck gauged the determination etched on his friend's face. They had had falling-outs in the past, but always resolved them short of violence. They were equally skilled in hand-to-hand combat; Rebuck's catlike quickness rivalled Ike's bearlike strength in effectiveness. As they squared off in deadly silence, their respect for each other's abilities stifled their moment of willingness. An unspoken mutual understanding cooled their blood.

Having won the right to be heard, Ike searched for the words to describe exactly how he felt. Sensing the impatience building within Rebuck, he spoke in an earnest tone of voice. "Little Brotha, you know I've never bullshitted you, and man, I'm not shittin' you now. There ain't no way to reason with you 'cause somethin' heavy has landed on your head."

"Bottom line, Ike. If you got one."

"You don't cross the captain without gettin' your lights burned. But you're doin' it, and you'll keep doin' it 'til he comes for you. An' when he does, 'cause the motha will, our blood-brotha friendship is *over*."

"And how will he come for me? With an army of hit men?"

"Little Brotha, super-bat flies a-lone."

Rebuck smiled.

*　　*　　*

192

Jessica Towne wished the mission director would come to the point. She sat rigidly in his tiny, cluttered office, wondering when he would ask if she was the girl with the man who had trespassed on Amish land. But he had yet to mention the Amish elder's unprecedented visit. Instead he was asking her questions about Ron Rebuck and Ike Vesper—what were they doing out there? What did they do for a living? She didn't know, and told him so.

She watched him rise slowly from behind the old desk and walk to the window, where he gazed out into the night. She felt his silence as a condemnation, that he thought she was lying. "Mr. Ragonese, I'm sorry you don't believe me, but I really don't have any answers for you."

He turned from the window. "I believe you, Jessica." He moved back to the desk and sat on the edge of it. "But surely you must have some idea."

"I don't. I *really* don't."

He leaned forward. "Names, Jessica. Have you heard them mention any names?"

She shrugged. "A captain. They talk a lot about a captain."

"Does this captain have a name?"

"No, just Captain."

"Anyone else? *Think*, Jessica."

"Yes, someone called Hans—I heard Ron tell Ike he didn't want to hear about him anymore. Mr. Ragonese, why are you asking me these questions?"

The mission director began slowly drumming on the desk with his fingers, and she looked away, hoping he would break the trying silence with a response.

"Jessica, do you know why the Amish elder paid us a visit today?" Without waiting for an answer, he said, "Is it true, Jessica?"

She bit down on her lip, then nodded softly.

"Why, Jessica? Why would he do what he did?"

"I don't know. He . . . he just went wild."

"Without any provocation?"

Jessica was silent.

"You're a bright young girl, Jessica. Someday you'll make a man a wonderful partner in life." His eyes pierced her. "Our founder's son is not that man." He paused for a moment before continuing. "In a few months, you shall graduate and leave the mission. Until then, you are not to see him again. Will you promise me that?"

Jessica stared at the threadbare carpet. "Mr. Ragonese, I can't make that promise."

"Jessica, I know you wouldn't break your father's heart. And I, myself, am very fond of you. No one has ever been expelled from Michael's Mission. I hope you shall not be the first."

She would not let him see the tears welling in her eyes. She rose from her chair and fled from the office.

The mission director stroked his wiry beard. He walked over to a painting depicting the body of Christ fused with the soul of the Archangel Michael. Taking it from the wall, he opened his hidden safe, removing several documents before returning slowly to his desk.

He spread three papers on the desk and reread the fine print of a real estate option for the mission's five hundred acres. There were two signatures under the last line of the agreement. The line read "American Realties, Inc." Below a signature which he could not make out, and that of his own, a notary's seal had been affixed. Ragonese looked next to the mission's deed, where the one name which appeared was that of the founder, Ron Rebuck, Sr. After Rebuck's death, Ragonese had become the sole administrator of the mission and the property on which it stood. The third document contradicted it. It was a codicil to the founder's will, and it had muddied waters he had thought were crystal clear. It was all becoming legally quite complicated, and the thought of the twenty-five thousand dollars he had already received for the option only darkened his mood.

From a desk drawer, he took out his personal telephone directory and address book. He leafed through the pages and found the Washington, D.C., listing for American Realties, Inc. A finger traced down to the third set of numerals. His hand went for the chipped black phone and he dialed the number. After three rings, someone picked up.

"Hello, this is John Ragonese," said the mission director. "May I speak with Sam?"

CHAPTER 21

TUCKED AMONG the hunter-green North Carolina hills, the Billy Hale Bible College glowed with sunshine. The college, named in honor of its founder and chief benefactor, could not have had a better day for its commencement exercises.

Billy Hale was housed in the brick and stone residence of the college president. He sat in a chair by a window, overlooking the peaceful campus of the institution which he regarded as the most enduring monument of his worldwide ministry.

He had not slept even an hour the previous night. The telecasts of Harley Lombard standing in front of the House of Representatives in Washington, D.C., surrounded by born-again Christian politicians, were etched on his troubled mind.

"The man is either obsessed with power or plain mad," he said aloud.

Doris Hale had chosen a summer dress suitable for the occasion and came to his side for approval. "How do I look, Billy?" she asked.

"Fine, just fine," he said. "You would be lovely in a potato sack."

His thoughts returned to Lombard and his first public appearance as the spokesman for Virtues, Inc. "Doris," he said, "I feel I know Harley better than anybody on earth, with the possible exception of Wilma Mae. His drawbacks have always involved his impulsiveness, his failure to look before he leaps. But this Virtues, Inc., business is insane. The man has no idea what he's gotten himself into."

"Billy, he's not the son you've always thought of him as. Harley has never done anything for anyone but Harley."

"Jimmy Christian can go to the devil. But with Harley, I can't help feeling somewhat responsible. He only went by the book *I* wrote."

"Worrying will be the death of you. If it's not worrying over when Dan Kaiser will get in touch with you, it's waking up with nightmares about Christ Town. Last night it was Harley. What will be next, Billy?"

He attempted to stand, but the sharp pain in his knee stiffened him. Doris brought him his cane and he leaned heavily on the marble head. A pained smile creased his wrinkled face. "You're right again, Mrs. Hale. I've done all the worrying I intend to do. From today on, I'm going to start making *others* worry."

Tiered stone steps rose to a field where three hundred spectators viewed a stage set among evergreens and flower beds. The graduating class, who had earned their doctor of divinity degrees, was comprised mostly of young men, although there was a higher percentage of women than usual. The graduates, along with their families and friends, applauded warmly as the world's most famous evangelist limped to the podium.

There were a few raised eyebrows when Billy waived the traditional invocation and went directly to his address.

"I say to you who will soon become ministers, who will preach from pulpits in churches throughout this land, that the greatest challenge you face is not in the morality of your parishioners, but a challenge from *within*."

He then spoke fiercely against the building of Christ Town. Without mentioning Jimmy Christian's name, Hale accused the creators of being profiteers who were ripping off God himself.

Faculty members seated on the dais looked at each other in disbelief. Even Doris Hale was taken by surprise. Publicly attacking a fellow evangelist was a violation of unwritten laws. But Billy Hale had ceased to play by the rules.

197

The graduates leaned forward in anticipation and Billy forged ahead. "Look upon the face of the world. Are we so infected with apathy as not to recognize the religious scars of yesteryear? I speak of the so-called holy wars, the shedding of blood in God's name. I speak of nations in desperate strife because of the religious leaders who are their heads of state."

He paused and there was total silence. There was no sound of creaking chairs, no coughing, no clearing of throats. It was as if even the birds had stilled their chirping to hear the importance of what he said.

"A religious organization," Billy continued, "yes, I said religious, has come upon the American scene. I speak of what the newspapers, radio, and television find worthy of headlines in the hope of creating flaming religious controversy. You all know it as Virtues, Inc., I call it demagoguery. And I strongly oppose the actions of misguided members who crusade against the separation of church and state; men and women who, without the grace of God, have elevated themselves into the roles of false judges."

He paused and lowered his eyes as if deep in prayer. Only his wife understood how difficult it was for him to condemn someone he had considered a son. "I ask you all to pray for Harley Lombard. Pray that he may realize the error of his ways.

"Today we find ourselves in the midst of a crisis. Our Christian leaders have come to represent little more than blind greed and ambition. While there are still men of God among their ranks, too many of them are frauds, charlatans, and deceivers who have broken every one of the Lord's commandments. In doing so, they have broken faith with their millions of followers, and handed the shield of moral rectitude to those who would destroy them."

A hopeful smile creased Billy's face as he eyed the graduates. "You, each and every one of you, must be united in body and soul to face the great temptations that have infiltrated the vocation you have chosen. You are the core of a new beginning. Build not monuments to greed.

Flaunt not your Christian ideologies upon those who seek peace through their own. Help those with searching minds who cannot truly justify fundamental Biblical beliefs. Rely not totally on the Holy Book, else you shall drive those who seek knowledge into God-forsaken cults. Harass not the elderly, the sickly, and the depressed with additional burdens of fear. Permit them to enter the last great adventure without thoughts of hell and a punishing God. Encourage their spiritual rendezvous with an all-loving Being. I ask you today to accept a challenge—the challenge to be of the givers—not of the takers. Return the Ministry of Christ to its rightful course!''

They jumped to their feet: graduates, parents, friends, and faculty alike. Their tears were those of hope and joy rather than sorrow. It was as if Billy had resurrected their faith and cast away the dark shadows. The standing ovation persisted and they stood proud—proud to be Christians this very day.

In the last row, wearing dark glasses, Dan Kaiser made good on his promise to Billy Hale. He was in touch.

CHAPTER 22

JESSICA TOWNE'S ROOM reminded her of a cell. A small cell, at that. Her new quarters in the mission house's third story might at one time have been a sewing room or, more likely, a walk-in closet. There was barely space for a single iron-framed bed and a four-drawer chest. Such a room would have been claustrophobic even for a Trappist monk, and Jessica felt sure that her change of lodging was more than an attempt by the mission director to prevent her from seeing Ron Rebuck; the smallness of the cubicle was intended to break her down. The director had put her here, she was certain, because he thought it would make her beg forgiveness and flow contritely back into the mainstream of mission life. But he would be disappointed. She would not bend, no matter how deep her depression or sense of isolation.

If anything, her yearning for Rebuck had intensified. But she knew that any further attempt to see him would result in her expulsion.

The mission was an interdenominational seminary which offered no degrees, a retreat where young people were afforded the opportunity to study the genesis of all religions. Michael's Mission represented no creed; it attempted to refute religious myths, hypocrisies, and man-made dogmas. The mission challenged the brainwashing approach of born-again movements and personality cults, and the "Bible tells us so" mentality of the Christian fundamentalists.

She had made the decision to come to the mission primarily because of a fascination with mythology and world religion. She'd also felt a need to leave home, to seek challenges and new experiences in life while she was young and strong. Living with her family—her mother, father and nine brothers and sisters—on the edge of poverty was no way to spend the rest of her life.

She had learned of Michael's Mission while browsing through the public library in her home town. Happening upon Ron Rebuck Sr.'s inspirational book, she had become enchanted by his portrayal of the supremacy, and particularly interested in his theoretical reasoning for the birth and death of mankind. It had taken a week to finish a letter which she felt adequately expressed her feelings, and a month of summer had passed before she received a response.

A graduate of the mission living in Charleston paid her a visit. Jessica was immediately impressed by the sincerity that emanated from the young woman, only a few years older than she. There was no hype, no cult-like recruiting technique, and no religious ideology forced upon her. Jessica, like the other seminarians, would be able to meet her personal needs by working on the mission's farm. It would require only one year of her life and would be an excellent transition from high school to whatever path she would choose to follow the rest of her life. Until now, Jessica had never once regretted her decision to come here.

She stared into the cracked mirror above the scarred dresser, tears welling within her sky-blue eyes as the image of Ron Rebuck's handsome face thrust itself before her. For three days she'd fought the urge to see him, trying to convince herself it was all a mistake—a case of her naiveté and his overwhelming effect upon her. She had encountered a strange breed, indeed . . . a man whose worldliness was far beyond her grasp, and whose intense hatred of all things religious both intrigued and frightened her.

She had come to the conclusion that she was living a fantasy. She had read about characters like Ron Rebuck in popular novels, fiction that allowed women to safely fantasize. He was that particular kind of male, fast slipping into extinction, that only the bravest, most reckless of women could love. She thought of the vast majority of women who dared not venture to love a man in conflict with a sheeplike society, content instead to marry the safe-bet type. Hadn't she left West Virginia to avoid exactly that? No, she could not follow her mother's example, devoting herself as the wife of a hard-working coal miner, raising children, and in later years watching as her husband withered away from black lung disease.

She could hear the students breaking up from their evening recreation in the room below, and her feelings of not belonging progressed to an insurmountable loneliness.

She went to the bed, struggling against the tear gates which threatened to burst open. As she lay there, a saving thought came to mind. She would enlist in the military. It was an option she had once considered in West Virginia. Yes, first thing in the morning she would make the arrangements. She would request to be stationed abroad— oceans away from Michael's Mission and Ron Rebuck.

A door closed down the hall, reminding Jessica of her isolation. She threw her legs over the side of the bed and sat up, suddenly no longer able to resist the rising desire which had become uncontrollable. There was something she had to do, and now she drew deep down within herself to summon the courage it would take.

Jessica removed her slippers, pulled on her sneakers, and walked over to the dresser where she snatched a light blue sweater from a drawer. Draping it around a white blouse tucked into jeans, she moved decisively toward the door. She would see Ron Rebuck one last time.

She stepped cautiously into the dimly lit hallway, her ears tuned for living sounds. Her eyes cleared the corridor and froze on the staircase ahead. For a tense moment she contemplated retreat, but the driving compulsion was too great as her heart pounded in rhythm with her quick-moving feet. Reaching the stairway, she tiptoed down the creaky old steps. Above, the door to the director's bedroom creaked open.

Jessica moved soundlessly from the porch into the dark under a crescent moon partially veiled by a thin overcast.

She walked eagerly under gently swaying trees toward the trail. The night air was heavy with the smells of freshly mowed grass and the rich Lancaster County soil, and she finally felt alive, free from the entrapments that had been tightly binding her young life. The thought that she had chosen a firm course of action lifted her spirits.

She soon reached the spot where the vehicle path Vesper and Rebuck had cleared split off from the paved road, and she jogged the final one hundred yards. The Doberman pinschers snarled at her intrusion, but she quieted them as she had many times before and moved past the kennel into the heart of the compound.

She did not need a light to find Ron Rebuck's motor home, but as she hurried toward it a sudden realization brought her to a restrained walk. Her eyes moved to Ike Vesper's trailer, and she could see no sign of life there either. Looking around for the black van, she realized it was gone.

As she turned and moved back past the kennel and onto the trail, she kept telling herself that perhaps it was better this way. In time, Ron Rebuck would be reduced to a memory. Still, a tear escaped her, and she silently cursed the ineffectiveness of logic at times like these.

As she moved down the trail, a feeling, a vibration, struck her senses and brought her to a sudden halt. Her ears perked, she stood motionless, listening to the sounds of the night: a rustling from nearby bushes, the distant hoot of an owl, the busy anthem of crickets, and then—a human voice. Her anxious ears sought out its origin when again it came, ever so faintly, as if carried by the gentle wind.

She reversed her path and ran across the cornfield, past an irrigation ditch, moving toward the area of the mission grounds many considered to be the most beautiful. Only once, during her orientation, had she set foot on the unfarmed land where the mission's founder was buried.

Within a rock's throw of the grotto delineated by pines, Rebuck's voice brought her to a halt. She listened closely, but his words were garbled. She did not run to him, respecting an inner voice urging caution. Avoiding the grotto's access, she crept through the pines to where she could see him in the glow of a kerosene lamp.

Ron Rebuck sat at the foot of his father's grave under an immense statue of the Archangel Michael. The orange glow of the lantern cast ominous shadows on the statue's face. Having finished well over half a bottle of tequila, his drunkenness had encouraged an emotional monologue directed at his father.

"Nothing," he said, shaking his head. "You proved *nothing*. Didn't even make any money out of it." He took another swig from the bottle of tequila. Close to the point of total stupor, his faltering body was driven by a relentless soul. "Crazy. The whole thing was crazy. Telling people there's no killer God . . . Telling 'em someone else thought up mankind . . . writing a new Bible. Didn't you have any idea where it was at? Where it'll *always* be? Didn't you know that *fear* is inevitable?"

He wiped his mouth on his sleeve and looked at the small stone marker fronting the base of the impressive statue which bore his father's name " 'I'm defending God,' you'd tell me. But did you stop 'em, Dad? Did you put even one sleaze-bag evangelist out of business? You'd have done better taking on the fuckin' U.S. government."

Burning memories which had long lain dormant now burst forth through his bitter words. "My father, the martyr. Champion of a cause doomed from the start. For Christ's sake, Dad—a loving, neutral God *doesn't* build churches, *doesn't* fatten bank accounts. Were you really blind to that?"

He had trouble raising the bottle to his lips, and the potent liquor ran down his chin. "Trying to change the whipped minds of people . . . did you really think they even wanted to hear—hear about a fight between two mythical angels? Did you expect the assholes to believe *their* destiny was the result of *that?*"

His sudden heaving rid him of the poison in his gut, but not the venom in his mind. He wiped his mouth with his forearm and returned his attention to the grave. "Man, you should've taken the time—the time to understand how those religious creeps make it work for them: the unknown, life after death, Judgment Day, heaven or hell, eternal bliss or Armageddon. *That's* where the fuck it's at!''

His face had lost all color, and his forehead was clammy with sweat. "What was your great antidote, Dad? Taking away the hopes of brainwashed people believing—believing their sufferings on this rotten earth would be made right by an avenging God?" Bile dribbled from the corners of his mouth. "Tellin'—tellin' those suckers that the corruptible rich, sinners and atheists, will not be punished in an eternal hell? You blew it, Dad . . .'' The words trailed off into a guttural moan as Rebuck doubled over and vomited directly onto his father's grave.

Jessica could not bear to watch any longer, and started to walk toward him. Then she saw him—watching Rebuck from behind a tree. The mission director's bearded face was partially veiled in the flickering darkness. It was possible, in fact likely that he'd seen her, if so, her expulsion from the mission was certain. But that no longer mattered to her. What did was her concern for Ron Rebuck. Still, the director's presence intimidated her. She decided to wait—at least until her emotions would let her wait no longer.

Rebuck was kneeling at the foot of his father's grave with the bottle of tequila tightly gripped in his hand. "Where are you now, Dad? Heaven, Hell, Purgatory? You been reincarnated? Have you talked to God? Told him what a raw fucking deal He gave man? Could you tell Him I never was asked—never asked if I wanted to play in His lousy game?''

His voice cracked. "Loved the SEALs, the navy. Had a career, an *honorable* career.'' His deadened mind jammed the words, yet he continued his confession. "It—it was all behind me, Dad. Wakin'—wakin' up all those nights, seein' you nailed to that cross.''

He stumbled to his feet and staggered to the foot of the ten-foot-tall statue, whose luminous marble eyes were cast down upon his father's grave. "You were news for a while, Dad. Month, maybe two. The newspapers and TV showed you on that cross. Know what I would hear, Dad? That's Ronnie Rebuck—his father was the Antichrist. And Mom—she just couldn't take it."

The thought of his mother made him shake his head with bitterness. "It was all behind me and then it happened, like a bad dream. Either enlist in his conspiracy or . . ." He began to tremble. "What would you have done, Dad?" His entire body shook convulsively. "But it doesn't matter because I'm not you. I'm not a martyr. I'm not a fool. I'm a survivor!" He wailed into the night. *"I'm a survivor!"*

"Oh, my God," Jessica called out, wringing her hands as she shared his pain. Surprised at her own outburst, she looked for the mission director in the shadows. He was gone.

Ron Rebuck's hazy eyes rose from the ground. His words were disguised by calmness as he went on, apparently oblivious to her presence at the edge of the grotto. "Know what I do now, Dad? I mean, for a living? Every three months I'm paid twenty-five thousand dollars to waste people, or set them up to *be* wasted—people who did me no wrong."

Tears dripped from his eyes. The words came slowly, shamefully. "Look at me, Dad. Your son, the *assassin.* Aren't you proud?" He stiffened as if coming to attention before an invisible power. The hate festering in his mind surfaced through his crazed eyes. "Don't worry. I'll make you *real* proud. Your death won't go unavenged . . . I promise you."

He had nothing more to say. The alcohol would soon take him into a drunken sleep. He looked at the statue's face lit by an eerie glow, and memories were vividly relived in his mind. He recalled the visitations his father claimed to have had. Visitations by only a voice, so far away, as if it had come from another world, and speaking in a tongue none but his father understood. Now, as he looked at mortal man's image of an eternal spirit, an angel named Michael whom his father had called man's champion and his mother had cursed as a mythical ghost which had obsessed and ultimately destroyed her husband, his feelings of shame and disgrace were swept away by anger. A sudden rage sounded in his temples. Incensed to destroy, he approached the statue and struck it over and over with his naked fists, his attack ending quickly as he fell hard against the concrete base.

He did not feel the pain in his bruised hands and shoulder. He strove helplessly to rise, only to fall again. On his knees, he looked hatefully up at the marble face. He blinked his eyes. Again. And still again. He kept telling himself that what he saw was not there and that the light reflecting on the statue's face was creating an illusion. For how could a cement sculpture suddenly come alive with eyes that now glared at him?

He would not be tricked as he thought his father had been. He was drunk, and drunks saw things that were not real. He would not let himself be tempted into believing in supernatural happenings. Tears dripping from the faces of religious icons, holy statues that spoke to the faithful, and Lourdes, which his father called "the Catholic Church's great carnival," were, in his belief, the kind of miracles manufactured to pump religious juices into the minds of stupid people. Yet the more he denied what he was seeing, the more bizarre it became.

"Speak, you son of a bitch! Speak to me like you did to my father! No, you can't . . . you damn well can't now, and you never could!"

Rebuck heard a sound not unlike the opening of an ancient stone crypt, marble grating against marble, and the illusion intensified. The angel's wings suddenly shot out like gigantic fans. They began to flap, at first slowly, then faster and faster until they created great gusts of wind accompanied by booming claps of thunder. Its hands turned into enormous claws with razor-sharp tips. The face began to melt into a shapeless mass until the statue was headless. From within the neck's gaping black hole, a volcanic eruption of fire burst violently into the night.

He felt the wind beating against his face and the fiery tongues licking at him. Through burning eyes, he saw the winged and headless demon hovering over him as if to scoop him up with a talon and soar off with his body and soul to Hell's dumping grounds. The bottle in his hand became a knife. Out of desperation, he hurled it at the beast, and collapsed onto his father's grave.

No force on earth could stop Jessica. She ran toward Ron, calling out his name. She reached his prone body, laid her folded sweater under his head and tenderly, lovingly stroked his hair.

For the second time that night, she felt a third presence. She looked up and saw a man standing in the shadows behind the statue. As he moved forward a step, there was just enough light for Jessica to make out a man she had never seen before, a hollow-eyed man whose scarred face was contorted in an evil smile.

Then he was gone.

PART II

IN GREED WE TRUST

CHAPTER 23

BILLY HALE ASSAILS VIRTUES, INC.,
AS DEMAGOGUERY:
CALLS CHRIST TOWN A RIP-OFF

That was one of the milder headlines which appeared in newspapers across the country.

The telephone calls began at 6:00 A.M. The language melted the wax in Jimmy Christian's ears. He cursed the telephone operators and their supervisors for giving out his nonpublished number. But Jimmy's cursing accomplished nothing more than blowing off steam. As for the callers, Jimmy accused them of being enemies of God and condemned them one and all to everlasting hell.

Already troubled by Christ Town's progress—it would take a five-star miracle to complete the theme park by the Fourth of July—Jimmy's problems didn't end there. G.L.E.E. Club collections were at an all-time low, and losing the invaluable services of Beth Staples had him popping tranquilizers as if they were aspirins.

He sat morosely in the circular bed mulling over whether to take a sedative before or after breakfast when out of the corner of his eye he saw the sleeping Cora Lee with black patches over her eyes and plugs in her ears. Bounding from bed, he scurried to the bathroom and gobbled two Valiums like a junkie needing a fix.

It was Sunday and the domestic staff was reduced to kitchen personnel—a European-born cook and his wife, who also doubled as the housekeeper. The latter, a hefty woman with prominent features, sat reading the front page of the Virginia paper while her slender husband read over her shoulder. Jimmy's unexpected entrance wiped the amusement from their faces.

"Is that *my* paper?" Jimmy demanded.

The woman began to reassemble the Sunday paper, but Jimmy scooped it up and snatched the section she was holding from her hand.

"I will have my usual breakfast by the pool. And another thing," he added as he stopped at the door, "let Cora Lee answer the stinking phone."

Jimmy found refuge from the telephone calls by the cross-shaped pool in the rear of his million-dollar Virginia colonial, which overlooked a picturesque body of water he called "Lord's Lake." Over soft-boiled eggs and his daily apricot juice, he read the newspaper article for the fifth time. Its prominent display on page one led him to believe that Billy Hale still had some clout. But then, he reconsidered, newspapers thirsted for controversy, and religion was getting plenty of ink.

Jimmy detested the tabloids. Whenever he heard of another newspaper folding, he joyfully cheered the paper's demise. His contempt for the Fourth Estate dated back to the time an enterprising reporter for a Virginia paper had written a series of articles about him that were less than complimentary.

"Words without a face to speak them are not to be trusted," he combated this reporter over his G.L.E.E. Club television ministry. He never pursued it after the reporter fired back in bold print, "If what Jimmy Christian says is true, then how can he preach the faceless words of the Bible?"

Cora Lee appeared at the top of the stairs leading to the pool attired in a flowing peignoir, her hair in curlers. "You've got a phone call," she shouted in her shrill voice.

"Legitimate?"

"What do you mean, *legitimate?*"

"Is it another kook or someone I know?"

"Is C.D. Pittman a kook?"

212

"C.D. Pittman!" Jimmy said, springing from the chair and sprinting toward a yellow-striped cabana. Once inside, he plugged a white phone into a wall jack and changed his doomsday expression into instant cheerfulness. "C.D., what brings you to call me on Sunday morning? . . . You knew I wouldn't be at church? That's funny, C.D. . . . Sure, I read it. Not to worry. Billy's a senile old man shooting off sparklers . . . C.D., I certainly wasn't referring to *you* being old . . . What? My fault? I started a war with Billy? . . . Beth Staples? C.D., I didn't fire her . . . C.D.? *C.D.?"*

He stormed from the cabana too incensed with rage to notice Cora Lee carefully negotiating the steps in her high heels. A large glass of orange juice sloshed in her hand.

"The bastard," he said aloud. "The old bastard, hanging up on me!"

Cora Lee lowered herself into a lounge chair across the pool, oblivious to his concern. Her indifference only provoked him further.

"First Billy Hale, and now C.D. Pittman. I've been attacked by the ancients," he shouted. "Crickety-boned, old, old men," he moaned. "But if that atheist Pittman thinks he can screw with me, he's jerking off! Did you hear me, Cora Lee?"

"Jimmy, must I listen to your problems?"

"No, I didn't hear that."

"Yes, you did, and if you like, I'll say it again."

"I don't believe you," Jimmy said, walking around the pool toward her, his face fuming. "All of a sudden *you're* not involved? The Mercedes, the Continental, this house, ten fancy-priced dresses a week, and you can tell me you're not involved?"

"Billy didn't call me names in the paper. Matter of fact, I've heard he enjoys my singing."

Jimmy slapped his forehead with his hand. "Who can reason with you?" He threw up his hands in disgust. "Why do I *try?"* He began to pace, circling the pool. He tried to think, but nothing would take shape in his mind. All he could focus on was his frustration and rising anger. Suddenly, he stopped and turned around. "Cora Lee, that linebacker, that bufforilla I let you hire to take Beth Staples's job, she *goes!*"

"Uh-uh, Jimmy. Remember the probation agreement."

"*Ha!* The probation agreement."

"You can't worm your way out of that, Jimmy."

"The probation agreement," he kept repeating, working himself into a frenzy.

"Jimmy, what in a pig pen are you doing?" she asked, watching him drop his pajama bottom.

"Cora Lee—" He bent over, sticking his white rump in her face, "—here's what you can do with your probation agreement."

Before Cora Lee could activate her vocal cords and shatter his eardrums, Jimmy dove into the pool.

Wilma Mae Lombard drew the bedroom curtains open with a yank and admitted a flood of morning light. With a newspaper tucked under her arm, she moved to the bed where Harley lay sleeping.

"What the . . ." Harley yawned, sneaking a look at the alarm clock on the table next to the regal bed. It was six forty-five and he was not due at the World Cathedral until an hour before his eleven o'clock Sunday morning television service. He could have slept another hour; he glared at her. Then he buried his head in the soft pillow.

"Wake up, Harley. There's something you should read."

"Later, with coffee."

"It says in the newspaper that you are a demagogue and a false judge."

Harley sprang to a sitting position and grabbed the newspaper from her hand.

"Page one," she clued him.

The headline drove the last vestiges of sleep from his eyes. "How could he? How could he do this to me?"

"Undoubtedly, to stop you from making a fool of yourself."

He rose from the bed with his eyes still riveted to the

story. "Billy's been like a father to me. Why would he do this?"

"Might it occur to you that the man *believes* in what he says?"

Harley began to pace the length of the huge master suite. "Spite. He did it out of spite. He's jealous, Wilma Mae. Jealous of Virtues, Inc., of what I'm doing."

She laughed. "Billy Hale has never been nor will he ever be jealous of anything you do."

Harley's eyes brightened. "*The Republican Convention*! Billy must have caught word I'm giving the invocation and benediction. That's it."

She shook her head with great effort and Harley anticipated a crunching sound. Moving toward the door, she said to herself, "My father told me someday I'd come to realize what an asshole I married."

Harley threw the paper onto the floor, sending a shower of sections onto the thick carpet. "That's right, Wilma Mae, drive the spike into a wounded man. Billy blasts me for all the world to read and you've got to bust my balls."

She stopped at the door without looking back. "Such an act, Harley," she said. "Save it for the telecast. You'll need it."

"Goddammit! What is it with you, anyway? I'm becoming a household name, yet you keep trying to beat me down."

"Someone has to—you're in way over your head."

"Is that what you think?"

"Obviously Billy Hale does."

"*Billy Hale?* Who'd Billy ever elect president? He was a friend of Richard Waters, but he never got him elected."

Wilma Mae moved through the doorway and into the hall leading to her bedroom. Harley chased after her, stopping at his bedroom door. "The election of the next president of the United States is in *my* hands. Did you hear what I said?"

"Harley, you're a fool."

"No, Wilma Mae, not me. Your *father* was the fool. The pastor of a bunch of derelicts and poverty-mouthed,

215

lazy bastards. He was nothing, Wilma Mae, nothing. But I'm somebody and that burns your cold ass."

Wilma Mae stopped at the entrance to her bedroom and turned with surprising agility, her eyes puddling with tears. "At least my father stood on his own two feet. He was a man, Harley. He didn't need any advisors telling him what to do."

"No one tells me what to do. No one! I make all the decisions. *I am* Virtues, Inc."

She slammed the door in reply.

Harley paced angrily about his bedroom. "That douche bag calls me a fool? The goddamn pope couldn't pull off what I'm doing." He kicked the newspaper from his path. "Billy this, Billy that. He'll be sorry. He'll come begging for forgiveness."

Harley moved from one chair to another, but he could not remain seated. Finally, his eyes fell on the telephone. His lividness left him as he pushed the phone's buttons. His face melted into a smile as the connection went through. "Sue?"

CHAPTER 24

THE BENEDICTION was given for the Democratic National Convention. The president was renominated by his party, and most of the TV experts predicted he would not be evicted from the White House by the as-yet-to-be-confirmed Republican candidate, Senator Bartley Sinclair.

Jimmy Christian turned off the news report on the TV in the back of his limo and got out. He looked past the harbor at the two hundred feet of super-luxury anchored in deep water. There was virtually no ocean wind along this part of the Virginia coastline and the sweltering July sun drained energy from even aggressively spirited people like himself. He took off the light tan suit jacket and displayed a blue shirt soaked with perspiration about the collar and armpits. His unorthodox rendezvous with C.D. Pittman was something he felt could have waited. Construction of the Hell-Bent Express, Christ Town's featured amusement ride, was nearing completion and Jimmy thought his daily supervision was essential.

A swift motor launch knifed through the windless waters. "You Christian?" the driver yelled as he approached the dock.

Jimmy ignored the question and waited for the boat to dock alongside the pier.

"Are you Christian or not?"

"I'm *Reverend* Christian. Who are you?"

"From the *Morning Star*. I'm to pick up a Mr. Christian. No one said nothin' about Reverend."

"A little late, aren't you?" Jimmy said, stepping aboard.

Jimmy had not seen Pittman since the "Night of the

Disciples" telethon, when the billionaire had saved him from Christ Town's long list of creditors. Actually, he had spoken to C.D. Pittman only on two occasions, the latter being that Sunday morning at Lord's Lake he would have liked to forget. After Beth Staples's departure, there had been no communication whatsoever with C.D. Pittman, and Jimmy had been free to raise havoc with the construction foreman. He had paid little attention to Beth Staples's initial warnings concerning his interference; he had paid even less attention to Beth's fear over the contract he had signed with Pittman Industries. For, despite C.D. Pittman's reputation as a man-eater in the business world, Jimmy saw him as more eccentric donor than astute investor.

As the launch drew closer to the triple-decked floating mansion, Jimmy's eyes were drawn to the ship's smokestack. Painted in fiery red letters within the orb of a golden sun was the name *Morning Star*. It filled him with a vague uneasiness he could not explain. "Morning Star," he mused, searching his mind.

The launch reached the port side of the superstructure, looking like a codfish next to a whale, and Jimmy's eyes rose topside. A canvas-covered lift, the kind used to unload freighters, appeared over the side and slowly descended towards the launch. Surely, he told himself, this could not be the way he was to be taken aboard. Thinking there had to be a more conventional way, he asked the sailor, "Is *this* how I'm getting aboard?"

"Yeah," sneered the sailor, "like a piece of cargo."

No sooner had Jimmy stepped onto the lift than the cables jerked, causing the lift to lurch, and Jimmy clung for dear life to the hand rails. The electric winch was set to ascend at top speed and Jimmy looked down to see the grinning sailor shrink before his eyes. He could look no longer, and felt a weakness in his legs. Not until he reached the deck did he open his eyes.

A single deckhand, dressed in red bell-bottoms and a black tee-shirt bearing the ship's golden crest, helped him aboard and indicated that Jimmy should follow him. As he tried to keep up with his guide, Jimmy took notice of the recreation area which featured a deck-tennis court, Jacuzzi, and a swimming pool large even by cruise line standards. He took special notice of the swimming pool and was not impressed; the pool was only slightly larger than his own at Lord's Lake. But what he did not know was that the swimming pool's mosaic floor, at the touch of a button, could be converted to a dance floor.

Jimmy heard the sound of the crew's activity below and at points forward, yet there was not a soul to be seen. The swimming pool, sundeck, and a thatch-covered open bar surrounded by umbrella-shaded tables and chairs were deserted. Where were Pittman's guests? Surely he had guests. Family? Friends? Jimmy wondered. Perhaps the scorching ninety-six-degree temperature had chased them to the comfort of air-conditioned quarters below.

Unanswered questions continued to nag him. Why this meeting? Why had Pittman been so insistent, so adamant for it to be today? And why on his boat? Jimmy didn't like it, not one bit.

They approached an elevator and Jimmy noticed the life rafts set above the elevator's roof and held in place by metal clamps. He froze again on the name, *Morning Star*. "*Lucifer*," he gasped.

The deckhand looked at him peculiarly, then pushed the elevator button.

That's it, Jimmy thought—the name of this ship is a name given Lucifer. An eerie chill stole his breath. A disembodied voice spoke within his mind. Get out! Get away, lest he drag you into the pits of Hell. His body stiffened. His heart pounded in defiant protest of the warning voice. Nonsense, he reasoned. Hokum! Pittman was only a man, a mortal like himself. And that voice—that damned voice—it was Billy Hale's, he was sure. The words of an old and senile man, he told himself as the elevator door opened, awaiting him.

Jimmy slipped into his suit coat and wiped the sweat from his face with a damp handkerchief, feeling shamed and stupid. He was allowing himself to be intimidated. It was all beginning to fall into place. He should have known what was happening from the moment he was picked up on the dock by Pittman's surly employee, then brought aboard like a sack of provisions for the next cruise. Now, to be escorted by a mulish escort who acted as if he, Jimmy Christian, seen and heard by millions over his G.L.E.E. Club television ministry, the creator of the soon-to-be dedicated Christ Town, certain to be the talk of the religious world, was nothing more than a piece of meat being delivered to the great butcher, C.D. Pittman.

He could only figure that Pittman wanted him humbled, but he no longer cared. The fighting spirit which had brought him through many tough scrapes to the top of the evangelical ladder provided a psychological transfusion. His adrenalin was still pumping when the elevator opened two decks below.

Following the silent guide through a narrow hallway, Jimmy glanced at the original paintings with their themes from Early American folklore. When he searched among the gallery for something of a diabolical nature, the closest thing he could find was a witching scene of an autumn night with a full, glowing orange moon in a blackened sky above a pumpkin field. He had begun to doubt that Pittman had chosen a seldom-used theological name for Satan for his vessel intentionally, when they came to a large oak door with *C.D.* meticulously carved in script. Jimmy drew a deep breath as the burly guide pressed down on the silver door handle.

The vast stateroom was as elegant and lavishly appointed as any room Jimmy had ever seen on land. It ran the width of the yacht and was furnished with contemporary American furniture of the most expensive woods, metals, and fabrics. Oddly, Christian thought, nothing was nautical. They could have been in a penthouse suite.

He was captivated by the sight of the grandiose spiral staircase leading to what he assumed were C.D. Pittman's private quarters. He, himself, had such a staircase in his home at Lord's Lake, but somehow, he felt his to be inferior. As he further examined the extravagant fixtures, he compared them to those in his own living room. Why

220

did these seem so much better? Cora Lee, he reasoned, had a flair for making everything look like a toilet.

The gentle sound of running water shifted his curiosity. He looked at his guide, but the man seemed frozen at the foot of the staircase, as if he was waiting for God Himself to appear. Jimmy ventured farther into the room, to a corner where two marble columns served as the framework of an arched, hidden alcove. He looked between the columns and was not surprised to see the man-made waterfall with its crystal-clear water splashing down over fern-covered rocks and spilling into a black marble pool.

C.D. Pittman descended the staircase slowly, trailed by a valet bearing an enormous bath towel. Jimmy felt his presence as though a sudden current of electricity had streaked through the room, and he stepped back from the columns to see C.D. conferring in hushed tones with the man who had guided him to the stateroom. Jimmy realized the man was C.D.'s personal bodyguard and he took a deep breath. As C.D. approached, the evangelist flashed his best TV smile.

The sight of Pittman's nakedness as his valet helped him remove his robe filled Jimmy Christian with revulsion. His body was bloated, completely without muscle tone, the skin sagging and hideously wrinkled.

"Young man," Pittman said as he stepped gingerly into the pool, "you truly nauseate me."

"Is that right?" Jimmy replied angrily. "Well, you're not one of my favorite people either, and I didn't come here to watch you dog-paddle in a toy pool."

Pittman laughed so heartily he swallowed a mouthful of water. A fit of coughing cut short his mirth. *Choke, you old bastard*, Jimmy thought to himself.

"Speaking of dogs," Pittman said, regaining his composure, "I once had a dog when I was a child. Damned thing was always begging. You remind me of that dog."

Jimmy was not accustomed to such castigation. It was usually he who did the insulting and condemning, and he was unable to defend himself with words which did not include vulgarity. As the naked Pittman came out of the

221

pool, Jimmy's steaming eyes shifted to the valet who obediently handed the old billionaire the towel.

"Alfred, I shall delay having my Bloody Mary. I only drink with friends."

The valet assisted Pittman into his robe, bowed, and left the stateroom, as Jimmy wondered what kind of friends the industrialist really had. Fellow buccaneers of industry, he thought, bracing for a confrontation.

Pittman brushed past him and headed for a green wingback chair. Jimmy slowly turned to follow, but realized there were no chairs close to where Pittman was seated.

"Do you *mind* if I sit down?"

Pittman pointed to a straight-backed wooden chair of Federal Period ancestry, a good distance from him. It was a museum piece, not a chair to provide comfort for a guest. Jimmy was hesitant at first, then sat down stiffly and studied the face of his belligerent host. Pittman had no beard or mustache to cover the flaws of a drooping chin and tightly pinched mouth. Except for those bushy white eyebrows, Christian thought, there was nothing at all distinctive about Pittman's face: it was simply old.

Pittman broke the awkward silence. "I hear the gimp, Billy Hale, whipped you with his cane."

Christian squirmed. Only Beth Staples could have told him that. "Yes, he did," Jimmy admitted. "Fortunately for Billy, he's an *old* man or I would have hurt him."

Pittman slapped his right knee. "Ha, *you?* As much as I loathe Hale, he would have beaten you into the ground. Old as I am, I believe I could clean this room with you."

Jimmy laughed to himself. Jesus, he thought, the old geezer was actually challenging him to a fist fight.

"Speaking of Hale," Pittman continued, "I'd dance on his grave, yet I respect him. You I neither like nor respect."

"Look," Jimmy said threateningly, "I don't give a hoot in hell what you think of me. I suggest—"

"*You* suggest? You suggest nothing! Is that clear?"

"No," said Jimmy, coming out of the chair, "it's not clear. I don't have to sit here and take this crap from you, you godless heathen."

"Well, well," Pittman smiled. "Didn't think you had it in you."

"You sent for me and I'm here. So why not get to the reason."

"Very well," Pittman said, reaching for a silver humidor and withdrawing a long, hand-wrapped Cuban cigar. He removed the wrapper and bit off the tip, then pointed the cigar at Christian like an elderly schoolmaster lecturing a laggard student. "As of midnight last night, you owe me five million, two hundred and three thousand, four hundred sixty-five dollars and eleven cents. Did you bring a cashier's check?"

"*What?*" Jimmy gasped.

"I'm referring to the interest on my loan."

"C.D., you're not serious."

"Young man, I'm deadly serious. Surely you're not so foolish as to expect me to disregard what is mine?"

"C.D., c'mon, you're kidding."

"Apparently you are not familiar with my reputation as an astute businessman. You borrow from me, you adhere to my terms. Just like a bank."

"Jesus, C.D., when Christ Town is completed, it will be *bigger* than Disney World."

"I hope so."

"There'll be enough for your damned interest one hundred times over."

"*Mister* Christian, I am not in the charity business. I learned at a tender age that to involve oneself in charitable organizations is a sure-fire way of going broke."

"Dammit, Pittman, I'll sue!"

"Sue, you say? Well, anything's possible. You might have your day in court. But I'm afraid you gave up your rights to litigation, as well as arbitration, when you failed to pay the interest at the designated time."

"My lawyers won't see it that way."

"Your lawyers," C.D. mocked. "Your lawyers were fools for letting you and your wife sign the contract in the first place. As of this moment, I own everything in Christ Town. That includes your new Glee Club communications

223

center and the rubber bands on your desk. Also, Mr. Christian, in a monetary sense, I own everything you and your wife possess, including the second-rate mansion you so ostentatiously call 'Lord's Lake.' "

The toughness had melted from Jimmy's voice. "C.D., *please*. For Chrissakes, you can't do this to me."

"You're begging. Just like that dog."

"All right, I'm begging. But give me a week, *three* days. I'll get the money."

"How, Mister Christian? By selling the grave sites belonging to people you've already fleeced?"

"You can't just ruin someone's life. Everything I've worked for. Christ Town is *mine*. I created it. I'll . . . I'll stop you, Pittman! I'll burn Christ Town to the ground before you'll own it."

"Unfortunately, the insurance would not cover my investment or time. Therefore, be warned: if you set one foot inside Christ Town, you shall be arrested for trespassing."

"Billy Hale was right all along. You are the devil."

"I am only protecting what is mine. However, since Billy Hale saw fit to advise you, perhaps my suggestion will provide a remedy for your troubles."

Jimmy wore the relieved expression of a man facing a firing squad and learning there were no bullets in the rifles. His ears strained to hear words of mercy and he leaned forward, ready to clutch at any straw Pittman extended.

An evil grin appeared on the old man's thin lips. "There is always suicide," Pittman recommended.

"You . . . you stinking fiend! You no-good son of a bitch!"

At the sound of Jimmy's outburst, the door opened and Pittman's muscular bodyguard appeared, ready to strike at the snap of his employer's fingers.

"Garrett, get this con man off my yacht. I can no longer stand the sight of him."

Despite his bantam size, Jimmy pushed the larger man's hand from his elbow and walked to the door.

"Garrett," Pittman called after his man, "I hope the crew has been alerted. We wouldn't want it known that we didn't give the Right Reverend Christian a proper salute."

Christian was nearing the elevator when a familiar voice stopped him in his tracks. He turned and was shocked to see Beth Staples standing in the passageway. She was wearing a red, one-piece swimsuit, and held a white terrycloth coverup. She had been the object of his dreams, a woman he had truly lusted for, but he now saw her as the enemy, a turncoat. As she approached him, her graceful sway was met by an expression of contempt rather than desire.

"Et tu, Brute?"

She did not answer. Instead, she spoke in a whisper to Pittman's taciturn bodyguard, who reluctantly yielded to her request. As he passed, he shot Jimmy a warning look, then went to stand guard by the elevator.

"You sold me out, huh, Beth? You sold me out to the devil."

"No, Jimmy, you have only yourself to blame. How many times did I warn you about that contract?"

"What kind of contract did *you* make?"

"I don't have to apologize for anything I've done. Can you say the same, Jimmy?"

His pain was too great for him to reflect on old wounds. The thought of losing Christ Town was too overwhelming to evoke false courage. "Beth, he can't do this to me. He can't, Beth. I'll be ruined."

"You must believe it was not my idea for you to come here. I had hoped C.D. would reconsider and give you an extension. Apparently, I was wrong. But there's still a chance."

"Beth, don't build me up unless you know something."

"Stay at home and, for God's sake, don't go near Christ Town. I'll get in touch with you through Bucky."

"Beth, can you really save me?"

Save him, she thought. As if he deserved saving. "I don't know, Jimmy. It might depend on whether I'm willing to sell *my* soul."

His look was one of confusion.

"I can't promise you anything, Jimmy. I can only try."

Jimmy took the elevator to the upper deck. The heat was still oppressive, but a wall of angry clouds had rolled in from the southwest and thunder grumbled in the distance. He was too emotionally devastated to notice the gathering storm. He also failed to notice the ship's company gathered around the waiting cargo lift. Walking after his guide with eyes fixed on the deck's polished planking, he was unaware of the final humiliation Pittman was about to inflict.

As Jimmy approached the lift, a deckhand stepped in front of him waving a five-dollar bill. "Reverend," the man leered, "what kind of prayer can I get for this?"

"Hey, Rev," another said, flashing a ten-spot, "whatever he gets, I want double."

The men hooted derisively as Christian made his way past them, his pride crushed. All of them were waving money.

"Listen, Preacher," said another, "there's this great piece of ass in Nantucket. I'll give you twenty for a prayer that I get into her pants."

A breeze came up suddenly as a severely depressed Jimmy Christian stepped into the lift. Lightning flashed and a clap of thunder drowned out the jeering chorus. A gust of wind caught the lift and spun it against the hull. Jimmy looked down at the frothing whitecaps stirred by the sudden onset of the storm. He became gripped by an urge, an impulse to destroy himself. But the will to live was stronger. "No! *No!*" he shouted out—repeating the word again and again, until he had banished the suicidal urge and seethed again with hatred for the man who had brought him to the most humiliating moment of his life.

Standing at the rail of the second deck in the driving rain, Beth Staples realized the intolerable pain Jimmy was experiencing. She watched in agony as the forlorn figure finished his swaying descent to the tossing launch, and winced when he lost his footing and almost fell into the water while entering the pitching craft. The bitterness she harbored toward him was diluted by a growing sense of deep compassion. As she watched the pathetic figure being transported toward land, she was unable to suppress her emotions. Beth Staples quietly wept.

low, the man in the wheelchair. "Multiple sclerosis-uh?" he asked, as he watched the palsied hands. "Cal... California," Langly hissed, the sick brightening, the emotion flush upper lip-ah wept.

CHAPTER 25

IT LOOKED LIKE the waiting room in a medical clinic. A collection of people with diverse physical handicaps—the most conspicuous a man in a wheelchair—sat in folding chairs being coached by a neatly groomed young man who obviously had done this many times before. "Remember," he instructed, tucking his fingers into the vest pockets of a lightweight green suit, "Reverend Langly must speak to you first." His eyes went to the back of the room, where a circle of motherly ladies sat patiently. "Your *guardians*, sitting in the rear, will inform Reverend Langly of your respective afflictions."

Suddenly, the door swung open and all eyes turned towards a humpty-dumpty, middle-aged man with large, hanging jowls. "Prayyyy-zuh Gee-zus," he heralded in a quavering voice.

"Praise Jesus," the guardians responded over a chorus of murmurs from the "chosen" afflicted.

Reverend Wallace Langly, Jr., smiled and rubbed his hands together, surveying his selected props. "And what is your affliction-uh?" he asked a middle-aged woman.

She held up a gnarled hand.

"Arthritis," said the aide.

Langly's interest went to the woman's other hand. It appeared normal. He seemed disappointed and moved on. "And what is *your* affliction-uh?" he asked another.

The white-haired man pointed a trembling finger to a milky eye. "Blind," he said as if it were a curse from Satan.

"Yay-us," Langly gleefully exclaimed, then stood before the man in the wheelchair. "Multiple sclerosis? Muscular dystrophy? Brain tumor? Polio?" he rattled off hopefully.

"A massive stroke, Reverend Langly," the aide informed him.

"We shall *smite* the *stroke*," Langly said, drifting to the next candidate.

This particular man had no visible infirmities, and Langly assumed from the redness of his face and the bags under his eyes that the man was an alcoholic. "Fow-elll, wretched alcohol! The drink of the devil!"

"I drink a little," the man slurred. Pointing to a bulbous nose which began to run, he boasted, "I can make it drip any time I want."

Langly stiffened. He glared at his youthful subordinate. "You bring *me* a runny nose? A common cold?"

"Uh, Reverend," the aide added quickly, "this man is also stone deaf in one ear. *Aren't* you, sir?"

"Huh? Oh, sure. Sure I am."

"Righeeet," Langly said, drawing out the syllable as if it couldn't bear to leave his mouth. Turning, he left as he came, praising Jesus.

The aide had loosened his tie and let out a sigh when the man with the runny nose nudged him and whispered conspiratorially in his ear. "I still get the hundred bucks, don't I?"

Nobody had expected Wallace Langly, Jr., to follow in his late father's faith-healing footsteps. He simply lacked the tools of the trade—the essential qualities prescribed in the unwritten faith healer's handbook. Unlike his late father, he was not gifted with the booming voice that could chill one's blood, or the burning eyes to penetrate one's soul. Instead, he spoke in a voice which made children laugh, and his soft eyes were those of a puppy expressing a need to be loved. To his father's great disappointment, Wallace was sadly afflicted with the image of a clown.

The only thing he had in common with his father was that he became an accredited minister. But even with these credentials, he was unwanted. He was for a time the assistant pastor in Wheeling, West Virginia, but when the pastor was killed in an automobile accident, he had replaced him for only a month when his congregation urgently summoned another minister to relieve him of his duties. He was finally given a parsonage in a rural territory other ministers referred to as "Purgatory Junction." Langly was there when the news came of his father's violent death during Billy Hale's "Night of Life" campaign at the Hollywood Bowl.

His father's aunt was the person responsible for his becoming a faith healer. The idea came to her at her nephew's funeral, when Wallace gave the eulogy over his father's grave. The obvious, the incredible, and all the other reasons why he could not ever be successful were overruled by her recognizing something unique in this pathetic little man.

An avid television viewer, a soap opera fanatic, she reasoned that, with sufficient television exposure week after week, people became acclimated even to the asinine. She pursued the idea and saw that Wallace would not only be accepted, but could be a refreshing face among the pompous and pious evangelists in the growing electronic church.

Wallace Langly fulfilled his great-aunt's hope, and beat the odds with his outrageous brand of evangelical faith healing. His television fame surpassed that of his late father's to the extent that he was able to quietly drop the "Junior" from his name. His "Ministry of Miracles" televised healing services were seen in almost as many markets as Jimmy Christian's "G.L.E.E. Club" and Harley Lombard's "Ministry of Might." Though both Jimmy and Harley considered him a farce, he had become a major force in the world of televised religion. The membership of his ministry had increased sixty-six percent in the last eighteen months—twice as much as any other ministry of the airwaves.

A reporter writing for a national magazine best summed up Wallace Langly's success: "Wallace Langly's traveling

'Lourdes,' which heals everything from acne to leprosy with a hocus-pocus, forehead-zapping style, is the best sit-com TV series of the season. The professionals should be so funny. Langly might be the comedian of the decade. And if you're among those who believe Langly is just a fad, as Batman was to fraternities in the sixties, don't bet on it. There is, and always will be, a reservoir of sick and handicapped people for faith healers like Langly to tap. As pure theater, Langly and his religious road show rate four stars. How many stars the Almighty awards him is a matter for conjecture.''

The road show had descended on the upstate New York hamlet of McCrory. The citizenry of this scenic town, with its patriotic and God-fearing reputation, was rapidly filling up the newly furbished armory, with its seating capacity of three thousand, for the evening's event. But the promoter, a town councilman and Langly's cousin, was bitterly disappointed after hearing it would not be televised.

Wallace Langly was slumped in a chair in the armory's cramped backstage dressing room, speaking to the man who served as producer and executive director of his "Ministry of Miracles."

"I don't like it," Langly said. "I shouldn't have let you talk me into coming here. I don't like it, Jerry. Not a tidbit."

"Wally," soothed his tall, horse-faced associate, "we do Rochester Saturday and Sunday, then two days in Buffalo, and before you know it we're working our way back to Oklahoma City."

"Something's wrong, Jerry. I can feel it."

"Wally, relax. We're not taping. You can wing it without working up a sweat. It's the perfect opportunity for you to try something new——maybe even heal a heart attack victim on stage. Besides, you're doing this town for your aunt, not your cousin. You owe her that much."

"For how long must I be owing her?"

"You know she's a lifelong governor of the ministry."

"I know she's ninety-two years old. Most people die before ninety-two, but not Auntie. She lives just to remind me of how much I owe her. And I'm *not* staying at my cousin's home overnight. I can't stand the man.''

''You won't have to stick around here. I've arranged for transportation to take you to the Marriott in Rochester. It's only about forty-five miles away.''

''Jerry, something keeps telling me I shouldn't be here.''

''That's what you said about Albany and Schenectady. And what happened? Ten thousand new members and we sold out of merchandise.''

Langly moved to the dusty mirror above the dressing table and studied his long face with a nose like a curved blade. It was as if he was searching for the reflection of a guardian angel in his sad, soft eyes.

''Wally, want to tell me what's really bothering you?''

Langly continued to gaze at his reflection. ''The killings, Jerry.''

''Wally, you're letting Billy Hale's paranoia get to you.''

Langly spun from the mirror. ''Jerry, I want bodyguards. I *demand* bodyguards.''

''Now, Wally, bodyguards are bad for your image. You know that. You're a miracle worker. A man who cures people.''

''So did the Lord Gee-zus, and they crucified him.''

Jerry shook his head. ''All right, Wally, all right. I'll get you bodyguards.''

''When?''

The door opened and Wallace Langly's cousin, the last person in the world the faith healer wished to see, entered, smiling as if he had a winning ticket to the Irish Sweepstakes.

''A packed house, Wallace,'' the man said jubilantly. ''We can't put another soul in the place.''

''*Won*-derful,'' Langly said with forced cheer.

''I told you, Jerry. Didn't I tell you McCrory would do it? I told him, Wallace.''

''Yes, yes, you did.'' Jerry looked at Langly. ''He did tell me, Wally.''

''Prayyyy-zuh the Lord-uh,'' said Langly, fleeing to the bathroom and slamming the door behind him.

''Wallace?'' the man called after him. But there was no

reply from the bathroom and Langly's cousin turned to the producer with a puzzled look on his face.

"Your cousin needs time for concentration," Jerry explained.

"Concentration?"

"To commune with God."

"In a bathroom?"

"A spiritual idiosyncracy."

"Jerry, you should have televised tonight. I mean, I've got a lot of explaining to do."

"Next year, I promise," said Jerry, leading the man from the room.

"Never!" Langly shouted from the bathroom, as he opened his fly and interrupted his communion with God.

A brandy-colored limousine rolled along a narrow stretch of country road in a lingering summer twilight. It passed miles of orchards and vineyards characteristic of this region of New York State. Nearing McCrory's town limits, there were few "For Sale" posters along the road, indicating that perhaps the bulldozers of "progress" would not soon turn McCrory and its rustic surroundings into a galaxy of pre-fab homes and condominiums.

The limousine drove past block after block of stately white homes on elm-lined streets until it reached the small, quaint business district. As it circled the square in the center of town with its covered bandstand, a visitor could almost hear the strains of Sousa marches floating on the still night air. Unlike most towns, McCrory had remained a town. And the old, remodeled armory still housed the town's major indoor recreational and civic events.

The armory's parking facilities were filled and the entrance was blocked off with a long line of sawhorses. Across the street, the Lutheran Church's empty parking lot was closed off by an iron chain. The lot normally handled the overflow for armory events which did not conflict with church services. It was quite obvious that the church's pastor had not put his spiritual stamp of approval upon Wallace Langly's faith-healing business.

The limousine's chauffeur was not concerned about the shortage of authorized parking spaces. He brought the limousine to a stop directly in front of the armory entrance. The chauffeur, a short, wiry man attired in formal gray livery with matching cap, left the car and raced up the concrete steps, taking them two at a time. Each of the three doors he tried was locked, and he returned to the center door and began to pound on it with a gloved fist. A security guard cracked the door open and a blast of gospel music burst into the night.

"Sorry, no more," the security guard informed rudely. "Fire rules—"

"Get me one of Reverend Langly's people," the chauffeur said in a belligerent voice which matched a face bearing traces of a pugilistic past.

The guard gave the man a long, appraising look. "Wait a minute," he said, closing the door.

It was five minutes before the young man who had rehearsed the chosen afflicted peered out from the partially open door. "May I help you?" he asked politely.

From within the limousine, an old man with unruly white hair watched with interest as his chauffeur conversed with Langly's trusted aide. A smile rippled on his parched lips as he saw the aide become increasingly drawn into the conversation. The smile spread as he witnessed the twenty-dollar bill disappear into the young man's suit pocket.

Inside the armory, the Ministry of Miracles singers, backed up by a seven-piece band, concluded their musical solicitation, "Invest in God's Band and Be Rich in Heaven," as Wallace Langly merrily bounced onto the stage. "Did they laugh at Gee-zus when He raised Lazarus from thee dead? Did they scorn Him when He gave sight to thee blind? Fed thee multitudes? Cured thee lepers? *Noooooo-oo*-uh."

He thrust out his arms, wiggling his fingers. "Thee power from Heaven works through these blessed fingers. Those, *yah-us*, those who laugh, who spread lies, who slander me, who mock me, are in big—I mean *big* trouble." He dropped his arms and shook a finger as if only he knew of his skeptics' eternal fate. "My friends-uh, members of this ministry, there is no laughing in Hell. *Noooo-uh.* No-*sireeee.*"

The audience thundered its approval as the slow-footed old man walked down the far aisle following the bribed aide, who carried a folding chair. On stage, Wallace Langly's spur-of-the-moment decision to shorten his lengthy sermon on Hell pushed the ministry's singers into service with "Better to Believe than Burn."

Wallace Langly noticed the old man and sailed to the rampway where the afflicted would come on stage. Crooking his neck like a pigeon, he waited for the old man to sit, then signalled for his aide to approach the ramp.

"What is that old man's affliction-uh?" Langly whispered.

"Megabucks," said the aide.

Langly smiled warmly at the old man, then strode toward center stage, ready to roll with his "mind over matter" religious magic show. It was time for the main event—what row after row of the sickly, the depressed and handicapped had come for. All were in need of fast miracles, and not the kind prescribed by the medical profession.

Several of the sturdier male singers remained on stage to act as catchers, in case any of the miracle-seekers fainted from the cosmic force of Wallace Langly's healing hands. The show would begin with the chosen afflicted. Their awed testimony usually generated enough mass electricity to charge deadened nerves and aching muscles. A guardian, posing as a wife, led the blind man on stage. "The doctors say the eye is inoperable," the woman said, her voice breaking.

Langly looked gravely at the man. "Are you born a-gain?"

"I . . . I believe."

"If you are not born a-gain, you shall go to everlasting Hell. Do you wish to go to everlasting Hell?"

"No." The man shivered at the thought.

Langly's hand covered the man's eye. "In thee name of Gee-zus, I command Satan to abandon theeee-uh!"

The man blinked prematurely. "Yes, yes, I can see. I can see!" He shouted like an actor in a third-rate movie.

"Praise God," said the guardian, wiping away her tears.

"A miraculllll," Langly exclaimed blissfully as he turned to the crowd and spread his arms.

The audience applauded, but the old man sat impassively.

"Do you love Gee-zus for the great miraculll He has given you?" Langly asked with a nervous laugh.

"Yes, I love Jesus," the "healed" man replied.

Langly waved his arms in glory. Again the audience applauded. The old man smiled smugly.

Next, he healed the woman with the arthritic hand, at least to the extent that she flexed it, then straightened out a man's curved spine, cured an ulcer, and relieved a woman of her migraine headache. Then it was time for the evening's big-ticket miracle, the stroke-smitten man in the wheelchair. "Has he given up on God?" Langly asked the guardian, woefully shaking his head.

"At times," she confessed.

Langly frowned at the man. "Do you think God is paralyzed? Nooo-uh," he exclaimed before the man could part his lips. "Are you a partner in the ministry?"

"Yes," the guardian cut in. "He has filled out his membership card and given his tax-free twenty dollars to the Lord."

"Yay-us, a membership to the Ministry of Miracles is a passport to Heaven."

"I bought your healing towel," the crippled man volunteered, much to the dismay of his guardian, who thought he was mute.

"And it shall wipe the sins from your mind," Langly quickly replied, as he placed his hands upon the man's balding head. "Gee-zus, make this man walk a-gain." His hands pressed harder into the man's scalp. "Let him walk among the non-believers as standing testimony." He pressed even harder and the man winced from the pain. "Heal!" he commanded. "Oooo-uh," he shouted, tearing his hands away from the man's bruised head. "Did you feel the power of Gee-zus?'' Langly asked in a tone that precluded a response.

The man looked blankly at Langly as if he had missed a cue.

''Why do you sit in that wheelchair? The Lord wants you to riiiise-uh.''

The man sprang to his feet and Langly's face soured. If this had been televised, it would certainly be edited from the tape. But as the man romped about the stage without the slightest indication of ever having been paralyzed, the audience clapped louder than before. The old man in the first row quietly left his chair.

Langly had just finished healing a club foot when the half-deaf man who could make his nose run at will stood before him with the last of the guardians. He was smiling, and Langly was disturbed by it. In less than an hour his case history had changed to stone deafness, and the man stood, staring vapidly.

Provoked by the silly grin, Langly hurried the miracle and stuck his index fingers into the man's ears. ''Come owwwwt,'' he demanded shrilly. Retrieving his fingers, he then spoke into the man's ears. ''Ma-ma. Say, ma-ma.''

The man's dumb grin widened.

''Say ma . . . ma,'' Langly went from ear to ear, but there was no reply. As Langly mouthed the word so that an imbecile could read his lips, the guardian grasped the soft flesh under each of the man's arms and pinched hard. ''Ma-ma!'' the man shrilled.

''Praaaayyyy-zuh the Lord-uh,'' Langly exulted. ''He hears. A miracullll!'' He then proceeded to zap the grinning man's forehead with such force that the loud thud could be heard throughout the hall.

''*Holy shit*,'' yelped the man as he collapsed backward into the arms of the catchers.

The faith-healing crusade was over by 9:30 and the Ministry of Miracles treasury was forty thousand dollars richer in new memberships. An additional twenty thousand dollars was collected from the sale of healing towels, healing face cloths, healing coffee mugs, and Wallace

Langly's new healing book, *With These Hands*. The two thousand people who paid for their annual membership cards would each, in the course of one year, spend an additional fifty to one hundred dollars for various ministry merchandise and fund-raising programs. As one of Wallace Langly's many critics wrote, "Once your name, address, and social security number are fed into Wallace Langly's Ministry of Miracles computer, you have been *religiously* had."

Wallace Langly slipped unobtrusively out the back exit and into a raven-black vintage Cadillac which would take him to Rochester. It was a contented faith healer who sat back and closed his eyes. He was pleased by his quick getaway. The fact that he wasn't being chauffeured in some plush, streamlined limousine did not faze his ego. In his frame of mind, he would have accepted a ride on a moped. McCrory was now behind him, along with that ominous premonition of lurking danger. The last time a man of God was murdered now seemed a long time ago.

His driver, a full-blooded Mohawk Indian, need not be told to refrain from initiating conversation. He was quiet by nature, and, from the way he grimly looked into the rearview mirror, he either did not like or did not trust people with born-again religious affiliations. Perhaps it had something to do with his Indian heritage.

Wallace Langly would be forty-five next month and he yearned for a change in his life—something that might broaden his horizons. He had reached the top in the faith-healing profession, with no serious challengers. He had considered expanding his ministry to Europe or Asia, but his pony-puss advisor, Jerry, spoke convincingly of the numerous drawbacks. His unusual style, the natural comedic delivery which was accepted in America, might not do well in translation. In many foreign places, the citizenry took their religion quite seriously, some fanatically so.

He was more in a quandary over his dull personal life. He had never married. Rejection by women was routine, yet Wallace Langly continued to have eyes for only the most attractive. He narrowly missed marriage on two sepa-

238

rate occasions, years apart, when each of the women had similar second thoughts about spending the rest of their lives with a fat, insipid faith healer.

Finally, he had given up his pursuit of a mate after his experience with an attractive divorcée who had hidden ambitions. She called off the wedding after learning his wealth was tied up in the ministry. Less his modest salary, the ministry's assets were secure from any divorce rulings. Wallace Langly could not produce the miracle she expected.

Langly's thoughts dimmed as he rode on into the night. Suddenly, an explosion from the rear tire thrust him forward, his shoulders smacking against the front seat. Another jolt knocked him to the floor. The Mohawk cursed in his native Amerind as he fought for control of the careening vehicle, which skidded off the road and tilted heavily to one side before it came to a crashing halt against a grassy embankment.

Wallace Langly struggled to the window and peered out into the moonlit, desolate countryside. Blood trickled from a cut lip and his face was ashen. The Indian sat motionless in the front seat. He seemed in no hurry to check the damage.

"Have you a gun?" Langly asked, trying to keep his voice from shaking.

"No gun," said the Indian.

"Do you have a telephone in this car?"

"No phone."

"You have no gun, you have no telephone. Are you going to just sit there like a cigar-store Indian?"

The bright beam of headlights from an approaching car reflected in the rearview mirror. "A car's coming," the Indian said, opening his door. "You—stay here."

Wallace Langly stared ahead as the brandy-colored limousine slowly passed the arm-waving Indian, then pulled to the side of the road onto the narrow dirt shoulder. The old man looked out from the tinted rear-door window and watched his chauffeur following the cursing Indian to the crippled vehicle.

The men scanned the mangled wheels and the Indian

went to the rear door to relay their findings. "You, get out!" the Indian instructed Langly curtly as he opened the bent door.

Wallace Langly scowled at the Mohawk, then turned to the smartly uniformed chauffeur. "What is this stupid man saying-uh?" he asked him.

The chauffeur kept drifting farther away from the car. "I think he's telling you there could be another bomb."

"Bomb?" Langly choked on the word, bruising a knee in a desperate exit from the car.

The faith healer did not need to be convinced that someone had just tried to kill him, and he moved quickly to the limousine. He sighed in relief as he recognized the old man. "Praayyyy-zuh Gee-zus," he said, scrambling in beside him.

The old man seemed not to hear. His eyes were fixed intently on Langly's hands.

Poor devil, mute and deaf, thought Langly as the limo pulled onto the road. Leaning forward, noticing the telephone in the front, Langly spoke to the chauffeur. "Driver, have you notified the police-uh?"

"The line was busy," the chauffeur said. He held up a small metal device. "This little bugger is what did you in."

Langly's face went white. "Stop this car!" he demanded.

"Shut your fuckin' mouth!" the chauffeur shouted.

Langly reached instinctively for the door handle, but the sight of the .357 Magnum in the old man's hand paralyzed him.

"Face it, you're a dead man," the chauffeur said over his shoulder.

"Shut up and drive," Ron Rebuck commanded, holding the gun on the terrified faith healer.

The limousine sped past the expressway entrance and went another three miles before it pulled onto a dusty trail flanked by shrubs and dense with trees. Ahead, the reflection of a half moon shone upon a dilapidated barn where Ike Vesper waited beside a royal-blue sedan.

The limousine rolled into the doorless barn, bumping

240

into cast-off farming equipment. As the chauffeur turned off the lights and engine, Wallace Langly could feel his blood rushing to his head. His eyes glittered feverishly in the blackness. He was unable to secrete the saliva needed to soothe his dry throat, and his healing hands were wet and clammy. With the Magnum's barrel poking into his side, he stumbled out of the car and smelled a musty odor thick with decay. All at once, he thought of his late father.

Seeing Ike Vesper, handcuffs dangling from one hand and a roll of tape clutched in the other, Langly thought he must be looking at a demon from the depths of hell. "Mercy," he begged, looking up into Ike's fierce black eyes. "Mercy," he whined as Ike cuffed his wrists behind his back. *"Mercy!"* he screamed into the silent night, before Ike slapped the tape over his mouth and muffled his pleas.

The blue sedan bypassed downtown Rochester and headed in the direction of Lake Ontario's New York shoreline. Ike manned the wheel. Next to him, the old man was no longer old; Ron Rebuck had tediously peeled the latex from his skin and removed the scraggly white wig from his head. Behind Rebuck, with his feet braced against the bound and gagged Wallace Langly, the chauffeur had also shed twenty years. Golden haired and deeply tanned, he had the look of a California surfer.

Unlike Rebuck and Vesper, who had changed into summer slacks and sport shirts, Golden Boy wore faded jeans and a black tee-shirt printed with a pierced Valentine heart dripping blood. His shiny black boots ground into Wallace Langly's chest whenever he felt the faith healer becoming too restless.

Ron Rebuck was thinking deep within himself, unable to extract a reason for his and Ike's limited participation in "Operation Heel." Upon reaching their destination, it was Golden Boy's responsibility to deliver the faith healer to someone. What was the captain telling him? Rebuck wondered. And what had the faith healer done? And to whom? The captain? The pun in the code name, "heel" as in "heal," had not escaped Rebuck. He puzzled over the riddle; the captain's riddle, he was sure.

The sedan cruised past summer homes and cottages clustered along Lake Ontario's beaches. Langly's manacled hands were numb, he was frightened, and the tape had pulled open the cut on his lip. Yet his will to survive would not negotiate with alien death. The hopeful thought that he would be held for ransom and eventually released ran through his mind. Jerry, reliable Jerry, his trusted director of the ministry, would *surely* be contacted. Jerry would give them whatever money they wanted. Jerry was loyal, a good Christian man. Yes, Jerry would take care of it. Unless, unless Jerry—and *Auntie?* Oh, how she would love to see her grandson take over *my* ministry. Could they? Would they? Were they *all* involved? "Noooo," he hollered through the gagging tape, only to receive a vicious kick in the ribs.

The sedan had reached a deserted stretch of lakefront. Ike's eyes had momentarily left the road to look at the map for his landmark when Golden Boy shouted in his ear. "Slow down, you dumb ape. You'll miss the turn."

Ike felt Rebuck's hand on his elbow. "It's okay, Little Brotha. I read this turkey. I've seen his act before."

The dark road was once an access to a public boat ramp and came to a dead end. Ike flashed the high beams three times.

"Well, this is where we say goodbye," Golden Boy said, dragging Wallace Langly from the car. As Rebuck and Vesper watched, he shoved and kicked the faith healer in the direction of the narrow path. When the sobbing Langly stumbled, a kick to his spine drove him face first into the weeds and brush.

"Brave punk," Ike hissed. "I'd like to meet up wi' that garbage, one on one."

The helicopter was five thousand feet over Lake Ontario, midway between the United States and Canada, maintaining its blackout. Harnessed tightly into his seat by belts across his waist and chest, Wallace Langly had been freed of the gag and was begging for his life.

"It wasn't me," he sweated in his defense. "I've never been in Elkton, Maryland, or Greensburg, Pennsylvania. As Geezus is my witness, you have the wronnnng man-uh." His sweat thickened. His voice grew hoarse. "Pleeeez-uh believe me. I never stole money from your mother. I never tried to cure her cancer. It couldn't have been me. Twelve years ago I was an assistant pastor. It had to have been my father, Wallace Langly, *Sr.*"

Captain Claude Gemmer passed sentence.

"Can you fly?"

Thirty-six hours passed before Wallace Langly's bloated body was discovered bobbing in Lake Ontario by fishermen. Once more, the media decried it as another religious killing. Editorials made Langly out to be either a clown of Christ or a saint. A born-again U.S. senator called for an immediate Senate investigation into the rash of murders of religious people. A New Orleans evangelist did his preaching holding a shotgun. Harley Lombard was unavailable for comment and a selected spokesman for Virtues, Inc., told how deeply saddened Reverend Lombard was when given the news. In fact, Harley's precise words to Sue Bergman were, "Who gives a shit?" No one from the press spoke to Jimmy Christian because no one was able to contact him. Schools did not close; flags were not lowered to half-mast. In Europe, Lourdes did not close in memorial. No one really seemed to care.

Billy Hale cared though. He cared plenty.

CHAPTER 26

BILL HALE'S FAMOUS guest was no stranger to his Shenandoah home. When he was president, Richard Waters would occasionally fly in by helicopter from the White House to spend the day. "Camp Billy," his aides called it. The security people had a less flattering name.

They spoke of times past, reminiscing over when their paths first crossed. There was nothing maudlin about their memories as they recalled their first meeting at a communion breakfast for the newly elected Senator Richard Waters. The junior senator had relinquished his claim as heir to the family-owned Great Pacific Ship Builders Corporation to enter politics. In his first outing, he won a split decision over a former governor in the Oregon U.S. Senate primary, then went on to upset the favored Democratic incumbent. At the time, Billy's star was also rising. His syndicated column appeared in two hundred newspapers and he was the only notable evangelist on television. After Billy had given the communion benediction, Waters had taken amiable exception to a Biblical occurrence Billy had mentioned, calling it an example of the pure myth which occurs in the Bible. The fundamentalist Billy gave no ground, yet found Waters to be a learned tactician who was able to construct his basic arguments by quoting from the Book of Genesis and using its strictest interpretations. Hale defended the passage in question with skill, but found Waters had a sound fundamental knowledge of the Bible. Their spirited discussion established what was to become a long and cordial debate. Their friendship developed through the years, and when Richard Waters was sworn in as

President of the United States, Billy became his unofficial spiritual advisor.

Doris Hale prepared Richard Waters's favorite meal of meat loaf, mashed potatoes, and creamed corn, yet he ate sparingly. To Billy's surprise, the former president consumed three stiff bourbons as if they were water. Billy knew him as a man who smoked too much, but never as a heavy drinker. He remembered how Waters could nurse a drink as well as anyone. Billy had often heard him tell close advisors and staff, "One of the great obstacles a president must overcome is to avoid becoming a drunkard."

Their after-dinner stroll was turning into a tour of the hundred-plus-acre property. Billy fell behind, failing to keep up with the former president, who seemed caught up in the serenity of the estate. A secret service man assigned to ex-President Waters came to Billy's rescue by picking him up in the golf cart Billy used to get around the estate.

They sat on matted wooden chairs in a gazebo and looked out at the spectacular twilight view of the Shenandoah's green valleys and the mountain crest lit by a purple glow. "Intoxicating," said Waters. "That, before our eyes, is truly America the beautiful."

"Doris's and my favorite spot," said Billy.

"It was here, right here, where I decided to negotiate with the Russkies over nuclear disarmament."

"Perhaps you should have come here more often. As I recall, that decision proved quite successful."

"Well, I can't take all the credit." His eyes moved toward Billy. "I was blessed with fine advisors, like yourself."

"*Spiritual* advisor, Richard."

"Many thought you were much more."

"Many?"

Waters lit up a king-sized cigarette and hacked loudly. "You must admit there were times when your valued advice was not so spiritual. I'm sure you recall the bill to tax church-owned properties."

"I seem to remember it died in committee."

"True. However, convincing you at the time of its merits was no simple task."

Waters rose from the chair and began to peel the paper from the cigarette, his fingers so deft that he disturbed not a shred of tobacco. Billy watched him fascinated, then remembered Waters's great knack for using something as a prop before making his point. Obviously, Billy thought, Waters was about to reveal the purpose of his visit. "Do you happen to remember when, on your behalf, I had that little chitchat with the FCC people?" Waters remarked.

"The first or second time, Richard?"

"When I forced them to open up on religious broadcasting."

"Richard, would you mind disposing of that prop?"

Waters laughed heartily and let the tobacco slip through his fingers. His Gucci shoe crushed out its fire. "Then, of course," he went on, "there was the time when you urged me to put a ban on contributions made by American citizens to the Irish Republican Army."

"Catholics and Protestants are still killing one another."

"Nonsense. The media made it into a religious war."

"I beg to differ," Billy argued.

"What was the great religious difference? Confession?"

"Richard, regardless of how you have expertly managed to word things, any advice I gave you was *spiritually* oriented."

"How about when you asked me—fervently, I might add—to use my influence on Supreme Court justices in the case against prayer in public schools?"

"What have you done, Richard, made a list?"

"Israel. How can we ever forget your advice about Israel?"

"Said in a fit of temper," Billy said defensively.

"Make Israel into an international religious state, wasn't it?"

"All right, Richard, I surrender. You made your point. What I would now like to know, is why?"

Waters drew another cigarette from his silk shirt pocket. The lighter's flame threw light upon his face, reminding

Billy how much the former president resembled the actor Sir Laurence Olivier. Yet such a resemblance was never mentioned during Richard Waters's second term. Billy happened to have been on hand when a reporter made the mistake of telling the president how much he looked like the English actor. He would long remember Richard Waters's reply: "Actors must be excellent liars. Are you inferring that your president is a liar?" The reporter lost his credentials, and Olivier movies were thereafter banned from the White House theater.

"William, I am going to confess something which shall not be written in my memoirs."

"If it is of a spiritual nature, I'm afraid I won't be much of a father confessor. It so happens I am doing quite a bit of confessing of my own these days."

Waters dragged long and hard on the cigarette. He was unconcerned by Billy's response and spoke through the rising smoke. "As president, the one thing I wanted to do more than anything else was to take the torch from the Statue of Liberty's hand and point her finger toward the sea."

"My God, man, you would have been impeached!" Billy laughed.

"I damn well knew after I left office, future administrations would become so caught up in human rights, they'd make this country the ward of the world's scum."

"Richard, I do not believe what I am hearing," Billy said, trying to keep the conversation light.

"I possessed the foresight and the cure, but I did nothing. It just was not realistic at the time."

"Old friend, why do I suddenly acquire the distinct feeling there is a parallel here?"

"William, your article was—ill timed."

Billy cleared the laughter from his throat. "You are truly the master of manipulating the human mind. I often wondered why you ever needed a secretary of state. Next you will have me convinced that little newspaper story is the real reason for your visit."

"The word 'little' can hardly apply to something read by millions."

"And shortly forgotten by the same."

"Not in a presidential election year."

Billy was amused by the serious expression on the world-famous face. "Richard, tell me why I have the feeling I am about to be convinced I did something wrong?"

"As an evangelist, no. As a good Republican, don't you believe you did?"

"Most certainly not," Billy said, a little ruffled. "But what I do believe is that for the first time in my life, I find myself strangely in need of a very stiff drink."

They retired to Billy's den and sat opposite one another in deep overstuffed chairs. A bottle of bourbon supplied from Richard Waters's traveling stock, a pail of ice, and a crystal pitcher of water sat on a small hickory table before them. Billy poured himself a double, straight up, and eyed the alcohol in his glass with great uncertainty.

Waters's attention roamed across the familiar high-ceiling room which Billy referred to as "Daniel's Den." He scanned the overwhelming array of religious busts and took notice of the portrait of himself centered among the gallery of pictures hanging over the massive fieldstone fireplace. He was distracted by a choking sound. Billy had downed the drink in a single gulp and now sat with his face flushed and eyes watering.

"Another like that, William, and I shall be deprived of your company."

Billy pointed a damning finger at the bottle of bourbon. "Surely you can't *enjoy* that."

"One develops a taste."

"If it doesn't kill you first."

Richard Waters left his chair and strolled toward one of the many busts. He went from one to another and paused before that of Moses. His hand traced the lines of the sculpted face. "Tell me, William, do you honestly believe these men ever existed?"

Billy endured the burning sensation in his stomach. "The Bible tells us so, Richard."

"A lame reply. Lame indeed."

"There is nothing lame about the Bible, Richard, only the minds of people who don't believe it."

"Like atheists and agnostics?"

"Among others."

"Amazing," Waters said, pouring himself another drink and returning to his chair. "Amazing," he repeated to himself. "How odd . . ."

"Go on, Richard. Don't stop now."

"I was thinking of how we both prospered from one very particular component which religion and politics have always had in common."

"Which is, Richard?"

"Pure, unadulterated horseshit."

"I see," Billy said, undaunted. "A new twist, Richard? Rather than merely pick apart the Bible and its authors, you have now included politics in your strategy. Interesting, if nothing more."

"At least we American politicians exploited our horseshit from a reliable foundation."

"Meaning, we in the religious field deal in myth?" Billy said as the liquor began to warm him. "Richard, we have been through all of this many times before. Why do you continue to persecute yourself?"

"It fascinates me. It's like reading a mystery thriller only to realize at the end that the author cheated the reader."

"Of course you are referring to the Bible."

"I'm referring to the greatest hoax ever perpetrated upon mankind."

"Old or New Testament?" Billy encouraged him good-naturedly.

"From Genesis through Revelations. From the absurd to the sublime."

"I do believe I shall have another," Billy said, reaching for the bourbon.

249

Waters quickly snatched the bottle from Billy's grasp. "This time, dear friend, *I* will do the fixing."

Billy watched his guest drop ice cubes into the glass, followed by a half-shot of bourbon and plenty of water. The word "hoax" began to haunt his mind. He remembered someone else long ago calling the Bible the same.

"You know, William, if Jesus Christ were around today and preached what the Bible said he preached, he would be arrested as an enemy of the state."

Billy was too darkly preoccupied with a ghost from the past to reply.

"William? Still with me?" Waters asked.

The distant gaze left Billy's eyes. He leaned forward and accepted the drink.

"Dwelling on something I said?"

"What? No, Richard, it was nothing."

"Out with it, man." He raised his drink in toast. "This shall be a night for revelations."

Billy swirled the glass beneath his nose, hesitating to divulge an innermost secret. "I was thinking of a man . . ." His voice trailed off as if he were ashamed to speak the words. "A man I now believe I once defamed."

"An enemy of Christianity, no doubt."

"I'm no longer sure."

"Might the reason for your defaming this man be his not believing what righteous Christians would have him believe?"

"Almost, Richard, but not quite."

"What did you call him? Devil worshipper? Or was it a lesser charge, like atheist?"

"There were times, Richard, when I was inclined to believe *you* had atheistic tendencies."

"My definition of an atheist cannot be found in the Bible or a dictionary."

"Richard Waters, another Moses? I am most anxious to hear."

"Since you insist. My definition of an atheist is an intelligent person who has read the Bible in its entirety and comprehends all of which he or she has read."

Billy frowned. "On second thought, maybe my inclinations were correct."

"In truth, William, those sermons of yours, particularly when you spoke of eternal damnation and the fiery pits of Hell, were they merely to keep the sheep in line? To frighten them into parting with their money?"

"Why do you ask? Are you frightened, Richard?"

"Fortunately, my mind was never programmed to believe all of that damnation business when I was a child."

"There is a great deal more to the Holy Book than fear."

"The major things I have extracted from the Bible, besides hypocrisy, are that it breeds prejudice and has kept women in a subservient role for centuries."

Billy sank back in his chair. A smile came over his face. "Not nice, Richard," he said, raising his drink in a mock toast. " 'Vengeance is mine, sayeth the Lord.' "

"Ridiculous! Why would an avenging God avenge Himself?"

"Say that again?"

"Hell, if I am to believe Genesis, a supreme God started it all. No one volunteered to play His game."

Again Billy smiled. "You old fox. Taking me on in my own field, are you?"

"What, and risk being attacked by chapter and verse?"

Billy felt he detected a certain concern in Waters's voice. "What is behind all of this, Richard? Has meditating on the inevitable finally caught up with you?"

Waters drank deeply. The sparring was over. "I am in need of a favor. I wouldn't ask, but as you know, over the years I have done a few for you."

"Yes. Yes, that is certainly true, Richard. C.D. Pittman does come to mind."

"God-fearing jurists would have found you guilty in the largest libel suit in history."

"I'm wearing my chest protector, Richard, so why not shoot for the bull's eye?"

"Lay off Virtues, Inc."

Billy's immediate reaction was a sharp frown. "You missed, Richard. The arrow is sticking in my arse."

"You've upset many important Republicans with that public statement."

"Have I?" Billy began to stand up, but felt a sudden rush of lightheadedness. "I fail to understand why I have suddenly become the Republican party's bad boy."

"The party needs whatever votes Virtues, Inc., can produce."

"My God, Richard, the clunk we have for president has made enough blunders for the party *and* Bartley Sinclair to capitalize on."

"The power of an incumbent is an awesome thing to overcome. After all, I should know—I was one. The Democrats will capitalize on Bart having been a general. The networks and the papers will portray him coming to Washington in a tank, shooting down blacks and liberals."

"Richard, I suggest you advise the party to discourage any relationship with Virtues, Inc."

"That sounds like a man who has taken the sword from its scabbard."

"I haven't the energy to carry it."

"What is so evil about Virtues, Inc.?"

"Everything, Richard."

"Wanting to restore morality to a country up to its neck in trash is wrong?"

Billy set the drink aside. "Richard, I can appreciate your concern for Bartley Sinclair. He will make a fine president. After all, he was taught by an expert. And he will be elected *without* any votes from Virtues, Inc."

"It's more than that. The party has an opportunity to capture enough Senate seats to give us the majority. I *need* this favor, William."

"Preposterous," Billy said, stumbling to his feet and grabbing the back of another chair. He spoke in a disbelieving tone. "Here you are, a man of history, asking *me* to refrain from speaking out against something I know to be wrong, as if the presidency depended upon it."

"It just might—and you needn't look at me as if I have

lost my mind. Strange as it may sound, the power from the pulpit might possibly swing this coming presidential election.''

''Maybe in Israel. But in the United States? Richard, *please.*''

''The timing for Virtues, Inc., is excellent. Most Americans are wary of a spendthrift Congress and an inept Supreme Court. Along with the increasingly deplorable state of the economy, the majority of Americans is plain fed up. And what is it they say about troubled people, William? How they suddenly find Jesus?''

''Richard, please do not make it difficult for me. I must say what I honestly believe.''

''Then do so, William. The day after the November election.''

Unable to decide what bothered him most—the pain from his aching knee, the alcohol's buzzing effect in his head, or Richard Waters's burdensome request—Billy stumbled towards his favorite chair.

The former president watched him struggle to seat himself. He remembered the Billy Hale of yesteryear: the vibrant Billy Hale, the indestructible Billy Hale. And now he watched him hobble about in ailing health and, like himself, a victim of the unmerciful aging process. Waters downed his drink and waited for Billy to respond to the verbal fast ball he had thrown him.

''As you undoubtedly have already assumed,'' began Billy, ''I intentionally planted that story. And yes, I knew it would upset, even anger, some people. But my purpose, then as now, was more than to get into the newspapers. As you understand Bartley Sinclair, I understand Harley Lombard. Virtues, Inc., was not his idea. He is being used. And I intend to find out who is using him.''

Richard Waters toyed thoughtfully with his glass. ''Here we are, two old men acting like doting fathers over the welfare of our prodigies. How ironic.''

''Then that should make it easier for you to understand.''

''I do understand, but apparently you don't. Virtues, Inc.,

is nothing more than a gift horse you neither feed nor whip."

"A *Trojan* gift horse, Richard."

"I'm asking you as my truest friend not to rock the party's boat. Bart needs the votes Virtues, Inc., can deliver."

"You know I would do nothing to impair Bartley's chances, but Virtues, Inc., *must* be stopped."

"Do so, William. *Do so*—after the election."

"*You* don't understand, Richard. By then it will be too late. By then, Virtues, Inc., will have destroyed the careers of innocent people."

"Innocent? All of a sudden you have become a bleeding heart for liberal politicians? Pornography, abortion, and abolishment of Christian prayer in public schools were not the doings of conservative Republicans. How can you, of all people, be so against Virtues, Inc.? All they're doing is acting from the script *you* authored."

Although he did not say it, Billy knew what Waters was implying. Since he came out of retirement, the word "hypocrite" seemed to greet him at every turn. "I have never authored or encouraged a conspiracy."

"Virtues, Inc., a *conspiracy?* Is your argument against Virtues, Inc., so weak you now have to rely on sensationalism?"

"It is sensational, Richard."

Waters laughed, freshened his drink, and spoke with a patronizing smile. "Tell me all about this conspiracy."

"There is nothing humorous about it."

"A conspiracy against whom? Non-Christians? Atheists?" Waters took a hard swallow of his drink, lit up another cigarette, and spoke of the past. "When I was president, I grew sick of the word. Conspiracy this, conspiracy that. Everyone knew of a conspiracy."

"Do you have the stomach for another?"

Richard Waters's voice was even more condescending. "If for no other reason than to appease you."

"You needn't appease me, Richard. Not when Virtues, Inc., is tied into the rash of terrorism which is presently occurring in this country."

Richard Waters's eyes met Billy's. "I find *that* absurd."

254

"So did I, at first."

"What happened, did you have one of those famous revelations of yours?"

"No, Richard, it was nothing more than a hunch."

"Merely a hunch?"

"It started with Cody Walker's death."

"Cody Walker?"

"The cult leader—a former electronic preacher—whom our government officials conveniently reported to have committed suicide."

"You mean the man who held those Americans prisoner?" Waters asked. "Central America, wasn't it?"

Billy's adrenalin was pumping as he took the offensive. Waters's vagueness concerning Cody Walker disturbed him. "Cody Walker's death, the kidnapping of Reverend Tho, and the killing of his followers were not 'accidents,' Richard. Jason Everson, an evangelist, was not killed in an accidental fire. And you can bet that the faith healer Wallace Langly, Jr., didn't just happen to fall out of the sky."

"*William*! William, you are sounding like a chairman of a crime commission."

Billy ignored Waters's comment. "Furthermore, *none* of these violent acts has been solved by the authorities."

"And *that* constitutes a conspiracy? Just what is the connection between these killings? Though there is, admittedly, a common thread—evangelism—running through this rash of deaths, I don't see any conclusive connection between them."

"There *is* a connection. I am not sure at this moment what it is, but I am sure it exists and that there is a link to Virtues, Inc."

"Your personal grievances toward Virtues, Inc., are one thing, but for you to accuse a religious organization of being involved in murder and terrorism is ludicrous."

"Ludicrous, you say? Hardly a day goes by without the newspapers and television headlining religious killings. Haven't you heard it has now become quite fashionable to kill in the name of God?"

"You're saying Virtues, Inc., is in the business of Bibles and bullets?"

"Virtues, Inc., may not be directly involved, but there *is* a connection."

"Tell me, then, in what capacity? As an accomplice? How, William?"

"I know Harley Lombard. The man is a born coward. He'd run like Satan was after him if he knew what was transpiring around him."

Richard Waters rose from the chair and stretched his legs. "I don't wish to crowd your market on hunches, but I seem to have one of my own."

"I respect your right, old friend."

"Mine is far less dramatic. It doesn't have the pizazz of a conspiracy, but then, hunches do cover a broad spectrum." Waters moved farther away from the chair without looking at Billy. "I've the feeling you are feeding my tired old mind with incredible thoughts so as to avoid the purpose for which I came." He turned back towards Billy. "Would such a feeling be realistic?"

"I would like to believe you happened to be in Washington and decided to call on an old and trusted friend."

"How can you seriously expect me to believe this conspiracy of yours?"

"I wish you would stop referring to it as *my* conspiracy."

"Then, if it isn't yours, who in blazes composed such nonsense?"

Billy had to catch himself to hold back his reply.

"Tell me, William, has retirement become so unbearable?"

"That was uncalled for."

"Then be practical, man. *If* what you've told me has an inkling of truth to it, don't you believe the media people would have exposed it by now?"

"No, not necessarily. They could be suppressed."

"Suppressed? The media? By whom, *God?*"

"Did I note a strain of anger in your voice?"

"The inevitable bottom line, old friend," Waters said, examining his empty glass. "Let's pursue your conspiracy. Shall we start with proof?"

"No, Richard, I do not yet have sufficient evidence to prove my allegations. But I can tell you that my information comes from a most reliable source."

"Reliable, as in irrevocable trust?" Waters asked, pouring himself another drink.

"The man is living a daily hell. He doesn't know where to turn."

"Apparently he has turned to you."

"No, Richard, it was I who first turned to him."

"With your hunch."

"Yes."

"Then presto! Two hunches make a conspiracy."

"Richard, I would appreciate it if you would dispense with the levity. It is no joking matter. I don't think he can live with what he knows much longer."

"Why haven't you convinced him to go to the proper authorities?"

"He is the— He believes this network of terrorists includes the proper authorities."

"Is there no *end* to this conspiracy?"

"I believe this man. His credibility is without question."

Waters did not seem convinced. He folded his arms and looked skeptically at Billy. "Have you given thought to the times you said things you later regretted having said?"

"Not this time, Richard. Not this time."

"Very well," said Waters, who went to a telephone on the desk by the bay window.

"Richard, what are you doing?"

"If for nothing more than to satisfy myself, I am about to set up a meeting for you with Bingo Bridges of the Senate Judiciary Committee."

"Richard, *no*. Please hang up the phone. I *cannot* jeopardize the man's identity."

The pleading tone in Billy's voice was too sincere. Waters replaced the receiver in its cradle and returned to his chair, deep in contemplation. "William, if perchance there is some truth, *substantial* proof, to this preposterous conspiracy theory of yours, either you or your informant must divulge the information to someone besides me."

"Richard, why do you persist in referring to it as *my* conspiracy?"

"It is impossible not to. You have become a willing accessory. This informant of yours has filled your mind with incredible ideas and you have propagated them into stark lunacy."

"I will know a great deal more at the convention."

"The convention?"

"Yes, Richard, the Republican National Convention."

"You will know a great deal more?"

"From what I have been told."

"By your informant."

"Richard, must you banter?"

"I'm *afraid* to ask."

"No, Richard, I do not believe the party is involved, nor have I been told as much."

"That's comforting, even though such comfort is derived from what I perceive as fictional foolishness."

"Call it what you may, but until I learn the contrary, I cannot turn my back. God knows I have tried. And I can promise you, I will not be going to the convention with the attitude of a prosecuting attorney."

"I suggest you not attend."

Billy was astonished. "Am I hearing right?"

"Save yourself the embarrassment, William, and watch it over TV."

"Richard, *why?* Surely not because of that article?"

"The party has adopted a gung-ho theme of 'No Guts, No Glory.' It already has set the mood for the delegates. From what I hear, you are *persona non grata*."

"Damn it all, Richard! I am as good a Republican as anyone who will be at the convention and better than most."

"I know it and you know it; however, unless you publicly withdraw your statements against Virtues, Inc., too many of the party's hard core will believe you sold out."

"*I* sold out? For the party to *associate* with the likes of Virtues, Inc., is nothing less than criminal. Oh, no, Richard, I will be there. And I fully intend to speak out against Virtues, Inc., with everything I—"

"You won't reach the platform. And if by some miraculous power you do, you will be driven off."

"Richard, you must clear it for me to address the delegates."

"You will have to go it alone, William. I'm sorry. You see, I will not be in Houston."

"You not there? Not on hand to witness Bartley Sinclair's nomination? I should think that nothing on earth could prevent you."

"And in Heaven?" Waters asked.

The finality in Richard Waters's tone was unmistakeable. "What is wrong, Richard?" Billy asked anxiously.

"Life's temporal clock is running out for me, old friend."

"No, Richard, *no*."

"The cancer in the prostate will eventually spread to the bones," Waters said flatly.

Billy had to look away. "I should have known something was terribly wrong when you spoke of religion."

"William, you are among a trusted few who know. It must not be leaked. I don't want anything to detract from Sinclair's day in the sun, no wash of party sentiment."

For a man who had prepared so many to meet their deaths, Billy was speechless. Tears began to fill his eyes.

"Hell, William, I have had a wonderful life. Other than seeing Bart become president, I have little left to look forward to. Besides, my life has reached the stage where it is becoming rather boring."

"Dear friend, what can I say?"

"You can say some nice things over my grave, but nothing flowery please." Waters smiled at his old friend.

"Richard, are you right with God?"

"You have it wrong. The question should be, is God right with me?"

"You are incorrigible," Billy said with fondness.

"William, I can only hope you decide not to attend the convention, but I know you will. Just like I know you won't deny a dying man a last favor."

There was no evading the issue. The scale was too weighted down with favors the former president had granted him in the past, and Billy feebly nodded.

"Do I understand your gesture to be affirmative?"

"Yes, Richard, I will refrain from saying or doing anything against Virtues, Inc., until after the election."

Waters stood and extended his hand. "I am pleased, William, extremely pleased."

"There is one condition."

"Must there be?"

"For better than forty years, we have always called each other by our proper given names. I do believe it is time we drop that formality."

The former president retrieved his hand. A radiant smile warmed his face. Then, as if drawn by a magnetic force, the two men embraced. There was no holding back their deep affection for one another and no shame in their tears.

"Thank you, *Billy*."

"God bless you, *Dick*."

CHAPTER 27

RON REBUCK'S DARK brows were knotted in thought. He sat away from the picnic table, where Ike Vesper and Jessica Towne were engaged in after-dinner conversation, the light from a kerosene lamp playing on their faces. He was looking into the moon-bright August night at the silvery stars which indented the heavens, entranced by the mysterious vastness of space where Earth was but a dot. Billions of people inhabiting a dot.

The more Rebuck stared, the more he realized the insignificance of his plight on Earth and of life itself. Weren't the joy of birth and the tears of death really the total extent of it? And weren't the years in between only to survive? But to survive for what? To die?

Captivated by the countless objects floating through the cosmos, his thinking centered on the supernatural, the mystique of the unknown. He wrestled futilely with the greatest interrogative of them all: "Why?" Those he considered to be the jackals of man's sorrows and fears, the same who preached of an almighty deity, responsible for all of man's blessings and curses, were an army with plastic faces marching through his mind. They formed a sea of mouths chanting doom to all who disobeyed the laws of God. God's law? Not God's law, Rebuck thought, but the laws of fallible, corruptible, self-serving men made revered by the passage of time. Faith's ageless sword slashed at his reasoning, but arrows of logic shot back. Faith in what? In whom? Faith in an all-knowing supreme being who created an imperfect existence called Man? *"Who asked Him?"* Rebuck shouted.

Ike and Jessica looked at him with alarm. "Ron, are you all right?" Jessica said.

"Fine," said Rebuck, "just thinking."

"About the universe, infinity?" she anticipated.

"More or less."

Given the rare opportunity to share in his thoughts, and despite Ike's facial warning not to do so, she said, "Ron, do you believe in life after death?"

Rebuck's head turned slowly and she could barely see his face. "When you're dead, you're dead," he said flatly.

"Little Girl," Ike intervened, "religion's not the man's bag."

"I'm asking because I'm doing my final report on the plausibility of a hereafter."

Rebuck frowned. "Based on theology?"

"Yes, but not in the fundamentalist vein."

"So?" said Rebuck.

"Do you believe we're born just to die?"

"We're nothing more than part of a giant food chain. Just a link in the nitrogen cycle."

"Really? Nothing more?"

"Until someone can show conclusively that they've come back from the dead, who can believe anything else?"

"I can," Jessica said boldly. "I believe there's more, much more. I mean, take television. Look how a person's image can be beamed electronically over the airwaves. Applying that kind of logic, why should it seem impossible for man's spirit or soul to travel into infinity?"

Without a word or so much as a glance at Jessica, Rebuck left the lounge chair and retreated hastily to the refuge of the motor home.

She looked disappointedly at Ike. "He could have said *something*."

"You stung 'im, Little Girl. Made some sense outta somethin' senseless."

"I've got to talk to him, Ike."

"You gave 'im enough religion for one night."

"It has nothing to do with religion."

"You wanna run it past Uncle Ike?"

262

"I wanted to tell Ron what the mission director threatened."

"*Threatened?*" Ike grew stiff on the bench.

"He said if I ever saw Ron again, I would be expelled."

"Figures," Ike said with relief.

"But he *hasn't* expelled me, and it's not like Mr. Ragonese to change his mind."

"When did Spooky Dude tell you this?"

"The day the Amish elder came to the mission. When Mr. Ragonese asked me all those questions."

Again Ike's interest sharpened. "What questions?"

"About you and Ron. What you do for a living. Who you talk about."

Ike rose suddenly from the bench. "Little Girl, maybe you better talk to the man."

She watched Ike rush to the motor home, and let out a deep sigh. Since that June night at the cemetery, she had kept to herself what she had learned about the man she loved. But she could no longer allow it to fester inside her mind. Knowing he was an assassin had devastated her. She had to tell him what she knew. Tonight, away from Ike's trusted ears.

The loud conversation inside the motor home ceased. The screen door swung open, and a ruffled Ron Rebuck moved quickly toward her, trailed by an equally unsettled Ike.

"What's Ike rambling about, Jessica?"

"I told him the mission director threatened to expel me if I saw you again. But Ron, he hasn't, and he knows I'm coming here. He hasn't said a word to me."

"Is that all?" Rebuck asked.

She lowered her head.

"Tell 'im, Little Girl. Tell 'im 'bout the questions," Ike prompted.

"He asked what you and Ike were doing out here, and what you did for a living."

"The mission director," Rebuck clarified.

"Yes, Mr. Ragonese."

"What did you tell him?"

She looked up from the ground. "That I didn't know."

Rebuck could sense she had more to say and was holding back.

"Let it run, Little Girl," Ike coaxed.

"Ike, will you let her speak for herself."

She hesitated before answering. "There—there is something else. That terrible night at your father's grave . . ."

"What, Jessica," Rebuck encouraged.

"I think I saw a man standing next to the statue."

"The mission director?" Rebuck probed.

"No. He didn't have a beard and his face was badly scarred. And he was smiling—an awful smile."

Ike's jaw dropped. His eyes closed. A nightmare jammed his mind.

"Are you sure, Jessica? Sure you're not imagining this man?"

"Imaginin' nuthin'," said Ike. "It was *him.*"

Rebuck pivoted toward Ike. "What makes you so damn sure?"

"The night I couldn't find you, I received a code."

"What code?"

"Crucifix."

"Crucifix," Rebuck muttered as he moved toward Ike. "You should've found me," he whispered.

"Man, how'd I know yuh'd be freakin' out in a graveyard?"

"Ron," Jessica pleaded.

Rebuck held up his hand to silence her. His voice was troubled. "We've had codes ordering us to leave the area before. How could the captain know you wouldn't find me?"

"You've been talkin' 'bout readin' the captain's mind. *You* tell me."

Jessica would not be excluded from their conversation. "Ron, what are you talking about?" She turned to Ike. "Tell me, Ike."

"Man, tell 'er. She got a right to know."

"Tell me what? Ron?"

"Nothing. *Nothing.*"

"Ron, please, you can tell me."

"Man, you got 'er into it—nobody else. Tell 'er or I will."

"When I'm damned sure and not before."

"Yeah," Ike said, walking away. "After the captain slits 'er throat."

Rebuck, determined to get Jessica away from the complex before Ike frightened her further, took her hand. She gave little resistance as they walked in silence past the kennel and the whining dogs, and onto the trail.

He did not know how to start or how to explain it all to her and wondered if he should even try. But he knew she had not imagined seeing the captain—her description of the scarred face and evil smile left no doubt in his mind that she'd seen him. And he'd seen her.

When they were a good distance from the complex, Jessica broke the silence. "Ron, I was listening that night at your father's grave. I know what you do."

"Damn!" he cursed. That fact alone solidified the danger in which he had placed her.

"Ron, who is the captain and what is his hold on you?"

"Jessica, I want to tell you. I really do. But you must believe me—the more you know, the greater the danger. I can't let anything happen to you, of all people."

"But why would he want to hurt *me?*"

He could see the dark outline of the mission house ahead and stopped to look at her apprehensive face. "Jessica, I've made a terrible mistake. But no matter what, I won't let anything happen to you." His hands went to her waist. "I've got to get you away from here. I'm taking you home to your family first thing in the morning."

She moved closer and fell into his arms. Her body softened at his reassuring touch and she looked up at him. "Ron, I can't leave now—in a couple of weeks I graduate from the mission."

"Jessica, you *can't* stay here. You have no idea—"

She broke away from him. "Ron, I can't leave with graduation so close. I've worked too hard for it. Besides, as long as I'm with you I'm safe. Please don't try to make me go . . . because I won't." Her lower lip quivered slightly and she pressed her face to his chest. "I love you, Ron. I love you more than anything."

He watched her run toward the house until she became a blur in the darkness. All at once, he felt a tightness in his stomach. Ike was right; he had made a costly mistake. He had played into the captain's hand. His concern for Jessica's safety had now ended his independence, his ability to act for only his own survival in the mad captain's sordid game of life and death.

His attention went aimlessly to an upstairs window of the mission house. A light burned softly and the evening breeze parted the curtain. The silhouette of a bearded man looking down upon him was not a figment of his imagination. It was the mission director, John Ragonese, and Rebuck knew he could ill afford to ignore his suspicions. The captain had his informant. The mission director had been bought or intimidated, and Rebuck would spend most of the night thinking of a plan to counter the captain's telling move.

CHAPTER 28

"NO GUTS, NO GLORY," painted in blood-red letters and encircled by blue and white stars, dominated billboards and posters from Houston Intercontinental Airport to the sprawling site of the Republican National Convention. The spirited theme sparked an aggressive mood as delegates from the fifty states and U.S. territories gathered in Houston to nominate Senator Bartley Sinclair as their Republican candidate for President of the United States.

Billy Hale stood at the registration desk of the Shamrock Hilton Hotel, convention headquarters. Doris Hale waited by the bellman's desk, watching her husband's mounting annoyance. After ten minutes of foot-dragging and computer terminal consultation, the young desk clerk condescendingly informed the evangelist that there was no record of his reservation.

Billy insisted there had been a mistake and politely asked the clerk to check again. The results were the same. The computer would not read out his reservation, and the young clerk became insolent. Billy forced a smile, refused to surrender his position at the counter, and turned to speak to the smirking and foot-shuffling delegates waiting their turn to register. "Ladies and gentlemen, what we have here is a perfect example of what is wrong with America today. Perhaps the party's platform would do well to include a pledge to improve the competence and integrity of the American worker."

"You tell 'em, Billy," rang a friendly voice that went unappreciated by the long line of impatient delegates.

"Now which is it, son?" Billy leaned forward, buttonholing the adamant young clerk with the power of his voice. "Integrity or competence?"

A diplomatic room manager was finally summoned and America's most celebrated religious leader was given lodging at a convention to which he had not been invited.

The Shamrock, once the crown jewel of Houston hostelries, had been restored to its original elegance years before and was a hotel of oversized rooms and extravagantly appointed suites. But the Hales's suite consisted only of a moderate-size bedroom featuring two double beds, a bathroom, and a small adjoining parlor. It was not the type of accommodation usually afforded someone of Billy's international prominence, and Doris was infuriated by the cost—$275 per day. Nothing, not even a basket of fruit, was complimentary. "There was a time," she said as she unpacked, "when hotels around the world would pay for everything. How could things change so much in two years? You're still the most famous religious figure in America."

Billy stood glumly before one of two windows and looked out from the fourteenth floor. Outside it was a sweltering Houston afternoon, the kind which causes sweat to gather at your Adam's apple and trickle down your chest, with more of the same predicted for the next three days.

"That clerk was intentionally rude," said Doris, "and all of those people in the lobby pretending not to recognize you—people we have known for years, acting as if we didn't exist."

"Richard Waters told me what to expect should I attend this convention."

"I wish you would have taken Richard's advice."

"Must I again explain the purpose in our coming here?" Billy said, turning from the window.

"To look for conspirators? Terrorists? At the Republican Convention?"

"Dan never said the party was involved; he only warned me to be on the lookout for certain special-interest groups the convention would attract."

Doris removed a shirt from the leather suitcase and paused before asking, "Might Dan be wrong? I mean, could he be misleading you?"

"Willfully?" Billy stepped from the window to watch her sorting clothes on the bed. "Why would Dan purposely give me false or misleading information?"

"I don't know, Billy. I guess I'm talking to hear myself talk."

"We have known Dan Kaiser since he was a child, Doris. He comes from fine stock. No one could persuade or force Dan into doing something he knows to be wrong. The man would resign from the FBI first."

Doris shook her head ruefully. "How this whole thing has mushroomed."

"And it's still growing," Billy said grimly. "This morning, before we left for the airport, I received another tape from Dan."

She clenched the blouse she was holding. Every time he heard from Dan Kaiser, he got so excited that she worried about his heart.

"Dan seems convinced that a secret government is building within the government. Besides the Pentagon, the CIA, and his own FBI, he now smells the stench of a conspiracy within Congress as well."

"Billy, it sounds so incredible."

"It is all beginning to fit into place, Doris. Especially the reason why these conspirators are so in need of a religious outlet like Virtues, Inc."

"Billy, I can understand why you were driven to take out after Harley and Jimmy Christian, but not this. Each time Dan gives you information, I see how it eats at your insides. Billy, you're not well enough to cope with it all. Let Dan do his own investigating. He's a trained professional. He knows—"

Hale suddenly pressed an index finger to his lips. "Doris," he whispered, "get your purse and the room key."

Hale escorted his wife into the corridor and stood leaning heavily on his cane. He nodded politely to a passing group of delegates and waited until they were well down the long hall. "I have the feeling our suite is bugged," Billy whispered.

"Why would anyone do such a thing?" Doris asked, shock in her voice.

"Woman, have you forgotten so quickly how I was welcomed to this convention?"

"But who? You can't think Harley would."

"The man would electrocute himself trying," said Billy, who switched the cane to his other hand while Doris recognized the worried expression beginning to line his face. "Doris, if what I believe is true, I have seriously jeopardized Dan's anonymity, maybe even his personal safety."

"Billy, could it be that you're overreacting?"

"Possibly." He wearily shook his head from side to side. "All this spy business is wearing on my mind."

"Billy," she pleaded, "there is a cure. Let's go home."

"It's tempting, Doris, but even if I am tilting at windmills, I must see it through."

"Even if it drains the last bit of energy from your body?"

"And then some." He mustered a smile. "Now, be the understanding wife you are and go back into the room. But don't answer the phone. Just let it ring."

"Billy, where are you going?"

"To reserve myself a box seat in the lobby."

"What about the press, the TV people, and your promise to Richard Waters?"

"For me to break my promise would take an act of . . ." He could not bring himself to implicate the Supreme Being.

Harley Lombard stretched out on the curved maroon sofa with a glass of champagne dangling from his hand. Across from him the porcine evangelist, Veep Siler, was seated in a wooden armchair with only the chair's front legs visible.

"Top floor, suite fit for a visiting king, expensive champagne. My, my, Harley, quite impressive," Veep said as though tantalized.

"Jealous, Veep?"

"Astonished, Harley. Simply astonished."

"Get used to it," Harley said as he drained his wine glass, " 'cause it's only the beginning of things to come."

The Florida evangelist had noted the two men standing idly at the far end of the room. Not one to forget a face, Veep remembered the taller man as the one he had belly-bumped off the elevator during his visit to the Cathedral Towers building in Charity, Ohio. "Those men your new traveling team, Harley?"

"Fuckin' robots," Harley cursed, trying to reach the bottle of champagne.

"I gather Andy Gaines no longer makes the road trips?"

Harley sprang to a sitting position, pouring more champagne for himself. "Look, Veep, you really should have called. Set an appointment like everyone else. You can't just pop in unexpectedly and think I'll see you. I'm a *busy* man." He glanced at his wristwatch. "And right now, I've got to get ready. There's a shitload of politicians needing to kiss my ass."

Veep Siler's laugh was more of a snort. "I'm honored by this special audience, Harley. However, if you'd returned my calls, you could have saved the expense of my coming to Houston."

"What calls?"

The fat man blinked like an owl. "Communication flaws with your minions, Harley—or might it be a suppression by a higher power?"

"*You people!*" Harley shouted at the two men who he felt were eavesdropping. "Take it to a bedroom. And *shut* the door."

"Such leadership," Veep mocked, casually inspecting the champagne bottle.

"Now what the hell were you saying about higher something?"

"An assumption, Harley. Merely an assumption."

Harley's attention was drawn toward Veep Siler's feet. The longer he looked, the wider his eyes grew.

"Searching for something, Harley? Perhaps a misplaced bugging device?"

"Veep, the chair—the one you're sitting on—where the fuck is it?"

"Ah, yes, the proverbial insults to my bodily person. Feel better now, Harley?"

"What is it, Veep? But before you tell me, if it pertains to money, *forget it*. You get the big stuff on the come and only on the come."

"The come," Veep repeated. "Such a disgusting usage."

"Veep, the time, the time," said Harley, tapping his wristwatch.

"Yes, Harley, I know. The bitching time. But first, may I ask, are you satisfied with the job on Senator Lollar?"

"Jesus, Veep, couldn't you have drummed up something else against him?"

"Did you have a specific type of slander in mind?"

"A scam—like a political payoff. You didn't have to make him out to be a fag."

"Homosexuals may get elected in California, but *not* in Florida," Veep said defiantly.

"Okay, okay. I don't have the time to argue. What *is* your problem, Veep? And why in hell did you have to come to Houston?"

"A case of business ethics."

"*You*, business ethics?" Harley guffawed.

"I have laid out a considerable amount of capital for expenses, Harley, and—"

"*No way*. No fucking way, Veep," Harley said, waving his arms. "You're not weaselin' out of our deal."

"May I have the opportunity to finish?"

"Go ahead, but save the bleeding tears. If Senator Lollar loses, you win. I gave you a plum. If it rots, you still eat it."

"Dearest Harley, so far you have given me nothing. Not a dime."

"We made a deal, Veep."

"True, but only you have benefited."

"What kind of horseshit are you dumping on me?"

"To be explicit, how am I to be assured I shall ever get paid?"

"You're guaranteed fifty thousand. The two hundred thousand is on the come when Lollar—no, *if* Lollar loses."

"And who, may I ask, is the guarantor? Virtues, Inc.? You personally?"

"Goddamn it, Veep, you've always been a thorn in my side. Don't be a spike."

"Harley, Harley, where is your sense of fair play? I have expended a significant sum of money with only your word as assurance that I will be paid."

"The election is not until November. How can you be asking for money before Lollar wins or loses?"

Siler's eyes narrowed. "From what I've heard, memberships to your Virtues, Inc., have surpassed two million. Twenty-five dollars per membership amounts to fifty million, Harley. What is a paltry fifty thousand between such good friends?"

"For your information," Harley said, "I've better than three million memberships."

"All the more reason for you to arrange the disbursement of such a pittance as fifty thousand dollars."

"I can't," Harley said flatly.

"Why, Harley, I thought you were the hammer, the sovereign pontiff of Virtues, Inc."

"I *just* can't," Harley said obstinently.

"The infallible, the king, can't?"

The telephone rang twice before it was answered in the bedroom. Veep grunted. Telephone interruptions were *too* routine when meeting with Harley.

"Reverend Lombard," a man poked his head out from a bedroom door, "your, ah, wife is on the phone."

Harley scurried from the sofa to the phone. "Calling to apologize, Wilma Mae? . . . Huh? . . . Oh. Oh, yes. Yesssss," he purred.

"Do give Wilma Mae my regards," Veep said peevishly.

Harley turned his back on the fat man and spoke in a whisper. "Yeah, he's here. Who told you? . . . Happened to be in Houston . . . Sure, I'm sure . . . Listen, when are you leaving Washington? I need you something terrible . . . Who? . . . Billy's in the lobby? Who gives a shit? And how could you know that? . . . All right, I'll dodge him . . . Don't *you* forget . . . You know what I mean. The stuff. The kinky stuff . . . Tomorrow night. Right. And it won't be so easy this time."

"And may I ask how Wilma Mae is these days?" Veep asked when Harley returned to the sofa.

"Huh? Oh, she's fine," said Harley. "Look, Veep, we can't be seen together. I mean, not here at this convention."

"Orders from the top?"

"What do you mean, orders from the top? We just can't be seen together. As a matter of fact, Billy Hale is sitting in the lobby like some house detective."

"Such an informative call, Harley. Is Wilma Mae into reading crystal balls these days?" Veep laughed, his great belly rolling.

"Veep, go back to Florida *tonight*. I'll see what I can do about the fifty grand. No promises. I'll try."

The fat man rose. "Mind if I take a hostage while you try?"

"A what?"

"Is Andy Gaines still on the slave block?"

"You want him, I'll pay *you*."

"Only for a couple of weeks."

Harley was relieved when Veep finally waddled toward the door. But he could not see the scowl which had replaced the fat man's perpetual smile.

"I'll be in touch after the convention," Harley said reassuringly.

"I'm concerned, Harley, and when I'm worried, my appetite becomes ferociously carnivorous."

"I told you, I'll try to work something out. Don't push me."

"A most revealing visit, Harley. Most revealing."

* * *

274

Billy Hale settled into an overstuffed chair a little too close to the lobby's crowded bar area and its loud cocktail-hour conversation. But the location afforded him a view of the elevator area, the registration desk, the entrance doors, and the long corridor which stretched from the pool patio to a mall leading to Trader Vic's. He could see everything but the shadowy interior of the Shamrock Pub, but at least he could note that room's comings and goings.

The evangelist felt like a man in the terminal stages of leprosy. Few delegates acknowledged his presence with even a wave or a nod. Old associates paused when they saw him, then gave him a wide berth. Those too embarrassed to detour around him pretended to be looking for somebody.

For the past seven Republican National Conventions, Billy had enjoyed an insider's role. He had often mediated intra-party disputes and he had persuaded the Rules Committee to adopt his code of moral behavior for Republican candidates. For almost thirty years he had been the party's unofficial chaplain, far more influential than Boston's Cardinal Cushing had been during the Kennedy administration. He had reached the peak of his behind-the-scenes power during the administration of his longtime friend Richard Waters. He had always had the respect and trust of friend and foe alike. Now Hale was an outcast for his public criticism of Virtues, Inc. Widely condemned as a turncoat, Billy felt as if his exile had been decreed by some fascist tribunal.

The media, he discovered, was immune to his leprosy. The lobby was filled with local and network mini-cam crews waiting for the imminent arrival of Senator Bartley Sinclair. Newspaper types identifiable by their note pads and tape recorders stood in hostile clusters. Most newspaper reporters were Democrats, Billy had learned years and conventions ago. He noticed three of the journalists leave the pack and approach him warily.

"Billy Hale, sitting alone in the lobby?" said a veteran field reporter who Billy knew.

"One of the luxuries of retirement, Ted."

A younger man of the new breed of journalists dispelled

the mood of familiarity and was direct. "Are you here to speak out against Virtues, Inc., Dr. Hale?"

"I am here as a good Republican, attending the convention."

"Your name's not on the list of speakers."

"Young man, I was never under the impression I was to be a speaker," Billy replied with a dash of annoyance.

A brazen, middle-aged woman with a wide mouth and flaming red hair followed the young man's line of questioning. "Dr. Hale, your attack upon Virtues, Inc., *and* Reverend Lombard won't make you many friends at this convention. Don't you agree?"

"I am not aware of Virtues, Inc., being a part of the Republican Party," Billy replied.

"The very man you called a false judge and demagogue happens to be delivering the convention's invocation and benediction," interjected the young man.

"The party has always been free to select who they choose," Billy said curtly.

"But, Dr. Hale, that role has always been reserved for you. Shouldn't that really tell you where you stand with the party?" snapped the woman.

"Miss?"

"*Mrs.* Bagwell, Dr. Hale. From the *Atlanta Constitution.*"

"Well, Mrs. Bagwell from the *Atlanta Constitution,* I fail to see the significance."

"The significance, Dr. Hale, is that Reverend Lombard and Virtues, Inc., have a great deal to offer the Republican party, namely *votes.*"

"I believe you are putting excessive emphasis on an invocation."

The young man seized the opening. "Are you saying that prayers at political conventions are insignificant?"

"Nice try," Billy said as he visualized the morning headlines. "No, young man, I did not say that at all. What I *said* was that Mrs. Bagwell puts too much emphasis on Reverend Lombard's giving the invocation, not that the prayers are insignificant." He looked at the veteran reporter. "You heard me, didn't you, Ted?"

The network reporter smiled. "I heard, Billy."

"Dr. Hale," the woman continued, "hasn't Reverend Lombard often been referred to as your protegé?"

"I've heard as much."

"Apparently your protegé has turned against you," the woman goaded.

"Mrs. Bagwell, I would rather believe the prodigal shall return."

The smile broadened on the seasoned reporter's face. Knowing his peers would be unsuccessful in their quest to trip Billy into speaking out against Virtues, Inc., he changed the subject. "Billy, what can you tell us about these religious murders?"

Hale's expression turned cold. "I can tell you there is nothing religious about murder."

The reporters bolted toward the bank of glass doors. Senator Bartley Sinclair had arrived. Surrounded by his large entourage, the senator moved into the lobby. A phalanx of secret service men, eyes roving automatically over every inch of the lobby, had moved into positions on either side of the center doors.

Bartley Sinclair's erect carriage expressed his military heritage. His rugged face was dominated by a pug nose and a jutting chin. His blue eyes were clear and alert, and his voice brought parade grounds and ramrod-stiff cadets to mind. He believed in maintaining a sound and trim body and the proof lay in 170 pounds on his six-foot, one-inch frame.

The campaign professionals had failed in their efforts to change Bartley Sinclair's military demeanor. The senator scoffed at the Madison Avenue image maker who wanted his short sandy hair to grow long and appear free and wind-blown. Sinclair would not hear of wearing store-bought suits. His suits were hand made by one of London's finest Saville Row tailors. He had no interest in looking like a common man. He was always the General. And today, even with the overbearing Houston humidity, he appeared dressed immaculately in a light gray suit with a conservative matching tie neatly adorning the robin's-egg-blue shirt.

The most influential person in Bartley Sinclair's life was former President Richard Waters. Unlike Harley Lombard, Bartley Sinclair continued to seek the wisdom of his longtime counselor. They enjoyed a father-son relationship, and although Richard Waters had two natural sons, according to Mrs. Waters Bartley was her husband's favorite.

Most of Bartley Sinclair's friends and colleagues had considered him foolish to forsake his military career. He had graduated from West Point, then rose meteorically from second lieutenant to the rank of brigadier general by the age of forty-two. He had given up a career with the almost certain potential of becoming a four-star general in order to become a politician because his advisor, Richard Waters, had forseen things to come. After Vietnam, the former president was certain that American military might would erode, Congress would cut the defense budget to the bone, and Bartley Sinclair would become a frustrated general in a deteriorating army.

He was Governor of Oregon at the age of forty-three, elected U.S. Senator at forty-seven, and now, at forty-nine, all but officially nominated by the Republican party as its candidate for President of the United States. Bartley Sinclair's zooming political star found critics regarding it as nothing more than a copy of Richard Waters's run for the presidency. Longtime opponents of Waters portrayed Sinclair as a marionette with the former president pulling the strings. Bartley Sinclair never denied the role Richard Waters had played in his life and readily admitted that he would continue to seek his invaluable advice should he be elected. But in answering their accusations, he tersely disclaimed being anyone's puppet. He was his own man, he said, although few, if any, of his adversaries would believe it. For Senator Bartley Sinclair, ex-general and ex-governor, the trip to Houston was not for nomination by the Republican party, but for coronation.

The swarm of television, radio, and newspaper reporters converged upon the senator, slowing his passage. The secret service men resisted the shoving of the reporters, and the senator nodded to an aide that he was willing to be interviewed.

"Just a few questions, please," the aide said to the throng of media personnel.

"General Sinclair! General Sinclair!" a bearded, shaggy-looking scribe for an avant-garde newspaper shouted.

"*Senator* Sinclair," the aide corrected politely.

The shabby reporter asked, "Senator, do you anticipate problems from the handful of black delegates within your own party?"

"Why do you people continue to refer to minorities by the color of their skin? As president, I intend to relate to people, not their color."

"How about religious persuasion, Senator?" another questioned.

"The same applies."

"Is Virtues, Inc., the exception? You do accept their endorsement, don't you, Senator?" asked another.

"I have not, as yet, been nominated. However, should I be, I would gladly accept the endorsement of any law-abiding organization whose primary concern is to restore morality to this country."

"Senator! Senator!" a well-known female television news personality called out. "Can you tell us your feelings as to Senator Lollar's claim that he is being slandered by Virtues, Inc.?"

"If it's true, I'm sure the distinguished senator from Florida will prove it. I understand he was once an exceptional criminal lawyer."

"That's all!" the aide shouted over a volley of questions.

Turning, Sinclair saw Billy sitting alone, looking forsaken. "Keep the reporters away," he said in a voice only the closest secret service agent could hear.

Billy was surprised to see the onrushing agents making a human cordon around both him and the approaching Bartley Sinclair and attempted to rise.

"No, please, Billy. Please sit," Sinclair insisted, sitting next to him.

279

Billy returned the warm smile and looked upon the face that made Richard Waters beam with pride.

"Billy, how have you been?"

"Oh, still hobbling about, Bartley."

"The old man was sure you wouldn't be here."

"And miss your nomination?" Billy said, sensing a hint of sadness in Sinclair's eyes. "How is Richard?"

"Unfortunately, a little under the weather. He thought it best to remain in Portland and watch it on the tube."

"I'm sorry to hear that. I know how much your nomination means to Richard. You will give him my fondest regards when you speak to him?"

"Without fail . . . Billy, have you been made comfortable? Anything I can do for you?"

"Actually, you can. I find myself without an invitation to the convention."

"Incredible," Sinclair exclaimed. "George!" he called out to a burly man, who obediently broke through the blockade and came to his side. "I want you to see to it, personally, that Reverend Hale has invitations to *all* of the functions." He reached for Billy's hand. "Wish I could stay longer."

"I understand," said Billy, taking his hand.

"Billy, I had nothing to do with that newsletter sent to the delegates. I know what you said about Virtues, Inc., came from your heart."

"I had no idea a newsletter was sent."

"Well, I just wanted you to know."

"Good luck, Bartley."

"God's will, Billy. God's will."

The words "God's will," so loosely bandied about for centuries and still loosely defined, were the very words Billy himself offered to the bereaved who had lost a loved one or when scripture was inadequate in explaining tragedies frequently referred to as "acts of God." The phrase now smoldered oppressively in Billy's mind.

That night, Billy went alone to the Astrodome and sat in an upper box seat with a bird's-eye view of the delegates assembled in their sections arranged according to state.

Harley Lombard was introduced by the speaker, and Billy's attention centered on the man he had personally groomed for evangelical stardom. Harley made his way to the platform atop the triple-tiered stage where two giant helium-inflated red, white, and blue latex elephants gently floated at each side.

Billy was unable to hide his apprehension. He grimaced as Harley stepped before the podium's bulletproof shield and piously asked the convention's body to bow their heads. To Billy's great surprise, Harley's invocation was not an adulating tribute to himself. He spoke well and made no mention of Virtues, Inc. Billy was equally surprised by the brevity of his prayer. The fact that Harley swallowed his pride and adhered only to the words composed by another were, in Billy's opinion, a miracle almost comparable to Jesus' raising the dead.

Billy could not remember when he had last witnessed a convention of politicians so united. There were the usual blowhards making their speeches, those who played to the TV cameras, and a few minor disturbances when someone advocated an issue deemed liberal, but on the whole the Republicans seemed stoutly uniform.

He wearily left the dome and returned to the hotel. He had little to say to a sympathetic Doris. She knew how his status at the convention was tearing at his nerves. She could see how his health was swiftly deteriorating.

Billy tossed and turned in the bed. When sleep finally came, it provided little solace before his mind was attacked by another of his recurring nightmares. He saw himself limping through dense and darkened woods pursuing the sound of a human moan. At a clearing, he saw a steep and unusual hill, barren of trees and grass. It was composed of neither dirt, rock, nor sand, but appeared to be a sheet of blackened ice. Driven on by the persistent moan, he stepped into the clearing and wearily approached the strange hill. He raised his eyes to the hilltop where, under a beam of hallowed light, the cause of these moans became clear. A man in street clothes was kneeling before a tribunal of skeletons attired in monks' robes. The man's head was lowered as if he were repenting. His sickly moans deepened. His trial had ended. The judges were also his prosecutors, and they rattled their shields—each emblazoned with the symbol of a great world religion. Their bony hands gripped the golden handles of flashing steel swords, and Billy bleakly identified this scene from a book he had read—a book written by a man he could never forget. Suddenly, the judges raised their sabres in a salute to the summoned executioner. A dark, hooded figure towered over the judges, and Billy shuddered. A snow-white cloud with blood-red letters forming the words "IN THE NAME OF GOD" loomed above the ghostly hill. The faceless angel glided forth and swung a mammoth sword from side to side, creating gusts of wind. The condemned man's moan swelled into a frenzied scream as the slashing blade severed his head cleanly from his body. A chorus of heinous laughter was emitted by the skeletal judges as the decapitated head rolled down the icy hill and lay motionless at Billy's feet.

"Noooo," Billy shouted, bolting upright in the bed with sweat pouring from his terrified face.

Instantly awakened, Doris flicked on the table lamp. "Billy, are you all right?" she asked, fearing her husband was having a heart attack.

Billy lifted the bedcovers from his legs as if they were blankets of steel, then slipped off the bed and limped to the bathroom. Doris brought him a lightweight bathrobe and helped him remove the drenched pajama top from his quivering body.

"The hallway?" she softly asked.

"No. If our words are being heard, so be it."

She watched him collapse into a chair, noticing the terrible strain on his face.

"These nightmares," he moaned, "must they persist?"

"What was it this time?" she asked.

Billy took a deep breath. "Dan Kaiser—I saw his decapitated head lying at my feet."

"Billy, we're going home. You must get away from it all."

"I cannot get away from myself." He brought a hand to his face and his fingers massaged his furrowed brow. "It is more, Doris. God knows how much more." His words now came with confessional truth. "The Trinity, God's will, I now find myself questioning the very beliefs I have so vigorously defended, so righteously preached to people who have gone to their graves believing in what I said."

"It's no wonder. You're frustrated over this conspiracy business, you're not able to fight off bad thoughts."

"I am supposed to be a man of unfaltering faith."

"Billy, the devil is feeding on your wounds."

"The devil? No, Doris, I am afraid not. For even Satan is no longer colored red."

"Billy, surely you're not losing your faith?"

"Maybe I'm gaining in faith. Perhaps I am now able to see things I never before wanted to see."

"No, Billy, your mind is so terribly weakened. Worrying so much has confused you."

"Quite possibly. Regardless, I cannot help but question."

"It's the devil. It has to be. How he would cherish a victory over you."

"I am inclined to believe it *is* a spiritual force. However, it is not a force of Satan."

"If not the devil, who?"

"If I am to believe my conscience, it is from the soul of the man I defamed."

Doris could see the color gradually returning to his face, and she was surprised by his rising from the chair with new-found vigor.

"From here on, Dan will have to follow his own leads while I concentrate my efforts on something I should have taken care of the moment we arrived."

"Harley?"

"His narcissistic self."

"He'll only keep avoiding you."

"Harley's leisure habits are not as unfamiliar to me as he might presume. Tomorrow, if I have to camp in front of his door all night long, I damn well shall get to see him!"

*   *   *

Harley Lombard was drinking too much. Without Sue Bergman's guiding presence, he was out of control and feeling mightier than ever. The guests invited to Senator Sinclair's cocktail party—mostly high-level campaign workers, political allies, and a few heavyweight financial backers who mingled in the expansive living room of the senator's presidential suite—found Harley rude and bordering on the obnoxious. In return, Harley found them utterly inferior to his grand self.

Sue Bergman's hand-picked successor to Andy Gaines, a man named Deek Ashburn, brought Harley another scotch, but only after Harley threatened him.

"That little guy," said Harley, "the one watching television by himself, he looks familiar. Find out who he is," he ordered, plucking the drink from the man's hand.

"Reverend Lombard, I think it ill advised."

"You think *what?*"

"Ms. Bergman left instructions you were to meet with her before coming to this cocktail party."

"Is she here, dummy?"

"As I told you, her plane was late leaving Washington. Reverend, I think we should return to your suite and wait for her."

"Did she arrange this meeting with Sinclair or not?"

"I wouldn't know."

"Don't you think I can handle it?"

"Reverend Lombard, you've already had too much to drink."

"Consider yourself fired."

Annoyed, Harley brushed past a group of people and approached the man he thought looked familiar. "You're ah . . . ?"

"Dooley Law, Reverend Lombard."

"Of course. You're running against Senator Lollar."

"There is the matter of winning the primary."

"You will, won't you?"

"I expect to. But then, only death and taxes are certain."

"I don't know about taxes," said Harley, rocking from

side to side. "What I do know is that we've spent a lot of money kicking Lollar's ass. Understand?"

"Mmmmm, no. I'm not sure I do."

Harley drew closer, searched the smaller man's face, and took particular notice of Dooley Law's unusually large ears.

"Is something wrong, Reverend Lombard?" Dooley Law asked, somewhat annoyed by Harley's close inspection of his head.

"No offense intended, but were you called Dumbo as a kid?"

Senator Lollar's likely Republican opponent was not amused, nor was he willing to let it pass as words from a man influenced by liquor. He was greatly offended, and stepped backward like a bantam rooster about to attack. "Large ears do have their advantages. One can hear the words of a drunken jackass miles away."

The appearance of a Sinclair aide aborted Harley's nasty reply. "Excuse me, Reverend Lombard, the senator will see you now."

Dooley Law murmured, "Stupid, stupid man," as he watched Harley follow the aide through a crowded room to a closed door where two secret service agents stood sentry.

For someone who had never met the senator, Harley acted as if they were old school buddies. But the senator's attractive wife did not buy Harley's familiarity, nor his bright smile and glad hand. Concealing her distaste, she graciously excused herself from the sitting room to leave her husband and his veteran campaign chairman braced for the unexpected.

"Senator," said Harley, "it'll be a landslide."

"From your lips to God's ears, Reverend Lombard," the campaign chairman interjected amiably.

"And I can tell you, when I speak, God listens," Harley countered gravely.

"Have you seen Billy?" Sinclair inquired.

"Billy who? Oh, Billy."

"He is here at the convention. Or didn't you know?"

"Yes, I've been told."

"He is a great man, remarkable and sincere. Wouldn't you agree, Reverend Lombard?"

"True, Senator, quite true. And Billy deserved his retirement."

"Richly and honestly earned, Reverend Lombard."

"Senator," Harley said, eager to change the subject, "I want you to depend on Virtues, Inc., for five—no, make it ten million votes."

"*That* is a staggering number, Reverend Lombard. Isn't it, George?" the senator said to his burly campaign chairman.

"Really? And I'm thinking *conservatively*," Harley laughed.

The senator failed to smile, and it was difficult to read the reaction of the savvy chairman who had once served as Richard Waters's press secretary. Harley spoke boldly on. "If I were you, Senator, I'd alert the fumigation people. Get 'em ready to clean up all that donkey shit in the White House."

Suspicion glinted in Sinclair's eyes. "You do have a certain flair for saying what is on your mind, don't you, Reverend Lombard?"

"Senator, if Harley Lombard tells you he can deliver, you can bet your Bible delivery is assured."

"You are, of course, referring to votes," said George.

"Ten million of them. And the count goes on."

"I was not aware that Virtues, Inc., was such a powerful entity," the senator said.

"Entity, Senator?"

"Forgive me. I meant to say I didn't realize it had such an influence on the American voter."

"Enough to put you in the White House," Harley said. "And another thing, Senator; the way I see it, forget wasting valuable time on the Jews and niggers. Hell, you don't need their votes. God-fearing Americans will get you elected."

The campaign manager cleared his throat nervously and looked at his watch. "Uh, Senator," he said, "I believe Senator Bridges is waiting."

"Senator Bridges!" Harley belittled. "Is he more important than ten million votes?"

"Why, no, it's only that Senator Sinclair is on a very tight schedule, and—"

"Reverend Lombard," Sinclair interrupted, glaring at Harley, "I believe you omitted the Hispanics when you referred to minorities. Was it simply an oversight?"

"The *Spics?* Hell, most of them don't have birth certificates."

"I see," Sinclair said, extending a reluctant hand for Harley to shake.

"Just remember what I said, Senator."

"Reverend Lombard, I can promise I will not soon forget."

No sooner had Sue Bergman entered her reserved room—connected to Harley's suite—then successive messages informed her of Harley's damaging performance. She snapped at the man Harley had fired in a rare outburst of temper. "Why did you let him go?"

"Ms. Bergman, unless I used force, there was no way to stop the man."

"Maybe you should have," she muttered as she kicked off her shoes and plopped into a chair.

"Ms. Bergman," Deek Ashburn held out two cassettes, "here are the tapes of his phone calls and his meeting with one Veep Siler."

"Not now," she said, pondering her predicament. She needed to regain her power over Harley. Her endeavors to fill Harley's mind with visions of papal power had backfired, for Harley was living the visions. The fact that he had attended Sinclair's cocktail party told her that she could no longer count on his obedience. A confrontation with him was imminent. "Find him, Deek!" she ordered.

Harley left Sinclair's suite praying Sue Bergman had arrived. He was totally oblivious to anyone or anything else. The fact that he had called a potential U.S. senator "Dumbo" and made bigoted remarks to the man who would soon receive the party's presidential nomination—

these matters had no place in his mind. He had no after-thoughts or regrets.

Anticipating pure bliss, he made the turn to his wing, where he saw Andy Gaines's successor coming toward him. "Why aren't you in Siberia?" he hissed.

"Ms. Bergman wishes to see you in *your* suite."

"Not as much as I wish to see her," said Harley.

The door was locked and Harley was without a key. He felt that carrying heavy metal keys was undignified for a man of his stature. "The only key the pope carries is the key to the treasury," he had told Sue Bergman after she admonished him for locking them out of several hotel rooms during their extracurricular activities.

"Well?" Harley said pompously. "Open it and *maybe* I'll consider your reinstatement." However, once inside, rehiring the man was out of the question. "Get lost!" Harley threatened.

"When Ms. Bergman tells me," came the crisp reply.

Harley was enraged by his unwelcome escort, who followed him into the master bedroom. Before he had time to explode, Sue Bergman appeared at the connecting door, changing his fury to fervor. She came through the door, dismissed the man with a nod, then slipped back into her room with Harley at her heels like a dog in heat.

She removed his hand from her arm and sat in a chair opposite a drab sofa.

"Sue, no kiss?"

"Sit down, Harley. We've something to talk about."

"Later." He moved clumsily toward her.

"I *mean* it, Harley. Sit down."

She was showing a side he hadn't known she possessed. "What are you so mad about?" he said indignantly.

"When you sit down, you will find out."

He did not have the patience or will to argue. With a growing bulge in his pants, he sat down on the sofa submissively.

Momentarily, she was unsure where to begin. "Harley, we have to do something about that mouth of yours."

"Speaking of mouths," he said coyly.

"You made a fool out of yourself in front of Senator Sinclair and his campaign chairman. Fortunately, and I do mean fortunately, no reporter was present. And what possessed you to insult Dooley Law?"

"I just told Dumbo where it was at."

"*Dumbo* happens to be a very important industrialist who *knows* where it is at."

"Elephant Ears needs my clout. I just reminded him."

"*Your* clout?"

"Who else's?"

"Harley—"

"Sue," he interrupted, "without Virtues, Inc., Sinclair doesn't become president. Isn't that what you've been telling me?"

She would not deny it and create doubt in Harley's mind. He had become the ultimate egomaniac, and she would need to use great delicacy in handling him. "Harley," she began, "a great deal of money has been spent by my clients. Understand that, while they are God-fearing patriots, they are excellent businessmen as well. What I'm saying, Harley, is that they would neither appreciate nor forgive seeing their dollars given to a cause which could lead to bad headlines in the papers."

She rose from the chair and moved deliberately away from him. "Therefore, tomorrow morning you will hold a press conference. You will speak about the constitutional rights of Blacks and America's support for Israel."

"Sinclair doesn't need the damned nigger and Jew vote. He knows it, I know it, God knows it, and so do you."

"For everyone's benefit, you *will* have that press conference."

"You're making it sound like *I* have to kiss Sinclair's ass."

"Harley, who more than anyone else wants you to fail?"

"I don't know. The devil?"

"What if Billy Hale finds out what you said about the Blacks and Jews? Think, Harley. He would waste little time in destroying your credibility. Virtues, Inc., would collapse. I would have some serious explaining to do and *you* would have some serious problems of your own."

"Well, maybe the bit about Israel. But bullshit on the Blacks."

"From this moment on, you are the great defender of the Constitution. And that includes constitutional rights for all *Black* Americans."

"Damned spades."

"Harley, if they crucified Christ, surely you are not invulnerable."

"All right," Harley surrendered bitterly.

"Tomorrow, you will have the press conference?"

"Yeah, I'll do it."

"Is that a promise?"

"Jesus, Sue, I *said* I'll do it."

She was still not totally convinced as she returned to the chair and warned, "This is one promise I'm going to hold you to."

"Really?" said Harley. "Oh, really? And I'm holding you to yours."

She looked at him oddly, then that silly, stupid grin on his face became all too enlightening. "Tomorrow, Harley, after the nomination. After you give a splendid benediction."

"Uh-uh, *tonight*. Merry widow, nylons, garter belt, the whole bit." He sprang off the sofa and sank to his knees before her. "I'm ready for you, Sue. It's not going to be so easy."

She looked down at the determined face and sighed. "Harley, I'm awfully tired."

"I'm *ready*. You'll get lockjaw before I come."

She knew further attempts to postpone his desire were futile. "Must I wear that stuff? I mean, it takes longer to put on those garments than the act itself."

"Not tonight!"

A disbelieving smile creased her full lips. "Sure, Harley, sure."

It took precisely forty-nine seconds for Harley to dash into his master bedroom, shed his clothes, splash musk cologne on his face, spray deodorant under his armpits, and use mouthwash. Sue Bergman took twice as long just to brush her teeth.

Ridiculous! It was insane, she repeated to herself. How could she have allowed this to happen? How could she be intimately involved with a man she utterly deplored? She had not been as thorough in her investigation of Harley as she had once believed. Providing him with sexual favors was one thing she had never anticipated.

Normally, true to the ethics of the legal profession, she would avoid getting sexually involved with her clients. Intelligent conversation, an evening at the opera, or an afternoon at a horse show would weed out the men who had sex as their first priority. But the first night she dined with Harley he was constantly feeling her knees and thighs under the table, telling her how horny he was getting. She thought his conduct vulgar and especially unbecoming a man of God, yet at the same time somewhat refreshing. The latter feeling was her downfall. Ever since that night, Harley had become addicted to her mouth.

In her bedroom, wearing the outfit Harley had prescribed, she stood before a dresser mirror. Her fingers ran across her full breasts where they rose above the bustiére. Her hands slipped to a tight waist which indented above full hips and shapely thighs, then moved to check the garter clips which held up black nylon stockings. Black spike heels added inches to a figure Lombard once said would have driven even the most incorruptible of saints to sodomy.

"Jesus, Sue, what a rod I'm getting," Harley called from the other room.

As a young girl, her first sexual experience with a man was like something out of a novel with incest as its theme. She was only twelve, growing up in suburban Atlanta, when her respected southern-judge grandfather went beyond his usual fondling and took her virginity.

Her only marriage had lasted five days short of one year. Her engineer husband blamed the breakup on her career as a lawyer in her father's prestigious Atlanta firm. She was too caught up in her own career, he said, to be the

291

loving wife he needed. In truth, his appetite for oral sex was more than she could endure.

"Sue, you got it on?"

The more she looked into the mirror, the more depressed she grew. A self-analysis only deepened her shame. How could she, a professional woman, a lawyer, the executive director of the A.R.A., trusted by some of the biggest names in American industry, be compelled to submit to a deed whores on the street did for a living? Furthermore, how could she, a woman of such limited experience, obsess Harley with her lovemaking? While she could not answer the latter question, she knew the answer to the first—ambition.

"Sue, what's keeping you? Damn, I'm horny!"

She resisted the temptation to shatter his vanity and tell him how she detested the very sight of him; how it had become impossible for her to conceal her contempt for him. Now she was locked into a predicament reserved for kept women and whores. But she would not express her outrage for fear of compromising the ARA's game plan, not to mention her own plans. She had only herself to blame.

"Sue?"

The only thing which put her into motion was the thought of finishing him off fast, followed by a hot shower and sleep. Stepping from the mirror, she quietly appeared at the doorway to his bedroom and saw Harley busily stroking his engorged organ.

"Sue, you're driving me crazy. Will you hurry up!"

"I'm here, Harley," she whispered.

He could not find words to give meaning to how he felt; how her shapely presence in the semidarkness had stolen his breath; how no price was too high for the pleasure she was about to give him. He beckoned for her with outstretched arms.

Contrary to her resolve, she suddenly felt a need for time, for conversation. "Harley, why me?" she asked.

"What an ass," he marveled.

"I'm curious, Harley. Why me?"

"Sue, will you come here?"

"Not until you tell me."

"You're kidding!"

"I'm not. And I need to know."

Harley laughed. "You're the best. *Okay?*"

"Surely you've had better."

"Sue, if you think you can get me out of the mood with all this talk, you can forget it."

"What about your wife? Doesn't she, as you say, blow your brains out?"

"*Wilma Mae?* If I gave her the chance, she'd bite it off."

"Why would you even say something like that?"

"Why? Because it's true. She hates me. She's got a screwy complex over her father."

"How so?"

"She tells me constantly that I'm not the man he was."

"What kind of man was he?"

"He was a peckerwood preacher in a broken-down church who preached to broke parishioners—Sue, goddammit!"

She realized there was no point in stalling the inevitable, and walked over to the side of the bed furthest from him. He sat there, entranced by the gyrating movement of her hips, until she swung her legs onto the bed.

"Sue, let me suck those beautiful tits."

"Relax. Lie back," she said, fighting off his hands.

"I want to feel that ass."

"Just lie back. Enjoy."

"Sue, sit on my face."

"Shhhhush," she pacified, placing a finger to his lips.

"No," he protested.

Having managed to position her knees between his legs, she softly pushed his chest until his head rested on a pillow. Bending forward, she caressed his face with her warm lips, yet avoided his wet and open mouth. She then nibbled at his ear, breathed heat into its cavity, and repeated the same in the other ear in a slow, seductive manner; her darting tongue generated electrifying chills which raced to his wriggling toes.

Working downward, she stroked his chest with her fingertips, then licked and nipped at his hardening nipples. The soft, delicate touch of her fingers played along his sides as she eased her face toward his swollen penis.

"Aw, no," he groaned, tossing his head wildly about the pillow as he felt the warm approach of her mouth to his throbbing erection. "Noooo," he feebly uttered as she cupped his balls in her hands, arching them towards her parted lips.

She examined his fully expanded glans with the dispassionate gaze of a woman looking over cuts of meat in a supermarket counter. But while she felt neither ardor nor desire, she was fully programmed to complete the act. She knew it would all be over in three minutes or less. She would reduce him to a state of total helplessness. He would have his orgasmic fix and she could return to her room and worry about tomorrow.

He felt her hot, wet lips lathering his cock and gripped the bedspread in anticipation. Her snaking tongue titillated his nerve endings, forcing him to squirm, when she took the head into her mouth. And then came that suction. She took an inch more—and again that suction. Another inch and the juices began to curdle in his balls. With another swallow, she took his entire prick deep into her mouth.

"I love you, Sue," he kept repeating through the grinding of his teeth.

She released an inch at a time until only the head was inside her constricting mouth. She went down again, swallowing and sucking, and when she took him full, her deft right hand left his balls and he could barely feel her finger until it probed deeper into his ass. Despite his boast of control, he was nearing an explosive climax that would leave him whimpering, and she was furiously driving him towards it when her mouth froze. She became breathlessly still.

"Sue, for God's sake, don't stop!"

The sound of door chimes became clearer and she raised herself upward with semen dribbling from the corner of her mouth.

"Sue, do it. Don't stop. Jesus, *suck me!*"

"Someone is at your door," she informed him coolly.

"Who gives a shit? I was coming!"

The chimes persisted, and she slithered to the edge of the bed, away from a face gripped with frustration.

"Sue, you can't leave me this way. I'll have blue balls for a month!"

The chimes gave way to a loud knocking.

"Whoever it is will go away," Harley dismissed desperately.

"I don't think so, Harley."

"Shit! Who the hell would be banging on my door this time of night?"

"I don't know, Harley, but it must be important."

"Who? Who, Sue? *Who?*"

"Why not look through the peephole and find out?"

"Shit," said Harley, getting off the bed. "Piss!" he cursed as he took her advice. "Corruption!" he bellowed with scatological rage, leaving the bedroom.

The knocking intensified as he bounded nude across the living room, then tiptoed to the door. As he peered through the peephole, the red drained from his flushed face. A palish gray took its place as he streaked back to the bedroom.

"It's Billy Hale and his fucking cane."

Sue Bergman did not look surprised.

"What right has that old man to come here at this hour and bother me?"

"You won't know unless you open the door."

"The hell with him. He can stay out there all night."

"That wouldn't be smart, Harley. If the press gets wind of Billy knocking on your door, we're likely to read about it."

"Goddamn nosy old man. Got nothing to do but bother people."

"Harley, where are you going?"

"Where the hell do you think? To let him in."

"Nude?"

In the hallway, heads were popping from rooms. Curious faces focused their attention on Billy Hale. Undaunted, he continued to rap the cane's marble handle against the wooden door frame with increasing urgency.

"Harley," Billy shouted, "this disturbance will only worsen."

"Coming, Billy! Coming!"

The door opened and Billy took in the sweat rolling down Harley's face.

"Sorry I took so long. I was taking a shower," said Harley. He beckoned Billy in, then quickly shut the door behind them.

Billy saw the redness on the tip of Harley's nose brighten. "I would think it was a sauna by the way you're perspiring," he said, moving past Harley.

"A *hot* shower," Harley defended weakly.

"I can imagine," said Billy, taking notice of the oriental silk robe draped over a chair.

"Something wrong, Billy?"

"Oh, yes. Something is wrong. But first I want to know why you have been ducking me for the past two days."

"You know how it is, Billy. Interviews, newspaper reporters, the TV people."

"Spare me the B.S., Harley. The red spot on your nose is blinking like a neon sign."

"What—what do you mean?" Harley protested meekly as he watched Billy move further into the living room and casually inspect the furnishings.

"Quite a place, Harley. You could fit my entire suite into this one room."

"Ah, Billy, I've got a busy day tomorrow. What's this problem you wish to talk to me about?"

With the aid of his cane, Billy turned to face him. "Son, *you* are the problem."

"*Me?*" Harley shook his head. "No. No, I don't think so. It wasn't me who said terrible things about *you* in the newspapers."

Billy's nose twitched. "Perfume, Harley?"

"Huh?"

"Pleasant fragrance. Is Wilma Mae here?"

"Ah, no. No, she—Billy, where are you going?"

Billy was too far into the room for Harley to stop him. The bedroom had been plunged into darkness and Billy looked from corner to corner searching for a presence. He stepped further into the room with ears perked to hear the slightest sound, and suddenly likened himself to an exorcist seeking out a demon.

"Ms. Bergman?" he called softly.

There was no response nor any sound. And he called again in a firmer tone, "Ms. Susan Bergman?"

A blur passed before his eyes, leaving a warm wind in its wake. A creaking sound preceded a ray of light, and Billy saw her standing in the doorway that connected the suites, dressed in her exotic undergarments and seemingly unruffled by his presence.

"Let Harley be," said Billy Hale as if he was commanding Satan to be gone.

She smiled triumphantly, then vanished into her room.

It was an embarrassed Harley who was hard put to explain upon Billy's return from the bedroom: "It's not what it appears to be."

"Never is."

"She has the room next door."

"With a connecting door."

"We were talking. Just talking."

"About lingerie, no doubt."

Before Harley could object, Billy was seated. "Really, Billy, why don't we discuss this problem of yours tomorrow over breakfast. Say, eight o'clock?"

"Thanks, but no. And it's not my problem, it's yours."

"Really, it's late, Billy. How's lunch tomorrow?"

"No breakfast. No lunch. And why do you persist on using the word 'really.' I can assure you, it will not appease a guilty conscience."

"Billy, I'm really not in the mood for a sermon."

"Sit down, Harley."

"Billy, really, this is—"

"*Sit* down!"

Nobody pushes Harley Lombard around, he thought, especially not now when he was being touted as Mr.

Morality, the pontiff of Virtues, Inc. Yet he still could not muster the courage to tell Billy what he really thought. He slumped grudgingly into a chair directly across the large room from his old benefactor.

"Son, you've been so busy riding the glory train that you have not taken the time to deal with reality."

"Is this going to be another one of your attempts to frighten me?"

"I must try. I owe it to you, Harley."

"It won't work, Billy."

"Unless you give up this Virtues, Inc., nonsense—"

"*Nonsense?* You call Virtues, Inc., *nonsense?*"

"I repeat, unless you give up this Virtues, Inc., nonsense, you will be dead and buried within six months."

"*Jesus,*" Harley jumped out of the chair, "there you go again."

Billy pointed a finger to the bedroom. "That woman will eventually destroy you."

"What woman?"

"Ms. Susan Mai Bergman. Age, thirty-five. Occupation, lawyer. Present status, executive director of the American Recovery Association. *That woman.*"

"Sure," Harley nodded. "it figures. What now, Billy, are you going to tell Wilma Mae? Tell her whom I'm sleeping with?"

"You damn fool, do you think I was blind to your affairs with women?"

"Andy Gaines is a liar!"

"I did not come here to discuss your adulterous activities."

"You're assuming, Billy."

Billy once again pointed to the bedroom. "She has drugged your mind with so much false power that you are oblivious to the great danger surrounding you."

"It's not going to work, Billy, and I know the reason why you are trying this."

"Do you?"

"It troubles me to say it, but you're jealous, Billy."

298

"Of *you?*"

"I've surpassed you, Billy. I've surpassed the great Billy Hale." Harley returned to his chair, sparkling with confidence. "I'm accomplishing things you never did."

"If perchance you are referring to Virtues, Inc., I have never robbed a bank either."

"You know what I mean, Billy. You *know* what I mean." Unable to remain seated, he paced the room. "Harley Lombard, that's right, Billy, Harley Lombard controls the national elections. *I* say who becomes president of the United States. Oh, you think not? You'd be surprised to know the names of the politicians begging for my endorsement."

"I am sure Senator Lollar is not among them."

"Lollar is *finished.* Along with the rest of those liberal give-away heathens."

"The Bible is quite precise when it refers to fraud and defamation as non-virtuous acts. Yet you have the unmitigated gall to call your organization Virtues, Inc.," Billy condemned.

"Virtues, Inc., is America's modern-day crusade against—"

Billy interjected, "How much are you paying Veep Siler to ruin Senator Lollar's good name?"

"Veep's got nothing to do with Virtues, Inc."

"What have you promised the man?"

"I—I don't know what you mean."

"Yes, you do, Harley. You are no match for Veep Siler. The man dreams of devious schemes. He will swallow you whole."

"*No one* swallows Harley Lombard!"

"Get off that throne and listen to me."

"To the words of an old man? A jealous old man!"

"Old, I am. Jealous? No, Harley, caring."

Harley felt momentary shame. "I'm—hell, I'm sorry, Billy. I shouldn't have said what I did."

"I have been called the same by another; he too is blinded with false power. The difference is, Jimmy Christian knowingly accepted his pact with his devil."

"Jimmy *who*? From what I hear, he's become a hermit. Half of his Glee Club network has joined mine."

Billy knew it was useless to continue. Only an appearance by God Himself could penetrate the wall of megalomania which surrounded the evangelist. He rose with difficulty. Harley was most anxious to see him out and frowned when Billy paused at the door.

"For how long, Harley? How long before the media decides to crush you? Before the ARA—yes, Harley, the American Recovery Association and that woman—no longer need you? How many more evangelists will be murdered before it is your turn?"

"Not *that* again."

Billy's face softened; the fight had left him. Harley had been brainwashed with delusions of grandeur. There was nothing Billy could say that would bring Harley back to reality, but nevertheless he tried once more. "Regardless of your present faults, I have come to you because I truly care. I am as concerned as a father would be for a son."

"Billy."

"Allow me to finish. There may not be another time."

Harley's face dropped. He could not deny Billy from speaking the words which came from his heavy heart.

"I am deeply worried over your personal welfare. If ever you respected my advice, now is the time. Son, get out and far away from Virtues, Inc. Take that vacation—a very, very long one."

"The next President of the United States, Senator Bartley Sinclair," announced the speaker amidst tumultuous applause.

The band played a Sousa march while thousands of red, white, and blue balloons lofted towards the Astrodome's roof. From the mouths of two giant inflated elephants came trumpeted blares befitting a Caesar, as Bartley Sinclair stepped before the podium with extended arms waving to the deafening approval of the delegates.

300

Far out in the audience, Billy Hale sat in silence. Next to him, Doris was caught up in the festive pandemonium. "Billy, isn't this exciting?" she leaned over and asked.

His reply was drowned out by the blaring horns nearby. She did not hear him mutter, "The only thing missing is 'Heil Hitler.'"

CHAPTER 29

GRADUATION CEREMONIES at Michael's Mission bore little resemblance to the traditional pomp and circumstance of academe. There were no caps and gowns, no awarding of honors or diplomas. The mission students had undergone 350 days of intensive instruction on the religions of the world. Now it was time to leave this sectless seminary and apply what they had learned in their daily lives.

Jessica Towne stood in a soft, late-summer drizzle, away from the students gathered in front of the porch steps leading to the main house. She had survived the silent scorn of her classmates and the threat of expulsion, she thought— but what now? To live like a gypsy with the man she loved, a man stalked by palpable danger? A man whose heart was an unfathomable pool of hate?

The mission director, John Ragonese, came out from the old house and stood on the porch. It was a tradition for the director to bid each class farewell with a few encouraging words. Resting his bony hands on the porch rail, he searched among the students for Jessica. He saw her standing by herself almost out of range of his voice. ''Well,'' he commenced, ''you have spent a year of your lives studying the various religions of the world. No religion or sect has been presented to you as superior to any other, including the beliefs of our founder. We have attempted to teach that, while no religion is inherently corrupt, all religions are self-serving and capable of engendering the evils which have befallen man. Now the last day is upon us and so too is the inevitability of moving ahead with your lives. I sincerely hope that, as you do, each of you will understand and benefit from your stay at Michael's Mission.''

A ripple of applause caused the mission director's voice to quaver with emotion. "Ron Rebuck founded this mission twelve years ago. Since that time it has survived his untimely death, weathered prejudicial challenges against its charter, and endured vindictive assaults upon its property. It has withstood libelous accusations of being a cult molded by the devil, and lived with the ill will of its neighbors. Michael's Mission survived it all.''

This time the applause was loud and long. John Ragonese drew a deep breath. He had lifted their spirits only to beset them now with gloom. He raised his hand for silence. "But now,'' he continued, "our longtime benefactor from Rome has decided to discontinue her support. Our graduate messengers are sorely pressed with economic hard times of their own.'' He paused to scan the solemn faces, then rushed his closing statement. "I am sorry to say Michael's Mission is unable to support another class.''

His commencement address had become a eulogy. Michael's Mission had run its course. And he would not appease their feelings with a false hope or vague promise of reopening the mission in a metropolitan area or under a different economic format. Nor would he inform them of the November real estate closing on the mission's land.

He remained on the porch as the students disbursed and headed for the yellow school bus that would take them to Lancaster's terminals. He could hear a few disgruntled remarks, none of which were personally directed at him. He turned away, swept by a wave of regret, and saw Jessica standing alone, looking lost and confused. She was caught between the urge to leave and the desire to stay, and he picked up on her struggle. If anything, he thought, could be salvaged on this day of mourning, he would do his best to reason with her, convince her to get on that bus. But the moment passed as the black van rolled down the circular drive and pulled up to the porch steps.

Ike Vesper barreled out of the van and bounded up the

steps to where Ragonese stood. "The girl's stuff—where is it?" he growled.

Ragonese pointed to a battered brown suitcase lying to the side of the screen door, and waited for the mumbling Vesper to pass him, then descended the stairs. Jessica saw him approach and turned away.

"It's not too late to change your mind," he said gently.

"I'm afraid it is."

"You're making a terrible mistake, Jessica."

Jessica turned and saw Ike throw the suitcase into the back of the van. He was eager to leave, for he always felt uneasy in the director's presence. "Little Girl, let's go!" he shouted.

"Jessica, what can I say or do that will make you leave these men and go home?"

"I think you've said enough already."

Jessica was startled by a crack like a pistol shot and almost fell into the director's arms. She turned and saw a cloud of blue smoke floating toward them. The old school bus had backfired as it groaned toward the entrance to the main highway.

"I can always drive you to Lancaster," he said.

"Mr. Ragonese, it's partly because of you that I'm not going home."

"Hey, Little Girl!" Ike shouted impatiently from the van.

"Tell him to go," the mission director pleaded. "*Please*, Jessica."

The hopeful expression on his gaunt face would not be denied. "Go ahead, Ike. I'll walk. It's okay. Really."

Vesper grunted an obscenity and pulled away, leaving them in a shower of gravel.

The soft patter of rain fell on the leaf-strewn trail as Jessica and the mission director walked together in silence, she confused, he curious. "Jessica," he said finally, "what did you mean when you said that it was partly because of me you weren't going home?"

"Ron doesn't trust you."

"That's not surprising. He's unable to see through all of his hate."

"I told him what you said to me that night . . . the questions you asked about him and Ike."

"I only asked those questions because I was concerned for your welfare."

"No, Mr. Ragonese, that's not true. That night at the cemetery, I saw you. You know something about Ron. And you know about the other man who was there too."

"What other man?" Ragonese registered genuine surprise.

"Why do you keep lying to me?"

"I admit I went looking for you that night and found you in the cemetery. But I left. I didn't want to hear that man's soul crying."

"You didn't see another man? A man with scars on his face?"

"Jessica, I only saw you and Ron Rebuck, Jr. This I swear."

Jessica folded her arms as if to ward off a sudden chill in the air. "Everything is so confusing," she said.

"And frightening?"

Yes, she thought to herself.

He spoke to her in a fatherly manner. "You are so young. You have so much to look forward to. There can be nothing here but unhappiness for you."

"You don't understand."

"I understand how a young girl can fall under a bad influence."

"Mr. Ragonese," her voice was breaking, "I *can't* go home."

He watched her run—running to the compound. To *him*, to Ron Rebuck, to the very man who had given him so many sleepless nights.

Ike Vesper looked through the binoculars, calling himself a fool for going along with an order he was sure had nothing to do with his job. The night before, Ron Rebuck had come to his trailer home instructing him to get up at the crack of dawn and take up a position in the loft of the red barn, from where he would have a bird's-eye view of the old house and its circular drive. He was to report back to Rebuck *only* after the mission director had left in the bus.

"Fool's messin' with Captain Death," Ike said aloud. "Ain't shittin' me. Him and his operation ultra-mad. Operation *Doom's* what it is." He lowered the binoculars and continued speaking to himself. "Screwin' up that little girl's life . . . he couldn't party with me. Naw, he had to have Little Red Ridin' Hood. But he ain't gonna get me involved in his crazy scheme. Not this nigger. The captain ain't gonna tear out my guts and shake 'em before this mothafuckin' face."

Jessica Towne had spent a restless night in her new home. She sat in a terrycloth robe drinking her second cup of coffee and watching Rebuck put a small plastic pouch into a blue canvas tote bag. "Ron, is my being here going to be a problem?" she asked.

"Nothing is going to happen to you," he replied, closing the bag.

"I didn't ask you that. I want to know if you're happy being with me."

"It's been a while since I've been happy."

"Ron, about last night . . . I'm sorry."

"For what?"

"The things I said. The way I felt. I didn't mean to burden you."

"You were disappointed. Some graduation. At least you could have received a diploma."

She did not miss the edge of suspicion in his voice. "Ron, do you really believe Mr. Ragonese is the captain's informer?"

"What did that night in the cemetery tell you?"

"I know, Ron, but he swears he didn't see anyone but you and me."

"*Swears?*" Rebuck slighted.

"But why? Why would he be involved with the captain?"

"That's what I intend to find out."

The dogs alerted them to Ike's return, and she watched him slip the tote bag over his shoulder and head for the door. "Ron, where are you going?"

"To answer your question," he responded without looking back.

Outside the mobile home, Ike told Rebuck what he wanted to know. He was about to add his feelings about spending the entire morning in a hayloft when Rebuck motioned for him to follow.

"Where we goin'?" Ike asked, disturbed.

"For a walk in the noonday sun," Rebuck said, starting towards the trail.

"Wonderful," Ike muttered to himself, wondering what the hell Rebuck was carrying in that tote bag.

Not until they reached the point in the trail where they could see the old house did Rebuck elaborate. "Once we're in the house, you take the upstairs and check out every room for weapons. Closets, drawers, under mattresses, everywhere."

"What kind of weapons am I looking for?" Vesper grunted. "The dude's a spook. He's into mojos, not weapons."

"I said weapons, Ike."

"How about a fuckin' slingshot?"

All the doors to the mission house were locked and Vesper forced open a porch window, ripping the clamp on the lock from the seventy-five-year-old frame. They scrambled through the window and looked around the large parlor with its bare, dusty floor and worn furniture. Rebuck pointed to a hallway which he believed would lead Ike to the second floor, but Ike had sauntered toward the portrait which hung over the fireplace, entranced by the striking resemblance between Ron Rebuck and his father, particularly in the eyes. He turned to say something and found himself alone in the room.

Rebuck, rummaging through desk drawers in the director's spartan office, found nothing in the clutter of records and correspondence relative to what he was looking for. There was no filing cabinet or safe in the tiny office and

Rebuck dropped into the wooden chair in a gesture of defeat. His instincts had been wrong. The director was not quite as disorganized as he appeared to be. Seeing what seemed to be a black, leather-bound religious missal on the desk next to the battered telephone, he casually picked it up.

Ike clumped down the creaking stairs and entered the main room, whisking past the portrait of Rebuck's father. Standing in the doorway to the small office, he saw Rebuck seated behind the desk reading what he assumed was a holy book.

Rebuck looked up. "What did you find?"

"Shotgun. Twelve gauge. Plenty of shells. Found it inside Spooky Man's bedroom—in a closet."

Rebuck tossed the book to Ike. He caught it with one hand. "What page does Moses whack off on?"

"Under American Realty. The last telephone number. Read the name."

Ike turned to the last page of the book and ran his finger down the numbers. It stopped on a single name: "Sam." Vesper felt a burning sensation in his finger, and a cold wash of fear raised gooseflesh on his massive arms.

"Interesting?" asked Rebuck.

"Man, it could be someone else. There's a whole lot of guys named Sam."

Rebuck leaned forward in the chair, pointing to the phone. "Why don't you call that number and find out?"

"Man, I'd call hell first." He flipped the directory back to Rebuck.

"Ike," said Rebuck, slowly rising from the chair, "I get the feeling there's a safe hidden somewhere in this room."

Vesper had an immediate vision of the Reverend Cody Walker, of that night they had walked away from a fortune. "A safe like the one we never saw?" he asked. "The one they say had a million bucks stashed in it? Man, if I had known there was a motherfuckin' safe in that turkey's den, I'd be in Tahiti now, instead of up to my ass in ulta-matums."

308

"Think back, Ike. Where did they say the safe was?"

"Behind some holy . . ."

Their eyes went simultaneously to the only picture in the director's office, a stylized portrait of the body of Jesus Christ in fusion with the soul of Michael the Archangel. Rebuck lifted the large oil painting off its wall fastening, revealing a small safe. He removed the plastic pouch from his carry bag and molded two small charges of C-4 explosive, then inserted a thirty-second timing detonator in each. It took only a moment for Rebuck with his expertise to wire the safe to blow properly and not destroy its contents.

The explosion ripped the safe's door from the hinges, smashed the lone office window, and sent a creaking shudder through the old house. They waited for the smoke to clear, then re-entered the office. Vesper ripped the dangling door from the splayed hinges and peered inside. "Shit," he said, "ain't nothin' in here but a bunch of papers."

"Put them on the desk," Rebuck ordered.

Cursing their luck, Ike placed several legal documents on the desk for Rebuck to read.

While Vesper paced in and out of the office, Rebuck spent the next twenty minutes methodically poring over the papers. Ike grudgingly admitted to himself that most of Ron's hunches concerning the mission director and the captain had been on the mark. Once again he stuck his head through the office doorway. "Those papers tell ya anything, Little Brotha?"

"All I need to know."

"What's Spooky Man's connection with the captain?"

Rebuck pushed back the chair and stood up. "About one and a half million dollars," he replied.

John Ragonese returned to the mission driving a 1980 Plymouth he'd bought with the money from the sale of the school bus in Lancaster. For the first time in twelve years, he would be the sole occupant of the old mission house. He had deposited his three staff members and the cook at the bus terminal; now, with no new class of students to occupy his attention, Regonese knew he would finally have time to concentrate on affairs of an urgent nature.

He smelled the acrid odor of the C-4 explosives the moment he unlocked the front door. Hurrying to his office, he discovered the shattered window, the blown safe, and its contents—piled neatly on his desk. Ragonese did not need a degree in criminology to identify the recent trespassers. In a way, he had almost expected it, but he had no intention of immediately confronting Ron Rebuck, a man whose hatred filled him with terror.

Through the evening hours and deep into the night, Ragonese sat in his creaking chair considering his options. The codicil Rebuck held to his father's will seemed to be an insurmountable barrier. He knew Rebuck would turn down his offer to buy the two hundred acres of the mission grounds and that it would be useless to try and influence him through Jessica; she was too much under his spell.

It was understood that if Ragonese could not deliver the entire five-hundred-acre parcel to American Realty with a clear title, there was no deal. He would be forced to return the twenty-five-thousand-dollar down payment, money he had already spent to nurse the mission through its final term. He could probe for a solution until sunrise but the answer would not deviate. He would have to sell all but Rebuck's two hundred acres to another. But to whom? His Amish neighbors had condemned the mission's land as unholy. The mortgage payment for the students' building was a month in arrears, and the Lancaster Bank had sent the second letter demanding payment. Foreclosure was imminent.

Opening his personal directory, he found the phone number of American Realty for after-business hours. It was the only way, he thought. Perhaps he could convince American Realty to either negotiate separately with Rebuck or accept the land without his two hundred acres. Exhausted from his own mental gambits, he dialed the number. "American Realty? . . . Yes, this is John Ragonese calling from Michael's Mission in Pennsylvania. I must speak with Sam.

*   *   *

The codeword "Crucifix," the alert for Rebuck and Vesper to promptly leave the area, was received by Ike over the portable communication system at precisely six minutes and six seconds after 6:00 P.M. Ike disconnected the radio with its electronic scrambler, carried the equipment out of his trailer, and rushed to the motor home. Entering, he heard the running water, swept past Jessica, who was preoccupied with cooking, and shook the shower curtain. "We got a 'crucifix,' Little Brotha. Move it!"

Rebuck calmly shut off the water and stepped out from the stall. "It figures," he said to himself, reaching for a towel from a cabinet. "Go ahead and hook up the radio in the van. We'll be there in a minute."

"*We?*"

"We're taking Jessica."

"Are you crazy?"

"Ike, we're *taking* Jessica."

John Ragonese drove the white Plymouth at a speed even the most patient motorists found exasperating. His slow driving along the winding, heavily traveled truck route had caused a long procession of fellow travelers to form behind him, flashing their high beams in his rearview mirror, honking their horns, and risking high-speed passes in the short passing lanes of the dangerous three-lane artery. He finally reached King of Prussia and coasted into a gas station for directions to the Hilton Inn. The clock inside the station's cubicle read nine o'clock. Ragonese drove the final miles to his destination more briskly. His instructions were to wait by the pay phone inside the Hilton lobby for a call which would be placed at precisely 9:30 P.M. He was to ignore the ring and wait for another call which would come at ten o'clock. If Ragonese was puzzled by the cloak-and-dagger routine, he would be completely baffled before the night was over.

Ragonese answered the second call and was instructed by a voice he could not identify to proceed to the nearby Valley Forge Sheraton. He was handed written directions by the Hilton bell captain. At the Sheraton registration desk, he asked for the key to room 666 according to his instructions. "You've been pre-registered," the clerk said, handing him the room key.

John Ragonese sat in room 666 for the better part of an hour, waiting for still another phone call. The phone jangled and he let it ring four times, again according to his instructions. Unlike before, he was not cordial to the caller and demanded to know the reason for his dashing from one place to another. All he heard in reply was a loud click in his ear.

His next destination. The Sting Restaurant, was a short distance from the Sheraton, and John Ragonese had resigned himself to play out this game of intrigue. He was determined to accomplish what had taken him from the mission as he swung the Plymouth into the half-filled parking area. As he entered the restaurant, he wondered if its name was telling him something.

Ike Vesper pulled the black van into The Sting's parking lot and cut the lights. "What now, little Brotha?"

"We wait. Just like before."

"Ron," Jessica said from the back seat, "what is he doing?"

Rebuck looked at his watch: 11:29 P.M. "We'll soon know."

"How soon?" Ike asked. He was wary about following the mission director without understanding the reason.

"If my guess is right, before midnight," Rebuck answered.

They sat in silence, each with his own thoughts, until Ike suddenly said, "Spooky Man's visual."

Ragonese had emerged from the restaurant holding a sheet of scribbled instructions which he read while he walked to the car. He was still staring intently at the paper when he guided the car back onto the highway.

"Closer, Ike," Rebuck urged.

"Man, the spook'll know we're followin' him, if he don't already."

"I want him to. Just like I know a gray sedan is following us."

It was 11:50 when Ragonese drove through the main entrance to historic Valley Forge National Park. Ahead, dappled in the light of a three-quarter moon, he could see the wooden huts which had housed George Washington's bedraggled Continental Army during the bitter winter of 1776. Ragonese crumpled the paper in his sweaty hands. There were no more directions to follow. He was to park the car in front of the seventh hut, then walk back. At the stroke of midnight, he was to enter the fifth hut.

"He's stoppin'," Ike alerted.

"Pull over," Rebuck ordered.

Ike brought the van to the side of the narrow road fronting the third hut and looked into his rearview mirror. Fifty yards behind, the gray sedan did likewise.

"Spooky Man's footin' it. Comin' towards us, Little Brotha," Ike whispered.

Rebuck saw the silhouette of the mission director, and Jessica could feel the tension building in his body.

"He's stoppin'. Standin' before a hut," Ike informed.

"Why?" Jessica asked, no longer able to silently observe. "Who's in there?"

"Tell her, Ike."

"Man, tell her what? I don't know who the spook's meetin'."

"Who else would pick out a location like Valley Forge for a midnight meeting in a darkened hut?"

"Uh-huh, sure," Ike responded to Rebuck's rhetorical question and straightened up in his seat. "And if you're right like I think you are, they don't need our company."

Rebuck did not protest as Ike let out the clutch and threw the van into a squealing U-turn. The two occupants of the gray sedan looked straight ahead as the van sped past them.

Only through a great exercise of willpower did John Ragonese summon the courage to enter the darkened hut. He immediately had a sense of having entered a forbidden place. Faint rays of moonlight flickered through cracks in

313

the ancient logs and he could dimly make out the rows of double bunk beds which had held the bodies of American patriots on those freezing nights more than two hundred years earlier. All his instincts told him to flee and forego this meeting, but he was struck by a terrified paralysis. His feet were locked onto the sacred ground.

A sudden sound of movement from a corner of the cabin stole his breath. He squinted, trying to focus on the shadowy figure crouched in the darkness. "I'm John Ragonese," he said, praying for an answer. He was greeted by silence. "I'm to meet with someone from American Realty." Still, the figure made no sound or movement. "Are you their representative?"

"Were you ever a soldier?" came a raspy whisper from the darkened corner.

John Ragonese was too frightened to recognize the voice. "Ah, no. No, I'm afraid not."

"Do you hear them?"

"Hear who?"

"Soldiers! The soldiers of the Continental Army. Their spirits pervade this dwelling. *Do you hear them?*"

All Ragonese heard was the trip-hammer pounding of his heart. "I'm sorry, but no, I really don't."

"Have you ever spilled a man's blood in combat?"

"As I said, I was not in the armed forces."

"Religious reasons? *Conscientious objector?*" the voice thundered.

"Sir—sir, this is all very strange. I've been told to go to hotels, a restaurant, and now here to a historical shrine. Sir, are you—"

"You were followed."

"Followed? Excuse me, but am I speaking with an authorized representative of American Realty?"

"Who did you call?"

"Sam. I called Sam."

"Get on with it, then."

"Yes. Yes, of course, then I take it you are Sam."

"Call me what you please. Just get on with the purpose of your request."

314

Ragonese was not sure where to begin. "I have a certain problem concerning the sale of the mission land. It is a problem I felt I had to discuss with a representative of American Realty."

"The codicil?"

"Yes, that is the problem, but I don't believe I ever mentioned it to anybody at American Realty."

"Go on."

Ragonese fought back his increasing uneasiness. "You are obviously aware of the difficulty I face in selling a two-hundred-acre portion of the tract."

"For every problem, there is a solution. And if you can't find a solution, then change the problem."

"I was thinking that perhaps you or some other representative of American Realty might have a talk with the young man who holds the codicil to his father's will and can, therefore, block the sale of the entire property."

Ragonese was buffeted by a sudden storm of manic laughter. "Denied!" the voice bellowed.

"Then would American Realty consider purchasing the land less the young man's two hundred acres?"

"Denied!"

"Then I am left with no alternative. I am unable to honor the contract. I will be forced to return the option money."

"You don't have it."

"No, not right now. But I do have until November 7 to raise it."

"Then raise it—one hundred thousand dollars."

"Sir, I believe you're mistaken. I was paid only twenty-five thousand dollars."

The voice now had a hard, businesslike edge. "If you fail to execute the contracted sale of the land by virtue of default, you are obligated to pay all legal costs and expenses, plus interest which has accrued since the date you signed the option. By November 7, that amount will be exactly one hundred thousand dollars."

Ragonese swallowed hard. He moved warily toward the

doorway. "I see no point in further discussion," he said, trying to match the man's icy aplomb.

"Mission Man, you hold a contract worth three thousand dollars an acre. Is that man's life worth one and one-half million dollars?"

"What are you trying to say?"

"You have a solution. A prosperous one."

Ragonese suddenly remembered Jessica telling him of the man in the cemetery with the scarred face. "Who are you?" he asked, petrified.

"I am who I am!" Captain Gemmer's thunderous voice rattled the ancient hut, sending the tiniest of insects fleeing to their shelters.

CHAPTER 30

CHRIST TOWN U.S.A. REQUESTS THE HONOR OF YOUR PRESENCE
AT ITS PRIVATE OPENING

Billy Hale read the ornate, gilded script of the invitation, then re-read the letter of confirmation.

To the Right Reverend Billy Hale:
    We will be honored by your presence at the private opening of Christ Town. I have reserved the Manger Suite in the Bethlehem Inn for you and Mrs. Hale for September 7th arrival and September 10th departure. I am pleased to inform you that Frank Buckmaster will serve as your personal guide.

Yours in Christ,
Elizabeth Staples
Director of Operations

P.S. Your itinerary is enclosed with your personal Christ Town information packet.

The conditions of Hale's acceptance had been defined explicitly. He would not attend press conferences or photo sessions, nor would he take part in any ceremonies or activities which could be interpreted as being personal endorsements of Christ Town. He was puzzled by the apparent ease with which his strict conditions had been accepted.

Billy had purposely neglected to inform Ms. Staples that

317

he would be arriving at the hotel not the night of the seventh, but after the opening ceremonies the following morning, and he secretly hoped his reservation would be cancelled. However, knowing Frank Buckmaster, the chance of that was slim. He was sure Bucky would barricade himself in the reserved suite until he arrived. Billy smiled at the thought.

Returning the invitation and letter to the packet bulging with brochures, Billy found his itinerary and winced at the first entry on the long list of activities.

RIBBON-CUTTING AND OPENING CEREMONIES AT THE
CHRIST TOWN ENTRANCE. TEN A.M.
INVOCATION BY RABBI ABRAHAM MARGOLIS.

Billy's veteran chauffeur, Emile, glanced into the rearview mirror and saw the scowl on his boss's face. "That bad, Chief?"

Billy flipped the program to the side and dropped the scowl. "Emile, do you know what a Messianic Jew is?"

"Are those the guys who wear their hair in pigtails?"

"No, Emile, a Messianic Jew is one who believes Jesus Christ is the Messiah."

"Don't that make him a Christian?"

"Messianic Jews cling tenaciously to their roots in Judaism. Yet they do believe Jesus fulfilled the Old Testament's prophecies."

"Don't make sense, Chief."

Billy smiled. "You have a point, Emile."

Billy leaned against the soft backrest of the Lincoln, unable to dismiss Abe Margolis from his thoughts. The man was high on the growing list of people he disliked. Although he despised C.D. Pittman for his professed atheism and predatory business ethics, Margolis was nothing more than a sleazy opportunist. Neither the Star of David nor the Cross of Christ made any real difference to the man, they were interchangeable symbols. Margolis pinned his loyalty to whichever faith provided the largest profit margin. He was, in Billy's opinion, a religious whore.

318

As Emile drove through the rolling Virginia country-side, Hale's thoughts drifted to his wife, Doris. He wished now that she had come with him. Her decision to remain at their Shenandoah home was prompted by a reluctance to watch him endure the kind of emotional stress which had wracked him during the Republican National Convention. Christ Town promised to be an equally demanding ordeal.

Billy ended a twenty-mile silence. "Emile, what good reason could I possibly have for attending the opening of something I have publicly denounced as a religious sham?"

Emile shrugged. "Maybe it's something you have to see for yourself."

"Maybe you're right about that."

"Chief," Emile said after a few moments of silence, "maybe you being who you are, the Christ Town promoters just want to use you."

"Exploit my presence?"

"Why not? Having Billy Hale at Christ Town's opening could sure work in their favor."

"I think, Emile, it might be more to their disfavor."

Billy was certain the Christ Town opening would be a three-ring media circus covered by the major networks. The press gallery would be filled with columnists, special assignment writers, and religious reporters, particularly representatives of the liberal East Coast newspaper giants, institutions Hale himself had fought for more than thirty years. Whatever the tone of their commentary, Hale knew they would fulfill their purpose; fundamental Christians would be unswayed and the religious theme park in southern Virginia would receive millions of dollars of free publicity, including a bonanza of prime-time TV exposure. Yet, unlike Virtues, Inc., which he was bound by his promise to Richard Waters not to criticize, he felt free to publicly express his opinion of Christ Town. In fact, he fully intended to.

Still, the invitation made no sense to him. Jimmy Christian was certainly aware of his feelings. To put his blessing on Christ Town would be to approve of C.D. Pittman, something a legion of angels sent by God could not coerce him to do. "Emile," he said, more for his own benefit than anything else, "Jimmy Christian sold his soul for thirty pieces of silver, and damn C.D. Pittman for being the banker of hell."

"If you say so, Chief."

The marker on the interstate indicated that Christ Town was still ninety miles away. Billy looked at his watch. It was 9:30 A.M.

The clock in Jimmy Christian's study at Lord's Lake chimed the half hour. An unshaven Jimmy Christian stood at the bay window looking out at the September morning with a nip of approaching autumn in the air. The early light glinted off the lake below and the pristine rolling hills of rural Virginia.

Christian felt like a shell of the brash evangelical dynamo who once could do no wrong. Since his humiliating confrontation with C.D. Pittman aboard the yacht *Morning Star*, he had lived the life of a semi-recluse, brooding, plumbing the depths of his troubled spirit to find why everything had gone so terribly wrong. He was past the point where he could dodge the truth through self-serving lies. His grandiose dreams had been torpedoed because he had failed to heed a sincere warning from Billy Hale and the sound advice echoed by Beth Staples. His treasure ship had run aground on C.D. Pittman's reef of hell.

Cora Lee bobbed her head into the doorway. She had a new hair style, her fifth in two weeks, and the cut complemented her pert features. She called to him, but he stood trance-like at the window, wrapped in the cocoon of his thoughts. "Jimmy," she repeated, "you can still watch the opening ceremonies over the monitors at the Glee Club Studio."

He turned and looked at her blankly with hopeless resignation.

"Don't blame Beth because you weren't invited, Jimmy. She did the best she could."

"I know. She sold her soul."

"Instead of feeling sorry for yourself, you should be

grateful. God knows she certainly didn't owe you any favors."

"Cora Lee? What world have you been living in?"

"Don't start with me, Jimmy. Beth saved our house. She saved the Glee Club. And you might as well know, people no longer believe you're ill. If you weren't so stubborn, you'd accept the offer Beth got for you."

"I won't be Pittman's carnival barker. He's destroyed me, damn it! Can't you get it through that hummingbird brain of yours?"

"I haven't the time to argue with you, Jimmy. It's bad enough most of the help quit because of your temper tantrums. If you chase off the cook, you'll fix your own meals." She glanced at her diamond-studded Piaget watch. "I mustn't be late for the opening ceremonies."

"By all means, don't be late, Cora Lee." She left the doorway so swiftly she failed to hear his final words. "Sing, Cora Lee . . . sing for your stinkin' supper."

The European cook and his wife heard the moans coming from Jimmy's den. They stopped their kitchen inventory and read one another's minds. They would leave a note with an address where Cora Lee could send their final check.

A green sign shaped like a stone tablet read, "Christian Boulevard." Appropriate, if nothing else, Billy Hale thought as his limousine moved down the six-lane highway with its north- and southbound lanes divided by an island of perfectly manicured Virginia foliage. He wondered if this freeway leading to the theme park entrance was named after Jimmy Christian. He was inclined to think not. Had Christ Town been Harley Lombard's brainchild, Billy could only guess what name Harley would have chosen to immortalize himself.

Emile spotted a smaller sign of the type one sees while driving into the nation's major airports. The chauffeur turned on the radio and winked the digital display to the assigned 1610 AM frequency. The cheerful voice of a young woman filled the limousine, riding a strong, static-free signal. "Welcome to Christ Town. You are now traveling north on Christian Boulevard, the only public access highway serving Christ Town U.S.A."

Had they incorporated the place? Billy wondered, thinking immediately of the tax advantages and the potential pork barrel of state and federal aid.

"The first exit is located a quarter of a mile before the first overpass," the voice continued. "The exit ramp will lead you to Pilgrim Avenue, a four-lane, divided highway. If you follow the Pilgrim East exit, you will arrive at the Wilderness Campground. The campground is on a twelve-hundred-acre tract and is America's finest outdoor recreational facility."

The recorded voice described the campground's features: six thousand hookups for RV's; boating, fishing, and swimming in the clear waters of Lake Gethsemane; backpacking and horseback riding on miles of wilderness trails. She did not fail to mention the full line of supplies and camping equipment available at the Last Convenant General Store. "It sounds more like Abercrombie and Fitch," Billy grumbled.

"The wilderness," Emile spoke over the voice. "Isn't that where Jesus was tempted by Satan?"

"That it was," Billy confirmed.

"Will they show that?"

"Emile, I'd imagine for a fee they would show Jesus walking on water."

"The Pilgrim West exit," the recording continued, "leads to the Evangelical World Center. Visitors may attend the famed Glee Club television services, tour the International religious library, or visit Rock of Ages Village."

Rock of Ages Village, the recording informed them would be the closest thing to heaven on Earth for Christian couples who had reached the golden years. "Rock of Ages will eventually expand to a planned retirement community of ten thousand Christians." She then went on to mention that the Christ Town Bank would provide mortgage money and full banking services. Billy had heard enough. "Emile, turn it off. I have yet to see a thing and I'm already feeling pinched."

Emile drove past the Pilgrim West exit and Hale saw the huge blue and gold hemispheres which marked the entrance to the Evangelical World Center. Billy remembered the day he had visited Jimmy Christian, when the evangelist had assured him that Christ Town would be only part of an expanded Evangelical World Center. But the center and its buildings occupied less than five percent of Christ Town's total acreage, if Hale could believe the map which came in his VIP packet. Billy had more than an idea of who was responsible for the radical change in Jimmy's original concept.

"Look, Chief," Emile said, making no attempt to hide the excitement in his voice, "it looks like the entrance road to Disney World."

The broad median strip was landscaped with exquisite topiary, each sculpted shrub standing precisely eight feet tall. There were thirteen plantings and they had been pruned with professional skill into the unmistakable shape of human figures. The first twelve were obviously intended to represent the Apostles, Billy thought, because the thirteenth shrub had been trimmed into a representation of Christ on the Cross. As they drew abreast of the striking montage, Hale could see that the name of each apostle was written in brightly colored stones.

"They forgot some," Emile said as they passed the shrub of Christ on the Cross.

"I counted twelve."

"I didn't see Paul and Luke."

"Nor Mark," Billy included.

"They screwed up, huh, Chief?" Emile said with a grin.

"I'm afraid not, Emile. Paul, Luke, and Mark were never with Christ."

"You're kidding me! They never met him?"

"Not personally, no."

"Then how could they write so much about him in the Bible?"

"Emile, would you mind if we postponed this Sunday School lesson for another time."

"Sure, Chief. But I'll bet money that half the Christians in this world don't know Paul and Luke never met Christ."

It was a wager Billy would not take.

Another huge sign, representing an opened book with Roman lettering, read, "Resurrection Towers, Bethlehem Inn—Next Exit." With the exception of the radio hustle, everything Billy had seen so far was in good taste. Christian Boulevard was not, as he had expected, lined with motels and fast food restaurants. Could he be wrong about Christ Town? Had his hatred for C.D. Pittman prevented him from attending the preview with an open mind? Or were the spacious, tasteful perimeters of the attraction a facade? He would find out soon enough, he thought, as Emile steered the Lincoln onto the exit ramp leading to Hallelujah Trail East and the Bethlehem Inn.

Stately pines, birches, and oaks cast a canopy of shade along Hallelujah Trail and partially obscured the striking high-rise, a contemporary building of glass and steel towering fifteen stories. Emile turned right onto a circular drive and stopped the limousine at the entrance. Two young men clad in the flowing robes of Biblical shepherds ran smartly to the auto. One opened the door for Hale, the other waited for Emile to push the button to unlock the trunk. A third young man arrived clad in the tight-fitting tunic of a Roman centurion. Handing Emile a claim check, he whisked the Lincoln to the "chariot" parking lot.

"Feel like one of the Three Wise Men, Chief?" Emile asked.

"More like one of the wary men," Billy answered, following the porters to the entrance, where a doorman holding a shepherd's staff bowed deeply upon recognizing him.

Bethlehem Inn's lobby was a dazzling architectural marvel. Thousands of rough-cut crystals were imbedded in walls and ceilings which appeared to be hewn from quarried granite, and they glinted like mica in the sunlight. Billy was gaping at the grottolike effect, captivated by the most beautiful manger he had ever seen. Mother and child reposed in a lean-to, surrounded by miniature Virginia pines. Golden trumpets were pressed to the lips of cherubs that seemed to float above the manger, cleverly suspended by transparent wires. The Three Wise Men surrounding the manger regarded the infant with expressions of rapture.

"Hallelujah! Praise the name of the Lord!" Frank Buckmaster shouted from across the lobby.

Billy smiled, watching the heavy-footed Buckmaster, dressed in a blue blazer and a typically flamboyant bow tie, clumsily make his way past a group of curious spectators. "Bucky, my boy," Billy said, embracing his one-time aide affectionately.

"Where is Mrs. Hale?" Bucky inquired, shaking Emile's hand.

"She thought it best to wait for my report."

"Glad tidings, to be sure."

"Tell me, Bucky, how did the opening ceremonies go?"

Bucky made a clucking sound and grinned broadly. "Blessed are they who promote the glorious deeds of the Savior."

Billy was trying to place the origin of the Biblical phrase when an excited Emile unexpectedly stuck his face before Bucky's. "Did you know Paul and Luke never met Jesus Christ?"

Before the dumbfounded Buckmaster could respond, Billy prevented the potential filibuster by placing a gentle hand on Bucky's shoulder. "There will be time enough for your religious erudition," he said. "Suppose we start seeing the things I have been invited to see?"

Bucky glanced at his watch. "How about beginning the tour with an early lunch in The Loaves and Fishes? They have a fabulous seafood buffet."

Billy declined. He would not chance indigestion until after seeing what Christ Town had to spiritually offer the world.

Buckmaster led them through the lobby doors to a covered platform, where they boarded a tram similar to those in use at the nation's most modern airports: a smooth, silent, air-conditioned people-moving conveyance. Billy noted with satisfaction that the cars were devoid of unnecessary decals and religious graffiti. Bucky ushered him to the front of the car, where the view was best. Emile, who knew the place of a chauffeur, took a seat in the rear.

The shuttle glided away on its four-hundred-yard run and Bucky began the singsong spiel of a tour guide. "Over there, Billy. See that high-rise? That's Resurrection Towers. Has twenty floors. Five more than the Inn. A little too commercial, if you know what I mean."

"And the Bethlehem Inn is what? *Mildly* commercial?"

Bucky grinned broadly, exhibiting his rabbitlike front teeth. "Like it says in the brochure, 'There's always room at the Bethlehem Inn.' "

"If one can afford to pay the bill, that is."

"The *tithe*, Billy. At Christ Town there are no bills, only tithes."

"Mandatory tithes, of course," said Billy, adding, "with all major credit cards accepted."

Bucky jabbed his stubby finger against the glass window. "Apostles Parking, Billy. Twelve sections. Each holds fifteen hundred cars."

Hale let his eyes roam over the vast blacktop, realizing that this private opening would be the first and last free day in the history of Christ Town. Only one section was filled with cars belonging to VIP's, and attendants dressed like Roman guards stood idly in front of stone booths. "I see the toll collectors are having a final dry run," Hale remarked.

"Collectors of tithes, Billy," Bucky corrected.

"Forgive me. Those 'tithe collectors,' are they students from the Bible college?"

"Right you are, Billy. Eighty percent of Christ Town's employees are either students from the International Bible College or senior citizens from the Rock of Ages Village."

How economical, Billy thought.

"See those long tramways leading into the lot, Billy?

Each section has its own station. Every tram carries one hundred and fifty people to the Christ Town Express."

Billy noticed a sleek red-and-white train speeding along an elevated monorail. "Is that the Christ Town Express?"

"That's it. Streamlined, isn't it? Besides taking people to and from Apostles Parking, it travels in and out of the lobby to the Resurrection Towers Hotel."

Hale had heard all he wanted to hear about the Christ Town Express. "Is Harley Lombard here?" he asked.

"He was invited, Billy, but somebody from Virtues, Inc., called Beth Staples and told her he had a previous commitment."

"What about Senator Sinclair?"

"No, his staff said he's tied up with campaign business. But there's a slew of senators and congressmen, governors and mayors, too. The press is all over the place, Billy. And you can't believe the TV coverage. Praise God! Yup, everybody who's anybody in evangelism is here, even a couple of Catholic bishops."

"Does the exalted list include an evangelist named Jimmy Christian?"

Bucky's jowls sagged. Billy had his answer. He understood Bucky's loyalty, his most admirable trait, and he would not press the issue. He would find out about Jimmy's strange absence later.

The shuttle glided to a smooth stop, and Bucky's almost childlike enthusiasm was back at full boil. "We're here, Billy!"

At first glance, Hale thought they had arrived on a movie set constructed for the filming of a Biblical epic. But as they walked closer to a twenty-foot wall of weathered, irregular stones pocked with ten wide portals, Billy could not help but feel impressed.

"It's a walled city!" Emile exclaimed.

"Christ Town," Bucky said, his voice trembling with pride.

A Biblical town, Billy thought, feeling a sense of apprehension as they entered an eerie re-creation. And when they passed through a turnstile manned by more Romangarbed employees, Billy's senses were assailed by a sight he felt was fascinating and at the same time sacrilegious.

"Look, Chief," Emile bubbled. "It's a holy flea market!"

"Matthew's Market Place," Bucky corrected, pointing to a prominent sign over the entrance.

Overwhelmed by the spirited activities unfolding before him, Billy went unaware of the brewing personality clash between the skeptical Emile and the Bible-spouting Buckmaster. While they glared at each other, Billy stood transfixed by the sight of shepherds walking behind freely moving flocks; braying jackasses struggling under the burden of packs and scolding drivers; a caravan of camels kneeling stupidly before brightly colored tents while Arab traders haggled furiously with flinty-eyed Hebrew merchants. There were jugglers and magic acts, snake charmers, and filthy beggars seated amidst the choking dust and offal of the market place. A wild-eyed man obviously impersonating John the Baptist preached with fervor of the coming of the Messiah, while Roman foot soldiers gestured for him to move along. A first-rate performance, Hale thought, although the man posing as John the Baptist seemed a little too aware of the battery of TV cameras.

The Bible college students and senior citizens who composed the cast of Matthew's Market Place wore tunics woven of unbleached muslin, the headdresses of white or striped material encircled by two bands of heavy cord; the women wore scarfs on their heads and simple dresses with loose, flowing sleeves. Everything worn was the authentic attire of that turbulent period in the Roman Empire's rule over a remote nation of nomads, shepherds, and tradesmen.

Billy further noted that the Roman soldiers were clothed in short-sleeved woolen shirts and cloaks; they wore bronze helmets with crests of dried horse hair and were armed with small, double-edged swords and javelins tipped with lead spearheads. Carrying oblong shields on their right forearms, they marched in perfect cadence to the pulse-quickening beat of drums. Billy felt a rush of adrenalin in his veins.

Bucky had slipped away during Billy's reverie and now

328

reappeared driving a small, electrically powered vehicle with four seats and a canopy shaped like the wings of angels. "Your personal chariot," Bucky said.

"Is this the mode of transportation for the elderly and the infirm?" Billy asked.

Bucky chose to ignore the obvious reference to Hale's pronounced limp. "We even supply a driver," he said.

"For a tithe, of course."

"Just a small tithe, Billy."

Driving slowly through the teeming marketplace, with lively Near Eastern music adding to the atmosphere, Billy prepared himself for an assault from reporters converging on his cart He repeated again and again that he had not yet seen enough of Christ Town to make a public statement. But the media mob was not easily dissuaded; Billy's page-one denunciation of the project had made his reaction a mandatory follow-up piece. Hale sat impassively through the salvo of controversial questions, but there was no way he could avoid being photographed seated next to Jimmy Christian's lieutenant, a shamelessly mugging Frank Buckmaster.

When they had finally cleared the gauntlet of reporters, Billy decided to dismount and walk alone. Emile handed him his cane and he hobbled bravely into the tumult. The majority of the merchants who recognized him keyed on his movements. They were most eager to show their wares and seemed not a trifle embarrassed by the prices, which Billy considered way out of line for even captive buyers.

The man posing as John the Baptist saw him and slunk away, fearful he would issue a false prophecy under the scrutiny of an acknowledged Bible scholar. Billy's fellow evangelists greeted him politely, but with aloofness.

A somber Abe Margolis watched Billy from a distance.

Although they were outrageously overpriced, Hale thought the hand-wrought miniature Roman soldiers and centurions were exquisite, as were the gold- and silver-bound New Testaments printed on parchment stock. He carefully examined the portraits of Christ depicting various events of His life and found them to be tastefully well done by unknown but talented artists. Each was a signed original and they ranged in price from a modest fifteen dollars for a small charcoal drawing of the Man of Sorrows to five hundred dollars for a superb oil of The Last Supper. He approved of the Hummel-style statues of the Apostles, fifteen to a set, including Paul, Luke, and Mark. The myriad of bumper stickers and Christ Town pennants were, Billy thought, tacky but inoffensive as were the bread and fish bracelets along with the forbidden fruit charms. But as Billy moved from stand to stand, he began to see ample evidence of what he instinctively feared was festering at the root of Christ Town.

Billy was shocked by the sight of Jesus dolls: dolls topped with crowns of thorns, others with pierced palms, still others bearing the wounds of the stigmata. There were battery-powered Jesus dolls—one which stumbled along under the weight of a plastic cross and others that spoke in hollow computer-synthesized voices, uttering abbreviated parables and holy phrases. Billy felt the rising of his gorge, a sour bile in the back of his throat, and it took an act of willpower to keep from lashing out with his cane when he came upon a display board of Jesus wigs.

He managed to choke back his anger and made a closer inspection of the merchandise displayed in row after row of tented stands. He fingered a multicolored Jesus robe decorated with a bleeding heart circled by an olive wreath and doves. What he first thought to be handwoven wool was actually a clever polyester blend.

He hobbled on, passing tiers of shelves stacked with bath towels featuring a gaudy iron-on Jesus walking on water; beer steins depicting Jesus at the Last Supper drinking from an identical vessel; and "Jesus Jams," with their illustration of Christ blessing a harvest of fruits and berries. But when he came to the head of an aisle marked "Sweet-Smelling Jesus," Billy was reaching the end of his strained emotional tether. Grabbing a bottle of Christ Cologne, his temples pounded as he read the trademark on the label; "Christ Town Products, Inc., a subsidiary of C.D. Pittman Industries."

"Sacrilege!" Billy thundered, looking wildly in the direction of a gaping shopkeeper.

Billy gripped his cane with both hands and, before the befuddled merchant could react, cleared the display with one well-aimed sweep.

Emile sprang from the cart to see his boss acting like a man gone berserk. He could not chance making a preventive move while the crazed Billy wielded the cane like an ax, striking down upon the "Prince of Peace" aerosols and powders. When Billy finally dropped the cane to tip over a stand, scattering the "Trinity Toiletries," Emile rushed forward and restrained him from committing further havoc.

A startled Bucky watched from the cart, recalling what the Bible said another had done on the temple steps two thousand years earlier.

Having escorted the trembling Billy safely to the cart, Emile was alerted to the mini-cam crew setting up to shoot and the rush of photographers galloping toward the scene like Italian paparazzi. "Get us out of here," the chauffeur snapped at Bucky.

Standing in the background, Abe Margolis had witnessed it all.

They drove in silence past rows of flat-roofed, one-story structures with sidings of baked brick and vines supported by trellises twining gracefully to the roofs. "Bartholomew's Bazaar," Bucky announced, breaking a long, nervous silence.

Billy was still trembling and stared straight ahead, reliving his recent performance with mingled feelings of shock, shame, and lingering anger.

"Hungry, Billy?" Bucky asked as he stopped the cart at the entrance to the first of the bazaar's strip of fast-food restaurants.

Billy surveyed a crowded patio shaded by a roof of thatched palm fronds, and winced when he saw the name of the establishment. "Bethlehem Burgers?" He frowned.

"Best burgers in the Christian world," Bucky boasted.

Billy gestured harshly for him to drive on.

They passed Nicodemus Knits, Mary Magdalene Mochas, Pontius Pilate's Pizza House, The Big Fisherman Fish and Chips, John the Baptist Barbeque, Peter's Pottery, Paul's Pecans, Simon's Shrimp and Salad, and Thomas's Tannery. Finally, a famished Bucky could stand no more and pulled up in front of Herod's Hoagies.

"Good as Philly hoagies?" Emile asked.

"Better meat and more cheese," Bucky replied with authority.

"Chief?" Emile pleaded, pinched with hunger and one foot out of the cart.

"All right, if you people must," Billy reluctantly consented.

"Anything for you, Billy?" Bucky asked.

"Absolutely not! . . . And, Bucky, let Emile get what you want."

Bucky twice repeated his order to Emile, handed him complimentary food tickets, and climbed back into the cart. "Well, Billy, what do you think of Christ Town so far?" he asked with an uncertain grin.

Billy shook his head. Bucky's naiveté truly bordered on the saintly, and he was forced to crack a smile. "Bucky, I think there is no other place on earth where you can eat a Pontius Pilate Pizza, then only yards away purchase a Lazarus Curing Cloth for the body's afflictions."

Bucky's face saddened. "You can't blame that on Jimmy."

"No? Then who is responsible? Satan?"

"Jimmy's original plans were much different," Bucky said. "Jimmy's so . . . so sad, Billy. He never leaves Lord's Lake. He hasn't taped a Glee Club service in months."

"I gather this Elizabeth Staples woman has taken charge?"

"Beth is a good woman, Billy. A Christian to the bone. She's trying to help Jimmy, but . . ."

"But she has to answer to another?"

Bucky agreed with a weak nod.

"Is that rogue Pittman here?"

"Mr. Pittman hardly ever comes here. Beth handles everything for him. Poor Jimmy."

"And you, Bucky, how are you holding up?"

"Okay, Billy. I guess."

Before Billy could pursue the topic, Emile returned with his face steaming. "The religious war debt! That's what I paid for these Herod hoagies and Salome sodas."

"A small tithe to the glorification of God," Bucky halfheartedly defended.

"Glorification of greed," Emile responded sarcastically.

Suddenly, Billy's senses signaled an alarm. Turning, he saw a swarm of reporters coming his way, trailed closely by a TV crew. "Can you people eat those things elsewhere?" Billy asked in a rush.

"Onward," said Bucky. "We shall dine at Kingdom Come."

"Kingdom Come" was a wildlife park, and among the most ambitious of Christ Town's satellite attractions. Designed along the lines of contemporary zoological gardens, an impressive array of African, Asian, and North American wildlife lived in an environment which included rock formations, caves, grassy savannah, and man-made marshes and swamps. A monorail ran back and forth above Kingdom Come continuously.

Billy Hale appreciated the pleasant change of pace Kingdom Come represented, but looking at wild animals in a re-creation of their habitats was an activity for a leisurely afternoon. He wanted to take in as much of Christ Town proper as his stamina would permit, yet the large, oddly shaped building looming behind a grove of trees continued to fuel his curiosity. And Bucky, slobbering down his Herod's hoagie and slurping the Salome soda, was getting on his nerves.

Emile had eaten hardly half of his hoagie when Bucky drove the cart to a walkway leading directly to the huge building. "Do you see what it is?" Bucky asked.

Billy shrugged. "It looks like a very large building to me."

"Don't you see? It's a modern-day Noah's ark."

Billy had difficulty seeing what constituted an ark's design in the building. It was encircled by a canal with several drawbridges providing access to the entrance, but he had to press his imagination before noticing more than a vague likeness. "Bucky, I was under the impression Christ Town's theme centered exclusively on the life of Christ."

"Billy, Christ is God, isn't he?"

"In a manner of Christian belief," Billy hedged.

"The Trinity is three in one, right?"

"Jesus is an intricate part of the Godhead, yes."

"Then didn't Jesus, as God, say to Noah, 'Come thou and all thy house into the ark, for thee have I seen righteous before me in this generation?' "

"That don't make a damn bit of sense," Emile said, entering the conversation. "Why would an all-knowing God destroy something He knew to be bad before He created it?"

Buckmaster glared at Emile. Weary of the impertinent interruptions, he decided to silence Emile once and for all with his favorite haymaker from Genesis. " 'And all flesh died that moved upon the earth, both the fowl, and of cattle and of beast, and of every creeping thing that creepeth upon the earth, and every man.' "

"Yeah?" Emile challenged. "What about the fish?"

World-class circus acts, booked through the Mary and Joseph Talent Agency, dominated the upper portion of the multilevel building. Below, an aquarium with a dazzling variety of fish and marine creatures, including cruising sharks, glided among irregular crags and contours which could have passed for a Bahamian reef. On still another level was a serpentarium featuring the world's largest collection of reptiles, including a giant anaconda wrapped around a tree with boughs bearing golden apples. Surrounding the vast arena was a petting zoo with elephant and pony rides, and a marvelous collection of small furry creatures for the children to feed and pet. Scattered among the attractions were every conceivable type of concession stand, souvenir shops, and strolling vendors hawking their wares.

Billy Hale had drifted in deep thought, ignoring the

many people who, recognizing him, stopped and stared. Every yard he had covered since they had driven onto Christian Boulevard bore C.D. Pittman's unmistakable signature. Everything he had seen so far reflected the industrialist's avarice, hatred for religion, and yes, Billy admitted grudgingly, the man's organizational talent and financial clout. In the past he had tried everything he could possibly think of to bring C.D. Pittman down. Planting devious stories with the IRS, convincing the FBI—particularly Dan Kaiser—to investigate Pittman's activities in interstate commerce. Lambasting Pittman on national television and in print had backfired, leading to the libel charges. Now, in the twilight of his life, Billy was forced to admit with bitterness that his old nemesis had successfully invaded his own field of endeavor.

Once again, Bucky had left the cart. Billy spotted him at the far end of the serpentarium, talking to a gaunt-looking man with a head that seemed too large for his body. It was Rabbi Abraham Margolis. He had Bucky cornered against the wall and was poking an index finger into Bucky's chest.

"I wonder what that's all about," Hale said.

When Bucky rejoined them a few moments later, he climbed into the cart without a word. In silence, he drove them back to the ark's center, where a trapeze act was nearing conclusion. Before he could shake off his doldrums and continue in the role of consummate tour guide, Billy said, "Bucky, I believe I have seen enough of Kingdom Come."

"But," Bucky sputtered, "you haven't seen the Evangelists' Hall of Fame yet."

"The what?" Billy asked.

"Up there, in the balcony, behind the VIP seating, is the Evangelists' Hall of Fame. From John the Baptist to yourself, Billy."

"An evangelistic hall of fame in a *zoo*?" Emile interrupted.

"Bucky," Billy said, looking up at the balcony with its

335

theater seating. "This Evangelists' Hall of Fame—what is next to it?"

"Next to it . . ." Bucky had to think. "Christ Town Chicken," he rémembered.

"Sure," Emile perceived, "and I'll bet there's a toilet on the other side."

"There is," a perplexed Bucky confirmed.

"Get it?" said Emile. "One side chicken, the other a toilet."

"I have definitely seen enough," said Billy.

Still Bucky persisted. "The Hall of Fame honors you, Billy."

"No, Bucky, it is meant to embarrass me. If I were to so much as step onto that elevator, C.D. Pittman would laugh all the way to Hell. Now, what say we leave?"

"But the train ride to Gorilla Gorge?"

Billy reached for Bucky's hand. He paused long enough to select words Bucky would fully comprehend. "No train ride. No Gorilla Gorge. Do I make myself *commandment*-clear?"

Bucky drove the cart in silence down the winding trails of Kingdom Come. Sensing the hurt in Bucky's silence, the evangelist tried to buoy his spirits. "Well, what is next on our agenda?" he asked, hoping to restore Bucky's importance as tour guide.

"Billy," he whispered so Emile could not hear, "what *about* the fish?"

Corinthian columns of Italian marble gave Billy a feeling that he had finally come upon an attraction not defiled by fast-food restaurants, overpriced retail shops, or Halls of Fame with hidden meanings. Christ Square would hardly disappoint him.

Security guards dressed in ornate uniforms of Roman palace sentries waved Buckmaster through the towering archway, and they entered a subterranean grotto where concrete pillars supported a high ceiling constructed of roughly hewn stones.

"Some hole in the wall," Emile said.

Robed figures moved about the shadows away from the lighted passageway Bucky drove through. Billy could make out the dark entrances to caves and was reminded of what this dreary catacomb symbolized. He often wondered how he would have fared as an early-day Christian, hunted and persecuted. Would he, like the Christian martyrs, have possessed the unyielding faith to give up his life for a belief? Would he have made the sacrifice not even Jesus Christ had in common with these courageous Christians: to die without a true knowledge of the hereafter? His thoughts returned to the present. How simple it was to be a modern Christian, Billy thought, in a nation founded under God, when no brave deeds were required. He wondered what it would have been like for Jimmy Christian, Harley Lombard, and the rest of the TV evangelists. Had they lived in those perilous times, would they have stood in a public square and preached the gospel of Jesus as easily as they now faced the red light of a TV camera?

Bucky pointed above. "We're now directly under the Last Supper Restaurant, Billy."

Hale noticed a series of tubular, glass-enclosed lifts. "I presume those elevators take you to the restaurant," he said.

"Right, but not today. Electrical problems, Billy." Bucky's face sagged. "It's Jimmy's favorite place. The only thing in Christ Town they didn't change on him."

They emerged into the glare of the midafternoon sunlight and the full dimension of Christ Square unfolded before them, dominated by a north wall which ran one hundred yards and towered forty feet above the square. Individual alcoves, actually miniature amphitheaters, were enclosed by heavy tinted glass which served as curtains and glided open on aluminum tracks. Billy's attention turned to the largest of these stages, one centrally located over the one arched exit.

"From nativity to resurrection, Jesus' life is re-enacted!" Bucky exclaimed.

"Clever," Billy remarked softly.

"At night, the lights are really beautiful. And tonight

there's a special production of the passion play." Bucky pointed to the arched exit. "Out there, on Crucifixion Trail and Calvary Hill, will be a giant fireworks display."

Emile was more concerned with an enclosure which jutted outward and extended to the western end of the wall. "More restaurants?" he asked snidely.

"Christ's Cafeteria!" Bucky shouted out. "The largest cafeteria in the Christian world."

"Not until it makes the *Guinness Book of Records,*" Emile countered as if it wouldn't.

"Stop it!" Billy ordered. "Both of you are acting like bickering schoolchildren."

Bucky turned his back on the smirking Emile and looked at his watch. "Everything happens in one minute—and twenty-six seconds," he said, strictly for Billy's benefit.

"May I see your watch?"

He held his watch under Billy's nose, and the evangelist saw twelve miniature crosses marking the hours. He noted that Jesus' short hand was pointing to the third cross and that his long hand rested one dot before the hour. "We expect to sell them out in no time."

Before Billy could reply, men dressed in Roman togas and carrying long trumpets appeared on the north wall above each stage. They brought the gleaming instruments to their lips and blared out a fanfare reminiscent of "Hail to the Chief."

The sliding glass door to the main stage opened. The effervescent Cora Lee Christian strutted forward. Accompanied by the G.L.E.E. Club Orchestra and Chorus, she waded into her song, "Christ is Born."

Billy shuddered through the ear-piercing discomfort of her high notes and was thankful for the distraction of the alcove on the far left, where the opaque glass curtain had opened to reveal the scene of Christ's birth.

The nativity was followed in the next alcove by Christ's baptism, while Cora Lee bounded to the foot of the stage, thrusting a warning finger at the gathering audience and singing, "You Must Be Born Again."

"When did I die?" Emile muttered to no one in particular.

An abbreviated version of the Sermon on the Mount was next and without Cora Lee. Billy was taken in by the man portraying Jesus. "He has an excellent speaking voice," Billy commented.

"It's not his," Bucky said. "It's a recording, Billy, made by a Shakespearean actor. There are twenty-six Jesuses at Christ Town and the voice has to be the same."

Another alcove presented yet another Jesus protecting an adulterous woman from her rock-bearing accusers; Cora Lee assailed the crowd with a strident chorus of "Sin No More."

"Is she here *all* the time?" Emile groaned.

"Cora Lee has sold over a million records," Bucky defended.

"To whom? Deaf people?" Emile laughed.

Bucky's face turned the color of a boiled Maine lobster. "Next week, when Christ Town opens to the public, Johnny Clay will be the featured attraction in the square. Is *he* big enough for you?"

"Yeah," Emile grunted, "Johnny Clay's big, if you're into turd-kickin' music."

Billy quieted them with a wave of his hand. He wished to hear without distraction the recorded words of Jesus commissioning the seventy disciples. Yet the more he listened, the more doubt tightened its hold on his thoughts. It was not Jesus' deed that produced such skepticism, rather the accuracy of its author, St. Luke.

Saint Luke? Was he? Billy tumbled deeper into doubt. And Paul and Mark, were they truly saints? He wondered. Or were they opportunistic men who obtained their information from secondhand sources for reasons never revealed? Could they, these revered men, who never witnessed Christ's trials or tribulations, have perpetrated a religious hoax? Had they conveniently extended the Old Testament with the incorporation of Jesus' life to establish credibility in their efforts to propogate a new religion called Christianity? But why? For what reason? He pondered. For personal gain? For glory? Yet hadn't Paul died for the very cause he eloquently drafted? Was he not a martyr? But who told of his demise? Who actually witnessed his death? Billy knew it was never verified that Paul suffered martyrdom in Rome about 67 A.D. Loud music blaring from the center stage spared him further doubting thoughts.

The daughter of the infamous Herodias danced to the delight of Herod and his court. The raven-haired beauty moved about the stage slowly, seductively, as the music's tempo built into a furious crescendo. Her bumps and gyrations heated the glands in Emile's groins. "*That* is some Salome."

"There is no mention in the Bible of Herodias's daughter being named Salome," Bucky retaliated with authority.

"I saw the movie!" Emile responded, as if the film was unimpeachable.

The spotlight now belonged exclusively to Cora Lee, and her distinctive voice had lost none of its shrill. Billy was polite enough not to say it, but too much of Cora Lee's singing was hazardous to one's ears. "Bucky, I feel it is time to push on."

"But, Billy, there's eight more acts before the crucifixion," Bucky insisted.

"And I am quite sure each of those acts is splendidly performed. However, I no longer possess the stamina I once enjoyed. An afternoon nap has become a necessity at my age."

"Just a few more things, Billy," Bucky implored.

"Specifically, *please?*"

"The Miracle Mile—an entire mile of Jesus' miracles."

"Including Jesus walking on water?" Emile asked.

Fifteen Christ impersonators performed their wonders within appropriate settings. It did not take much to convince Billy Hale that he had wandered into a graduate school for future faith healers. Nor did he need Bucky to tell him the "cured" were chosen afflicted from the Bible college and Rock of Ages Village. The more Billy took in what he felt were religious sideshows, the clearer he could picture it all. C.D. Pittman would spring a new horde of faith-healing specialists to further saturate religious television networks. They were sure to have a bone man, Billy thought, watching a young woman rise nimbly from a wheelchair to kiss the hand of the Jesus who would heal her six nights a week and twice on Sundays. There would be a cancer man, an ear, nose, and throat man, of course. As Billy watched with revulsion, a Jesus cast devils from a man who bellowed obscenities and twitched with rehearsed insincerity. Ah, yes, the top of the line, Billy concluded; the *special* specialist who dealt exclusively with the possessed.

They pulled away from what was constructed as a leper colony, where an acting Jesus beckoned the incurable to come from their caves, and drove down a path lined with white pine. They approached a cove on Lake Gethesemane, and Bucky stopped the cart before one of three docks, harboring a fleet of sightseeing boats. The largest vessel was named *Ship of Saint Paul,* and Emile frowned. "Never met Jesus," he said half aloud.

"Not true," Bucky objected. "Jesus spoke to St. Paul on the road to Damascus."

"Never met him." Emile grew bolder. "And where does Jesus walk on water?"

Billy had heard enough. "Right now I would like to know where those boats go?"

Bucky explained that the craft navigated along the shores of the lake, visiting inlets and coves where Christ Town visitors could hear the water-related parables of the Savior, including the Pearl and the Net. Visitors would also witness his baptism by John, his calming of the storm, and—the highlight—an enactment of his walking on water.

Billy's attention was diverted by the swift, silent passage of a gleaming monorail. "Where does that go?" he asked.

Bucky pretended not to hear him and spoke on, explaining how the boats entered a miniature Sea of Galilee and how its fingers indented the Wilderness Campground and the bathing beaches serving both the Resurrection Towers and Bethlehem Inn.

341

"Bucky, is there something out here you do not wish me to see?"

Bucky lowered his head so that his triple chin touched his bow tie. "Bethesda," he replied with a hint of shame.

Emile would have to see Jesus walking on water another time. Despite his fatigue, Billy would visit Bethesda.

They traveled a quarter of a mile from the docks through scenic grounds lined with evergreen paths, over small bridges where the water below appeared too blue, and Billy searched his memory for the Biblical meaning for Bethesda. It came to him like a computer readout: A pool or reservoir near the sheep market in Jerusalem. The water possessed curative powers. It was where Jesus healed an impotent man.

Elegant Lebanon cedars framed a large, round building supported by marble columns. The sleek monorail Billy had noticed hummed from a tunnel and stopped with a soft hiss of air brakes at a wide platform next to the building. A hesitant Bucky led Billy and the trailing Emile toward the entrance.

A hint of frankincense and myrrh accented the air of a circular foyer with a white marble floor. Billy noticed the busts of Biblical greats rimming the room, much like those in his own Daniel's Den. As he examined them closely he was shocked to realize that they were identical in number and form to his own. Billy had always taken great pride that no one on earth had such a collection. How had Pittman acquired such exact information on his statuary? It would have to have been from someone who had access to his den—but who? Billy wondered. Jimmy Christian? He pushed Pittman from his mind.

Emile came upon a bust isolated from the others. "Look, Chief, it's you!" he said loudly.

Bucky was quick to explain. "Billy, your bust wasn't Jimmy's idea."

"You needn't defend Jimmy. I am beginning to understand."

They moved on to a vast room dominated by a massive pool of bubbling water, where a group of senior citizens

342

from Rock of Ages Village soaked their bodies in the supposedly curative effervescence.

"The water is just water," Bucky confessed in a whisper. "We expect a million bathers the first year and to sell five million bottles of Bethesda curing water," he concluded, adding to Billy's disgust and desire to leave.

Emile caught up with them in the lobby. He was holding a tinted quart of the blue curing water. "Six and a half bucks for this," he said, handing it to Billy.

"You didn't have to buy a bottle," Bucky scolded. "You could have drunk a cup from the fountain for only a quarter."

Hale read the name of the manufacturer on the label and smashed the bottle on the marble floor, leaving behind him a spreading blue stain and the startled stares of attendants.

Billy had seen all of Christ Town he intended to see— today or ever. After a solemn ride back to Matthew's Market Place, Billy ended the edgy silence. "Bucky, would you please take me directly to the Inn?"

"Sure, Billy, but—"

"No buts, please."

"All right, Billy, but you haven't seen the most exciting thing in Christ Town."

"Exciting?" Emile's fading interest revived.

"It's worth seeing, Billy. *Honestly*. When Jimmy got mad at me, he made me go there. Seventy-six times!"

"And just what is it that is so exciting?" Billy inquired.

"The Hell-Bent Express," Bucky said somberly.

"What the hell is the Hell-Bent Express?" Emile laughed.

"A ride into Hell."

St. James Amusement Park was compressed into a considerably smaller area than either Kingdom Come or Miracle Mile. Yet it was by far the busiest of Christ Town's three satellite attractions. Trams with linked people-carriers designed in the style of San Francisco cable cars roamed the midway, stopping to unload and board passengers. Many were going to or coming from Andrew's Arcade, which, according to Bucky, boasted the world's largest assortment of video games. Bucky, who had a childlike fascination with electronic gadgets, had become addicted to one game in particular, which featured an increasingly difficult gauntlet of lions chasing Christians. But when word reached Beth Staples that Bucky was spending a fortune in quarters, she protected his salary by banning him from the arcade. In addition to video games, pinball machines, and other electronic money-eaters, the arcade housed the more traditional dart games, baseball tossing, basketball shooting, and gong ringing. The object of each game was to prick, knock down, sink, hang, or otherwise humiliate either Judas or Satan. Prizes ranged from cheap sunglasses bearing the Christ Town logo to life-sized Jesus dolls.

From the moment they had entered the park through a portal in the east wall, Billy's gaze had been riveted on an oddity at the opposite end of the long midway. It resembled a vast oil tank painted midnight black, and rose at least three hundred feet into the late-afternoon September sky. It stood in eerie contrast to Christ Town's well-ordered architectural motif. Hale could think of nothing it resembled in either the Old or New Testaments.

They rode past one attraction after another, including the merry-go-round and Ferris wheel bearing the names "Christian Carousel" and "Wheel of the Trinity." "Serpent's Tail" was a whirling, whipping, neck-snapping ride which hurtled through undulating passages. The "Ascension Lift" cable cars moved in slow symmetry above them and served as an alternative to the trams which hummed along the midway. It also carried people over the wall for a breathtaking view of the Wilderness and Sea of Galilee.

Emile seemed totally disinterested and Billy kept staring at the strange structure while they moved through the carnival atmosphere of the midway. Emile's spirits revived somewhat when he saw "Bump Beelzebub Bumper Cars." Bucky slowed the cart so they could see the object of the attraction: attendants dressed in the traditional horns-and-pitchfork image of the devil trying to dodge a surge of criss-crossing bumper-car jockeys. The "Bible Bullet" appeared to be an outstanding ride, rivalling the best of any in the nation's major theme parks. Traveling at great speeds, it made turns as tight as those on an Olympic bobsled run.

They drove past "The Den of Disciples Wax Museum," which housed likenesses of the great and revered men and women of Christianity. They had driven closer to the mammoth black tank and Emile noticed from the corner of his eye that Billy seemed totally absorbed by the fluorescent lettering which girdled the top of the cylindrical structure. The letters read, "Hell-Bent Express." Both Emile and Bucky sighed with relief when Billy missed an unflattering wax replica of himself near the wide entrance to the wax museum.

Buckmaster drove the cart past another major attraction of the amusement park, the "Colosseum of Champions," an outdoor arena seating five thousand people. By day it was the scene of mock gladiatorial combats and the re-enactment of Christians enduring martyrdom at the teeth and claws of carefully tranquilized lions. By night, however, it was something quite different: a licensed track with parimutuel wagering on a card of one-mile chariot races. Billy read the sign above the main entrance: "Big Trinity Wagering Every Race!" Bucky informed them that the races were expected to handle $250,000 a night. The biggest lure, Bucky added: "Losers will be able to receive tax credits under the religious donations laws."

Buckmaster braked the cart to a halt at a designated waiting area in front of the sinister black structure. Only when they had dismounted and moved to the rear of a line stretching between polished aluminum railings did Hale realize the sheer size of the building. Laid on its side, he thought, it would rival one of those enormous hangars at Cape Canaveral. As the line inched along, a large, boldly lettered sign came into view. "Warning," it said, "Children under 18 Will Not Be Permitted to Ride the Hell-Bent Express Unless Accompanied by an Adult."

A flyer was thrust into Billy's hands by a serious young

woman dressed in a pleated skirt and Christ Town blazer. "Please read this carefully, Reverend Hale."

Billy scanned the official-looking page. "Dear Christ Town Visitor: You are about to ride 'The Hell-Bent Express.' Due to the intense nature of what we hope will be a memorable religious experience, all persons must go through a CPR blood pressure and pulse screening, and must sign a wavier at the bottom of this sheet. Any persons with a history of high blood pressure or cardiovascular disease are advised to avoid this ride. Thank you."

Hale then read a disclaimer at the bottom of the sheet releasing Christ Town U.S.A., Inc., from all liability. Beneath the signature line, it read, "Special 3-D glasses may be purchased for an additional $2.50 to enhance the visual effects of the Hell-Bent Express."

The trio approached a file of efficient, white-jacketed attendants who swiftly checked their vital signs and wrote the readings in a space at the bottom of the release sheet. "*Again*, Mr. Buckmaster?" said a young man at the panel of a console that flashed digital readouts of blood pressure and pulse. Billy extended his left arm. "Pulse 80, blood pressure 150 over 85. You're well within our parameters, Reverend Hale. Sign here, please."

Billy scrawled his signature, feeling a swell of curiosity and genuine apprehension. He was not a squeamish person. But why the CPR team and explicit warnings? Was it just more of Christ Town's incredible hype?

There appeared to be no entrance to the Hell-Bent Express. Bewildered, Emile asked, "How do you get in? By helicopter, or by saying 'Open sesame'?"

Bucky didn't reply and fumbled inside his breast pocket, withdrawing a clean white handkerchief, while Billy shared Emile's irritation over the extraordinary preliminaries leading to what he figured was just another rip-off of something Disney's people had been doing for forty years.

A remote camera picked up their presence and there was a grinding, crunching sound as the panel of a concealed entrance yawned open as if the building had opened its mouth.

346

Emile looked nervously at the ovoid entrance and the blackness behind it. "How do people get out of this place?"

Bucky managed a mirthless grin. He would let the Hell-Bent Express answer all further questions. He led them over the threshold past the unmanned turnstiles, where next week it would cost the public an incredible eight dollars per ride. They trailed a group of people that included a reporter from the Associated Press, a rumpled man wearing his best look of bored disdain. A black wrought-iron gate topped by sharp spikes lifted silently to admit them.

They proceeded down what was called "The Glory Road," a tunnel lit by torches that illuminated the walls with a flickering red glow. At the end of the tunnel, they stepped onto a moving walkway and were slowly transported upward past cavelike openings bathed in a myriad of colored lights and strobe effects. Large stone tablets materialized from the wall and what appeared to be tongues of moving fire etched the Ten Commandments as if they were chiseled by the omnipotent hand of God.

Through a long day of buffeting commercialism, Billy Hale had used the word "impressive" sparingly and then only in his private thoughts. Now the word formed freely on his lips. Bucky glowed and searched Emile's face for a similar expression of approval. The chauffeur remained silent, but his snide expression had vanished.

The escalator continued to ascend toward a massive, electronically controlled door. Above it was an inscription which foreshadowed what was to come. "Ye who have obeyed my laws shall not be consumed by what lies beyond."

A great, smooth-surfaced door opened with the explosive sound of a giant bolt being unlatched, and the escalator continued to climb through a passageway which meandered like a river through a flood plain. Entering a swirling mist, they approached what Billy perceived to be a graveyard pocked by freshly dug graves. Just beyond the hovering fog laced with human moans, the escalator slowed

347

and leveled off, and they approached a dimly lighted boarding platform where attendants dressed in hooded black robes beckoned the passengers to Hell with glowing lanterns that illuminated the station with a spider-web tracery of light and shadow.

"We're coming to the station for departing souls," Bucky explained. "This is where we ascend."

"Ascend to Hell?"

"Jesus did, Billy."

Hale had no wish at this point to debate the geography, astronomy, or precise whereabouts of Hell, nor would he challenge the Good Book on the findings of Jesus' visit.

A hooded attendant approached them and bowed with respect. Billy stepped carefully onto the platform, and the attendant led him to the first of twelve open cars which were linked in roller-coaster style. Each car had four seats, two in front, two in back. Hale heard Emile's breath catch behind him. "What the . . . ?" the chauffeur sputtered as he realized that the cars were shaped like coffins.

Billy handed his cane to Bucky, who wedged into the seat next to him. Emile shared the seat directly behind them with the AP reporter, giving the safety bar which locked them into place a derisive thump. He began to remove the 3-D glasses, but decided not to; if nothing else, this ride on the Hell-Bent Express might prove to be an interesting light show. Leaning forward as much as the safety bar would permit, he caught sight of the handkerchief clutched tightly in Bucky's hand. "Why are you holding that hanky?" he asked. Bucky's grin overflowed with vindictiveness.

The spectral necklace of coffin cars moved slowly out of the station and began an immediate and steep ascent into a sea of gray mist. The sound of weeping and despair which had filled the station subsided to a distant moan, an eerie surf of lamentation. They emerged from the swirling tentacles of fog and burst into the majesty of outer space. Billy felt a sense of exaltation and release, as if he had been freed from earthly cares and now stood on the threshold of the starry firmament. He knew the sensation of space and timelessness was created by laser beams and speed-room projections. Still, he could not help but feel he was on a weightless journey through galaxies undiscovered by man.

They climbed to a dimension of infinity where nothing was left in the heavens above them but a solitary star of awesome dimension and luminescence. The car finally leveled off, and they looked back with wordless awe at the worlds they had left behind.

"The gates of Hell," Bucky whispered, bringing the handkerchief reflexively to his mouth.

Looming ahead, Billy saw a circle of fire rimming another cavelike entrance. As they drew near, the flames suddenly arranged themselves into the fiery script of a message. "Only by the Grace of God shall ye depart the Kingdom of Doom," the words glared, and they smelled the pungent odor of sulphur.

"Here we go," Bucky said, a tremor of panic in his voice.

The illusion that they were being pulled into the fiery entrance by some cosmic force intensified. Hale felt a sudden clogging of his ears and realized he had braced himself against the safety bar. He felt they were being drawn by some invisible undertow through Hell's opening. Only as the string of cars lurched into the fiery maw did he realize that what had been a compelling visual experience thus far had also become an aural one. They were swept by a sighing anthem of moans, and diaphanous wisps materialized into the shapes of men. These wretched beings, which appeared to drift just ahead of them, were suddenly dominated by the head of a massive serpent with eyes like glowing coals. Smoke billowed from a mouth that lashed at the entering souls with a multitude of whiplike tongues, tearing away strips of flesh.

They entered the glistening cave of the serpent's mouth and, as if the powerful illusion needed further enhancement, Billy felt a blast of hot, dank air. His nostrils were violated by a fetid stench. The cries and moans of the damned rose to a caterwaul of despair. Suddenly, they began a rushing descent into a darkness accented only by a distant glow which brightened imperceptibly as they appeared to plummet deeper and deeper into the very bowels of Hell. "My God!" Billy gasped as the motion slowed abruptly and the cars settled into a more gradual descent.

Billy knew the entire effect was achieved by the magic of motion picture projectors, stereo sound, and a drop of no more than fifty feet. But he had been frightened. In fact, not since that terrible night eleven years before in the Hollywood Bowl had he been gripped in such a vise of sheer terror. Sweat dripped from his face; he was trembling. He stole a look at Bucky, whose face was buried against the bar, eyes closed. Emile's face was the color of ashes. A feeble grin was frozen on the face of the reporter, but the man was green around the gills.

The lamentations of the doomed souls had become a cacophony of misery. The moans of despair were caused by indescribable suffering inflicted upon the souls by a society of demons. Enormous winged creatures, some colored soot black, others the green slime color of a stagnant pond, stood on cloven feet, watching through dead eyes the horrific punishment inflicted on man's immortal soul by subordinate demons.

The cars crept through a deep valley flanked by cliffs and jagged escarpments. Looking upward, Hale saw a horde of souls cowering at the feet of a ranking jailer whose nostrils emitted jets of fire and choking clouds of sulphurous smoke. Having been assigned to the place where they would be doomed to remain forever, the souls were cast screaming off the cliff into a lake of molten lava. Hovering demons waited until they surfaced, hair and flesh aflame, then swooped down and held them afloat with grappling talons while enormous batlike creatures ripped at their smoldering flesh and plucked out their sightless eyes. once consumed by liquid fire and shredded by the beaks and talons of the winged predators, the souls miraculously achieved human form once again and were lifted back to the cliff by the winged demons, where the excruciating torment and degradation would be repeated—like all punishment in Hell—throughout eternity.

The landscape grew flat, taking on the lunar appearance of the great deserts. At a patch of desolation, where the sand became an expanse of salt, scores of souls were nailed to crosses of wood so rotten they were acrawl with giant flesh-feeding worms and maggots. Demons moved in leisurely fashion from cross to cross, dismembering a finger here, a toe there, ripping out a tongue or gouging out an eye. Billy looked away only to see the souls of the damned being whipped, then dragged up a hillside littered with jagged splinters of glass. Once at the summit they were tied to a railing honed to scalpel sharpness, then shoved headfirst on a long slide toward a ghastly heap of severed torsos.

Still deeper in the bowels of Hell, they passed row after row of pits where the damned repeated their earthly acts upon an eternal stage. The first pit consisted of a throng of mankind slaying one another by every possible means in a perpetual blood-letting enacted before a gallery of wildly cheering demons. Another pit revealed men's bodies entwined with one another, locked for eternity in a macabre dance of obscene death. The largest pit was clogged with those condemned for greed, who wallowed in the filth and stench of their own waste. On the rim of that pit, a mammoth devil with great, gleaming black horns sat on a throne constructed of coiled serpents. An honor guard of demons held the devil's enormous penis aloft while he showered the souls in the pit.

Deeper still, the cars descended to a plain of darkness pocked with smoldering fires and patrolled by hooded ghouls. There, souls were constantly rousted from their open graves and forced to crawl on their stomachs over fiercely glowing embers. And as they howled, the emotionless sentries mounted their blistered, charred bodies and chewed the flesh from their backs.

The message of Hell was clear, Hale thought, trying to suppress his rising terror and the dull ache in the center of his chest. There was no immunity in Hell, neither surcease nor solace. There was no compassion and no hope, no right of appeal or parole. Hell's only currency was despair, agony, filth, destruction, and eternal degradation. Billy had used many of these same words and depictions in some of his most memorable sermons. Now, as they glided through this computerized, synthesized netherworld, the evangelist found himself thinking he had helped to perpetrate and perpetuate a great fraud. At that moment, he felt he could no longer accept the belief that God would absolve Himself of his role in the sins of man and pronounce so harsh a sentence on that which He had created. "It can't be," he muttered to himself, as they began another dizzying descent. "It mustn't be," he prayed, as the string of coffin-shaped cars plummeted toward a flaming gorge.

Masses of souls were being cast from an unseen precipice into the blazing abyss. Hale thought that they too would be consumed when the cars appeared to enter the roaring flames. He was deafened momentarily by a great roar of sound. He opened his eyes in time to see a ragged streak of livid green lightning criss-crossing walls of raging fire. The intense blaze of heat he feared would ignite his clothing changed suddenly to an icy blast as the coaster made a final, violent dip, then spun from the infundibulum of fire to a celestial expanse highlighted by planets similar to those in Earth's solar system. The four men sagged back in their seats, relieved by the sudden scene of quiet and peace. But the respite was brief. One by one the planets exploded, filling the heavens with a terrifying vision of the apocalypse. Fiery meteors appeared on a collision course with the coaster. Dodging the streaking balls of fire, the coaster zoomed downward to the final level of Hell and into a stench so foul they gasped for breath.

Billy cupped a hand over his nose and mouth. He knew the ride was building to its climax and that they would soon confront the Prince of Darkness, the King of Hell. They skimmed a body of polluted water blotched with pools of blood, water infested with sewage, scum, and a flotsam of tormented souls, all being swept by a raging current toward a featureless horizon.

The waters parted in front of them with the deafening

roar of a tidal wave. The ultimate monster rose from the depths to tower above them and Billy was mesmerized by the sight of a head topped by a rack of incredible horns, lightning flashing between their tips. The beast's eyes, as cold and passionless as an arctic landscape, seemed to look directly into Billy's before it crouched to devour the soul-infested swill. As the beast salivated with savage hunger, gusts of foul wind from its cavernous nostrils buffeted them, trapping the souls in bizarre whirlpools of tangled flesh.

There were no lips on the ancient beast's face. Rather, crevices oozed pus from never-healing sores teeming with vermin. There was a rumbling sound, then an explosion like that of an erupting volcano as the crevices yawned open to their fullest extent to become one, emitting a stench so vile that Billy was felled by nausea. While Hale slumped, Emile and Bucky involuntarily relieved themselves of their Herod's hoagies.

The whirlpools were sucked into channels which swept the shrieking, clawing souls into a malodorous cavity where jagged teeth festooned with human rot tore them into digestible pieces. Billy gasped as his eyes locked with those of the great beast. His body stiffened in convulsion. He tried to cry out, but terror had constricted his vocal cords. The Fallen Angel was staring at him and him alone. Not even God could tell him otherwise.

Billy did not feel the pulling of the coaster as it was drawn into the sucking mouth amid the debris of brutalized souls. Once more they were plunging, circling in a series of tightly wrapped turns; glistening red membranes sped past as they followed the intestinal tract of the beast. Now they were whirling, the centrifuge violence plastering them against the padded sides of the car. Hale realized with terror that they were out of control.

But the violent spinning stopped even more suddenly than it had begun. The ride settled smoothly into a slow, straight run down a slight incline. Billy had cleared his head and realized that, somehow, they were not traveling backward. The cars jerked to an abrupt halt. Up ahead, they heard the amplified flatulent sound of expelled gas. Again they jerked into rapid motion, and Billy threw up his hands in terror and disgust. He felt weightless, as if he had been catapulted from the car. He was blinded by a sudden flash of sunlight and found himself looking up at the unmistakable folds and crevices of a gigantic rectum.

Billy Hale realized with a mixture of shame, anger, and humiliation that they had been defecated onto the platform. He rarely used profanity of any sort, but he allowed himself the luxury. "I've been shit by the devil," he said aloud, ignoring the rasp of Bucky's dry-heaving.

At that moment, the evangelist promised himself that for the rest of his life he would preach that Hell is but a rumor, man's greatest lie. Ashen-faced but composed, he permitted a white-jacketed attendant to assist him from the car. "To whom do I write the check?" he asked in a mocking tone. "I'm sure many life's savings and pensions will be pledged on this platform in the years to come."

Bucky lurched from the car and threw his soiled handkerchief into a trash barrel. "Donations are made over there, Billy," he said, pointing a shaking finger at a huge mail drop nesting under a Jesus the Savior poster.

For the first time that day, Emile did not offer a sarcastic response. The chauffeur had fainted dead away.

354

CHAPTER 31

THE TEMPERATURE AT Michael's Mission was ten degrees cooler than Christ Town's reading of sixty-eight. But one couldn't tell it by the sweat pouring off Ron Rebuck's lean and muscular body. Since dawn, he had labored over the digging of a deep hole.

Careful not to disrupt the formation of dirt bordering its perimeter, Rebuck emerged from the pit in time to see the sunset pull a lavender blanket of dusk over Michael's Mission. He permitted his mind to relax and felt the ache of weary muscles, the demands of an empty stomach. Slipping a navy fatigue shirt over a sweat-drenched chest patched with the rich loam of Lancaster County, he fastened the cartridge belt with the empty canteen to his waist and shoved the retractable metal tape measure into a pocket of his cut-off jeans. Slinging the combat pick and shovel over his shoulder, he took a long look at the dusk-shadowed statue of Michael the Archangel and began to walk wearily from his father's burial ground toward the compound.

Ike Vesper reclined in the hammock outside the trailer home watching Jessica Towne take her turn peeling potatoes on the redwood table next to the sturdy brick grill he had constructed. She should never have gotten her naive little ass involved, he thought. He'd warned her from day one to stay away from Rebuck. It wasn't his fault she didn't listen. His conscience was clear. It's Rebuck who's got the guilt trip, he reasoned. Him and his goddamn searching for innocence. "Him and his goddamn eye magic," Ike grumbled.

As Rebuck emerged from the woods, Jessica sat expectantly, watching him stow the pick and shovel under the motor home, then walk to the well, where he gulped three cups of cool, spring-fed water and poured a fourth over his head. He approached the table with the flicker of a smile on his face. He leaned down to kiss her, thinking she'd refuse to allow him the privilege in his filthy condition, and was surprised when she put her arms around him and gave him a deep, passionate kiss in return.

But then, she'd been surprising him a lot lately.

"Ron," she said, "thank you for letting me stay."

Rebuck unwrapped her arms from his waist and sat down next to her on the bench. "Jessica," he began, "we've got to talk about that. Now that you've graduated from the mission, if I can get you out of here safely it's something I've got to do."

Ike rolled over in the hammock, turning his broad back to them both.

"Ron, I can't leave you. Please don't try and make me."

He looked in her eyes and saw the depth of her feeling, but knew he could not give in. "Jessica, you don't understand," he said. "There's nothing but danger for you here. The cap—"

"The captain," she interrupted. "Yes, I know the captain is a killer, Ron. You've made that clear. But I still won't leave you—I just can't leave you . . . not unless you make me leave."

Rebuck was about to answer when he heard it. Jessica watched him as his eyes narrowed and he peered into the gathering darkness.

"Ike," he whispered, "south . . . ten o'clock."

Ike merely glanced in the coded direction, rolled silently from the hammock, and walked to the door of the trailer home. "Little Girl," he called back in a loud voice, "I'll cook up the steaks after I shower."

"Jessica," Rebuck said softly after Ike had slammed the door shut behind him, "in the motor home, there's a blue button next to the switch for the spotlights."

"Blue button," she repeated.

"Count to fifty and push it. Then get the pistol under the dashboard. Put it on the top step of the motor home and close the door."

"Blue button . . . count to fifty," Jessica repeated to herself, heading for the motor home.

Ike had left the trailer through a back window and now moved soundlessly into the woods of the compound's northeast sector. Armed with a twelve-gauge automatic shotgun, he moved with the stealth and grace developed during his SEAL training, homing in on the crackle of sound which had alerted Rebuck to the presence of an intruder.

Flattened against the leaf-carpeted earth, peering over the dense foliage of the ground cover, John Ragonese felt his body stiffen at the sound of a snapping twig. His hollow-cheeked, almost skeletal face was the washed-out gray of his shirt. Another crackling sound sent him slithering from the bushes to a small knoll, where he crouched breathless.

Inside the motor home, Jessica pushed the blue button. Eighty yards away, the gate to the kennel slid open with a soft whirring sound.

Ike heard the released Dobermans as they bounded into the complex. They paused with uncertainty near the fenced-in portable generator. Vesper let out a soft but piercing whistle that directed the dogs into the woods.

John Ragonese stiffened when he heard the panting approach of the dogs. Faced with being torn to pieces by the attacking beasts, he promptly decided his fate. Jumping to his feet, he held his arms aloft, fingers spread wide. "I am not armed," he shouted in a desperate voice.

For a fleeting instant, he saw the deep brown blur of the leaping canine which toppled him to the ground. He felt the animal's hot, stale breath in his face, then a sharp pain as the dog's stiletto-sharp teeth punctured the flesh of the forearm he had thrown in front of his face and throat.

Another searing flash of pain added to his hysteria as the second dog sank its fangs into his leg.

"Still!" Vesper commanded, and reluctantly the dogs backed off, snarling through teeth mottled with crimson, circling the mission director, who lay on the ground in the fetal position.

Ragonese slowly uncoiled to see the oozing indentation on his right arm and the blood staining the uneven tear in his denim trousers.

"You got a thing about suicide, Spooky Man?" said Ike, the dogs straining at his side. "Stay," he ordered the dogs as he approached the mission director. He stooped to frisk the man's cadaverous form.

"I'm not armed," Ragonese quavered.

"Man, you shoulda come in a tank."

"I need medical attention."

"For what? Once the man sees your spooky ass, he'll only hang you from a tree."

In fact, Ron Rebuck displayed neither concern nor anger. He hardly looked at Ragonese, yet he did nothing to prevent Jessica from tending the man's wounds. But the moment Ragonese attempted to engage him in conversation, Rebuck turned his back and entered the motor home.

When Ike returned from securing and feeding the dogs, he was surprised to see Jessica alone with the mission director. He wondered just how real Rebuck's hatred for the man really was. If the captain had caught Ragonese, he would have already torn out his tongue and cut off his hand.

Ike eased his hulking frame over to the well, where Jessica was cleaning the man's wounds, and casually watched her swab the punctures with dabs of alcohol from a first-aid kit. "Looks like rabies to me," Ike diagnosed. "You'll probably go mad, Spooky Man."

Jessica frowned. "Ike, the man is injured."

"The man's lucky he ain't dead."

"Mr. Ragonese, I think you should get to a hospital for proper treatment."

358

"I shall, Jessica." His eyes went to the motor home. "Right after I have spoken to *him*."

"*Him?*" said Ike. "*Him* ain't gonna talk with you, fool. You're stinkin' up his air."

"He'll speak with me. It is in his best interest to do so."

"Mr. Ragonese, why have you been spying on us?" Jessica asked.

"It wasn't a very good idea, Jessica—but then it was hardly proper of them to break into my safe." He paused. The burning sensation from his wounds gripped him with a moment of intolerable pain. "Jessica, it's vital that I speak to him—vital to us all."

She finished wrapping the bandages around his arm, unwilling to look at his face. "Mr. Ragonese, I can't help you."

"But you *must*."

"Man, what's this *must* shit?" Ike demanded. "You wanna talk *must*, you talk *must* to me, sucka."

Ragonese had not risked life and limb to negotiate with the second string, but under the present circumstances he could see no alternative. "I want to buy the two hundred acres. And since you and your partner have obviously read the contracts that were in my safe, you know the value of the property."

"Didn't the dogs teach you a fuckin' thing? The man hates your guts. What makes you think he'd sell one foot of the land to you, turkey?"

Ragonese twitched his scrawny shoulders in a shrug of resignation. "If he refuses to sell me the two hundred acres, there will be trouble."

Vesper snorted. "What could a candy-ass like you know about trouble?"

"The police might be interested in your activities out here."

Ike reflected upon the mission director in a new light. "Police? . . . Uh-huh," he said, moving rapidly to the motor home, where he banged a fist against the siding.

"Little Brother," he shouted, "Spooky Man's gotta threat workin'!"

Fresh from a shower, Rebuck emerged from the motor home dressed in a khaki shirt and pants. He walked to the picnic table and sat across from Jessica and the grimacing Ragonese.

"I've done all I can," Jessica said. "Ron, he should really go to a hospital."

"That's up to him," Rebuck said with indifference.

"Man, he's talkin' police," Ike protested.

"I don't have to," Ragonese said, an assured calm settling in his voice. "There is no need for any trouble between us. Not when the codicil you're holding is worth more than a half-million dollars."

"Six hundred thousand," Rebuck replied. "And nine hundred thousand for you," he added.

The taut lines in the mission director's face relaxed. Emboldened by Rebuck's reply, he ventured on. "Why can't we work this out?" He couldn't detect even a glimmer of reaction on the young man's face as he studied the piercing, hypnotic eyes. Strangely, Ragonese felt an unexplained compulsion to confess. "Yes, I was spying. But only after you broke into the mission and blew up my safe."

"And you lied to me, Mr. Ragonese," Jessica said.

"Jessica, I have *never* lied to you."

"The man standing next to the statue that night, you're doing business with him. So stop lying to me!"

"Jessica, I swear I don't know what you're talking about."

She spun from the table and began to walk rapidly toward the motor home. "Jessica," Rebuck called after her. "Come back, I want you to hear it all." She hesitated, then returned and stood by his side.

"Sell me the two hundred acres, Ron Rebuck," Ragonese said impatiently, wincing from the pain of his wounds. "We both stand to gain a great deal."

"By November seventh?"

360

"You are well aware of the closing date on the sale of the land."

Rebuck smiled. "Your deal with American Realty?"

"Yes, American Realty is the purchaser," Ragonese said curtly, unnerved by Rebuck's derisive grin.

"And if I don't sell you the two hundred acres, then what? You'll go to the police?"

"I would really prefer not to."

"And what would you tell them?"

"Only recently did I begin to put two and two together . . . I've finally reached a disturbing conclusion."

"Which is?"

"I don't believe that your absence from the mission grounds each time a religious figure has been assassinated is a coincidence. Your hatred for people with religious vocations has been well established, not only in your treatment of me but in your unprovoked attack on an Amish elder. That in itself may not constitute sufficient evidence for your arrest, but it will certainly be enough to cast you and your partner into the light of an investigation."

Vesper tensed. Jessica felt a knot of fear in her stomach, reliving in flashback that night when Ron Rebuck stormed nude from the motor home to hold a gun at the head of the Amish elder. Now he had been threatened by another religious person, and she felt certain the words of John Ragonese would provoke another firestorm of wrath. But Rebuck's noncommittal expression did not change. "Do you know *why* those people were wasted?" he asked calmly.

"No. But I'm inclined to believe you can tell me."

"But you *ain't*!" Ike Vesper broke in.

Rebuck hushed him with a wave of his hand. "They were wasted because a certain man ordered their deaths."

"Man, put a lid on it!" Ike pleaded.

Rebuck ignored Ike completely. "Do you know who that man is?"

"How could I possibly know?" Ragonese said.

Rebuck deliberately prolonged the scenario, the suggestion of a smile playing on the corners of his mouth. "It's

361

the same man you met at midnight in a hut at Valley Forge.''

Ragonese felt his knees grow weak; he was no longer aware of the pain throbbing in his wounds.

"That's right—the same man who holds an option to buy the mission's land.''

Ragonese stared at the ground, but his eyes refused to focus on the tangible, and what he saw flickering into his consciousness was a vision of his personal Armageddon— his lofty plans, his careful, deliberate sacrifices consumed by flames. "Sam,'' he gasped. "Is he the man you call the captain? The man Jessica believes I saw in the cemetery?''

"Tell him, Ike,'' Rebuck said.

"You've gone to fuckin' far, Little Brother. Too fuckin' far.'' Ike walked away.

Jessica placed her hands gently on Rebuck's shoulders.

Ragonese struggled to stand, then fell back on the bench. His deep, sunken eyes, rimmed now with a pain which went far deeper than his flesh wounds, darted first to Jessica, then to Rebuck. "What have I done?'' he said, chiseling each syllable, "for you to destroy all that I have worked for?'' The man let his eyes wander to the dying orange glow beyond the wavelike ridges of the Alleghenies.

"All these years,'' he moaned, "all these empty years since your father died, I had to work like a field hand to keep the mission open. Living on potatoes and beans . . . wearing clothes unfit for sale in a flea market . . . borrowing from one bank to pay the interest on a loan from another . . . bearing the scorn and constant harassment of my Amish and Mennonite neighbors . . . scorned like a leper . . . forced to live for a year on what even an impoverished minister spends in a week. For what purpose? To be ruined by the mission founder's own son?''

"Ron has done nothing to hurt you,'' Jessica said.

"Jessica, can't you realize the man you have turned to for love and protection has schemed with this captain to take all the mission land? Everything I've worked for.''

"You worked on it—but only because you planned to sell it,'' Rebuck concluded.

362

"What of it? Don't I deserve some compensation for my years of labor here?"

Jessica's frown was all too revealing; she'd lost all respect for John Ragonese. She turned and walked slowly toward the motor home. This time, Rebuck didn't try to stop her.

"If you weren't so greedy," Rebuck said, "you would have sold the land years ago."

"You speak of greed, but what have you done but swindle me out of what is rightfully mine?"

The anger Rebuck had been controlling since he heard the mission director blundering in the woods finally boiled over. "You're in a box, Mister. Time has run out on you. The bank in town has a fifty-thousand-dollar lien on the property. You're months behind on your payments. You can't make any miraculous deals with new investors, nor can you give the land away to your neighbors. And the worst of it is that you've taken twenty-five thousand dollars from a maniac who wants it back in blood."

"You failed to mention the codicil to your father's will."

"It won't matter in the long run. You're only the bait for bigger game."

John Ragonese slumped. He wore an expression of total defeat. "What now, Ron Rebuck? Will you turn the dogs loose again?"

"Ike," Rebuck called over his shoulder, "get him to a hospital."

"Hospital," Ike mocked, rising from the trailer steps. "Why not invite the spooky sonuvabitch to dinner? I got a better idea. Invite the dogs to have dinner on *him*."

A leery John Ragonese watched Vesper stride to the black van, mumbling obscenities to himself. Suddenly, it came to him that he would never reach the hospital. His body trembling from a combination of pain and fear, he turned to Rebuck and said, "Is this how you do it?"

"Listen, and listen good, Mister. If we all survive the next sixty days, you just might come out of this with your greedy ass intact. Until then, I don't want to see your face."

Rebuck stormed into the motor home, leaving Ragonese staring into the early night, groping for a meaning to his departing words. Ike's gruff voice cut into his erratic thoughts.

"Hey, Spooky Man. Move it!"

As the devastated John Ragonese limped to the van, it all came to him like bright morning sunlight burning away a gauze of ground fog: he had been wrong about Ron Rebuck and the land. The bigger game Rebuck had mentioned was Rebuck himself. And the man called Sam, Rebuck's "Captain," was the hunter. Suddenly, the solution suggested to him in that musty Valley Forge hut had begun to make sense.

Inside the motor home, Jessica was unable to focus on the evening news. She turned to Ron, who had taken a seat across from her. "Ron, I can't believe I was so naive as to believe in that man."

Rebuck's attention was on the television reporter speaking from the grand opening ceremonies of Christ Town, U.S.A.

"Who would believe he was in it just for the land?" Jessica went on, unaware she had lost her audience. "For all those years, he worked so hard to keep the mission running just for the money the land could bring him." She looked over at Rebuck. "Ron, how did you manage to see through him?"

He had not heard a word she had said for he was engrossed in the coverage of Christ Town's centerpiece, the Hell-Bent Express.

Rebuck's intense observation drew her eyes to the television screen, where she saw an old man telling a swarm of reporters to be patient until he'd seen enough of Christ Town to make a substantive evaluation. Not until the reporter identified him as Reverend Billy Hale did she recognize the famed evangelist.

There was a sudden chill in the air of the motor home's

cramped parlor, and Jessica again turned to Rebuck. What she saw raised ridges of gooseflesh on every inch of her body.

As he stared at the screen with unblinking concentration, Rebuck's face was locked in a maniacal glare of pure hate.

CHAPTER 32

THE PHONE JANGLED insistently, fists beat on the door. But Billy Hale heard neither summons, and an alarmed Emile sent a disoriented Frank Buckmaster waddling to fetch a bellman with a pass key.

Billy was finally awakened from a deep and dream-tortured sleep by Emile's insistent shaking. "What time is it?" Billy asked, blinking at the ceiling light the chauffeur had turned on.

"It's eight o'clock, Billy," Bucky said before Emile could look at his watch.

"Are you all right, Chief?" Emile asked.

Hale rubbed his aching limbs. "Apparently, I have survived that dreadful ride." He sat up and lifted the quilt from his legs.

"It's okay, Billy," Buckmaster said, consulting the watch that had ruled his day, "we still have time."

"Time?" Hale had to think for a moment before he remembered his promise. "I'm sorry, Bucky. I did say I would have dinner with you, didn't I?"

"Chief," said Emile, bringing him a lightweight bathrobe that was draped over a chair, "maybe you should eat in the room."

"But Billy promised—"

Emile spun and faced Buckmaster. "It's your fault the chief is so exhausted."

Billy raised a hand. "If you people will stop your incessant arguing and give me a few minutes, I believe I will be able to make my own decision about dinner."

Billy hobbled past Emile, pausing at the bathroom. "Have you eaten your dinner?"

"I ordered from room service, Chief. It's in my room."

"For heaven's sake, go and finish it."

Emile hesitated. "Can I do anything for you before I go?"

"Yes, you can open the drapes," said Billy, shutting the bathroom door behind him.

The chauffer drew open the heavy brocade drapes, exposing the nighttime glitter of Christ Town. He then escorted Bucky to the door, fighting off the urge to order him to lighten the demands he was heaping on his employer.

Freshly shaved and showered, Billy entered the spacious living room, shaking his head in wonder at the polished mahogany staircase leading to the elaborate loft that comprised a master bedroom regally furnished in manger decor. Billy had declined to sleep in the luxurious bed fit for a commercial King of Kings. He moved deeper into the heart of the immense suite and was surprised to see Bucky coming out from one of three bathrooms.

"You're not getting dressed, Billy?" Bucky asked, panic edging his words.

Bucky's forlorn appearance and agitated mood were the symptoms of a man in deep trouble, but Billy was in no mood to hear someone else's problems. He dropped into an overstuffed chair.

"Bucky, Emile is probably right. I'm quite tuckered out. Would you have any objection to ordering something from room service? We can have ourselves a pleasant chat right here."

"But, Billy, we're long overdue at the Heavenly Gate."

"The Heavenly *what?*"

"If I don't bring you to the Heavenly Gate Restaurant, I'm in big trouble."

"What kind of trouble?"

Bucky didn't know where to begin. He looked at Billy uncertainly.

"Would this trouble have anything to do with the conversation you had with Abe Margolis this afternoon at the Serpentarium?"

"He told me I had to bring you, Billy."

"*He* told you? I was under the impression that your orders came from that woman, Beth Staples."

"That's true, Billy. And I went to see her."

Billy waited patiently for him to continue, but his mumbling wouldn't develop into words. "Bucky, what *did* she say to you?"

"She told me I had to."

"Had to bring me to the Heavenly Gate Restaurant?"

"Yes. But don't blame her, Billy. She's been good to me. And she's trying to help Jimmy. She's—"

"An angel of mercy, I know. But tell me, did either she or Margolis tell you why?"

"Not really."

"Well, did you ask?"

"Ask?"

"For a reason, man!"

"I . . . I don't remember. Just that I had to bring you—or else. Billy, where would I go? What would I do? Don't let them fire me, Billy. Please don't let that happen to me."

"Calm yourself, Bucky. No one is going to fire you because of me."

Bucky's face brightened. "You'll go then?"

"I believe I know the reason," said Hale to himself.

"Billy, you'll go?"

Billy heaved wearily from the chair. "All right, Bucky. I'll slip into a suit and we shall go to this Heavenly Gate Restaurant."

"Thank you, Billy. Thank you," said a jubilant Bucky, rushing to kiss the old evangelist's hand in an emotional show of gratitude.

Cora Lee Christian fluttered from the G.L.E.E. Club in a rage. She had gathered the members of the chorus and orchestra to watch the evening news on the battery of giant color monitors. To her horror, however, not one of the television networks included a single frame or mention of her performance during their lengthy coverage of Christ Town's opening events.

She pushed her Mercedes convertible fast enough to motivate a highway patrolman to give chase with its siren caterwauling and dome lights flashing. But he gave it up when she pulled into the long drive to her Lord's Lake home. With so many of the county police moonlighting as security guards at Christ Town, he knew a losing proposition when he saw one.

Cora Lee whirled into the house, promising herself she would make a list of the corporations who sponsored the network news and, in the name of God, intitiate a movement to boycott their products. She bustled into Jimmy's den, anxious to give him a blow-by-blow account of her woes, but he was not there as she expected and she marched up the stairs, thinking he would be brooding in the bedroom. To her dismay, he was not in the bedroom; she considered adding his name to her boycott list.

She barged into the kitchen and found not a soul. Torn between anger and confusion, she noticed a note pinned to the carving block with a boning knife. Her kitchen help, the last of her domestic staff, had quit, citing in the crudely composed note Jimmy's strange and intolerable behavior of recent weeks. Cora Lee threw up her arms, outraged that the day could have been so unbearably cruel to her.

Multicolored lights played on a thirty-foot waterfall feeding a stream winding through a lush, tropical garden, flowing under graceful bridges garlanded with jacaranda and flowering Judas. The light reflecting off the fine mist from the waterfall produced a rainbow effect, the bands of color dancing with the even flicker of the concealed spotlight. What made the effect unique was that it was happening in the Resurrection Towers lobby.

Billy Hale stepped from the Christ Town Express and limped to the escalator connecting the monorail station with the main lobby.

369

"The Garden of Eden," Bucky informed him, the enthusiasm gone from his voice.

Billy could see that there wasn't anything tacky about the motif and that a great deal of money had been creatively spent in order to bring out a lavish Garden of Eden theme. There was no penny-pinching here, he thought as he followed Bucky through the crowded lobby. But the more he saw of the seductive verdancy, the harder it became to free himself of the ancient message underlying the garden of all gardens. The countless times he had preached of "original sin" now returned to him in sundry rebuttals. Who truly wrote Genesis? he wondered, allowing himself to dwell on the question. Contrary to what he had preached to millions, and despite the celluloid propaganda of C.B. DeMille's *The Ten Commandments,* he realized the flaws in crediting Moses. But had it been truly conceived by authors with merely letters for names?

They passed the waterfall and the terrace of the Garden of Eden Restaurant, and Bucky winced when a shapely cocktail waitress clad only in a loincloth and halter top waved at him from the entrance of the cocktail lounge.

"Hi, Bucky," she called. "Three for the price of one tonight." She blew him a kiss.

Bucky kept his eyes straight ahead, pretending not to notice the young woman. The truth was, following Jimmy Christian's banishment from Christ Town he had fallen off the wagon. The Adam and Eve Lounge had become a frequent haunt. He did not steal a glance at Billy until they were standing at the express elevator serving the Heavenly Gate Restaurant.

"Why would God impose such a test on virginal man when He already knew the result before the deed?" Billy harshly questioned.

Bucky's mouth fell ajar.

The elevator door opened, and Billy stepped into the glass-enclosed lift followed by a still baffled Buckmaster. The evangelist was so caught up in the detailed re-creation of the infamous Biblical garden that he was oblivious to anyone or anything. Free will, he thoughtfully reasoned.

370

But man never asked to be created . . . was never given a vote when the rules of the game were drafted. Original sin? Yes, but who was really the sinner? he dared to wonder as the elevator door glided shut.

The Heavenly Gate Restaurant did, indeed, have a gate, a golden one at that. The ornate latticework served as a divider between the entrance to the restaurant and a spacious waiting area fronting the reservation desk. They were approached by an imposing St. Peter, a large man with a flowing white beard attired in a long white robe. An enormous gold key swung on a chain around his neck. He waved Buckmaster and Hale past a group of people waiting to be seated. They followed the bizarre maitre d' into the marble-columned restaurant and through a large dining area which completed one full revolution every forty-eight minutes, affording a gradual 360-degree view of Christ Town. There was not an empty table in sight, and Billy saw many familiar faces. He paused to regard one in particular.

"Well, well—the mountain has come to Mohammed." Veep Siler raised his wine glass in greeting. "You remember Reverend Patrick, don't you, Billy?" Siler gestured to a man so tiny he required three cushions to bring his chin to table level.

Billy nodded slightly at the midget evangelist Barney Patrick, a morose man whose area of expertise was Doom and its cousins, Despair and Sorrow.

"You couldn't wait for me to be out of the way, could you, Veep?"

"Billy, you must try the rack of sacrificial lamb; it's scrumptious."

"How much money is Harley paying you?"

"The word 'paying' is hardly applicable. What Harley *owes* me would be more accurate."

"Don't play on words with me, Siler. I know you're behind the smear campaign against Senator Lollar and other liberal Florida politicians."

"Reverend Hale," the fat man said, laughing, "I do

371

believe you have me mistaken for Virtues, Inc.—Harley Lombard's crusade of righteousness.''

"Let Harley be, Siler. Lest you become a beached whale.''

"Is that a threat, Reverend Hale, or merely the words of a caring father? Commendable loyalty indeed, considering that Harley has publicly denounced you.''

"Harley is only a minnow. I'm sure you've found much bigger fish here in Christ Town's waters to feed upon.''

"The so-called minnow has become a plump tuna fish, Reverend Hale. And there is nothing you can do to save him. I'm afraid it is already much too late.''

"Later than you think,'' added the midget evangelist, between shoveling peas into his mouth.

Billy refrained from pursuing the conversation. He would not waste his energy sparring with a noncontender like Siler when he had come for a title fight. He moved on toward the entrance to a private dining room where Bucky and the maitre d' were waiting.

The intimate room, overlooking the midway of St. James Amusement Park, was not part of the revolving section of the rooftop complex. Hale shuddered at the looming bulk of the Hell-Bent Express and noted a line of people which stretched nearly a hundred yards. He was not surprised that the woman who rose to greet them was Beth Staples.

"It was good of you to come, Reverend Hale,'' she said, extending a soft, perfectly manicured hand. "Thank you.''

"I don't believe I had much choice in the matter,'' Billy said, ignoring her offered handshake and hanging his cane on the back of his chair.

"I'm sorry Bucky had to be involved in this,'' she said, sliding gracefully back into her seat. "Like Bucky, I also have to follow orders.''

"From a heathen?'' Billy was direct.

She paused, selecting the proper words for her reply. "It's not contagious, I promise you.''

"Tell me, Ms. Staples, what has become of Jimmy Christian? Why has he vanished from his usual position in the limelight?''

"I'm afraid Jimmy has fallen on hard times," she said, a slight flush interrupting her aura of poise.

"Could you be one of the beneficiaries of Jimmy's bad luck?"

"I guess you could say I have prospered in a way."

"Bucky tells me you have been trying to help Jimmy."

"Beth saved Jimmy's home," Bucky interrupted. "The Glee Club, too."

"So you have told me at least four times today, Bucky. I believe I'm thoroughly familiar with that phase of Ms. Staples's rescue mission."

"Unfortunately, I have reached the limit of what I am able to do for Jimmy," Beth said.

"What about Bucky here? Will you be able to help him?"

"Bucky?" She gently touched Buckmaster's folded hands. "Bucky will always have a home."

"From what I've heard, he was threatened with an eviction notice."

"That would never have happened."

"As you have previously said, Ms. Staples, you do take orders from another."

"My employer and I have understandings about many things. Bucky's future is one of them."

Billy was about to ask about Abe Margolis's threatening Bucky, but thought better of it. Instead, he said, "Is that a promise?"

"As I recall you once saying during a . . . shall we say, minor altercation with Jimmy, 'Bank on it.' "

Billy smiled inwardly, remembering the eventful day.

Beth Staples glanced at her watch. "I must get down to Christ Square. The passion play will be starting in a few minutes. Don't bother to get up, Reverend Hale." She was a bit surprised when he offered his hand; a faraway expression had replaced his glacial dignity. "Is something wrong, Reverend Hale?"

"Wrong? The entire day has been wrong! No, actually I was thinking of something my father said many, many years ago: 'When beauty departs, watch for the beast.' "

373

Beth Staples retrieved her hand from Billy's. There was nothing phony about her smile. As Billy watched her depart, he felt confident that her personal relationship with his mortal enemy C.D. Pittman was strictly platonic.

Bucky had raked his memory for a passage or parable in the Bible which would relate to what Billy had quoted. "Billy, there's nothing about the beauty departing and watch for the beast in the Bible."

"No? Well, maybe if you look again real hard, it might come to you in a manner of interpretation."

No sooner had Beth Staples left the private dining room than Abe Margolis appeared, escorting the small, wrinkled old man who had caused Billy so many sleepless nights. Bucky's sudden restlessness told Billy the "Beast" had arrived.

Billy had not seen Pittman since the years of Richard Waters's presidency. The ruthless industrialist had slapped Billy with a hundred-million-dollar slander suit, and Waters had induced Pittman to drop the suit on the condition of a personal apology. The "I'm sorry" Billy had muttered to Pittman in the oval office had been the two most difficult words of his life.

Margolis jerked his thumb at Bucky rudely. "You may leave, Buckmaster," he said with authority.

"And you may do likewise, Margolis," Billy returned, refusing to call him rabbi and galled by the fact that Margolis publicly referred to himself as such.

Margolis had no intention of leaving and sought approval for his staying from Pittman.

"You lose, Rabbi," Pittman ruled, his eyes colliding with Billy's.

The two old men, finally alone, sat across from each other, studying each other's face as if to check every line, every wrinkle. It was Pittman who finally broke the edgy silence. "I have taken the liberty of ordering champagne from my private stock. However, if you have a particular beverage in mind . . ."

Billy held up a hand. "I shall settle for ice water. Might I suggest arsenic for you?"

The industrialist accepted Hale's first insult stoically. He picked up a knife from the gold table service and scrutinized it like a marine officer performing a white-glove inspection. But his hand trembled with quavering, palsied spasms.

"Now I understand why in all these years you have been unable to cut your throat," Billy said, letting his gaze linger on the unbidden dance of Pittman's hands.

Returning the knife to the table, Pittman let his eyes wander along the deep ridges and furrows of Hale's Appalachian countenance. "From what I see, time has been equally unkind to you," he said.

"Every line in my face has been honestly earned. Can you say the same?"

Pittman leaned back in his chair and looked through the glass at the carnival atmosphere of the midway beneath him. "Honesty: an intriguing word. Its only barometer is conscience. Don't you agree?"

"Apparently, the good Lord neglected to give you one."

Their caustic exchange was interrupted by the appearance of a man dressed in a purple robe trimmed with silver. He wheeled the champagne cart to their table and rotated the bottle of Dom Perignon lovingly on its bed of shaved ice, then popped the cork with the easy grace of the professional sommelier. He filled the two glasses with all the proper flourishes, then replaced the bottle in the sterling silver bucket. It was all too rehearsed, Hale thought. And if the man was such a master of his craft, why had he failed to summon a bus boy to remove the place setting at the unoccupied third seat?

"Has another person under the anvil of obligation to you been invited to join us?" Billy said to Pittman, nodding toward the extra setting.

Pittman laughed, a dry, mirthless cackle which made Hale think of a child molester soliciting children in a park with a bag of candy. "I have reserved it for our guest of honor," he replied. "You see, we have been joined by a conscience which is neither biased nor bought."

Billy was not amused. "Spare me the theatrics, Pittman, and say whatever it is you have to say."

"Theatrics? Hardly. I invited you here—"

"Invited?" Billy sneered. "I wouldn't call having your stooge, Abe Margolis, threatening Bucky an invitation."

"I *arranged*," Pittman went on, "to bring you here so that I could personally express my gratitude to you."

"For what? For despising everything you stand for?"

"For opening my eyes. All these years my contempt for you had blinded me to the realization that the business of religion could be so lucrative. My other enterprises struggle to make a profit due to competition. They are so heavily taxed. But this . . . this is incredible!"

Pittman pointed to the bustling midway. "Pure profit. The born-again Christian robots you helped create work for minimum scale. The tax laws exempting religion that your self-serving lobbyists fought to keep on the books put me under the protective umbrella of the United States Constitution. And I learned it all from you, from your books, each and every one you ever had published."

"They certainly could not have helped you," Billy said.

"Ah, but they did. You see, there is nothing in Christ Town that you have not publicly endorsed."

"I find that absurd."

Pittman assessed Billy's hasty denial, and a devious grin lit the cadaverous pallor of his face. "Shall we start with the Hell-Bent Express?"

He couldn't have picked a more sensitive subject, and Billy squirmed in his chair.

Pittman did not hesitate. "I have become, you might say, a dedicated biographer of your life. I have in my possession a collection of every interview you've given, every book and every article you have written, and even videotapes of every one of your television campaigns. Do you recall the first article you wrote?"

Billy would volunteer nothing and eyed Pittman with a mix of skepticism and hate.

"The very first column you wrote, some forty years ago, was titled 'Armageddon and You.'"

Billy remembered it well. It had helped to establish the power of his ministry almost overnight. The editor of the newspaper syndicate had instructed him to make it juicy and frightening, to open up with a bang to grab the readers. Within a month, Billy was featured in *Time* magazine's Religion section. Six years later he graced the cover of that prestigious publication—the first American evangelist to be so honored.

"But let us not stop here, Billy. All those books about Hell you wrote . . . what were those titles?"

At this point, Billy was sure Pittman could rattle them off at will, and he was beginning to sense that a significant segment of his life was about to be dredged from the past merely for the sake of a devious old man's argument.

"*Eternal Doom*," Pittman began. "*Custody of Lucifer, Wailings of Repentment, Ultimate Despair, The Bleak and the Blackness, The Fires of Forever.*" Pittman leaned forward and smiled slowly. "Do those titles have a familiar ring?"

The crafty Pittman had named them all, every book Hale had written with hell as the theme. All of a sudden, the champion evangelist Billy Hale felt like a weary boxer, helpless on the ropes in the late rounds of the fight, unable to block his challenger's furious combinations. But unlike at a boxing match, there was no referee to step in and stop it.

Still, Pittman went on. "Let us not forget your famous TV specials. One in particular does come to mind. I believe the theme was 'The Price of Immoral Pleasure,' wasn't it? I'm sure you have relived that memorable night in Australia so many, many times."

Billy had. He could never forget the better than one hundred thousand Australians who were so captivated with his preaching of fire and brimstone; many felt as if the stadium seats they sat upon were on fire. Yet that night had proved to be the most embarrassing of his career as a TV minister. When he described the coming joy of a

377

former prostitute who had just stepped forward weeping to welcome Jesus into her previously immoral heart, Billy trumpeted the words, "You shall wake up one morning in the arms of Jesus." At that moment, a drunken Aussie in the fifth row had staggered to his feet and bellowed, "Right on, sister, fuck 'em all!"

"And what about your war against Satan?" Pittman was throwing his verbal punches at will. "The time you described with such vivid phrases the punishment inflicted upon souls in Hell. How eloquently you spoke, with such passion, with such vigor that you actually collapsed on stage and had to be rushed from the Los Angeles Coliseum to a hospital."

"Enough! You . . . you . . . you . . ." Billy's sputtering rage could not conjure a phrase pungent enough to express his loathing. His voice melted into a moan.

Pittman sat reveling in the mental anguish of a man who had been his nemesis for nearly four decades. He had one more haymaker to deliver. "The Hell-Bent Express was constructed under my direction," he said. "But you, sir, were the architect. I merely followed your blueprint to the most minute detail."

"May God damn your heathen soul," Billy cursed. But the match was over.

Pittman's laugh was part chortle, part wheeze, and total malice.

"You are the most corrupt and sadistic being to ever come from the womb." Billy spat the words.

Pittman addressed the empty chair of Conscience like a defense attorney making his summation to an impartial judge. "I stand accused of being both corrupt and sadistic. Yet let us examine my accuser. A man whose words drip with hypocrisy, a faker and a charlatan, a man whose total contribution to society has been to intimidate millions of the gullible with the world's oldest ghost story."

With his fists balled and his face a crimson mask, the anger erupting within Billy was rising to an uncontrollable peak.

Pittman looked directly at the livid face before him.

"Through my widespread endeavors, thousands of people have benefited. My annual payroll is in the hundreds of millions of dollars. Dollars which constitute a substantial part of the economy. Because of me, my workers purchase homes, buy cars, put food on the table, clothe their families, and send their children off to college. My employees pay taxes which support the needy, build schools, hospitals, roads, and bridges, and provide for this nation's defense. What am I? I am a ship of commerce!" he bellowed, ". . . and what are you?"

Enraged, Billy grasped Pittman's wine goblet and flung its expensive contents into his face.

The ugly sneer of triumph never left Pittman's mouth. Raising his goblet high at Billy Hale's retreating figure, he shouted, "I propose a toast to the Right Reverend Billy Hale . . . The ultimate huckster of holiness."

The words had come to Billy Hale too late. All the things he should have said to C.D. Pittman in a fiery but controlled rebuttal raced through his battered mind. He had been cleverly reamed, outfoxed by his greatest enemy, who had targeted in on the subject of Hell with indisputable facts from Billy's crusading past. As he stood listlessly at a window of the Manger Suite, he could see in the distance the torchlight procession of the passion play along Crucifixion Trail as it snailed upward toward Calvary Hill. But it was not enough of a distraction to chase Pittman from his thoughts. It took a sharp rapping on the door to bring about a welcome solace to his doldrums. What now, he wondered, limping to the door.

It was Bucky, dressed in the brown hooded robe of a monk. The only thing he had not changed was the hangdog look on his meaty face.

"Whatever it is this time will have to wait until morning," Hale said, blocking the entrance. "And why are you wearing that robe?"

"We all have to wear them during the passion play. Billy . . ." He paused, trying to remember the message which had been entrusted to him after a half-hour of power-drinking in the Adam and Eve Lounge. "Billy, Jimmy wants to speak with you."

So the ghost of Christ Town had finally materialized, Billy thought. Interesting, but he didn't possess the stamina to find out why. C.D. Pittman had devastated him, and his exhaustion had reached a dangerous plateau. "I will gladly speak with Jimmy," he said. "But it will have to wait until tomorrow."

"But, Billy," Buckmaster stepped back from the door, pointing down the hall, "Jimmy's right here."

Billy's brows furrowed as he brushed past Bucky to see the hooded, robed figure standing in the hall. The unkempt beard, the drooping shoulders and vacant stare, belonged to a man drowning in despair. "Come in, Jimmy," Billy invited, shocked by the man's gaunt appearance.

"I'll be waiting in the lobby," Bucky encouraged. "And don't worry, Jimmy. Billy will help you."

One thing was certain, Billy thought. There would be no need tonight to flog Jimmy with his cane.

They were alone and Billy sat quietly watching Jimmy pace the floor, patiently waiting for him to speak. But the man who had regaled millions with his up-tempo TV sermons was either unwilling or unable to divulge whatever was tearing him up inside.

"That bad, son?" Billy cracked the silence.

It was the icebreaker Christian needed. "He ruined me, Billy. He destroyed me."

"You can't say you were't warned about the man."

"All the time he was waiting. Waiting for me to make a mistake, to fall. Then he sucked out every drop of my blood and picked my bones clean. He humiliated me, Billy. You were right, Pittman *is* the devil."

"You'll get no argument here. But why have you come to me, Jimmy?"

"Advice, Billy. I came for advice. Anything that will help me stop Pittman."

"If you will recall, I have given you my advice."

"I know. I lost my temper. I was on such an ego trip, I

felt I could do no wrong. I apologize for what I said to you, Billy."

"Speaking of temper, I believe it was you who got hit with the cane."

"It should have knocked some sense into me."

"Now that we have put the apologies to rest, what kind of advice do you seek from me?"

"Anything. Anything to stop the man."

"Have you exhausted all legal means?"

"Billy, we're talking about taking on Fort Knox. He could keep me tied up in court forever. . . ."

"I did hear he left you the house."

"Beth Staples saw to that, Billy."

"And your ministry? The Glee Club?"

"You mean Pittman's ministry."

"Pittman's ministry?" Hale flinched. "How in blazes can an atheist possibly take over a ministry of God?"

"Maybe not in name, but Pittman controls it. He gives the orders and makes the bottom-line decisions."

Of course, Billy thought, quick to realize how Pittman had insured that Jimmy could not attack him over the G.L.E.E. Club network. "Tell me, Jimmy, just what *is* your role with the ministry?"

"I'm still the nominal minister. Pittman's too shrewd to fire me. He would have too many questions to answer."

"But he has taken away your TV pulpit."

"He may as well have. Sure, I can do my preaching, but with his script. Don't you see, Billy? That's why I won't do any more Glee Club shows. I'll be damned if I'm going to be Pittman's religious barker and bag man."

"What about appearing on other TV ministries?"

"Whose? What the Glee Club network hasn't picked up in syndication, your man Lombard has tied up. But even so, what could I say?"

Billy smiled. It had come to him like a flashbulb flaring in his mind. "There is a way, Jimmy."

"What, Billy?" He hungered to know.

"Much will depend on how badly you wish to stop this man."

"With everything that is left of me."

"Would that include your soul?"

"The man has *stolen* my soul."

"Has he? Well, I have a plan to help you get it back."

"How, Billy? Please tell me how."

"With the national media already here in droves, we shall hold a press conference. They have been dogging my footsteps all day, so I rather think it will be well attended."

Jimmy's face sank deeper in despair. "Billy, you don't understand. Without Bucky getting me this robe I would have been recognized, and Pittman would have had me arrested on the spot."

"Arrested for what?"

"For trespassing, Billy. There's a court order which prohibits me from setting foot in Christ Town's theme parks and hotels."

Billy weighed the problem of Jimmy's visibility. "Does that court injunction include the Evangelical World Center?"

"No. But that's only because Pittman believes I'll come crawling back to the studio and become his damned puppet."

"All right then, we shall hold the press conference at the Evangelical World Center. You can stay in the upstairs bedroom tonight, and first thing in the morning we will summon the media people."

"But, Billy, even if you manage to pull it off, what do you expect me to say?"

"I expect you to say that Christ Town is a cynical sham, a sacrilegious rip-off conceived and orchestrated by an atheist."

"Billy, *I'm* the creator of Christ Town. Construction was half completed when Pittman became involved."

"That will lend even more credibility to your words."

"You're asking me to denounce my own creation?"

"No, I'm suggesting a way for you to expose Pittman for the fraud he is."

"How will that help me get Christ Town back?"

"Can't you see it, man? You have a chance to be a true disciple of Christ, an opportunity few men in our profession have in a lifetime. Think of yourself as being chosen."

"Chosen for what?"

The word "saint" came to mind, but wouldn't flow from Billy's mouth. He was struggling in search of something less reverent when the jangle of the phone became a welcome interruption. He was sure it was Doris. The unexpected and hellish meeting with Pittman had so agitated him, he had forgotten his promise to call her.

Billy rose from his chair, limping past the ringing phone located upon a desk before a large window, choosing to take the call in the bedroom. He turned to Christian at the door. "Son, you have a chance to be truly reborn. Think about it. Think about it real hard."

There was a strange, almost eerie smile on Jimmy Christian's face as he watched Billy close the bedroom door behind him. His grievous ordeal had taught him the value of meditation, he had come to realize that he could never have been the king of evangelism. Billy Hale had retired the crown.

The ringing of the phone had stopped, and so had his meeting with Billy. He lurched to the door leading to the hallway, then looked back in the direction of the bedroom through tearing, bloodshot eyes. His words came in a voice heavy with doom. "I'm sorry, Billy, I no longer believe in God."

Two hooded figures passed in silence through the flickering torchlight of the tunnel leading to Christ Square. The slapping sound of their sandals echoed on the cobblestones as they walked past the catacombs and mounted the fire stairs beyond the twin elevators serving the Last Supper Restaurant.

"Did you remember to bring the key?" Jimmy Christian asked.

Bucky fumbled under his robe and found the key in a trouser pocket. He produced it proudly and offered it to Jimmy, who looked at it with grave uncertainty before taking it from Buckmaster's hand.

"I better wait for you," Bucky said.

"No, you go ahead. I'll meet up with you at the foot of Calvary Hill."

"But, Jimmy, you might need me."

"Need you?" said Jimmy. A smile thawed his grim lips. "How right you are, Bucky. The shame is, I never realized it."

"I've always been loyal to you, Jimmy."

"I know, Bucky. And all the while I treated you like dirt . . . can you find it within yourself to forgive me?"

Bucky shuffled his feet on the cobblestones in embarrassment. He was not accustomed to receiving apologies.

"I want you to know you're the best friend any man could ever hope to have," Jimmy said, his voice thick with emotion.

"Don't worry, Billy will help you."

"I'm afraid not, Bucky. The time has come when I can only help myself."

In a sudden, dramatic surrender to his emotions, Jimmy embraced his enormous disciple, then quickly climbed the emergency stairs to the Last Supper Restaurant.

"It's going to be all right, Jimmy," Bucky called into the long shadows. "Everything's going to be fine."

The Last Supper Restaurant was Jimmy Christian's favorite place in Christ Town. He had designed it from the germ of an idea and it was the only attraction in the park which had not been gouged by C.D. Pittman's ruthless revisions. Due to undiagnosed problems within the restaurant's computerized circuitry, it was not yet open to public scrutiny. Having the place to himself brought a lightness to Jimmy's heart.

He moved slowly down an aisle and stood before the thirteen mannequins seated at a long, rectangular wooden table. The lights from Christ Square below and the distant torches being borne up Calvary Hill reflected through the elongated picture window and streaked across the mannequins' fleshlike faces while shadows danced on the ceiling like ghostly witnesses. Feeling neither a sliver of remorse nor a resurgence of faith, Jimmy drew closer to the mannequin representing Christ. His eyes locked on the likeness of a man whose existence he had decided was a myth.

Jimmy reached under the table for a switch installed

exclusively for his use. He flicked it on, activating a computer located in a small control room marked by a hand-scrawled sign that read DANGER—FAULTY WIRING. He then stepped back and waited for the mannequins to perform their holy act.

There was a high-pitched whir while Christ and each apostle were programmed by the mainframe computer. Then, as if awakened from the sleep of centuries, the figures came alive with rigid motions. There was no bread for Jesus to break, no wine for him to drink, but Christian waited eagerly for the mannequin's lip movements to synchronize with the audio. Lips opened, but no words were spoken, and Jimmy cursed the ineptitude of man.

He heard a faint hammering sound and drifted from the mechanical men, stopping at the picture window where he could see the web of humanity circling Calvary Hill. The mass of torches illuminated the crosses of the two thieves, soon to be joined by a third cross bearing a Christ mannequin as lifelike as the one seated at the table.

Jimmy turned away from the window and dragged a chair from a nearby dining table, seating himself across from a mannequin at the far end of Christianity's famous scene. Unlike the others, this mannequin was not responding to the computer's commands. It was motionless and, this time, Jimmy cursed Pittman for the electronic flaw.

Ever since that dreaded day when C.D. Pittman brought him down to the lowest ebb of his life, Jimmy had gradually lost his fighting spirit. Not even the thought of revenge could spark his will any longer. He was reduced to self-pity. And as his eyes fell to the tile floor, once more man's greatest battle, the conflicting arguments between two warring factions, bitterly commenced within him.

There is no God, no Heaven, no Hell. What you see, feel, hear, taste, and smell is all there is, the advocate of Doom charged in opening argument.

Faith, eternal reward, the Spirit of Life defended.

Once dead, forever dead, Doom proclaimed.

Eternal life, unyielding paradise, Life combatted.

Misery, strife, despair, Doom challenged.

Joyfulness, peace, hope, Spirit countered.

Punishment, both jointly echoed for differing reasons.

With his mind walking the swaying tightrope which separated life from death, Jimmy felt a sudden, chilling sensation that he was being observed. He looked up from the floor and what he saw made the hairs on the nape of his neck bristle. He stared in awe at the mannequin which had failed to respond to the computer's commands. The robot's eyes were spinning wildly in their electronic sockets when the mouth suddenly sprang open. "I am not in Hell!" it proclaimed in an unnaturally deep, hollow voice as if it came from another world.

Jimmy was rooted to the chair. He couldn't tear himself from the mannequin's eyes, which had stopped their spinning movement and now seemed to penetrate his very soul and siphon away his most secret thoughts. Only now did he connect the mannequin with its identity—he whom Christians for centuries had called the great betrayer.

He managed to look away from the searching Judas and saw yet another of the apostle mannequins leering at him. Its lips began to move and it uttered the word "sin," first quietly, almost in a whisper, then more loudly in a voice which suggested a truckload of gravel being unloaded on a sheet of tin. Jimmy attempted to rise, but he seemed shackled to the chair by invisible irons. "Give . . . Give . . . Give," another mannequin wailed. "Heal . . . Heal . . . Heal," yet another thundered. "Hallelujah . . . Hallelujah . . . Hallelujah," still another took up the chant and bellowed, assailing him with the monotonous litany.

Rivers of sweat poured from Jimmy's face. He was locked to what was becoming a super-horror revival show. All at once, the throng of living mannequins, with the exception of a solemn-faced Jesus, glared at him, while their rondelet of "Sin, heal, give, and hallelujah," fiercely assaulted his reeling conscience.

The apostles now assumed the ringing, beseeching tones of television evangelists soliciting funds. Advancing along the table like a slowly breaking wave, their gravel voices shouted in turn. "Five thousand dollars for cables! Ten thousand dollars for lights! Twenty-five thousand dollars for sound! Fifty thousand dollars for cameras! One hundred thousand dollars for TV time! . . . Two hundred thousand! Four hundred thousand! Eight hundred thousand! One million dollars for Jeee-sus!"

Amidst these ecclesiastical auctioneers, Jimmy saw the face of Christ sinking in silent shame. Tears dripped from his eyes, and Jimmy gasped when he saw the tears were turning to blood.

Eleven mannequins rose suddenly as one and the evangelist's trembling lips framed the word "Mercy." They began to move in slow, stonelike fashion, their arms rigidly outstretched. In single file they left the table, abandoning the grieving Jesus and the leering Judas. The shuffling of their feet along the restaurant's tile floor produced an unearthly scraping sound. They began to circle him and Jimmy was frozen in a state of helplessness. His terror intensified as they proceeded to clap their hands, slowly at first, then building to a room-shaking cadence which suggested the amplified beating of a giant heart.

A crescendo of music from an invisible chorus swept into the room as if cued by the clapping. The re-enactment of Christ's death upon Calvary Hill had transpired. The thunderous explosion of fireworks blistering the night sky and sending flashing lights throughout the Last Supper Restaurant only added to Jimmy's silent hysteria.

It was now a scene of total mayhem. In a frightening chorus which overpowered their human counterparts on Calvary Hill, the apostles were now chanting Jimmy's requiem. The explosive bursts of fireworks punctuated their shrieking wails and hand-clapping cacophony as they began to dance in stiff-jointed unison, circling the catatonic evangelist in a macabre ballet of despair.

Like a frantic carousel out of control, they became a collage of flailing arms. Through the racing blur of automation gone mad, Jimmy noticed the sudden movement of the lone disciple across from him. Judas was no longer leering at him.

387

"I am not in Hell," Judas shouted. "I am not in Hell," he repeated, begging for Jimmy to believe him.

The evangelist's horror was elevated to a new summit when the head of Judas began to turn in a slow, crunching full circle. Each time the mannequin repeated that he was not in Hell, the whirling motion of his head intensified until it was a blur which merged with the tempo of the runaway circle of disciples. And the words, "I am not in Hell," echoed like an endless record in Jimmy's tortured mind.

Jimmy Christian did not smell the thin wisp of white smoke which seeped under the sill of the computer room door, nor did he see the small tongues of flame licking at the console. Overwhelmed by the accumulation of horror, he had collapsed unconscious to the floor.

Billy Hale, dressed only in his blue bathrobe and slippers, stood in a crowd of gaping spectators which included Emile, Beth Staples, and a totally numb Frank Buckmaster. They watched the Christ Town Fire Department bring the last flames under control. The fire chief emerged from the smoldering building, his face blackened by the fine, telltale soot of an electrical fire. "The damage could be a lot worse, Ms. Staples," he said, removing his heavy asbestos gloves.

"How much worse, Chief?"

We were able to save half the structure. But I'm afraid the half that was saved is the wrong half."

"The Last Supper scene?" Beth asked, disappointment in her voice.

"I'm afraid so." A quizzical expression crossed the chief's face. Seeing Billy Hale, he turned to him. "Reverend Hale, didn't Christ have twelve apostles at the Last Supper?" he asked.

"According to scripture," Billy replied.

"He has thirteen now."

CHAPTER 33

"A SPIRITUAL ASSASSINATION," read the headline of the New York *Daily News*. The source for the paper's story was none other than Cora Lee, who in the aftermath of her husband's death had succeeded in making the network news.

"It was the devil who killed my poor Jimmy," she sobbed. "But then it could've been Judas. No, it was the devil *and* Judas who started the fire."

An insurance adjuster muttered that he could find nothing in the fine print of Christ Town's policy that covered spiritual arson.

Beth Staples, who found herself in the unexpected role of Christ Town spokesperson, was unsuccessful in her attempts to isolate Cora Lee from the throngs of reporters. She had better luck with a severely depressed Frank Buckmaster, confining him to the infirmary. She could not risk the probability of Bucky's corroborating Cora Lee's incredible tales of the supernatural, undermining Christ Town's "family" image and frightening off potential visitors.

The massive media coverage of Jimmy Christain's bizarre demise had its run once the exhaustive investigations conducted by the authorities ruled out foul play. Faulty wiring was without doubt the cause of the flash electrical fire which had incinerated Christian. Both the devil and Judas were exonerated. Ironically, C.D. Pittman's name was never mentioned.

Billy Hale left Christ Town while the gauntlet of cameras and microphones was aimed in the direction of the smoldering Last Supper Restaurant and Jimmy Christian's charred remains. When a convoy of reporters caught up with him at his Shenandoah estate, Hale answered their far-ranging questions with deliberate vagueness. But in the seclusion of his den Billy confessed to Doris that he did not believe Jimmy Christian's death was accidental. She watched him cover his face with his hands in a gesture of self-disgust. "I failed him, Doris. I might have saved him . . . instead, I failed him in the hour of his deepest need."

"No, Billy. Jimmy Christian failed himself."

"He came to see me . . . so desperately in need of help. And all I could see was an opportunity to boycott Christ Town and bring that bastard Pittman to his godless knees."

"Billy, you can't allow these feelings of guilt over Jimmy's death to consume you."

Billy's hands slipped from his face. "I have no intention of doing so. No, if anything I feel closer to the truth than ever. There's a solid link now between Pittman and this wave of religious killings, and you can bet I won't rest until I've gotten to the bottom of it."

"Billy," she said after what seemed to be a long silence, "I was just thinking."

"About what?"

"The last time we laughed."

Another had deep misgivings about Jimmy Christian's fiery demise. For the past week, Ron Rebuck had thought of little else. The various stories he read in the newspapers of the eerie circumstances surrounding Christian's death made him think of Captain Gemmer's flare for the macabre.

Rebuck had scourged his mind for a credible motive. Where was the connection, the common denominator between Christian and the others Gemmer had targeted for execution? Unlike Reverend Tho, Christian was apparently not involved in political blackmail and payoffs. But then, he reminded himself, neither were Everson or Langly, as far as he could tell. There was only one thing Rebuck felt reasonably sure of: if Claude Gemmer *was* behind Christian's death, it would appear that the captain had decided the special team he and Ike Vesper represented was no longer viable. If this was indeed the case, Rebuck knew they were now expendable. There was no more time to think about it—he had to try and get Jessica to safety. It was now or never.

Ike and Jessica climbed into the black van with no idea where Ron Rebuck was taking them, though Jessica had her fears. Ron refused to enlighten them, and they drove in silence over the freshly graveled make-do road which Ike had resurfaced for the second time in three months. When the van's suspension bottomed violently against the frame, Rebuck turned to Ike.

"What did you fill the ruts with, quicksand?" he grumbled.

"Hey, I was a Seal, not a fuckin' Seabee," Ike said testily as they fishtailed toward the bend and the mission road.

As they approached the old house, Vesper put his concerns about its lone occupant into words. "Clippin' that buzzard's wings ain't enough, Little Brotha. Spooky Bird can still run."

"In a circle," said Rebuck, not worried.

Jessica stared at the ramshackle building which had been the fulcrum of her life; how dreary it looked without the mission students lounging in the shade of the porch. But her life had changed so dramatically since the arrival of Ron Rebuck on the mission grounds that she rarely thought of the four happy months she had spent before that fateful January day—a period of time when she had felt that Michael's Mission was a godsend and its director, John Ragonese, the closest thing to the second coming of Christ.

Once more Jessica's mind was assailed by negatives; if only she had never looked deeply into the fire in Ron Rebuck's eyes; if only she had never walked uninvited down that trail; if only she had comprehended the depth and sincerity of Ike Vesper's initial warning to her; if only she had never heard of Michael's Mission; if only the man she loved wasn't trying to send her away; if only—"Fuck it," she said aloud.

Rebuck glanced with disbelief into the rearview mirror, and it took Ike a full ten seconds to recover from hearing a word he'd thought her incapable of using. She made no effort to apologize for her outburst. Instead she said, "Ron, I'm on the team."

The team, Rebuck thought. She made it sound as if she had joined a high school volleyball squad. But he knew right then that if he failed to get her away from here now, he would have to tell her everything, that she would have no alternative but to be a player in a game where the odds against their surviving were a thousand to one.

Vesper hunched down in the swivel seat. He thought less of his own commitment and more about to whom it was made. Regardless of the bizarre circumstances, he had been hired by the captain to do a job, one he knew would involve activities that would take him beyond the law. And there was nothing Rebuck could say or do that would produce an inkling of mutiny in his mind. The captain had no quarrel with him, and he would give him no reason. His name was Ike Vesper, not Gunga Din.

Just before Rebuck slowed the van for the turn onto the main highway, he withdrew a Heuer digital stopwatch from his windbreaker pocket and concealed it in his left hand. At the precise instant the van turned onto the highway, he jabbed the stem with his thumb and began the drive toward Lancaster on the deserted country road. They didn't have to wait long for the expected to materialize. Rebuck saw the vehicle in the side-view mirror and depressed the crown of the watch. Forty-five seconds had elapsed.

"Company?" Ike asked, looking back at the gray sedan following them at a discreet quarter-of-a-mile distance.

"Who are they?" Jessica asked.

"The captain's hawks," Rebuck said.

"The mothafuckin' police," Ike said to himself, not wishing to engage in another polemic with Rebuck.

But Rebuck overheard and challenged, "You think so?"

"Man, I *know* so."

"Well, let's find out," said Rebuck, as he flattened the

gas pedal against the van's shag carpeting, inviting the driver of the sedan to give chase.

"Man, they ain't gonna throw the book at you, they're gonna make you eat it," Ike protested, looking at the speedometer pegged at eighty. At eighty-five, Ike was speechless and sneaked a look into the rearview mirror. The gray sedan had fallen far behind.

In the back seat, Jessica Towne closed her eyes and fought off the image of strangers gaping at her mangled body.

Rebuck had broken most of the Commonwealth of Pennsylvania's motor vehicle statues by the time they reached the REDUCE SPEED AHEAD sign which marked the outskrits to the picturesque hamlet of Intercourse. As they reached the town's twenty-five-mile-an-hour zone, he slowed the van to fifty and proceeded to run a four-way stop sign.

Crossing the double lines in the two-lane road, he sped past a horse-drawn buggy, narrowly avoiding a collision with an oncoming produce truck, and Ike wondered whether there was a Tahiti in the afterlife.

Close to the center of town, Rebuck shot through a red light, forcing a family of "plain people" to retreat to the safety of the sidewalk, then roared through the small business district with flashing lights and blaring horn. Not until they were beyond Intercourse's town limits did he end the reckless run and bring the van to a halt on the shoulder of the country road.

Turning to Ike, Rebuck coyly asked, "Where's your police?"

"Right there." Vesper pointed directly ahead.

A county sheriff's car was traveling in the opposite direction, and Rebuck smiled at Ike, exhibiting no concern. He waited until it drew closer before pushing the pedal to the floor, causing the van to skid out from the shoulder and onto the road in a cloud of burning rubber.

"Man," said Ike, looking back, "he's made a U-turn."

Rebuck kept the speedometer at eighty.

"He's got his blue light flashin'."

Rebuck maintained high speed for another half mile,

then took his foot off the gas pedal and let the van slow to a long, gradual halt onto the shoulder.

Ike was nearing exasperation and the sweat was beading on his forehead. "Man, do you know what you're doin'? I mean, do you *know* what the fuck you're doin'?"

The police car had parked a hundred feet behind them, and the lone officer was speaking into his radiophone. "He's checking us out," said Rebuck, watching in the rearview mirror.

"He's checkin' with the county jail, where they're gonna dump our asses." Ike turned to Jessica. "Do you bake pies for jailbirds?"

The husky deputy sheriff swaggered from his car and approached the van. Ike sank down in the seat, cursing Rebuck under his breath. The deputy twirled a finger for Rebuck to open the window, and he obligingly cranked it down.

"Goin' a bit fast, weren't you, Mac?" the deputy asked from a safe distance.

"I have no license," Rebuck informed him, "my registration's expired, and this man is in possession of cocaine."

"Whutchu sayin', *fool?*" Ike blurted. Wide-eyed, he looked past Rebuck at the officer peering into the van.

The deputy smiled down at Rebuck. "Keep it close to the speed limit," he said casually, then turned and walked away.

Rebuck waited for the deputy to make an unhurried U-turn in the road and head for Intercourse before turning to Ike. "What does that tell you?"

"It tells me the captain's got a lotta people watchin' . . . watchin' you, Little Brotha—not me."

"Let's be sure," Rebuck said, driving off toward Lancaster.

The quaint urban hub of Pennsylvania Dutch country was still a melting pot of diverse cultures. Even though Lancaster had fallen victim to the contemporaries of shopping centers and cable television, the Amish horse and buggy hitched to a parking meter next to a Cadillac was not an unusual sight. But the town's rich history was far from Rebuck's thoughts as he drove the van into the city limits, wondering if the captain's surveillance network was as extensive as it appeared.

When he spotted the gray sedan in the side-view mirror, he drove on without mentioning it for several blocks, then pulled into a metered parking space in front of the First Pennsylvania Bank building. With the engine still running he turned and spoke to Ike. "No questions. Just do what I say."

Ike produced the frown he used whenever he thought Rebuck was about to play games with his head.

"The gray sedan with the two men is back," Rebuck said. "They're double-parked behind us. Watch for one of them to make radio contact after I leave." As he opened the door and got out, he added, "If they make a move on you, drive as fast as you can to the mission."

Ike slid his large frame into the driver's seat. "He's doin' it . . . shittin' on my dream again," he groaned, looking into the rearview mirror.

"Ike," said Jessica, peering through the back window, "one of the men is speaking into a phone."

"I see 'im," Ike confirmed.

"What is Ron doing?" she asked.

"You can bet he ain't' makin' a deposit."

"Ike . . . does the captain plan to kill us?"

The gravity of her question and the blunt manner which she'd asked it found Ike groping for words. "You shoulda never gotten involved, Little Girl."

"But I did."

At that moment, Ron Rebuck sprinted from the bank. Avoiding eye contact with the occupants of the sedan, he climbed into the van through the passenger side. "Yes or no?" he asked, shutting the door.

"Yeah, they made phone contact," Ike said.

"Right after you entered the bank," Jessica added.

"Drive, Ike."

"Where?"

395

"Drive and I'll tell you."

Ike jerked a thumb to the rear. "Shake 'em?"

"No. I want them to follow us."

They drove deeper into downtown Lancaster, and Ike kept the gray sedan in his side-view mirror. "Ah'm just followin' orders," he spoke aloud to himself. "Got nothin' to do with the fool's scheme."

Rebuck paid no attention to Ike's commentary as he searched up ahead for a parking space.

"Doin' my job, gettin' my money, trustin' in the *main* man, an' it's crashin' in Tahiti," Ike babbled.

"Pull into that tow-away zone," Rebuck said.

"Shit," said Ike, thinking Rebuck was pushing it a bit too far with the local law, "why not in front of a fuckin' fire hydrant?"

"Why not just do as I ask?" Rebuck demanded in a cutting voice.

Ike swung the van into the no-parking zone, turned off the motor, and folded his arms. "Now what?"

"That travel agency across the street—see it?"

Ike scanned the row of storefronts. "Yeah, I see it. So what?"

"Go and check out a ticket to Tahiti."

Vesper whirled to face him. "Man, you gonna start messin' with my—" He cut himself short when he saw Rebuck's attention focused to the rear and on the men in the gray sedan.

As Ike dodged the traffic and crossed the street, Rebuck said, "They're not interested in Ike. If they were, they'd be on that phone."

"What about me, Ron? Are they interested in me?"

His eyes strayed from the rear window, picking up Ike leaving the travel agency. "We'll soon know," he answered.

Ike stopped to leer at the men in the sedan before climbing back into the van. "Where to now?" he asked.

"The bus station," Rebuck said.

Jessica felt frozen to her seat.

Ike spotted an unoccupied space close to the main entrance of the bus terminal, but was waved off by Rebuck.

They double-parked directly across the street and, as Rebuck expected, the gray sedan followed suit.

"I hope you ain't thinkin' on doin' somethin' crazy, Little Brotha," Ike commented, drumming his fingers nervously on the steering wheel.

Rebuck didn't reply and looked straight ahead, weighing the merit of his next move. Ike knew what was on Rebuck's mind, and hoped he'd strongly consider the danger involved. It was a little late in the game to be trying to send Little Red Riding Hood home through the woods.

"Jessica," Ron said. "I want you to go into that bus station."

"Alone?" she asked in a small voice.

"I'll be watching you." He handed her an envelope. "In here is enough money for a ticket to Philly, and the name and number of someone—a friend of mine—who will help you when you get there. When you get into the station, I want you to go directly to the ticket window and get a ticket to Philadelphia." Rebuck looked at his watch. "There's a bus leaving in seven minutes, and you've got to be on it, so hurry. When you get in, call this number. You'll be given directions where to wait, and you'll be picked up within ten minutes by a man who will use the code word 'Michael.' Don't speak to anyone else."

"Ron—" she started, but he cut her off.

"Jessica, I'm sorry it has to be this way, but there's no choice. Now hurry! And remember, don't talk to *anyone*!"

"But when will I see you? How will I know you're all right?"

"Right now, you've just got to trust me, Jessica, and do exactly as I say. I'll be in touch as soon as possible. Now go!"

Vesper watched her walk toward the terminal and shook his head, looking at Rebuck who had also climbed out of the van and was standing by it, just staring at the two men parked in the car behind them. It was as if he was daring them to get out and go after the girl, Ike thought. "Man," he said to Rebuck through the open window, "you are one crazy motherfucker!"

Suddenly, the two men got out of the gray sedan and walked casually toward the terminal. As Rebuck moved to block their way, the smaller of the two men grabbed and held him, and the other, a swarthy man in a green suit, delivered a crunching blow to his midsection. As Rebuck doubled over, still in the grasp of the smaller man, the man in the suit raced into the terminal.

Ike was quickly upon the scene. With the strength of a mad bull, he pulled the man off Rebuck and threw him to the ground. When Ike looked up, Rebuck had already disappeared inside the terminal.

Jessica was standing her ground in line at the ticket counter inside the small terminal. Her wide eyes were pinned to the schedule she held in her shaking hands. She did not see the green-suited man as he approached her.

"Miss," he flashed a silver badge attached to a leather case, "I'm with the police department. Would you please come with me?"

The officious show of the badge confused Jessica. As she stood dumbfounded, he grasped her wrist and roughly dragged her away from the ticket window toward the buses in the rear of the terminal.

Ron Rebuck stepped from the side of a public telephone booth and blocked them at the turn. "Let her go," he said evenly.

"Don't interfere," the man warned, tightening his grip on Jessica.

"Ron, he's a policeman," Jessica blurted.

"Show *me* that badge," Rebuck demanded.

"I'll show you my foot up your ass," the man said, extending an arm to push Rebuck aside.

Rebuck's blow to the man's chin was quick and solid. As her would-be abductor tumbled onto the tiled floor, Jessica stood stunned by the swift action, and Rebuck had to take her hand and pull her from the scene. Together, hand in hand, they raced from the terminal just as a uniformed policeman burst through the rear entrance.

The ride back to the mission was without incident, and Rebuck had molded his assumptions into irrefutable facts.

It was obvious to him that the captain had directed his dogs to follow him whenever he left the mission grounds. What wasn't obvious was the degree of Gemmer's interest in Jessica. Rebuck didn't think her kidnapping had been an unconditional mandate from the captain; the attempt had been clumsy, too amateurish, unworthy of the captain's calculating style. Still, his intentions had been made clear. He wanted Jessica within his grasp.

They turned off the main road and into the mission property, passing the old house. As soon as Ike had braked the van, Jessica got out and fled to the motor home.

"Poor kid," Ike said, looking glumly after her. "Probably had to puke her guts out." He turned to Rebuck, fixing him with an accusing scowl. "You're lucky the captain didn't get her."

"If he'd really wanted her, it would have been handled better. It's obvious he doesn't want her leaving, but he's playing out his hand to the end."

"Man, you knew the rules, but you had to go messin' with a mission female. Didja think the captain wouldn't know?"

"I made a stupid mistake, but I'm not about to make another," Rebuck said. "We should keep a close eye on Ragonese and the mission house . . . it could help us stay one step ahead of the captain." He looked Ike in the eye and said, "Pack up your personal gear."

John Ragonese picked up the plain brown packet which had arrived in the afternoon mail and looked suspiciously at the Washington, D.C., postmark. It contained the latest edition of *Time* magazine, and the arrogant visage of the Right Reverend Harley Lombard stared at him from the cover.

Ragonese finished his early-evening meal of a cheese sandwich and glass of milk, then opened the magazine he had laid on the scarred kitchen table before him. With mounting interest he read of Lombard's rapid rise from evangelical obscurity to his current position as a major religious and political power. He was particularly interested in the role Billy Hale had played during Lombard's early career. The cover story, entitled "Virtues, Inc., and the New Morality," made Ragonese reflect on his own religious past.

Scenes from a dozen years ago projected like a movie in his mind. He saw Ron Rebuck, Sr., vigorously denouncing Billy Hale on a syndicated talk show, calling America's most revered religious personality a sanctimonious liar who had deceived the Christian masses for personal gain, accusing Hale of living comfortably off the fears and traumas of people he and his colleagues intimidated with the threat of everlasting Hell. He saw Ron Rebuck, Sr., sitting in the mission office, drained of energy, talking to him. "Logic and common sense are forbidden factors in organized religion, John. Billy Hale and his kind want you to stumble in the dark, and my putting on a light is not the way the religious game is played."

Ragonese remembered the elder Rebuck's frustration during a series of unsuccessful attempts to lure Billy Hale into a televised debate. For reasons unexplained, Rebuck was persona non grata as far as the network talk shows were concerned. While they continued to book wild-eyed leaders of bizarre cults and off-the-wall authors of obscure or ludicrous religious "works," Rebuck was ignored.

With a shudder, Ragonese's thoughts turned to that terrible night in the Hollywood Bowl, when a mortar shell fired by a religious fanatic still unknown turned Hale's "Night of Light" into a horror of death, the stage erupting in flames just moments after the evangelist had denounced Rebuck as the Antichrist. There was the final, chilling vignette of Rebuck's crucifixion, which would haunt John Ragonese's harrowed mind forever.

Ragonese cleared his head and rose from the table, tossing the magazine to the floor. Thinking of the past only magnified his depression. All he knew was that Harley Lombard was dining on gourmet food tonight, while he ate processed cheese spread on stale bread; Billy Hale would probably live forever, but Ron Rebuck, Sr., had been dead and buried for twelve years. What did it all prove? He flushed duskily. That he, John Ragonese, had bided his time for the past eleven years of his life, waiting for a financial windfall—a deserved legacy—which had been suddenly threatened by complications created by the appearance of the founder's embittered son and the menace of a sinister man known as the captain.

"Damn Billy Hale!" he shouted. "Damn Ron Rebuck, Sr. . . . and goddamn his son!"

The sound of car doors slamming pulled Ragonese from his wallow of self-pity. He moved cautiously from the kitchen and down the hallway to the large common room. Two men were standing at the screen door, silhouetted against the fading twilight. His mind raced to the shotgun in his office when the men walked in without knocking. Ragonese noticed with slight relief that the intruders were well dressed and did not appear to be muggers or burglars. The taller of the two, a younger man in a dark green suit, appeared to have a badly swollen jaw.

"Are you John Ragonese?" the shorter man asked as if he already knew.

"I am. Who are you?"

"Sam sent us."

"If he sent you to collect twenty-five thousand dollars, the money is not due until November seventh."

"Hey, look," said the man, "you wanna talk here or in your office? Personally, I don't give a shit."

Ragonese eyed the man with the swollen jaw with caution. If there was anything physical he could do in life, John Ragonese could run. "Right here will be fine."

The man reached into his jacket and handed Ragonese a neatly typed document. Ragonese accepted the paper with grave skepticism.

"Read it carefully," said the man. "I got no time for any explaining."

Ragonese read the document twice, then looked up at the man, confounded. "American Realty is going to pay me eighteen thousand dollars to *rent* this house for the month of October? I don't understand."

The man took a check from the same inside pocket and handed it to him. Ragonese found himself staring at a cashier's check for $18,000. He no longer worried about his safety; men who brought him such a large sum of money had not come to harm him. "Why don't we go into my office?" he said, forcing a warm tone into his voice and gripping the check so firmly between his fingers that his forearm shook.

Ragonese sat behind the old desk, captivated by the strange circumstances unfolding before him, and was not alarmed by the man in the green suit, who was examining his shotgun.

"Sign at the bottom over your name," the man acting as spokesman directed.

Ragonese looked down at the unfolded document before him. "If you don't mind, may I have a little time to think this proposition over?"

"What time? Tomorrow the bank calls in that fifteen-thousand-dollar interest payment you owe. Your phone is about to be disconnected and there's nothing in this shithouse a flea market would buy. So stop with the stalling and sign it."

"May I have a word?" Ragonese implored.

"Make it short," the man relented. "Just don't bullshit me."

"I have found out that American Realty is indeed a legitimate firm located in Chevy Chase, Maryland. However, I would like to know this cap . . . I mean, Sam's connection."

The man rose angrily from the chair. "Gimme the fuckin' check!"

"Wait! I was simply making an inquiry."

"Then sign!"

Ragonese fumbled for a pen. "I'll sign it, but I want it understood by your employers that I'm only agreeing to what is in this document—nothing more."

The man thrust a ballpoint pen into Ragonese's hand, and he scrawled his signature under those of the American Realty signers. Before he could make a final inspection of the paper, the man snatched it from his hand.

"Shouldn't I have a copy?"

"Sam don't give copies," said the man, nodding to his silent companion and leaving Ragonese to ponder the numbers on the second largest check he had ever seen in his life.

John Ragonese had little time to reflect on his startling windfall, for no sooner had the gray sedan vanished into the deepening twilight than he heard a fresh squeal of brakes. He started to rise from the chair but gave up the effort. Whatever would come, would come.

There was the wet-wash sound of a large suitcase or canvas bag thudding onto the driveway, followed by the loud breathing of somebody carrying a heavy load up the porch steps. The leaden footsteps grew closer, and Ragonese flinched when he heard the screen door clatter open. He pulled himself to his feet and waited with both apprehension and fear to face his latest visitor. What he saw at the doorway gave him a new run of chills.

"Spooky Man, you got yourself a new boarder."

Ike Vesper's duffel bag crashed heavily to the floor.

CHAPTER 34

HARLEY LOMBARD'S ANGER had left him speechless. The evangelist slumped behind his pontifical desk, fuming over the startling information revealed to him just moments before. He stared morosely at the bearer of the bad tidings, who was seated across from him on a velveteen couch. "All on videotape? *Everything?*"

"Everything," Sue Bergman replied with bitterness.

"The fat sonuvabitch won't get away with it. *Nobody* blackmails Harley Lombard."

"You were stupid, Harley."

"C'mon, Sue, I feel shitty enough. Don't rub my face in it."

"I should have put my foot down the moment I knew about it."

"You knew?"

"Of course I knew," she said crossly.

"But how? Who told you?"

"Don't be so naive. You made a dumb mistake and I let it slide by."

"Christ, have you got people spying on me?"

She ignored the question. "Tell me, *truthfully*, why did you have to get involved with Veep Siler?"

Harley shook his head. "It's a long story."

"Condense it."

"I owed him, Sue. Veep once helped me out of a jam." He moved out of the thronelike chair and paced the gracious penthouse office. "It happened years ago. At divinity school."

"What kind of trouble were you in *then?*"

404

"A girl . . . goddamn hussy."

"How old was she, Harley?"

"Sue, I swear, she looked twenty. She had knockers the size of cantaloupes."

"How *old*, Harley?"

"Thirteen. But, I'm telling you, she misled me."

"Did you have intercourse with her?"

"Hell, she knew more about sex than I did. Christ, Sue, she acted like a pro."

"And, of course, Veep Siler was your alibi. What did he tell the authorities, that you were with him, studying the Bible?"

"It's Billy Hale's fault, Sue. He never let me cut Veep into any deals."

The man who had replaced Andy Gaines as Harley's Chief aide and caretaker, Deek Ashburn, slipped into the office and walked directly to Bergman. "He's on his way," he said, ignoring Lombard.

Harley overheard him and pounded a fist into a fleshy palm. "I'll kill the bastard when he gets here."

She motioned for Ashburn to leave them and waited until the door closed before speaking. "You will keep your mouth shut. You've already done enough damage."

"Hey, I'm on the cover of *Time*. The country's 'Mr. Morality.' No one talks to me like that. Not even you, Sue."

She jabbed a finger in his direction. "Don't come on to me with the high-and-mighty crap, Harley Lombard. Your mistake has seriously jeopardized Virtues, Inc., credibility—something I have worked long and hard to establish." There was no doubt about the glare in her eyes as she rose from the couch and strode briskly to the door, turning to fire a final salvo. "Don't make this predicament any more difficult than it already is."

"Where are you going?"

"To the eighteenth floor. I need some time alone to think of a way to get us out of this mess with the least amount of damage."

*   *   *

Andy Gaines drove his dilapidated Volkswagen toward the cutoff that would take him to the Cathedral Tower building in downtown Charity. He had received a phone call from Deek Ashburn ordering him to drop everything he was doing at the World Cathedral and come directly to the Tower building. It was a vague summons and Andy could not fathom the reason.

During the past three months, Gaines had been able to make a gradual adjustment to his diminished importance as the new chief custodian of the World Cathedral. He had taken heart in that there had been no reduction in his already paltry salary—until he had learned that his assistant custodian made more.

He still saw Harley Lombard on rare occassions, most often at the tapings of the "Ministry of Might" television services he once produced. Harley would acknowledge his presence with a grunt or a slight nod, but they had not spoken since the day of his unceremonious eviction from the penthouse office. Andy hadn't seen Sue Bergman since, nor did he have the slightest desire to see the person directly responsible for his life changing for the better. He no longer had to serve as Lombard's pimp and procurer, be at Lombard's beck and call, and be continually insulted and victimized by Lombard's wrath. For the first time in twenty years, he felt a breath of freedom, and he was finding the courage to sever his ties with Harley Lombard and the ministry altogether. Veep Siler's Florida offer was sounding better each passing day.

He pulled up before the tower entrance and immediately saw his successor scrambling toward his car. Deek Ashburn opened the passenger door and Andy recalled the stoic expression which seemed glued to the man's face.

"Leave it here and come with me," Ashburn instructed.

"You pay the tow-away charge," Andy replied harshly.

He followed the man through the lobby and felt a twinge of uneasiness when he realized they were walking toward the private elevators servicing the eighteenth floor. What, he wondered, had he done to rate a summons to the eighteenth floor? Had Veep Siler made his offer of employment known to Harley? No, he figured, something as mundane as that would have been handled with a phone call. Besides, Bergman would have already sent her goons to supervise his eviction from the apartment over the World Cathedral.

Andy came out of his funk in time to see the rude escort waving him past a stone-faced guard and into the waiting elevator. Access to the building's mystery floor, a place he once thought unattainable, was too quick for him to have time for further speculation. Yet he knew the answers were forthcoming as he watched the floors flashing past on the digital readout above the doors. Then the elevator braked silently.

The doors glided open and Andy found himself staring at an expanse of large bronze letters spelling "Virtues, Inc." across a wall painted pale green. The impatient escort nudged him toward a reception area where two uniformed guards wearing sidearms sat behind a rectangular steel desk topped with closed-circuit TV monitors and other electronic gadgets. Andy could not help but notice the blown-up copy of the *Time* cover with the rearranged headline, "Mr. Morality." If the world only knew, he snickered to himself.

Given a red, white, and blue visitor's badge by one of the guards, Andy stood several feet behind the escort and the heavy steel door, aware of being scrutinized by an overhead camera. Suddenly, there was an electronic buzz, the door whirred open, and they entered the sanctum of the eighteenth floor.

The sound of busy fingers racing across computer keyboards and the manic chatter of high-speed printers counterpointed the hubbub of activity which unfolded before Gaines's startled eyes. Everywhere he looked, high-technology hardware was in view—banks of mainframe computers, desk after desk topped with powerful microprocessors either interfaced to the IBM heavyweights or using their own software to run the diverse affairs of Virtues, Inc.

Andy followed his guide down one of two hallways

which strangely appeared to have no end. So this is the mysterious eighteenth floor, he said to himself, unable to take everything in at once, especially when the pace of his escort was like that of an entrant in a walkathon.

Men and women wearing gray blazers scurried in and out of the tinted glass-fronted offices lining both sides of the hall. About halfway down the long corridor, Andy saw a large room dominated by an electronic wall map that looked like something out of the Strategic Air Command headquarters. He stopped to watch the operators feeding input into the banks of a giant computer that transferred readouts onto the wall map, state by state. Virtues, Inc.'s, nerve center, Andy thought. Bull—it's a super collection center, he corrected himself. He found himself thinking back to the times at the leaky auditorium where Harley first preached, when the method of bringing in the bucks was to go into the audience and collect God's loot in a gold-painted tin pail. A burning glare from the impatient Deek Ashburn moved him along.

Virtues, Inc.'s, in-house public relations, security, publishing, TV and radio programming, national advertising, donations, and mail order departments, each with its name stenciled in gold on the door and served by a battery of computer terminals, color monitors, disk drives, and laser printers, were among the divisions Andy Gaines took note of in passing. He could only guess at the functions of the departments located along the second hallway, though *slander* and *blackmail* came instantly to mind. If nothing else, Andy could not help but admire Sue Bergman's running of the tight and efficient organization of malice, knowing that Harley was merely its titular head.

At the end of the hall, they came to another lobby similar to the one they had first entered. Two more guards sat manning an airport-style metal detector in front of a pair of matching doors. Ashburn was waved through immediately, but even after being cleared by the detector Andy was subjected to a body search.

A buzzer droned and the door to the right slid open, revealing a hallway carpeted in red cut pile. They walked past a series of large rooms, a library and conference suite, and Andy noticed that they were deserted. As they moved farther down, the doors were shut and marked PRIVATE. By the time they came to the end of the hall, Andy was more concerned than puzzled as to why he had been summoned —to the sinister eighteenth floor's projection room.

An indefinable sense of danger seized Andy as he cautiously followed his escort into Virtues, Inc.'s, theater. As he quickly scanned the ten rows of soft leather reclining chairs, his eyes froze on the scowling personage of Harley Lombard. He was trying to decide whether Harley's sneer was from habit or due to some specific annoyance, when he felt a tug on his arm and was led to a middle seat in the front row.

He felt another's presence in the room and looked back, avoiding Harley glaring at him from a far corner of the last row, to see Sue Bergman taking a seat behind a glistening black console and firing orders to the projectionist. Deek Ashburn stood at her side and pointed for him to face front. A moment later, the lights dimmed and the smaller of two screens appeared by the magic of a pushed button.

The early frames of the videotape shook Andy Gaines with stark reality. The reason behind Veep Siler's inviting him to spend two weeks at his Florida panhandle estate was being vividly projected on the screen. And Andy heard Harley Lombard's unmistakable grumbling behind him.

Harley Lombard was now biting on his hand as he watched Andy and Veep Siler's blond chauffeur locked in a passionate embrace. But when Gaines disengaged from the long kiss and flicked his tongue against a pierced ear lobe, Harley could no longer control his disgust and raging anger. "Homo sonuvabitch!" he shrieked. "Limp-wristed dick-licker!"

Andy refused to look back. He would not subject himself to a shouting match with a man he knew had no right to cast stones. Nevertheless, he found himself framing his defense.

The screen was filled with more zealous lovemaking.

Andy had slipped to his knees and his mouth had become scabbard to the blond chauffeur's blade.

"Will you look at this?" Harley stammered. "The fag's taking him right down to his tonsils!"

Andy bit his lip, wondering why there was no sound track to accompany a film indictment which left nothing to the imagination. He knew the scene that was coming next and closed his eyes.

"No, I don't believe it," said Harley, bug-eyed. "Jesus Christ, he's cornholin' him!" he bellowed.

Through his anger, terror, and shame, Andy heard Sue Bergman issue a command. The screen faded to dark. Although the lights had not come up, Andy felt Lombard's elephant rush down the aisle and braced himself to meet the onslaught. Before he could escape from the seat, the evangelist was upon him, spouting various yeasty diminutives and raining blow after blow on Andy's head and shoulders. Letting himself slide from the seat, Andy absorbed the shock of Lombard's fury until he could find room to run. But when he reached the floor, Harley's attack switched to his lower extremities, and he howled in pain when the evangelist's busy feet found his groin, kidneys, and lower back. He struggled again to rise, Lombard's manic bellows lending urgency to his task. "You no-good, dick-licking, fudge-packing faggot sonuvabitch! I'll kill you!"

Sue Bergman had motioned to Deek Ashburn, who moved deftly to pull the men apart. Staring into the enraged face of this man who had the gall to condemn him, Gaines found the few words he needed to defend his homosexuality.

"What's worse," Andy rasped, "me engaging in sex with a consenting adult, or your weekly molesting of a fourteen-year-old girl, *Reverend* Lombard?"

"I'll kill him! I'll kill the shit-plumbin' cocksucker," Harley shouted, trying to break away from Ashburn's hold. Harley continued to rant and rave as Ashburn surrendered him to a squad of security guards, who dragged him from the theater with the practiced ease of Bourbon Street bouncers.

Sue Bergman jerked her head for Ashburn to leave, and Andy felt the cool attention of her eyes.

"What now, a sermon from *you?*" he asked.

"Hardly, Misss-ter Gaines."

"Is this how you get off, by humiliating people?"

"I did everything in my power to keep Harley from viewing that tape."

"Not *everything*, Ms. Bergman."

She ignored the inneundo. "Mr. Gaines, we both know Harley Lombard is a fool."

"Not according to *Time*."

"And what would he be if a copy of that tape showed up in the offices of *Time?*"

"And how would that happen?"

"Come on, Mr. Gaines, do you think Veep Siler dropped his chauffeur in your lap as a tip? I'm sure you can recognize a blackmail setup when you see it."

"How much does Siler hope to get out of this?"

"One million dollars in unmarked bills."

Andy forced a laugh. "Good for Veep. Justice has been served."

"Justice, Mr. Gaines, also has a way of compensating the injured."

He was puzzled by her sudden detour. He couldn't think of any reason why Virtues, Inc., would want to compromise him. "You surely aren't referring to me as the injured party."

"But I am."

"Forget it, Bergman. You don't have to worry about buying me off. I loathe Harley Lombard, and I dislike you immensely. But it's not my style to tell the world what I know."

"Most commendable, Mr. Gaines. However, I would like to help you. Though you might not believe it, I am quite interested in your future."

"You're right. I don't believe it."

"Would I be right in saying you've worked the past twenty years for Harley?"

"*Slaved* would be a more appropriate expression."

"And would I also be right if I said you were insufficiently paid for your services?"

"Embarrassingly so."

"I have not known Harley as long as you have, but he has confided to me his innermost secrets. Can you say the same?"

"There's a difference. He told you his secrets in bed."

"Mr. Gaines, I have not assailed your character and I see no reason for you to condemn mine."

"Why don't you just tell me what you're driving at, Bergman?"

"Are you familiar with Harley's home?"

"With the exception of Wilma Mae's bedroom, I know every nook and cranny. Why?"

"Interesting," she said through a devious grin. "Mr. Gaines, I believe I can make you an offer God will endorse."

It was past midnight when Harley Lombard left the strategy briefing with Sue Bergman and her personal staff. She had convinced him that sexual blackmail had gone out of style in the 1920s. Besides, Andy Gaines was a single man. What control could Virtues, Inc., have over his sexual proclivities? He would be fired, of course; his overt homosexuality had come as a deep shock to Reverend Lombard, who abhorred such sexual perversion.

By the time he pulled the Porsche into his driveway, Harley no longer felt intimidated or wronged by Veep Siler's blackmail threat. He had full confidence in Sue Bergman to work it out. She always did. And what the hell, he figured Virtues, Inc., had tons of money. Paying off Veep Siler would be a debt paid in full. Billy Hale was to blame, and Veep was only getting even.

He left the car parked in front of his house, knowing it would give Wilma Mae miserable moments. *Wilma Mae*, he thought, remembering it was her bridge night and wondering if she was home. God, how he wished she would meet a man who measured up to her father's qualifications and shack up with him for the night. He recalled the words of a woman-hating pastor he had argued with once on the subject of marital fidelity, and the man's rebuttal to Harley's assurance of Wilma Mae's unquestionable faithfulness. "Bullshit, Lombard. She has and does." If it were only true, Harley thought.

It had been a taxing day of discovery and he was too gripped with anxiety for sleep. He tiptoed into the kitchen, planning to make himself a substantial snack and the hell with his diet, but a perusal of the refrigerator and pantry turned up a slim menu. Either Wilma Mae had forgotten to make up the grocery list, or the domestic staff was hoarding his food. He was forced to settle on a handful of chocolate chip cookies and a glass of milk.

Although Veep Siler had been exorcised from Harley's mind, Andy Gaines would not let go. "Twenty years," he said to himself, "and I find out he's a three-dollar bill. After all I did for the ungrateful bastard, he's been a raging fag behind my back." He thought of the Vatican's Swiss guards, wondering if some of them were on the *swish*y side.

Stuffing his mouth with cookies, he decided that what he needed to relax his nerves was a prolonged soak in his giant Jacuzzi. He was not prepared for the revelation—which caused him to choke on his cookies—when he arrived at the entrance to his religious spa. The massive oaken door was open.

Wilma Mae's eyes sprang open. She had been awakened from a dreamless sleep by the distant yet unmistakable sound of a man cursing. Coming off the bed, she stood erect, negotiating a move to fetch her housecoat. The sound she heard turned to great cracking sobs.

Harley Lombard was squatting inside the lone alcove across the pool. Its iron grating had been retracted into the ceiling. With each new stack of ten thousand dollars he discovered missing, he could not decide whether to curse or weep, and the veins in his neck appeared about to burst.

"How disgusting!" Wilma Mae ridiculed, her voice echoing in the vastness of the Holy Spa.

Harley spun so quickly that the armload of bills he was

carrying fell to the tiled deck. "I've been robbed!" he wailed.

"*You've* been robbed?" she said, referring to the manner in which he'd acquired the million dollars he had stored in cash.

"Two hundred thousand so far. Two hundred thousand of *my* money."

She laughed to herself and refrained from telling him what she thought of *his* money. It would only infuriate him further.

"Don't think I don't know who the thief is that stole my money. I know, Wilma Mae. I know."

"Who? If I may ask?"

"That faggot Andy Gaines, that's who."

"So it finally dawned on you. Even if it did take twenty years."

"Who else could it be, Wilma Mae? Who else?"

"And what if he did steal the money? What can you possibly do about it?"

"What can . . . are you totally crazy? As soon as I finish counting, I'm going to make a phone call that will put that dick-licking screamer behind bars for twenty years."

"You'll make a call," she mimicked him. "Who are you going to call, you damned fool—the IRS?"

CHAPTER 35

ALONG THE BANK of the Willamette River in Portland, Oregon, an old woman carried her life's possessions in a large shopping bag. She had just moments earlier eaten her evening meal from the scraps of a dockside restaurant's garbage bin, and now she planned to retire for the night—not in the public park or a downtown alley, but in a cemetery overlooking the river, where she could see the twinkle of the city lights and the lumber barges working slowly upstream.

The old woman struggled up a hill, leaning into a phantom wind, cursing each time she stumbled. At the top of the hill, she skirted a fence of wrought-iron pickets and entered the cemetery through an opening where the fence joined a high stone wall, unaware of the man in the dark turtleneck sweater who stood in the shadows of a large headstone watching her painful progress.

She trudged down a flagstone walkway flanked by a well-manicured hedge and lit by the reflection of an early October moon. Passing a seemingly endless line of tombstones, she came to a row of mausoleums nestled under large and spreading trees. Padding along on shapeless bedroom slippers reinforced with cardboard, the old woman paused in front of a family crypt with the name "Huntington" chiseled into its marble face. She knew the rusting entrance gate would be open; she had slept here many times and it was safe from the insults of winos and the ugly menace of marauding teenagers. The hinges squealed in protest and she slipped into the mausoleum with the nonchalance of a proper grandmother returning from a long day of shopping.

Moonlight projected a surreal pattern of light and shadow through the bars. The old woman rummaged through her shopping bag, removing first a candle, then a plastic holder to set it on, and, after a lengthy search, a box of matches. She lit the candle with the fingers of her arthritic hand, making the flames dance on the walls of the crypt, and sat propped against a damp corner, oblivious to the vaults of the entombed.

She had no conception of the hour. Darkness meant looking for shelter to sleep in, then awakening before dawn to begin another scavenging day of her life. Time had no relevance to her, only the hard actualities of hot or cold, night or day. They were the variables of her life; the only constants were the pain and the shame, and it had been many years since she had thought about the shame. But the pain was now, and she moaned from the throbbing in her joints.

Suddenly, the cast-iron door whined open, and she snarled like a dog at the shadowy figure of a man entering the tomb. Through squinting, bloodshot eyes, she watched him close the door, then limp slowly toward her. By the candlelight, she saw the scarred face and clutched the shopping bag to her chest.

Captain Claude Gemmer crouched to where his hard, gray eyes peered through the candle's spastic flame. "Are you a mother, bag lady?" His voice was almost tender.

The woman continued to hug the shopping bag to her withered bosom and stare at him, a mixture of puzzlement and terror in her rheumy eyes.

"Have you been forsaken by the bastards you brought into this world?"

She tucked her wrinkled chin into the ragged, filthy scarf wrapped around her neck, still staring at him, unblinking as an owl.

"My mother," Gemmer said in a reverent tone, "died of cancer." His eyes suddenly narrowed. "Her life's savings were depleted by a religious charlatan." He paused, sinking deeper in reflection. "My father was a military man to the bone. Major Carl Gemmer," his voice quivered with pride. "He fought the Germans in World War II . . . earned two Purple Hearts and was awarded the Silver Star. A real American hero . . . not some POW or gutless bastard of an embassy guard returning home to a ticker-tape parade." His voice had risen during the soliloquy. His eyes were now wild. "Do you know how he died, old woman? This man of uncommon valor? . . . Sitting on a toilet!" he bellowed in shame as he whirled and kicked the wall of the mausoleum with his game foot.

Regaining instant composure as only he could do, he again crouched and looked into the flame of the burning candle. His words darted in a new direction. "We are the victims of a grave injustice. We are born without choice, and *not* by any divine proclamation. We compete, fight, lie, cheat, even kill to survive. And for what? We survive to die!" he again clamored. ". . . And you, old woman, you, who are not even a statistic. Who cares for you in your suffering? Who tends to your needs while you rot away? You have been abandoned. No one will remember that you ever lived on this miserable Earth. Why, old woman, why do you struggle to survive?"

The toothless hag's lips parted. She finally had something to say. "Because that's the way it is, sonny," she replied.

Gemmer's smile lit the mausoleum. He was intrigued and amused by the old woman's simple-minded but sound philosophy. She had wrapped the whole secret into a cliché which somehow rang with sage truth on her parched lips. He began to laugh, at first a rumble originating in the pit of his stomach, then a raucous guffaw echoing into the night and blending with the woman's sudden, wheezing cackle to form an obscene, demented duet.

Gemmer pulled himself erect, staring down at the ancient gargoyle. "I shall treasure your words of wisdom, old woman," he said, dropping a crisp one-hundred-dollar bill which fluttered to the floor beside her. Limping from

417

the crypt, he was gone. He would not be a second late for that which had brought him to Portland.

Sue Bergman was getting nowhere. She felt as if she had been beating her head against a wall for hours, a disconcerting turn of events for a woman used to playing her Virtues, Inc., staff like a harp. This was her second meeting with Senator Sinclair's campaign chairman since her noon arrival in Portland. And for this evening's encounter, George Whipple had brought in a hired gun from New York, a noted troubleshooter named Red Meaher.

Meaher, a slender man with hair more brown than red and an easy smile which contradicted his toughness, stood at the bar in the lavish Benson Hotel suite, listening to Sue Bergman fence with George Whipple. He fixed himself a double scotch on the rocks and swirled it in the glass, waiting for an opening. There came an unsettling pause in the conversation, and he grabbed his opportunity.

"Ms. Bergman, we're already getting plenty of flack from the media about religious influence. We can't afford any more editorial attacks from the liberal press. To have Senator Sinclair address Virtues, Inc.'s, convention would be an open endorsement of Virtues, Inc. Not only by Senator Sinclair, but by the Republican Party. It's too risky."

Sue Bergman bristled and waited for him to sip his drink before firing back. "Mr. Meaher, I have yet to hear of one Republican candidate, including the senator, who has publicly refused Virtues, Inc., endorsement. Have you?"

"She has a point there," Whipple said.

"A point like a stiletto," he rebutted. "I've been in the political campaign business for twenty-five years. I've worked every level, from the wards to presidential campaigns. I've seen and been involved in some big-league mudslinging in my time, but what this Virtues, Inc., is doing is pure criminal slander . . . Salem witch-trials stuff."

"I haven't observed a stampede to the courts."

"You know better than that, Ms. Bergman. When you accuse a public official of being a Communist, fag, wom-

418

anizer, or drug addict, it's up to the injured party to prove it's not true. And the minute they go to court and file suit, your attorneys are going to subpoena their tax records of the past ten years. Look, Senator Lollar is not one of my favorite people. I hate everything the liberal bastard stands for, but your people have him sounding like a cross between Alger Hiss, Benedict Arnold, and Jack the Ripper.''

''Ms. Bergman,'' Whipple interjected, ''have you come to Portland as the executive director of the American Recovery Association, or as the ambassador for Virtues, Inc.?''

''The ARA has a large stake in Virtues, Inc. We see it as a potent, perhaps pivotal, force in the election. With that as background, I have been delegated by the ARA to oversee the day-to-day operation of Virtues, Inc.''

''I'm sure you have,'' Whipple said sarcastically. ''However, the other major problem we're dealing with here is that Senator Sinclair wishes to stay as far away from Reverend Lombard as humanly possible.''

''I can personally guarantee you that Reverend Lombard will be on his best behavior.''

The veteran campaign chief shot an inquiring glance at his public relations expert. ''Red?''

''If my input means anything, I'd pass on this one, George.''

''I'm sorry, Ms. Bergman, but unless a miracle changes my mind, I'm inclined to go along with Red.''

She looked at her watch. It was 9:52 and a limousine was scheduled to pick her up at the hotel entrance at 10:00 sharp. This was one appointment where tardiness would not be forgiven, and she rose from the chair. ''Mr. Whipple,'' she said, turning at the door, ''miracles are not exclusive to religion.''

The gleaming black Rolls Royce muscled into the light traffic of Broadway. The driver and his matching partner in the front seat were dressed in dark three-piece suits, and ''secret service'' was written in every mannerism. A soundproof, tinted-glass partition separated them from the pas-

419

sengers in the back—Sue Bergman and Captain Claude Gemmer, who were propped on jump seats facing the man who had summoned them to the meeting.

There was little of the famed diplomatic smoothness in the voice of former President Richard Waters. "How could you have let this happen?" he demanded, glaring at Sue Bergman.

"I was careless, Mr. President."

"The goddamn election is five weeks away and you were careless?"

"I just didn't believe it would ever come to something like this."

Waters pushed a button on the recessed console in his armrest, and a fully stocked bar emerged from a burled walnut cabinet. He poured a liberal belt of his favorite sour mash into a glass bearing the seal of the presidency in twenty-four-karat gold, and knocked back half of the hundred-proof bourbon. He seemed to ignore Gemmer's presence and focused his attention on Bergman.

"Susan," his voice lost its hardened tone, "have I ever told you how the concept of the ARA was born in my mind?"

"No, Mr. President, you haven't."

"It happened during the fourth year of my first term. I was dining with Charles de Gaulle at the Madrid Summit. I asked him what his greatest wish was. He thought and thought and finally, he drew himself up like a ramrod and looked me right in the eye and said, 'President Waters, my greatest dream has always been to be dictator of the United States.' "

"Fascinating, Mr. President," said Bergman.

"Later on, I often thought of de Gaulle's words while I was taking shit from those liberal pansies and the Jew-controlled media bent on destroying me. I knew the goddamn Commies were behind those civil rights movements. Yes, the thought that de Gaulle's dream might someday become a reality for the right American gave me the patience to bear with those ACLU lawyers making the country into a land of lawsuits. All the things I was unable to do as

420

President of the United States, I can damn well do now. But not if people I have entrusted with sensitive projects are careless. Do you understand, Susan?''

"I do, Mr. President.''

"All right . . . now let's rectify this blackmail matter. The first thing tomorrow morning, Susan, you will make arrangements to pay this Veep Siler the million dollars from our special funds account. However, you will demand that the bastard turn over the original tape and every copy of it. When our experts are satisfied that he has done so, Captain Gemmer will take over. Won't you, Captain?''

"As you say, Mr. President.''

"As I say,'' Waters repeated with notable sarcasm. He lit up a king-sized cigarette and leaned forward, exhaling the smoke into the captain's face. "When did I order the termination of that faith healer?''

Gemmer's lips tightened. "You didn't, Mr. President.''

"Yet you took it upon yourself to eliminate him. What the hell do you think I've provided you with, your own personal death squad?''

"The opportunity of ridding the country of scum presented itself, Mr. President.''

"You damn fool! They're all scum! But I say which ones are to be taken care of and when. God knows I couldn't stand that fat, miserable holier-than-thou faith healer, but so help me, Claude, you'd better not pull another stunt like that one.''

Gemmer started to speak, but the former president cut him off. "I'm calling the shots here, and this is a perfect example of why. I've personally planned every phase of this operation, with great attention to *timing*, Captain. This is just the sort of thing that could ruin everything.''

Waters blew another cloud of smoke at Gemmer before continuing. "I think I explained it to you clearly enough once, Claude, but at the risk of repeating myself I'm going to tell you one more time.'' He paused and stuffed out his cigarette. He leaned closer to Gemmer and fixed him with a piercing gaze. "The plan is to win mass support for evangelists . . . to create so much sympathy that when that

421

asshole Harley Lombard gets up at the Virtues, Inc., convention and makes his stirring call for all religious-minded people to come together, to unify in the face of the godless left-wing terrorism being perpetuated against religion in America, they'll jump into line for the Lord's candidate—the Virtues, Inc.-backed candidate. *My* goddamn candidate! We're talking thirty, forty, fifty million votes riding on it. Maybe more. Now don't give me any more of that bullshit about ridding the country of scum. I can't believe you'd even try something like this!''

"I did have certain . . . personal reasons, Mr. President."

"Personal reasons, huh? Well, Captain, if you ever cut your own orders again, you can kiss that admiral's flag goodbye after Bart Sinclair is president. And another thing, what is this fetish you have about cemeteries?"

"I wouldn't really call it a fetish, sir, it's just—"

"No more graveyards! You're a senior officer in the United States Navy, not a goddamn gravedigger."

"With your permission, sir, I will need to visit one more place of burial. I can promise you that it will be in the line of duty."

Richard Waters shook his head and turned his attention back to Sue Bergman. "What about the two principals in that videotape?"

"The chauffeur is no longer employed by Veep Siler. He is presently working on a fishing boat in Panama City, Florida. The other man, Andy Gaines, is no problem, Mr. President."

"As long as the man can talk and write, he's a problem." Waters nodded to the captain. "Get rid of them."

"Sir," she protested, "I can assure you that Gaines is no problem. He has been well compensated."

"Compensated by whom?"

"We arranged for Mr. Gaines to help himself to a quarter of a million dollars from Reverend Lombard's, uh, personal funds."

Waters was not amused. "Very well. But, Susan, I'm going to hold you responsible for this man Gaines . . . now, what's left?"

"I'm afraid I didn't have much luck persuading George Whipple to have Senator Sinclair address Virtues, Inc., convention."

"October fifteenth is only two weeks off . . ."

"I'm really sorry, Mr. President—it's because of Reverend Lombard's public comments, and I know it's my responsibility to keep him quiet."

"Don't worry about it, Susan. I can handle Whipple and Sinclair. You just keep Lombard out of sight. And for God's sake keep working with him on that speech. I spent a lot of time writing it, and that jackass better be inspired when he addresses the convention."

"It is a brilliant speech, Mr. President, and for all his other shortcomings, Reverend Lombard really does have a way of moving an audience. We're working on his delivery several hours a day now, and I can't believe how well it's coming along. When he takes the stage at Christ Town, he's going to knock them dead."

"I'm counting on it, Susan," Waters said, adding, "And while we're on the subject of Christ Town, how are the preparations for the convention coming along?"

"Everything is moving along on schedule. Mr. Pittman has been most supportive."

"Hmmmph," Waters snorted, "Mr. Pittman damn well better be supportive. He's got a damn good stake in the new order." He smiled faintly. "But I have to say he's made Christ Town into a real winner. It's exceeded all my expectations as a money-maker. Because of that religious Disneyland we're well subsidized through the national elections. Now, are there any other matters either of you wish to discuss?"

"There is the problem of Billy Hale's informant." Gemmer's tone had a sharp, cutting edge.

"Perhaps this will come as a shock to your ego, Captain, but I have already given orders for that file to be closed."

"That still leaves Billy Hale, Mr. President," Gemmer pushed further.

"There is no reason to concern yourself about Billy,

particularly now that his source of information has been silenced. Besides, Billy has pledged to me that he will refrain from making any inflammatory statements about Virtues, Inc., until after the election. By then, the ARA could care less.''

''What if he breaks his word?'' Gemmer goaded.

''Kill him,'' said Waters, freshening his drink with a very steady hand.

PART THREE

A TIME TO LIVE,
A TIME TO DIE

CHAPTER 36

THE PHONE RANG with the sound of an old sea bell. At the desk in his naval-decor den, Rear Admiral Lester Church, Judge Advocate General of the U.S. Navy, looked up from the legal brief he was reviewing to the ancient maritime clock on the wall. The hour was past 11:00 P.M., and he'd given orders to his aide, Captain Hamlin, that except in an emergency he was not to be disturbed at home.

"Church," he grumbled, running a hand through his silver-thatched hair. As he identified the voice, his attitude changed dramatically. Listening intently to what his caller had to say, he responded respectfully. "I understand. A wise decision . . . A lesson, of course . . . Yes, I will attend to it immediately . . . good night, sir."

Less than a dozen miles from Admiral Church's fashionable Chevy Chase, Maryland, home, a Citation jet dropped from a starless sky. It touched down on the runway, streaking past the blue ground lights, then braked with a reverse thrust of power and taxied to a designated area fronting a small terminal. The engine whined down into silence. The exit door sprang open.

Billy Hale took a good look at the deboarding steps. He waved off Emile's offer of help and carefully stepped down from the hired jet. As he entered the waiting limousine, the uniformed chauffeur at the wheel noticed how haggard Billy's face was. It had nothing to do with the arthritic pain shooting through the evangelist's steel-plated knee.

The limo eased out of the executive air-pack, picked up

427

speed, then rolled onto the Maryland highway. Billy heard the chauffeur tell Emile it would take between ten and twelve minutes to reach their destination. He looked at his watch. 11:22 P.M. Pushing himself deeper into the rolled leather of the seat, Billy wondered what kind of hell would unfold before the night ended.

The minutes seemed to pass like single grains of sand falling through an hourglass. Finally, the limousine pulled off the Rockville Pike and veered into the quarter-of-a-mile semicircular driveway. The sight of an imposing tower rising nineteen stories into the night sky stimulated Billy's sense of danger. The ghostly, dimly lit white structure looked ripe for evil games.

The tower, once the principle facility for the hospitalization of naval personnel and political leaders with navy ties, had been converted to offices. All that remained from the glory years was the rotunda lobby with its black marble columns and mezzaninelike balcony, which continued to serve as the main reception area for the "Naval Medical Command, National Capitol Region"—more commonly known as Bethesda Naval Hospital.

Billy's eyes climbed to the tower's penthouse. The flashing beacon atop its roof flung his mind into the deep past. There was something about the tower, something significant which had made newspaper headlines. A scandal? A kidnapping? He could not remember. Nor could he jog his memory further, for what had taken him from his Shenandoah home, what he had all along feared and foreseen in a nightmare during the Republican National Convention, now gripped him with apprehension and smothered him with guilt.

The limo pulled up short of the six steps leading to an island of cement. Off to the right, four additional steps led directly to the tower's entrance. With the exception of a U.S. Navy patrol car—occupied by two rent-a-cop security guards—no vehicles lined the drive.

Emile cut into Billy's thoughts. "Don't see any Ford station wagon, Chief."

Billy offered no response.

428

"Should I look around for her?" Emile offered.

"She's not here."

"Maybe she went to the bathroom."

"She's not here!" Billy snapped.

"Chief? You said she was upset when she called you. Maybe she got the numbers of the buildings confused."

"No. Someone made sure Cynthia Kaiser would not be here when I arrived."

"But who'd want to stop her from seeing you, Chief?"

"The same people who put her husband in this hospital— the ARA."

Emile flinched, but he'd no conception as to why. "Chief, where did she say her husband was?"

"Neuro Psychiatry One," Billy said gravely.

Neuro Psychiatry 1, commonly referred to as NP 1, occupied the entire first floor of a three-story building. It stood slightly behind and to the immediate left of the tower, a short walk from the looping drive. A copper-plated sign near the front entrance identified the building as "Number 3." Another sign advised visitors that the door was locked at 1800 hours.

The hospital's dental department conducted its business in the building's basement, while the second and top floors handled various classes and the overspill of offices. All were served by the same front entrance, where a long hallway connected with the tower. The building had no elevators; stairwells provided the only access from the top floors to the basement. At 2345 hours, Neuro Psychiatry 1 appeared to be settled in for an uneventful night.

Twenty yards from the entrance to Building number 3, a frustrated Billy Hale stirred restlessly inside the parked limousine, then reached for the door handle.

"Chief, where ya goin'?" Emile jumped from the car before Billy's feet touched the ground.

The evangelist angrily nosed the cane toward the glass door above and beyond the six steps. "There!"

"But, Chief, it's locked. You had me check it three times."

"If I must break in, I damn well shall," Billy threatened, limping off.

Headlights reflecting from the glass door stopped Billy short of the entrance steps. A blue Audi braked abruptly to a stop behind the limousine, and a slender man, casually dressed in gray slacks and a yellow sport shirt under a lightweight red sweater, slithered from the car and peered over the roof. Satisfied that the old man at the steps was truly the legendary Billy Hale, he flashed Emile a defiant look in passing and moved rapidly toward Billy in a gait that was distinctly military.

"Reverend Hale, I'm Commander Roeper."

Billy draped the cane over his left forearm and warily accepted the man's hand.

The commander picked up on Emile's approach and Billy noted the peculiar, jerking motion of the man's head. Roeper's eyes flashed here and there as if he were fearful of someone watching him. His smile as he turned back to Billy had a calculating quality to it. Here was a man, thought the evangelist, who could be extremely nasty.

"Commander, this is my associate," said Billy, introducing Emile.

The commander ignored Emile's outstretched hand. "I'm sorry, Reverend Hale, but my orders state that only you are to be allowed inside."

"Orders?"

"This way, sir," Roeper said, removing a set of keys from his pocket.

"Commander, may I ask how you knew I was coming here?"

"I understand you wish to see patient Kaiser."

"Yes, but who told you?"

"If you will please follow me."

"Just one moment! Why are you evading my questions? I asked how you knew I would be here?"

"Reverend Hale, it's almost midnight and I've had a long day. Do you wish to enter this building?"

Billy took pride in his uncanny ability to read the truth behind a face and extract a lie from the tone of one's

430

voice, but Roeper was an enigma. "I'd like to have a word with my man first," Billy said.

Roeper shrugged, then bounded up the steps to unlock the door.

"Chief, I don't like this," Emile said slowly, shaking his head.

"Nor do I. However, I must get into that building." He reached into his jacket pocket and retrieved a small personal phone directory. Handing it to Emile, he said, "Call Cynthia Kaiser and tell her to get here as quickly as possible. The number is listed under *K*. If you have any trouble getting through, get help from the Reston, Virginia, operator."

"Reston, Virginia," Emile repeated for memory. "Chief, what if I can't reach her?"

"Try every five minutes until you do. Use the car phone. And Emile . . . hurry!"

"Chief . . . ?"

"Well, what *is it*, man?"

"Just a feeling, Chief. A bad feeling."

Billy heard the impatient commander tapping the glass door with his key. He shook off Emile's offer to assist him and slowly mounted the stair under the commander's intense scrutiny. At the top step, he paused to catch his breath before following the agile commander inside.

Beyond a second entrance of double doors, Billy took a look down a long and cheerless marbled hallway, which appeared to end in a vacuum of darkness. But the commander veered left toward a pair of orange doors, and Billy hobbled after him faster than he could work the cane.

A posted notice hung to the side of the access doors, and Billy took in the signature affixed to the printed rules and regulations. It read: "Wm. Roeper, Cmdr. M.C. U.S.N. Acting Head, Psychiatric Department."

Roeper unlocked the orange doors, but before he could retrieve the key from the lock Billy barged past him and into the inner sanctum of Neuro Psychiatry 1.

"You needn't hurry, Reverend Hale. Patient Kaiser isn't going anywhere."

431

"The hell he isn't," said Billy, as he looked down the narrow hallway lined with doors that had small red lights over their entrances.

"Reverend Hale, before we go any further, I think it best I understand where you're coming from."

"Is that supposed to be some kind of stall, Commander?"

Roeper smiled nervously. "Are you aware of the reason for the patient's admittance?"

"He's not a patient. He's a victim. And yes, Commander, I am *well* aware."

"This is a man who attempted to kill one of his peers at the FBI."

"That's utter nonsense. Either it's a trumped-up charge or Kaiser was acting in self-defense."

Roeper ignored Billy's accusation. "Patient Kaiser arrived early this afternoon. He was hallucinating and considered extremely violent. He had to be heavily sedated."

"With what? Insulin? Narcotics?"

Roeper's eyes flared. "That's absurd!"

"That's attempted murder. And unless you wish to be named in a conspiracy, I insist you take me to Dan immediately."

Roeper glared at the older man. "As acting head of this hospital's psychiatric department, I can tell you that no one is going to be assassinated here. And I also don't mind telling you that there is a limit to my hospitality."

"It will take more than the marines to drag me out of here."

"If you will keep these unfounded accusations to yourself, that shouldn't be necessary."

"Then stop avoiding my questions. I demand to know who told you I was coming here. Furthermore, I want to know where Mrs. Kaiser is, and who's giving your orders."

Roeper's pale complexion turned beet red. Stifling a biting urge to toss the legendary evangelist out on his ass, he shot Billy a triple birdlike movement of his head and tersely fielded the incriminating remarks.

"My information in regard to you coming here came

432

from a superior officer who had been contacted by patient Kaiser's wife."

"Who is this superior officer?"

"I suggest you ask patient Kaiser's wife."

"I intend to."

"Fine. In the meantime, as long as you adhere to our rules and regulations, you are welcome to stay. If not, then I suggest you take your fears to the county sheriff's office." Roeper then turned and headed down the hall.

"Roeper!" Billy called, following him. "Should what I fear happen—should Dan Kaiser die before I am able to get him out of here—I can promise you there will be the most extensive inquiry and autopsy ever conducted in this hospital's history. Have I made myself clear?"

Roeper smiled arrogantly. "Tell me, Reverend Hale, do all your sermons include threats?"

The narrow corridor terminated at a wide berthing area with row upon row of unoccupied beds. A dispensing station bordered a brightly illuminated hallway which was in marked contrast to another hall at the opposite end of the huge room. From a distance this appeared cavernous, gloomy, and forbidding, closely fitting the common conception of the inside of a mental asylum.

Their presence sent a mild wave of curiosity into the doldrum mood of NP 1. Billy went oblivious to the faces of the medical personnel, and the wall clock's hand stroking the midnight hour was no longer a barometer in his race against time. Nor did he pay attention to the female officer heading their way. Roeper did. In fact, he welcomed her presence.

The hard-line look she displayed in her approach softened as she recognized the famous celebrity. "Problem, Commander?" she asked, with a smile aimed at Billy.

"Reverend Hale, this is Lt. Commander Bolt. She is the duty officer and—"

"Where are you keeping Dan Kaiser?" Billy spat the words into her bland face.

She stood unnerved, unflappable, as if immune to such

volatile outbursts, countering Billy's hostility with the dead-pan gaze of a professional poker player.

"One moment, Reverend Hale," said Roeper, repeating that odd jerking motion of his head as he took the woman off to the side.

There was no "one moment" for Billy. Scanning the wide room for a clue, the shrouded entrance to the rear hallway excited his senses, and he moved toward it.

The woman officer looked away from Roeper in time to see Hale vanish into the darkened corridor. "Excuse me, Commander, but our distinguished visitor has more than a vivid imagination. He apparently is blessed with a blood-hound's sense of smell."

Including the nurse's station, there were seven rooms off both sides of the hallway. Inside the first cubicle Billy opened, a man sat on the edge of a bed, rocking slowly back and forth in endless motion. The darkness prevented Billy from making out his face.

"Dan?" he whispered, approaching the pathetic figure gowned in what looked more like a burial garment than a hospital gown. "Dan?" he called again, this time in a firm voice.

The rocking ceased. The man's head rose ever so slowly and Billy could see the gaunt face, white as the walls, with yellow and purple crescents under lost and despairing eyes. His contorted, slightly parted lips screamed silently.

Billy backed away, but was unable to tear his eyes from the wretched soul.

"Did God send you?" the man asked. "Does He want to see me?"

"Not yet," Billy replied, retreating to the door.

In the next room, Billy's sudden appearance startled a young corpsman holding a bedpan briming with steaming feces.

"Where is Dan Kaiser?" Billy demanded.

"Who are . . . hey, ain't you Billy Hale?"

Commander Roeper appeared at the doorway. "Rever-end Hale, this area is completely off limits. These are patients with serious problems, and they must not be disturbed.''

"Then stop stalling and take me to Dan."

Roeper gestured and moved back into the hall. Billy followed him.

A few yards behind Roeper, Billy saw him pause in a pool of light spilling into the bleak corridor. In a blinking moment the nimble commander had vanished, and Billy trudged toward the light, each hobbling step keeping beat to an anxious heart.

At the threshold to the nurse's station, an Hispanic chief petty officer jumped on Billy's presence. He called to Roeper. "Sir!"

"Yes, I know," answered Roeper, who continued to read a medical chart. "Get on with it, Chief," he ordered.

The ward chief gave Billy a wide berth in passing. He did not recognize the man most white Anglo-Saxon Americans called "Mr. Religion." But he was no more than a passing blur to Billy, whose attention had locked onto a glass wall which separated the station from what was obviously an observation room. Through the one-way mirror, his eyes fixed on a man strapped to a bed.

Roeper looked up, eyed Billy with a scowl, tucked the clipboard under his arm, and without a word glided past him. When Billy's anxious penetration receded to the point where he realized he was alone, his urge to chase down the elusive Roeper had to wait until the smarting of light left his pupils and his eyes again adjusted to the dim passageway.

Through squinting eyes, Hale saw Roeper standing before a door at the far end of the shadowy ward. Billy had not gone ten pain-filled steps when his rampant curiosity, compounded by an instinctive distrust of Roeper, made him detour to a heavily framed door with an eye-level shutter the size of a postcard. Roeper, observing him, grinned.

The door was locked, and Billy jerked open the steel shutter. What he saw sucked the breath from his lungs and dried the saliva in his gaping mouth. The maniacal eyes staring back at him chilled his skin from the top of his skull to the tip of his spine, the bloodless face instantly recalling those of whom he preached when describing the damned souls consumed in Hell's demonic depths.

Billy closed the shutter, but he could not so simply shut out the vivid image of that face. The thought that at least, thank God, the unfortunate soul was not Dan Kaiser reminded Billy of his purpose for being here. "Roeper," he said, looking around for the psychiatrist. He had vanished.

Billy renewed his determined search for Kaiser, moving quickly, more quickly than even he thought possible. *The door at the far end—the open door. Before the first exit—across from the stairwell—Roeper's in there. He's in there, all right.* "Dan," he gasped as the sweat broke out on his forehead.

A clicking sound froze him as if it were a cannon shot.

The door to what was identified as the "Treatment Room" burst open. Light poured into the hall, and Billy heard Roeper's harsh voice as if it was projected in its glow. A man darted out of the room toward Billy, cloaked in shadows. Billy raised his cane on impulse, then felt the breeze as the fleeing chief petty officer moved past him and proceeded swiftly down the corridor.

From the time he had received Cynthia Kaiser's desperate telephone call, he had filled his mind with hope-filled scenarios. But now, as he heard the terse commands reverberating from the nurse's station, he was unable to suppress the feeling that Dan Kaiser was dead.

Billy dragged himself forward but stopped short of entering the room, unwilling to endure the visual shock of what he expected to see within.

"Oh, do come in, Reverend Hale," said Roeper, his tone sarcastic as he came back down the hall and walked past Hale into the treatment room. "Our patient seems to have vanished."

Billy's eyes flew past the commander to the sight of an empty bed.

"Surprised, Reverend Hale?"

Billy stared at the bed, then looked back to Roeper, his mind seething.

"You know, Reverend Hale," Roeper said, "you almost had me believing all of that terrorist nonsense. But then, you've been telling convincing stories for years."

"Are you expecting me to believe that Dan Kaiser rose from that bed and simply vanished?"

"Oh, he left all right. If not to your limousine, then to the plane you have waiting. But we'll find him. And when we do, you can tell it all to a judge. And I don't mean the immortal kind."

"You!" Billy shouted. "Stop your lying! You're part of this conspiracy, and you know I know it."

"The only conspiracy we have here, Reverend Hale, is the bamboozle you somehow pulled over on me."

Roeper's mouth twitched as he took the full brunt of Billy's burning glare Just then, the duty officer, Lieutenant Commander Bolt, entered, ending their silent duel. She ignored Billy and strode to Roeper's side. "The limousine's not going anywhere," she said.

Roeper raised his eyebrows. "They must have more people in on this."

"Security's questioning the chauffeur and another man."

"Hale's associate," Roeper said, recalling Emile.

"He's demanding to see Reverend Hale, and he threatened to call Richard Waters if he can't."

Billy's impatience boiled over. "Roeper, I demand to use a telephone to contact the police."

"The proper authorities have already been notified," said Roeper, handing his duty officer the clipboard.

"I don't believe you, Roeper," Hale said angrily.

"Reverend Hale, unless you make with one of those miracles you're famous for, and I do mean bring the patient back, you've bought yourself one helluva nightmare."

"I've heard enough of your lies," said Billy, stabbing his foot with the tip of his cane in his eagerness to leave the room. He had managed two steps when the fleet-of-foot Roeper stood before him.

"Your stay here at NP1 will be longer than you planned, I'm afraid."

Billy was undaunted by the brutish change which came

437

momentarily over the man's face. "Get out of my way," he threatened, raising the cane.

"He's not going anywhere security won't find him," the duty officer said, stepping between them. "I'll get the ward chief to escort him to his limousine."

Roeper's stonelike semblance gradually thawed. Life blinked in his eyes. Displaying neither apprehension nor anger now, he backed away.

Billy Hale had never left the scene of a confrontation without having the last word. At the doorway, he turned, pointing the wavering cane at the commander's expressionless face.

"When Cynthia Kaiser arrives, the truth will tear you down and put you where you belong."

"The truth? Reverend Hale, at this moment I wouldn't believe you if you swore on all of the Bibles at the Holiday Inn."

In times past, Billy would have sent an antagonist like Roeper reeling with a verbal onslaught, but at this moment, as he stumbled down the hall, he felt worn, very old, very tired. Beaten. The fighting spirit and unlimited energy he once could call upon at will had abandoned him. Despair, with all its allies, had overcome his body and spirit. Nothing remained for him but to return to the haven of his mountain home and bleed—thoughtfully bleed.

He passed the nurses' station, oblivious to a trailing escort.

Approaching the wide berthing area, he looked directly ahead at the narrow hallway leading to the orange doors. He ignored the passing faces and those who pointed and stared at him, but he could not avoid a gangling, black orderly, who left his patient and came at him like a windmill of legs and arms.

"Billy Hale! Man, I musta wrote you a dozen letters."

Billy forged on, but there was no escaping the excited orderly and his size-fifteen feet.

"Billy, I know sumthin' those holy turkeys neva wrote about in the big bad book," he said.

Billy took long limping steps.

438

"Man, I *knows* where it is," he squealed.

"I'm sure you do," Billy patronized.

"I'm talking heat, man . . . motha-grabbin' evalastin' Hell. The eternal D," he said with a knowing smile. Then he waved a bony finger about like a prophet of old. "The great ball of fire," he said, "billions of souls burnin' in the big heater!"

Billy had to wonder who needed psychiatric help more, the pathetic soul left standing in the vast open area with his head bowed, or this man with his bony finger and shuffling feet.

"Man, doncha see? God put the big zapper in plain view."

The trailing chief petty officer lurched forward, grabbing the arm of NP1's black Moses.

"Man, your damned patient is pissin' on the floor!"

Emile sprang from the limousine's side, hurtling up the steps two at a time. "Chief, are you all right?"

Billy clutched Emile's arm.

"Chief, what happened in there?"

"Please—just help me to the car. I need—need to sit for a spell."

Emile waved the curious security guard aside and completed the awkward task of getting his boss into the limo. The paleness of Billy's face and his irregular bursts of breath gave Emile reason for grave concern. Billy's recent visit to the family doctor had not found his employer to be "in the pink of shape"—rather the color of caution's yellow.

The instant Billy leaned against the soft backseat, the intolerable pain he had managed to suppress flared from every joint of his body. A long and heaving groan escaped through his lips and he lifted bloodshot eyes as if imploring help from above. A comforted smile crept on his lips. For the one thing which had kept him going, the thought which had enabled him to endure it all, would not be caught in the whirlpool of his depression. Hope glinted in his eyes.

"Emile, you did reach Cynthia Kaiser, *didn't you?*"

The sagging of Emile's shoulders made a spoken answer unnecessary, and Billy fell back against the seat in total despair.

"Chief, I must have called a hundred times . . . didn't I?" He nudged the chauffeur, who begrudgingly confirmed it with a nod.

Billy laid his head in his hands, his heart thumping rapidly in an aching chest. What he had always preached as the antidote for despair, the miracle cure for man's body and soul, would not go beyond the "Our Father who art in Heaven." For the first time in his adult life, he found himself unable to pray—something as routine to him as the drinking of his coffee in the morning and his glass of warm milk at night.

Had he done the right thing? Might he have fared better if he had taken the time to track down Richard Waters? No, he dismissed the thought. The former president would have treated his "life-or-death" information with more regard as to who really belonged in a mental ward. Besides— Billy grimaced—Waters most certainly would have reminded him of his damned promise.

"I'm onto something, Billy—something to shatter your faith in the human race." Dan Kaiser's precise words, spoken a week ago from a D.C. phone booth, returned to haunt his battered mind like the sound of distant sirens.

Hot blood rushed to Billy's face. His head rose from his hands and the expression in his eyes conveyed knowledge of a cold and irrefutable fact. Dan had finally pieced the missing parts of the conspiracy puzzle together. He had discovered the ARA's blueprints, and more—the architect who drew them.

It was all suddenly very clear to him. He had ventured into a dense field overgrown with lies and deceit. The tenders of the poisonous crops had strung him out from the moment he'd arrived. Roeper, Bolt the duty officer, and perhaps even the black orderly, were all part of the charade. And the power behind "The Secret Society," as Dan Kaiser had code-named the ARA, had given him warning not to swim in their bloody waters.

He leaned toward the open window and gulped in the cool evening air. Having had his fill of Building number 3, he looked off to his right. The sight of the imposing tower did more than spear his attention. What he had earlier been unable to remember now returned from the past like a shooting star.

"*Forrestal.* Secretary of the Navy Forrestal," he said in a tremulous voice.

Emile turned in his seat. "Say something, Chief?"

"Get me to the tower. At once!"

"No keys," the chauffeur said gruffly.

"He's right, Chief. That security guard took them," Emile confirmed.

Billy stared at the tower, at the long shadows streaking the building. Chills ran down his spine. His body trembled. The taste in his mouth was stale and sour. His words came in a forlorn whisper . . . "Dan's up there."

His breath now came in painful gasps. Determination filled his eyes. His trembling hand reached for the door latch.

"Chief!" Emile called after him as Billy limped off into the October night. With Emile close on his heels, they passed the security guard, who paused to deliberate over whether or not to give chase. For a man in searing pain, Billy traveled an incredible distance in a short time. But the six steps to the island of cement in front of the tower appeared insurmountable.

The guard moved to assist. "He'll fall on his face," he said to Emile.

Emile blocked him with an outstretched arm. "He'll make it," he said softly.

Between muffled expressions of pain, Billy climbed the last step and shakily stood on the leveled cement. His eyes lifted slowly, as if he were counting the nineteen floors. When they reached the top, he was sure the darting shadows he saw were human.

Billy blindly took one step forward, then another, and yet another . . . then something told him to take no more. The intense, concentrated effort of looking up caused a swirling in his head, and his legs began to wobble. He had to tear his eyes from the tower and, in that moment, that fleeting moment, death trumpeted its ugly presence.

"*Look out,*" Emile screamed, as he saw the bizarre fall of a gowned figure hurtling through the stillness like a dying condor.

Billy looked up and saw the body as if it was suspended in midair—the arms outflung, the face frozen in terror, the mouth opened in death's grip. Then a blur, followed almost simultaneously by the sickening thud of flesh and bones smashing against cement.

A petrified Billy Hale stood splattered with Dan Kaiser's blood as the night was filled with sirens and swirling lights. The island before and below the tower began to swarm with humanity—just as it had once before, so many years ago, when Secretary of the Navy Forrestal had lain in a crumpled heap almost in the identical spot where Billy Hale now sat by Dan Kaiser's mangled remains.

Billy no longer pounded the pavement with a bleeding fist. His hysteria had subsided to quiet sobbing. The proud evangelist, who many believed could make a peacock envious, had been reduced to a wretched figure.

Several miles away, in a place where a slope in the Virginia hills hid a mean curve in the highway, rescuers worked to free a woman trapped in an overturned station wagon. They, too, were too late. Cynthia Kaiser had bled to death.

CHAPTER 37

OCTOBER FOURTH—the feast day of Saint Francis of Assisi, the commemorative birth date of a Catholic saint, founder of the Franciscan order and holy patron of birds and animals—meant a whole lot of nothing to Jessica Towne. Today was her birthday. Her nineteenth.

Jessica's special day brought bright sunshine, temperatures in the high sixties, and a soft wind that caressed the changing leaves of early autumn. There might just as well have been a monsoon, she thought. Ron had become progressively more difficult for her to communicate with, and though she'd asked him time after time, he'd still not told her all the facts. He had promised her that she could stay with him, that there would be no more attempts to send her home, but his attitude, clearly, was still, "The less Jessica knows, the better." Even though she knew he was thinking of her safety, he was wrong. If this crazy captain was really planning to kill them, the more she knew, the better prepared she could be. But Ron's chauvinism had blinded him to this, and she was at the end of her rope.

The lie she'd told her family was eating at her. She felt she'd broken a trust with her father when she'd written about enlisting in the "Women's Army Corps"; about becoming a nurse; about being unable to contact them again until she'd completed basic training. That the letter had been composed out of "necessity," as Ron had put it, had not made it all right. Maybe if she knew the *whys*, she thought, she could live with it—but the fact that she was living the lie in total ignorance of the truth was so frustrating, so upsetting, that she didn't think she could stand it for even one more day.

The compound had become her prison. The move from the mobile home to the trailer meant only more living space. Gradually, she'd fallen into the rut of becoming a live-in maid. She cooked the meals, washed the clothes, overcleaned the trailer home, fed the dogs, even fixed the generator, and then she waited. Lately, it would be after sunset before Ron Rebuck came out from the surrounding woods, and she'd idle away the hours reading books Ike Vesper brought her when he delivered the groceries. But not today. Her suitcase was packed. Somehow, one way or the other—captain or no captain—she was going home.

Another had found the inspiration to make a drastic move. But unlike Jessica's, his motivation didn't manifest from a fortitude within. John Ragonese had been shot at with dye pellets, victimized with miniature explosives, forced to endure obstacle courses set up through the mission house, and harassed by moans and the rattling of chains at ungodly hours. But when he was awakened in the middle of the night by the acrid smoke of a burning cross under his bedroom window, the haggard director of the defunct mission surrendered to Ike Vesper's antics and willingly took up residence in the vacant students' dorm.

His last attempt to reclaim the house had ended when Ike Vesper appeared as a Zulu warrior and chased him off the porch. But today, he came armed with an eviction notice he was assured Ike could ill afford to ignore. Exuding a confidence at odds with his character, he entered the house.

He didn't have to wait long for a confrontation. Ike came lumbering through the hall and stepped into the large parlor holding a mug of black coffee laced with tequila.

"Yes, Mr. Vesper, it is I. And what I have to say will most surely interest you."

"The only thing I wanna hear from you is your movin' feet."

"Mr. Vesper, when I told you the mission house was

rented for the month of October, I neglected to tell you to whom."

Ike pointed to the portrait of Ron Rebuck's father. "Spooky man, you're jus' dyin' to meet up with him."

"Not I, Mr. Vesper, but perhaps you are. For you see, I've rented this house to the man called Sam. The same man you call—Captain."

"Aw . . . shit," Ike moaned as the mug slipped through his shaking fingers and smashed upon the wooden floor.

Jessica tore up the pages of the letter that had taken her an entire afternoon to compose. What she thought would pour from her heart, spill from her soul at the strokes of a pen did not read the way she felt. Deliberating over starting all over, she realized her inability to make the right words materialize on paper.

She would not simply abandon the man she loved. The only alternative left to her was to find him. Tell him why she had to leave. Make him understand. But when the portable transmitter screeched out a coded message, it touched a nerve and something burst inside her.

She picked up her suitcase and left what had been for her, more often than not, a place of nightmares. Determined, she moved toward the trail, telling herself that nothing would prevent her from reaching the Lancaster bus terminal. If Ike or the mission director refused to drive her, then, by God, she was ready to walk the entire distance.

She had hardly moved onto the trail when Ike drove the black van recklessly past her and into the compound. She dropped the suitcase, brushing the dirt and dust he'd raised from her blue sweater. She watched curiously as Ike unloaded his personal belongings from the van.

"Where's the man, Little Girl?" Ike shouted with urgency.

"Where else?" she said, and pointed toward the woods. "What is it, Ike?"

"What it is—is survival."

She waited for him to approach and then asked, "Would you please drive me to the Lancaster bus terminal?"

"Little Girl, didn't you hear me? I'm talkin' *survival*."

She would not beg or argue. Picking up her suitcase, she continued on her way.

Ike quickly caught up and stripped her of the bag. "What's the matter with you, Little Girl? Didn't that last trip to Lancaster tell you anythin'?"

"I can't stand it any longer, Ike—just waiting for something terrible to happen, without the slightest idea what's going on. And *please* don't tell me about the captain. I've heard enough about him in Ron's nightmares."

"And you think leavin's gonna get everythin' right?"

"I don't know what everything is."

"How you gonna get to the bus station?"

"Walk, if I have to."

"Little Girl, you won't get a hun'erd yards down the road before you're snatched."

"That's a chance I'll have to take."

"Chance? What chance? The dice are loaded and you ain't the shooter. An' if what Spooky Dude just told me is true about rentin' the mission house to you know who, *everythin'* will be comin' down before the month is done."

"Ike, may I *have* my suitcase?"

Ike could see that living with Rebuck had toughened her. She was no longer the starry-eyed teenager he'd played Uncle Ike to on that cold winter night . . . the night he'd done a half-ass job trying to convince her to forget Ron Rebuck.

"Little Girl, go and find the man. Let him know how ya really feel."

She shook her head and tried to take the suitcase from his grip. Ike held fast.

"Little Girl, I can't let ya go takin' a hike into Hell."

"I'm leaving Hell. Ike, *please* don't try to stop me."

"Listen, Little Girl," he said. "You go talk with the man in the woods. And when you do, be sure ta ask him to tell you *everything*."

*   *   *

Ron Rebuck stared at the statue of Michael the Archangel. For the past week, he'd spent from sunrise to sunset on this acre of ground, its shade trees guarded by thick, tall hedges—a green oasis amidst the golden corn and pumpkin fields. Tomorrow, he would pay close attention to the weather and especially to the phase of the moon, for he had no doubt that when Captain Gemmer came, he'd come with the darkness.

The trip he'd made to Lancaster with Jessica and Ike had proved what he had all along surmised. As for the challenge, it had been made that snowy February night in a Maryland cemetery when Gemmer asked him if he was "the best."

So far, he had correctly anticipated the captain's moves, and he'd studied the master assassin's text on guerrilla warfare until it was etched in his memory. With each passing day he became less concerned by the insurmountable odds against his survival in the inevitable rendezvous with Captain Doom, and more sensitive about the captain's predictable flair.

A rustling of leaves violated his concentration. He spun from the statue and reached for the hunter's knife at his hip. But his hand relaxed when he identified the intruder. Jessica Towne had broken her promise, and he carefully skirted the new grass adjoining his father's grave to cut off her advance.

"Dammit, Jessica. I told you not to leave the compound."

"Yes, you did. But you never told me why."

He took her arm but she pulled away, meeting his scowl with her own. He knew this time it would take more than soothing words to calm her down.

"Jessica, if you want to talk, let's go to the trailer."

"No. Right here, Ron. Here at your confessional."

"What is it? You've been talking with Ike again? He's been telling you more horror stories about the captain? Telling you I don't stand a chance?"

"Chance with what?"

"Jessica, go back to the trailer. We'll talk tonight."

"No, Ron. *Now*."

She was shaking, and he expected a run of tears. But her eyes were dry. Wild, but dry.

"Why can't we leave here, Ron? What do you do out here in the woods? And what does Ike mean by 'everything'?"

Her new-found tenacity, the absence of tears, had him at a loss. Her determined gaze told him that he had no choice but to tell her what he had so far tried to keep from her for her own good. Now, he couldn't see that it made any difference what she knew anyway.

"Jessica," he began, "through my stupidity, you've become a hostage to the captain . . . but you aren't his only hostage."

She raised an eyebrow. "Go on," she said.

"I probably should have told you this sooner, Jessica, but I really thought that I was protecting you. I was wrong, and I'm sorry."

"You were talking about hostages . . . who, Ron?"

"The captain has been holding my mother, Jessica. He knew it was the only way he could enlist me in his plot, and now, even though he's through with my . . . services, he's using her to keep me here for some kind of insane showdown."

Jessica was stunned by his revelation. "Ron," she said, taking his hand, "I had no idea. This is terrible." The words sounded so clumsy, so trite and inadequate as she spoke them.

Ron said nothing. He squeezed her hand, but his eyes were locked to the ground.

"Ron, we have to do something . . . you can't go on like this. You've got to trust me and tell me everything— *please*."

He looked up and saw the strength in her eyes, and he knew she was right. Still holding her hand, he told her everything. Beginning with the killing of Cody Walker, he went on to describe his ejection from the SEALs and his and Ike's odd indoctrination into the captain's machine of religious terrorism. He told her all about his mother, and everything about his father she hadn't heard before. He told her everything he knew about Gemmer, and about the people—like Trudy Ballin—who worked for him. Jessica listened carefully and without flinching as he described the assassination of Reverend Tho and the kidnapping of Wallace Langly.

When he was through, he looked deeply into her eyes and said, "Jessica, it's only a matter of time before the captain comes to kill us." She was silent, thoughtful, and he looked away, at the spectacular colors of russet gold and rich scarlet in the autumn foliage. His gaze then fell to the ground that a religious service had made sacrosanct.

They strolled from the statue in silence, moving toward the shade of a storybook chestnut tree.

"Jessica," he said finally, "I should never have set eyes on you that first day. I should have turned back when I saw you walking on the trail. I should have. But I didn't!"

He paused and she didn't press. He was coming from the heart, and she craved more.

"I wasn't thinking of the captain and his damn trap. And even when I knew I had made a mistake, I let it slide. Figuring graduation, and you'd be gone. The captain would never know. But all the while, he was counting on my making that mistake."

He stopped to pick a chestnut off the ground, flipping it from hand to hand.

"Ron, it's so incredible. So—so crazy. We're actually going to die."

"Don't be so quick to bury us."

"But Ike—"

"The captain is Ike's super-ghoul."

"Ike says the captain takes his vacations in Hell."

"He's only a man. For sure, the captain's not incapable of making mistakes."

"Ron—hold me."

She flung her arms around his neck, and he felt the wetness on her cheeks.

"Ron, what will it be like?"

"What will what be like?"

"Death. What will it be like?"

"Jessica, don't talk that way."

"I mean, will there be great lights? Beautiful music? Will we really see God?" She suddenly broke away from his arms. "You know what I think? I think we'll never remember this place. Like it never existed."

"Stop talking like that."

"No suffering. No *impositions*, Ron."

"Jessica, *stop!*"

Her eyes sparkled like blue crystals. "I know why no one truly knows anything about eternity—God doesn't want us killing ourselves to get there."

"Then why did this God think up the whole stinking mess in the first place?"

"Maybe he didn't." Her eyes went to the imposing statue of Michael the Archangel, now streaked with the golden glitter of a descending sun. "Maybe your father was right," she whispered. "Maybe it *was* another's idea."

CHAPTER 38

"ET CETERA, ET CETERA, ET CETERA," quipped the distinguished, silver-haired man into the phone. "Now, would you mind telling me why you had me go through the trouble of getting this report?"

At the parsonage of the Shenandoah Hills Baptist Church, a rapt Billy Hale had not missed a word spoken to him by his personal attorney of three decades.

"Billy, are you there?" Gabe Stillman asked with rising impatience.

Billy's lips pressed to the phone's mouthpiece. "Gabe, why wasn't I summoned to appear at the coroner's inquest?"

"Apparently, you were not considered a material witness."

"Gabe, I was right at the scene. I saw it happen."

"If that's so, why didn't you tell the detective?"

"What detective?"

Stillman opened a plastic folder containing the coroner's findings. "A Detective Baroni said he interviewed you inside a limousine prior to your leaving the scene."

The fingers of Billy's free hand tapped absently on the old leather-bound Bible which lay on the quaint desk before him. The night of Dan Kaiser's death and its connecting details were to him as muddled as an abstract painting.

"Gabe, for the life of me, I don't remember speaking to *anyone*."

"You were probably in shock."

"I don't know. Maybe to some extent. What I do know is that Dan Kaiser did not take his own life."

"The medical examiner of Montgomery County, Maryland, disagrees."

"I'm telling you, Gabe, the man couldn't even walk, let alone climb to the top of that tower and jump off."

"According to the coroner, he jumped all right. Nineteen floors."

"No, Gabe. Dan was murdered."

The attorney leaned back in his chair. He stared blankly at the rain pelting against the windows of his spacious Richmond, Virginia, law office, and weighed the ramifications of his famous client's accusation.

"Billy, are you in some kind of trouble?"

"I saw Dan Kaiser's killers."

Stillman moved a steady hand to a pencil-thin moustache. During his many years as counsel to Hale he had become accustomed to listening to some outlandish, if not bizarre, testimony.

"Billy, did you say killer, or killers?"

"I didn't actually see who pushed Dan off the tower, but Roeper and that—that duty officer, whatever her name is—are accessories to the crime."

Stillman searched the pages for the duty officer's name and found it. "Her name is Bolt. Lieutenant Commander Lucy Bolt."

"They're both part of the terrorist organization that killed Dan and Cynthia."

"Cynthia Kaiser's accident was no accident?"

"Gabe, I *know* it wasn't."

Stillman's interest was captured by the report he held. He zeroed in on a name.

"Do you know of this Captain Hamlin?" he asked.

"No."

"Captain Hamlin from the Navy's Judge Advocate General's office?"

"Gabe, I never heard of the man until you mentioned his name."

"That night, before you left your home, did you call anyone?"

"The only call I made was to arrange for the jet and the limousine."

"That was the *only* call?"

"Gabe, I just told you it was."

"Think, Billy. In your hurry to get to Bethesda Naval Hospital, could you have called a senator? The governor? Naval Intelligence?"

"Just what in hell are you getting at, Gabe?"

"Bear with me, Billy. The head, or acting head, of the hospital's psychiatric department, this Commander Roeper, testified that he told you a superior officer had informed him of your estimated time of arrival. Is that true?"

"Yes, he did. But—"

"Commander Roeper also claims to have told you that Cynthia Kaiser had telephoned a superior officer."

"Gabe, Roeper—"

"*Roeper* goes on to reveal that the superior officer was Captain Hamlin. What's more, Captain Hamlin has verified Roeper's testimony."

"What does that tell you, Gabe?"

"It tells me that this coroner's report would be difficult to dispute."

"Open your mind, Gabe! They killed Cynthia Kaiser to prevent her from contradicting their damned lies."

The judicious Stillman would probe no further. "Billy, I must believe you, but getting bits and pieces over the phone won't do. Unless you fancy coming to Richmond, I could be at your home, say about . . ." He looked at his Rolex. "Say . . . three this afternoon?"

"No, Gabe. Let it be."

"Excuse me?"

"You're not to get involved."

"Billy, I'm on my way."

"No! You *must not come here*. I'm all right."

"You're not all right. Not if there's truth in what you've told me."

"Gabe, if they wanted me dead, I'd never have left that hospital alive."

"Now you listen to me, Billy Hale. The moment I get

off this phone, I'm making arrangements for your and Doris's safety."

"No! You are to stay completely out of this. As it is I'm feeling responsible for two people's deaths. For God's sake don't make any telephone calls on my behalf. You could only make matters worse."

"Billy, you're tying my hands."

"*Steh gesund,* Gabe."

"Billy, listen to me. Billy? . . . Billy?" Stillman pleaded into a dead phone.

The findings of the coroner's report had come as no surprise to Billy. The ARA covered its bloody tracks with practiced expertise. The only new light shed by the report was the identity of Roeper's senior officer—one Captain Hamlin. Captain Hamlin from the Navy's Judge Advocate General's office; yet another high-level office which had been infiltrated by the ARA's "secret society." It would take Dan and Cynthia's resurrections to dispute the report. And Billy Hale had neither the resources nor the energy to chase after miracles.

Billy's attention drifted to the old Bible before him. He glanced at the inscription and ran the tips of his fingers across the book's fine leather. *"To Reverend Porter 'Scrappy' Dews. Within this holy book are all the answers. A fellow warrior for Christ, Billy Hale."*

As he shut the bible with a loud thud, he didn't hear the door to the low-ceilinged room squeak open. Nor did he see, at first, the rugged and weathered face peering at him. When he did, a smile forced its way through a dogged depression.

Reverend Porter "Scrappy" Dews was one of Billy's favorite people. As a World War II infantry sergeant, he had earned the Silver Star for valor. He would have remained in the peacetime army if Billy hadn't recruited him to do his fighting in the army of God. The nickname "Scrappy" had carried over from his military tenure, and indeed, at least in the earlier years of his ministry, the feisty pastor had rarely turned the other cheek. More than

454

once Billy had voluntarily interceded on Scrappy's behalf when a clash with the bishop had gotten out of hand.

Billy limped around the desk and took a seat in a wooden chair that was a Civil War antique. Admiration shone in his eyes for the man who had made less money in his life as a rural pastor than Billy had given away in tips.

"Thought you might like some tea," said the barrel-chested Dews, setting a tray down on his coffee table.

"Since when did Miss Marge trust you in the kitchen?" Billy said good-naturedly.

Miss Marge, as the folks in the Shenandoah hamlet affectionately called her, organized her pastor-husband's religious services, principaled the Crockett Elementary School, and was one of Doris Hale's closest friends.

"Scrappy, I was touched by your service for Dan and Cynthia."

"I got the impression most of the folks were disappointed that you didn't conduct the service," Scrappy said. He poured Billy and himself some tea.

"It's a shame, Billy. They just don't come any better than Dan and Cynthia. Two of the finest people ever to come out of Cullinan County."

"I married them, Scrappy. Right here in this church, before you were pastor. I baptized their children. Doris was Cynthia's Bible School teacher. And Dan . . ." His voice cracked, and he quickly turned from his host to hide the collecting tears.

"Billy, are you okay?"

"No, Scrappy, I'm not okay. I'm bitter. Terribly bitter."

The country pastor studied the expression gripping Billy's face, and he searched the misty blue eyes for unspoken thoughts.

"Billy, you don't believe Dan committed suicide, do you?"

As Hale looked into Scrappy's soulful hazel eyes, the words sprang from his mouth before he could trap them. "Dan didn't stand a chance, Scrappy, and the horrible truth is that he knew it." He tightened his lips to keep

455

them from trembling. He held the teacup with both hands, fighting to keep back the tears.

"I'm responsible, Scrappy," he went on. "It's my fault Dan is dead. And Cynthia . . . oh, my God." His words trailed into a sob, and then the tears ran freely.

"Billy . . . shall we pray?"

"Pray?" Billy recovered, wiping the tears away with shaky fingers. "Prayers have never brought back the dead. And what I don't need now is self-serving comfort."

Scrappy Dews maintained a respectful silence for the man he believed God had personally anointed.

Billy slowly began to surface. He'd spent all the tears he intended to. The spirit to act, to contemplate ways and means to publicly expose the ARA, filled him. But he would have to sit a while longer with his old and trusted friend to regain the physical strength to support his desire.

"Scrappy," he cut through the long and heavy silence, "I see you still have this Bible I gave you."

"Haven't made a trip to the pulpit without it."

"Do you believe everything it says?"

Scrappy Dews smiled playfully, as if modern history's greatest defender of fundamental Christianity was being facetious.

"Do you believe the Bible is the total truth?" Billy asked again with unabashed sincerity.

"Old and new?"

"From Moses to Malachi. From Matthew to Revelation."

"They're the words of God," Scrappy replied emphatically.

"The words of God, or the words of man?"

"Billy, is this some kind of quiz? Would you be testing my faith?"

"No, Scrappy—mine."

Emile drove the limousine through the sleepy Shenandoah town, then headed toward the foothills for the upward climb to Billy Hale's estate. They passed the cemetery where the fresh sod lain upon two graves had yet to take hold, then cruised by the old Hale farm, where a teenaged

456

Billy had forsaken a life behind a plow for evangelical greatness. When they reached a section of straight and level road, Emile glanced into the rearview mirror and said, "Chief, there's a blue car following us."

Billy's weary eyes met Emile's furtive gaze in the mirror.

"When you were visiting Pastor Dews, that car went by too many times. . . . Two men, Chief. And they ain't lost."

Billy knew who they were, and the purpose for which they had come. "Emile, do you have a weapon?" he asked.

"You mean a gun, Chief?"

"Precisely."

"You told me never to own one. You said, 'Those who live by the sword, die by the sword.' Remember?"

"I lied."

For the next forty consecutive hours, Billy Hale struggled with his conscience. Each time he'd formulate what he thought to be a workable plan, a red flag hoisted in his mind. He knew the key to attacking the "secret society" and its killer force lay in exposing the ARA's link to Virtues, Inc. But doing so would mean breaking his word to Richard Waters.

Dressed in cotton pajamas and wearing a red velour robe, he sat brooding in his den at the far end of the highly polished conference table. Unshaven, fatigued, tormented by relentless frustration, his bloodshot eyes slowly scanned the surrounding busts of Bible greats, which appeared to be silently mocking him.

"Where is the justice?" he pleaded, the anger showing in his eyes as they raised to the cathedral ceiling. "You! God! Do you revel in man's misery? Have you no compassion? Does suffering amuse you? What are you? *Who* are you? The God of Heaven . . . or Hell? Answer me!" he shouted, bringing the palm of his free hand crashing down upon the table.

The word "sacrilege" droned in his head, and he sank deeper and deeper into his frustration. He looked to the sculpted busts of the Old Testament's legends, who seemed to mock him with their scowls. Turning in his chair, he found no relief from the faces of stone, for he now beheld the signatories of the New Testament. The collection of hardened faces, starting with Matthew and ending with John, seemed like their counterparts to regard him with scorn. But Billy felt no remorse. He would not fall to his knees and beg forgiveness. Instead, their holier-than-thou expressions aroused his rebellious spirit. Rising defiantly to his feet, he assumed the role of an arrogant prosecutor about to deliver his summation to a jury of ghosts—and one supreme judge.

He pointed his cane first to the bust of Moses, then directed it deliberately to each of the conspiring religious heads, making a full circle. His opening statements were more than prosaic, and included them all.

"The ridiculous to the sublime. Authors of absurdity. The great conceivers of pure conjecture. Your boundless revelations and holy epistles are nothing more than the conception of man's imagination."

Billy smirked and addressed the bust of Moses. "Adam and Eve . . . come now, Moses, couldn't you have thought of something better? And what of their children? Were you too ashamed to reveal how Cain found his wife?" He paused to channel his anger into refined sarcasm. "Ah, but the tale must incorporate sensationalism. The violence of man, for all its reasons, would not suffice. No, Moses, you have to introduce the wrath of God into the mind of man."

He brought the cane down with a loud crack onto the table, his voice pitched with unequivocal scorn. "The great flood, the raining of hail and brimstone upon Sodom and Gomorrah, sending an angel of death to kill the first-born of Egypt, splitting the Red Sea to drown the pursuers of the so-called 'Chosen'—these are not the actions of a merciful and understanding God. These are the deeds of an ultimate monster. But then, Moses," his voice lost some of its disdain, "are you truly the author of such madness?"

Billy limped to the next in the line of busts. "Ah, yes,

Joshua. The great warrior and leader, who killed so many in the name of God. Well, nothing has changed, Joshua. We're still murdering and plundering in God's name.''

He moved on from Joshua to Samuel, and a quote immediately sprang from mind to tongue. '' 'And the Lord sent pestilence upon Israel, killing 70,000.' All because he was *mad* at David?''

Limping on, he paused reluctantly before Job. ''What is there to say to a *myth?*''

Billy now stretched his arms outward to encompass them all. ''Floods,'' he spat, ''fire—pestilence—plagues—hail—brimstone—angels of death; these were not enough. No, you great architects of the truth had to add lice, frogs, flies, and locusts to the manners in which God slaughtered man. And which of you takes credit for Chapter Two, Verses twenty-three and twenty-four in the Second Book of Kings?'' He looked directly at the bust of Ezra, then at Jeremiah.

''Tell me, what type of inspiration did it take to write of how two she-bears tore up forty-two children when the prophet Elisha cursed them—in God's name—for making fun of his bald head?''

He returned to the chair and sat in brooding silence, thinking of the uncountable times he had so vigorously preached the words he had now come to believe were pure nonsense. Richard Waters suddenly sailed into Billy's mind. His lips moved in silent sync to a definition that suddenly acquired credibility. ''An atheist is an intelligent person who has read the Bible from cover to cover—and understood it.''

Billy's attention quickly shifted to the busts representing the authors of the New Testament. Again the taste in his mouth grew bitter. The prosecution had yet to rest.

''The gospel boys,'' he said, totally disregarding the sworn religious vows he had once made. ''The Saints. The Emperors of the Epistle.'' He saluted them with a mocking sweep of his hand. His eyes sped to the busts at the far end. ''St. Matthew,'' he said as if making his acquaintance. ''The Publican of the Gospel. Another profiteer?

No. Biographer. And with the right credentials.'' The appeasing, lauding sound in his voice changed drastically. ''Matthew the Opportunist. Traitor to Israel . . . the most clever of the lot.''

He found the strength to rise and inched his way along the elongated table, positioning himself at the center of the Christian busts. His eyes never left the target of his attention. ''You used them, Matthew,'' he accused, pointing a sweeping finger at the other sculptures behind him. ''Historically aware that the biography of Christ would fall terribly short without a credible introduction, and realizing the Hebrew books would not be fulfilled without their Messianic promise, you and your alliance produced the candidate.''

Resting his hands on the cane's head, Billy sat on the table's edge. ''The candidate,'' he said with forced skepticism. ''A man who lacked or evaded directness and spoke in strange parables. A man who told of a life hereafter, and went unconcerned by the daily needs of physical man. A man who spoke of himself as the Son—who came to Jerusalem on the back of a jackass—who was tried as a heretic and put to death on the cross. The candidate . . . a man who never wrote a paragraph—a sentence—a word.''

He stared at the floor as if waiting for a spiritual ruling from the Supremacy. The hissing in his ears produced a weak objection, and he spoke on. ''After the candidate came you composers of contradiction. You masters of misinterpretation. You teachers of the holy triune.''

A swell of anger induced combativeness as he moved threateningly towards the busts of Matthew and John. ''The principle architects of assumption,'' he accused. His eyes flared upon Matthew. ''Chapter twenty-eight, Verse nineteen;'' his eyes shifted to John, ''Chapter ten, Verse thirty; and Chapter fourteen, Verse twenty-six, do not, I repeat, *do not* constitute the makings of a trinity. Not even by a liberal interpretation could a Godhead be reasonably established. Yet you conceivers of confusion pulled it off.''

He stepped back, feeling the weight of a belief that a

billion or more people considered to be gospel. But the cold, dead masks of Mark, Luke, and Paul provoked a necessity to go on. His voice now took on a hateful tone.

"Paul, Luke, Mark—you apostles of the aftermath, scribes of second- and third-hand information. Yes, the trio of theologians who never met the candidate, who never witnessed his acts, never heard his spoken words—acclaimed saints all."

Fury swelled within him, his face began to tremble, and the hatred in his voice poured from his eyes.

"Am I but a victim of the world's greatest hoax? Have I spent half a century of my life preaching the words of fabrication? Have I only added to the blindness of man's faith? Answer me, you three sons of sensation! Speak to me, you ministers of myth!"

Inflicted with a rage that until now only C.D. Pittman had been able to arouse, Billy struck the bust of Luke with his cane, chipping its nose.

"Fifty years," he groaned through a maddened stupor, turning to the bust of Mark and striking its face over and over. "Billy Hale, the fool!" he bellowed, wielding the cane in a series of blows upon the pompous image of Paul. "Billy Hale, the hypocrite!" he cried out, as a sudden, stabbing pain in his back came like an invisible blow and stole his breath.

"What on Earth?" Doris Hale gasped at the sight of her husband doubled over and struggling for breath. "Billy!" She panicked, rushing to his faltering side.

"It . . . it's okay . . . I'm all right now," he rasped.

She picked up his cane and helped him to his favorite chair before the fireplace.

"Doris, my pills. Please."

As she went to get his medication, Billy sat in the chair, wondering if he'd cheated death. Something that had been festering inside him for so long had finally freed itself from tradition and penalty. He felt neither shame nor guilt. And he savored this moment of inner peace.

Billy's eyes floated aimlessly to the portrait centered among the glossy photographs of world notables who had crossed his road in life. Suddenly, he stiffened. A gray pallor again stained his face. But it was not from a tug in his chest and back. This time, he buckled under a severe blow to his mind. For as he stared at the portrait of former President Richard Waters, it all came to him in a revelation dripping with betrayal.

At long last, Billy Hale knew his Judas.

CHAPTER 39

A SLEEK POWERBOAT planed across the calm Gulf waters. A man with field binoculars, standing at the window of a Panama City beachfront high-rise, watched the speedy craft bank to the south, heading away from the spectacular Florida sunset. As he trained the glasses on the setting star, the lenses reflected a flash of light coming from the mouth of the fiery ball, as if the mighty sun had burped.

The man lowered the binoculars, pivoted from the window, and went to a bedside phone. He calmly dialed, entered his credit card number, and waited for a connection. When it came, he said, "Deep six one—confirmed."

Veep Siler appeared to have seen his last sunset. And not from the porch of his lakeside Florida panhandle home. The evangelist's thick wrists were tightly secured by heavy line that was tied to the corner poles of the dock where two frogmen chatted leisurely while awaiting orders. Forcibly seated in the stern of his twenty-one-foot Bass boat, Veep stared at the young man standing at the bow within easy reach of the throttle. The man was giving no consideration to Veep's insistent pitch, and the obese evangelist wondered what kind of numbers it would take to free himself.

"Speak to me, boy!" Veep pleaded.

The young man jerked the bill of his soft cap and let out a short, ugly laugh.

"C'mon, boy, what does it take? Stop playin' possum and tryin' to jack up the price on ol' Veep."

"If I were you, fats, I'd start praying."

"You're not thinkin', boy. Piddley-ass prayers didn't build all those holy mausoleums. Money did, boy. Big money. The kind ah'm prepared to offer you."

The young man shook his head in disbelief.

"How does a million sound, boy? That's a million divvied up by you and your friends. But mind you, not a quarter more."

The young man chuckled to himself, then scanned the vast and uninhabited acres of woods that Veep had fleeced from property owners by virtue of a heavenly claim.

"Thinkin' real estate, boy? You're gazin' at five hundred acres of God's chosen land."

The young man looked toward the horizon as if searching for something just out of sight.

"Speak to me, boy," Veep wailed. "You might hit the jackpot. A million *and* the land."

"Forget it, fats." The young man was no longer amused. "Where yer goin' you'd better be cookin' up a deal with the devil."

"Ah've been talkin' to a fool," Veep moaned. "It's insane. Letting a million in cash and more in valuable real estate slip away, it's . . . why, it's *criminal*. Where's your greed, boy? What kind of pissy-ant Christian are you?"

Away from the dock, inside the screened-in porch, a man with slits for eyes, dressed in a loud Florida sport shirt, hung up the telephone. A bull-necked sheriff helped himself to a can of Budweiser from an old fridge used to store bait and beer.

"Yeah, what's the story?" the sheriff asked, collapsing onto a wooden rocker.

The man ignored him and retrieved a small wireless communication device from his breast pocket. He pushed the same digit three times, then waited for a response.

"Speak until you're through," came a muffled command.

The man quickly obliged. "Sir, the fat man's ex-chauffeur is food for the fish. We have the video copies made from the blackmail negative. The two you expected are no-shows. Countdown is at your leisure, sir."

An abrupt click terminated the conversation, and the

narrow-eyed man pulled an envelope from his hip pocket, tossing it to the observing lawman.

"You can release your dogs, Sheriff."

Checking the bills in the envelope, the sheriff asked, "What about your two renegades in Pennsylvania?"

"They think Florida sucks."

"Too bad. Me and my boys would have shown 'em some of our panhandle hospitality. 'Specially that black buck. We'da given the nigger a good old roast."

"Sure you would, Sheriff. Just like taking on a tank with a fucking BB gun."

Across the lake, an aluminum outboard motorboat puttered from around a clump of cattails. Veep Siler eagerly watched a man dressed in fishing attire steer the small outboard toward him.

"Neighbor," he called out.

"He ain't your neighbor," the young man corrected.

"Who is that person?" Veep demanded.

"God," the young man said with a strange reverence, straightening his posture.

"Can we deal, sir?" Veep asked, unable to make out the face shadowed by a wide safari hat. "Does a million in cash and the deed to my property interest you?"

A wry grin trickled across the fisherman's lips.

"I said a million and the property. Did you hear me, sir?"

The fisherman's smile vanished, replaced by a snarl.

"Ah'm talkin' about a million dollars in cash, and a great deal more. Surely you can't turn down so much for so little."

The fisherman didn't answer, and Veep felt himself drawing toward futility. Still he would not believe he had come upon a hopeless situation, that he'd come to a dead end in his lifelong dealing.

"You there," he shouted, "ah'm talking to you! Are you deaf? A million dollars and the deed, you damn fool!"

"Sink the blimp," Captain Gemmer hissed.

The young man thrust the throttle and Veep Siler tumbled backward, flipping into the water like a trained orca. He emerged as a great hippo, still cursing man's ineptitude to deal.

The two frogmen slipped from the twilight and disappeared into the blackness of the lake.

CHAPTER 40

THE BLAT-BLAT-BLAT of helicopter blades broke the stillness of an autumn afternoon. The chopper came down in a clearing beyond a curved ridge, and the passenger door sprang open. A short, stocky, middle-aged man wearing a brown tweed suit and matching hat stepped out. The man gazed at the spectacular Shenandoah Valley awash in fall color, and sneezed. Ned Worthy, the multi-Emmy-awarded producer of the prestigious "Up to Now" television show, was not into nature.

The late-afternoon visitor to Billy Hale's estate was responding to an unexpected telephone call which had aroused a long-dormant craving for adventure. Billy had promised him a scoop on "the conspiracy of the century," and the newshound in Ned Worthy was on the scent.

Worthy had been asked to leave more countries than Russian ambassadors had, and his earlier career as a foreign correspondent had more to do with creating news than covering it. Eventually, when his passport restricted him from traveling anywhere but to the North and South Poles, Worthy had dug up skeletons in the closet of his own past. Becoming a producer was inevitable.

Worthy noticed Emile storing the two white signal flags in the rear of a golf cart. But it was the shotgun resting on an improvised rack that brought a smile to his meaty lips.

"Hi, I'm Ned Worthy. Where's the great one?"

"Waiting for you at the gazebo."

"Sure he is," said Worthy, entering the cart with a wide smile.

"It's not far . . . just beyond those dogwoods," said

Emile, swinging the cart away from the chopper and its bored pilot.

"Why the shotgun, my man?" Worthy asked.

"Reverend Hale will have to tell you."

"Sure he will," Worthy said, enjoying the drama.

Billy Hale felt the chill from the mountain breeze. It whistled through the trees, put color in his cheeks, and made him feel alive.

No longer bound by a promise to a man with honest eyes and the devil's tongue, Billy had developed what he believed to be a workable plan, and the very person he needed to make it work was just now coming into view.

The cart pulled up to the foot of the gazebo, and Ned Worthy climbed the steps wearing a hearty smile. Billy made no effort to rise from his chair as he extended his hand. Worthy took it with both of his own.

"Been a helluva long time, Billy."

"Certainly has, Ned," said Billy, inviting him to sit beside him. "When was it—ten, eleven years ago when I gave you that scoop about Richard Waters firing his secretary of commerce?"

Ned Worthy grinned.

"You were a network field reporter then, weren't you, Ned?"

"What a memory," said Worthy.

"And now you're among the most important television producers in what—the country? The world?"

"You will always have my eternal gratitude, Billy."

Hale turned to Emile in the cart. "We'll be a while," he said.

"When do you want me back, Chief?"

Billy turned to Worthy. "How good a listener are you?"

"If it's news*worthy?*"

"Make it an hour, Emile," Billy instructed, then turned back to his visitor. But before he could dangle additional reminders of past favors, Ned Worthy threw up his hands in mock surrender.

"I owe. I owe already," he conceded. "So now, Billy,

now that you've had me drop everything and jet to D.C., then chopper in to your mountaintop, what's this conspiracy of the century all about?''

"Ned . . . it's about the falling of the eagle and the raising of the cross.''

A silver-and-black Mercedes cruised down Billy Hale Boulevard, through the village of Crockett, then onto the state road. It rolled into the entrance of the Full Moon Motel and eased to a stop alongside a blue sedan with Virginia rental plates. Tall, redheaded Trudy Ballin, dressed in a form-fitting gray designer pantsuit, stepped from the convertible, adjusted her dark glasses, and studied the room numbers on the doors of the one-story structure.

Captain Gemmer's personal representative moved decisively to the room at the farthest end of the motel and knocked twice on the door. It cracked open and she brushed past a young man with a full, groomed black beard, taking in the unmade double beds and cot. Ignoring the lascivious stare of another young man seated at a coffee table drinking beer, her attention turned to an older man emerging from the bathroom, zipping up his fly.

"Why isn't someone at Billy Hale's estate?'' she demanded.

No one spoke. No one budged.

"I *said*, why isn't someone at Hale's?''

The two younger men looked to their apparent leader. His stunned reaction, caused by her sudden appearance, gave way to suspicion. "Who wants to know?'' he finally responded, inching toward her.

"Kingdom Come,'' she snapped, and the man took a short step back.

His face registered surprise, and now he stood erect. Only Captain Gemmer's troubleshooter owned the code name "Kingdom Come.'' She was the handle to the captain's knife and had earned no little respect from the ARA's strike force.

"Your orders were to keep a constant surveillance on Hale's estate. Why haven't you?''

"No need," he said, and jerked a finger for the young man to vacate the table. "Everything is under control." He motioned for her to be seated.

"Is it?" she said, ignoring his concern for her comfort.

"We've rigged a laser device at the exit to Hale's estate. The laser beams a wave to a receiver which sends an impulse to a relay a mile away." He moved to where a small electronic component lay on a table separating the twin beds. "The signal is transmitted to this black box. When this buzzes, we're off."

"To Hale's?"

"No need for that. There's only one way down the mountain. It takes between eight and ten minutes from Hale's place to the crossroads, but it's only a two-minute drive for us."

"How many vehicles does Hale have?" she asked.

"A custom Lincoln limo and a station wagon. The chauffeur drives a new-model pickup when he's not driving the old man around. Mrs. Hale uses the wagon."

"And how many times has Hale left his home?"

"Twice. Both times he visited a pastor named Dews. Got a church a half-mile down the road."

"And what does that tell you?"

A man who gave the impression of having all the answers, he was obviously stumped for a reply and looked at her peculiarly.

"It should tell you that Hale is aware his phone is tapped. He's obviously making all his calls from that church."

"I suppose," he shrugged.

"That's not good enough, Mister!"

"My orders are to follow Billy Hale. When he leaves, I know about it."

"Do you?"

"I'm tellin' you, the man would have to be invisible to get by me."

"Or over you?"

He'd obviously given no thought to Billy Hale's taking to the air, and retreated into a shell of embarrassment.

470

When he finally looked up from the floor, it was as if he could feel the heat of her glare right through the dark glasses. Her words came like ice.

"I want your asses on Hale's property. Around the clock. And *you* will take the midnight to dawn watch. Is that clear, Mister?"

The man nodded slightly.

"Is that clear?"

"It's clear."

Satisfied with his repentant tone, she spoke to all of them. "We've reason to believe Hale might leave tonight or tomorrow morning for a trip south. If so," she turned to the man she'd belittled, "you will alert checkpoint and receive your instructions. Any questions?"

"And if Hale *does* leave by helicopter, then what?" the man asked.

"You just report it. Checkpoint will decide how to handle it."

"What about the sheriff in this goat town?"

"He is under the impression that you people are federal agents staking out a dope drop."

She passed by the attentive young men, who saluted her with their eyes. At the door, she turned and pointed a slender, deadly finger at the older man. "Be warned that Red Thunder has a strong personal interest in Billy Hale's surveillance. Don't make it necessary for me to come back."

Sixty minutes had passed. Emile had returned and had been sent to stand guard at the helicopter. Ned Worthy had chewed a pack of gum and was two sticks into a second pack as Billy put an amen on his story.

"Incredible," said Worthy. "Impossible. Harder to believe than *The Greatest Story Ever Told*." He couldn't remain seated and walked about the gazebo. "Jesus, Billy, this thing goes in more directions than a road map."

"Ned . . . I need your show."

471

"Names, Billy. I *need* names."

"And you shall have them. Including the demon behind it all."

"*When*, Billy?"

"When I do your show."

"I can tell you right off, Billy, I can guarantee a segment. Maybe even two."

"Not enough, Ned. I want it all."

"The full sixty minutes? You must have me mistaken for someone who walks on water."

"There's more, Ned."

"More," the producer moaned, plopping into the chair. "There's always more." He took off his hat, revealing a head like a shiny egg.

"I must do the show which airs on November fifth."

"We've already taped the show for November fifth."

"I'm talking live, Ned."

"*Live?* Billy, you're putting me on!"

"I can assure you I'm not."

Worthy jumped out of the chair. Again he paced from one end of the gazebo to the other.

"Live, November fifth . . . Billy, you must understand that I don't have complete control over the show. When I gotta take a leak, I have to ask a network V.P. for the golden key to the john."

"Don't give me that Madison Avenue crap, Ned. 'Up to Now' is your brainchild."

"Sure, but I don't run the network. I can't just preempt an air date with another show. Besides the big guns at the network, there's sponsor involvement. Legal problems. Billy, you're asking me to do a shuffle that no one could have the hutzpah to do."

"Ned, I called you because you can do more with mirrors than anyone I've ever known."

"Billy, the mirror you're giving me is cracked. Forget a live show and maybe—"

"No maybes, Ned. It's live and November the fifth or nothing."

472

Worthy returned to the chair, running a hand over his bald head. "Why the fifth?"

"November fifth is the Sunday before the national elections. If I'm going to effectively expose this secret society, it must be then. And don't tell me 'Up to Now' has never gone live. You've aired live shows before. The Libyan crisis, for one."

"Billy, the Libyan crisis almost triggered World War Three."

"Are you saying that what I've revealed to you is not war, Ned? We're talking about a secret society with unlimited resources. We're talking about highly organized terrorists who are far beyond the grass-roots stage. We're talking about lunatics who send out death squads, Ned—death squads to eliminate anyone whose assassination their war judge deems useful. And this isn't war? Is that what you're saying?"

"I'm saying . . . aw hell, Billy, I don't know what I'm saying."

"Have we wasted each other's time, Ned?"

"Did I say we did?"

"Mind you, I won't beg or banter, Ned. The only reason I haven't made contact with the Washington *Post* or the New York *Times* is that I received my fame through television, and that is the manner in which I intend to give it back. But . . . if you can't handle it . . ."

Worthy once more shot out of the chair, his adrenalin pumping. "All right . . . *okay* . . . I don't know how. It'll take one of those serious miracles you've preached about. But we'll go for it."

Billy disguised his relief. He had successfully worked the man's sense for adventure and intrigue: something he'd counted on.

"Today's Friday," said Worthy. "I'll call you next Tuesday. No, make it Wednesday. Wednesday afternoon. About four o'clock."

"Ned, I'd better call you."

"Your phone's tapped?"

"I suspect."

473

Worthy's eyes swept over the grounds just being touched by the reaching fingers of twilight. "Billy, if I were you, I'd have more than a chauffeur patrolling your property."

"Right now my concern is more for your welfare. Ned, I cannot stress enough how dangerous these people are. They killed Dan Kaiser's wife just to prevent her from speaking with me. If they get wind of what you're up to . . ."

"What? They'll toss me off a building? Drown me? Hell, Billy, death's given up kissing me. But just how do I keep something like this secret?"

"Ned, no matter what, it mustn't leak during your negotiations with the network people."

"Billy, it's *you* who's killing me. The network zombies I deal with aren't into pantomime. The kinda number I've got to run past them involves words. The *spoken* word."

"You're clever, Ned. You'll find a way. That's why I called you and no one else."

Worthy let out an exasperated sigh. "November fifth," he moaned. "Two days before the election . . . *live* . . . Can't let it leak . . . a secret society with eppus for names . . . Where's the flash? The sting? Billy, how do I convince a bunch of corporate nutcrackers this conspiracy is not out of cuckoo'sville?"

"Why don't you just let it all digest? Perhaps then you'll see a way."

"You know what I'm seeing? White coats and a straitjacket."

"Ned, call me if you have second thoughts."

"Bullshit! You think I'm gonna let those pussies of print beat me out of a Pulitzer? You called me because you know Ned Worthy's a winner. Right?"

"I've always thought so, Ned."

"Do you know why for the past five years 'Up to Now' has never dipped below second in the ARB and Nielson ratings? I'll tell you why. No interference with the show's format, that's why. *I* call all the shots. Know what hangs over my office door? 'Improve or Approve.' "

"What about the network honchos?"

"I'll handle them, Billy. Like I always do. After all, they don't call me *Balls* Worthy for nothing."

"Then I take it you're not overly concerned about your safety?"

"I should be frightened by this secret society? Billy, are you aware that some Middle East countries still have a bounty on my head? I'll make the deal, Billy. Jesus Christ Himself couldn't stop me. You can bet your tax-free ministry holdings on it."

"Are you superstitious, Ned?" Billy asked, changing the subject.

"Maybe a little during ratings periods. Why?"

"Well, today being Friday the thirteenth—"

"Friday the thirteenth! I had two shows cancelled on Friday the thirteenth. Someone stole my brand-new Maserati on Friday the thirteenth. Billy, I don't get out of bed on Friday the thirteenth!"

Billy threw his head back, and for the first time in a very long time, he laughed, a deep, hearty laugh.

The helicopter lifted into a darkening sky, and Billy left the gazebo feeling new hope. Ned Worthy had the hide of a rhinoceros. Once he was in action, nothing fazed the man. Equipped with mulelike stubbornness, relentless optimism, and singleminded determination, Ned would hurdle over thorny obstacles ordinary wheeler-dealers would retreat in terror from. Billy had the greatest of confidence in his abilities.

As a long-faced Emile drove the cart toward the house, he could no longer keep what was troubling him to himself. "Chief, I wish you'd let me call the sheriff."

"Did you see someone on the grounds?"

"No. But I sure felt a presence. As if we were being watched. And I don't mean by God."

"If you are referring to those men in that blue car, the sheriff says they're federal agents staking out a dope deal."

"You called the sheriff, Chief?"

"Pastor Dews did."

"Chief, they *ain't* no federal agents."

"Emile, about tomorrow—about Christ Town . . ."

CHAPTER 41

ACCOMPANIED BY THE G.L.E.E. CLUB orchestra and chorus, Cora Lee Christian sang her very own composition, "A Vote for Sinclair Lights Up Jesus' Heart," highlighting the entertainment for the five thousand delegates who'd come to Christ Town for the Virtues, Inc., National Convention. To say that Cora Lee wasn't universally appreciated by the crowd jamming Christ Square would probably not be putting it strongly enough; many if not most of them had already observed that her singing resembled most closely the howling of a coyote.

Seated on the dais of the main amphitheater and perched high above the arched exit, Harley Lombard looked down upon the crowded audience like a king surveying his loyal subjects, occasionally wincing as Jimmy Christian's widow hit a high note.

The animosity which had long existed between Harley's Ministry of Might and the G.L.E.E. Club had died with Jimmy, and the world's two most powerful Christian fundamentalist organizations now enjoyed a peaceful co-existence as the two main arms of Virtues, Inc. While Lombard's ministry concentrated on snatching up the independent evangelical shows riding the airways, using them to carry Virtues, Inc.'s, message, the G.L.E.E. Club's main efforts were directed into the production of extravagant shows and specials, buying massive blocks of air time and showcasing Christ Town on all the major networks.

The hyperactivity at center stage wasn't allowed to let up for a moment. Peter Paul, a youthful evangelist with golden hair and wide blue eyes, had been chosen by C.D.

Pittman as the new G.L.E.E. Club host and master of ceremonies for the convention. Lombard, who had tried unsuccessfully to oppose the fair-haired lad's assumption of Jimmy Christian's role, had to admit he ably handled the parade of celebrities and quasi-celebrities which entertained the audience. These included two former Miss Americas, several retired football stars, a handful of B-movie actors, and a much-decorated war hero, who thanked God for giving him the strength to singlehandedly annihilate sixty of the enemy in Vietnam.

Inside the Last Supper Restaurant, C.D. Pittman, Beth Staples, and Abe Margolis dined by the massive picture window, studying with occasional interest the action in Christ Square below, grateful to have control over the volume of noise wafting in over quadrophonic stereo speakers. Nursing a rare wine from a golden goblet, Pittman's expression was one of amusement.

Beth had been taken by surprise by Pittman's invitation to dine, but she certainly wasn't worried about job security. She'd piloted the Christ Town ship with uncontested efficiency, while Margolis, whom she detested, had run the merchandising end of things with results that were far better than had been anticipated. Through their efforts, the bottom line continued to show steady growth, and Beth had been highly praised by Sue Bergman and other Virtues, Inc., executives for her faultless preparations for the convention. Therefore, she guessed that Pittman, who had avoided Christ Town since the proceedings had begun two days ago, was here merely to satisfy his curiosity about the outcome of this, the big final day of the convention.

"It's a true marvel," Pittman said, breaking a long silence. "In fact, it's hard to believe what we've accomplished already by harnessing the energies of fanatics, lunatics, freaks, hypocrites, and faith-healing buffoons."

"You forgot to mention mental defectives and certified nutcases, C.D.," Margolis smirked.

Pittman chortled.

"I'm surprised you didn't mention blatant opportunists, Rabbi," Beth said, unable to suppress the thought.

"Now, now," said Pittman, raising his goblet. "There must be no bickering on a day that promises us all so much."

Explosive sounds like gunshots thundered across the grounds of Billy Hale's estate. From his lookout point at the edge of the surrounding woods, a bearded young man gazed through powerful binoculars toward the source of the sudden noise; what he saw made him laugh softly to himself.

Jerking down the long driveway toward Hale's mansion, Reverend Porter "Scrappy" Dews gripped the wheel of the backfiring, battered white Ford as if holding on for dear life. With a squealing of brakes, he rolled to a stop near the front entrance, cut the engine, climbed out, and strode sprat-legged to the oaken doors.

At that moment, the bearded youth observed a pickup truck loaded with furniture backing out of the three-car garage. He watched as Emile, dressed in work clothes, hopped from the cab and returned a wave to the visiting pastor, then walked around to the back of the truck and checked to make sure the tailgate was locked. As the front door to the house swung open and Dews was admitted, Emile climbed back into the cab and began the drive down the long driveway.

"The dude's on his way," the bearded man said into his transmitter as Emile turned onto the road. "He's all yours."

Emile maneuvered the pickup down the winding mountain road, bringing it to a stop at the flashing red light of the first intersection. There, parked by the embankment, was a blue sedan that the chauffeur recognized immediately. He reached down and touched the shotgun on the seat beside him, then swung the truck onto the highway and headed south.

In the rearview mirror he saw the sedan pull onto the highway some hundred yards behind him.

"I *knew* it wouldn't work, dammit!" he cursed under

his breath, wishing Hale had listened to him and taken a helicopter out. But another look in the mirror gave him hope; the sedan had fallen back, seemingly giving up the chase.

Six miles farther down the road, Emile pulled into a rest area and got out. A broad smile lit his face as he walked to the rear of the pickup and lowered the gate.

"We did it, Chief! We pulled it off!"

Wedged between several pieces of furniture, Billy Hale grunted a reply as he pushed down the tarp covering him and allowed Emile to assist him out of the truck bed.

"I *knew* we could do it, Chief," Emile went on enthusiastically. "They just couldn't imagine the famous Billy Hale buried under a bunch of chairs in the back of a truck."

"Let's go," Billy said. "We've got no time to waste."

"You got it, Chief," said Emile. "Next stop, Christ Town."

With just a few hours left in the official program, the long-awaited moment of the Virtues, Inc., convention was heralded by a mighty fanfare from the G.L.E.E. Club Orchestra. The media swarmed around the stage and the delegates held their breaths—if not their tongues—in expectation of the promised moment. Inside the Last Supper Restaurant, C.D. Pittman hissed at a waiter to turn up the volume, and from another vantage point near the front of the stage, Senator Bartley Sinclair, surrounded by aides and secret service men, fidgeted nervously in his seat.

Peter Paul took the stage, coughing twice in the mike to get the attention of the crowd. As silence fell over Christ Square, the young evangelist summoned his most awe-inspiring tone. "And now, ladies and gentlemen, delegates and distinguished guests, the moment we have all been waiting for has at long last arrived. It is my great privilege to introduce the man who has unified millions upon millions of Christians of all denominations into a force for righteous change in the land . . . the man who has sparked a revolution of Christian conscience in America . . . the man who will lead us into a new era of Goodness, Grace, and Enlightenment in our Lord Jesus Christ, and the man who has changed the entire course of modern history . . . Ladies and gentlemen, I give you—Reverend . . . Harley . . . Lombard!''

The crowd exploded in thunderous applause, completely drowning out the orchestra, which had launched into a frenzied rendition of "Amazing Grace." Harley—who had risen onto the stage through a trapdoor on a hydraulic platform—was suddenly standing at center stage, as if by magic, beaming in the glow of the powerful spotlights. Showing no immediate interest in restoring quiet, he raised his arms above him in a victory salute to a wildly cheering crowd.

"A *truck?*" Bucky gasped. "Billy Hale in a *pickup truck?*" It took the befuddled Buckmaster a full thirty seconds to get out of the angel-winged golf cart and waddle over to the passenger side of the idling pickup.

"Billy," he said incredulously. "You've come in a *truck?*"

Emile leaned over and said, "Jesus came into Jerusalem on the back of an ass, you know."

"That will be all, Emile," Billy said before Bucky had a chance to respond. "Bucky, get me to the convention immediately, please."

"Well, you're going to need a badge, and—"

"I already have one," Billy said curtly, showing Bucky his authorized badge complete with photo. "They gave it to me back at the guard station. Now, let's get moving."

Bucky was taken aback. "I don't understand, Billy. I didn't authorize that badge. It was less than an hour ago that your friend Pastor Dews called to say you were coming. I hadn't had time to arrange for one yet. And I didn't say anything to anyone about your coming, I swear."

Emile looked at his boss. "*Somebody's* expecting you, Chief," he said ominously.

Harley Lombard pranced about the stage, whipping the long cord to his microphone whenever the spirit moved him to emphasize a point. Sue Bergman, seated immediately behind Senator Sinclair, noted with approval that so far he had been true to the script they had been rehearsing and re-rehearsing for days. Occasionally he threw in a "God told me so," which made her cringe, but it didn't seem to faze Sinclair, so she told herself not to be overly concerned.

"The present liberal administration has done nothing to stop the erosion of America's highest ideals," Harley repeated dutifully. "The current crisis of leadership has brought the greatest country in the history of the world to its knees, crying out for spiritual guidance that can never come from those who pay only lip service to God." He paused for a roar of applause to die down. "This administration has done nothing to stop a wave of violence, including assassinations of our greatest Christian leaders, and I say to you here today, and to every American man, woman, and child who can hear my voice, that we must never forget the inspired message of men like Jimmy Christian—" he waited out a wave of applause at the mention of his one-time nemesis, "—who held out a light for all mankind in an hour of terrible darkness and despair." As the audience again cheered wildly, Harley said under his breath, "a pretty dim light, like the dimwit he was."

As the cheering continued, Sue Bergman bit her nails, waiting for Harley to continue. He'd gotten through the part of the speech he'd had the most trouble with—praising Jimmy Christian—but she sensed from the look on his face that something was wrong.

"*Sinclair*, Harley," she said to herself, "now the pitch for Sinclair and the Republican Party."

"Virtues, Inc., is strong," Harley said, shaking his fist. "We are Geeee-sus' chosen people, and we shall not rest until this nation is proclaimed the United States of Christianity!"

Sue thought she was going to faint. Bartley Sinclair turned around in his seat and said to her in a voice shaking with outrage, "The United States of *what?*"

In the Last Supper Restaurant, Abe Margolis said to a bristling Pittman, "I think our boy has just gone off the wall, C.D."

But the crowd in Christ Square clearly loved it, and as the cheering wound down, Harley felt inspired to free the torrent of his own thoughts.

"*Sinclair*, Harley," a mortified Sue Bergman repeated, this time loud enough to prompt her assistant beside her to view her with alarm. "Talk about *Senator Sinclair*, you *asshole*—for *God's sake*!"

"We are talking of a nation free of filth and corruption. We are talking of ridding from our Christian shores those who prey on our children's minds with their fow-ell movies, evil books, and violent television programming. Christian prayer will become mandatory in *all* schools, and mark my words: pornographers and abortionists shall feel the wrath of Virtues, Inc.—this is Holy War!"

Delegates rose *enmasse* from their seats, bursting with cries of "Praise Jesus!" and "Hallelujah!"

Harley had bounded back to center stage, his eyes looking up to the heavens as he continued to whip the microphone cord about violently. Sue Bergman was torn between running to the back of the stage, where she might be able to get Lombard's attention, and staying to soothe Sinclair, whose face was beet red now as he conferred with his campaign manager, George Whipple. Several of Sinclair's people were already on their feet and starting to move down the aisle.

"Virtues, Inc., will control the elections," boomed Harley. "We, Geeee-sus' chosen representatives, shall elect the next president." He raised his right hand to quell another rising cheer. "But this is only the beginning, my children, only the start of what is to come as we build—build toward the glorious day when the Holy Bible is *law*!"

At their table overlooking the stage, Margolis leaned over toward Pittman. "He just shit-canned the Constitution, C.D.," he said with an I-told-you-this-would-happen smirk.

482

Beth Staples looked at Pittman, who was trembling violently now, one hand gripping the table, the other his steak knife, the knuckles on both as white as the silk tablecloth. She thought he was going to be sick.

As Sinclair and his entourage began their exodus, Harley raved on into the microphone. "Virtues, Inc., is the party of truth! Ordained by God, inspired by the Holy Ghost, chosen as the ultimate mouthpiece for Christ! We shall not rest until every maggot-minded, Godless heathen has been driven from political office!"

Sue Bergman had planted herself in front of George Whipple, who was trying to clear the way for the senator's departure. "Please, George—now more than ever it's crucial that the senator stay and make the closing address to the convention."

"I'm sorry, Susan, this man Lombard is a complete lunatic. Bart's made up his mind to leave, and I have to concur with his decision. There's nothing, I'm afraid, that could change things at this point."

The chanting of "Harley, Harley, Harley!" had swelled to pandemonium heights. Sue looked at Whipple in desperation and said, "Not even the direct instructions of Richard Waters?"

Whipple put two hands on the shoulders of the ARA chief executive and physically moved her to one side to allow Sinclair to pass. "Ms. Bergman," the campaign manager said, "though you no doubt have his unlisted phone number, I'm afraid it's a bit late in the game even for that."

Billy Hale's face darkened as he and Emile followed Bucky into the underground passageway which led directly to the convention site. The noise from the crowd drummed in his ears with a warning beat. *Am I heading on a collision course with a nightmare?* he wondered.

As they entered the square, Billy squinted into the bright late-afternoon sunlight, mesmerized by the vast body of humanity pledging its allegiance to a man he suddenly regretted having sprung upon the world.

483

Clutching his cane, Billy moved toward the stage. As he did, Bucky tugged at his sleeve. "Billy," he said nervously, "maybe we'd better stay here. I'll get you a chair."

"Do you think I came here to sit on my rear end?" Billy said, withering Bucky with his eyes and continuing to move toward the front.

Turning heads and gaping mouths greeted Billy Hale's trip up the main aisle. Word of his presence spread quickly, and as Sinclair, who'd almost reached the farthest exit, got the word from an aide that the father of modern evangelism was approaching the stage, he stopped in his tracks. After a brief consultation with his staff, he took a seat at the back. Meanwhile, the supercharged Lombard had yet to take note of Hale's presence.

"We are the Guardians against the Godless, the Vicars of Virtue, the Missionaries of Morality," he intoned. "Our rightful place in history will not be denied us!"

As Billy reached the stage, the spontaneous roaring of the crowd, the praising of God and Jesus—the very same response he had nurtured during his own "Campaigns for Christ"—sickened him. With no way to ascend to the speakers' platform, he stood in the center aisle and raised his cane toward Lombard just as Harley was bringing the microphone back to his lips.

"Demagogue!" cried Hale, then again, "Demagogue!"

Lombard squinted down at Hale in disbelief. "It's you! It's really you!" he said, wiping the sweat off his brow with his free hand.

"Demagogue!" Billy repeated even more loudly over the rising murmurs of the restless delegates.

Peter Paul had rushed to Harley's side. "It's the great Billy Hale," he told Lombard—as if Harley didn't know.

Covering the mike with his hand, Harley threatened, "If you had anything to do with Billy coming here I swear I'll cut your little pecker off!"

Peter Paul smiled, then retreated to backstage.

The crowd had begun to quiet as Harley stood there

gazing down at Hale, stunned and momentarily lost for words.

Once more Hale charged: "Demagogue!"

Harley took a few steps back and spoke quickly into the microphone. "Our destiny is clear! The approaching election is . . . only a stepping stone toward our glorious future. It has been revealed to me that the Lord seeks a new address. It has been revealed to me by the highest of the high, by our Lord Jesus Christ, that not until Virtues, Inc., sends forth its own candidate . . . will God truly reside at 1600 Pennsylvania Avenue. It is written! The Bible tells us so! Prayyyyze Geeeee-sus!"

Peter Paul broke back onto the stage, a microphone in his hand. "May I have your attention, please! Ladies and gentlemen, may I *please* have your attention!"

Harley rushed to the diminutive young man's side. "What are you doing?" he demanded through clenched teeth. "What . . . the . . . fuck . . . are . . . you . . . doing!"

The words spilled through Peter Paul's live mike, and the words came booming through a dozen speakers. The silence was instantaneous.

Peter Paul took advantage of Harley's aftershock and spoke quickly into his mike. "Ladies and gentlemen," he said, "I give you . . . Billy Hale!" He tossed his microphone over the front of the stage, where it clattered to the ground.

"Traitor! Traitor!" Lombard shouted into his mike, but the sound had been cut off. He raced to the side of the stage where Sue Bergman was standing, arms crossed, a murderous look in her eye.

"Who the hell cut my sound?" Harley demanded.

Meanwhile, Peter Paul's mike had been picked up by a dumbfounded delegate. Billy snatched it from the man's hand and turned toward the delegation, almost knocking Frank Buckmaster over in the process.

"Speak, Billy, Speak!" Bucky implored him.

"Delegates of this convention," Billy began, and the moment the familiar voice came over the loudspeakers, almost total silence descended over Christ Square.

"I have not come here as a destroyer, but rather as an old man who has earned the right to offer constructive criticism."

At the back of the crowd, Bartley Sinclair hushed his staff and tuned his ear to the sound of Hale's voice.

"I once preached that if you are not born again . . . if you do not believe Jesus Christ is truly the Son of God . . . then you will never know Heaven. Today's evangelists have taken this Biblical wisdom one step too far. They threaten that if you are not born again, if you do not believe in Jesus as the Son of God, you will know Hell."

There was a scattering of catcalls before he could continue.

"Once, during a debate with a prominent tax reformer, I said that to tax a church or a ministry was to tax God. I also said, often, that prayer is the solution for all problems, and that God's will is not for us to judge. More often than I can recall, I spoke of miracles, and of my conversations with God. You see, in my zeal to convert the world to Christianity, I said many things under the guise of Divine Revelation—things which only the ignorant could possibly be expected to believe. Unfortunately, the ignorance I abetted—perhaps even increased—still prevails. In fact, it grows in great swells."

A rolling wave of boos now crashed through the square. Billy Hale took a deep breath and went on.

"During one of my early crusades, I preached that the Earth we live upon is six thousand years old. My source of information was, of course, the Bible. Starting with the book of Genesis, I had done a mathematical calculation of the 'begats' and 'begots' to arrive at my conclusion. Archeologists have since discovered the bones of dinosaurs which lived upon this Earth two hundred million years ago. You would think science had blown a sizeable hole in my theory. You would think that we fundamentalist preachers would stay clear of that issue. But only a short while back, Harley Lombard appeared on a national television show and defended the exact creationist theory I had propounded. Harley Lombard refused to accept the documented findings of scientists, who he labeled atheists and communist sympathizers. This is a man who speaks of virtue? This is the man who asks for your total *trust?*"

There came a sporadic rallying to Harley Lombard's defense—vocal and vicious denials to Billy's charges. He went undaunted and spoke above their protests.

"We evangelists do not stalk in darkness, or depend on secrecy. No, we are highly visible and quite, quite legal. The media has helped our cause, giving us even greater prominence, the same media people who call wars between countries 'Holy Wars,' who call terrorist acts 'religious killings.' TV reporters and newspaper journalists continue to bestow the title of 'Reverend' upon us. But then, if Satan himself were to stand for an interview, perhaps they would call him *'Reverend'* Satan."

The outbursts from delegates were scattered and leaderless. Billy had his way with the mike.

"Our heads are bowed, our eyes are closed. We hold hands. Our faces are gripped with piety. Our voices are strained with righteousness. We are the merchants who have made religion a product. And I am the one who wrote the sales guide."

In the Last Supper Restaurant, C.D. Pittman raised his goblet. "No greater truth," he toasted.

"Tears," said Billy. "Yes, tears are a requisite of our trade. We evangelists can turn on the weeping at will, especially when we solicit. Testimony from born-again celebrities is vital. Sports figures are the 'in' thing. Football players who talk of Jesus being in their huddle—baseball stars who pray for strikeouts and home runs—and, of course, boxers who credit God for the unmerciful beatings they have bestowed upon their opponents. Music is a must. Today, we evangelists depend on large orchestras and back-up groups. New songs with titles like 'God Told Me So' and 'I Saw Jesus Peeking through the Clouds' have replaced standard Christian compositions."

Billy paused to take a breath, and the silence in Christ Square was almost total.

"Whenever we evangelists make mistakes, it is never our fault—we simply blame it on Satan. And we know how to make the Bible work for us, selecting passages which are not remotely related to the contemporary matters we are discussing. Above all, we evangelists are never wrong. To suggest that is to call God a liar.''

Many of the delegates were uncertain as to whether they were hearing Billy's confession or an attack on *all* evangelists. Billy kept them guessing.

''Previously, I mentioned that I have spoken with God. I did. Many times. Unfortunately, it was always a one-sided conversation. But then, perhaps God speaks in our minds.''

''The devil's speaking in yours, Billy!'' a man's voice shot out from nearby.

It was hardly enough to fluster Billy, and he went on.

''Speaking with God is now considered old-fashioned. Contemporary evangelists have *discussions* with God. I also mentioned that I have witnessed many miracles. Actually, the only miracle which I can definitely attest to is the one which has been repeated time after time: how we evangelists are able to take money from the pockets of the public, and put it into our own.''

Backstage, Harley Lombard had run out of people to unload his frustrations upon. All but Sue Bergman, Peter Paul, and the bearded director had stayed clear of his raging warpath.

''Conspiracy! It's a fucking conspiracy!'' he shouted, kicking a prop out of the way.

Sue Bergman glared at him. ''If you must use filthy language,'' she hissed, ''do it in the men's room.''

''Who's responsible?'' Harley cried. ''Who let that old elephant into *my* convention?''

''Harley, I'd like to hear what Hale has to say. Run your mouth off someplace else.''

''You can't talk to me like that, Sue. You're just my advisor.''

''Wrong, Harley. Your caretaker.''

Billy Hale continued to ride over the dissident murmurings from the hostile audience.

''We television evangelists are well served by so-called 'acts of God.' The worse the disaster, the more our minis-

488

tries produce record contributions. How many of these tax-free donations ever reach the victims of floods and earthquakes? How much money actually goes to the starving people in the poverty-stricken hellholes of the world? More often than not, less than ten percent. How can this be? *Expenses*," he said with shame. "Ninety percent to cover *expenses*!"

Strangely, there was not a protest to be heard, and Billy continued.

"What do I hear?" he said, searching the blue sky. "What did you say? God wants more satellite Christian broadcasting? More Christian bookstores? Jesus—Jesus wants what? A playground? Christ Town? You say it's time for Christian banks, Christian candy stores, bakeries —an airline? What was that last thing? The franchising of Christian fast-food restaurants?"

The silence was broken by angry shouting, but Billy forged on.

"Who was I speaking to? The Holy Spirit, of course. the Holy Ghost, that mysterious member of the Trinity who informs evangelists of the Lord's earthly needs."

As charges of blasphemy sounded from every sector of the square, Billy went on.

"How can there be a dollar value placed on prayer? The God of all the people needs no financial brokers. Still, we manifest ourselves daily on television as religious revenuers."

With the blind rage of a rhino's charge, a burly middle-aged man rushed toward Billy. He shoved Buckmaster out of his way and grabbed the microphone.

"Condemn the Catholic Church," he growled. "They're the holy hoarders of wealth!"

Before the man's voice became an echo, Billy quickly rebutted.

"The Catholic Church deals in time. Income from their patronage is derived from baptism to burial. We evangelists want it *now*."

Another man's voice lifted above the melee. "You took yours, Billy. You damn well took yours!"

Billy declined to make a public admission. He would not be sidetracked. He'd more to say. Much more.

"Harley Lombard talks of filth and violence in the books our children read and the movies they see. But are we not guilty of far worse? We, who create and sell Biblical books depicting the acts of an unmerciful, killer God? Haven't we ourselves made frightening, lasting impressions in the minds of children?

"We, the protagonists of the electronic church, have had more revelations than did all of the prophets combined. Where others have dreams, we have revelations. In the course of one year, I personally alluded to twenty-six spiritual revealings. The vast majority of these dealings with divinity involved a price tag to the public. *God* wants, *Jesus* needs, the *Holy Ghost* demands. These assertions produced record donations of tax-free dollars to my ministry. Yet, in that very year, I crusaded against the revelations of a man who dared to suggest a theory of the conceivement of man that was not consistent with the Book of Genesis. I vigorously, publicly condemned this man for attempting to shed a new light on sacred, fundamental beliefs. I maliciously spoke out against this man for his efforts to raise religion from the dark ages and bring about a positive hope for all men."

In the heart of Christ Square, a man stood on a chair and yelled, "Down with Billy Hale!"

The delegates had found their war cry. As the contagious chanting picked up momentum, Billy knew he had to speak quickly and firmly to finish revealing what had festered so terribly long in his conscience.

"I'm speaking of a man many of you will remember. A man I publicly defamed in the name of Christianity. A man I judged unworthy of being inspired by God."

Billy never saw the first object hurled at him, but he felt the next one—a silver dollar, which grazed his temple and started a ringing in his ears.

Bucky watched the cane fall from Billy's hand. He looked in horror as pain seized his hero's face, confusion rendering him helpless.

490

Billy fought off the shock of the blow. He stood, wobbling, clutching the mike with both hands, and swore that nothing short of a coronary would stop him from concluding his unwelcome confession.

"How in the name of sanity can we set an example to a world seeking truth, not dogma? How long will it be before we are exposed for what we truly are? We, who refuse to think—who place our credibility in ancient, written words? We, the parrots of an infallible Bible—we, the clowns of Christianity—we, the hucksters of holiness?"

An ugly roar came in swift response. Those who had not previously found it within themselves to turn on a man they had once emulated now freely joined their ilk in vocal condemnation.

Frank Buckmaster moved from one angry face to another, pleading, begging for them to stop. Pushed, cursed at, and spat upon, he continued until a sharp pain sent him yelping in a circle like a wounded dog. The midget evangelist, Barney Patrick, had climbed down from his observation ladder, wormed his way through the crowd, and bitten Bucky on the ankle.

The hostility had reached fever pitch, and the physical assault on Billy Hale continued.

"They're *stoning* Hale, C.D. Stoning him with coins," said Margolis with merriment in his voice.

"They'll crucify him," Beth Staples said in fear.

"Not yet," said Pittman, signaling for Margolis to hand him the blue phone.

Having received his orders through the headset, the stage director stepped in front of the furiously pacing Harley Lombard.

"Get outta my face!" Harley threatened.

"The mike at the podium is live," the unruffled director informed.

"What about Peter Pricks?"

"Reverend Peter Paul's microphone is dead."

"And Billy Hale's?"

A sly grin slowly spread across the bearded director's face.

Deeply engrossed in her phone conversation, Sue Bergman did not notice Harley's fast break onto the stage. Seconds later, the clamorous ovation and chanting of Harley's name grabbed her attention and she put former President Richard Waters on hold.

Glorying in the applause, Harley strode menacingly toward a smug Peter Paul.

"You little prick with earlaps, get off my stage!" Harley threatened. "No one fucks with my thunder!"

Retrieving the microphone at the podium, and now in search of bigger game, Harley bounded to the center edge of the stage and pointed an accusing finger down at the man who had ruined his coronation.

"Traitor!" he cried.

Billy tapped a finger onto the mike. It was live, and he raised it to quivering lips. "Tell them, Harley. Tell them how Virtues, Inc., was not your revelation."

"I'll tell them that you are the Benedict Arnold of evangelism!"

"Tell them how they're being used, Harley. Tell them how you are no more than a puppet of a ruthless organization with a blatantly political goal."

"Turncoat!"

"Where is Veep Siler today, Harley?"

"Your faith has abandoned you, Billy."

"Who is the true power behind Virtues, Inc.? Tell them, Harley."

"Satan has claimed your soul, Billy."

"For once in your life, stand tall, man. Tell the people the truth."

"You have turned your back on the Almighty, Billy. By your own admission, you have alienated the Lord. Your soul shall know Hell!"

Five thousand delegates voiced a unanimous verdict. Billy Hale had committed the unforgivable: he'd bastardized the Bible. The defrocking of the world's best-known evangelist had commenced.

On the service road to and from Christ Square, a caravan of carts awaited Senator Sinclair's orders to roll. The senator was engaged in a heated debate with his campaign manager, George Whipple.

"Are you finished, Whip?" the senator said harshly.

"Bart, be practical. Billy Hale is poison."

"I want to speak with the old man, and I want to speak to him alone. So either you arrange it with the secret service people, or I will."

Billy Hale's trail of humiliation offered no compromise. Jeered and mocked by those he once called "brethren," he left their insults unchallenged. Each limping step he took became that of a martyr's march. Every person he recognized, many of whom had come to him in their times of need, now looked upon him as a heretic to be taken to the rack and flogged until his faith returned.

Relentlessly scorned and abused, Billy quickened his pace. Suddenly, he lost his footing and tripped over his cane. The harsh impact with the concrete jarred the back of his head. Blood trickled from his nostrils and he gasped for breath.

A swarm of delegates pushed past the guiding Buckmaster to form a wall of humanity around the fallen Hale. Bucky's attempts to break through were met by punishing blows from elbows and fists. Another desperate try brought him a rush of new pain: once again Barney Patrick had a lock on his leg, and was gnawing on his calf.

Beth Staples watched in silence as the long, late-afternoon shadows crept down from the themed Calvary Hill. She watched in horror as the looming cross cast its eerie shadow over Billy Hale.

"Where's she going?" Margolis sniped.

"Perhaps to wipe Hale's face," Pittman laughed.

Beth Staples commandeered the angel-winged cart she'd found at the tunnel's exit. With reckless abandon she drove down the center aisle, narrowly missing slow-to-move delegates. She rapidly approached the outer circle of neck-stretching and toe-standing onlookers. If not for a fast-reacting man's warning shout, her mission of mercy would have ended on a collision course with numerous legs and spines.

Unnerved by the angry comments and stares directed at her, she stopped the cart beside the fallen Billy Hale.

". . . my cane," Billy muttered between groans of flashing pain.

A false perception motivated the arriving Buckmaster's hysteria. "He's blind. Billy's blind!"

Beth Staples kneeled at Billy's side. "It's all right," she soothed. "I've brought a cart, Billy."

"No," he said.

"Billy, I have to get you out of here." Her eyes raised to the sobbing Buckmaster. "Bucky, give me a hand!"

"No," Billy said. "If I don't walk on my own two feet, evangelists yet born will preach of the day when I was struck down by the Lord."

The eyes peering down from the restaurant window danced with glee. Never had C.D. Pittman enjoyed such fulfillment.

"Give us Barabbas!" Margolis shouted.

Only a few yards remained to Billy Hale's purgatorial procession. He had endured, weathered the intolerable harassment, and made the most difficult and painful journey of his life. For the first time in his career as an evangelist, action, not a gifted tongue, had brought him through a grueling ordeal. Billy Hale had never felt more satisfied as he experienced a feeling long dormant: he liked himself.

The mass assailment on Hale suddenly gave way to song. Led by Cora Lee Christian and her choir, the aroused delegates sang out Virtues, Inc.'s, anthem, "War on Wrong." From section to section, Christ Square filled with the lyrics dealing with sundry "thou shalt nots" and designed to bring the convention to a close.

In the tunnel, Beth Staples helped Billy Hale into the cart's passenger seat. Apologies stuck in her throat as he fondly took her hand in his own. At that moment, Beth knew she had never respected anyone more.

Bucky drove off into the dimly lit catacombs, and Billy

reached into his pocket for the pills that he hoped would bring down his blood pressure and arrest the spasms coursing through his body. Only morphine would deaden the pain in his throbbing knee.

"They had no right," Buckmaster blurted out.

Lacking saliva, Billy forced the pills down his burning throat.

"They had no right," Buckmaster repeated.

"I was a fool, Bucky. A fool for coming here."

"But they had no right, Billy. No right."

"He knew," Billy said. "All along that devil knew I would come to this convention."

"The *devil* knew, Billy?"

Crucial thoughts chased C.D. Pittman from Billy's mind. What he'd done called for serious contemplation. He'd made the mistake of publicly referring to a ruthless organization and its ties with Virtues, Inc., revealing a clue to the ARA's identity. What's more, he'd connected the killer force with Veep Siler's death. He had become a positive threat to Richard Waters. Suddenly, Billy knew the feeling which came to a hunted man.

Confident that Doris was safe with Scrappy and Marge Dews, his primary concern now was to reach Emile and escape from Christ Town. But how? He was troubled in thought. In a truck? On the open road? All at once, resolving his predicament tumbled into futility. What gave him reason to fear now stepped out from the near shadows a short distance ahead.

"Stop here, Bucky," Billy commanded.

Buckmaster brought the cart to a halt about thirty yards from the two men dressed in business suits.

"Just security, Billy," he said.

"All the security personnel I've seen were in uniform. Run, Bucky!"

"Run?"

"Damn it man, run! Get out and run for your life!"

In his haste to obey, the hefty Buckmaster lost his balance getting out of the cart and fell to the ground. Climbing to his feet, he ran with tiny steps, like a man going nowhere.

The two men approached the cart, and Billy struggled for dignity. One of the men was about to speak, but Billy silenced him with a hand.

"All that I request is to be permitted to stand."

The man shrugged to his partner and they watched Billy climb painfully out of the cart. With a slight tremor to his lips, Billy grittingly stood before the men he believed to be his executioners.

"I would appreciate it if you would do the deed swiftly, for I have endured enough pain this day for a lifetime."

The man to Billy's left spoke first. "Reverend Hale, Senator Sinclair wishes to speak to you."

Billy closed his eyes and muttered the words most people do when taken with relief. "Thank God."

The caravan of carts entering Apostles Parking had been reduced by five. They moved in a wedge formation and came to a stop alongside the angel-winged carrier where Emile and Buckmaster stood sentry. Senator Sinclair held back the half-dozen secret service men. He'd talk to Billy alone.

Emile and Bucky gave the Republican nominee for president a clear path to the pickup. A wary Billy Hale greeted him through the open passenger's window with a worn smile.

"Billy, I'd like very much to hear what you *didn't* have a chance to say."

Billy studied the stern face. The determination in Sinclair's eyes and the stubbornness of his chin encouraged a trust which diminished his suspicions.

"May I?" Sinclair smiled, pointing to the driver's seat.

Billy waited for a long moment before nodding.

A cordon of tight security surrounded the pickup through the twilight and into darkness before a somber Sinclair finally emerged. Shortly thereafter, searchlights from a descending helicopter shone down on the dusty truck.

CHAPTER 42

HALLOWEEN—the eve of All Saints Day.

Ron Rebuck had awakened before dawn. The first rays of light found him inspecting the fronts he'd prepared within the skeletal woods and fields to the mission property. Come nightfall, he foresaw, the peaceful settings would be battlegrounds.

Totally convinced that the captain had chosen this night of witches and goblins, Ron Rebuck had prepared for his fateful rendezvous with a "vampire." The firepower he'd collected from past operations provided a formidable arsenal to throw against a company of "crazies." Still, Rebuck knew it would take something more than his heavy firepower to bring down the great destroyer. Without question, the captain *was* the ultimate assassin.

For Jessica Towne, the passing night ran long and her train of thoughts ran short. The more she pondered over her bizarre circumstances, the less she could understand. She was guilty of nothing. She'd killed no one, nor was she a threat to society. All she'd done was fall in love. And although Ron Rebuck had told her everything, she would not, could not, accept the reason she'd become a victim, an innocent pawn in a madman's game.

Ron Rebuck returned and heard the muffled sobs coming from the far end of the mobile home. He carefully opened the bi-fold door and saw Jessica lying on the hideaway bed, crying softly into her pillow. A wave of guilt swept heavily over him.

He drew closer and sat on the bed's edge. An urge to touch her went no further. Frustrated by his ineptness, he silently cursed the man he held responsible. The son of a snake, Gemmer, had perceived it all. It was a preliminary move to the maniac's game plan—psychological warfare before the battle.

All at once, Ron Rebuck felt wounded—and the captain had yet to fire a shot.

Three pistols told Ike Vesper that the men bearing them had not stormed into the mission's kitchen to interrupt his breakfast for the business of trick or treat. He quickly recognized two of the faces as belonging to the men who'd attempted to snatch Jessica from the Lancaster bus terminal.

"Strip," said the oldest and shortest of the men.

"Do *what?*" Ike said, rising from the kitchen chair.

"Take off your clothes!" the taller man snarled.

"Wuchu mean, take off my clothes?"

The taller man shook with rage. "Lemme pistol-whip the son-of-a-bitch."

Ike countered the man's threatening move with a hostile glare. But his real concern was due to the youngest of the trio standing at the kitchen's entrance. The expressionless face, the way he stood, and his manner of indifference, all were markings of someone trained in special forces.

The tall gunman tired of Ike's stalling. "Are you gonna take 'em off, or do we?"

Ike reluctantly shed the woolen shirt, exposing a custom-designed flak jacket strapped snugly to his broad chest.

The tall man's eyes flooded with distrust. "What's in them pockets?"

"Your momma!"

The leader wisely stepped between them. "Take it off—real easy."

Ike silently, daringly refused. By the glare in his black eyes, it would take nothing short of death to confiscate the life's savings stuffed into the bulging pockets that were sewn shut with heavy thread and a cobbler's needle.

The man shrugged, regarding physical force as unnecessary, and motioned for Ike to strip downside.

Ike dropped his pants, revealing navy-issue skivvies and

a small Beretta strapped to his lower calf. Before he could free his booted feet, the man stooped and yanked the piece from his leg.

"Let's go," he ordered.

"Where?" Ike asked.

"Somebody wants to see you."

"*Him?*" Ike rasped.

"Her."

Conversation somewhat alleviated Jessica's depression. She sat across from Ron Rebuck in the kitchenette's booth, trying not to watch him feed bullets into the chambers of various handguns.

"Ron . . . what about your mother?"

He pretended not to hear and went about his task.

"I mean, do you think the captain will kill her?"

Rebuck held a bullet in his fingers. "I don't know the answer to that, Jessica. But it's a moot point, since he has her and I don't."

"If you kill the captain, won't his people . . . want to get even?"

"Jessica, I just don't know. I don't even know if she's alive now. All I know is that he's coming for me—for us—and I've got to kill him." He jammed the bullet into the chamber. "Now, if you must talk, change the subject."

She found no difficulty with this. "What makes people like the captain the way they are?"

"No one's like the captain."

"But what makes him do these terrible things?"

"Insanity."

"He was born insane?"

"Madness runs in his blood."

"Does he have a wife? Children?"

Rebuck had to think. He really didn't know. It was one part of the captain's make-up he took no interest in exploring.

"Does he, Ron?" Jessica persisted.

"I doubt it."

"Then he has no family, no one?"

"Jessica, what's so damn important about a crazy man's family tree?"

"Don't you think it's natural for me to want to know something about a man who wants to kill me? Kill *me* for no reason?"

She hid her tears, but not the trembling in her voice.

"Yeah . . . yeah, I guess so," Rebuck pacified, hoping she'd turn it off. But she didn't.

"Ron, what makes the captain kill people?"

"It comes as natural to him as eating."

"Why hasn't anyone killed him?"

"They've tried. Maybe a thousand have tried. He challenges death. It's a game with him. For some reason, he thinks I'm a worthy challenger."

"Are you, Ron?"

"I said, *he* thinks so."

"But why? Is there something he knows?"

"With the exception of the God in the Old Testament, he knows more ways to kill than anyone."

"I'm talking about you, Ron. What is that something special he knows about you?"

Rebuck's face turned grim. Again she had struck a nerve. This time she pursued.

"Isn't that something special—hate? The kind you showed that night against the Amish elder? Ron, who is it you really hate? The captain—or someone else?"

The barking of the dogs aborted her search for the truth. Rebuck met her frantic eyes. They read one another's minds. What was to come had begun.

"Little Brotha!"

"That's Ike," Jessica said.

"And talking through a bullhorn." Rebuck searched his mind for a reason.

"Little Brotha, come out on the trail!"

"Ron, what's happening?" Jessica said.

"I'm about to find out." He rose from the table and placed a loaded 9mm Browning into her trembling hand. "Anyone comes to that door, squeeze the trigger."

Moving to the door, Rebuck scanned the compound

500

through the screen. Slipping out of the trailer home, he moved briskly to the trail. The reason for Ike's using the bullhorn became clear to him—he was somewhere behind the bend, within sniper range of the mission house. Quieting the whining dogs, Rebuck moved along the trail, alert to any movement in the flanking brush.

Reaching the bend, Rebuck left the trail and crouched behind a small cluster of bushes. From here he could see Ike, stripped to his skivvies, standing in the middle of the trail some seventy yards from the highly visible mission house.

"What's coming down, Ike?"

"It ain't cool, Little Brotha."

"Do I talk from here?"

"The trail. But don' go reachin' for anythin'. There's two sharpshooters at the windows."

Rebuck rose from the bush and cautiously stepped onto the trail. Using Ike's massive frame as a shield, he stood directly in front of him.

"Little Brotha, the place is crawlin' with crazies. They got the grounds surrounded. An' the red-headed bitch is callin' the shots."

Trudy Ballin. It didn't surprise Rebuck. She was as bloodthirsty as the captain. "What are the ground rules, Ike?"

"It's between you an' the man."

"What about Jessica?"

"Hostage bait."

"I don't see it that way."

"Man, I go back without the little girl an' the bitch'll send out a goon squad to whack her."

"Not likely. That would spoil the captain's Halloween party. The way I read it, Jessica's the prize. If I survive, she lives. If I don't, she doesn't stand a chance."

"Man, read this. The bitch is holdin' my bank. They got me down to my skivvies. An' when I go back they're gonna look up my asshole ta see if you gave me sumpthin'."

"Care to exchange problems?"

Words clogged in Ike's throat. All of his problems now seemed infinitesimal.

"Go back and tell Ballin the trailer home must be respected as sanctuary for Jessica," Ron said. "She stays there until it's over. If she can't accept that, the war starts without the captain."

"Man, this ain't some UN negotiation."

"I want her answer delivered by you. Alone. And with your clothes on."

"Man, she didn' come to deal. She's the mothafuckin' funeral director."

"Thirty minutes. And not here. In the compound. At the picnic table."

Ike shook his great head. "Little Brotha," he shouted after him, "whyn't ya just ask the bitch to surrender?"

Ron Rebuck found Jessica where he'd left her, sitting in the booth, staring at the weapon in her hand. He mercifully relieved her of the pistol and gradually the color returned to her face. He knew she'd have been incapable of squeezing the trigger.

Rebuck wandered over to the chair before the TV set, and she followed his movement with rising interest.

"What is it, Ron? What happened?"

"Unless I'm wrong about everything, we're about to win round one."

"How?"

"I've just put a wrinkle into the captain's game plan. Something for him to think about. And she can't take the chance I'm bluffing."

"She?"

"Gemmer's lieutenant, Trudy Ballin."

Rebuck's eyes suddenly narrowed. He placed a finger to his lips, and they listened as the sound of a motor became more and more pronounced.

Rebuck searched the midafternoon sky and sighted the single-engine prop plane diving out of a cloud. It dipped its wing, banking left, and descended to an altitude Rebuck

502

gauged as two thousand feet. It then proceeded to make two full circles over the mission land.

Ron Rebuck now knew how the captain would arrive.

Ike Vesper got back his clothes, but not his bank. He stood before Trudy Ballin inside the dingy mission office, gawking at his flak jacket spread across the ancient desk.

"Chief," Ballin ran a finger along the stitches of a bulging pocket, "I know you won't do anything stupid."

"Never," said Ike, grimly watching her fingers caress the pocket.

"Ten—twelve thousand?" she asked with a teasing grin.

"Right," Ike agreed, not about to tell her that every bit of thirty-six thousand dollars was stuffed into the multiple pockets.

"Fine." Ballin rose from behind the desk, dismissing him. As he reached the door she said, "Chief, do give the handsome lieutenant my final regards."

Ike bounded from the office, unaware of John Ragonese slumped in a chair below the portrait of Ron Rebuck's father.

Two men carrying Uzi machine guns escorted Ike to the trail, and with Ballin holding his bank, he was sure that they needed only the slightest provocation to blow him away.

He stepped onto the trail and looked over his shoulder. The escorts stood watching him, and he moved steadily along. "Fuck cameraderie," he said to himself. "Survival ain't got no friends. I warned his ass. Him an' his thinkin'. The fool thought himself right into a box."

In his present circumstance, sentiment meant suicide. He would have to stifle his true emotions. It was Ron Rebuck's nightmare, and he played no part in it. But as he approached the kennels, ignoring the yelping Dobermans he'd groomed and fed, something shifted in his mind. And when he saw Ron Rebuck standing beside the picnic table, his caring for a brother would not be so easily compromised.

They stood across the table from one another, and Rebuck's patience waned with Ike's failure to speak.

"She bought it?" Rebuck asked.

"Yeah," Ike muttered, turning his back on the penetrating eyes.

"Yeah, what?"

"She bought it. Ain't that what you asked?"

"Do you believe her?"

"Man, it ain't for me to believe the bitch."

"Lighten up, Ike. I'm just asking for your opinion."

"*Opinion?*" Ike turned about, slamming both hands onto the table. "You're askin' *my* opinion? When the fuck didja eva listen to *my* opinion? How many times did I tell ya not to go messin' with the man's head? How many times did I warn ya to play it straight? But you hadda come on with that jive imposition shit. An' what did it get ya? Waitin' an' wonderin' where the man's gonna stick his blade?"

"I'm glad intimidation isn't contagious."

"Man, it didn' have to come ta this. It shudda neva happened."

"Ike, I *made* it happen."

"Thinkin'. All that thinkin' made ya crazy."

"It would take a thousand years for you to understand."

"I understan' you're gonna die, fool! . . . Ya got no chance. Not a zillion ta one. Ya bought nothin' with that sanctuary shit. The *Man* makes the rules. Not the bitch."

Rebuck swung his legs over the bench. The action distracted Ike enough for Rebuck to take the lead in their conversation.

"Save the last rites bit, and tell me when you think he'll come."

"Man, there's no tellin'. Jus' know it'll be in the mothafuckin' darkness."

"Alone?"

"For sure. But ya'll think there's ten of him."

"And you don't believe the captain will go along with the trailer as sanctuary for Jessica?"

"Shhhhit."

"Meaning you think the captain will try to get to her."

"What *try?* The man wants her, he gets her."

"What do I do, watch?"

"You'll never know he snatched her till ya see her hangin' from a tree."

Rebuck sensed Jessica's presence behind the screen door and cautioned Ike with his eyes.

"Shit!" Ike cursed the heavens and straddled the bench.

"Ike," Rebuck spoke into a building silence, "there's never been a man who didn't have a weakness."

"Weakness? Is that what you're countin' on? Ain't ya once listened ta what I said? Super Bat sleeps in Hell. It'll take some thunderbolt comin' outta the motha sky ta do him in. An' ya can forget that eva happenin'. 'Cause the big cat with that kinda power ain't into helpin' no mothafuckin' atheist."

Rebuck had heard all the doom-filled predictions he could bear. His concern turned to Ike's welfare.

"What does it look like for you?"

"The bitch didn' say. Jus' ta do what I'm told or kiss mah bank and black ass goodbye."

"You'll come out of this okay, Ike."

"Yeah." Ike slumped.

"It never was your war."

"Man, you're blood. The best friend I eva had." Moisture collected in his black eyes. "Man, ya knows I love ya, Little Brotha. Ya know that. But there ain't nothin' ah can do."

"Ike, you made that clear from day one."

"But man, ya gotta expect sumpthin' from me."

"I expect you to catch that dream."

For the second time in the same day, Rebuck was unable to free heartfelt emotions: to tell Ike how much he cared for him, how much he loved him as the brother he'd never had.

"You had better get back, Ike, before—"

"Ah'm stickin'."

"Forget it!"

"Ah'm stickin'. Someone gotta bury your ass."

"It's not your war."

"It's mah life."

"Ike, you'd only hold me down."

"Man, ya can't get any more down but six feet."

Jessica had come out from the trailer, and to Ike's eyes she'd seemed to age ten years. He rose slowly from the bench and was surprised when Jessica focused her attention on him.

"Ike, do you remember that first night?"

She need not elaborate. "Yeah, Little Girl, I remember."

"The advice you gave me."

Ike forced a nod.

She moved away from Rebuck's side and stood before him. He looked down at her face, at the dark circles around her eyes and the paleness of her skin.

"Ike . . . please don't stay," she said.

Standing on her tiptoes, she kissed his cheek. Before Ike could react, she was halfway to the trailer home.

Rebuck led Ike toward the trail, and neither spoke until they'd reached it.

"This is it?" said Ike, knowing.

"This is it," Rebuck replied in a strained voice.

"Man, how come I don't feel like John Wayne ridin' off inta the sunset?"

"Maybe because you're not wearing a white hat." Rebuck cracked a nervous smile, extending his hand.

Ike smothered it with his own, and their locking eyes said things words could not. Then that confident, arrogant grin appeared on Rebuck's face. But Ike saw the stirring of a troubled soul.

"I'm going to make it, Ike."

"Sure. Sure ya are, Little Brotha."

"Jessica and I will survive."

" 'Cause yer heads are together," Ike retrieved his hand.

"The captain can't intimidate me."

"You're untouchable, Little Brotha." Ike backed toward the trail.

"The captain is vulnerable."

"You'll find his weak spot."

"I'm ready for him, Ike."

"Ready and waitin'." Ike turned, breaking into a slow trot.

"I'm going to kill the bastard!" Rebuck shouted after him.

"He's a dead man," Ike shouted back. "A dead man!" Breaking into a brisk jog, he repeated, "Dead man," in a weakening voice. "Dead man," he uttered between winded breaths, as tears flowed freely down his face.

The spirit of Halloween came with darkness. Across America, nightfall entered laughing. Orange and black colors were predominant in every city, town, and hamlet. Children dressed in their costumes and masks went trick-or-treating throughout the nation's neighborhoods. It was a time for sipping cider and telling tales of witches on brooms and black cats perched on wooden fences, goblins and skeletons prancing among the pumpkin and cornfields under a harvest moon. Halloween—when the living laughed at the dead.

But not everyone observed the October night as an evening of frivolity and folklore. The mission's neighbors regarded it as a religious commemoration: All Hallows, the eve to All Saints Day. For the inhabitants occupying the mission home—Trudy Ballin, her two executioners, and a petrified John Ragonese, it was a period of waiting—waiting for the arrival of "Red Thunder."

Halloween night for Ike Vesper was a room in a Philadelphia hotel, a bottle of tequila, deep depression, and much self-recrimination. For Ron Rebuck and Jessica Towne, final preparations for an encounter with a homicidal maniac had been completed.

At dusk, Ron Rebuck took up a commanding position atop a hill and searched the clouding night sky. At his side, the panting Dobermans, splashed by intermittent moonlight, presented an eerie warning to Halloween trespassers.

Hatless, dressed in khaki fatigues with dark tennis shoes replacing combat boots, Rebuck had decided not to apply cami-paint to his face and hands. He had a reason for not adhering to this and other instructions in the SEAL manual of guerrilla warfare: the captain was its author.

Armed with a Stoner machine gun, sufficient ammo for a close-range firefight, golfball-sized grenades, and a 9mm Beretta tucked into a shoulder holster, Rebuck at this very moment would trade it all for a rifle with a starlight scope. Not once had a rifle been included on the list of weaponry he and Ike had used in their missions for Gemmer. Rebuck knew that by now the captain had made a detailed study of the stolen firepower and equipment he'd disobeyed orders to destroy.

He's *only human*, Rebuck spoke silently to a doubting mind. He's no vampire. No Super Bat, as Ike called him. He's neither endowed with supernatural powers nor even truly unique. What he is, Rebuck convinced himself, is a ruthless destroyer. Yes, a man who flirts and walks with death. But as all living things sooner or later come to realize, the reaper knows no favorites.

As he waited in the night, flanked by the attack dogs with their stiletto-sharp canines flashing in the darkness, Rebuck gave final thought to Jessica's safety. His bluff to start the war without the captain had worked. Whether or not the captain would respect the trailer home as sanctuary for Jessica was now inconsequential. Jessica's fate depended solely on his own now.

He suddenly became aware of a light flickering in the distance. It came from beyond the perimeter of the mission property. A flashlight or the beam of a headlight, Rebuck couldn't tell which.

More lights, and he shifted his weight, stirring the dogs from their book-end rigidity. The holy people—with lanterns—praying in the fields—prayers for the dead, he was convinced. But when the lights began to scatter, forming a wide circle, it all took on a new meaning. "He's coming," Rebuck shivered in whispering, his ears tuned for a particular sound.

It came. First, ever so faintly. Then louder and louder until Rebuck felt the vibration in the night air and searched for the source of the harsh sound of blades slashing the ghostly sky.

He looked up at the moon and saw its light penetrate a wisp of cloud, giving off a diabolical haze. And then—as if by the devil's trickery—the cloud unmasked the moon and for a moment, for a breathtaking moment, a human figure streaked across the spectral sky as if it had tumbled from a star.

Rebuck crouched low to the ground. A chill reached his bones as he made out the silhouette of a man dangling from a darkly veiled chute, sailing over treetops and descending toward the circle of lights. The great assassin had landed.

After months of tedious preparation for this encounter with the devil's mortal twin, Rebuck now searched the recesses of his mind for possible flaws. There was only one potential weak spot that concerned him. Intimidation would mean certain death.

"Go!" Rebuck commanded, and the Dobermans bounded down the hill in search of the legendary invader.

A face painted in orange cami with black streaks under deadened eyes and across a rebuilt nose peered over thick brush at the abandoned cornfield ahead. A ghoulish smile spread slowly across Captain Claude Gemmer's face as he identified the disturbance in the cornfield.

Placing the "hunter's ear" sound device at his side, he released the backpack from his shoulders, removed the cartridgelike belt from his waist, and slipped off the infrared binoculars from around his dark turtleneck. Then he calmly rose and stepped into a clearing patched with moonlight, waiting for the killer dogs to pick up his scent.

They came at him with mouths frozen in killing snarls: four-legged nightmares anxious to sever his jugular with slashing teeth. The captain merely awaited their approaching fury with the feral smile of a grinning death's head.

"Hello, puppies," he greeted them, with razor-sharp steel flashing in both hands.

*　　*　　*

Rebuck listened to the savage sounds. The violent struggle seemed to be coming from the mission property, where he'd daily trained the dogs to seek and destroy. The fact that gunfire didn't materialize led his mind to the unthinkable. Had the dogs achieved what so many mortals had failed to do?

The raging below ceased with abruptness. Rebuck stiffened. Then a lone animal sound shrilled into the night. Rebuck's blood chilled as he suddenly remembered what Ike Vesper had said about the captain after a kill . . . how he would wail like a dog—or was it like the howling of a wolf?

Forced to assume the captain had survived, he would not deviate from his plan. He would now take the initiative. Flush out the captain and lure him toward the next trap. Unless, of course, he could kill him first.

Timing the cloud cover of the moon, he moved down the hill, his finger caressing the trigger of the Stoner with its banana clip of fifty rounds. With his eyes darting everywhere, his ears programmed to detect the slightest sound, he stopped short of the cornfield's perimeter. Here, he crouched behind a grassy knoll, and scanned the rows of cornshucks, looking like challenging sentries tipped with silver light.

"The man's everywhere, Little Brotha," Ike had said. *"An' before ya can swallow spit, the blade's cuttin' at your throat."* The warning, prompted by fear as it may have been, made sense. Rebuck knew he must not create a lull by staying in one place too long. He moved ahead, infiltrating the field, his instincts finely tuned, his blood on fire.

Reaching a point where the compass in his mind arrowed right, he scampered across a bald area to another row of forsaken corn. Squatting between dying shocks, he would now wait and listen. He had gone far enough as the hunter. It was time for the captain to take up the hunt.

Moonlight came and went a dozen times before he noticed something peculiar. Shifting his weight ever so gradually, he took a longer look at two cornshucks directly ahead, alongside a dried-up irrigation ditch. They appeared to him to be wet. But it was too early for dew. And why were the rest of the shucks as dry as parched bones?

An illusion, he reasoned. Nothing more than nightfall's trickery. Yet he waited in the stillness for the moon to once more break from the clouds and sprinkle the field with a spectrum of light. When it came, what he identified made the blood surge from his heart and pound in his brain. A weakness came to his knees as he stared at the color of crimson glinting in the moonlight.

Stay! Stay put! A voice within warned. *The captain is nearby.* But where? He shuddered with apprehension, listening for telling sounds of a presence. There was none. Not a murmur from the underbrush.

With each passing second, he began losing control of an unmanageable curiosity. The temptation to rise from a trained freeze position became a feverish obsession. Abandoning his programmed caution, he rose and waited breathlessly for another strike of moonlight.

What he saw in the first glimmer of light numbed blood and bone. Spiked to the tops of the two cornshucks were the heads of the Dobermans: both decapitated at the jugular, their eyes rolled back, their blood-dripping tongues hanging from death-gripped jaws.

Rebuck was frozen, shock crippling his trigger finger. Fear ate freely at his brain. Then it came—living, breathing, evil incarnate.

"Trick or treat!" the familiar, unmistakeable voice came from somewhere behind him.

Sweat burst from every pore and Rebuck felt his flesh burning. A choking sound stuck in his throat. The urge to whirl about blindly firing the machine gun turned in a moment into a sense of futility. He realized the pointlessness of any attempt to escape and closed his eyes. But not to pray. Above all, not to pray. Not to God—or man.

Was that it? Is that what the captain waited for? Expecting him to pray? The reason for the delay of pain, death, and oblivion?

"*Never*, Captain!" he swore through gritting teeth.

There was no response. Nothing but the fading echo of his voice to disrupt the gravelike stillness.

He waited for the light of the moon before venturing a deliberate about-face, the Stoner dangling at his side. His vision encompassed nothing human, and the unexpected stunned him as it would a condemned man who opens his eyes to find that the firing squad has vanished.

He sank to his knees, waiting for the feeling to return to the finger locked to the Stoner's trigger. He gave little thought as to why the captain had spared him—more to how a man with a limp had disappeared without the slightest sound. As if the captain possessed ghostly gifts—as if he were a man whose feet never touched the ground.

Right now he had to break out of the cornfield, lure the captain toward the next of his prearranged fronts. But just as he readied himself to sprint the distance, again came the unexpected.

"Trick or treat!" the captain called out again.

Rebuck spun to his right and fired, spraying the area with bursts of repeating rounds, whittling down the cornshucks to their starving roots.

From yet another direction the captain's voice boomed, "Trick or treat!"

With lightning reaction, Rebuck stood and fired, punishing the area from which the captain's voice had emanated with a devastating barrage. Dirt and cornshucks flew everywhere. And the crazed Rebuck kept firing until his clip went dry.

There came a total silence. The dreaded voice had been stilled. Confidence shone in Rebuck's eyes, for no one could have escaped the torrential hail of heat. Not man, beast—or ghost.

You're dead—you intimidating bastard! Rebuck said to himself, releasing the empty clip of the smoking Stoner. Still, doubt restrained his pent-up exuberance. Not until he saw the captain's body stiffening with rigor mortis would he truly believe the captain had "made the final trip."

He'd move on to the next front, and wait. Wait until

dawn if necessary. But when he turned eastward, a thousand ghosts shouted "Beware!"

"You missed, Lieutenant."

"You bastard," Rebuck screamed into the night.

What Rebuck had thought impossible deadened his brain. A loss of feeling in his legs buckled his knees and he slumped to the ground. The dank and repulsive odor Ike Vesper had referred to sucked out all the breath from his lungs. The taunting voice came again.

"Running out of tricks, Lieutenant?"

Regaining his breath, Rebuck took a bearing on the captain's voice. He was close. Too close.

"Are you the best?" the captain thundered.

For the second time, the captain's unwillingness to make a quick and easy kill gave Rebuck a chance to recuperate. His mind jolted into gear. The sweat drenching his body cooled. From a kneeling position, his hand went to the shoulder holster.

"Are you the goddamn best?"

Thirty . . . thirty-five feet. Front and center, Rebuck silently measured, steadying the 9mm Beretta.

"Will you disappoint me like the others?"

Rebuck rose an inch at a time. He would not be tricked by the dark shadows crossing his line of vision, and held his fire. *Once more, you bastard.*

It came with the swiftness only light could bring. What the black heavens surrendered to moonlight presented Rebuck with the ultimate Halloween sight of fright. All he could do was stare at his grotesque foe, standing between the cornshucks which held the decapitated Doberman heads, a sickly, inhuman grin fixed to the orange face which glowed in the night like some luminous and hellish pumpkin.

Screaming, Rebuck fired off round after round until the Beretta was empty. But the light had faded, and with it the bizarre target. That among the debris, bullets had further desecrated the Dobermans' gave the attending ghosts little to cheer about.

Rebuck had failed to react physically before the mind commanded—something which had been drilled into his subconscious throughout BUD and SEAL training. He had done precisely what the intuitive captain described in his required text when referring to men engaged in battle being confronted by a far more powerful enemy.

Frustrated by being intimidated by a man who mocked him with nothing short of suicidal courage, Rebuck reached for one of the grenades tucked safely inside a fatigue pocket. Pressing a thumb down on the luminous red dot to activate a delayed firing mechanism, he held it firmly in a sweaty fist, listening for a sound. Any sound.

Laughter, the kind to chill the most fearless, rang out. Rebuck homed in on the maniacal outburst. Eleven o'clock. Two hundred feet.

"What else, Lieutenant? What else do you have for me?" The captain's voice came from a point far from where the laughter had originated.

Rebuck adjusted his bearing to a closer point, and flung the grenade. The explosion ripped into the night. The time which lapsed between the voice and the miniature bomb's concussion was too fractional for anyone to have possibly eluded the razor-sharp, flying shrapnel. It would seem to have been a direct hit. The witnessing ghosts knew differently.

The maddening laughter erupted from still another area, and Rebuck's hand went instinctively for a second grenade. Suddenly, he paused. *The bastard's throwing his voice*, he connected. It was time to move onto the next front, where intimidation had no place.

Under the heckling of ghoulish laughter, Rebuck sprinted, dodging, sidestepping cornshucks and stumps without any loss of speed or balance. He broke into the clear and raced over open ground toward the mission pond, surrounded by trees vivid with streaking moonlight.

The captain emerged like a great snake from its hibernation hole. And, like the reptile, he now hungered.

Entrenched in a fortified bunker, Rebuck waited. Having survived the cornfield, the shifting of battlegrounds restored his perspective. Not a trace of fear lingered—in fact, he felt strangely content.

Peering out from the bunker's vantage point, he could barely make out the shapes of the surrounding trees. Directly to his front the pond was lost in a cavity of blackness. It didn't matter to Rebuck. Moonlight—or the lack of it—would have no effect on what had taken him months of meticulous preparation to achieve.

Dark shadows slithered down the trunks of trees. Ghostly forms rose from the depths of the quiet ground. Images of cloaked figures seemed to congregate on the pond's surface. Behind every nook and crook they appeared: faceless, formless, breathless, *apparitions all*. Ron Rebuck was aware only of the darkness and the whispers of a rising wind.

Suddenly, a fierce howling, as if the devil trumpeted the presence of a beloved son, shook the ground under Rebuck's feet. The demonic bellowing caromed from tree to tree, spiraling into the Halloween night, ending like the clashing of cymbals. Ron Rebuck smiled.

"You failed, Lieutenant!"

This time, the sound of the captain's voice did not tear up his insides and reduce him to a helpless state. He welcomed it.

"The moment of truth, and you failed, Lieutenant."

There was a sad, choking quality to the captain's voice. Rebuck noted it, and sat completely still, in total silence. Waiting.

"Thou shalt not survive!" the captain boomed.

Rebuck again felt himself drawing to a climax; one that he trusted would send the captain to the lowest ebb of the Hell which had given birth to him. Every breath he took trembled with anxiety as he listened intensely for a particular sound.

A humming, buzzing drone streaked from the trees and snaked across the ground. Almost simultaneously, the area was alive with light. A hidden array of spotlights, some deftly concealed in the trees, others ingeniously placed at ground level, lit up the battle site. Rebuck saw Gemmer standing by the pond's bank, motionless as a rigid deer, his face showing his bewilderment. It was the captain who now tasted the unexpected.

Claymore mines burst one after another in a domino effect, creating a hurricane force carrying chunks of metal, shards of steel, and thousands of ten-penny nails. Trees fell, lights popped, and foliage flew, as Rebuck anxiously awaited the finale to the sheer devastation he'd prepared. It didn't fail him as he felt the quaking of the concussions in the pond.

When it ended, there came stillness; a provocative calm, as long, pallid beams of moonlight revealed the mutilation of a once-tranquil scene.

Ron Rebuck rose from his protective pit and looked over its ridge, taking in the destruction of the grounds where mission students had spoken of love, peace, and a world without conflict. Now, Ron Rebuck thought only of death—the captain's.

The last of the spotlights, dangling from a high branch, dropped to the ground, hissing upon impact. Above, menacing clouds again blanketed the moon. Veiled in darkness, Rebuck crawled out of the bunker. He walked to the next front.

Shadows moved furiously throughout the scarred and brutalized ruins. They appeared to be grouping, gathering en masse, circling the pond as if summoned by death's call. A thousand ghosts.

The murmuring heard only by the dead ceased with a rippling of the water. A head slowly surfaced from the blackness, and a sudden streak of moonlight creased the face smudged with orange paint, creating the effect of a ghoul rising from the slime.

"Magnificent," said the captain, over the wailings and moans of embittered souls.

Ron Rebuck sat in pitch darkness. Propped against a corner wall inside the mission barn, once more he had to deal with time. Everything had worked. The generator in the compound had held up. The sensors detecting the captain's body heat had set off the lights, and the clay-mores had done the rest. Nothing that lived could have survived the shelling. But the temptation to return to the scene, to see for himself, went no further. No, he would remain in the barn's tomblike stillness, his mind geared for the incredible, awaiting the dawn when vampires lost their bite.

The night was young: a shade past eight. There was ample time for the captain to accomplish what he had dropped out of a witching sky to do before the stroke of midnight—if he still lived. Rebuck rejected the possibility, but . . .

Suddenly he heard a sound . . . a distinct sound of movement from outside. Again it came, and Rebuck clutched the weapon he'd hidden in the barn, certain that what prowled in the night was no four-legged beast. The incredible had happened.

The bizarre possibility relentlessly picked at his brain: needling, piercing, converting the heat to steam inside his body as if sweat poured from clamoring cells. His eyes shot sparks into the darkness as he listened feverishly for further proof of a stalking presence. All he heard were the faint barking of a dog, the creaking of the old and tortured wood, and the sound of his own breathing.

A tapping—or was it footsteps? He couldn't tell. He felt a draft of cold night air and lifted his nose, using it as a sensor to probe the chilling black silence. He knew almost at once the origination of the draft: having covered the barn's windows with tape, sealing cracks and openings on its entrance and sides, he had left only the roof unattended—and that, purposely.

His eyes rose in the darkness with alerted expectation. At first, he ignored the drifting apparitions he saw, but when a conglomeration of shadows manifested into a swirl-ing black mist, every nerve ending in his body torched with terror.

Before his disbelieving eyes, a storm arose from no-where. Ike Vesper would have sworn the twisting, whirling fury was created by a gale of icy breath blowing from the land of the forever doomed. Rebuck saw it as an illusion. But when the illusion revealed two faint beacons of light surfacing from layers of torrid blackness, Rebuck saw them as eyes—insane eyes that stared at him from a lightless Hell.

Captivated by the demonic glittering, Rebuck dared not close his eyes. He struggled for an explanation, something to tunnel his vision through the horrific scene, something to arrest a runaway mind. It came to him in an ironic manner, for what he had rejected as pure myth, a warning from Ike Vesper's portfolio of super-spookery, now returned to him with blessed enlightenment.

"He'll throw some unbelievable shit at ya, Little Brotha. Make ya panic and waste your load."

Rebuck's eyes danced irrepressibly upon the absurd whirlpool of blackness. He now saw it for what it was, nothing more than a magical smoke screen: unexplainably concocted, yet nevertheless an illusion. He rose to his knees.

"You must be the best!" the captain's voice erupted from the whirling abyss.

Rebuck carefully raised the steel casing of a weapon familiarly used to flush out eluders in caves and concealed bunkers. Determination gripped him with a fanatical yearning.

"Burn . . . burn, you bastard, burn!"

Awakened by strange sounds in the night, a neighboring Amish farmer held back his brood and looked down the hill upon the blazing barn. The contempt he held for the mission people pervaded his deeply lined face. God's will, he silently praised, but then his eyes narrowed. What he saw standing on the roof, encircled by flames, stole his breath. His entire body rippled with chills. For what howled above the roaring fire bore little semblance to mortal man: rather, it appeared to be a multihorned gargoyle immune to the fiery tongues. Totally bewitched by the awesome spectacle, a Biblical name for the devil came from the depths of his soul, passing through trembling lips . . . *"Beelzebub."*

* * *

518

Ron Rebuck had had his fill of darkness, ominous shadows and hellish illusions. Contrary to his plan, the compound blazed with light. Every bulb burned inside the trailer home.

He sat in the kitchenette booth, withdrawn into himself. Two 9mm Brownings and a Magnum .357 lay before him, but it was the half-empty bottle of tequila he reached for. A swig of the Mexican madness worthy of Ike Vesper gave no relief from an evening of violence and terror. It had now come down to a final stand . . . one last chance to overcome a seemingly indestructible foe.

The hum of the generator ceased abruptly. The compound went dark. The hunter had come for his kill.

"No sanctuary!" the captain shouted with maddening glee. "No sanctuary for the girl! . . . No sanctuary! No sanctuary!" he repeated over and over, throwing his voice as if there were ten of him surrounding the trailer home.

Ron Rebuck calmly reached for the tequila. He took a moderate swallow and let it settle before rising from the booth.

Moonlight struck the compound, and Rebuck sensed the deadly presence at the window. He looked up to see the ghastly face, the frightful eyes and sardonic smile. Yet he merely regarded the unearthly presence with exhausted silence. His deadened nerves gave fear no place to feed. He was now ready to take on the relentless maniac in a most unorthodox manner.

The captain's fiendish leering changed abruptly to an odd and startled look. His thin, cruel lips twisted with perplexity. Confusion touched his devious mind as he studied the sight of a naked Ron Rebuck.

With his hands behind his head, the fingers entwined in a prisoner's lock, Ron Rebuck stepped out into the moonlight. The chilly night air prickled his warm flesh, causing a slight rattling of his teeth. From the corner of his wary eye, he saw *him* standing next to the silenced generator.

"No sanctuary for the girl!" the captain shrilled.

Rebuck dared not speak. He moved brazenly toward the

519

trail, leaving the gaping captain convulsed in frustration and fury.

Rebuck had crossed the trail and was heading west when the explosions thundered in the night. He'd set the timing device to give him ample time to get clear of the devastation of the trailer home. The thought that Gemmer's corpse lay among the debris was wishful thinking. Maintaining the awkward position of surrender, he continued on, and soon became aware of the pursuing captain, who darted from tree to tree, keeping pace with him.

Rebuck came out of the thick woods and saw his destination. The far trees beyond the open field stood in a luminous mist. Knowing his only chance of surviving was to reach the mission cemetery, he moved onward.

"Not another step, Lieutenant!" the captain commanded.

Rebuck kept moving. He would not falter—to do so would surely end his life. The moon had sided against him. Regardless of the stories telling of the captain's kills in the darkness, tonight was the exception. *He* was the exception. The great assassin's predictable flair called for an execution witnessed by the heavens and by the hell of Earth. With death at his back, his heart roaring in his ears, Rebuck lengthened his stride and ventured farther into the moonlit field.

There came no follow-up to the captain's command, but Rebuck did not look back. Nor above, where the rolling clouds splashed across the moon like black waves. He stared straight ahead, where the silhouettes of encircling high hedges and lofty trees appeared as a life-saving oasis. With his arms pumping in rhythm to his legs, he realized that he was running—fleeing from a demon with a limp.

The sudden loss of moonlight caught him racing blindly in the blackness. Naked, he ran, his feet sailing over rough terrain. He was actually out of control when his foot hit a rock and he hurtled forward, tumbling onto the hard, cold ground, somersaulting to a stop.

He lay motionless in a fetal position, consumed by intolerable pain. The nasty gash on his toe felt as if it were on fire. Blood oozed from the surface wounds at his elbows and knees, and red sparks shot off in his head. Struggling to his feet, he suddenly felt terribly cold. Worse, he'd lost his bearings. He looked around him, into the impenetrable blackness, and listened—listened for the merciless hunter.

Naked, bleeding, he felt helpless, lost in some God-forsaken maze. About him, nothing stirred; there was neither movement nor murmuring from the underbrush. As if life had stopped—or never existed. As if death had forever claimed this spot in the world. Was this what Ike Vesper had meant when he said, "You'll be dead and never know it"?

A sound penetrated the strange void. Rebuck groped for the identity of the welcome sound. "Bats," he whispered. "No, crows," he said, recalling their nests in the trees around the burial grounds. Over the sound of the blood pounding in his ears, he heard the flapping of their wings, monitored the direction of their flight, and once again navigated through the darkness.

A long beam of moonlight sifted through the running clouds, touching down upon the cemetery grounds. A mist seemed to gather from out of the ominous darkness; twisting, whirling into a thousand ghostly forms.

From the farthest corner of the memorial acre, Ron Rebuck's eyes were glued to the glinting sword pointing toward the heavens. He watched the light trickle down the stainless steel of the statue, touching the marbled muscular arm, then slowly unveiling a face that was virile, rugged . . . so unlike that of a pious Christ.

The awesome statue of Michael, the Archangel, had no spiritual effect upon him. He saw the impressive symbol as a Biblical fantasy created by man; a myth which had obsessed his father—a myth which had led to his murder. The effect was to awaken his senses to the realization that he'd truly beaten the odds. Guided by the crows, he'd arrived at his final destination. There would be no retreat from here.

The crackling leaves under his feet set off the crows

from their treetop nests. Their caws of protest filled the shadowy grounds. Surrounded by the dark, misty apparitions, Rebuck moved to the side of his father's grave, away from the hovering, marble-winged goliath, and waited for the dealer of death.

There came a sudden shower of moonlight, and an illusion flashed before him. It manifested itself in the person of the captain, who appeared to have stepped out from the statue, staring at him with tiger's eyes.

The captain drifted from the statue and stood across from Rebuck, regarding his nudity and position of surrender with an expression that was both puzzled and excited.

"You are not tricking me, Lieutenant?"

Rebuck's expression betrayed nothing.

"No, Lieutenant." Certainty rang in his guttural voice. "Your hate is too great."

As if sensing something hidden, the captain looked back at the statue, then at the ground adjoining the grave before him. His eyes rose to look at Rebuck. An expression of malevolent cruelty replaced the suspicion on his face.

"You have bloodied me, Mister!"

Rebuck took note of the dark, wet stains where shrapnel had torn through fabric and into the captain's arms and thighs.

A bitter smile crossed Gemmer's lips, and Rebuck braced for another blast of wrath. It came with both anger and shame.

"Did you think I was always a cripple?" Gemmer shouted.

Aware as he was of the man's unpredictability, Rebuck was stunned as the captain's body was suddenly wracked by violent spasms. Then, in the blinking of an eye, the convulsions had ceased, and Rebuck saw that sardonic smile spread across Gemmer's face with quiet ferocity.

"You failed, Lieutenant. Twice I gave you the opportunity to strike me down. *Twice* death was at your command, and you floundered like a quivering sheep."

He paused to further examine Rebuck's nudity and prisoner's stance curiously. Then, as if seized by an uncontrollable passion, his face contorted with rage. "You shall not surrender!" he bellowed.

Rebuck fended off fear, holding his unwavering position.

"Where is the girl?" the captain shrieked.

Not a muscle quivered on Rebuck's face as he took the full brunt of the captain's demonic glare. They continued to stare at one another until a sweeping calm came over the captain.

"You see, Lieutenant," Gemmer said softly, "I chose you as I had chosen him. An officer, like yourself. A major in the South Korean Army. An R.O.K. Ranger. An ally in Vietnam . . . a most worthy challenger." Again his face reverted to anger and contempt. "You shall not shame the brave!"

What now concerned Rebuck was the heaviness of his arms, the growing numbness of his clasped hands, and the coldness of his feet. Would he be able to move at the necessary moment?

The captain snorted and went on. "He was good, Lieutenant. Exceptional. Trained from childhood to kill." He paused, eyeing Rebuck with craft and malice. Rebuck was expressionless, completely still. But he was braced to react at the slightest advance toward him.

"Unlike you, Lieutenant," the captain continued, "I found him lacking. The enemy to him was abstract, a matter of politics. Nothing more. He lacked that precious venom which blackens your heart. Which runs so pure in your veins." His eyes now lingered on every moonlit feature of Rebuck's face; a deep and piercing scrutiny which found no answers, no clues. "Pure hate is never tainted! It conquers the impossible!" He whirled around, his face contorting as if he'd been seized with great pain.

The captain's wrath left as it came, mercurially. He now spoke calmly and deliberately. "Eternally in search of a worthy challenger, I had to find out if this valiant man was truly the best. However, it became necessary to create a potent motivation for him to accept my challenge. Yes, Lieutenant, I had to instill in him the hatred which burned into your soul at the time of your father's death. I am talking about the purest of all emotions, that which motivates the mortal to accomplish immortal deeds. The unyielding fever which only a vengeance satisfied will cool.''

He paused—a lengthy pause. When it became apparent Rebuck would not break his silence, Gemmer's face flushed with rage. Heat roared from his throat. ''You shall not disgrace the honor of that brave man!''

As Rebuck expected, the fiery indignation consuming the captain left him with the release of a deep sigh. The confession of a morbid deed came without remorse.

''I once told you in a place of hallowed ground how I made a study of pure hatred—what makes such a passion so volatile, untainted, and true. Realizing it must stem from man's vulnerability, and knowing that love represents the most vulnerable aspect of man's nature, it was quite easy for me to make that valiant man rise to superhuman heights of hate. I merely slit the throats of his wife and children.''

Leaving Rebuck to dwell upon this horrid revelation, the captain limped toward the statue. Rebuck's moment had come, but he failed to react swiftly. The command from brain to feet came too late. The captain eyed the statue with suspicion and hastily returned. Amidst the witnessing ghosts, the dark shadow of the reaper loomed forward to make another claim.

The captain's hand went slowly to his throat. From under the tattered turtleneck, he yanked a gold chain from his neck.

''The memoirs of an honorable confrontation, Lieutenant.''

Rebuck forced a glance at the two shiny ornaments encased in separate glass cases dangling from the chain.

''The sacred remains of that fighting man who first bloodied me.''

As Rebuck looked past the ornaments being held out toward him, it took all his courage to study the face only Hell could produce.

The captain now held the chain in both hands and looked down at the glossy ornaments as if cherishing precious stones. ''I learned much from him, Lieutenant.

So very much . . . he used the environment with a prowess I had never before encountered. A true master of the silent freeze—a wizard of illusion. Half man, half leopard, he did so much damage with so little.''

The captain now spoke in a lower voice, yet with great emotion. ''He left his mark, Lieutenant . . . and I honorably carry the scar.''

Like an unexpected wind, the captain's body quaked with unharnessed rage. Then, as he had in that Maryland cemetery, he kicked the ground with his bad foot. Harder and harder he kicked as he let out an appalling howl which broke into a tremulous quivering and ended in his wounded cry, ''He made me a cripple!''

Rebuck's arms dropped heavily to his sides. His mind more than his body was weary . . . weary from the ordeal of witnessing the changing, bizarre actions of this deadly madman.

Repulsion spread across the captain's face. He now looked upon the naked Rebuck as prey reduced to a helpless and frozen state. Yet his disgust was momentary; the climax to a night which had promised him so much would not be prematurely terminated by a quick and unchallenged kill.

He found solace in the ornaments in his cupped hands. Fondling them, he began mumbling to himself. The incoherent muttering continued until clarity shaped his words. ''So long . . . so very long . . . for so many years I've worn these medals—these badges of honor.''

Rebuck heard only the monotone of the captain's gibberish.

''Yes,'' the captain agreed with himself. ''Yes, there were others—valiant men with serious potential. But none equaled this brave man.'' His voice fell off, his eyes dropped softly to the ornaments in his hand. Just as he appeared to be lost within himself, his face hardened like gleaming marble. His hand closed over the ornaments, squeezing tightly, then he shook his fist at the blackened heavens and bellowed, ''Only he brought me to the brink. Only he!''

The captain's eyes returned to Rebuck. That sinister smile curved his lips.

"Then came you, Lieutenant—then came you."

Rebuck felt a strange sense of submission, a withdrawal like never before. There was a lightness, as if he were floating. As if the very life of thought and will would shortly leave him. A yearning soul called for its release.

The captain's smile vanished. He held out the ornaments for Rebuck's review. "Yes, Lieutenant, this brave man made me a cripple—and I took his eyes. What shall I take from you?"

Suddenly, the captain held two knives, as if he had plucked them out of the night air. He juggled them from hand to hand. The blades, stained with dog's blood, glinted in the reflecting moonlight, but failed to bring any change to Rebuck's even gaze.

The hurled knife came as a blur to the naked eye. It lanced into the fleshy part of Rebuck's thigh. The shock activated his senses. His pain-filled cry shot into the night, titillating only the grim reaper and his mortal ambassador.

Rebuck pulled out the blade, widening the wound. There would be no tourniquet to stop the bleeding.

"Go for it, Lieutenant. Rid yourself of at least one object of hatred," the captain goaded.

Rebuck tore his eyes from the gaping wound and met the captain's arrogant sneer.

"Do it, Lieutenant. Finish the task so many have failed to."

Rebuck's bloody hand relaxed. The dagger slipped to the ground. His obvious unwillingness to accept the challenge enraged the captain.

"You shall not disgrace the valorous men before you! Here, you will live or die!"

As if the intolerable pain from the clotting wound was not enough, Rebuck felt a building nausea and dizziness.

"Pick it up, Lieutenant!"

Rebuck's clouding eyes stared in rebuttal.

"You must be that special human my destiny foretold

of. That particular mortal to end my future in a world of mediocre men. You *must* be the best!''

Cold paralysis gripped Rebuck's naked body. Despair cast its long shadow upon his lifeless face.

"Damn you, Lieutenant. Deliver me!''

No greater desire possessed Ron Rebuck.

The fury within the captain ran with such turmoil that every nerve flamed, every muscle spasmed. Madness warped his face. Saliva foamed at the corners of his mouth. Yet the hand holding the dagger was rock steady.

The observing ghosts no longer voiced their windlike murmurs. Even the darkened trees appeared to hang in cold silence. The vigilant reaper drifted into the eerie light, ready to claim the dead.

Rebuck's eyes suddenly livened. The captain's one vulnerability—his flair, his need for drama—had presented itself. The ghoulish captain limped to the statue and stood leering at the Archangel's great marble face. Rebuck knew there would be no other chance. He had to act. *Swiftly.*

The captain began to rant in an unknown tongue: strange and incoherent words known to the formless witnesses, who awaited their revenge on one who dared to speak out his soul. Driven by a savage bitterness, he kicked the statue's base. Again and again he kicked at it, howling from the self-inflicted pain, his rage out of control.

Rebuck looked down at the ground with the fixed stare of the hunted. He saw the quivering, silver-tipped blades of grass as beckoning fingers. But desperation moored in his eyes, futility in his nerves. The signal from brain to feet was seemingly smothered by a mutinous soul.

The captain's insane fury receded. He leaned back and glared at the awesome, hovering monument of strength and righteousness as if daring man's image of an archangel to breath with life.

"Call upon him, Lieutenant. Call upon your murdered father's champion. Let the great defender of heaven take up your defense.''

Rebuck did not respond, and contempt filled the captain's eyes. "Come to life, Archangel. Bring down that mighty sword. Prove you are not myth, or let it be known that Lucifer drove your cowardly soul from heaven.''

The cold, dead stare of the marble eyes, the hardened lips, seemed to further infuriate the captain. Bitten by frustration, he coughed up a glob of sputum and spat it high onto the glittering face. The bloody mucus dripped from the bridge of the nose, and for a moment, an illusionary moment, the marble eyes blazed with anger.

A quickness came to Rebuck. Strength rose within him. The night of treachery showed promise of one last trick.

The captain turned from the statue in disgust and looked down at the senior Rebuck's grave. He began to cackle; ghoulish-sounding laughter. With his free hand, he zipped open the fly to his fatigue pants. Releasing a doglike penis, he proceeded to urinate upon the memorial plot.

With an impetuous jerking of his head, the captain leered at the wavering Rebuck. He was now, and only now, ready to take his treat.

With a silent scream, Rebuck fell forward, caving through the rigged grass, vanishing into the ground.

Struck by the unexpected, the captain stood wild-eyed, floundering in disbelief. His eyes raced to the statue, and slowly returned, brightened by knowledge. A smile, bare of evil, exuding an inner peace, eclipsed the cruelty of his scarred face. Finally he'd encountered the best.

The statue burst with blinding light. The deafening explosion blew mythical angel and man into bits and pieces. The horrible finale to the witching night rained mortar, marble, flesh, and bones. The captain had been reduced to carrion for scavenging beasts, and a thousand dancing ghosts jubilantly celebrated their revenge.

A tongue of moonlight lapped into the pit. An exhausted, wounded Ron Rebuck felt only the beating of a liberated heart. Shifting his weight off the detonator he'd activated in his fall, he took the quivering and blanketed Jessica into his arms. Here they would remain, locked in embrace until the breaking dawn.

PART IV

IN THE NAME OF THE FATHER

CHAPTER 43

NOVEMBER FIRST—ALL SAINT'S DAY.

Six men carrying a large rubber bag converged upon the battle-scarred compound. Ron Rebuck looked out from the motor home's front window, past the smoking remains of the trailer, and watched them place the bag onto the picnic table. He knew there was nothing saintly about its contents.

A curious Jessica Towne peered over his shoulder. "Who are they, Ron?"

"'Pallbearers."

"The captain—"

"What's left of him," Rebuck concluded.

Jessica laid her head against his shoulder. "When will this ever end?"

From the corner of his eye, Rebuck saw a flash of sunlight on chrome. A moment later, the familiar black van pulled down the dirt trail and came to a halt.

"It's Ike!" Jessica said excitedly, rising.

"No, Jessica—it's not Ike."

Trudy Ballin stepped out of the van. Followed by two male escorts carrying Uzi machine guns, she moved rapidly from the trail to the picnic table. The awaiting men fanned out and she sat down on the bench. Her bodyguards flanked her like deadly bookends.

"Loo—tenant!" she sang out.

Jessica's hand went to Rebuck's arm. "Is that her?" she whispered.

Rebuck turned from the window, flinching from the pain of his flesh wound. "Jessica, no matter what happens out there—don't say a word."

531

Trudy Ballin eyed the limping Rebuck's approach with wary admiration. She barely glanced at Jessica.

"Sit down, Lieutenant. At this wake, you are the guest of honor."

"I'll stand," said Rebuck, averting his eyes from the body bag.

"We thought it best not to show the corpse. The remains are in too many pieces. But take my word for it, the captain is quite dead."

Rebuck's attention shifted to the two men with her. He could feel their eyes on him.

"Which brings us to the will, Lieutenant. You're the sole beneficiary."

Rebuck looked at her in surprise. "What could he possibly leave to me?"

"First and foremost, your life—as well as that of all of those . . ." Ballin's glance swept over Jessica, "near and dear to you."

"My mother—where is she?" Rebuck demanded.

"She is safe, you have my word on it," Trudy said. "However, there is one condition you must satisfy before you can see her."

"Which is?" Rebuck said, bristling.

"You and the girl must remain here until after the national elections—that's a mere six days."

"So that's the catch," Rebuck said. "And if I don't agree?"

"Then your great victory will have been in vain."

"And what about Ike Vesper?"

"Chief Vesper no longer concerns you, Lieutenant."

"Is he alive?" Rebuck pressed.

"There is no mention of Chief Vesper in *this* will."

Rebuck decided not to push it any further. Knowing these people, his best strategy would be to keep silent—it would probably be the best way to bring an end to the macabre disposition of Gemmer's will. Anyway, Ike could take care of himself.

Trudy Ballin smiled. "The motor home is yours, Lieutenant," she said. "The bill of sale and registration will be given to you before you leave. Everything else, remains. I have a complete list of the items which must be turned over to me, including passports and other identification.''

As Rebuck studied her wickedly alluring smile, he saw the fangs behind the sensuous lips.

''Do you recall the captain's promise, Lieutenant? What he promised you one cold night last February?''

The memory of his first meeting with Gemmer was something he'd never forget.

'' 'A gift more precious to you than wealth'—wasn't that it, Lieutenant?''

Jessica felt the adrenalin running in Rebuck's body. Her hand slipped from his stiffening arm.

''The captain often spoke of you, Lieutenant. He'd refer to you as someone special. I remember the time he ranted and raved over your calling him 'Claude.' But deep down, he admired your guts. Actually, if the captain had been capable of liking anyone, it was you.''

Rebuck was aware of her tactical spiel. She had perfected the captain's technique of speaking in gibberish before making a deadly point.

''Tell me, Lieutenant, did you really know what was going on? I mean, how were you able to counter the captain's every move?''

While Rebuck kept his silence, Jessica found herself hungering to know. Hoping to discover what Rebuck had *not* told her.

''Cody Walker, Reverend Tho, and Veep Siler—what *didn't* they have in common with Langly, the faith healer?''

Though Rebuck had reasoned that Langly's death was not authorized by the captain's superiors, he saw no reason to answer her. He shrugged.

''Langly was a gift the captain took for himself. Unfortunately, a pressing priority kept the captain from presenting you with your gift—your very special gift.''

Her pause was too obvious, her smile too revealing. Ron Rebuck gritted his teeth in anticipation.

''I've never known the captain to break his word. A promise was sacred to him. So, Lieutenant, as sole executor of the captain's will, I find his promise an obligation which demands satisfaction.'' Her smile tightened. ''Consider it done, Lieutenant. I will take great pleasure in cheating that old bastard out of a natural death.''

Rebuck was too exhausted to react. Having survived the night of All Hallows, endured the hellacious workings of a maniac, Trudy Ballin was too soon a demon to encounter. He turned from her deadly smile, limping away from an individual he judged to be as sick, or perhaps even sicker than the captain.

''We're not finished, Lieutenant!'' Ballin snapped.

Rebuck half turned to see one of her armed guards double-time to the black van. As he reached in and pulled a man out, Rebuck's interest was instantly renewed. An alarmed Jessica drifted to his side. Both watched the captive, gagged and bound at the wrists, dragged toward them, then forced to his knees at their feet. Ron Rebuck looked away from the gaunt and agonized face of John Ragonese.

''This man owes a great deal of money,'' Ballin charged. ''He blames his failure to pay on you, Lieutenant. He keeps talking about a codicil to your father's will. I told him it was a fake. The captain took the names of the witnesses from tombstones.''

Rebuck had all along assumed the codicil to be phony.

''Still,'' Ballin continued, ''the codicil played an important part in the captain's initial strategy. What better place for you to live, Lieutenant? So close to your father's grave. A masterful plan, don't you agree?'' Her eyes fell upon the pathetic, kneeling figure. ''The captain gave this gutless coward every reason to kill you.''

Rebuck had yet to look down upon the bearded, sweaty face of John Ragonese. His eyes remained fixed on Ballin, his expression inscrutable.

''Have you a solution to this man's problem, Lieutenant? It must interest you. After all, the money this faker owes, he now owes to you.''

Rebuck refused to say anything which might delay Ballin's

departure. He ignored with effort Jessica's concern for the mission director.

"Ron, please?" she whispered, breaking her silence for the first time.

Rebuck looked down at Ragonese. Everything he hated was represented by the petrified man groveling at his feet.

Trudy Ballin rose from the table. "That's all—for the moment," she said. "It will be necessary for me to meet with you again, Lieutenant, to discuss a few . . . details. In the meantime just remember that as long as you both remain here for the next six days, you are free. My sincere congratulations."

Rebuck became caught between her departure and the pallbearers gathering at the table to carry off the captain's remains. Jessica's attention was drawn to the lone man hovering over the wild-eyed John Ragonese. She froze in terror when the man pulled out a pistol and held it to the back of Ragonese's skull. "Do I blow this wimp shit away?" he asked.

Trudy Ballin stopped halfway to the van. "That pleasure belongs to the lieutenant."

535

CHAPTER 44

NED WORTHY told his story. The first reactions from the four men who had gathered in the elaborate office of the president of International Broadcasting Corporation were unanimous. Worthy was out of his mind. But the veteran television producer had not taken it this far to be rejected without a good battle. Before he surrendered, it would take the man seated behind the curved desk to shoot him down.

Yale Norman never felt far from his growing-up years in Brooklyn. Under the hand-tailored suit and silk shirt was a stomach that had taken many a blow during his boyhood on the mean streets. At forty-three, he was named president of the network, and for the past seven years his stewardship had been impeccable. With an education from both the streets and the university, he was known to be tough, demanding—and unmistakably fair.

Norman's eyes had not left Worthy. It was as if he read the man's soul. When he finally looked away, his words were directed to the white-haired man seated to his left. "What is Ned really telling us, Austin?"

Austin Branch, president of the IBC network news, smiled expansively. "It's preposterous," he said.

Ned Worthy's face reddened. "The story of the century, Austin, and you call it preposterous?"

"Ned, let's be practical."

"Three days to air time and you expect Sales to tell the sponsors we're shelving a ready-to-go show for a live telecast?"

"Hey, what are we talking about, some stupid sitcom?

'Up to Now' is number one. You lose a sponsor, you've got ten waiting in line.''

"Ned, even if I liked the idea, the affiliates would pre-empt our pre-empt with 'Leave it to Beaver.' ''

"Austin, I think you're getting senile. Have you forgotten about the Libyan crisis? How many sponsors did you lose on that one?''

"Ned, just what do you have? *Billy Hale?* His last testimony? His last hurrah?''

"Haven't you been listening? Billy's sitting on a time bomb!''

"Fine. Tell Hale to give us a list of the names, and I'll do more than reconsider.''

"What am I, some rookie producer to hammer on?''

Austin Branch threw up his hands. "He's all yours, Legal.''

Ned Worthy's attention focused on the two men seated off in a corner. The elder man, chief counsel for the network, took up the challenge.

"Mr. Worthy, from what I can deduce, you intend to pre-empt the show scheduled to air on November fifth with Billy Hale.''

"Jesus, how'd you know?''

"Mr. Worthy, feel free to jump in whenever you like. But tell me, does November fifth have a special meaning to you?''

Worthy rose from his chair and turned to Austin Branch. "Do you get a cut in his retainer for stupid questions?''

"I can assure you, Mr. Worthy, my question is quite relevant. What I am referring to is the date. It happens to be two days before the national elections.''

"So?''

"It gives little or no time for the recipients of Reverend Hale's charges to make their rebuttals.''

"They're fucking conspirators! Killers!''

"Now, hold on, Ned.'' Austin Branch exercised his departmental authority. "Counselor has a valid point.''

"Like a damned needle, he does!''

"Ned, perhaps there is a way,'' Branch said, to everyone's surprise. "What if you made it a challenge match? A debate between Hale and Harley Lombard?"

"Harley Lombard is Virtues, Inc. Virtues, Inc., is sponsored by the conspiracy."

"All the more reason for Reverend Lombard to appear."

"Austin, if word gets out that Billy Hale is doing 'Up to Now,' he's a dead man."

"And just when do we tell the viewing public—five minutes before air time?"

"The day before. Flood our TV and radio promo spots. Even some special-bulletin stuff."

Yale Norman cleared his throat to interrupt. "Your final opinion, Counselor. And please be brief."

"The network could be subpoenaed with a conspiracy count of its own. At least to the extent of a Senate investigation. Not to mention the FCC."

The younger lawyer looked up from his yellow pad. "May I ask Mr. Worthy something?"

Norman waved a hand to proceed.

"Mr. Worthy, where is Reverend Hale presently?"

The blood rushed to Worthy's face. Distrust splashed in his eyes. "None of your goddam business where!"

"You lose," said Norman, turning his attention away from the young lawyer and upon Austin Branch. "Any change of mind?" he asked.

"Religion's hot."

"How hot?" Norman pressed.

"God is a hot property today. Religion's become a potent product over television. Hell, we carry some of those evangelical programs over our cable subsidiary."

"And?" Norman pushed him to conclude.

"Unless it's a debate between Hale and Lombard, it's not for us, Yale."

Yale Norman sat back in his leather chair and inspected his carefully manicured fingernails. "Ned, how long did Billy Hale promise to sit on this?"

"Until the day before the telecast."

"And if you tell him you were unable to sell the boys in the ivory tower?"

"I won't have to. If he doesn't see any promo of his appearing on 'Up to Now,' he gives it to the New York *Times,* or the Washington *Post.* And we've blown a broadcasting blockbuster."

"If you were to get the green light, which of the 'Up to Now' reporters would host the show?" Norman asked.

"Crown, Browder, or Vanderhaven. It doesn't matter."

Austin Branch took the cue. "Vanderhaven would be the best choice . . . hell, he's heard it all. Billy Hale would have to do some magic act to convert Vandy."

Yale Norman took a long, hard look at Worthy, like a judge weighing his sentence. Tall and lanky, he got out of the chair and went to the large window to peer out at the Hudson River. At first, his words seemed to be for himself.

"There is so much religious bullshit being dumped on people these days. God knows we in the media have rolled out the royal carpet for these televangelists. Hell, if Billy Hale, the father of them all, will come down on those sorry sons of bitches, it just might give people—the silent majority—something to cheer about." He turned from the window, looking at no one in particular. "I don't know about you, but I get sick to my stomach seeing those pious, evangelizing bastards stinking up the airwaves." He turned to Ned Worthy. "Go for it, Ned. Shove it right up their holy asses!"

CHAPTER 45

IKE VESPER licked the salt from his quivering lips. The straining of his stomach muscles relaxed. Wishful thinking set sail in his mind. He could cry a river, curse until hoarse, yet nothing would alter his deep, tortured, anguish. Ron Rebuck, Jr., had made the ultimate trip. The captain had done Little Brotha in. He would now have to get on with his own life, and pursue that dream.

Holed up in a Philadelphia motel room for the past two nights, he suffered from claustrophobia which fed off his despair. Trudy Ballin's vague instructions did not restrict him to the motel, though someone with the code name "Trapper" was supposed to deliver information on an assignment there. Feeling suddenly daring, if not rebellious, Vesper decided that "Trapper" would have to track him down.

So Ike spent the remaining daylight hours traveling from one movie theater to another, most of them nearly empty, staring down oddballs who chose to sit next to him. Following a barbecued sparerib dinner in a run-down eatery, Ike was off to Cool's Cabaret with its connecting and sleazy motel, located in the heart of a combat zone. Frequented by sailors and merchant marines, Cool's featured bad booze and fast women. No stranger here, Ike had made half the line of girls who paraded their bodies on a dilapidated stage to soul music provided by a four-piece band whose only claim to fame was failing a screen test for a movie called *Pete Kelly's Blues*.

Although fights here were as common as the cockroaches climbing the walls, Ike kept adrift from the riffraff: drunken

540

sailors running off their mouths and Cool's generally scab patrons. He had come strictly for female companionship—tonight more than ever. But what he failed to notice, as he scanned Cool's clientele, was a wiry, fair-haired man in his early thirties, seated off in a far corner and partially hidden by the stage—taking interest in Ike's every move.

The weasel-eyed man who handled Cool's transactions gave Ike the lowdown on a new dancer, a soft-eyed, silky, brown-skinned girl. She was diminutive but big-busted, with a slight overbite—characteristics which all of Ike's ex-wives had possessed.

Making the arrangements for a condom, a bottle of tequila, and the girl, Ike followed her through a back door and into the motel's raggedy entrance. A black man of Ike's proportions gave them a key and they stopped at a door midway down the poorly lighted hall.

The dingy room had no windows. The walls were painted a murky, peeling brown. The feature event was a large bed.

Ike watched her slip out of a cheap, slit dress. She was without panties and bra, and her tits were even larger than he'd imagined. She wasted no time in informing him that she was into things which "Cool's" price list didn't include. If he had something kinky in mind, she was quite amenable. But when Ike came out from the pigeonhole of a bathroom, she quickly introduced limitations. That he was big, black, and enormously endowed, she could handle. But the flak jacket with its bulging pockets, and the small Beretta strapped to his shin, gave her reason to wonder whether he had come to fuck or to fight.

"I ain't into commando shit, honey," she ruled out, shaking her head.

Ike bent over to unstrap the Beretta from his shin. Suddenly, some inner sense shouted danger. Motioning for the puzzled girl to move into the bathroom, he pulled the gun from its holster. Catlike, he moved to the side of the door.

The bolt to the door tore loose under an expert and savage kick. The wiry man who had been watching Ike in the cabaret burst into the room, dropping into a military stance, his weapon aimed at the unoccupied bed. Before he could react, Ike had the barrel of the Beretta held against his throat.

"Drop the load—on the bed!" Ike demanded.

Instead, the man carefully tucked the Walther PPK into his belt. "Chill down, Chief. Code name's 'Trapper.' "

Ike eased the Beretta from the man's throat. "You gotta dangerous way of deliverin' orders."

"The word on you is that you're into whores. Had to find out for myself just how vulnerable my new cadre chief really is."

"Sheeeeeit," said Ike, returning his piece to its holster. The word "cadre" had clued him as to Trapper's military background. "Army?" he asked, sizing him up.

"Special forces."

"Green Beret?" Ike soured.

"Black."

Ike shrugged with mild approval.

"Get dressed," Trapper ordered.

"Man, I'm paying by the hour. What's the deal?"

Trapper stopped at the broken door. "Before that whore in the bathroom scrambles your brains, we'll talk in the bar."

Ike grabbed his pants off a chair and sat on the edge of the bed, grumbling to himself. As he cursed the timing of his future strike force commander, he was unaware of the girl creeping out from the bathroom and eyeing his flak jacket with interest. Drawn to the scent of money, she sat at his side.

Maybe a crazy, Ike told himself as he studied Trapper. *The dude's no Rebuck*, he thought. *For sure, he's no Little Brotha*.

The girl snuggled up to his flak-jacketed chest, running her fingers over a pocket's thick seam. Frustrated by her failure to gain entry to a pocket, she bit at the stitches Ike had sewn with his cobbler's needle.

"What the—?" Ike grabbed her by the hair, separating

542

her sharp teeth from his bank. "*Girl*, you'd do better goin' after Fort Knox."

Muttering, Ike moved out into the hall, rambling to its end, pausing briefly where the huge keeper of the bordello lay hogtied on the floor, moaning in pain. As he passed through the portaled archway and into the cabaret's back door, he immediately took in the unconscious, weasel-eyed man, crammed into a large rubber trash can.

Ike's eyes traversed the interior of the cabaret, searching for his new commander. He saw him occupying a far corner table, his back to the graffiti-ridden wall.

"Man," Ike dropped into a chair across from him, "you leave sum-kinda wake. Why'dja do a number on those suckers?"

"Pests," said Trapper, downing a jigger of straight gin.

"The orders?" Ike asked. "What and where?"

"Advanced training for new recruits. We're blowin' south tomorrow," Trapper said.

"South of Tahiti?"

"South of nowheres."

"You got it straight from Red Thunder himself?" Ike asked.

Surprise ran briefly in Trapper's eyes. "I ain't into communicating with the dead."

Confusion broke out on Ike's face. "What are ya tellin' me?"

"Red Thunder got his ass blown away. Kingdom Come's calling the shots now."

Ike's black eyes bulged with shock. "You bullshittin' me? Man, tell me you're not bullshittin' me!"

"Hey, freeze the heat. I got it from the inner guard. Had to be some piece of machinery to put out the captain's lights."

"Little Brotha," Ike gasped. "Little Brotha did it—he done Super Bat in."

Trapper eyed him with concern. "Don't get weird on me, Chief."

"He done it, man!" Ike shouted, rising to his feet. "Little Brotha did it!"

Sailors reached for concealed hardware and blades. The dancers quickly glided off the stage. The bartender went for a shotgun.

"Little Brotha *survived!*" Ike wailed.

CHAPTER 46

THE FIRST FROST came early to southwest Georgia. The sparsely populated Calhoun County was an area of the southland isolated from the hustle and the hassle, where neighbor truly cared for neighbor, where neither civil rights militant movements nor racist fearmongers disturbed the flow of peaceful coexistence between whites and blacks, where living in general was simple and sure. The man sitting on the porch of the Leighton Plantation's guest house remembered the lifestyle well. To Billy Hale, it was what America used to be.

He had watched the birth of another day as he had done for the past two and a half weeks. Except for the television news, Billy had been cut off from the rest of the world. The phones to the guest house had been disconnected, and only the lack of TV bulletins assured him of Doris's and Emile's safety.

Given sanctuary by an unlikely benefactor, protectively confined deep within the plantation grounds, Billy had never before felt so cut off, so isolated, so out of touch with the human race.

His nights had been spent in reflection. Only now did he experience a dimension of contemplation known to hermits and monks. Only now did he understand the damage that exponents of Fundamental Christianity could inflict on the nation. Only now did he actually feel guilty about his own past ignorance and greed. Only now did he see through the distant gaze of the elderly and infirm, and reflect on how evangelists and faith healers preyed on their fear of the unknown that lay beyond. Only now did he understand the search for spiritual values by the world's youth.

But in his sobering conclusions, he saw the future, when the idiosyncracies and ignorance of common religious theories would fall to heresy and hypocrisy. He saw a time when there would be no falling back on ancient scriptures and proverbs, no retreating behind the holy testimonies sounded in religious persuasion, when killing and plundering in the name of God would pass. He envisioned a time when the very Bible he himself had once believed to be infallible would lose its power—and those who continued to believe would be deemed by society to be Neanderthals.

Lastly, he saw the inevitability of religion's adopting a more scientific approach. Outer space would become the new source of religious knowledge. Man would move into the solar system and beyond, into space, infinite space, where he would forfeit his ego and truly begin to evaluate his own significance. In space, man's search for new religious meanings would not be jeopardized by dark and ancient Biblical legends.

The first announcement of Billy's special appearance on "Up to Now" came as a brief promotional spot during the evening news. It would build to a full day of media blitzing. Come noon on Sunday, November fifth, he would end this period of confinement. His flight northward on the Leighton Bottling Company's corporate jet would find him carrying a bomb Richard Waters had ordered his searching death squads to defuse.

546

CHAPTER 47

THE ADVICE came in one word—*Run*.

The recipient of this message brooded over its bluntness. John Ragonese was confused. He expected more from Ron Rebuck, and his pale, gaunt face blended with the dreariness of his cubbyhole of an office.

He'd received an offer through the bank for the sale of the mission's five hundred acres. It fell far short of the price he'd once quoted. It was hardly what he'd expected as compensation for his years of labor. But for a man blinded of direction, beaten down by the bizarre and living with daily dilemmas, the pending sale came to him as a blessed windfall.

Seated behind the scarred desk, silently cursing the birth of Ron Rebuck and his father, an inner voice warned him to waste no more time in self-pity. He would have to act, he knew, and it would not incorporate *running*.

Wandering into the mission's reception hall, he paced the wooden floor like a medieval monk contemplating the renewal of his vows. Desperation seized him. With or without Ron Rebuck's consent, he'd sell the land and keep it all. The hell with Rebuck and his phony codicil. But first, he'd go to the police—the county sheriff. He'd tell them where to find the assassins, and demand their protection.

Floundering for answers, his eyes turned to the awesome portrait of Ron Rebuck's father. As in times past, he felt that the mission founder's eyes followed him. What he didn't feel were the eyes of the living, watching him through a porch window.

*   *   *

The life-saving pit adjoining the lone grave had been filled with dirt and debris. The jagged remnants of the once-dominant statue of Michael the Archangel had been buried, the ground leveled. Ron Rebuck and Jessica Towne worked well into the brisk afternoon, restoring the mission cemetery so that no evidence of what had occurred on that horrific Halloween night remained.

Rebuck stood at the foot of his father's grave. Blood seeped through the bandages covering his wound and soaked damply into his denims. It would take a great deal more to distract him from what he was compelled to say.

An exhausted Jessica noticed the proud smile playing on Rebuck's lips. She understood, and went quietly to stand by the hedges marking the entrance. Here, she would wait—wait for Ron Rebuck to finally conclude his business with the dead.

His words came evenly, calmly. "I did it, Dad. I beat the odds. I survived."

The smile left his lips, yet brightened in his eyes. "And I didn't run."

An urge to leave, to go from this place immediately, stirred his feelings but went no further.

"I took on more than a maniac captain. I accepted the responsibility for another. I cared about Jessica. Would you have, Dad?" He slowly shook his head. "Not a chance. You were too obsessed with angels, with trumpeting a new religious belief to the world. Your madness left no room for caring about anyone but yourself . . . and for what? To become a little-known prophet, viewed by the leaders of established religions as a heretic?"

Jessica drifted closer.

"You know how I feel, Dad? How I truly feel? . . . I feel free. Like I've been reborn. As if I've entered a new world—in which you play no part."

He paused to reflect over his vow, the vendetta he'd sworn to keep.

"I'm sorry, Dad. It's left me. Everything's been purged. I don't hate any more. It's all buried with you now."

*　　*　　*

Darkness failed to alter Ron Rebuck's mood of exhilaration. His eyes danced with liveliness, and a teasing smile was on his lips. Jessica savored every moment of this dramatic change.

He spoke freely, talking about a new beginning, starting life anew in Canada, or Australia. He used the word *we* when he spoke of the future, and when he told her about the money which Ike Vesper had deposited into an international account, he referred to it as *theirs*.

Whether or not he was ever capable of loving a woman wholeheartedly had no immediate significance to Jessica. Right now, she was intoxicated by his magnetism, by his soaring spirit that she had always intuitively seen, though it had been smothered by hatred.

They showered together in the motor home's miniature stall, and when she applied fresh bandages to his thigh wound, her bathrobe parted, revealing her tanned, shapely legs. She noticed the excitement building on his face, the lust in his eyes, and she didn't blush. And when he gently removed her robe, she held back from rushing into his arms and ravaging his mouth and face.

His kiss was long, tender. His hands ranged everywhere over her body. She felt the throbbing of his penis and craved for his hardening organ to make its entry. Yet, unlike the times before, it was *his* desire, his foreplay, and he would not be rushed into reaching a climax.

His hands softly cupped her pointed breasts, and when he took a hardening nipple into the warmth of his mouth, she squirmed with uncontrollable sensations. But when she felt the heat of his breath upon her navel, she had had all she could possibly take of his foreplay, and begged him to drive his penis into her. He held her legs, restraining her wild rhythm, then entered—at first gradually, and she moaned for it all. His thrusts deepened and she went with the flow of his steady motion. The more he plunged, the greater her ecstasy, the louder her cries of love. And when she felt the climactic surge of his body, her legs broke from his hold, and clung to his lower back. Her move-

549

ments were like an erotic dancer's torrid thrusts, as she wildly met his orgasm with her own.

They were in no hurry to wash off the moistness or the scent of their lovemaking. Jessica had experienced multiple orgasms, and now the feeling which came to a woman fully satisfied. Ron closed his eyes, enjoying the solace of an inner peace. For the first time in their relationship they were free of concern. But concern was the nature of their habitat, and at this very moment, a deadly night visitor stalked the grounds.

As they ate a dinner of soup and bread, Jessica saw her through the window, standing next to the picnic table, bathed in the light of a full moon. Calmly, quietly, she told Rebuck.

Ron got up from the table quickly. He pulled on navy jeans, and slipped on a sweater and tennis shoes. As he reached the door, he stopped and turned to Jessica.

"There's no reason to be afraid."

She forced a nod. But he saw the glimmer of fear in her eyes.

"Believe me, if she wanted us dead, she wouldn't have waited until now."

"I'm all right, Ron. Really."

"Just stay inside and keep the gun handy."

She appeared to Rebuck even more beautiful than on that dreaded Christmas Eve when his nightmare had begun. Perhaps it was the moonlight, enhancing the lines of her sensual face. To his surprise, she was not attired in combat fatigues as she'd been a few days ago, but in a white wool sweater and tight-fitting designer jeans which showed off her shapely figure.

"Expecting me, Lieutenant?" she said, smiling.

Rebuck bit his tongue, and watched her silently as she sat down at the picnic table.

"Full moon—a night for lovers. Don't you agree?"

More a night for werewolves and vampires, Rebuck thought, taking a seat across from her.

"I've been thinking about you, Lieutenant."

Rebuck regarded her smile with uneasiness.

"The captain was right when he said you were special. But I knew it myself that night in Washington. You actually turned me on, Lieutenant. Few men have."

She drew a deep breath, clasping her ringless fingers together, and looked up into the moon-bright night. "If you're thinking the captain was my lover, you're wrong, Lieutenant. He preferred Russian roulette to sexual intercourse."

Rebuck took notice of what appeared to be a small bloodstain on the cuff of her sweater. But his scrutiny was fleeting, for her eyes had fallen from the heavens, turning upon him, and he felt drawn into them, as if bewitched by the way they glittered. Like emeralds, he thought.

"What are your plans?" she asked.

Rebuck said nothing, prompting her to continue.

"In a few days you'll leave here. What then? What will you do with your life?"

Rebuck studied her with deep penetration, then broke his silence. "What do you want from me?"

"I've come to make you an offer."

Rebuck smiled. A distrustful grin.

"No threats. No ultimatums. An offer, Ron Rebuck."

"An offer." Rebuck laughed. "What could you possibly have that I'd want?"

She fixed him with her eyes in such a way that there was no doubting her seriousness. "Myself," she said.

Rebuck's eyelids flew upward, and for a moment everything went blank in his mind.

"With me, Lieutenant, you could have a life of unlimited adventure. With me, you'd have a real woman in your bed, and not just some hayseed kid."

Her snide reference to Jessica got to him. "You're crazy," he said. "Crazier than the captain ever was."

"*Crazy?*" She pulled off the sweater, revealing her full, magnificently arched breasts. "Would having this body to use any way you desire be *crazy?*" She rose from the bench and Rebuck struggled to tear his eyes from her. Her hands dropped to undo the catch of her jeans. "Take off your clothes, Lieutenant, and I'll show you what it really feels like to have your brains fucked out."

Mesmerized by the awesome sensuality of her body, its curves touched wickedly by the moonlight, not a word rode on Rebuck's breath. He could not control the course of his eyes as they drank in the entire woman, moving down from her spectacular breasts to her tiny waist, then to her flawless thighs and the long, shapely legs. Then his gaze returned to her face, as he was captivated by the full, tempting mouth and imprisoned by her hungry eyes.

She was the most sensual, desirable woman he'd ever laid eyes on, but the knowledge of how she'd lured any number of unsuspecting men to their deaths kept him from blindly succumbing to her erotic wiles. With a great effort, he turned away. And when he saw the outline of Jessica's face observing them from the window, the meaning behind the temptress's invitation became all too clear.

"Forget it, Ballin. Wrong time, wrong circumstances, and the wrong world."

She laughed, and Rebuck curiously turned to see her pulling on her jeans.

"Again you prove to be special, Lieutenant. But then, I happen to be holding a wild card. Call it a joker." Slipping her sweater back over her head, she smiled, then tossed her mane of red hair triumphantly. "A joker—with Billy Hale's face."

The mention of the famous name blew into Rebuck's ears like a thunderous wind, spreading through his system and reawakening a raging hatred he'd thought was purged. She saw it glowing in his eyes.

"In my last meeting with the captain, he told me that the Right Reverend Hale was yours exclusively. I am to give you full support—if you make the commitment."

Taken by surprise, Rebuck just stared at her.

"We're talking about *Billy Hale*, Lieutenant—the man responsible for your father's murder."

A wild card of his own suddenly presented itself amidst the fury in his mind. "Produce Ike Vesper first."

The winning edge to her smile faded. "Your commitment first."

"No go. Unless Ike Vesper is alive and part of the package, the only commitment I'm making is to putting a lot of distance between us."

"I don't believe you, Lieutenant. Your flesh burns at the mention of Hale's name. And without your commitment, Billy Hale is not your kill."

Rebuck weighted the risks of provoking her. Behind that beautiful face were the workings of a mind as savage as that of her legendary predecessor—though she had far less patience than had the captain.

"Walk with me, Lieutenant," she said finally, in a soft voice that took him by surprise.

Rebuck stood his ground and watched her slowly break for the trail. Turning, Ballin quickly tuned into his concern for Jessica.

"There's no reason to worry about your girlfriend. The captain's will is irrevocable."

After considering the situation for a moment, Rebuck decided to take the chance and rely on the sanctity of the captain's will. Joining her on the trail, he told himself he'd limit their encounter to a brief conversation.

As they walked, she was silent for several minutes—as if, Rebuck thought, she could not bring herself to divulge secrets she had previously shared only with the mad. He purposely stayed within arm's reach of her, aware that in the event of an ambush, holding her hostage would be the only possible way to insure his and Jessica's survival.

"There is not one among those I command who can live up to his expectations," she said finally, adding almost wistfully, "How he despised mediocrity."

Rebuck saw the baleful gleam in her glittering eyes. "Where is the captain now?" she demanded suddenly, stopping and turning toward him.

"The captain is dead," Rebuck answered.

"No last great adventure? No spiritual journey of the soul?"

He stared at her. "When you're dead, you're dead."

"We survive to die, then—is that it?"

"That about sums it up."

"No, Lieutenant, there is more."

"There are only theories," Rebuck said.

"Like the bunk in the Bible? Like the words your own father wrote?"

Rebuck fixed her with an icy glare. She ignored the intimidating look. "Your father had much to do with your selection, Lieutenant. His book provided the captain with a knowledge—and gave you an advantage other candidates lacked."

Rebuck thought of his father's book. It was a curse, a lasting remembrance of an adolescence he'd tried desperately to forget. Now, a maniac was opening old wounds, resurrecting bitter memories, telling him that his father was a prime reason for his nightmarish association with assassins.

"Your father demonstrated the absurdity of the Book of Genesis. He proved there was no conceivable plausibility to Milton's 'Paradise Lost.' He presented logical reasons for Man's birth and death as no one else ever had. But his gift of spiritual insight failed him in the end, when he judged the master of the universe to be impartial."

Rebuck clenched his hands so tightly the nails cut into his palms. It was the captain all over again. And right now he felt he'd neither the strength nor courage to challenge her.

"The true God created places in the universe as battle-fields. Earth was selected for man. The almighty architect made no rules or regulations, did not harness man with commandments. It was Man who saturated his existence with beliefs, superstitions, and laws."

He looked into her eyes, eyes which seemed to burn with evil. As she spoke, her teeth flashed in the moonlight. "Only the brainwashed, the utterers of ridiculous prayers, the fearful and the ignorant retain a blinding faith in the God of false Bibles."

Rebuck had cried out within himself to deafen her words,

554

but a quotation from his father's book shot through his mind, expressing the madwoman's revelation:

"Who shall man's soul charge responsible for its bodily existence? You, Michael, who planned it? You, Lucifer, who fathered their death? . . . Or you, God, who allowed it all?"

The pallor of exhaustion spread over Rebuck's face. Perspiration gleamed on his brow as he struggled to prevent his silent agony from erupting into a volcanic rage.

"There is no afterlife for cowards and hypocrites!" Trudy Ballin thundered. "There will be no garlands of praise for the cowardly peacemakers. Only the strong, the fearless, *we*, the believers, the disciples of a supreme assassin, shall take part in the last great adventure!"

Rebuck grimaced in anticipation of yet another burst of evangelizing. But, instead, the flashing lightning of power left her eyes. She smiled, and Rebuck felt the sweat on his face run cold.

"Did my moment of revelation surprise you, Lieutenant?"

Rebuck first weighed his reply. "I've heard it before."

"That God is the greatest killer of all?"

"That if a supreme being created man, there is none more evil."

"From *whom?*" she demanded. Her body shook as if an unearthly wind had swept over her soul. "From whom did you receive that revelation?"

"From a fool."

Rebuck looked up from the ground and saw the instant change in her countenance. She stood as if turned to stone, gazing at him with dead eyes. She became dark and formless before his eyes.

As she gradually came out of her trance, Rebuck sensed that she had reached an understanding within herself.

They walked on in silence, passing the bend in the trail and moving onto the drive leading to the mission house. Rebuck's attention raced to the two men just ahead of them, standing by a black sedan. He recognized them in the moonlight as the same men who had stood guard by her during the reading of the captain's will. As he watched, several rifle-toting men filtered out from the woods and climbed into a van.

Approaching the house, Rebuck inched even closer to Ballin. The house was cast in darkness; not even the porch light burned. Along with the noticeable absence of John Ragonese's car, this gave Rebuck every reason to believe that the former mission director had forsaken greed for survival and *run*. In that split second, Trudy Ballin drifted from his reach.

As he stood there, unarmed and vulnerable, Rebuck knew he'd lost his only chance to continue living. The expressions he saw on the faces of the two men told him they'd enjoy nothing more than for him to make a sudden break for it. But Ron Rebuck was beyond fear. The numbness peculiar to the doomed pervaded him.

Trudy Ballin turned at the car to look at him. Then, as if regarding him as a lost cause, she shook her head and climbed into the car.

Rebuck moved cautiously toward the house, alert to the movements of the two assassins. As they reluctantly joined Trudy in the sedan, relief swept over him, and his breathing began to return to normal.

As he walked past the idling vehicle, she rolled down her window. Her words came without malice. "Lieutenant, I hope you won't decide to waste your future, but I suspect you will."

The window closed, shutting out the wicked sound of her laughter. The car's engine roared and Rebuck alertly stepped onto the porch, escaping the dirt and gravel kicked up by squealing tires. Not until the car had moved onto the state road and sped off into the night did he trust that she had finally left. Still, something more than a gut instinct told him they would meet again.

Needing time to allow the tension to wind down in his mind, he sat on the porch steps. Even his urge to return to Jessica would have to wait. Emotionally drained, he gulped in the chilling air as if it would cool his burning nerves, and soon became drawn into the silence of the night.

At first, what he heard failed to reach his troubled mind.

But a growing awareness of what sounded like the dripping of a faucet within the darkened house finally became an intrusion on his thoughts which he could not ignore. He slowly rose, then entered the house.

A stream of moonlight seemed to carry him inside the wide reception hall. It trickled through the pervasive darkness, its silvery tentacles reaching across the room. His eyes followed the path of the light to the point where it revealed a ghastly scene—the nude body of a man, hanging from a lower beam, his face grotesquely twisted in death, the eyes rolled back and bulging in their sockets, the tongue protruding from lifeless lips.

John Ragonese had not run fast enough.

Held motionless by the macabre sight, Rebuck's attention was drawn by a dripping sound to an old, rounded washtub. His eyes slowly raised to the dead man's crotch. He blinked at the gaping wound, and not until he forced another look did he realize the man had been castrated.

Ron Rebuck had reached the limit of his endurance. The nightmare life he'd been living since leaving the SEALs had not terminated with the captain's death. Another monster had surfaced to stoke the coals of his hate, to scar his mind with yet another horrendous act. He could no longer suppress the agony of his body and soul. He felt his whole being engulfed in tides of suffering, despair, weariness, and grief. To him, life was nothing but treacherous beasts, forever prowling.

"Where?" he shouted over the suffering of his soul. "Where is my *escape?"* He pounded the walls until all feeling left his hands.

Exhaustion gradually cooled the heat which fueled his fury. A reservoir of tears flooded from his eyes as he slumped against the wall, sinking slowly to the floor, his body seeming to melt into the gloom of the accursed room.

As he sat with his back against the wall, two glowing eyes penetrated his blurred vision. At first he saw them as his own, looking back at him with the despairing gaze of a dying man; but as his vision cleared he knew it was no apparition, no image cast by a demonic power. For too long a time, he looked upon the portrait streaked with eerie light. He was helplessly transfixed by his father's pathetic stare.

Within moments, he fell into a deep, coma-like sleep. He didn't open his eyes until morning, when he heard the distant calling of his name. Jessica was shaking him gently.

"Ron . . . Ron, are you all right?" she was saying.

His face registered instant surprise. Looking up, past her, what he *didn't* see held him speechless. The gruesome corpse from the night before was gone. There was no body, no washtub filled with blood. Nothing.

"What is it, Ron?" Jessica said, alarmed by the wildness in his eyes.

"It can't be," he muttered, getting to his feet, then walking over to the location of the death scene he was sure he hadn't imagined. Confident that he would find a clue, a close inspection betrayed him. Not a drop of blood had stained the floor, and there were no rope marks on the beam.

Looking over to the far wall, Jessica's eyes welled with discovery. "It's gone, Ron," she said.

"What's gone?" he said, half aloud.

"I suppose Mr. Ragonese must have taken it."

Ron Rebuck looked up to where his father's portrait had been, and felt his body tremble.

CHAPTER 48

THE NOONDAY visitor was sight-cleared by the post sentry to grounds which the media had once called "Camp David West." Entering the rustic lodge tucked into the Portland, Oregon, forest, he found his way to the impressive den with its cathedral ceiling and twin fireplaces. Senator Bartley Sinclair's campaign chairman smiled weakly at the chain-smoking Richard Waters, who sat in a recliner, watching television and nursing a straight bourbon.

Waters clicked off the TV by remote and motioned for his former press secretary to be seated. "Whip, Hale's appearance on 'Up to Now' is getting a lot of advance promo."

"The show is live. And not from New York—D.C." Whipple informed him.

Waters gouged the cigarette into an ashtray. "I let William slip away. I should have listened to Red Thunder."

"No word from the captain?"

"I'm afraid our Captain Gemmer is on permanent leave. And I don't believe his new employer will grant him a furlough from Hell."

Whipple flinched with surprise.

" 'Kingdom Come' and her people picked up what was left of him somewhere in Pennsylvania and buried the remains in a Maryland cemetery."

"Jesus, that's hard to imagine."

"Find time away from Bart and leak a story to Admiral Church at the Pentagon. Make it sound as if the captain was kidnapped by terrorists."

"No problem. The North Vietnamese still have a standing bounty on his head."

An electronic beeping interrupted their conversation, and Waters reached for the cordless phone at his side. He waited for the caller to be cleared before acknowledging, then sat back in his chair to listen.

Whipple observed the man he had seen almost every day for eight years. He knew the many moods behind the changing expressions which came to the former president's distinguished face. The one he identified now was that of revelation.

Waters returned the phone to its cradle and slumped in the chair, his arms hanging over the soft armrests. His words came in a slow and bitter voice. "It *was* Bart who provided the helicopter for William's escape from Christ Town."

"He never said a word about it to me," Whipple said. "I can hardly believe it."

Waters fixed him with a long and steady gaze. "I now know where my friend William is hiding."

"He has to have left the country."

The former president's reply came with a grim smile. "Georgia," he said.

"Fort Benning?" Whipple wondered.

"West—and further south."

Whipple thought for a moment. "Bart's in-laws. The Leighton Plantation. Where Bart was married. Of *course*."

Waters reached for the phone and pushed the numbers to connect him with an underling. "Call the damn thing off," he instructed. "Yes, the search for Hale . . . and be damn sure to make contact with Kingdom Come. She's standing by."

Whipple waited for the former president to lean back in his chair before speaking. "You're going to let Hale appear on that TV show?"

"I am."

"Mister President, he's sure to tell everything he knows."

"William's informer has been eliminated. Who besides theologians believe the hand-me-down testimonies of dead

560

men? Besides, the only person who could substantiate any of William's charges *won't*, by virtue of a deal.''

"It's still too risky. We could be talking disaster, Mister President.''

"Complications, but not disaster.'' Waters's lips pursed in thought. "When there appears to be no solution to the problem—you must change the problem.''

under President Hereupon cross-small began murmuring: the
on Wilhite's chances for reelection as an autocrat." on his
"It's still too early!" warned the voice against Many
President."

Crumm nodded, but observation . . . . If American aroused
enough . . . . Wanderhaven, suspect . . . politician in the
prohibit . . . won

CHAPTER 49

THE SUPER-HYPE had ended. Countdown to the award-winning television show "Up to Now" neared T-minus-zero seconds. The show's senior reporter, Curt Vanderhaven, shuffled his notes into order. On cue, he flashed a cosmetic smile, spoke of the program's unusual change of format, then introduced the show's only guest as "the dean of world evangelism."

Billy Hale entertained no last-minute reservations about telling his story to the millions of Sunday-night viewers. His words came unhindered. "I am not appearing on this live telecast as an evangelist—not in the usual sense. I am soliciting nothing. The fact that I am here is the only miracle to speak of. For, you see, there are people who have reason to kill me."

From inside the control booth, the show's producer, Ned Worthy, flashed a winning smile.

"It all started with a hunch," Billy explained. The story went on from there.

Hardly a vehicle moved in the village of Crockett. "Up to Now" beamed into the homes of the hill and valley people, and the natives of this region of the Shenandoah watched their favorite son. Inside the parsonage house of the Baptist church, Doris Hale, Emile, Pastor "Scrappy" Dews, and his wife, Marge, hung on Billy's every word.

Harley Lombard, favorite son of Charity, Ohio, paced his cross-shaped home bitching and moaning over his failure to reach Sue Bergman. His wife, Wilma Mae, added to his frustration with needling remarks.

562

In Portland, Oregon, the man hoping to become the nation's favorite son refused all incoming calls to his unpretentious suburban home. Nothing short of a family emergency would keep Senator Bartley Sinclair from watching Billy Hale's telecast. His campaign chairman, a darkly concerned George Whipple, sat below the portrait of former President Richard Waters at an angle where he could easily monitor the senator's reactions.

Earlier that day, Richard Waters had left Portland.

Billy Hale had craftily reconstructed the bloody trail he'd followed. Having prominently mentioned Virtues, Inc., he talked about the ARA, calling it the "Secret Society." To a defense attorney, it was nothing more than a fascinating story.

The show's director cut away to a commercial and looked back at Ned Worthy.

"Dynamite." He shot the producer a thumbs-up sign.

"That's only the sparklers," Worthy said, hoping.

So did Ned Worthy's boss. Watching the program from inside his Manhattan penthouse apartment, Yale Norman eased a vodka martini into his system, wondering if he'd contributed to the dumping of more bullshit on the American public.

The commercials ended. The stout and sixtyish Curt Vanderhaven, regarded as the Viscount of Viciousness by many of the multitude he'd interviewed, appeared most eager for the floor director to give him his cue.

"Reverend Hale," Vanderhaven began, "if we can, I'd like to separate truth from fiction. Do you have any evidence to substantiate the looming presence of this alleged secret society?"

The sharpness in Billy's mind dulled. His answer came lamely. "My evidence has been suppressed."

"There is no one who can corroborate your statements?"

"Only the guilty."

"I see."

"I don't believe you do," said Billy, reading the disbelief in the other's eyes. "Those who knew the truth have been murdered."

Vanderhaven blinked. "Can you tell us the names of these, as you say, murdered people?"

Billy paused for a moment before answering. "Daniel Kaiser—former assistant director of the FBI—and his wife."

Vanderhaven's memory was lightning quick. "There are reports which take strong issue with you, Reverend Hale. The county coroner and the FBI have called Daniel Kaiser's death a suicide."

"Dan and Cynthia Kaisers' deaths were sponsored and suppressed by a secret society that is attempting to influence American politics and the national elections in particular."

"Reverend Hale, are you asking the American people to believe that this evil force has successfully infiltrated the highest levels of government?"

"I'm not asking, I'm telling."

"You said in your opening remarks that religion is an intricate tool for this secret society to achieve their goals."

"Specifically, *fundamentalist* Christianity."

"And its practitioners—such as Reverend Harley Lombard."

"*Reverend* Lombard is being used. Virtues, Inc., is not a spiritual revelation of Harley's, as he has said. It's a vital tool for the secret society to elect or destroy political candidates—all in the name of God. In Harley Lombard, they found the perfect stooge."

Harley Lombard shot out of his chair. "What did the old goat mean by that?"

Wilma Mae Lombard's attention remained riveted to the wide-screen TV in her den.

"Was he defaming me?"

Annoyed by his pacing, she replied, "He called you incorrigible and destructive."

"I didn't hear him say that."

"If you need another opinion, why don't you try calling your advisor again."

Vanderhaven reflected. His thick brows furrowed. "Reverend Hale, I am sitting here amazed by much of what you've said. Have you, of all people, actually become disenchanted with modern Christianity?"

"More so with the ways and means of its propagators."

"Evangelists, Reverend Hale?"

"The mighty of mouth, among others."

"Like yourself?"

"It usually takes one to know one."

Harley Lombard gloated. "Didja hear him, Wilma Mae? Billy Hale the loser. Just like your father. He's abandoned Jesus. He's no longer worthy of receiving revelations."

"He received one, Harley. The very same revelation my father had. The one in which Jesus told him what an asshole you are!"

Vanderhaven had yet to live up to his reputation as the fastest gun in broadcasting. He seemed content with his probing tactics, as if he was dangling bait for Billy to nibble on.

"Reverend Hale, the Constitution does not prevent religious organizations such as Virtues, Inc., or clergymen like Reverend Lombard from publicly speaking out for or against any issue. Every citizen, including yourself, has this right."

"This *God*-given right?"

"However inspired, Reverend Hale."

"The right to defame honest men and women running for political office? The right to smear their characters? The right to suggest that God endorses certain candidates and damns the rest?"

"Virtues, Inc., has rallied a morality movement in this country. I should think that you, who have spent a lifetime preaching against decadence, greed, and corruption, would be the first to approve."

565

"Are you so naive as to believe that this is a matter of morality for Virtues, Inc.?"

"Do you have a case in point, Reverend Hale?"

"Surely you must be aware of what is happening to Senator Lollar."

"I take it you are speaking about the hotly contested abortion issue in the Florida Senate race."

"It's the *only* issue, Mr. Vanderhaven."

"Apparently the people of Florida think so."

"Doesn't that strike you as odd?"

"Hardly, Reverend Hale. The abortion issue is not isolated to the state of Florida. It happens to be an important national issue."

"I'm referring to the character assassination of an honest and caring man. I'm referring to Senator Lollar *and* others, who've become the targets, the victims of malicious persecution by the propagandists of the 'born again.' I'm referring to the despicable tactics employed against Lollar when those so-called moralists found it impossible to attack his political record. I'm referring, Mr. Vanderhaven, to billboards in Lakeland, Florida, showing Senator Lollar dressed in a surgical smock—depicting him as a baby killer!"

"In all fairness to the industrialist Dooley Law—Senator Lollar's Republican opponent—Mr. Law publicly denounced those billboards."

"How, in a whisper? A paragraph buried somewhere in the newspapers? A one-line mention over your network news?"

Vanderhaven feigned a smile. "Where else does this conspiracy wind on to, Reverend Hale?"

"It knows no boundaries."

"And you say that the ARA—the American Recovery Association—is behind it all, Reverend Hale?"

"That is correct."

Vanderhaven smiled widely. "I am familiar with the ARA, Reverend Hale. It is widely known as a super-patriotic organization. I am also aware of its executive director, Susan Bergman." Disbelief hardened his face.

566

"Are you suggesting that a Washington attorney is the mastermind behind this conspiracy?"

The inevitable fell upon Billy as he had all along expected it would. It came down to keeping one promise and reneging on the other. Precious prime-time seconds were passing, yet Billy deliberated.

Yale Norman envisioned "Up to Now"'s highest ratings ever. The recipients of Billy's promises, Ned Worthy and Senator Bartley Sinclair, sweated in suspense. All the nationwide media's machinery needed was a name.

Vanderhaven, impatient, prodded his guest. "Reverend Hale, when arrangements were made for you to appear on this television program, didn't you agree to reveal the names of *all* the conspirators?"

There would be no skirting, no sliding, no evangelical babble in Billy's reply. "I did, Mr. Vanderhaven. And at this very moment, one side of me screams out to expose the name of the true murderer. My better sense tells me it would be unwise."

Ned Worthy spit out his gum. "Billy, you can't do this! You can't cop out on me!"

Bartley Sinclair pressed his fingers together and closed his eyes. George Whipple now understood the deal Richard Waters had referred to.

"Reverend Hale . . ." Vanderhaven cleared his throat with much exaggeration. "Are we to assume the identity of this dastardly person will only be spoken from your lips to God's ears?"

"God has nothing to do with this. Whereas I no longer have the strength to pursue this monster, I have given the sword to someone who has the ways and means to bring the conspirators to justice."

Receiving his cue to break away to a commercial, Vanderhaven flashed a grim smile and intoned, "We will be back with more of the Billy Hale—story."

George Whipple felt Sinclair's hard stare, and shrugged. "How deep do you go, Whip?"

"I'm afraid to the bottom of the well."

"And all the while you've been double-dealing as my campaign chairman."

"Bart, I never took any active role."

"But you knew what was going on. Goddammit, you knew! You kept it all from me."

"I had to."

"And just what do you expect me to do about it?"

"Senator, I expect you not to blow the presidency."

Sinclair's temples were pounding. Anger steamed from his face.

The burly Whipple didn't need to be told his presence was no longer welcome. He turned at the den's door. "Bart, you can't fight it. Hale is only scratching the surface."

"Was that a veiled threat?"

"Advice."

"Right now, your advice stinks."

"Bart, I'm begging you—don't do anything rash. I think you should talk it over with the old man."

"I intend to. After the election—win or lose."

Sue Bergman sat staring at the TV set in her high-rise apartment overlooking the Potomac River, evaluating the damages. So far, Billy Hale's charges lay solely upon her. Not a person prone to panic, she had good reason to wonder how she now fit into Richard Waters's scheme of things. Past experience told her the former president regarded no one as indispensable. And she wouldn't fool herself into believing she was the exception.

Ned Worthy ran out of objections. Unable to persuade Billy Hale to reveal the identity of the conspirator of conspirators, he ambled back to the control booth muttering that he'd never again trust anything or anyone "religious." Billy Hale's growing distrust of Curt Vanderhaven had nothing to do with religion.

With thirty seconds and counting left to the commercial break, Vanderhaven had all the while kept to himself.

Reviewing a fresh batch of notes, he'd appeared oblivious to his producer's pleadings and Billy's apologies.

"That many questions left?" Billy asked, hiding his true feelings behind an attempt at lightness.

Vanderhaven collected the notes, deliberated, then shrugged. "Reverend Hale, that chair you're sitting on is likely to get extremely hot. Nothing personal."

"Isn't it?" Billy expressed doubt, studying a face that was even craggier than his own.

The next segment of "Up to Now" was on the air, and Vanderhaven wasted no time in making good on his warning that he'd heat up Billy's seat.

"Reverend Hale, the story you have told smacks of sensationalism. Filled with intrigue, crowded with unsolved, cold-blooded murders, it winds and twists with all the suspense of a bestselling spy thriller. You have accused the American Recovery Association of being super-conspirators, and made out its executive director as some modern-day Mata Hari. Frankly, Reverend Hale, your story reeks of fiction."

Billy checked a rising resentment for the man, remembering that he would have the last say. Unless Ned Worthy saw fit to get even and permit Vanderhaven to run through his promised closing monologue.

"Isn't it true you called Virtues, Inc.'s, principals, namely Reverend Harley Lombard and lawyer Sue Bergman, demagogues and false judges?"

"Frequently."

"Reverend Hale, why did you go to Virtues, Inc.'s, convention?"

"I have asked myself that very question a thousand times."

"Isn't it true you were called a traitor and the Benedict Arnold of Christianity?"

"Among other things."

"Isn't it true you were defrocked by your peers?"

"Defrocked?"

"And isn't it true that not only were you not asked to give the invocation and benediction at the Republican National Convention, but you were not even invited?"

"I would rather believe—"

Again Vanderhaven cut him short. "Isn't it also true you went to the convention with the express purpose of speaking out against Virtues, Inc., and, particularly, Reverend Lombard, who had replaced you?"

Suddenly wise to Vanderhaven's prosecuting device, calculated to make him out as the defendant, Billy sat back in his chair and smiled at the camera, waiting for the man to finish running off at the mouth.

"In raising these allegations of conspiracy, could you be casting shadows of suspicion over Virtues, Inc., and Reverend Lombard for personal reasons?"

"Are you quite finished?"

"For the moment, Reverend Hale."

"First of all, I went to the Republican Convention as a lifelong registered Republican. As for my not giving the invocation and benediction, the party has always been free to select whoever they wish. My ultimate reason for going to the convention was to warn the party to sever any direct or indirect ties with Virtues, Inc."

"No one listened to you, Reverend Hale. You never reached the speaker's podium."

"It would have taken an act of Congress to reach that podium."

"Certainly your inability to address the convention shouldn't have surprised you, Reverend Hale. After all, why should they give national exposure, at their expense, to a man whose new-found ideology is in direct conflict with their platform?"

"I am speaking of a national conspiracy. People have been murdered. Every level of government is being infiltrated by a society bent on controlling this country. This isn't a partisan issue, as you are making it out to be."

"Do you actually believe that something of this magnitude could go on in this country without drawing the attention of someone other than yourself?"

"It did. And Dan Kaiser and his wife were murdered."

"Reverend Hale, with all of the resources available to

the President of the United States, wouldn't it seem unlikely for him not to be aware of such a conspiracy?''

"*If* he is aware, and I do not know that to be a fact, what can he do? Order investigations that would be stonewalled by enemies within?"

"Incredible."

"And frighteningly real," Billy tagged.

"What I find even more incredible is how one of the most influential and respected religious leaders of modern times, a man who took evangelism out of the tents and paved the way for the electronic church, who formed the coalition of American religious broadcasters into a powerful lobbying force, a religious figure over whom only the popes have won more adulation, could possibly lose his faith."

"To the contrary. My faith has never been stronger, or clearer. However, I have broken the rules, so to speak. In fact, I've violated fundamentalist Christianity's greatest commandment: I have allowed myself to think."

Throughout, Billy had not been able to cut through Vanderhaven's tight, smug grin. But as Vanderhaven searched for a reference card from among those scattered before him, Billy's sense of distrust for the man deepened with anticipated alarm.

Vanderhaven looked up at Billy with the judicious expression of a prosecuting attorney. "Let's talk about some other claims you've made, Reverend Hale. Isn't it true that you once called a famous atheist 'Satan's daughter'? Isn't it true that during one of your worldwide television campaigns, you said all non-Christians would go to Hell? Isn't it also true that you once said it is better for a child to go ignorant than to be taught anything other than the Christian Bible? And isn't it true that you once said rock-and-roll music was composed by the devil? . . . Tell me, Reverend Hale, does the name 'Rebuck' bring anything to mind?"

Billy knew Richard Waters had reached the man.

"Eleven, twelve years ago, didn't you accuse this man Rebuck of conspiring against Christianity? Isn't it true you publicly judged this man to be the 'Antichrist'? And wasn't he the same man who, shortly thereafter, was murdered by crucifixion?''

Billy had to react—to hesitate would prove disastrous. He knew all too well of the viewing public's fickle judgment.

"Mr. Vanderhaven, as an evangelist, I spoke of many lame-brained conspiracies. And yes, most of them were blamed on the devil. However, your selecting this particular incident to discredit me and to distract the millions who are watching did not result from any research done by you or your staff. *Isn't it true*—this information was furnished to you by the ARA?''

Six miles off the Vancouver coast, the super-ship *Morning Star* flew its colors of a blazing sun. Below, inside the luxurious master stateroom, Richard Waters raised his wine glass and toasted Billy Hale's image coming over the large TV set. *"Touché*, William,'' he saluted.

His host, C.D. Pittman, abstained with a scowl.

Jessica Towne sat transfixed by the famous face filling the TV screen. She'd finally discovered the *almost* to the "everything" Ron Rebuck had told her. And she knew that neither intelligent reasoning nor personal persuasion could hope to lessen his thirst for vengeance.

She closed her eyes in an effort to rid herself of the terrible truth and drifted off to sleep. Waking after only a few minutes, she sensed Ron Rebuck's presence. She could not bring herself to look in his eyes, but the compulsion to hear from his lips what she knew in her heart was too great.

"Ron—are you going to kill Billy Hale?''

The final segment of "Up to Now" had been reserved for Billy to make his concluding statement—without rebuttal.

"I am sure there are many of you who do not feel threatened by a thing I have said. Perhaps you choose to believe that this conspiracy I speak of exists only in an old man's mind. As to this madness for morality, the movement of fundamentalist Christianity, perhaps you are secure in your lifestyle, and merely regard it all as a fad, a phenomenon which like so many trends will come and go. I can assure you it won't go easily, and whether or not you are a Christian, you have reason to fear.''

Billy bit down on his lip to arrest a quiver of anxiety. ''Do not be fooled by these fundamentalist Christian preachers when they speak of their support for Israel. It merely stems from their preference for Jew over Arab. Do not be taken in by the flowery and friendly words directed at Jews by Harley Lombard and the other fundamentalist Christian preachers of the electronic church. Behind their smoke screens, the persecution of Jews is considered correct. Where is the proof of my allegation? It resides with these fundamental contemporary crusaders, and their fanatical following of the 'born again.' Simply ask them of the Jews' place in eternity. Ask them of the final destination of the bodies and soul of those who do not believe Jesus Christ is God.''

Vanderhaven tapped his pencil on the table which separated them. It would take much more of a distraction to derail Billy's train of thought.

''Whereas I failed to make any headway at Virtues, Inc.,'s convention, and whereas I realize the futility of reasoning with the locked minds of those who travel that virtuous path of fundamentalist Christianity, I address you, the silent majority, who must not be influenced by these righteous moralists.''

Canals of sweat formed across his lined forehead. He had learned from experience that to perspire when appearing on television was a catastrophe—that sweating created not only a visual unpleasantness but an aura of distrust as well. But he was beyond regard for appearances and pushed on with the courage of his deep convictions.

''The phenomenal growth of fundamentalist Christian broadcasting, the steady influx of evangelists appearing on TV, is part of a well-orchestrated plan which respects no other opinions and knows no limitations. The boldness of this movement serves the dangerous conspiracy I have told you of tonight. In order to achieve their ultimate goal of

573

turning this nation into a super-conservative state, the alliance they chose was religion. In Virtues, Inc., the ARA has created the necessary tool—a propaganda machine.''

Billy was unconcerned now by the closeness of a camera which would pick up the slightest quivering or nervous twitching of his face. His mountain-blue eyes glowed with sincerity.

''The time has come when you, the public, can no longer remain silent and apathetic, or unwilling to tread upon what these demagogues profess to be sacred ground anointed by God. I implore you to take a stand against these evangelizing intimidators, these preachers of fear. You must openly, publicly, combat these fundamentalist Christian movements and their leaders, who interpret scripture to exploit human prejudices. Refuse to subscribe to television services which incorporate the programming of these misused electronic ministries. Take on the associations of Christian religious broadcasting. Fight them in courts. Flood the American judicial system with class-action suits. Lobby in great numbers to shake the halls of the ruling FCC. Fight to keep the electronic church from smothering the airwaves with fundamentalist Christian ideologies and deceit. Be on guard for disciples of the 'born again' acquiring control of major commercial television networks and radio stations coast to coast. Boycott their sponsors' products. For you, the silent majority, possess the true power.''

Billy was blind to the floor director's final signal and rolled on with the blessings of his body and soul.

''Listen not to the parrots of the 'born again'—the radical puppets of fundamentalist Christianity, who in their dark ignorance suppress theological growth. Let no man, woman, or movement tell you for whom to vote, and above all, do not allow them to dictate your life—in the name of God!''

C.D. Pittman turned to his guest. ''Mister President, I do believe you should be entertaining a bold measure to counter all of this.''

574

"A sacrificial lamb?"
"A martyr would be more appropriate."
"I agree, C.D. But *who?*"
Pittman smiled.

ing his phone. Lombard utilizing the act-dialed phone one of the major world communicating/inside of his office's personal Cable Box radio.

Wilma Mae Lombard

CHAPTER 50

REPORTERS, resembling yapping dogs, converged upon the gates of the Lombard estate. Uniformed guards kept them at bay. Inside the cross-shaped home, Harley Lombard's headache from the night before was something aspirin would not relieve.

Wilma Mae Lombard had left before the reporters arrived, and Harley cursed her for abandoning him. She had scoffed at his sudden need for her company. He would have had to crawl on his knees and admit her father was a better man than he before she would even have contemplated cancelling her trip to Africa to see their twin missionary sons. With experienced foresight, she had given the domestic help paid vacations, leaving Harley no one to take out his frustrations on.

What Harley had expected to be a day spent garnering last-minute homage from politicians endorsed and *blessed* by Virtues, Inc., had instead become marred by Sue Bergman's telephone call after Billy Hale's "tell it all" appearance on "Up to Now." Harley's interest in adhering to her demands was at an all-time low.

"Who does she think I am, some kid with his hand down his pants? Where does she come off ordering me—Harley Lombard—to stay out of the limelight until after the elections? It's *my* fucking limelight!"

His furious pacing in the sunken living room ended at the phone. "Don't call anyone—my ass!" he sputtered, pushing the numbers to his penthouse office at the Cathedral Tower Building.

No connection, and he tried again. "How can this fucking be!'' he raged, throwing the gold-plated phone onto the shag-carpeted floor. The red spot on the tip of his nose flamed. ''No one messes with Harley Lombard! Threatening me with that accessory shit. I'll show that suction pump broad who's an accessory,'' he ranted, storming through the kitchen en route to the garage.

Arm-waving security guards patrolling the grounds rushed to flag down the Turbo Carrera Porsche. Behind the wheel, Harley Lombard kept a finger on the trigger of the electronic device which beamed open the gates. On the other side a rowdy mob waited, and he was forced to drive the Porsche at a crawl. Besieged by the brigade of eager reporters thirsting for controversial rebuttals to Billy Hale's statements, which had made front-page headlines in all the morning papers, Harley put on the radio and blared his horn to drown out their shouting. Slowly, he plowed through to the freedom of the street.

Sitting in a parked blue Chrysler, Sue Bergman's efficient watchdog, Deek Ashburn, the man who had given Harley heartburn, reached for the car phone.

Billy Hale slept for ten hours. When he awakened a few minutes past noon it took a while for him to phase into the actuality of being home, and in his own bed. Doris brought him the morning papers, which Emile had rounded up. The various headlines pleased him. One in particular, ''BILLY HALE LINKS VIRTUES, INC., TO NATIONAL CONSPIRACY,'' summed up the damage he had intended to inflict.

Although the headlines indicted the ARA, its executive director, Sue Bergman, and Virtues, Inc., Doris Hale found some of the smaller print most uncomplimentary. The journalist from the Washington *Post* referred to Billy's testimony over national television as teasing, and tagged it with, ''Who is this mystery person behind Billy Hale's alleged conspiracy? You guessed it. The *devil*.'' Another paper paralleled Billy's presentation with the sermon on the mount, calling it ''the sermon on Mount Senility.''

''Doris,'' he placed a hand over the article she was

reading, "stop fretting. Who, today, actually reads more than a few paragraphs beyond the large print?"

But as the day rolled into midafternoon and reporters stopped calling, Billy concerned himself with why there had been no response from those he'd named.

His mind turned to his old friend, Richard Waters. Surely, he thought, Waters had to be worried over what effect the television program would have on the American voters. If the newspaper accounts were any indication, Waters's cause had been severely jeopardized. Billy reasoned that the former president would have to counter somehow. Something with shock value. But what? There was little time. The polls opened in less than twenty-four hours. Billy explored the possibilities, but could think of nothing other than "general denials."

The publisher-editor of the *Crocket Chronicle*, Cullinan County's leading newspaper, a friend of the Hales for years, received the latest information over the wire service and personally delivered the stories to a grateful Billy. His attention went first to Sue Bergman's statements.

"Reverend Hale's despicable attack upon Virtues, Inc., the American Recovery Association, and me as the ARA's executive director, is the true conspiracy. There is not one shred of evidence to support his outrageous charges. The collaboration between 'Up to Now' 's producers, the IBC network, and Reverend Hale in this flagrantly libelous attack only two days before the national elections was unprecedented, unethical, and totally irresponsible. We'll see them all in court."

Billy turned to the next story. The headline, "VIRTUES, INC.,'S HARLEY LOMBARD CLAIMS BILLY HALE IS POSSESSED," drove the remnants of sleep from his eyes. But as he read further, the vindictiveness he expected was strangely absent. Instead, Harley had portrayed himself as the forgiving Jesus and called upon all Christians to pray for the restoration of Billy's faith.

"Such a turning of the cheek," Billy mocked aloud. "Cleverly conceived—but not by Harley. The man never said a word of this." Suddenly he felt chilled to the bone.

578

Harley Lombard sat alone in his penthouse office desperately in need of advice. His promise to show Sue Bergman what she could do with her threat to name him as an accessory had fizzled the moment he entered the Cathedral Towers lobby. The vicar of Virtues, Inc., and self-acclaimed pope to the Christian morality movement suddenly found his headquarters without troops.

The entire eighteenth floor, Virtues, Inc.,'s nerve center, had been abandoned. The hi-tech computers, the sophisticated global communications system—it had all strangely disappeared. The executive offices on the penthouse floor were unoccupied, and with the exception of a few security guards, Virtues, Inc., task force of sixty people had vanished.

Harley had given up calling Sue Bergman's unlisted Washington number every five minutes. His call to Bartley Sinclair in Portland also proved unsuccessful. The senator was quite unavailable. Harley had to speak to someone. And that someone was sneering at him from the doorway.

Harley saw the face he despised. "You better have some fucking answers!" he shouted, demeaningly.

"You're not supposed to be here." Deek Ashburn entered.

"Where is everybody?"

"Maybe Billy Hale will tell you."

"*Billy Hale*—what the hell are you talking about?"

The man approached the desk. As if by magic he produced a Cleveland newspaper. Harley's suspicion bordered on tilt before he reached across the desk and snatched the early-evening edition from the man's hand.

"*Billy Hale possessed?*" Harley read aloud. He read on until he could bear no more. "I never said this shit about forgiveness. Who released this story to the press?"

"Maybe Billy Hale will forgive *you*. Call him."

"Call him? Are you fucking mad? I'd shine the pope's shoes first. But why am I sitting here talking to a piss-ant?"

Harley went to rise but was stopped in midmovement by an action he saw as a blur. With swift sleight of hand, Deek Ashburn had drawn a pistol.

The phone call came from Hell. At least that is what Doris Hale believed. But Billy was not shocked by Harley Lombard's telephone call. He had almost expected it. And seeing that particular look on his face, Doris knew he was contemplating another mission of madness.

"Billy, Harley Lombard is not the prodigal son."

"Perhaps not. But the man needs me."

"Let someone else save him."

"Who, Doris? Who else can he turn to?"

"I don't know. And I don't care. As long as it's not you."

"I can't help but feel responsible."

"Billy, you said it all over television. Your conscience is clear."

"Doris, it's because of me that Dan and Cynthia are dead. Jimmy Christian needed my help and I turned my back on him. I must leave for Charity. At once."

"Billy," she pleaded. "It's sure to be some kind of trap."

"Doris, I do believe Richard Waters's next move comes directly from a chapter out of my life."

Harley Lombard sat between two security men in the back seat of the blue Chrysler. When it became obvious that his abductor, Deek Ashburn, was driving towards his home and that his life appeared not to be in immediate danger, Harley proceeded to threaten Ashburn with punishment ranging from the medieval rack to twenty years of hard labor in a state pen. Sue Bergman's strong-arm said nothing.

The gates were manually opened by the two security men, who remained there, and the Chrysler moved down the drive. Harley took notice of the absence of the security personnel usually stationed at various places around his property. He'd little time to wonder as a threatening Deek Ashburn escorted him to the door.

"You don't leave the house until Ms. Bergman says so. And if you're wondering why there's no reporters hanging around, they've been told you left for Washington."

Harley snarled at Ashburn. "You're going to pay for this."

"The last thing Ms. Bergman said was to use force if necessary. So just try to leave, *Mister Morality*, and you will give me the pleasure of putting a bullet into your knee cap. Then you *really* will have something in common with Billy Hale."

For a good twenty minutes, Harley stormed from room to room cursing everyone who'd made his day miserable. His Africa-bound wife, Wilma Mae, headed the list.

"Goddam douche bag. Leaving me without a cook. What does she care? As long as she's busting my balls she's happy. Always talking about her saintly father . . . Saint Shitbum is what he was. And *Sinclair*—having some flunky tell me he's unavailable. Doesn't that asshole understand I'm worth *millions of votes*! . . . My nerves, my nerves," he moaned, plopping into a chair.

His face flashed angrily. "Bergman—the bitch had to be the one who released that bullshit story about me *forgiving* Billy Hale. She'll pay for that," he promised himself. "I'll give her something to choke on."

Rage again clouded his features. "That fucking Billy Hale," he cursed. "Billy started the war. And when he found out what kind of power he was screwing with, he had to make up that conspiracy shit. It's all that old man's fault. He couldn't just fucking retire."

Harley felt he could handle no more. His brain overburdened by the day's events, he escaped into the sanctuary of his holy spa.

If Harley could possibly find peace of mind and harmony within himself, it would be here, in the two-thousand-square-foot room with the high domed roof dotted with glittering stars above the giant Jacuzzi pool. This was Harley's escape from the world, a place he shared with no one.

He emerged from an alcove, slipped off a black velour robe, and stepped into the warm swirling water. Easing his portly nude body into the contoured marble Jacuzzi with its surface-level head rest, he looked up at the twinkling stars swarming above while the tranquil music caressed his ears.

Though it was after 6:00 P.M., time for his customary vodka martini, or two, it didn't concern him. He would attend to that a little later, he thought, before making himself a late snack. Of course, it would be like Wilma Mae to have put locks on the fucking fridge, he reflected with mild irritation. But he put it out of his mind as the Jacuzzi relaxed his every muscle and brought a sporadic titillation that only the magic of Sue Bergman's mouth could surpass.

Eventually, Harley's attention drifted to one of the seven Venetian tiled alcoves . . . the one he had had reinforced after his former aide, Andy Gaines, had helped himself to a quarter of a million dollars of his "hush money."

He came out of the pool and walked over to the alcove, his nude body dripping water on the tiled floor. "Blessed are they who help themselves," he said, and his vocal command activated the super computer. The two steel grids at the alcove's entrance lifted one after the other, and he entered, smiling.

He spoke his full name and a steel wall slid open with a crunching sound. The wizardry of the computer had accepted the authenticity of his voice, and the sight of one million dollars stacked in various denominations created an arousal in his mind not even Sue Bergman could rival. Lusting with a miser's greed, he'd reached out and picked up a stack of large bills when, suddenly, the lights went out. The music stopped.

Harley's jaw locked. Every nerve in his body tingled as he listened in the darkness. All he heard was the gurgling of the pool.

No one knew the passwords he'd programmed into the computer after the burglary, he told himself. No one could possibly gain entrance. Not even Wilma Mae. *No one* . . . but someone had.

With the caution of a hunted fox, he ventured out from the alcove, still clutching a fistful of hundreds. Suddenly,

582

he felt cold all over, as if a blast of icy wind had gushed into the darkened spa. Sensing a presence, his trembling lips parted. But all that came from his mouth was the sound of chattering teeth. Then his beady eyes became alerted to a darting shadow across the quieted pool.

"Who's there? . . . Is—is that you, Wilma Mae?"

There was no reply from the ghostly form across the pool from him, and Harley could only think of one other.

"Sue? *Sue?* Is it you?"

Again, not a word came in reply.

The Charity city cab pulled up before the high, wrought-iron gates to the Lombard estate. The driver, a rotund, middle-aged man, shifted the cigar from one corner of his mouth to the other. There was no guard on duty, and he'd no intention of getting out of the cab to check if the gates were locked; instead he turned to face his famous passenger in the back seat. "Don't see any call box. What now, Reverend Hale?"

Billy looked at the cheap clock rigged to the dash. It was 9:50 P.M. Almost seven hours had passed since he'd received Harley Lombard's brief and desperate call. Knowing the man's cowardly streak, he'd expected to find the grounds swarming with security—armed guards and attack dogs everywhere, floodlights, alarms, and every other form of protection known to man. Instead, except for periodic illumination by moonlight, the estate was in total darkness.

Billy fell back against the tattered seat, thinking of the effort it had taken for him to get here. Had the considerable expense of hiring a Citation jet and crew on short notice, the ordeal of soothing a worried Doris, and a shouting match with Emile now ended in his being stopped at these gates, only a few hundred yards short of his destination? The driver interrupted his train of thought. "'If ya ask me, I'd say nobody's home."

Suddenly, Billy knew different. "Someone is," he said, pointing to the gates—which were now slowly opening.

They drove down the elm-lined drive to the house and

pulled up in front. The driver eyed the darkened entrance. "Maybe I should wait here for you, Reverend Hale."

"That won't be necessary," Billy said, handing him a crisp twenty-dollar bill.

The driver pushed Billy's hand away, refusing the fare. "My wife told me that what you said over television last night made a helluva lotta sense."

Trickles of moonlight moved over the immediate area as Billy ascended the steps to the front door. He searched for the pearl button that, when pushed, activated a computerized ringing of bells throughout the vast, cross-shaped home. Since his last visit, the pearl had been removed.

Billy knocked twice and waited. All he heard was the sound of the departing taxi. He knocked again; still no response. Instinctively, he reached for the ornate gold door handle. To his surprise, it was unlocked. A strong vibration warned him to turn back. A stronger curiosity won out.

He stood inside the dark foyer listening for sounds which would reveal a presence. Over his own breath, he heard the faint yet distinct sound of music. Finding a light switch, he flicked it on and continued his search.

As he walked, he turned on one light after another, and followed the sound of music to double oaken doors with two angels carved into the wood.

No secret password was necessary. The mammoth portals were partially open, and Billy pushed against the bulky door. Cautiously, he peered into the immense spa facility.

"Har-lee?" he called out in a singsong voice which clashed with the soft classical music wafting from concealed speakers.

Once more, an intuitive feeling told him to beware, and he was about to turn back when, as before, curiosity overcame his better judgment.

Drawn by the domed ceiling with its hundreds of silver-blue stars shining like sequins on a black dress, Billy moved at a cripple's pace to the pool's edge.

584

"Harley?" he called in a firm voice. "Harley, where in blazes are you?"

A muffled sound came in swift response.

Billy keyed on the sound's direction. It came from one of the cavelike adjacencies. But all he heard was the music. All he saw at the blackened entrances were unbidden images. And the more intensely he looked, the more illusory the images became.

"Harley," he called again.

Another sound, louder and lengthier, drew his attention to the other side of the pool. He could barely make out the entrance to an alcove, eerily touched by an unknown light source.

All of this was for his benefit. He was sure of it. His best strategy would be to leave—and quickly. But no sooner had his brain sent the order to his feet than the dome's galaxy of stars lost their glitter. The music faded. The oaken entrance doors slammed shut with a thud, then locked with a click.

The trembling started in his fingers. Fear stole into his senses. Breath clogged in his throat.

Then the bizarre struck. A burst of incredible light blazed from inside the fourth alcove. Billy shielded his eyes from the brightness. The thunderous "Hallelujah Chorus" began hammering in his ears.

He knew the spectacle before him was no supernatural illusion—no awesome light from beyond—no gathering of angels, singing *en masse*. Mere mortals had anticipated his arrival. He'd been lured into a trap, just as Doris had feared. Harley Lombard's telephone call had been arranged by Richard Waters in order to get him here. The only remaining question in Billy's mind was whether or not he was here to meet his executioner.

Suddenly, magically, the room exploded into a myriad of colors, as wild strobe lighting accompanied Mendelssohn's "Hallelujah."

Moving under the flashing lights, his feet sinking into the deep velvet pile carpeting, the music assaulting his eardrums, Billy saw through squinting eyes a nude Harley

Lombard, seated upon his immense and pretentious toilet. His forehead and feet were tightly bound to the regal john by thick leather straps. His bulging eyes were fixed in a gaze of terror. Heavy tape covered his mouth.

"My God," said Billy in disbelief. He closed his eyes, hoping it would all disappear, but when he opened them, the bizarre had struck again: they were not alone in the outlandish lavatory.

A tall, naked woman glided into the dazzling center of the luminous and musical madness. Billy felt himself controlled, mesmerized by the voluptuous body vibrating in a sensually savage rhythm to the driving music. He was so overcome with amazement that at first he didn't realize the frightening oddity about her. When he did, a moment later, a chilling sensation swept down his spine. Her face was painted in a ghoulish green-gray cami, in demonic contrast to the beauty of her large, jutting breasts, the rounded buttocks, and the long, lithe legs. What Billy failed to notice in his trembling observation was the small, thin leather holster strapped to her right ankle.

"Stop this!" The words came out weakly.

She now danced with even greater intensity, a fervor of bodily bumps and grinds, all the while moving nearer to the petrified Lombard. Billy could not muster the strength to move, or even to scream the protest that raged within him.

The gyrations of her spectacular body ended with a flurry of torrid bumps. She stood motionless before Harley, a malevolent stare glittering in her green eyes. Then, slowly, seductively, she went to her knees and looked up at him with a wide and diabolical grin.

Harley's frenzied eyes shifted imploringly to his old benefactor, but nothing short of a miracle would free Billy from his viselike paralysis. Nothing less than a command from God could stop this macabre nightmare.

Harley's twisted face suddenly flushed as he felt the caressing touch of her fingers stroking his limp penis. The warmth of her breath on his deflated organ convulsed him with spasms. When he felt her darting tongue lashing out at his penis, the veins and muscles in his arms and legs bulged, straining against the unyielding leather straps.

The cane slipped from Billy's lifeless hand. His face was drenched with sweat. The numbness slowly spread to his brain.

Rising in a slithering motion, the nude Amazon straddled Harley's immobilized legs. Smothering his face with her breasts while rubbing his penis against her wet pubic mound, she brought about a rising to an impossible erection, and guided the organ into her. Holding onto the corners of the high backrest, her hips moved on Harley in a thrusting rhythm.

The music reached an incredible decibel level. The flashing lights threw off their colors with blinding intensity. Billy tried to call out, but could not find his voice in the depths of his despair.

The woman's hands left the backrest. She sat heavily upon Harley's crotch, releasing her breasts from his whitened face. Her right arm slipped from her knee, the long fingers reached for the ankle holster.

Billy saw a flash of steel amidst the collection of clashing lights, and his lips moved in a soundless incantation of terror. His legs failed him, and he stumbled backwards, falling against the padded wall, slumping helplessly to the plush carpet.

Tossing her head from side to side, her hips wildly working to the beat of the pounding music, she drove savagely toward her demented and ultimate orgasm.

Harley's maddened attacker dug her toes into the velvet pile. Her hips rose and the lips of her vagina rubbed against Harley's protruding belly. The arched breasts again smothered his face.

She was nearing a climax not to be denied, and her entire body quivered with sporadic convulsions. Then it came—her ultimate orgasm. With a wild scream, violence and passion embraced each other. Seizing Harley's hair with her left hand, she slit his throat with the other.

Billy's eyes were transfixed by the macabre sight. What

he witnessed next flooded his very soul with horror and anguish.

She ripped the tape from Harley's mouth, and blood gurgled from the throat, bubbling over lips that had opened in a final, horrendous shriek. Hungrily covering his lips with her own, she thrust her tongue deep into the blood-filled mouth. One last shudder coursed through her body as Reverend Harley Lombard's life drained away.

Half-conscious, Billy Hale was dimly aware that the mad music and dancing lights had ceased. Now, all he could see was a pair of tigerish eyes. Green, gleaming eyes which appeared to be floating toward him.

Billy had no strength to move or even cry out. No thoughts of God, eternal Heaven, or Hell entered his mind—only the thought that he was about to die. The slashing of his throat would be swift. He would suffocate in his own blood and be found with Harley in this outrageous place.

Suddenly, he felt her hot, dank breath on his face. He closed his eyes to avoid the painted, ghoulish face with Harley's blood smeared upon the wide mouth. Awaiting the blade that would sever his jugular, his entire body convulsed as he felt her arms drape around his neck.

In his ear, Trudy Ballin whispered, "Not yet," then covered his lips with a bloody, savage kiss.

CHAPTER 51

NOVEMBER SEVENTH—ELECTION DAY.

An autopsy officially determined Harley Lombard's death to have resulted from an act of foul play. The murder weapon was described as a sharp instrument like a surgeon's scalpel. The brutal slaying had occurred sometime before midnight.

A knowledgeable captain of homicide saw through the wet face cloth rinsed of blood which lay in the sink of the super-lavatory and the smudges of dried blood at the corners of Billy's mouth. He knew this circumstantial evidence was intended to frame Billy Hale and to make the headlines of the scandal sheets.

Minutes before reporters swarmed upon the murder scene, the veteran policeman whisked the devastated Hale off to the Charity Airport, where his rented jet awaited. Before boarding, Billy gave the patient policeman his eyewitness account of the brutal murder.

An ocean away, Wilma Mae Lombard heard the news of her husband's murder. Accompanied by her missionary son, she spoke briefly to the reporters crowding around her at the Dakar, Senegal, airport. She had to hold back from laughing in one reporter's face when he spoke of her—and the world's—great loss.

The first thing Wilma Mae did upon her return to the States was to put to rest misleading newspaper stories about Harley's funeral. It most definitely would not be held at the Miracle of Might's vast cathedral in Charity. Instead, the service would be a private and simple affair, to be conducted by her twin ordained sons at her late father's church in Cleveland—the very place Harley had always referred to as a broken-down church in a peckerwood parish filled with paupers. An adjoining cemetery would be Harley's final resting place. Wilma Mae richly enjoyed the final insult.

Andy Gaines presented the patrons of his exclusive "Cuts and Curls" beauty salon with the finest champagne. The man who had for twenty years borne the brunt of Harley Lombard's wrath culminated his day of rejoicing with a private party. Prancing about his plush Rio de Janeiro ocean-front apartment, to the amusement of his gay friends, he toasted Harley Lombard's memory with mocking and degrading eulogies.

Throughout Christ Town, flags were at half mast. Inside the vast studio, the taping of a tribute to Harley Lombard neared completion. Supported by the G.L.E.E. Club Chorus and Orchestra, Cora Lee Christian butchered Harley's memory with the singing of her own composition, "Harley's Happy in Heaven." Backstage, her unofficial fiance and co-star, the boyish preacher, Peter Paul, mimicked her singing with mocking facial expressions. Noticeably absent from the television taping was its announcer and perennial prat man.

Frank Buckmaster was a lost soul sitting in the Garden of Eden setting of the Resurrection Hotel lobby. Instructed by Beth Staples to gather all of his worldly belongings, the ruddy-faced Bucky's grief was compounded when he found the Adam and Eve Lounge closed during election hours and his concealed flask empty of whiskey.

Beth Staples, for whom he'd waited so long, finally stepped off the elevator.

"Well, Bucky, we are no longer associated with Christ Town."

"We're out of work?" Bucky quavered.

"New Employment. We're leaving for Ohio."

"I was born in Ohio."

"I'm the new general manager of C.D. Pittman's flagship television station in Cleveland, and you—are its new weatherman."

"A *religious* weatherman?"

Beth Staples laughed. "Why not?"

High above, inside the ornate Caesar's penthouse, a meeting was taking place. Much to Rabbi Abe Margolis's chagrin, the new executive director of Christ Town was exploring possibilities which he considered to be out of bounds. The aged emperor of Christ Town, C.D. Pittman, smiled approvingly.

"The way I see it," Sue Bergman concluded, "we should reach out for other convention business and not direct all of our attention to Christian organizations."

"You can't expect the likes of IBM," Margolis sniped.

"You are a Messianic Jew, aren't you, Rabbi?"

Margolis sneaked a look at Pittman, silently asking for relief. The elderly billionaire appeared totally fascinated with Bergman.

"A convention for Messianic Jews—put it together, Rabbi," she ordered.

"I have nothing to do with conventions," Margolis protested.

"You do now."

"But—"

"You are excused, Rabbi."

Margolis's pleading face turned to Pittman.

"Get out!" Pittman rasped.

Margolis shot out of the room and Sue Bergman took a seat across from, and closer to, the bemused billionaire.

"Am I going to have a problem with him?" she asked.

"Nothing you can't handle."

She crossed her silky legs and leaned back in the comfortable chair, studying the aging man who appeared to be dwarfed in an oversized lounger.

"C.D., you do understand that I will be making occasional trips to Washington."

"I don't think so."

Bergman faltered in confusion. "Surely, Richard Waters must have mentioned my need to be in Washington."

"My dear, your ARA business can all be conducted from here."

"Am I to believe my fate has been decided?"

"Fate, Ms. Bergman, forever roams as a parentless bastard which touches our lives with rewards or curses. When that hypocrite, Billy Hale, exposed you over national television, the former president considered you to be expendable. I, however, did not."

"Why should you take such an interest in me?"

"It's a combination of things, my dear."

"Would you elaborate?"

Pittman chuckled. "Whereas your predecessor, Elizabeth Staples, is intelligent and beautiful, she's still a girl. You, my dear, are a woman. . . . Now, tell me—how did you manage to keep that fool Lombard in line?"

"C.D., if you don't mind, Harley Lombard is a part of my life I hope to forget."

"Whatever it took?" he prodded, ignoring her comment.

"To handle him?"

Pittman smiled, nodding.

"Well, yes," she said. "I guess you might say that."

Excitement coursed Pittman's wrinkled face. His old eyes were alive with lust.

"Tell me, my dear," he said, "are the strokes of your whip softly lashed—or are you utterly merciless?"

Mercy played no part in Ike Vesper's new assignment. Stuck somewhere in the Louisiana swamps, bordering Cajun country, Ike looked out from his cadre hut at the squad of men milling about the soggy compound fighting off constantly attacking insects. In his mind he saw only the familiar sight of Tahiti, and the native girls attending him in his retirement. But the fulfillment of his dream now seemed light years away.

The man called Trapper—the same who had broken down the bordello door at Cool's Cabaret—entered cursing. "That bitch . . . that crazy bitch!"

Ike merely looked at him with a curiosity born of boredom.

"We're stuck here, Ike. No Central America. No Africa. Here in this shithouse of a swamp! That bitch, Ballin, has made us her *special* team." Trapper fixed Ike with an intense look, and he said in a near whisper, "We gotta kill her, Ike—before she kills us."

Ike had heard it all before. He grimaced with painful understanding. "Aww-shittt. Not again."

WELCOME TO OCEANIA. The sign reflected brightly from the motor home's passing headlights. Ron Rebuck barely noticed it. Jessica Towne stared at the nearing lights of the elevated West Virginia coal town. Her town. Her home town.

Rebuck turned onto the sporadically lit main street and braked to a stop across from the bus station. He opened the door for Jessica, then retrieved her only possession: a battered suitcase. They crossed the street in silence.

Rebuck watched as Jessica concluded her call and came out of the phone booth. She slowly approached him, her head bowed, as she struggled to hold back her tears. Rebuck put a finger to her trembling lips.

"No tears. No emotional goodbyes. That's what we promised—remember?"

She threw her arms around his waist, nestling her head against his chest. For a long moment they communed silently, each with an understanding of the other. But Jessica had to speak of her deepest fear.

"Ron," she whispered, "don't do it. Please—don't do it."

Rebuck gently forced a separation. He fixed her with a firm gaze before speaking. "Jessica, I have a date with destiny."

Billy Hale's eyes were glued to the bedroom television set. The reports that he had been a witness to Harley Lombard's murder had given way to news of greater consequence. The national elections took precedence.

593

Seated in a chair by his bedside, Doris divided her attention between her worn-out husband and the latest election results. The polls showed that the tide was turning. Senator Sinclair was pulling away.

Billy watched as the televised scene shifted to a Portland, Oregon, hotel ballroom filled with campaign supporters waiting for Senator Sinclair's arrival and acceptance speech.

"Billy, will he live up to his promises?" Doris asked.

"Who can say what happens to a man when he becomes president?"

"Only God knows."

"Doris, pardon my vulgarity, but I really don't think God gives a shit."

Senator Bartley Sinclair stood at the podium. He had just received the concession from the president and given his acceptance speech to the tumultuous cheers of the campaign workers who filled the ballroom. The secret service agents had grown in number and George Whipple had to force his way to a beaming Sinclair's side. Whipple whispered in Sinclair's ear, and the senator's face clouded with apprehension.

Led by Whipple and accompanied by the secret service agents, Sinclair found himself at the door of a private suite. The agents stationed themselves outside as Sinclair alone entered.

The suite's only occupant, former President Richard Waters, smiled from ear to ear. "Well, Bart, we did it."

Sinclair felt this confrontation had come too soon after victory. "Why?" was the best response he could manage.

Waters leaned back in the chair. "Questions are not part of the president-elect's arsenal. Demands are more suited to the office."

"Not when I feel like an accomplice to murder."

The former president studied him closely. "Hardball? Is that what you want, Bart?"

"I want the truth, the whole truth. . . ."

594

"And nothing but the truth, so help me *God?*" Waters laughingly concluded. "The way it appears, without Virtues, Inc.'s, swing of votes, your place in history might not have come about."

"Is that why Harley Lombard was murdered? To pump up Virtues, Inc.'s, following?"

"The damn fool finally did serve a purpose in life."

Sinclair keyed on the former president's self-satisfied grin. "What about Billy Hale?"

"What about William?"

"You must know of my promise to him." Sinclair said.

"I do."

"Then what do you expect me to do?"

Waters's eyes glittered as he spoke. "I expect you to be the greatest president in the history of this country."

"And you?" Sinclair asked.

Waters's words came with chilling reality. "Come that January day when you place your hand on that Bible and are sworn in as president of these United States, Bart, I shall remain quietly in the background—as dictator."

CHAPTER 52

DANIEL'S DEN. THANKSGIVING MORNING

The Billy Hale ministry's board of directors sat around the elongated mahogany conference table. The encircling busts of Biblical figures stood as symbolic, spiritual witnesses to an important meeting. At the head of the table, Billy Hale listened attentively to the portly man reading the financial report and carefully avoided eye contact with the lone guest in attendance.

The distinguished guest, Gabe Stillman—Billy Hale's attorney for almost four decades—had no idea why Billy had insisted on his presence. And on Thanksgiving, no less. Wise to Billy's ways, he ruled out the purpose of lending the Board his legal expertise. All he could think of was that something highly significant would soon transpire. The tip-off had come when Billy failed to give the traditional invocation and forged directly into the financial report.

Billy's attention drifted beyond the busts of Old Testament prophets and heroes to the noticeably vacant spot amidst the gallery of photos where Richard Waters's portrait had once prominently hung. With a bitter feeling of distaste, he thrust the former president from his thoughts. His gaze briefly touched upon each of the newly elected directors. Looking at his wife, Doris, Scrappy Dews and Miss Marge, and lastly, a gloating Emile, Billy recalled the ghosts of yesteryear who had sat in their very seats. He saw the faces of the prominent and powerful who had once made up the governing board.

Clarence Hickey, the board's treasurer, aptly nicknamed

Chub, who had inherited the seat from his late father, paused to adjust his bifocals. He then continued reading from a bound report. "Sources of income for the past two years have been limited to interest-bearing investments, monthly installment payments from real estate holdings, and royalties derived from Reverend Hale's books. With the ministry's inactivity, the liability picture is zero."

Hickey thumbed to another page. "The work force has been reduced to four mailing secretaries and, of course, Emile. Along with the upkeep for this estate, Reverend Hale's modest salary, professional fees, and incidentals, the expenses are less than twenty per cent of the gross revenues for the twenty-four-month period." He looked up to meet Billy's eyes. "Considering your semi-retirement, the ministry is in a very liquid position."

"How liquid?" asked Billy, anxious for the bottom line.

Hickey reached for a computer printout. "Including the installment receivables—six million, two hundred and sixty-three thousand."

"What does the ministry's pension fund tell us?" Billy asked.

Hickey picked up another glossy folder before him. "As of September thirtieth, the ministry's pension fund is in the amount of three million, two hundred and forty-one thousand dollars."

Billy allowed the figures to settle in the minds of the board members before speaking. "Tell me, Chub, how much money would you say I've raised in the name of God?"

"In your entire lifetime?"

"Yes."

"No telling, Billy."

"An estimate will do."

"Billy, we're talking about a period of over forty years."

"A guesstimate, *please*."

Hickey shrugged. "Two . . . maybe three hundred million."

"And how much of that do you suppose actually went to charity?"

Hickey searched the faces of the board's members. Their expressions matched that of his own: bewilderment. A knowing smile crossed Gabe Stillman's lips.

"In your tenure as treasurer, do you have an idea, Chub?" Billy pressed.

Hickey thought for a moment. "Offhand, let me see . . . there's the Billy Hale Bible College. The Hale wing to the Richmond Hospital. The Billy Hale Christian Scholarship Fund. The . . . Billy, there *is* a list."

"What percentage *really* went to charity, Chub? Ten percent? Twenty?"

"A great deal went for expenses," Hickey defended.

"Expenses. Blessed expenses. Of course," said Billy.

"Television time alone for your worldwide campaigns took a big chunk."

"Thank you, Chub," Billy said with finality. He then addressed the members as a body. "Are there any questions?"

No one replied.

Billy rose from the table and stood without the support of his cane. "What I am about to say might lead some of you to believe I have lost my mind. I can assure you that senility has not yet taken its hold on me. What I ask is for you to please reserve your questions and, perhaps, objections until I have finished."

Billy reached into his coat pocket and retrieved a large envelope. He held it up for examination.

"Inside the envelope is a check which closes out my and Doris's savings account. It is made out to the ministry in the amount of two hundred and twelve thousand dollars. Also in this envelope is a transfer to the ministry of all my stocks, certificates of deposits, and treasury notes. Their face value is well over one million dollars."

Billy handed the envelope to Doris and waited until she relayed it down the table to the puzzled treasurer.

Gabe Stillman ran a fingertip over his pencil-thin mustache. It sounded, to him, more like the making of a last will than a directors' meeting.

"Chub," Billy went on, "I want my share of the pension fund returned to the ministry's treasury. *Also*," he kept the fleshy Hickey from protesting, "come the first of the year, this entire estate will go up for sale."

Hickey put up his hand, but Billy shot him down. He would not be interrupted. "Everything, and I mean *everything*, purchased with ministry money—yes, the expensive silverware, china, the busts in this room, the limousine, down to the clothes and shoes I wear—will be sold. Those items which cannot be sold are to be donated to a nondenominational charity. All ministry credit cards are to be cancelled."

Billy then placed both hands on the table. Relief bloomed on his face. His constant battle with hypocrisy would finally end.

"Ladies and gentlemen of this governing board, as the Billy Hale ministry's final act—we shall declare a dividend."

"Declare *what?*" Hickey choked in disbelief.

"As far back as our records go, every person who has donated money to this ministry shall finally get something more in return than holy lip service."

Clarence Hickey looked at the faces of the board members, searching in vain for any signs of resistance. He understood the reason for Billy's selection of new directors. None of them would turn against him.

"Ridiculous?" Billy asked, bearing in on Hickey. 'How ridiculous was it when I went out to raise money in the name of God? Armed with faith, optimism, and ignorance, I solicited as much or more than any other evangelist in history. But now that I wish to give, such a deed brings a doubting and skeptical reaction. Is that it, Chub?"

"Billy, have you any idea how many of those donors are dead? We're talking about a period of over forty years. How many have moved?"

"I'm sure the Internal Revenue Service will know."

"Fine. Probably so. But what are we really talking

about? The return of a penny on the dollar? In some cases the postage might be more than the return.''

''Perhaps you have missed the point, Chub. What this old man is attempting to establish is that this ministry will not end among the takers—rather, of the givers.''

''Amen?'' Hickey forced his concession.

''Unless the members of this board say otherwise.''

All eyes fell on Billy as he slumped into the chair. There was a lengthy silence in the room. Only Billy heard the illusory bickering among the busts. Then—it started.

At first the applause was polite and scattered. It then swelled in unison. Gabe Stillman was the first to rise, Clarence Hickey the last. Billy had expected no such demonstration and was visibly shaken. He looked at the faces, beaming with pride . . . and more, *respect*. Doris tenderly took his arm and he looked down to see the deep affection in her tearful eyes.

''Billy Hale,'' she whispered under the continuing applause, ''I've never loved you more.''

Family commitments prevented Hickey and Gabe Stillman from staying for Thanksgiving dinner. A dutiful Emile was excused from driving Stillman to his waiting private plane. Hickey would take him to the valley airport on his ride back to Winchester. Their audience with Billy in the Hale living room neared its end.

''I want you to know, I will not accept any fee for the enormous task you have given me,'' Hickey announced.

''*You*—working without compensation?'' Billy was startled.

''I did not include expenses.''

''What on Earth has touched you, Chub?''

''Something contagious,'' Hickey smiled. ''Helluva nice way to start Thanksgiving, Billy.''

Gabe Stillman waited for Hickey to waddle out of the room before approaching his most famous and difficult client.

''You had to do it, didn't you?''

600

"Gabe, if you'd known what I was up to, you would have had me committed."

"Without question. However, I was referring to something else."

Billy recognized a certain look which came to Stillman's face. It always preceded something personal he had to say.

"I must confess, Billy, that as a Jew, I've often thought of Christianity as a crock. I've always believed fundamentalist Christianity, in particular, to be a ripoff. I mean, how you evangelists can come up with such cockamamie, lame-brained schemes to raise money has always been beyond my comprehension. Then you, Billy Hale, showed me how *true* Christianity is supposed to work."

"Thank you . . . my dear, dear friend."

"Well, today you have earned something more than my services, Billy."

"What's that?"

"My respect."

"You've always had mine, Gabe."

For the first time in their lifelong association, the two men allowed their feelings to run unhindered. Their embrace was warm and genuine.

"Gabe," Billy called after him. "You're not even going to ask where Doris and I will live, or what I'm going to do?"

"Not today, Billy. Not on this most revealing Thanksgiving day."

Thanksgiving dinner lay spread upon a hand-carved antique table. Doris Hale, Pastor and Mrs. Dews, and Emile bowed their heads, anticipating Billy's giving of the prayer. Instead, Billy tapped his ring on the wine glass, and the pinging sound quickly gained their attention.

"I cannot ask God's blessing for the food we are about to eat. Not when so many of our fellow men are starving. To do so would make God out to be, in my eyes, one who plays favorites."

Billy raised his glass, and all but Doris looked at him questioningly. Mystified, they yet followed his lead.

"I would like to toast a new beginning. To the Billy Hale Bible College, where Doris and I shall permanently reside—where I will return to the grass roots with the hope of teaching a new dimension in Christianity."

Doris followed suit and rose. "To my husband, who has found his true self."

Next came Emile. But the faithful chauffeur and "Man Friday" was unable to find words that would express his gratitude for what Billy had bequeathed to him.

Miss Marge's toast fell along the more traditional—"Thanks to God."

Under the watchful scrutiny of his wife, Scrappy Dews completed the toasting. "First and foremost, to Billy Hale, who this very day has rightfully earned the title Reverend. To Doris, and my wife, Miss Marge, who together have justifiably earned the Christian Medal of Honor. And lastly, to the American Indian, whom our forefathers royally screwed."

Came nightfall and a cold, strong wind blew upon the Hale estate. The temperature had dropped considerably and the forecast for this region of the Shenandoah called for snow to follow the high winds. Nature's climatic conditions had no effect on Billy Hale. He had never felt more at peace with the world. And more—with himself.

"Doris," he came out of the bathroom and into the cathedral-ceilinged bedroom, "I cannot tell you just how good I feel. Even the pain in this blasted knee of mine is tolerable."

She placed his warm milk on the night table separating their beds and smiled.

"All I ever knew was the feeling that comes with taking. The power—the righteousness of acting in the name of God which dismisses all guilt."

"It is better to give?" Doris hinted at a Biblical phrase.

Billy remembered the full verse so very well. The countless times he had used it when soliciting big bucks in God's name! "How ironic," he marveled. "Only today have I truly experienced the opposite side to taking."

602

She saw the deep frown invade his pleasant mood. "Is something wrong, Billy?"

"Have I gone too far, Doris? I mean, do you think I let myself get carried away?"

"Wasn't it you who felt the title *reverend* to be a misnomer as applied to members of the clergy? Well, today, Billy Hale, I concur with Scrappy. You earned it."

"But do you realize that in giving the Hale farm to Scrappy and Emile we have nothing left of our own?"

She would not tell him that neither Emile nor Scrappy would accept the deed to the multiacre farm. Nor would she make him aware of the savings which foresighted wives kept secret from domineering husbands. "You have made two deserving people very happy."

He shook his head in agreement. "I did right, by golly. Can't you picture Emile's face when he learned of his pension? And Scrappy—his lifelong dream has been to own a farm."

He moved about the bedroom, exuding an energy he thought had long dissipated. "Maybe one last campaign, Doris."

She sat up in her bed, quick to remind him of a binding promise. "The only campaign you will be launching is at the Billy Hale Bible College, William Hale."

He looked at her with sleepy eyes. "It's been one hell of a Thanksgiving—hasn't it, Mrs. Hale?"

She didn't have to tell him to come to bed. And when he rejected his warm milk, she offered no objection. His day deserved to end without any reproaches. She turned off the table light and they lay in the darkness, each with his own thoughts, until sleep rendered them oblivious to time and the howling wind.

An hour had passed when a loud, thumping noise roused Doris. "Billy? . . . Billy, are you awake?"

"It's nothing, Doris. The wind must have loosened a shutter."

When the noise came again, she turned on the light and reached for the bedside telephone.

"Emile's at Scrappy's for the night," he groggily informed her. "I'll fix it."

"Billy . . . it doesn't sound like a loose shutter."

Billy opened the bedroom door and listened. The noise was louder and clearer. It came from downstairs, and sounded as if someone was knocking on a door—the Daniel's Den door. Suddenly, Billy knew. What he had long expected had finally come to pass.

He turned from the door and slowly came to the bed, sitting down at her side.

She saw the gravity of his concern. "What is it?" she asked, probing the distant gaze of his blue eyes.

"Doris, I must ask you not to leave this room. Will you give me your promise?"

"Billy, what are you talking about?"

"There is someone downstairs."

"Who? For God's sake, *who*, Billy?"

"God has nothing to do with it. I've long expected this visitor."

"The noise, Billy—it stopped. Whoever—"

"*Promise me*—you will not call anyone, or leave this room. I beg you, Doris."

"You're frightening me."

"There is nothing to fear. Everything will be all right."

"Someone has come to kill you. I know it. Billy, you . . ."

He tenderly placed a hand over her trembling mouth. "Allow me to end this wonderful day in even greater glory."

She began to shake uncontrollably, and he held her trembling body with the deepest of affection. He then gently lifted her chin to look long and lovingly at her face, as if storing her lovely features in eternal memory. Then he kissed her.

"Promise you will do as I ask?"

She bit down on her quivering lip, and nodded.

He sighed and came off the bed. Taking her hand, he kissed it, avoiding her tearful eyes.

604

He could not look back; he shut the door behind him. He would now keep his date with destiny.

As Billy moved down the stairs, with each step he thought of eternity. Another life . . . a new beginning . . . or was it all nothing more than a hoax? He stopped before the door to Daniel's Den. Inside, death waited. He was never more sure. With a heavy sigh and a steady hand, he opened the door.

He was not surprised that only two dim bulbs burned at the far corners of the room, nor at the failure of the main lighting when he flicked on the switch. His gaze traveled the full circle of the busts, and took in no sign of mortal man.

He limped to the conference table and slumped into the leather chair at its head. His eyes drifted aimlessly, his ears pitched to the slightest sound. But all he heard was the angry wind beating against the storm windows. His attention became drawn to the gallery of photos above the fieldstone fireplace.

The portrait of the man who haunted him hung where the painting of Richard Waters had been removed. He stared at the eyes of a face he'd seen so many times in his nightmares. But this was no time for illusions. He need not be concerned with the dead, rather the living.

"I expected you," Billy said, in a calm and deliberate tone.

There came no reply, nor did Billy anticipate any.

"I often wondered, with all the killing of evangelists, when you would come around to me. But then, I knew when Harley Lombard was brutally murdered that you would soon appear. Your accomplice, that woman, gave it away."

Again Billy waited for a response. Only the wind answered.

"Show yourself and be done with it!" he shouted angrily.

He thought he heard a movement from behind one of the Biblical busts. Peter's, or Paul's—he couldn't distinguish.

"Surely you cannot contain your hate, your vengeance. How many years have you waited for this moment? Come out, damn you, and face the man you hold responsible for your father's murder.''

As Billy waited for another sound, a deep, enveloping calm came over him. He was totally prepared to die—with dignity.

"Beg your forgiveness? Is that what you expect? You wish to see me crawl on my knees? Plead with you to spare my life?'' Billy shook his head. A peaceful smile touched his lips.

"I'm sorry to disappoint you, young man. But I have done all the begging and pleading I intend to in this life. As for forgiveness, I'm afraid it is going to take someone or something much greater than you to light my candle.''

Suddenly, what sounded like the cocking of a pistol hammer reverberated through the shadowed room. Billy's mind fled back to the past with fleeting vignettes of his life. He heard his mother calling him and saw himself as a child picking apples in the Hale orchard. He saw his ordination, with his proud parents looking on. Then came his marriage to Doris, and the growth of an immortal friendship. The loss of his only child, a son bearing his name, and those terrible days of bereavement merged into the chanting of his name in jam-packed stadiums all over the world.

The flashing-back of his life abruptly ended with a blur from the present. Billy saw her coming out from behind the bust of Paul, those demonic eyes gleaming, a glint of steel clenched in her fist. He closed his eyes, awaiting her death-strike, when in that frozen instant he heard the muffled sounds.

His eyes flew open, and in that moment, that fleeting moment, he saw the crazed Trudy Ballin hurtling onto the conference table, chunks of flesh exploding from her face, an eye dangling from its socket.

Bathed in the dead woman's blood, he looked away from the crumpled figure sprawled before him. What he now saw stole his breath. From the shadows, a man holding a pistol came forward. Billy sat in further shock as he recognized the eyes of a dead man—reborn.

"Why? . . . Why?" Billy cried out.

"In the name of God?" a forgiving Ron Rebuck, Jr., said with a smile.

THEIR LIVES, THEIR LOVES, THEIR LEGENDS

Their movies still delight us, their romances continue to thrill us and their tragedies hurt as deeply as those that happen to members of the family!

Here they are! **MARILYN, ELVIS** and **JIMMY**—each in a handsome magazine packed with informative articles and glorious color photographs, many not seen in years!

Plus, each magazine contains 8 giant color pin-ups, which unfold to become 16" x 22" posters. Rare! A collector's item!

50 pages + pin-ups. 8" x 10 7/8" flexible cover.

MARILYN MONROE $9.95   ELVIS PRESLEY $5.95
JAMES DEAN $10.95